WILD CARDS

HIGH STAKES

Other titles in the Wild Cards Universe
published by Gollancz:

THE ORIGINAL TRIAD
Wild Cards
Aces High
Jokers Wild

THE PUPPETMAN QUARTET
Aces Abroad
Down and Dirty
Ace in the Hole
Dead Man's Hand

THE AMERICAN HEROES TRIAD
Inside Straight
Busted Flush
Suicide Kings

THE FORT FREAK TRIAD
Fort Freak
Lowball
High Stakes

WILD CARDS

HIGH STAKES

A MOSAIC NOVEL

Edited by

George R.R. Martin
& Melinda M. Snodgrass

And written by
David Anthony Durham
Stephen Leigh
John Jos. Miller
Melinda M. Snodgrass
Caroline Spector
Ian Tregillis

First published in Great Britain in 2017 by Gollancz
an imprint of the Orion Publishing Group Ltd
Carmelite House, 50 Victoria Embankment
London EC4Y 0DZ

An Hachette UK Company

1 3 5 7 9 10 8 6 4 2

ISBN: 978 1 473 22198 7

Printed in Great Britain by
CPI Group (UK) Ltd, Croydon, CR0 4YY

www.georgerrmartin.com
www.orionbooks.co.uk
www.gollancz.co.uk

To Ty Frank,
for all the horrors,
and Jayné Franck,
for art deco wonders

Editor's Note

Wild Cards is a work of fiction set in a completely imaginary world whose history parallels our own. Names, characters, places, and incidents depicted in *Wild Cards* are fictitious or are used ficticiously. Any resemblance to actual events, locales, or real persons, living or dead, is entirely coincidental. The works contained in this anthology are works of fiction; any writings referred to within these works are themselves fictional, and there is no intent to depict actual writers or to imply that any such persons have ever actually written or published the fictional essays, articles, or other works referred to in the works of fiction comprising this anthology.

MONDAY

BARBARA BADEN—THE ACE Babel—stared through the open window. Overhead, the Milky Way arched in a glorious, multicolored stream through the night sky—dusted with more stars than Barbara had seen in ages. In New York City, they were lucky to spot even such luminous constellations as Orion in a sky fouled by city lights and haze. Here in Peru, at Machu Picchu in the mountains far from any city lights with the air thin around them, the stars cavorted in all their glory. Below Barbara, on the steep slopes, a new city of tents was spread, many of them alight from the inside, all of them bright in the silver light spilling from the half-moon crawling up the slope of the mountain Huayna Picchu, the peak looming over the Incan ruins.

Down in those tents were several of the Committee aces: Earth Witch, Bugsy, Tinker, the Llama, Brave Hawk, and Toad Man, as well as UN troops. But Klaus and Barbara, being who they were within the Committee, had—like Secretary-General Jayewardene of the UN—managed to commandeer actual rooms in one of the reconstructed buildings high up the slopes. It was one of the perks of being in charge.

"It's lovely here, isn't it?" she heard Klaus—Lohengrin to nearly everyone else here—say behind her, and his arms went around her as she leaned back into his embrace. She could feel the scratch of his eye patch against her scalp as he bent his head down, and see his arms. His skin was dry, and there were already faint wrinkles netting the back of his hands. They were both now well in their mid-thirties, and the dreaded "forty" could be glimpsed in the distance, a thought that had seemed impossible when Barbara had first met Klaus, some eight years ago. Her own hands, on top of Klaus's, no longer looked as young as they once had, and she was fight-ing both weight gain and the occasional grey hair in her short, dark brown hair. She'd already given up on holding back the lines around her eyes. "You can see why the Inca wanted this place to be their capital. And haven't I done a lovely job to bring this together?"

"You mean 'we,' don't you?" Barbara told him, and she felt more than heard his laughter.

"Of course. We."

The Committee had become involved in Peru as it became apparent that an internal squabble was about to boil over into loss of life. On one side were the New Shining Path rebels, advocates who wished a return to the structure of the Incan empire and an overthrow of the official Peruvian government and the military cabal that propped it up. The rebels were led by their own aces: Lorra (or as she was more popularly known, Cocomama) and Curare, a frog-like ace-joker who exuded poison from his skin and tongue.

The official Peruvian government was headed by President Keiko Fuji-mori, the daughter of former president Alberto Fujimori, who was sup-ported by the leaders of other South American countries as democratically elected, especially those presidents who worried about coups and upris-ings themselves. The Peruvian government, of course, had the military complex behind them, a well-equipped force with weapons that, if not entirely modern, were more than capable of creating mass numbers of casualties, and President Fujimori's recent speeches had made it clear that she intended to use that capability if she must.

The UN forces, with Jayewardene in command of the team, had landed two weeks ago, just as the first major battle erupted between the two forces, near this very place. The rotors of the UN helicopters had thrashed the foliage around the clearing, whipping greenery into a frenzied dance. Below, they could all see the narrowing no-man's-land between a Peruvian army company and the rebel forces. Tinker's armed drones were already hovering above the opposing lines, whining and threatening and drawing fire.

Babel was wielding her wild card before the first helicopter touched ground. Her ability to render speech incomprehensible had quickly sown confusion and fear into the ranks of both sides, visible in the uncoordi-nated reaction to the UN troops' arrival. It was impossible for armies to fight when their commanders couldn't make their orders understood, when officers couldn't pass the orders down the line and sergeants couldn't communicate to their squads, when no one knew what they were supposed to do or where they were supposed to go. Even radio communications seemed to have been spoken in some incomprehensible nonsense language. Compounding the confusion on both sides was the fact that the UN troops and the Committee aces with them didn't have that problem and could still coordinate their actions quite effectively. The line of eight copters— two UH-1Y Venom choppers with the Committee aces inside, and six huge, double-motored MH-47G Chinook troop carriers—banked in like roaring, menacing raptors, the Venom "Super Hueys" spraying a line of warning machine-gun fire to chew up the ground between the two forces as they approached. Through the glass cockpit, Babel saw one of Tinker's drones explode into a shower of plastic shards and baling wire from the "friendly fire" as Tinker cursed loudly behind her and the chopper performed a stomach-dropping turn and landed.

Lohengrin's ghost armor appeared as he leapt out of the Committee copter, his sword waving threateningly as both Peruvian soldiers and rebels retreated from the wind of the rotor blades and the blue-helmeted UN soldiers who poured from the other copters. The Committee aces with Lohengrin and Barbara followed him. Tinker's remaining drones swooped down, racing along the lines. The earth shuddered under the opposing sides as Earth Witch quickly dug out a wide ditch between the two forces, which Ana banked high with rich, dark soil. The Llama, a well-known and popular South American ace, stepped to Lohengrin's right; he spat once, warningly, the slimy mess traveling a good ten yards to land near the end of the Peruvian company's line. Buford Calhoun stepped down after the Llama, transforming as he did into Toad Man, his tongue flicking out like a grotesque whip—those nearest the copters on the rebel side quickly retreated at the sight, too frighteningly similar, perhaps, to their own Curare. Tom Diedrich—Brave Hawk—hovered menacingly above the other aces, his black wings flexing. Glassteel stood at the rear of the aces, a crystalline, glittering presence.

And behind the aces, two companies of UN troops arrayed themselves in blue-helmeted lines, their own weapons at the ready.

There'd been some initial automatic weapons fire between the two sides as the copters first approached, but now it had just . . . stopped. Babel stepped out last from the copter as the rotors slowed. She took the microphone offered to her by one of the UN soldiers and spoke, her voice booming over loudspeakers mounted on the copter, her words now comprehensible to everyone who heard her, regardless of the language they spoke.

"This is over now," she said. "You will all put your weapons down. You don't want to face the consequences of continuing this fight."

The physical battle ended with minimal casualties on both sides, and with the power that the aces and the UN troops represented, Jayewardene quickly brought both sides to the negotiations table, though there were a few sporadic incidents with recalcitrant rebels or army squads, all quickly settled by ace intervention. Jayewardene led the talks, though it was Babel and Lohengrin who, each night before, consulted with Jayewardene as to what he needed to say, what concessions to ask for, and where there could be compromise and where there could not. They slowly, over the next week, brought the Fujimori delegation and the New Shining Path advocates together.

The movement of a moth's fluttering wings brought Babel back to the present. The creature that came to rest on the curtains of the open window was beautiful: a dark-winged apparition easily the size of one of Lohengrin's hands, its wings swirling with multicolored whorls that looked like huge staring eyes. She knew what the moth was and what it represented, of course: their briefings had told them about the mysterious Messenger in Black, whose body could only appear in a whirling cloud of these moths, how he could hear and see what those individual insects observed, and how his prescient mind informed the rebel forces even if he himself never called himself the New Shining Path's leader or took part in the fighting.

Babel gave the moth a quick, wry smile. She shook the curtain and it rose and banked away as Babel closed and locked the window. She leaned back against Lohengrin once more. When his hands went to cup her breasts, she didn't stop him, just turned so they were facing each other. She stared up into his face.

"Not here," she said. "Too many eyes—of all kinds—and cameras with long lenses."

Klaus grinned at her and touched his eye patch with a finger. "I only have one eye, and it's looking at you."

She gave him a halfhearted, sad smile at that. "We have an early morning tomorrow, you know. It's already late."

"Does that mean we can't have an even later night, *meine Liebe*? After all, tomorrow's just for show. As for our infestation of voyeur moths, we'll just close all the curtains."

"You're impossible."

"Nothing's impossible. Not as far as I'm concerned."

"As long as we work together, you mean?" she asked him, and he gave a sniff of amusement.

"As long as we're working together, then," he growled. *"Yah."*

She took his hand, smiling back to him, and led him to their bed.

The moon had climbed well above Huayna Picchu before they went to sleep.

Marcus Morgan slid out of the barn. Normally, he was smooth and powerful, propelled by serpentine muscle that began at his waist and stretched twenty feet to the tip of his brightly ringed tail. He cut an impressive figure, snake on his lower half, a well-muscled young African-American man from the torso up.

He didn't feel impressive now, though. He tried not to wince with the pain of moving, but he couldn't help it. Getting shot was a bitch. He was hurt. Bad. He knew that now even if he hadn't fully understood it in the chaos of the arena or in the exhilaration of fleeing from it. If he had to fight now he wasn't sure he'd be any good; the rage that took him over in the arena was gone. He hoped fighting was behind him. Now he just needed to stay alive and get home. That was going to be hard enough.

Looking around at the nondescript buildings and the dim, sputtering streetlights, he thought, *Would you look at this? Me, gunshot, stuck in Kazakh-wherever-the-hell-we-are . . .*

He turned as a young woman crept out of the shelter. She wobbled on her stilettos. Like everything she did, she made that wobble look sexy as hell. Marcus had fallen for her the first time he saw her, when she slipped into his cell back in Baba Yaga's joker gladiator compound. She'd looked like she'd stepped out of *Vogue*. She'd been too perfect to be real, with her light blue eyes and short black hair that reminded him of a movie star from the 1920s he'd once seen on a postcard. It was hard to place her age, except that everything about her glowed with the raw beauty of youth.

And I'm with her, he thought. He still couldn't quite believe it.

"I'm not dressed for this," Olena said in her Ukrainian-accented

English. It was an understatement. She still wore the clothes of her role in Baba Yaga's casino. Pleasure girl, given like a piece of exotic meat to victorious gladiator jokers. Her short red dress clung to her curves, skintight. It was so sheer Marcus could see the contours of her abdomen and the lines of her collarbones. He didn't let his eyes linger on her nipples, though they wanted to. She was gorgeous, but she wasn't a piece of meat to him. She was more than that. If they survived this he would prove it to her.

There was one thing out of place in her appearance. The Glock that she had shoved down under her belt. It pressed flat against her belly.

Earlier, he'd asked her, "Where'd you learn about guns, anyway?"

She'd answered curtly, "My father." That was all she would say about it.

"Are you ready?" Marcus asked, starting to slither away.

She fell in step beside him. "I still think we should—"

"I'm not going to the hospital! The hospital's going to be filled with people from the casino. People I sent there."

"Wasn't only you that did it," she grumbled.

"You saw the ambulances arriving as we left. The military vehicles. There must be cops all over the place."

"You've been shot. When people are shot it's hospital they go to! Why are you stubborn?"

"I'm a joker. If I wasn't stubborn I'd be dead by now." Marcus paused as a black SUV roared across the intersection in front of them. A moment later a police car flashed by, lights blaring but with no accompanying siren. Moving forward, Marcus asked, "What if Baba Yaga's there? We'd both be fucked then."

"She is dead woman. Who is afraid of her?"

They'd been through this all already. The hospital was out. Talas itself was out, what with Baba Yaga's thugs around, with no way of knowing who they could trust, and with him being the way he was—a black half-snake joker from New York. Not only that, the entire city seemed to itch with unease. While they'd hidden and tried to rest, sporadic gunfire kept jolting Marcus awake. Once an explosion went off near enough for Marcus to feel it through his tail, loud enough that the whoosh of the flames was audible. At some point sirens began to wail a monotonous message. They were still at it. Shouts and running feet, the sounds of fighting, helicopters chopping through the sky. He didn't know what all was going on, but they had to get away from it.

Olena said, "You should've killed Horrorshow as well."

"Horrorshow?"

"It's just one name for him. That awful old man always beside Baba Yaga." She made a sound in her throat, an exhalation of both disgust and fear. "Once I had to sit near him in the box." She shivered, flicking her fingers as if to shake some foulness off them. "God. He's horrible. He's . . . I don't know what. Some people said he liked the killing, that he enjoyed it and that Baba Yaga created the whole arena for him. Others said he was an ace who had crossed her. She'd made him like that as punishment, so that he would suffer and suffer, and everybody would see it. I don't know what's true. There were many rumors."

Remembering the deformed, drooling old man enmeshed in a confusion of tubes and respirators, Marcus said, "Who said all this about him?"

Olena walked on a moment without answering, and then said, curtly, "Guards. Sometimes they talked and talked."

Marcus immediately wished he hadn't asked the question. It didn't take much for him to imagine the worst. Guards, talking and talking because they had Olena alone, because she was a whore in there and they had just . . .

He cut the thought off and changed the subject. "Where are we headed anyway?"

"That way." Olena pointed through a gap in the buildings. A snow-capped peak rose in the distance, in shadow against the red-hued sky. "Toward that mountain."

"Why that one?"

She brushed her short hair from her face. "You know a better mountain? We go toward that one because it's outside the city. We're not. If we reach it, we are."

"I can't fault your logic."

"Come. We go." She took his hand.

Marcus slithered beside her. His tail was sluggish and aching. It shot jagged shards of pain through him. He hoped they'd be able to avoid people, to move cautiously and get out unobserved. It didn't take him long to give up on that.

Once out from their hidden back lot, they found a city alive with people and cars. It wasn't a normal busy, though. A driver careened down the street, swerving and cutting others off. He pounded on his horn and shouted out his window. As if racing with him, one boxy little car jumped the curb and whined down the sidewalk. Marcus and Olena barely managed to get out of its way.

"What the fuck's going on?" Marcus asked. "Nobody wants to get to work that much!"

Olena didn't answer. She waded into the crowd of pedestrians. Seeing his serpentine bulk, people cleared out of their way. Mouths gaped and eyes went wide. Marcus couldn't tell if they were surprised by his tail or his ethnicity. Either way, they parted.

The city would've been strange enough to Marcus's eye even in normal circumstances. The buildings were squat and ugly, cement facades that seemed designed to warn people away. The cars were different makes than he was used to, older-looking and shaped funny. He thought he'd seen just about every type of person—and every kind of joker—in New York, but he'd never seen people quite like these. Light-skinned and black-haired, Asian-looking but distinct somehow from the Chinese and Koreans Marcus knew from Jokertown. Their clothes were exotically colorful in some ways, drab and bulky in others, just normal sometimes. He registered all of this vaguely, but it was the chaos that really baffled him.

An old man yanked on a dog's leash, trying to get the frightened canine to move. It wouldn't, and the man began walloping it with his cane. Young men climbed into a truck already piled high with furniture and household items. One of them waved an ax above his head and said something sharp and threatening to Marcus. A girl stood on a street corner, turning around and around, calling for someone. A guy on a bicycle weaved one-handed through the traffic, a flat-screen TV perched precariously on his shoulder. There was something in the air, a panic that seemed to have touched everyone. That was obvious, but just what caused it Marcus couldn't figure out. It wasn't like they were running in any one direction, or like there was anything causing the chaos other than themselves.

Watching the cyclist weave away, Marcus realized another strange thing. "How come there are no jokers?"

"In cities," Olena said, eyes scanning the crowd, "they are not welcome."

A mother shouldered past them, crying baby clutched to her chest and an older child dragged behind her. The child, seeing Marcus, went wild-eyed and began crying. Olena caught the woman by the arm and spoke a rapid barrage of Russian words that meant nothing to Marcus. The woman tried to pull away, but Olena pleaded. Reluctantly, the woman answered, speaking even faster than Olena. She yanked her arm away and strode off, her baby crying all the louder.

"What did she say?" Marcus asked.

"Nothing that makes sense," Olena said. "She said the police are killing people. That Allah has turned his hand and—"

A car slammed into a lamppost beside them. The driver's head smashed against the windshield, cracking it and leaving the driver bloody and unconscious.

"Jesus!" Marcus cried. "What's going on?"

Olena finished her sentence, "—we are to be tested." She looked at Marcus for the first time since they'd entered the chaos. "Marcus, you look horrible. You're paling. I didn't know you could, but . . . You've lost too much blood."

"Don't start talking about the hospital again."

She exhaled. "We need to find someplace where they will help you. Away from here. We need to find it fast." She glanced around, lips pressed together in thought. Her gaze settled on a truck that had just pulled onto the street. "I'll be right back."

"What? Where you going?" Marcus asked.

Pulling the Glock from her belt, Olena stepped into the street, heading toward the truck.

Just how in the hell, Detective Francis Xavier Black asked himself, did he come to find himself in an elevator on the fourth floor of a Kazakh hospital while a cold breeze brushed his skinny ass exposed by his hospital gown?

Because someone stuck a gun in your face, and suggested you'd like to investigate the screaming.

The someone in question was one of the three thugs employed by the Russian crime boss Baba Yaga. Of course when you say "crime boss" the image of a wizened eighty-something-year-old woman with impossibly red hair didn't spring to mind. But once he'd looked in Baba Yaga's cold grey eyes Franny had no doubt about her ruthlessness or her resolve. She'd have her goons gun him down like a dog if he didn't comply.

Franny had been staring at his image in the bathroom mirror noting that his eyes seemed more bloodshot than blue, that he had two days'

growth of dark beard and his black hair formed greasy spikes. He was wondering when he'd be allowed to take a shower when a guy "no taller than
a lamppost, and no wider than a beer truck" had dragged him out of the
room. The fact the gorilla was wearing a two-thousand-dollar suit was off-
set by the fact he clearly wasn't a big fan of showers. The man's B.O. was
like a wave proceeding them down the hall.

In Baba Yaga's room there were two more goons, and a very well-dressed
man with a smooth expressionless face, manicured fingernails, a Rolex
flashing on his wrist, and sleek brown hair. Something about him made
Franny think of otters. Of the other goons one had a shaved head that
glittered under the fluorescent lights. The other sported a large ruby earring and a luxurious mustache. Franny started to say, *Hey, the seventies
called, they'd like their mustache back,* but didn't because Baba Yaga had
turned those dead eyes on him and scornfully called him a hero. Then the
screaming had started.

Baba Yaga's command had been short and succinct. "Go. Check it out.
Come back and tell me what you see."

Franny had tried to argue. "Send one of your damn bully boys."

"I'm not risking my guards and you caused this. Now go."

"If I caused this then you know what it should be . . ."

The old woman had nodded at the Baldy and Franny found himself
staring down the barrel of the guard's Sig Sauer.

"Okay, persuasive reason why I should go."

Franny had been dithering so long that the elevator doors started to
close. He threw up an arm to hold them back, and was forcibly reminded
that he had a recently sewn bullet wound in his side, and another in his
shoulder. The room seemed to be ballooning in front of him. He knew
he was pumped full of painkillers, but drugs alone couldn't explain the
creeping fear that was crawling up his spine and left his belly empty and
shaking.

Shouts and sobs were coming down the corridor. Franny shuffled off
the elevator, his paper slippers sussing and crackling on the linoleum. A
pair of security guards went past. They were muscling an older woman in
a nurse's uniform who was screaming abuse while she tried to claw at their
faces. Her face was a mask of rage, spittle formed white flecks on her lips,
and the front of her dress was spattered with blood.

Franny pressed himself against the wall. The screaming was still continuing. More voices, bellows of rage. "Fuck this," he whispered.

He was no longer under guard. He could just exit the hospital and find help. The absurdity of the plan soon presented itself. He didn't speak the language, didn't have any local money, or ID, and was dressed in a hospital gown. If he saw himself wandering around New York like this he'd arrest himself.

He forced himself back into motion. Heading toward the raised voices, the nexus of the uproar. Pressure tightened around Franny's skull and it felt like something was crawling slowly down his nerve fibers. A low grotesque humming seemed to fill the air. Anger at Captain Mendelberg back in New York who *hadn't fucking listened and wouldn't fucking help,* thoughts of Abby *constantly blowing him off even when he worked his ass off to help her.* His fucking partner *who left this pile of steaming shit on his desk and didn't help until he made a halfhearted offer when it was too fucking late.* The other cops at Fort Freak *who couldn't even give him one fucking little congratulation for making detective.* Jealous assholes, all of them . . .

What the fuck? He pushed aside the chaotic, angry thoughts, tried to focus. What had he come here for? Oh yeah. He continued down the hall and stepped into a room where doctors were frantically working on a man in a doctor's white coat who was lying on a gurney. A scalpel was embedded in his left eye, his face a mask of gore. A pair of nurses were hugging each other and sobbing. There was a babble of conversation in a language he didn't understand as several security guards seemed to be trying to interview the bystanders.

Several IV stands surrounded the bed, and tubes snaked down to— Franny recoiled. He had thought his years in Jokertown had prepared him for anything, but the figure in the bed was beyond grotesque. The arms and legs were twisted and skeletal, but the belly bulged like a woman on the verge of delivering. It was so bloated and distended that the gown couldn't hide it. It was also pulsing, shivers running across the skin, and there was the slow roil of deep purple and violent red beneath the surface as if something were swimming in the blood and viscera.

The thing had a mouth, but the lips were elongated, resembling the proboscis of a mosquito or anteater. Those rubbery lips were working like a blind baby seeking a tit. Grey stony growths shot through with gleaming red veins protruded from his cheeks and neck. The grating humming, like foil on gold filings, was emerging from that deformed mouth. There was a faint glint from beneath the wrinkled eyelids as if he was trying to wake.

The smell of blood, vomit, and fear-induced sweat overlaid the tang of disinfectants and bedpans. Franny memorized the scene as best he could, and then stumbled backward out of the room. He staggered down the hall. He passed an orderly leaning against the wall, his pants unzipped, dick in hand. He was energetically beating off while staring at a young nurse who was crying in the corner.

With each step away from the room the band around Franny's head loosened, and that maddening humming began to ease. He punched at the elevator button with increasing desperation. Finally he went to the stair- well. No matter how much it might hurt he had to get away. All the anger was gone. Only fear remained.

Mollie Steunenberg, still woozy from getting zapped with eight jillion volts right in her tits, slumped in the back of a squad car while the driver jab- bered on his radio in French. She didn't understand what he was saying, and she sure as hell didn't understand why the cops had tased her—they fucking *tased* her—just for swiping a few shitty earrings. Was that even legal? They could have given her a goddamned heart attack. Plus, the elec- trodes had pierced two little holes in her blouse. Right over her boobs, of all places, which now ached like they'd been set on fire. Fucking frog cops.

Oh, right, she remembered. *Gendarmes.* That's what they're called in France. Ffodor had taught her stuff like that. Which was how she also knew the streetlights glittering through the beaded rain on the car windows were the lights of the storied Champs-Élysées.

He'd also tried to teach her that a smash-and-grab was the province of thugs and petty criminals. And therefore beneath her. But she was faster than any nat thief, and she hadn't actually smashed anything. She, of all people, never had to do *that.* So it wasn't her fault she got caught. She'd explain it to Ffodor: what lousy luck that a cop car happened past at the moment she was reaching through—

She shook her head, clearing away cobwebs and uncomfortable thoughts, before testing the handcuffs again. The clink of a chain pressed cold metal against the small of her back. She could open an interdimen- sional doorway and leave right now, but then she'd go skidding out the other side with the same relative speed as the cops' car. Which, given her lack of a portal site conveniently located over a giant stack of pillows, would suck.

The car swung through a roundabout, leaning slightly on its suspension as it peeled away from the Champs-Élysées. The acceleration pushed Mollie away from the door. She toppled over like a sack of onions. Thanks to the Taser she had all the muscle tone of a jellyfish. The seat upholstery smelled like sweaty feet and stale cigarette smoke. Her wobbly stomach did a somersault. She tasted bile.

Given a pen or paperclip, she could pick the cuffs. She'd learned all sorts of things from Ffo—

Focus. Focus. Worst case, they'd stick her in a cell, and surely they'd have to take the cuffs off then. Worst case, she'd just have to be patient a little while. And then it'd be, *Au revoir, Frogs.*

They passed the Louvre, and then Mollie understood why the cops— gendarmes—were so trigger-happy with the Tasers. The glass pyramid, along with wide swaths of the surrounding buildings, was *still* under reconstruction years after some badass old-timey ace had practically leveled the place. Mollie didn't know the whole story there; she'd been busy at the time pinching a metric fuck-ton of gold from the treasury of a Central African dictatorship. Which is how she met . . .

She shook her head again, this time in frustrated anger. It was *also* how she'd met prissy Noel Matthews. Noel Fucking Matthews. He'd found her after her stint on TV, where her troubles had really started. Not least because that shitmuncher Jake Butler had cheated her off the show, but also because it was via *American Hero* that she got tangled up with Michael Douchebag Berman. Michael Grabby-Hands Berman. Michael Needle-Dick Berman.

By now she should have been living on easy street, but it never worked out that way because every single person she met turned out to be a flaming asshole.

Well, except maybe one.

Yellow halogen light and the silvery glow of a full moon kaleidoscoped through the rain-stippled windows when the car swung through another roundabout. Mollie watched the floor in the vague hope that a pen, paper clip, or other useful implement might slide conveniently from beneath the seat. No dice. She sighed. The residual tremors from the tasing had temporarily ruined her fine motor skills anyway. She couldn't pick the locks, nor could she break the chain.

Ffodor had insisted she could open portals within solid objects because it was no different from opening them on a wall or in midair. It was the closest they'd ever come to an argument. *Of course* it was different: air was invisible, and it moved. Her one attempt to visualize a portal inside something else had given her the worst headache of her life.

The handcuffs clinked. The second cop, the one in the passenger seat, Monsieur Electrocute-First-And-Ask-Questions-Never, shot a glare over his shoulder. It was a look of naked disappointment: they'd nabbed a short, slightly plump, twenty-two-year-old American with too many freckles to be cute and unnaturally coppery curls in blue jeans and blouse rather than a tall, leggy, teenaged heroin-chic Parisian runway model in a skirt that reached just below her pubes.

Mollie returned the glare. "Supermodels are all shrews and cokeheads, you know."

He said something to his partner. Everything sounded snide when you didn't speak the language.

The car swerved, pressing her face into the seat upholstery again. Her stomach lurched in response to a strong whiff of the foot stink. Mollie wormed upright into a sitting position before she upchucked all over herself. She resigned herself to watching a rain-soaked City of Light slide past the windows.

The car passed a fountain. She smiled.

Fine, she thought. *Let's do this the* really *easy way.*

Even with her brain half scrambled from the Taser it was easy as breathing. With barely a conscious thought, she opened a pair of twinned doorways: one atop the dashboard, and a much larger one in the fountain basin.

Cold water gushed into the car as though somebody had pointed a firehose through the vents. The frogs swore in unison—"*Merde!*" (even Mollie could understood that)—as the driver planted his foot on the brake. They skidded. The water, already over her knees, sloshed over the headrests. Mollie slammed her forehead against the Plexiglas divider. She closed her eyes, concentrating on holding her breath to feign unconsciousness.

The water kept coming. In seconds it was over her waist, but then it dropped as the befuddled cops bailed from the car. Mollie kept the doorways in place. Now the water gushing from the dash mostly poured out the open doors, but enough pooled in the backseat to pose a drowning hazard.

The hard part was maintaining the act while the gendarmes dragged her from the car like a sack of fertilizer. Her lungs were well and truly burning before the idiots realized they had to take the cuffs off before they could do CPR. Mollie abandoned the act as soon as the cuffs fell from her wrists. She leapt to her feet, stumbling a bit thanks to the lingering dizziness from the Taser and holding her breath.

"Thanks, morons," she said.

The driver barked at her. He didn't sound happy. His partner scrabbled at the Taser on his belt.

"Oh, yeah," said Mollie, "please try it again." He wouldn't catch her by surprise this time.

He aimed. She opened two new holes in space: one just past the end of his weapon, the other a couple feet lower. Between the darkness and the water dripping from his eyelashes he didn't notice the shimmer. He pulled the trigger, shrieked, and immediately collapsed into a quivering heap, having tased himself in the nuts.

Mollie made yet another pair of doorways. She flipped a double bird at the other cop as she leapt from a wet Paris night to the synchronized chaos of Shinjuku Station, Tokyo. She bowled into a salaryman with his nose buried in a manga featuring a cartoonishly buxom caricature of Curveball on the cover. He yelled at her. She put a portal under his feet and dumped the pervert in a smelly Venice canal. Then she sprinted through the crowd, snatching purses and billfolds along the way, leaving angry commuters in her wake. A transit cop tried to give chase but she leapt from the train platform and came to a soft landing on the sand of Cottesloe Beach, just outside Perth. Her cash dash had netted about twenty-nine thousand yen, or a little under three hundred bucks. Not great, but also not bad for ten seconds of work. She dumped the purses and wallets on the beach and stepped across the continent to a laneway just outside a Melbourne currency exchange. Five minutes after passing the fountain in Paris, she identified a suitable replacement blouse in a Sydney department store window. It was nicer than the one the gendarmes had ruined.

"Well?" Baba Yaga demanded when Franny returned to her hospital room. She might be old and frail, but the rap of command was in her voice.

Sucking in a breath, Franny gave a concise description as if he had been reporting to Maseryk or Mendelberg back at the precinct.

"Hmmm, perhaps you are not quite as stupid as I thought."

The old woman turned to the Otter and said something in what

sounded like Russian. The smooth-faced man pulled an incongruous evening gown out of the closet, helped the old woman out of bed and into
the bathroom. A few moments later they emerged. Baba Yaga was now
dressed. She wore the little slippers provided by the hospital rather than
the high heels that Franny could see in the closet.

All five of them headed for the door. It was clear they were blowing this
popsicle stand. Franny stood for a few moments reflecting on what he'd
seen on those fight videos. The unspeakable horror that had been unleashed on ordinary citizens by the woman who had just walked out.

"Yeah, fuck no," Franny muttered, and he went after them. It hurt to
run and he felt like a fool as he tried to hold the back of his gown together.
Baba Yaga and her thuggish entourage were at the front entrance.

"Hey! Hold it! You're under arrest!" People in the lobby were staring at
him. A woman behind a large desk stood and reached for the phone.

Baba Yaga ignored him. Franny gave up on modesty, pressed his arm
against the bandage on his side, and ran harder. There was a jostling crowd
on the sidewalk. Cops and Baba Yaga and her people. Franny assumed they
were responding to a 911 call. A limo was idling at the curb.

Franny grabbed one of the cops by the shoulder. "You've got to stop that
woman! She's a criminal. A kidnapper. A murderer." The officer frowned
and knocked Franny's hand off his shoulder. "Look, I'm a cop, too!"

Most of the officers had entered the hospital. A few were still outside.
They looked inquiringly at Baba Yaga and a stone sank into the pit of
Franny's gut. He recognized privilege and payoff when he saw it.

One of the cops said something. It sounded like a question. The Otter
leaned down and Baba Yaga whispered in his ear. He answered the cop,
who pulled out his baton.

"Ah shit. Really?"

The nightstick slammed into his shoulder. Franny spun away and the
next blow landed on the wound in his side. Pain pulsed through his body
and a burning light exploded behind his eyes.

Marcus could barely believe Olena had really stepped out into the street
to meet the oncoming truck. If he'd had the strength he would've grabbed
her. He didn't, though, and could only watch.

For a moment he was sure the truck was going to run her down. And then he was sure that she was going to shoot the driver. Neither happened. Instead, she walked right up to the moving vehicle, stepped onto the sideboard as it passed, and jabbed the pistol through the window. Marcus didn't hear what she said, but the gun made her pretty convincing. The truck stopped. Olena jumped down. The man climbed out, the Glock aimed at him the whole time. She made it look so easy.

She had turned her head, flicked the hair out of her face, and said, "It's probably better if I drive. Get in."

In the truck's bed, Marcus had asked her through the open window of the cabin just who she was. Her answer, "I'm Ukrainian girl," hardly explained it. Marcus was beginning to suspect that there was more to her than he imagined.

It embarrassed him that she'd gotten *him* out of this city, that she'd taken control. But it was a shallow level of embarrassment. He was relieved that it wasn't all on him. If it wasn't complicated enough, he was still ashamed of the things she'd seen him do in the arena. Ugly things. Murderous things. Some of that he'd done for her, but still . . . he didn't like the memories he had of it. He didn't recognize himself in them. He just saw a monster with blood on his hands and venom in his mouth.

Considering that, there was something about being nearly dead in the back of a truck stolen for him by a beautiful Ukrainian girl that seemed almost all right. Somebody cared, and if that was true there was still some hope left. If only he wasn't hurting so. Bleeding still, dizzy enough that he felt near to losing consciousness . . .

"Don't sleep, my hero," Olena's voice said, rousing him. "Stay awake, okay? Sleep later."

Marcus opened his eyes. The glare of the world flashed to life again. The valley floor stretched out below them, looking dry and scraggly as it dropped down toward Talas. Around them, the foothills of the mountains rose into a series of ridges, one piled on top of the other, growing in height. That mountain? It was there, miles away, towering above a desolate, foreign landscape like nothing he'd ever seen.

Olena stood behind the truck, holding up a jar of water for him. A little distance away a man, a woman, and several small children stood outside the door of a modest house, staring. At their feet sat the crates of cigarettes that Olena had said she was going to trade for clothes. Apparently, the barter had worked.

She had exchanged her slinky dress for a local getup. A colorful but shapeless sort of jacket, a woolen skirt so long it brushed the ground, and a hat into which her short hair disappeared entirely. He was going to miss the little red number, and she wasn't exactly going to pass for a local with her angelic features and high cheekbones and crystal blue eyes. But from a distance she looked the part. Kinda.

He tried to cover up the pain of reaching for the jar by smiling. The effort of it, and of talking, was almost more than he could manage. "I like the look," he said. "Doesn't . . ." He exhaled, wondering where his breath had gone. "Doesn't do you justice, but that's probably a good thing."

"You think I'm not so pretty now," she said.

"God, no, I don't think that," Marcus said.

She brushed him off with a motion of her head. "Anyway, now we are hidden."

He wanted to ask her how she could think a black guy with a twenty-foot striped snake tail could possibly be hidden anyplace, much less in rural Kazakh-wherever-they-were. But he didn't. He didn't really want to ask her. He wasn't sure what to make of the fact that she seemed to continue not to see him as deformed. He certainly didn't want it to end, though. He said, "You look great. Just like a local."

"I know where to go now." She gestured toward the watching family, and then waved at them. "They told me about a village. A good place for us."

She hefted a large metal gasoline can into the bed and then climbed back up into the cab. She turned over the engine and pulled the truck back onto the long, narrow stretch of dusty tarmac that had taken them out of the city. They kept on rising into the mountains.

"What's good about this place?" Marcus asked through the window.

"You'll see," she said.

Barbara's sleep was restless. A dream—a nightmare, truthfully—returned, one that she'd had several times when she was younger but which hadn't bothered her for many years now, a memory that inevitably morphed into a night terror.

She was barely twelve when her mother died.

As the only child without any other parent or siblings, she was acting as the *shomeret* for her mother, sitting watch in the funeral home. Relatives and friends remained with her that night as she sat near her mother's wooden coffin. Her mother had died only that afternoon: a suicide bombing in Shuk HaCarmel Market in Tel Aviv. The funeral would take place the next day.

The rabbi had come and intoned the ritual words: *"Barukh atah Adonai Eloheinu melekh ha'olam dayan ha'emet"* and torn the Kria, ripping the left side of her blouse.

"Such a terrible loss, a terrible day. How are you holding up, my child?" the rabbi had asked her, his eyes sad and kind. She could only shake her head.

"I don't understand," Barbara answered, and her voice broke with the sobs that had wracked her on and off ever since the news had come. "The police . . . they said that Mom told them before she died that she saw this young man walking into the market looking like he was sick or frightened, all sweating and pale, that she called out to him to ask him if he needed help. He only shouted back to her in Arabic and waved his hands at her, but Mom doesn't speak Arabic and she didn't know what he was saying. He ran deeper into the market, and she followed him, and that's . . ." She swallowed hard. The grief in her mouth tasted like ashes and tears. "That's when the boy, or someone else, set off the vest. Rabbi, maybe he was telling Mom to stay away. Maybe he was warning her, but she couldn't understand . . ."

"None of us can understand a tragedy like this," the rabbi told her, but his words and the arm he put around her shoulders were little comfort to her. She kept replaying the scene in her mind: her mother following the boy, wanting to help him, the light and heat and shattering concussion of the explosion, her mother falling amid the debris and screams . . .

In the nightmare memory of that night, she approached the coffin. She would be suddenly alone: the rabbi gone, her relatives and family friends all vanished. There was only the room and the coffin. She saw the lid lifting, her mother's blood-streaked hand and arm shoving it upward. Barbara could only stare, frozen, unable to move. As the lid was pushed back with a hollow thud, her mother's corpse slowly sat up. Her face turned toward Barbara: a visage of raw horror, strips of flesh falling away from a shattered skull, an eye dangling from its socket, half of her jaw gone and her tongue lolling down like a fat grey worm . . .

But this night, in Machu Picchu, the nightmare shifted and changed. It wasn't her mother's arm that lifted the coffin lid, nor her mother's body that appeared. The arm was Klaus's, clad in ghost armor that looked to have been cracked and broken. It was Klaus's shattered and ruined corpse rising up in the coffin, turning slowly to stare at her with its moldering, one-eyed face.

Klaus. Not her mother.

In the dream, Barbara screamed, as Klaus's body started to pull itself from the coffin that held it; as she found herself suddenly awake under the covers, shivering and terrified at the dream's lingering memory.

"What's the matter?" Barbara heard Klaus ask sleepily from his side of the bed.

She tried to calm her racing heart. "Nothing," she told him. "Just a dream, is all. Go back to sleep."

Klaus grunted. She felt him turn in the bed.

She'd been barely twelve when her mother died . . .

The nightmare of seeing the ravaged, shattered body of her mother rising from the coffin would haunt her teenage years. In reality, at the funeral the following morning as the coffin was lowered into the earth, Barbara's card would turn. As Barbara cried out in pain and anguish and fright, the chanting of the rabbi became nothing more than nonsense syllables, and frightened onlookers could only shout incomprehensible questions to the sky.

None of them could any longer understand the other. Like her mother and the young man in the market . . .

For long minutes, Barbara stared into the darkness of the ceiling above her, pondering what this altered dream meant, afraid for some reason that this was some portent, some warning. She wrestled with herself, insisting that to think such a thing was irrational and ridiculous, but the feeling persisted even under the logic.

When sleep—blessedly dreamless this time—finally came to her again, it was followed far too soon by the stern beeping of her phone's morning alarm.

The first thing Franny saw were large feet encased in heavy steel-toed shoes. His eyes felt gummy and his mouth tasted of blood. He had apparently bitten his tongue. Slowly he identified the noise he heard as a car engine.

He was on the floor of the limo wedged between the facing seats. They went over a bump and Franny gasped in pain. He looked up. Baldy, Stache, and B.O. were seated on the jump seat.

A hand twisted in his hair and he was rolled over to face Baba Yaga. His gown was twisted and hiked up over his hips. Bad enough to be in the custody of a psychopath but having his dick and balls exposed somehow made it even worse.

She tapped a forefinger against her lips and studied him. "You are a great deal of trouble," she said.

"So why bring me?"

"You might prove useful. If you aren't I will kill you. Clear?"

"Crystal."

They continued to drive. The Otter was murmuring into a cell phone. Everyone else was silent. Franny cleared his throat. "So, where are we going?"

"Shut up."

Ten minutes later he tried again. "May I get on a seat?"

"No." Baba Yaga was a woman of few words.

Eventually they came to a stop and Franny was pulled out of the car. He groaned as pain flared in his side and his shoulder. They were back at the casino. Not a place he'd ever wanted to see again.

Franny suggested they leave him in the car with the Otter, but Baba Yaga didn't seem to be the trusting sort. Baldy had shoved a gun in his back (it was very cold against his bare skin), and Franny followed the old lady into the casino. It was a mess. Overturned roulette tables, chips scattered across the floor, the garish colors clashing against the paisley of the expensive carpet. The faces on the strewn cards looked surprised as they trod across them. The blood also didn't look all that good on the carpet.

There were a couple of evidence techs going about their business. They straightened, and gave Baba Yaga respectful nods as she moved past them. Clearly the old criminal owned the cops in Talas. As if being beat like a drum on Baba Yaga's say-so hadn't been enough of a hint, Franny thought.

A skinny man dressed in a Gandhi-like diaper hurried through a door off the casino floor. The lights shone on the viscous slime that coated his body, and gleamed on his shaved head. A pungent odor had Franny's eyes watering. It was the joker Vaporlock, aka Sam Palmer, a well-known figure around Jokertown, a pathetic loser known to the cops as a small-time

thief, and a traitor to his fellow jokers. Based on Wally Gunderson's statement Vaporlock had helped kidnap jokers for Baba Yaga's fight club. That
accusation was now proved.

"Shit, Baba Yaga . . . ma'am. We thought you were dead. I mean, man,
were we *worried* when that big-ass snake whacked you. Some of the guys
believed that. But not me. I knew you'd be back. Nobody can take you
down." The words emerged tight and fast.

Baba Yaga didn't actually address Vaporlock. Instead she turned to Baldy
and said simply, "Bring him."

They started across the casino floor with Vaporlock twitching and
bouncing along next to the old woman. "So what's the plan, ma'am? We
gettin' out of here? Some of the guys have gone nuts to even think about
challenging you." Baba Yaga ignored him.

There were still bodies sprawled around slot machines and under tables.
Franny reflected that being dead in a tux didn't add any more dignity to
that state. Some of the dead sported bullet wounds. Others were just dead.
Probably victims of IBT's poisonous tongue.

Contemplating tuxedos brought to the fore Franny's most pressing concern. "Hey. I need some clothes," he said.

"We are not a haberdashery," Baba Yaga said.

Franny pointed at a dead man. "He's not using them. Can we take a
couple of minutes?"

Baba Yaga contemplated him in his open-backed hospital gown and
the tattered slippers on his bare feet. Something almost like a tiny smile
quirked her withered lips. "Fine."

He found a man who was roughly his size, and stripped him out of his
coat, shirt, trousers, socks, and shoes. Franny figured he'd go commando.
Wearing a dead man's underwear was a bridge too far.

"Bathroom?" Franny asked.

Baba Yaga didn't bother to answer. Just gave him a look. Franny turned
his back and dressed. The pants were too big and the shirt too tight, but
he felt far less vulnerable. He had barely tied the shoes, a painful operation because bending over pulled at the stitches in his side, when Baba Yaga
started moving again. A not-too-gentle push from B.O. propelled Franny
back into motion.

Vaporlock, having given up on any conversation with Baba Yaga,
dropped back to walk next to Franny. "Hey, I recognize you. You're a cop,

right? At Fort Freak?" Franny nodded. "So, if I help you out you'd put in a good word for me, right?"

"You're not very bright, are you?" Franny said softly.

"Huh?"

"You might want to rethink talking about cutting a deal with me while you're walking with *her*."

"Uh." Vaporlock raised his voice. "I meant only if she doesn't need me. I'm totally with her unless she wants me to leave—"

"Sam." Vaporlock looked up at Franny. "Stop digging," he said softly.

They went through another door at the back of the casino and up a staircase. The second floor over this wing of the building was living quarters. Franny didn't think much of the decor. It was cluttered with furniture in competing styles. Leather-covered armchair next to a Louis XIV chair with incongruous leather upholstery. Fringed-edged ottomans, and numerous knickknack tables.

Baba Yaga, trailed by two of the guards, went into the bedroom. A string of what were clearly expletives erupted from the bedroom. Franny went to the door to look. Baba Yaga was staring at an enormous jewelry case on the dresser. It was conspicuously empty.

She brushed past him, hurrying back into the living room. A nod to one of the goons and he threw back the edge of the oriental carpet to reveal a floor safe. She knelt and twisted the dial. Franny sensed the goon's eyes on him, and he made an obvious show of looking the other way. All this damn furniture crammed into such a small space . . .

"*She . . . changes people. And not in a good way. We're talking about furniture.*"

The words of the disgraced and now arrested Hollywood producer Michael Berman came floating back. Franny looked more closely at a large armchair. That didn't look like normal leather. He moved so he could see the front of the chair. The seat held a face. A terrified, openmouthed face. The feet of the chair appeared to be clawed hands, and human feet with the toes tightly clenched. Franny reeled back from the grotesque sight.

A chuckle like dried leaves across concrete. Baba Yaga was stuffing handfuls of various kinds of currency, gem-encrusted jewelry, and gold coins into a leather satchel, but her gaze was fixed on him. "If I kill you, boy, you won't die easy."

She's enjoying my disgust and distress, Franny realized. He schooled his features and gave a shrug. "Then I sure hope you just shoot me. Sucks to admit it, but I'm kinda getting used to it."

Franny tried not to look at the furniture, but it was like trying not to think about elephants. Clearly Baba Yaga was a wild card. He wondered how she did it. His desperately wandering gaze fell on Vaporlock. His eyes were flicking from the satchel to the three goons to the door of the living quarters. Franny tensed and felt the pull in his side and shoulder.

Baba Yaga was pulling out a stack of passports held by a rubber band. Before she could place them in her bag Vaporlock swept a hand across his chest and jammed the slick, smelly mess into the face of Baldy, who stood closest to Baba Yaga. As the man gagged and slumped Vaporlock grabbed his pistol and fired wildly at Baba Yaga while reaching for the satchel with his free hand.

Franny was in motion long before the shot. He knew better than to try to grab the slippery ace. Instead he snatched a heavy metal and enamel icon off the desk, and slammed the heavy framed edge down on Vaporlock's forearm. The shot went wild, slamming into a nearby sofa. Instead of pale stuffing the bullet sent up a cloud of red- and flesh-colored particles.

Baba Yaga's mouth was working, the wrinkled cheeks becoming even more sunken. Vaporlock looked terrified and he whirled and ran. A gob of spit hit the floor behind his heels, but he was through the door and slammed it shut.

Franny started to move toward the door. He was still clutching the icon. Baba Yaga's command cut the air.

"Stop!"

"I want to arrest that asshole."

"Always the noble hero," the old woman said and gave a nod toward the icon. Franny looked down and for the first time noticed the figures. It was St. George slaying a dragon. "Well, I want to kill him," Baba Yaga said in a prosaic tone. "But I think we're both doomed to disappointment."

There were male voices in the hall outside the living quarters. Franny couldn't distinguish what they were saying, but Vaporlock's voice came through shrill and angry. "Yeah, the bitch is in there." More murmuring. "Two. I took down one guy. Oh and a hurt cop. Don't worry. I heard about him back in New York. He's a pussy."

Franny pushed aside his irritation and focused on the more immediate problem. "Who are they? Do you know?" Franny asked.

"Crows come to pick at the corpse," she answered. She was placing a stack of old-style cassette tapes into the satchel.

"Very poetic, but that doesn't tell me much."

"Competitors who see their opportunity. Well, they'll be ruling in hell very soon." She said something to Stache and B.O., who were still on their feet, and they took up positions to either side of the door.

"I'm going to be very disappointed in you if you don't have an alternate way out of this joint," Franny snapped at her.

She gave him that cold, secretive smile again. "We cannot simply run before them. They must be forced to pull back and lick their wounds."

"You give me a gun and maybe I can help."

"I give you a gun and maybe you use it on me."

"As I recall I just saved you from a bullet. Also you're my ticket out of here."

Hand signals were being exchanged by the guards. One of them snapped off a shot and someone screamed. A hail of bullets came at the defenders. B.O. went down. The day was just getting better and better, Franny reflected.

Baba Yaga frowned, scuttled forward, and grabbed the pistol that Vaporlock had dropped. She returned to Franny's side, and slapped the gun into his hand. She shoved him toward the door. It hurt because it was his wounded shoulder.

"Make them regret the effort."

Franny duck-walked to the door. It pulled the stitches in his side and hurt like hell. He shook his head trying to concentrate. He risked a quick glance around the doorjamb. Big men in cheap suits with guns. A lot like Baba Yaga's big men in cheap suits with guns.

Franny's brief look had drawn another volley. He and Stache exchanged glances, then leaned out and shot down the hall, then jerked back into cover. The kick from the pistol hurt his wounds, and Franny had to take a few seconds to just breathe.

"Not sure I hit anything," he said aloud. "Not sure I want to." Killing the joker El Monstro was a fresh and horrifying memory. Stache gave him an amused look. "Okay, so you do speak English. Asshole," he added, but he said that under his breath.

There was a quick conversation between Stache and Baba Yaga. Stache started blasting down the hall. Franny joined in. He had a brief glimpse of Vaporlock at the back of the pack. The slide ratcheted back; he was out of ammo. He crawled to the body of B.O., and patted at the pockets looking for a reload. The gunfire slowed. Baba Yaga swung open a panel in the wall.

She snapped out something in Russian and Stache fell back. He grabbed Baldy off the floor, threw Baldy over his shoulder in a fireman's carry, and darted to the opening through which Baba Yaga had already vanished. Franny realized that whether he followed or not was going to be entirely up to him. He dropped the useless pistol, gritted his teeth against the pain, got to his feet, and sprinted after them.

His ears were ringing from the gunfire so he had no idea if their attackers were entering the room. Begrudging even the small second a glance behind might cost him, Franny leaned forward, and was through the panel. It was dark so he missed the steep staircase. He lost his footing and went tumbling headlong down the steps.

Playing hockey through grade school and high school had taught him how to fall, and Stache, acting more out of self-preservation than any kindness, grabbed him by the waistband and stopped the headlong plunge. Yanked to his feet Franny felt a warm trickle running down his side. Fortunately fear and adrenaline masked any pain from his torn stitches.

Through another door and he found himself back in the gladiator quarters where this nightmare had begun only the day before. He had a sudden memory of the handcuff swinging loose on his wrist, Mollie Steunenberg's mocking smile and upthrust middle finger. The bitch had abandoned him. Maybe if he'd treated her better? Or scared her more? He pushed aside the regrets and second thoughts. He'd find some way to get home and when he did Ms. Steunenberg was going to face a judge.

The bodies of Stuntman and El Monstro lay on the floor. There was a sweetish scent of flesh starting to decompose. Added to that was the stench of the rotting food on the buffet. The smell of death and corruption. It seemed the perfect analogy for what had formed the foundation of Baba Yaga's kingdom. Franny choked back bile.

Baba Yaga grabbed a napkin off the buffet table and wiped Vaporlock's ooze off Baldy's face. She then threw a pitcher of water in his face and started slapping him. The heavy jeweled rings cut his face. Baldy groaned and came around. There was a tense conversation in Russian. Baldy nodded and dabbed at his bleeding cheeks with his tie. He clambered to his feet and they were back in motion again.

Franny forced himself to look at Stuntman's face as he passed. One side was unmarred. On the other his eye hung grotesquely on his shattered cheek and his skull was depressed.

I'll see you home. I promise.

He fought down the urge to kick El Monstro's body. If not for the joker he and Jamal would be back in New York safe, drinking, and maybe not fired by the NYPD and SCARE.

Franny followed the old woman and her two guards down a hallway to a heavy metal door. She unlocked it and they stepped out into a garage. There was a van with New York plates parked in the docking area.

There were also four thugs waiting for them. Gunfire echoed off the concrete. Baba Yaga's guards were controlled and icy as they double-tapped, firing at the mob competitors, but there was enough lead flying that some of it found its mark. Baldy went down again and this time it didn't look like he was going to get up.

Franny was hugging the concrete. Baba Yaga's slippered feet went past his face. He looked up in time to see Stache shoot one of the two remaining attackers. The other received a spray of spit from Baba Yaga right in the face. He began to scream, clawing at his eyes. Then his head stretched, widening and elongating. His eyeballs popped from their sockets and burst, blood and intraocular fluid running down his deformed face. His arms jerked behind his head, and fused together while his legs did the same. His screams were punctuated by the sharp crack of breaking bones. His body stretched and widened until he was a tall rectangle. The blood and fluid from the burst eyeballs now stained the face of a clock.

Franny scrambled back toward the door. This was a fucking nightmare—Jamal's death, the violence at the hospital, and now this. Could he really stay in the company of this murderous old bitch? Baba Yaga and Stache walked past the dying man. He must have still had vocal chords because inhuman cries were emanating from the cutout moon that decorated the face of the clock. As she passed she put a hand against the deformed and suffering figure and shoved. He went over with a crash as the transformation concluded.

She looked back at Franny, who was huddled against the door to the casino. "Hurry up! And pick up some of these guns. You need to be useful now."

He wanted to refuse, but he was afraid how the old monster would react. She had decided she needed him. Better not to antagonize her. Franny darted past the transformed man. He didn't want to look but couldn't help himself. Please God, let the poor bastard be dead, he thought, then the long cabinet gave one final jerk, violent enough that it rolled onto its side.

He gathered up a couple of pistols and a small submachine gun. Stache was doing the same. They all piled into the van. Franny was surprised when Baba Yaga took the wheel. She threw the van into reverse and they went roaring up the ramp and out onto the street just as more mobsters erupted through the doors of the casino. Bullets wangled off the hood of the van. The guard leaned out and returned fire. Franny followed suit. The old lady hit the brake and spun the wheel, sending them into a violent spin. She righted the van, and accelerated away from the casino. As they roared past the limo he saw the windows were shot out, and the Otter had half his head missing. He was suddenly glad he hadn't been left in the car.

They went weaving through the traffic at speeds approaching seventy miles an hour. Franny wondered where she had learned to drive like this. Now that the immediate danger was past Franny felt that heat and trembling in his muscles that signaled the end of the adrenaline overload under which he'd been operating. Which meant he was suddenly very aware of his injuries. His shoulder was throbbing in time to his heartbeat and the wound in his side was a flare of agony.

He also had time to reflect that he was riding in a van that had carried kidnapped jokers to Baba Yaga's not-so-little-house-of-horrors. So why had she set up the fight club? Now that he had met the woman it was clear she was coldly practical. There couldn't have been enough money in bets to make it worth the risk. So why do it? He decided to just ask her.

She glanced over at him. "So now you think to ask. After you have come in and broken all the dishes. You're a fool, boy. You think you're a hero, but you may have destroyed the world. I hope it was worth it."

"What are you fucking talking about?"

"You'll see. Soon the whole world will see. Can it be stopped? Well, we'll see about that, too."

They were passing through the center of the city. They crossed a plaza with an equestrian statue in its center. Off to the left Franny saw the outline of the hospital etched against the setting sun. Sirens were converging from all over the city. A couple of police cars, lights flashing, barreled past them. Down a side street Franny saw steel barricades being set across the street by Kazakh policemen.

"So fast. I did not think it would start to happen this fast," Baba Yaga said softly to herself. "I think we will take a longer, slower, safer route to the airport."

She took them in a tight U-turn that had other cars blaring their horns at them. A few more sudden turns took them away from the city center. Franny sat tensely erect, a pistol clutched tightly in his hand. Periodically he had to switch off hands so he could wipe the nervous sweat from his palms on the fabric of his pants. Stache was whistling tunelessly in the backseat. Baba Yaga's lined face was expressionless, watching the road. Franny wondered what thoughts were whirling behind that wrinkled mask.

Michelle and Adesina dashed into the graffiti-covered subway car just as the doors were closing. Michelle grabbed two empty seats and they sat down. The car didn't smell like urine today—an improvement from yesterday's trip—and the hard blue molded seats were actually clean.

Michelle sighed with relief when she saw no one recognized her. Her baseball cap concealed her long platinum hair, and the oversized Ray•Bans had done the rest. Dressed down in jeans and a T, she looked like every other aspiring model in town.

"Mom," Adesina said, plucking Michelle's T-shirt with her claw. Adesina was the size of a Jack Russell terrier. Her body looked like a butterfly, complete with iridescent wings. Her face was that of a little girl.

"You said I could wear lip gloss to school." She gave Michelle her very best big-brown-eyes momma-please look. Under normal circumstances, this ploy would have worked. But Michelle was working on setting boundaries.

"You're right," Michelle replied, shifting her Prada hobo bag on her lap. "You can't wear makeup until you're thirteen." That sounded very mom-like to Michelle.

"You wore makeup when you were my age," Adesina said, using her trump card. *Oh, you little stinker,* Michelle thought.

"When I was your age I wore makeup because modeling was my job," Michelle replied tersely. "And it still is. Stop using that as an argument. It's not going to work."

Adesina pouted. "You're mean."

Michelle couldn't help but smile. Even pouty, her daughter was adorable.

They came to the next stop, and two men wearing Knicks T-shirts and

jeans got into the car. Despite there being seats still open, they made a
beeline to Michelle and Adesina. *Great,* Michelle thought. *Just great.*

"That your freak?" one of them said, gesturing with his thumb at
Adesina as the car started moving. A wave of crappy, overbearing cologne
flowed off of him.

Michelle didn't have to look at Adesina to know she was tearing up.
She reached over and touched Adesina's hair to comfort her. They'd gone
to the hairdresser and had it done up in cornrows. She looked beautiful.
How could anyone look at Adesina and see anything other than a sweet
little girl?

"Hey, do I know you?" the other man said. He didn't give off quite the
full-blown asshole vibe his friend did, but he was obviously in training.
"You seem really familiar. Did I ever fuck you?"

Wow, dude, she thought. *Big mistake.*

"First," she said calmly, and for anyone who knew her, too calmly. "Stop
making ugly remarks about my daughter. Second, do you kiss your mother
with that mouth? Third, you're boring me and embarrassing yourself. Also,
you really don't want to make me mad."

Both of the creeps burst out laughing. "Ooooo, she's so tough," the
overscented one said. He leaned in close, trying to intimidate her. It was
adorably stupid. She smiled coldly. He looked confused.

She glanced at his friend, who by now was staring at her as recognition dawned and he began backing away. "I think you'll remember me
in just a second," she said as she stood up. Her purse fell to the floor.

Then she let a bubble form and it floated above her hand. It wasn't one
that would explode, much as she wanted to let it. But it would hit him
heavy and hard as a cannonball.

Before he could react, she hip-checked too-much-cologne dude into the
center of the aisle. At six feet tall, she had about four inches on him and
was heavier than she looked. She let the bubble go. It caught him in the
gut and threw him off his feet. He hit the floor hard and slid backward five
or six feet. The other passengers lifted their feet as he slid by, then went
back to their tablets and phones.

She turned to his companion, her smile icy. "You remember me now?"
she asked, another bubble forming in her hand. "Or do I need to remind
you, too?"

The man held up his hands. "I'm very sorry, Miss Bubbles," he said.
"We were just trying to have some fun."

The bubble was the size of a baseball and getting denser by the moment. She wanted to let it go. She fairly ached to do it. "It's fun to be mean to children and say horrible things about them?" Michelle said, the anger making her voice more of a growl. "It's fun to bully and threaten women on the subway? You have an interesting idea of fun." She leaned toward him. "Do you know what I think is fun?" The bubble floated out of her hand, hovering there like a promise. And it itched and burned to be released. "Bubbling someone. Particularly punks. There's nothing like it." The second man paled, then staggered away from her. Michelle left the bubble floating between them. Until she decided what she wanted it to do, it was just a pretty ornament.

The car slowed and stopped at Michelle's exit. Adesina tugged on Michelle's jeans and held up her front legs. Michelle retrieved her purse from the floor, then picked up Adesina and walked to the open doors. The other passengers stood, but waited as she walked by, leaving her a clear exit. She turned and let the bubble pop. "You boys knock this crap off," she said. "You never know who you might run into. Also, manners."

She stood at the open doors and the rest of the passengers exited, flowing like a river around her.

Michelle stepped out of the car, and Adesina stuck out her tongue at the men as the doors slid shut.

The Midnight Angel hurried up the front steps of the Bleecker Towers, a Jokertown hotel that lately she'd become all too familiar with. She compressed her lips tightly in a peevish expression accentuated by a disapproving frown.

The usual desk clerk stood behind the reception counter. He was neatly dressed as always and was rather handsome for a Cyclops. The hotel, with outdated but clean and well-cared-for carpets and furnishings, was located on the edge of Jokertown. Most employees and guests were jokers of middle-class means, and hotel management tried hard to project a friendly, safe, and stolidly respectable atmosphere. They mostly succeeded, but then, the Angel reflected, this was Jokertown, where things could turn in a second and often did.

She caught his eye and he nodded deferentially.

"Is he in?" she asked, making no attempt to keep the exasperation out of her voice.

"I don't know, ma'am." The clerk knew she was talking about Jamal Norwood through previous interactions. "I haven't seen Mr. Norwood go out today, but then I've been away from the desk several times."

She hurried past, heading for the staircase that led to upper-floor rooms, her exasperation tinged with worry. *Maybe he's too sick to make the appointment,* she thought to herself. *And too stubborn to call for help.*

Norwood was a member of the team of SCARE agents the Angel ran, but lately things hadn't been going well for him. His power of invulnerability to damn near everything had been failing, making him weak and lethargic after physical encounters. It had gotten so bad that currently he was on medical leave and being treated at the Jokertown Clinic by Dr. Finn—so far to no avail. SCARE had arranged for several out-of-state specialists to consult on his case, and Jamal hadn't shown up for that appointment.

The Angel took the stairs at an effortless jog—it was her policy to get her exercise in everyday activities rather than waste time at a gym—worrying about her subordinate as she went up the five flights.

Norwood was brash—he'd hung her with the nickname of She Who Must Be Obeyed—borderline insubordinate, far too stubborn, and all too unwilling to ask for help. The Angel had grown up in the South, and she knew the difficulties a strong, intelligent black man trying to make a place for himself in the world had even today, so she was willing to cut him some slack. She allowed him his stubbornness and petty rebelliousness. In a sense Norwood reminded him of her husband. Loving and living with Billy Ray for a decade, she'd experienced many manifestations of both those traits over the years. She didn't, and never could, have children and although Norwood was only a few years younger than she, the Angel felt motherly toward him. Or at least big-sisterly.

She reached his floor, still breathing easily after her upstairs jog, went down the hall, and stood before his door. She raised a hand to knock, but something stopped her.

A feeling ran down her spine like the tickling of spider legs skittering on bare skin. The wild card virus hadn't given her precognition, but the decade she'd spent as a SCARE agent beside Ray had honed her senses to an almost supernatural sharpness. It had also taught her to trust her instincts, which now were whispering urgent warnings in her ears.

She paused at the door and listened. Initially it was quiet inside, but there came a brief murmur of low voices and then again silence. She frowned, staring at the hotel-room door. The Angel was not a subtle person. She felt a tiny pinch of guilt, knowing that Billy would moan when SCARE got the bill for this—they were always seriously underfunded—but she had to do what she thought was right. And the tickling feeling in her spine and the haunting whispers in her ears were telling her that this was right.

"Save my soul from evil, Lord, and heal this warrior's heart," she murmured. Her four-foot-long, flaming cross-hilted broadsword appeared in her leather-gauntleted hands and she plowed through the door, yanking it from its frame, shattering its wooden panels, and sending pieces flying before her into the room beyond.

"Freeze, Stunt—Jesus Christ!" a foreign-accented voice shouted. The empty bed and the aborted command that had come from one of the two men standing across the room both told her that Jamal wasn't present, though plainly expected.

They gaped at her, momentarily caught mid-draw. She knew that she had only a fraction of a second before they'd shoot. Her sudden appearance had disconcerted them, as had the flying pieces of shattered debris they were ducking. They raised their arms to shield their faces. The Angel knew the only thing to do was disconcert them further.

She cocked her arm and threw her blade sideways. It helicoptered across the room like a flashing scythe and as it left her hand the sprinkler system in the ceiling kicked in. The fire alarm hooted, adding to the chaos. Even more astonishing, at least to the ambushers, the flames dancing on the sword's blade were unaffected by the water spraying upon them. The Angel was not surprised. Like the sword itself, the flames were unnatural. Both were manifestations of the grace granted her by God and like her righteous anger neither could be quenched, broken, or even impeded by anything physical.

She followed the whirling blade, not breaking stride as she stooped low and in passing a desk single-handedly grabbed it by a leg and bore down upon the two men, waving the furniture over her head like an unwieldy club.

The men both seemed to be nats, but were as mismatched physically as a comedy team. One was short and round, the other tall and skinny. The skinny one was an inch or two taller than the Angel. The short, fat guy had long blond hair that was slicked back even before being soaked by the ceiling sprinkler, and was pulled into a lank ponytail.

Their pistols momentarily forgotten, both were ducking and cringing. They fell sideways to avoid the whirling blade that was exuding clouds of steam as the sprinklers pattered down upon it. The flames might not have been real, but they were as hot as hell and the blade was sharp as a serpent's tooth as it chunked solidly into the wall near them, neatly slicing off the tip of the fat man's ponytail as he fell on his ass trying to get out of the way.

The fat one fell to the Angel's left, the sword vibrating in the wall and impeding her access to him, so she swatted the skinny one with the desk as he desperately tried to bring his pistol into line. He got off a shot, but the bullet flew over the Angel's head as her ungainly club smashed into him on his head and torso. It was only cheap hotel furniture and it shattered as it drove him down to the floor, but it was more solid than he was. He had time for a single scream that segued into a choking gurgle as it passed his lips.

The Angel dropped the desk leg and pulled her steaming sword out of the wall. She slashed at the fat one, but he wanted no more of her. He vanished, sinking through the hotel-room floor faster than a boulder through water. He left no trace of his passing, except for a single gasped word.

"Gospody!"

The Angel sat down on the edge of the adjacent bed, sighed, and said automatically, "Don't blaspheme."

She glanced over at the skinny guy. He was still there and apparently alive and conscious. His arms and legs were moving feebly as he lay on the floor among the wreckage of the desk. She slipped the tip of her sword under the largest piece of debris and flipped it off him. His eyes were half closed. He was bleeding from his mouth and a nose that had once been rather sharp and prominent, but was now smashed flat. His gun lay on the floor by his side. On his chest, among the remains of the shattered desk, lay a closed laptop.

The Angel's eyes gleamed. "Jamal's computer," she said. It had been in a desk drawer that now also lay splintered on the man's chest.

She took her hands from the sword hilt and the blade disappeared. She arose from the bed, knelt down before her feebly groaning prisoner, and picked up his gun. She glanced at it. She had no idea what kind it was. She didn't like guns. She ejected the clip, checked the chamber (Billy had taught her how to do this; he didn't like guns either, but he used them if he had to), and she tossed the weapon onto the bed.

The man groaned. The Angel eyed him grimly. He and his fat partner must have been waiting for Jamal to return. Waiting to kill him. She didn't like hit men, either.

"Shut up."

The man fell silent. She took the laptop off his chest. She had one just like it. Government issued.

The Angel heard the sound of running feet out in the hallway and she stood, muttering her prayer, facing the doorway, sword again in hand as the desk clerk staggered into the room, breathing heavily. His eyes went wide.

"Jesus fucking Christ! What the hell is going on in here?"

The Angel looked at him sternly and pointed her sword at him. "First," she said severely, "don't blaspheme."

The clerk, who'd been frantically glancing about the room until he'd seen the apparent body and desk debris at the Angel's feet, snapped his eye back to her. He licked his lips and stood very still.

"Yes, ma'am," he said.

"Second," the Angel said, "turn off the water." She caught herself just in time to not say "damned water."

He nodded accommodatingly. The hit man at her feet let a groan out between his mashed lips. She looked down at him. He closed his eyes and pretended to be unconscious. The Angel sighed. As much as she'd like to have him all to herself for a while, she knew he needed medical attention.

"And third, you'd better call the police."

The desk clerk nodded hurriedly, turned, and dashed away.

"And bring me some towels," she shouted at his back.

When they got to the Carter School, the playground was filled with children. A number of them were jokers. All of them were wild carders. Some had been rescued from the People's Paradise of Africa eugenics program and brought back to America. Adesina had been one of those children.

Michelle saw Rusty and Ghost standing at the foot of the steps leading up to the school. Wally's iron skin was looking pretty good. There was no rust on him and he had a dull sheen in the sun.

Yerodin was noncorporeal at the moment and floated a few inches above the ground. Ghost and Adesina had been rescued from the PPA together. Wally had adopted Ghost and brought her back to New York as Michelle had done with Adesina. The girls had become friends after starting school together.

Ghost turned solid and pulled her tablet from her bag. The girls began playing the multiplayer version of *Ocelot 9* as they walked up the steps to the school doors. The game was ridiculously popular at the moment, and Adesina was fixated on all things Ocelot.

"Hey," Michelle said, using her best mom voice. "I thought we agreed, no games at school."

"It's only summer school, Mom," Adesina replied. She looked at Yerodin with an expression that said, "Parents." Ghost returned the look.

"Michelle is right," Wally said in his thick Minnesota accent. "You need to put those tablets away or we'll take 'em away." He was far too nice to make it sound even a little bit like a threat. The girls giggled.

"Oh, hell," Michelle sighed. "It *is* only summer school. They're mostly doing arts and crafts and playing music, anyway." She shoved her hands in her pants pockets. "But this counts as part of your six hours of games for this week, Adesina!"

The girls were already halfway up the steps, and Ghost just waved. Moto and Cesar were waiting for the girls at the top of the steps.

All of the children in the group had been in the PPA together, and all had been experimented on. Michelle couldn't believe how normal they seemed after everything they'd been through. They went into the building, and she turned to Wally. He was looking moodily at The Carter.

The building had been built in Gardener's memory: The Jerusha Carter Childhood Development Center. Gardener had died in the PPA, and Wally had been devastated. Michelle was grateful there was a place like The Carter for children like Adesina and her friends. Jerusha would have liked that.

"You doing okay, Wally?" she asked. He'd never been the same since Gardener died.

"Oh, I'm doing fine," he said. "Can't complain."

It was the same exchange they had every time they ran into each other. There was a kind of comfort in it. He lied and she let him.

"You got plans?" he asked. She liked that he always sounded as if he was really interested.

"Got a shoot for L'Oreal," she replied with a shrug. "Hair stuff. They'll do computer magic and make me look like my hair is the most impossibly beautiful thing ever. Oh, and the commercial is with me and Peregrine together! How awesome is that?"

Wally nodded and smiled. "She sure was nice on *American Hero*. And really pretty."

"I know. She was very nice to me, even after I got booted off."

She looked at her phone, checking the time. "I guess I should get going. I told Babel I'd come by and get caught up on Committee business after this shoot. Busy day. Oh, are the girls still having a sleepover at your house on Friday?"

"You betcha," he said, a real smile breaking out across his steam-shovel face. "We're going to make cupcakes, eat pizza, and play that *Ocelot* game all night. I even found some of those stuffed Cherry Witch toys." A baffled expression crossed his face. "I sure don't understand this game. Ocelots and witches. It makes no sense at all."

"It's a phase. Severe cuteness is a little girl thing. And your sleepover plans sound awesome, Wally." She gave him a hug, then began walking to the subway.

Franny didn't need to speak Russian or Kazakh to recognize expletives. Stache was raging. Baba Yaga stood very still. The engine of the van pinged softly as the engine cooled. They stood in the empty, echoing cavernous hangar at the Talas International Airport. There were a couple of tire blocks tossed off to one side, several tall lockers, and a workbench against one wall.

"I take it there's supposed to be an airplane in here?" Franny finally said. Baba Yaga just spun on her heel and walked back to the van. "Not very big on conversation, is she?" Franny said to Stache, who had seemingly run out of cuss words.

Before she reached the van the old woman staggered. Franny crossed the distance between them in time to keep her from hitting the oil-stained concrete. Small as she was it still hurt his shoulder and his side and he gave a hiss of pain. As for Baba Yaga her eyes were half lidded and she was very pale.

"Always the hero, eh," she rasped out.

"Let's settle for gentleman. My mom raised me right."

Looking worried, Stache joined them. There was another hurried conversation. Since Franny couldn't either understand or join in he decided to investigate the lockers. Maybe somebody kept a change of street clothes. Running around in an ill-fitting tuxedo was going to draw attention. They were locked, but the locks looked flimsy so he took a wrench off the work-table and using his good arm bashed them loose.

"What are you doing?" Baba Yaga called.

"Looking for something a little less conspicuous. I'm tired of running around like an action hero in a spy novel."

Her eyes raked him up and down. "Don't flatter yourself," was the dry response.

"Guess your mother didn't raise you right." He pulled open the doors, and got lucky. There were some clothes in one of the lockers. "Didn't she ever teach you the Thumper rule?"

"What is the Thumper rule?"

"If you can't say anything nice don't say anything at all."

"Stupid rule."

For some reason the exchange amused him. Franny stifled a smile. "So, what's the plan now?"

The old woman seemed to have exhausted the number of words she would allot to Franny and she didn't answer. Instead she climbed into the backseat of the van. Stache leaned in the door, and there was another quick, incomprehensible conversation.

An imperious wave brought Franny to her side. "Go to the terminal. Investigate the situation. And no, I can't send him." She nodded at Stache. "He is known to work for me."

Franny wasn't actually going to argue because it meant he could get away from Baba Yaga and he was at an international airport—a fact he found rather surprising, but was happy to roll with it. Moving to the front of the van he changed out of the purloined tux and into the jeans. The jeans were too short and the shirt was a no-go, it was way too small, which forced him to stay in the dress shirt, which sported a bloodstain. To hide the stain Franny slipped back on the tux jacket. Unlike the slacks with their formal stripe it didn't just scream tux but he was sure not making a sartorial statement.

He headed off across the tarmac toward the terminal. The air reeked of jet fuel and the sun bounced off the pavement, adding to his throbbing headache. He circled the main terminal building until he found the front doors. There was the usual flow of travelers, uniformed airline personnel, the expected security, and big men in dark suits with suspicious bulges under their arms. They were surveying everyone entering the building. It seemed that Baba Yaga's criminal competitors had anticipated her move. Still the old lady was right and they didn't know Franny. He could walk through those doors and—

His thoughts stuttered to a stop. *And do what?* He had no money, and no passport. Talk to the cops? The cops all appeared to be backing the various mobsters. Maybe somebody would let him use the phone? To make an international call? Yeah, like that was going to happen. No, he had to resign himself—he was not going to be boarding a plane out of this shithole. It appeared that for the moment Baba Yaga was his only ticket out. Maybe he'd find an opportunity to help himself to some of the loot in her satchel and then he could consider other options.

Once again he thought of Mollie and that flash he'd seen through the doorway she'd opened for her escape. She had gone to Paris. Fucking Paris.

He returned to the private hangar. Baba Yaga just stared at him. "They're waiting for you to show up," Franny said.

The old woman nodded and spoke to Stache. He started the van. Franny scrambled into the passenger seat next to him and they were on the move.

Once again they skirted the city until they hit the entrance to a modern highway. There was a cop car parked there, lights revolving, a uniformed officer leaning against the side. Baba Yaga snapped out a command, and Stache swerved away from the entrance.

Another hurried and incomprehensible conversation ensued. Stache pulled a hard U-turn and they headed back toward the airport, only this time they sailed past. The Belt of Venus formed a pink arch on the horizon. Above it stars littered the sky. It also told Franny they were traveling east, but to where?

"Where are we going?" he asked. Baba Yaga ignored him, and kept scrolling on the cell phone. "May I use your phone? Call my captain."

"No."

"How about my mother?"

"No."

They turned down a road that seemed to be heading for distant hills rising like dark blue cutouts against a paler sky. After another couple of turns it was clear that was where they were heading.

"So we're literally heading for the hills?" The smile he'd summoned at his own feeble joke curdled and died under Baba Yaga's gelid gaze.

The Angel sat on the desk chair, towel in hand, watching expressionless as the cop surveyed her handiwork. She'd mopped her face dry, but her long brown hair, tightly braided in a thick rope that hung nearly to her waist, was still soaked and dripping lightly onto the soaked hotel-room rug. Fortunately, the leather jumpsuit that she favored while in the field had repelled the sprinklers' advances and she was still dry underneath it.

"Andrei the Ice Man," the blond detective-inspector said as the EMTs lifted him, groaning, onto a dolly and wheeled him across the squishy carpet. "Nice work. How many times did you hit him?"

The cop didn't sound reproachful, just curious. She was a tall woman, almost the Angel's height but the Angel probably had forty pounds on her. She had a lean body and a lean, sharp-featured face. Her hair was long and blond, her eyes a mild blue.

"Just once," the Angel said.

The detective's left eyebrow quirked. "With what?"

The Angel gestured silently toward the remains of the desk scattered around the body.

"Nice," the female cop repeated. "I'm Inspector-Detective First Class Joan Lonnegan."

The Angel nodded. She'd heard of her. "I'm Bathsheeba Fox—"

"I know," Lonnegan said. "The Midnight Angel." Her intent regard, the Angel thought, was frankly curious. "If you don't mind a personal question, what's it like being married to Billy Ray?"

The question threw her for a moment. Was she serious, or just testing her in some way. "Endlessly exciting," the Angel finally said.

Before Lonnegan could reply they were interrupted as a tall, slim black detective in a nice suit entered the room.

"And this," said Lonnegan, indicating the handsome young man, "is Detective Third Class Michael Stevens."

"CSI is on the way," he said. He stopped before the Angel, turned to face her, and extended his hand. His features were expressionless as they shook. "Ma'am."

The Angel, startled as she was, also remained expressionless as she palmed the small folded bit of paper he passed to her.

"I checked with the desk clerk," he reported to Lonnegan. "This is SCARF agent Jamal Norwood's hotel room."

"Is, or was?"

"Is. But he hasn't been seen for more than a day."

Lonnegan turned her attention to the Angel. "Ms. Fox?"

"Call me Bathsheeba—or Angel, as you prefer," the Angel offered, and Lonnegan inclined her head.

"Yes. It's true. I've been looking for him." She wondered how much she should tell the detective, then decided that she couldn't expect to get info if she didn't offer any. "He missed a medical appointment today."

Lonnegan's eyebrows rose and Stevens's face took on a concerned expression.

"Was he ill?" Lonnegan asked.

The Angel hesitated. No sense in making this too easy. "I can't say. I will tell you that officially he was on medical leave."

With this news the detectives exchanged worried glances.

"So," the Angel said, "this Andrei the Ice Man . . . ?" She let her voice trail off.

Stevens looked at Lonnegan. When her expression didn't change he apparently took it as a sign of acquiescence.

"One of the Brighton Beach boys."

"Russian Mafia?"

Michael nodded in confirmation. "Hit man. One of the best—or should I say the worst? He was here alone?"

The Angel shook her head.

"Short, fat guy in a ponytail and loud clothes?"

She nodded.

"That's his partner in crime—and in life—Shadow."

"They're a couple?" the Angel asked. She was only briefly surprised. A decade by Ray's side made you receptive to the unusual.

"Marriage made in hell," Lonnegan volunteered.

"I'd like to be present when you question him."

"Well, in the state you left him, that may be a while."

The Angel shrugged. She stood, turned to drop the towel she'd been holding over the top of the chair, and slipped the note Michael had passed her under the cuff of her gauntlet. She turned and faced Lonnegan and Stevens.

"Nevertheless," she said. "I'd be very interested in why the Russian Mafia was trying to kill one of our agents."

"So are we all, Bathsheeba."

Lonnegan, the Angel realized, was going down the tight-lipped route for now. That was all right. She glanced at Stevens, who was studiously looking elsewhere.

"Thank you, Detective." She looked at Michael and nodded. "Detective."

She didn't look at the note that Stevens had passed her until she was alone in the elevator going down to the lobby. It read in hastily scrawled letters: "Meet me at Uncle Chowder's in three hours. Important."

She stopped at reception. The desk man handed her the computer she'd given him along with a fifty-dollar bill when he'd brought her the towels she'd requested.

"Thank you," she said politely.

"Anytime," he replied, and watched with great admiration as she sashayed to the front door.

In all fairness, the Angel thought, she could hardly expect Detective-Inspector First Class Lonnegan to show her hand when she was holding her own cards so close to her bosom.

"Miss Pond, Miss Sweet, please look over here." The photographer pointed toward the loft's south-facing windows, and Michelle and Peregrine immediately took his direction and started giving him pose after pose.

"You know," Peregrine whispered, "if they hadn't told me you were doing this campaign, I might not have done it. But 'Women of Power' looks like it's going to be good."

A jolt of happiness surged through Michelle. She had admired Peregrine for years. "Well," she whispered back, "I was thrilled when I found out you were going to be part of this, too."

"How would you feel about coming on Season Nine of *American Hero* and doing a guest shot? We have some interesting kids, and you'd probably kick all their asses."

"I don't know," Michelle said with a laugh. "I've got a lot on my plate right now. This campaign, and I'm still on part-time with the Committee. Also, as tempting as it would be to come back to *American Hero,* I'm not sure I'm the right fit."

Peregrine nodded and tossed her head a little. "I understand," she said. "I might have left myself, but they're paying me a fortune to stay."

They were both dressed in stovepipe black slacks, white shirts, and black platform shoes. Posed in front of a white backdrop, they were supposed to be showing off their wild card powers. And Michelle had made sure she had enough fat to bubble through the session.

"Miss Sweet, Miss Pond, can you give us some buddy shots? You know what we want: look like you've known each other for years. And Michelle, can you make those bubbles a little bigger?"

Amare gave the photographer an imperious look. "Dear boy," she said, "we *have* known each other for years. Ever since she was on the first season of *American Hero.*"

The photographer didn't look chastened at all. "Both of you have appointments after this," he said with a sigh. "And I promised I'd get you out of here quickly. Get off my back, Amare."

Peregrine laughed, and her wings fanned out behind her. "Oh, Jimmy, I do so love it when you get all businesslike. I remember snorting coke with you off some bar in Jokertown in the eighties."

Jimmy started taking more pictures while they chatted. "I don't know what you're talking about," he said, snapping away. "Besides, you'll give the kid the wrong idea."

Michelle draped an arm around Amare's shoulders and floated three cantaloupe-sized bubbles in front of them.

"Jimmy, you know very well I grew up modeling. Nothing surprises me."

Peregrine laughed and opened her wings wide, framing both herself and Michelle in white and brown feathers. Then she rose a little off the ground.

"That's the shot," Jimmy said.

The Angel had a room in a Holiday Inn Express right over the border from Jokertown in a slightly more respectable Manhattan neighborhood. It was small and not exactly luxurious, but it met her needs. It was nice, unostentatious, conveniently located, and cheap. For Manhattan. Anything more glamorous would have made her feel uncomfortable—her poverty-stricken small-town upbringing still affected her greatly—and although she was of course on an expense account her innate frugality always made her budget conscious. Although Billy kept telling her that one agent's expenses didn't make a gnat's ass worth of difference to the budget, she still liked to do the best she could to keep the notoriously underfunded agency in the black. The room was comfortable and cosy and she didn't need anything more.

She set Jamal's computer on the nightstand beside her neatly made single bed, sat down on the chair next to the deskette, took off her gauntlets and unlaced and removed her boots. She stood and shimmied out of her leather jumpsuit. It was a little damp and although it had been a warm early summer day, her finely-toned skin was clammy in places where the deluge from the hotel's sprinklers had eventually leaked through. She unbound her braided hair and feathered it across her shoulders and chest, and stood again, looking at her body in the deskette's mirror.

She'd been lucky enough over the years since she'd joined SCARE not to add any scars to it. She pulled her heavy-duty sports bra over her head and let it fall to the floor. She'd been lucky, too, with her explosive metabolism, that she hadn't gained an ounce, either. It'd only been since being with Billy—and it had taken several years, even then—that she could look at herself in the mirror and feel pride in what she saw instead of shame. Almost unconsciously, her hand traveled across her flat stomach and traced the long, curving scar that stood out against her pale skin just as clearly as it had the day her mother had caught her kissing a boy on the front porch and after running him off their property had taken a kitchen knife and cut out her uterus while screaming and calling her terrible names.

Her mother had been insane, of course, probably even before she'd met the college boy who'd seduced her, gotten her pregnant, and abandoned her. The Angel had forgiven her now long-dead mother, but it had been only the luck of the wild card that had turned her ace and saved her life that day.

Her life with her mother had always been hard. As a toddler and into her teens she'd been dragged from place to place and from church to church, her mother searching for the peace she'd never found. But her mother's terrible deed had made the Angel what she was and eventually had given her Billy Ray, which had completed her in ways she had never even imagined and had made all her prior suffering and misery worth-while.

God, she reflected for not the first time, worked in mysterious ways his wonders to perform.

She snagged a towel from the small bathroom and rubbed herself down until she was totally dry, then went to the bed and sat upon it cross-legged. She took Norwood's computer and said to herself, "Now, let's see what you've been up to, Jamal."

She turned it on. It didn't take any magic to access it. As Jamal's team leader she was privy to his password for both safety and security reasons. She scanned the files that popped up in the directory, and was pleased to see, superficially at least, that he'd followed rules and hadn't put personal info or data on the computer, just docs relating to business. Of course, he could be hiding things under innocuous file names, but she'd check that later.

She called up the most recently opened file and read for a good ten min-utes, a sudden frown deepening as she scanned the doc.

"Oh my God," she said, and the way she said it was a prayer not a curse. She read for a few more moments and stopped. She went to the soggy jump-suit that she'd hung over the chair before the deskette, extracted her cell phone from a zipped pocket, and speed-dialed the first number on her list. He answered after the second ring.

"Hello?" His voice was guardedly gruff. It felt so good to hear it again, although she'd already called him earlier that very morning.

"Hello, Billy."

"Angel!" Billy Ray was the baddest dude she knew in or out of govern-ment service and over the last decade or so she'd met a lot of bad dudes. He was the greatest martial artist she'd ever seen in action and over the years she'd seen a crap-ton of that kind of guy and gal. He was probably the only man or woman she herself would be afraid to take on because he was absolutely relentless and fearless and nothing but the hand of God, himself, would ever stop him if he was on your case. And, frankly, she was actually a bit unsure about that. She smiled as she heard the gladness in his voice when he realized it was her on the phone.

"How's your day been?"

"Ah." His voice turned edgy again. "These God—er—fucking budget meetings. I swear to—I mean, this crap just drives me batshit."

The Angel smiled to herself. She loved it when he was being sweet.

"Did you track him down?" Ray demanded before Angel could say anything.

She paused a moment to gather her thoughts. "No." She could hear him growl in frustration. "Billy, how long will it take you to get here?"

There was a moment of silence on the other end of the line.

"That bad?" he finally said.

"Yes."

"Two hours."

"Good. It's complicated and I'm not totally sure what's happening, but Jamal is in trouble. He—he seems to have gone to Kazakhstan with a detective from Fort Freak and the help of that teleporter who calls herself Tesseract."

There was a moment of silence.

"What?"

"Yes—it's about all the jokers who've gone missing lately. You've got to get here ASAP. As you see, it's beyond complicated—the jurisdiction issues alone are a nightmare come true. Call me once you get on the plane and I'll fill you in further. But get here fast—fast." She checked the small clock on the nightstand. "If you can get here in two hours you'll be just in time for the meet."

"Meet?"

"Yes. An admirer has been slipping me secret notes."

"We'll see about that," Ray said. There was more than a hint of menace in his voice. The softness of his tone told the Angel that he was angry and that anger, the Angel knew, was directed at her revelation about Jamal's situation and not her banter about a secret admirer that she'd hoped would divert him, at least a bit. Both she and Ray had been worried about Jamal's apparently deteriorating medical condition, partly because it paralleled what Ray had been going through himself lately. Partly because Jamal was under Ray's command and responsibility. And partly because they both liked the cocky young agent. Though, of course, Ray wouldn't come right out and tell him that.

"I hope so," the Angel replied.

"How's John?" Michelle asked. It was a touchy subject, but Michelle knew Peregrine's son from her early days with the Committee.

Amare was undressing and handing her clothes to Jimmy's assistant without an ounce of embarrassment. Michelle was doing the same. They'd both done enough runway shows that getting naked in front of assistants didn't seem peculiar.

"He's okay, I guess," Peregrine said, pulling on a floral-print sundress designed to accommodate her wings. "He doesn't call enough. But, well, he's never in one place too long. I keep getting postcards from everywhere. Occasionally we Skype. But he's not the same anymore. After . . . you know."

Michelle did know. John Fortune had lost all of his powers. She couldn't imagine living without her ability to bubble. The thought made her feel sick.

"You okay?" Peregrine asked. She reached out and laid a hand on Michelle's shoulder.

"I'm okay. Just, well, what John went through . . ."

Peregrine nodded. "I know," she said. Her voice trembled. "His life has been so difficult, and there's nothing I can do to help."

"I have the same problem," Michelle said. "I want to protect Adesina, but the older she gets, the more difficult it'll be."

Peregrine gave her a hug. "It'll be fine. At least that's what I keep telling myself." She took a deep breath, then smiled a little too brightly. "I think we're filming a commercial next week. I'll see you then!" She kissed Michelle on the cheek, then breezed out the door.

Michelle pulled her clothes on quickly, then looked in the mirror. She glanced at her phone. There was no time to take off her makeup. Fortunately, her hair looked halfway normal, but really it didn't matter. She coiled it up and stuffed it under her baseball cap.

Slowing the truck where a dirt road veered off from the highway, Olena pointed at a cluster of cottages nestled on the hillside above them. "There. That's it."

"You still haven't told me what's so special about this village," Marcus said. Certainly, from this vantage, it hardly looked like a prime destination.

"They will help us," Olena said. That was as detailed as she would get on the matter, though Marcus had been pushing her since she first mentioned it. Shifting the truck into gear with a jolt, she turned off onto the side road and began the ascent.

They crawled into the village with the big engine rumbling loud enough to announce them to anyone within earshot. Marcus was glad when she turned it off and climbed out of the cab. The place seemed deserted. Ramshackle. Simple, run-down-looking houses, a few barnlike structures, black windows, and closed doors. The hulk of an old car perched on blocks, wheel-less. The silence was almost unnerving in the high, thin air, whipped by gusts of wind that only made the place seem more like a ghost town. A raptor of some sort screeched in the sky, dipped and dove.

Marcus shivered. He'd gotten cold the last few miles, a bone-deep cold that seemed to come from inside him.

Olena called out in Russian. She tried a few different phrases, turning as she did so and projecting her voice.

Marcus whispered, "There's nobody here."

Olena pinched that thought between her teeth a moment and then said, "Come down so that they can see you."

"So *who* can see me? There's nobody here!"

At her urging he slid painfully from the bed of the truck. He rolled awkwardly to the packed dirt, head swimming from the motion. He leaned against one of the truck's large tires, panting from that small exertion.

Olena began calling out again. Something about hearing her lone voice in the place made his spirits dive. At that moment, dressed as she was and speaking as she was, she seemed completely foreign to him. It reminded him how lost he was, how out of his depth and so very, very far from the things he knew. And there was nobody here. It finally, fully bloomed on him—the understanding that he was going to die here. He could feel the life draining out of him. He wondered, for the first time, where he would go when he died. Father Squid knew. He was there already. Maybe, if he was lucky, the priest would be waiting for him on the other side of life. If they were to go to the same place. He hoped so. He truly hoped so.

"Look, Marcus," Olena whispered.

He opened his eyes. He hadn't realized he'd closed them. Olena's face swam before his. He lifted an arm to touch her cheek. She clasped his hand, brought it to her lips, and kissed it. Her eyes looked wet with tears as she turned and pointed. "Look, Marcus. I told you this was a place for us."

With effort, he turned. There, on the street a little ways away, shapes moved. They were strange shapes, and at first he didn't understand them. He thought his eyes were playing tricks on him. Then they came closer, and he saw what they were.

Jokers. That's what the shapes were. A man who limped on legs that weren't jointed right, that splayed out to either side as he walked. Another with a single horn that curled around his head like a turban. A woman with the face of a toad. Another—man or woman Marcus couldn't tell—that came on like a hunchbacked, hairy beast of some old horror movie. And still others with mutations small and large. They converged slowly on Marcus and Olena, a silent procession of the virus-twisted.

Marcus had watched them as his vision blurred, unsure whether what he was seeing was real or imagined. Unsure whether to fear them, or to reach out for them as kin. Instead of doing either he'd lost consciousness. Or most of it. He knew that Olena had talked with the jokers. He knew that they'd worked together to lift and move him. He knew he was inside somewhere warm and smoky, smelling of metal and oil. But all of this seemed far away, like none of it really had anything to do with him, until Olena woke him, for the second time that day, by saying, "Don't sleep, my hero. Soon you can, but not yet."

Opening his eyes, Marcus at first thought they were in a barn, as the rafters and walls were hung with tools. He could feel the rough contours of the floor through the old quilted blanket he lay on. With effort, he rose to his elbow, leaning back heavily on a sack.

Olena said, "Someone is here to help you."

The someone stood just behind her, a villager who looked ill at ease. He was a middle-aged man, short and round-faced and Asian-looking, like many of the people Marcus had seen since escaping the arena. Burlap sacks covered his hands, tied in place at the wrists. Behind him the glow of a furnace lit the room with soft yellow light.

"This is Jyrgal," Olena said. "Around here he is called the Handsmith. You understand? Instead of blacksmith. Handsmith. This is his forge."

Marcus wondered if the man's hands were covered because he had burned them. "I don't need a blacksmith," he said, his voice barely more than a whisper.

"And this is his son, Nurassyl."

Marcus hadn't noticed the boy. He stood mostly hidden behind his father's legs. His body was shaped like a child draped in a sheet, like a simple ghost costume. His flesh was gelatinous, glistening with moisture. His arms were chubby and he held his fists tight against his chest. He moved not on feet but on a wriggling platform of little nobules. Marcus couldn't place what they reminded him of for a moment, and then he did. Anemones. They moved him out from behind his father, a smooth glide accompanied by a squelching sound.

Despite all the strangeness of his appearance Marcus could see the boy beyond the deformity. The boy that he would've been if the wild card hadn't twisted him was there in the curious sparkle of his eyes, in the way they widened on seeing Marcus, and in the way he clutched at his father's leg and half hid behind him. Marcus had done that, forever ago when he was the boy that his father still loved. Before everything changed.

"You brought me to jokers?" Marcus asked.

Olena nodded. "This place is called a 'village of the prophet's abhorred.'" She glanced over her shoulder, as if worried the father and son could understand her. It didn't look like they could. To Marcus, she continued, "A village of jokers. In Kazakhstan they are not looked on kindly. They group together in secluded places and live quietly. They were nervous about coming out. Sometimes bad people come here and cause trouble. So they were careful until they saw you. I've explained everything to them. Jyrgal is here to help you. He will take the bullets out of you. He says that in Islam one does not turn away a man in need, especially when that person is a brother in curse."

With deliberate, careful motions, Jyrgal gripped one and then the other of his mittens in his teeth. He pulled them free and let them drop. Where he should have hands he had . . . flesh. Amorphous stubs that bulged and pulsed, shapeless and yet constantly changing. He picked up a metal bar from beside the forge. A small brick the size of a Snickers. He slipped it into his mouth. He tilted back his head and swallowed. Marcus winced as he watched the bar slip down his throat. The man rolled his head, worked his jaw to different angles.

The boy said something and the father responded with a word. He lifted the writhing lumps he had instead of hands. He stared at them and began chanting. A prayer of some sort. Or was it singing? The fleshy lumps flushed red, and then darkened. They took on a metallic sheen and shape. One became a thin sliver of curved metal. A scalpel. The other took longer to settle into shape. It became a sort of pliers, delicately pointed instruments that the man snapped open and closed for a moment, testing them. Jyrgal spoke to his son, gesturing toward Marcus.

With his wide, kind eyes, the boy slid toward the patient. He spoke and Olena translated.

"He asks that you trust him. He says that Allah made him as he is. He deformed him, but he also allowed him a way to serve others. He believes that if he gives his gift freely he will be welcomed in heaven one day. He'll have a normal body there. He'll be able to run, and chase kites, and play ball. He'll be uncursed. That will be heaven for him."

Olena paused a moment, listening as the father responded. Marcus watched emotion bloom in her eyes. Something like sadness, but not quite. She whispered, "Jyrgal says that his son may be right. But also it may be that in heaven Nurassyl will be exactly as he is here on earth. He may not be able to run after kites or play football, but he will still be just as perfect. Just as loved by his father. That, Jyrgal says, would be heaven for him."

The boy smiled. He peeled his hands from his chest and stretched them toward Marcus. Like his father, they were not hands at all. They were a writhing mass of tiny tentacles similar to those that he stood on. Marcus stared at them, transfixed and terrified at the same time. His fear vanished when the tentacles touched his scales. It was the gentlest of caresses, radiant with warmth, a strange, tingling feeling that, above all else, was comforting. It felt like each tentacle sang through him, telling him that everything would be all right.

"Being as he is," Olena whispered, close to his ear and translating Jyrgal's words, "there are many things my son cannot do. But who needs to do other things when he can relieve the pain of others? Because of him, you will feel no more pain."

So saying, the Handsmith went to work. And it was as he said. Marcus didn't feel the scalpel slicing into his flesh or the pliers probing for bullets. He just watched the large-eyed joker boy, awed by his healing touch and by the complete goodness of him.

The elevator doors opened with a sigh, and Michelle stepped out onto the Committee floor of the UN. There was the low hum of people working. It hadn't been like that when she'd started. Back then it had been just the eight of them in Jayewardene's office.

She didn't like the way it had blossomed into this bureaucracy. Now there were always new people she didn't know and people bustling from here to there, looking intent and purposeful.

The receptionist, Margaret, gave Michelle a winsome smile, and Michelle smiled back. There had been some minor flirting between them, but Michelle tried her best not to flirt back. It wasn't professional. Still, Margaret was really cute. But now Ink was working as Jayewardene's assistant, and it might be awkward if she discovered Michelle making sexy eyes at Margaret. Once again, Michelle wondered if getting Ink a job with Jayewardene had been wise. Former girlfriends just muddied the water.

"I'm supposed to meet up with some of the new kids, Margaret," Michelle said, walking up to the sleek metal and glass desk. Everything on the Committee floor was sleek and modern. It managed to look austere and expensive at the same time. "They still in the big conference room?" She was trying very hard not to be distracted by Margaret's pretty—and very soft-looking—red hair. It had been a long time since she'd been interested in anyone, much less interested in anyone in a very unprofessional way.

Except for Joey. Joey was always in the back of her mind. There were layers of complication being involved with Joey. What they might be to each other she didn't know. Michelle wanted to find out, but she knew it was emotionally dangerous for her. Also, the Ink and Joey thing—well, that was a mess.

"They were in the big conference room, but most of them left for lunch already," Margaret replied. "You look especially nice today. Those jeans are perfect on you. And do I smell Chanel No. 5? I *love* that fragrance." Margaret gave her a smoldering look, and then gestured toward the sitting area. *Why am I thinking about Joey when there's a perfectly nice girl who obviously wants me?* Michelle thought as she began digging through her handbag like she was trying to find something important.

"One guy came in after they'd all gone to lunch. That's him over there. His name is Cesar Antonio Clerc. Code name is Aero."

Michelle looked over and saw a man somewhat older than her who was sitting in one of the low-slung black leather chairs. He was reading on a tablet.

"Thanks, Margaret," she said.

Michelle walked across the wide waiting room toward him. He looked up at her and his eyes widened.

"Hello, Cesar," she said, holding out her hand. "I'm Michelle Pond."

He stood, took her hand, and gave a firm handshake. Not too hard, which was nice. A lot of men gave her the I'm-manly-and-my-handshake-is-super-strong. Those never hurt her—they couldn't—but it did make her wonder if they did that all the time to people it *might* hurt.

"I know who you are, Miss Pond," he said, releasing her hand. He spoke with a slight Spanish accent. His eyes were jade-colored, and his skin was olive; he was a few inches shorter than she was. "You've been in the news a couple of times," he said dryly.

Michelle decided she liked him. "It looks like you missed the orientation meeting," she said. "I'm late, too. How about we go get some lunch and I can answer any questions you have about Committee procedures. And about how much trouble you've gotten yourself into by agreeing to this."

"Trouble," he said in an amused voice. "Trouble I'm used to."

Machu Picchu now formed a glorious, cinematic backdrop for the press cameras. A large, open-sided tent had been erected on the terrace just outside the Three Windows Temple, protecting the gathering from the sun while leaving the stunning mountainous scenery visible all around. The terraces gleamed in the late morning sun, the polished drystone walls of the buildings around reflected the light, though many of the walls still showed the damage of the fighting that had erupted here two weeks ago, when the UN had first made the decision to send in the Committee to end the burgeoning civil war.

The two Peruvian sides were already seated under the tent. As Barbara and Klaus approached, they could see Secretary-General Jayewardene waiting for them, and behind him, conspicuously present, the other Committee aces were standing in a cluster. Blue-helmeted soldiers stood posted around the perimeter of the terrace.

"This will play well in the press." Klaus leaned in toward Barbara, whispering in her ear as he put an arm around her. She saw him nod in satisfaction. *"Das gut."*

She smiled back at him. "Yes," she told him. "It's good." She patted his hand, then moved it from her shoulder. She ran fingers through her short, dyed hair. "Appearances, love," she whispered back to him. "And it's time for yours. I'm already working, you know. And I'm tired—not enough sleep last night."

Klaus grinned at that, and Babel forced herself to remain smiling, but most of her attention was on making certain that everyone sitting at the table under the tent would be able to converse with the others; her concentration was there. The ghosts of German, English, Spanish, Sinhala, Quechua, and Aymara words wisped through her head, and she formed them all into a common language that everyone at the table could understand. It was like juggling: hearing the words in each person's head a moment before they were spoken and reshaping them as they emerged, twisting the sounds that they made in the air and placing a sphere of understanding around everyone in the tent. The task was second nature to her now, but it was still something that required concentration and energy, and which would leave her exhausted afterward.

This was more difficult than her other skill: that of making speech incomprehensible and communication impossible. That side of her ace was far simpler to handle. Confusion was always easier than understanding. She knew that too well.

They reached the Secretary-General. As they did, Klaus closed his remaining eye momentarily, encasing himself in the shining, white armor of ghost steel, though he left his head and long blond hair uncovered, displaying the black eye patch surrounded by the facial scars that had left him half blinded. He grounded the blade of his greatsword in the grass below. "Let's get this done," he said.

"Excellent," Jayewardene answered. "I had a dream last night that this went well, so the omens are good. Though other things, elsewhere . . ." He frowned and shook his head. "Well, that's for later, on the flight back. As you said, let's finish this."

The trio strode under the tent's shadow, Klaus ducking his head to get under the flap. The round table—as it had in the mythical time of King Arthur—promised that no person was more important than any other, but everyone here knew that for the farce it was. Barbara glanced around as the furious, muting clicking of cameras from the press section began.

Babel thought Curare, one of the two Shining Path leaders, more deuce than ace—his frog-like, thin body was clad only in ridiculous red- and yellow-striped spandex swimming trunks that clashed badly with his black-spotted, eye-searing blue skin. He sat on his haunches on a wooden platform made specially for him since normal chairs couldn't accommodate his body. His huge golden eyes shifted as he glanced from Cocomama, seated next to him, to the last arrivals to the table.

Cocomama was a young woman dressed in traditional Andean clothing with an intricately beaded and feathered headdress over long, raven-black hair just beginning to be touched with premature grey around the temples. At Secretary-General Jayewardene's insistence, she wore cotton gloves, even in the heat: her cocaine-laced touch was able to drug a person into submission.

Barbara smiled at the two as Jayewardene, Lohengrin, and she took their seats. Curare and Cocomama, from her observations and the intelligence on them that they'd been given, had a complicated relationship. The twin heads of the New Shining Path rebels were lovers, and their organization was funded by the seemingly unlimited resource of the cocaine Cocomama's ace could provide. Over the last decade and a half, they had shepherded the New Shining Path from a minor, fading annoyance to a full-fledged danger to the stability of Peru. In the Andes region, especially, the New Shining Path now controlled the roads and main towns.

Curare was the titular leader and spokesperson, but Barbara suspected that it was Cocomama who was the true head of the organization, that it was her will that dominated the group's decisions, and she had advised Jayewardene accordingly. Then there was the mysterious Messenger In Black, and no one knew his role with the New Shining Path at all. However, there were dark-winged moths flitting all around the terrace and under the tent's fabric: whoever the Messenger was, he would know what happened here.

Barbara wondered if the New Shining Path's leaders realized that their complicated, three-legged relationship mirrored that of the aces before them: Secretary-General Jayewardene, Lohengrin, and herself. Jayewardene had the legal authority, but it was the shining, ghost steel–clad Lohengrin who, in the eyes of the public, was the leader of the Committee that underlaid and supported the UN's power. As for herself . . . to most, she was a secondary figure, but with both men she often felt like the only adult in the room. Klaus, despite her love for him, had only one tactic: go striding in with sword blazing and dangerous aces arrayed behind him; Jayewardene was Klaus's opposite, bound tightly by rules and regulations and trying desperately to placate the agendas of all the countries and all the powers that had put him where he was, and as a result—at least in Barbara's opinion—often moving too slowly and too timidly.

It was Barbara who often had to hold Klaus back when he wanted nothing more than to jump into blind action; it was Barbara who had to prod and poke Jayewardene to move when the man wanted to sit and wait and ponder.

As Barbara and Klaus sat, flanking Jayewardene, her gaze moved across the table from Cocomama and Curare to President Fujimori, General Ramos of the Peruvian army, and the assorted high-ranking officers who sat with them. The Secretary-General remained standing. He tugged at his suit jacket as he took a long, slow breath, and one brown hand reached out to rest on the thick document placed on the tablecloth in front of him.

"I congratulate you, President Fujimori, and you, Curare and Cocomama," he said. With Babel's ability, each of them heard Jayewardene speaking in whatever passed for their own native language. "What we have accomplished here is nothing less than historic, and when this agreement is signed, Peru will be well on its way back to stability and prosperity, for everyone in your great country."

With that, he picked up the pen placed alongside the document, and with a flourish signed his name to the paper. He slid the document to Klaus, who also signed it, then in turn passed the bound papers down the line until the signature page faced President Fujimori.

The president had a polite smile plastered on her face. Cocomama's frown, Babel noticed, did not match President Fujimori's smile, while Curare's lipless, amphibian's face was impossible to read. The New Shining Path had been the most difficult of the opposing sides to bring to the table. They, after all, had the option to slide back into the mountains and the jungles from where they'd come and hide away once more. Babel wondered if Cocomama, especially, had reconsidered the agreement they'd finally hammered into final shape the night before.

Neither Klaus nor Jayewardene seemed to be aware of how Cocomama's frown deepened as President Fujimori now stood and returned Jayewardene's opening volley with her own flowery predictions of harmony and peace. Babel continued to regard Cocomama as Fujimori finished her speech, as the cameras chattered and video cameras panned the assembly. As the president finished her short speech and also signed the document, as her people in turn slid the document around the table toward Curare, in the myriad languages in her head, Barbara heard Cocomama whisper to Curare: "Fujimori is right there. You could reach her before anyone could stop you. Grab me, and leap through this tent canopy. We could be away before they know it."

The frog's golden eye flicked over to his companion. "We shouldn't . . ."

"We should. *You* should," Cocomama insisted.

Babel knew then: she saw the way Curare glanced toward President Fujimori, saw the muscles tighten under his slick, glossy body. Babel shifted the pattern on her power, still allowing the others to talk among themselves, but putting a wall around herself, Curare, and Cocomama. "Curare is right. You can't do that," she told Cocomama, as heads around the table, puzzled by the nonsense words they heard her speaking, turned toward them. "That's not a solution."

Cocomama's face twisted in a sneer. "We've given away too much," Curare told Barbara in a croaking, cartoon-figure voice. Barbara knew the words were likely more Cocomama's than his own—or perhaps those of the Messenger In Black. His tongue flicked out, as if tasting the air, and translucent eyelids slid over the globes of his eyes. "This isn't all we wanted. We asked for so much more. We *needed* much more."

"I understand that," she answered. "But diplomacy is the art of compromise, and you can have a portion of what you wanted now, gained with nothing more than your signature. You'll have a voice in the government, to which everyone will be required to listen. You and the New Shining Path will have immediate legitimacy."

They were all watching the three of them now, quizzical and unable to understand what they were saying. Jayewardene stared at Babel, puzzled but with a quizzical smile, his hands clasped before him as if they could hold him in his seat. Lohengrin did stand, a winged helm now covering his face, and Barbara saw his hands flexing on the greatsword as he glared at the New Shining Path aces through the eye slits. Cameras flashed all around them, everyone sensing that there was a problem. Barbara shook her head slightly to Klaus and Jayewardene as she continued to speak to Curare and Cocomama.

"If you falter now, if your great courage in taking this step fails," she told them, knowing that they too were seeing Lohengrin's growing impatience and anger, and must feel the tension increasing around the table, "if you choose revenge over compromise, you both lose everything. Believe me, I understand this situation better than you might think. Isn't it wiser to eat the meal offered to you than to shove it away and go entirely hungry? This way, you have the energy and the opportunity to gain all you wanted another day; the other, you will inevitably starve and die."

She realized that she understood Cocomama's feelings quite well. She understood wanting more. *All the times you have been the one with the negotiated solution, the diplomatic and correct answer, yet Klaus or Jayewardene was given the credit. All the times you were in the background of the picture, never the one on which the cameras were focused . . .*

"We should listen to her, Lorra," Curare croaked urgently. Curare's long tongue flicked out, then back. The sticky pads of his fingers touched the paper and pen in front of him as he stared hard at Cocomama.

A moth fluttered down from the canopy to land on the signature page of the treaty, its wings rising and falling; Barbara saw Cocomama stare hard at the insect. "If you want to win today, Lorra, you need to do so with ink, not blood," Barbara continued, using the woman's name to gain her attention, her voice urgent. "And if your victory isn't everything you wanted, well, you'll still be alive to strive for more tomorrow."

She looked significantly from Curare and Cocomama to Lohengrin. She narrowed the focus of her power, so that only the two Peruvian aces and perhaps the moth could hear and understand her. "Don't believe that you two alone can stand against Lohengrin's sword or the other aces here," she finished. "I know him well. He's not a patient man, I'm afraid, and the pen is right there in front of you. Ink is far less painful to spill than blood. Ink will give your people the chance to gain everything you want in the future. Choose otherwise, and you might kill President Fujimori, but you will also both die here. I know you think you won't. I know that you—like my husband—think your powers will always protect you and despite the odds, you'll escape. I know you believe that because you've always been able to do so before. But I'm telling you: *that won't happen here.* Look around; there are too many others with powers of their own—my people—and if you do this, they will all consider you enemies. I guarantee you won't leave this terrace alive."

A flock of moths entered the tent, settling around Cocomama's shoulders like a shawl. The open fury in her face slowly dissolved, and the moths flew away a few moments later, flowing down the slope of the terrace. Cocomama said nothing directly, but nodded to Curare. "Thank you," Barbara told the woman.

Babel dissolved the language barrier around them, bringing them back into the larger circle of understanding: as Curare clumsily picked up the pen in his large-padded fingers, as the moth on the treaty flicked its wings and rose from the signature page. Cocomama still frowned, but remained silent.

Curare scrawled his name on the paper as the cameras clamored and Lohengrin's hands relaxed around the hilt of the ghost steel sword. Klaus's helm vanished, his long blond hair falling around the shoulder of the white armor. Jayewardene applauded softly.

They both smiled into the flashes of the cameras.

The lenses paid little attention to the woman seated with them.

"That's basically it for procedures," Michelle said, sipping her coffee and then digging into her cheesecake. "Of course, there are the trickier bits. Like dealing with the press. They're slippery bastards."

Cesar wiped his mouth. "I had some experience with them when I was in Spain. It was . . . unpleasant."

"It's going to be worse here. At least in the beginning it will be. You're a good-looking guy with a sexy accent. That's like catnip. And you'll be fresh copy."

"I wear a mask," he replied as he began eating his dessert. "That should help keep them out of my private life."

"I appreciate your optimism, but—" She looked around the room. The deli was cramped like most of the restaurants in Manhattan. They had a booth and she was pretty sure they couldn't be overheard, but she dropped her voice anyway. "They will be crawling up your ass to try and figure out who you are under that mask." She leaned toward him. "Also, there are some topics that are flat out off-limits."

"I can imagine," he replied. "We can't talk about missions unless we have permission. At least that's how it was in Spain."

She shook her head. "Not just that. There are P.R. issues. Stay off religion and also leave out the politics of what we're doing."

"Yes, my religious beliefs would be . . . problematic." He took a few more bites of his cheesecake.

"Oh?" Most of Michelle's wild card friends just didn't talk about it. Then there was Angel, who was deeply religious and wasn't shy at all about expressing her beliefs. But by and large, wild carders had enough trouble without bringing faith into things.

Aero smiled wanly. "When the Black Queen took my sister I was still a believer, having been raised in the Catholic faith." His speech was slow and precise. "As a boy, the Sisters gave me a picture of Jesus in a plastic frame. I'd done well in my schoolwork and this was a reward. The picture frame had small doors that opened and closed. It was a trifle, but I kept it out of sentiment. The night my sister died I shut the doors and prayed to Jesus to open them so that I would know my sister was in heaven. Surely, such a small thing was not too much to ask to keep me from so much doubt and pain."

"I'm so sorry for your loss," she said, knowing the words were inadequate. "But I'm guessing God didn't open them for you."

"No, of course not." He shook his head. "It was the beginning of the end of my faith. My parents scolded me for testing Jesus, but I wasn't testing, I was begging. I truly wanted to believe."

Michelle didn't know what to say. Sadness and anger were etched across his face.

"We all have our losses," he said. "But there has been compensation. I've learned to value my time on this earth. There's a discipline, even an art, to enjoying one's life."

Michelle nodded. "I'm not a believer. Unlike your parents, my parents only believed in money." She gave a bitter smile. "You shouldn't tell that story to anyone you don't know or trust. If the press gets wind of it, they'll tear you to shreds. They'll take things out of context. You'll be fodder for the evangelical and anti-wild card movements. And you don't need any more pain."

"You're right, of course." He dabbed his napkin at the corner of his mouth. "They'd mine my pain for public consumption. They do it everywhere. I suppose . . . I suppose I just wanted you to know. I'm already feeling homesick, and I just arrived. I want someone to know me." Then he took a sip of his coffee. "The cheesecake is good," he said.

His sharing his story made Michelle surprisingly glad. "Hey, if you're not doing anything this evening, why don't you come to dinner at my house? You can meet my daughter, and then you would know at least two people in New York."

His eyes lit up. "I'd like that," he said. "What time?"

"How about seven? It should give you enough time to finish up your Committee business. Let me give you my information, then we can walk back to the office together."

He pulled out his phone. "Ready when you are."

Uncle Chowder's Clam Bar was a long-standing Jokertown favorite. The neon sign high on its front brick facade picturing a top-hatted clam had been tap dancing on rickety stick legs for decades. It currently enjoyed a reputation vastly more refined than in its initial years when it shared the building with a bottom-floor dive called Squisher's Basement. Squisher himself was long-gone and his basement now contained The Foxes Booze and Cruise, an upscale gay bar—though among jokers the distinction between sexes was sometimes blurred. It catered to a younger and, for Jokertown, a moderately sophisticated and upscale clientele, joker yuppies who were gentrifying nearby neighborhoods. At times both the gentrification and the gays were not, the Angel knew, totally welcomed by the locals, but in Jokertown money talked and the less fortunate, no matter how long they'd been living in the neighborhood, walked.

Chowder's was intimately lit, with a polished wooden buffet bar, a scattering of cloth-covered tables, and a row of plushly cushioned booths against the wall opposite the bar. The sound system was playing something from Lady Gaga, one of the current diva crop, a mystery chantreuse who refused to confirm or deny if she was a joker. The Angel only recognized the song because it was ubiquitous. She knew as much about Lady Gaga as she did about other current pop culture phenoms, or maybe even less. She and Billy didn't get out much.

She scanned the room. It was moderately busy with a late dinner crowd, mostly couples, quietly absorbed in their lobster bisques, raw oysters, and King Crab legs.

He'd be in a booth, she thought, and she was right.

The handsome young cop who was Franny Black's partner was huddled alone in a corner of a booth near the end of the row. He looked up when the Angel slid next to him into the booth. Despite the dim lighting, she could see worry, apprehension, even perhaps a bit of fear on his face.

"Officer Stevens," she said in a low voice barely audible over the music.

"Agent, uh—"

"As I said, call me Angel, or Bathsheeba, as you will."

"Yes, of course." He took a sip from the glass he held cradled in both hands, a thick, squat block of cut glass with a few ice cubes covered by a couple of fingers of dark amber liquid. "Can I get you a drink, Angel?"

She had the feeling that he was usually good with women, but he was too worried and otherwise occupied to try to assert what she assumed was considerable charm. She could see that part of him was still appreciative of her looks and her relative closeness. But she, too, was where she wanted to be. Not across the table from him, but next to him. Well within reach. She shook her head and just looked at him.

He nodded and glanced down at his drink, but didn't take a sip.

"I'm not," he said, paused. Obviously making an effort, he started again. She could barely hear his quiet voice over the music. "I am not a snitch," he said.

She nodded agreeably. "Where's your partner and Agent Norwood?"

"You know they're working together?" he asked, glancing up at her and then away again.

The Angel just nodded. She'd learned things from Jamal's notes on the computer, but there were still many missing details. One of the things she didn't know was how much she could trust Stevens.

"I should be with them," he said in an even softer voice that the Angel could barely discern.

"Why aren't you?" she asked reasonably.

"Franny"—he almost choked on the name—"wouldn't let me go with them. I have a family—two wives, a young daughter—"

The Angel's eyebrows rose.

"—I would have gone anyway, but Franny and your man left without me." The dam within him burst and Stevens looked right at her and spoke rapidly and almost pleadingly. "It was the jokers, the missing jokers. They were being taken off the streets—"

"Kidnapped?"

Stevens nodded. "Yeah, and something wasn't right. There was no . . . interest . . . in the case upstairs, but Franny kept pushing, kept gnawing on it. He went against orders, kept investigating. Finally he and Norwood caught a break with this TV guy, this Michael Berman. They disappeared, vanished. I don't know where and how, but this chick, Mollie—she was on *American Hero*—"

"The teleporter?"

"Yeah. And yesterday, a bunch of the jokers just reappeared, right in the middle of the precinct. It was a fucking circus. They kept babbling about the games, death matches. Father Squid—" Stevens choked and almost broke down.

"What about him?" the Angel asked. She had met the kindly old joker priest several times. He was, many said, the soul of Jokertown, and she believed that. She didn't know what denomination he was, but there was no doubt in her heart that he served the Lord.

"They say he's dead."

She felt suddenly cold. "And Jamal and your partner?"

Stevens shook his head miserably. "They weren't among the jokers."

"What happened to them?" the Angel asked, her jaw clenched.

"They're . . . gone. Vanished. Supposedly the Feds swooped them up."

"I would have heard,"

"I know," the cop said. "There's . . . something wrong in the precinct." He had to force the words out of his mouth.

"You think?"

He nodded. The Angel stared at him. He didn't avert his eyes. There was misery in them, and worry for his partner and Jamal, and more than a hint of shame because he wasn't with them.

"I think," the Angel said in a much louder voice, "we can trust him."

Stevens looked at her, frowning. "What?"

A man who had been sitting at a table with his back turned toward them silently stood, removed his lobster bib, and dropped it on the table, turning toward them. He was dressed in a finely tailored suit that fit his ordinary-sized frame like a dream. His shadowed face was half illuminated by one of the infrequent ceiling lights. It was lean and hard-looking, with an askew nose, and was generally too battered-looking to be handsome. He crossed to the table with a dancer's grace. The Angel smiled a little. Even in this difficult time, with the terrible news that she'd just heard, she never tired of watching him move. But she still kept an eye on Stevens, whose expression had turned uncertain and concerned. She didn't blame the policeman, what with the expression on the newcomer's face.

"If you say so," Billy Ray said, glaring at Stevens like a disapproving angel on Judgment Day.

Promptly at seven, there was a knock on the door, and Michelle answered it. Cesar stood in the hallway holding a bottle of wine and a small lavender gift bag encrusted with silver glitter.

"I come bearing gifts," he said with a smile. "The wine is for you. The other," he said, holding up the bag, "is for your daughter."

"What a lovely thing to do!" Michelle exclaimed, stepping backward and gesturing for him to come in. "I should warn you, I'm a terrible cook. So I've ordered in an insane amount of Chinese."

"Fortunately, I like Chinese."

Michelle led him into the living room, gesturing for him to sit. "Your home is lovely," he said with a smile. "I also like mid-century modern furniture. And your choice of colors is perfect for the period."

She looked around her living room with an enormous sense of pride. The walls were a creamy yellow and decorated with an eclectic collection of paintings, prints, and photographs. She loved the sofa and chairs. She'd had them upholstered in a retro grey-and-white coin pattern. Adesina's books and computer games were scattered across the coffee table and her school backpack had been tossed on one of the chairs. It all looked like something out of an idealized sixties TV show. Except that a flat-screen TV hung on the wall across from the couch. Pillows were still bunched up on the couch where she and Adesina had lain the night before to watch Adesina's favorite cartoons. It pleased Michelle to no end that she'd made a home for them.

She smiled at Cesar. "I wanted it to be normal. Nothing fancy. I grew up with all that fancy stuff and it didn't make me happy." A frown slipped across her face. "Her life isn't going to be easy for so many reasons. I want her to know what normal feels like. Not that I have a deep well of that to draw from."

Adesina came into the room. She'd changed from her school uniform into fleece pants and a T-shirt. They were specially made for her body. Michelle didn't think she really needed to wear anything, but she didn't want Adesina to feel even more different from other children.

"And this is my daughter, Adesina," Michelle said. "Adesina, this is Mr. Clerc."

Adesina half fluttered, half walked over. "How do you do?" she asked, proffering her claw.

Cesar smiled at her and Michelle was relieved. Though her daughter had a beautiful and sweet little girl's face, her insect body made some people nervous.

"How do you do?" he asked, taking her claw and giving it a gentle shake. "You may call me Cesar, if you like. I brought you something." He gave her the gift bag.

She pulled out the pink tissue paper and gave a squeal of joy.

"I don't have this one," she said, plucking the plastic figure of Misty Mouse from the bag. "How did you know I like *Ocelot 9?*"

He looked very pleased. "I met a woman called Ink, and I asked her what you might like. Apparently, your mother talks a lot about you at work."

Mollie stepped into the musty darkness of a one-bedroom apartment in central North Dakota. Months had passed since the last time she'd been to her Bismarck bolt-hole. The air was stale, and the odor told it'd been far too long since she ran water down the pipes. Mollie went through the apartment, turning on lights and running the faucets. The two-by-fours that she had installed in brackets behind the apartment door still barricaded the entrance. A considerable layer of dust dulled the glitter from the jewelry heaped on the battered card table in the kitchen. A pair of roaches scuttled down the drain when she swept the shower curtain aside.

These weren't the ritzy digs she'd always imagined for herself since the day her card turned—those had yet to materialize in a permanent fashion. But it was the kind of place where a person could pay a year's rent and utilities in advance with postal money orders. She'd done that under an assumed name soon after Ffodor had taught her how to get a decent false identity. Just because she was raised as an unsophisticated hick from potato country didn't mean she was *stupid*.

It was very quiet and very *very* private. Even Ffodor hadn't known about her place. She sure as hell never told Berman about it. And she'd never had

anybody over. Not because there was nobody to invite, she quickly reminded herself, but because she wanted it that way. If she really wanted
to bother with it she could easily find people to hang out with. Easily. She'd
just been too busy. For years on end.

She swept aside boxes and shopping bags until she'd carved out enough
room to flop on the bed. A pile of laptops and tablets teetered at the foot
of the bed, many still in their packaging. Mollie took one off the top,
opened it, and tossed the box aside. It landed on another pile of unopened
loot.

This was getting ridiculous. She had to start making time to pawn the
stuff she snatched, otherwise what was the point? Yes, indeed. What was
the point of all this? But that was a dangerous train of thought, so she
shied away from it. Instead she power-cycled her wireless router and got
comfortable on the bed while waiting for the tablet to find the network.
Web surfing wasn't particular exciting—everyone knew that half the people
on the Internet were trolls, the other half assholes—but it gave her something to do until her stomach growled.

She put the tablet aside, then opened a new pair of gateways: one in
the bedroom wall a foot away, and another inside the refrigerator of a
farmhouse a half-hour drive outside Coeur d'Alene, Idaho.

A sharp metallic *snap* echoed within the refrigerator, accompanied by
a stab of agony in her fingers. Mollie yanked her hand back through the
opening into her own apartment. She pried the mousetrap from her fingers and flung it aside. It bounced off the wall hard enough to leave a ding
in the drywall (*Great, another chip off the deposit*) before tumbling under
the bed.

It hurt so much that at first Mollie thought the fucking thing had broken her fingers. But she could still bend them. She flicked the portal egress
from her parents' refrigerator to the freezer and (after checking for another mousetrap) grabbed some ice. She used another opening to grab a
washcloth from the bathroom. Having made a makeshift ice pack for her
fingers, she glared into the Steunenberg kitchen while nursing her fingers.
It smelled faintly like sour milk but also like pot roast. The TV blared from
the living room; Mom and Dad were watching *Wheel of Fortune*. A pang
of homesickness caught her off guard. But then she inspected her fingers,
which were already swelling up like sausages, and remembered why she
didn't come home more often. She hadn't felt welcome at the farm since
Noel had killed her brother Todd, stabbed her brother Brent, and shot her

dad. Nobody ever came out and said it was her fault. (How could it be? Mollie just provided the opportunity. Dad and the boys were the Einsteins who'd come up with the actual plan.) Still, Todd's death had left an ineradicable pall on her family relationships. Including Mom and Dad. But they hadn't been the ones to set the mousetrap. They weren't that childish.

Mollie leaned through the hole in space, and shouted: "Brent, you greasy turd! You'll regret this!"

After closing the hole she went into the kitchen—her own kitchen, in her own apartment, walking there on her own two feet like a nat—and poured a bag of frozen stir fry into a skillet. While it simmered, she went into the bathroom and took a leak. She didn't flush.

Eating dinner beside a fist-high pile of stolen jewelry, some that she'd snatched over a year ago and never bothered to pawn, she couldn't help but wonder why she did this. She wasn't a kleptomaniac; she liked money, wanted money—wanted a metric crapload of it—and didn't steal just for the thrill of it. Her ace made stealing practically trivial. So why was it that without the drive to be a good pupil for Ffodor she'd become so lazy about turning the goods into cash?

Mollie wondered if mountain climbers ever felt like this after topping Everest.

She'd stolen an entire country's gold reserves. On her very first foray as a professional thief. Granted, there was a team involved . . . her thoughts skittered around Ffodor again . . . but she had personally handled millions upon millions of dollars in gold. (And, like anybody would have done, she'd seized the opportunity to widen her cut. Which would have worked out just fine and wouldn't have hurt anybody, fuck you very much Noel Matthews.) After that, almost nothing seemed worth the effort.

Which is why she'd pushed Ffodor for something fun, something challenging, something worthy of two kickass aces on a tear. She'd worked so hard to convince him she wasn't the clueless, immature naïf he'd first met. And it worked. Soon after that, word had come through the grapevine about a casino somewhere in Bumfuckistan, which led to—

No. She shook her head again.

She set the alarm for oh-dark-thirty before crawling under the sheets. At first she tried sleeping on her stomach, like she usually did, but the residual tingle in her chest made that impossible. Nearly an hour passed before the irritation with herself for being so careless as to let the gendarmes take her by surprise, coupled with the shame of acting like Ffodor hadn't taught her a goddamned thing, subsided to the point where she could fall asleep.

The alarm woke her. Mollie didn't bother to get out of bed. She created an opening at the bottom of the toilet bowl and twinned it to another about two feet over the head of Brent's bed. She held the fold in space long enough to hear a splatter, a shout, and disgusted sputtering echo from within the ceramic bowl in the next room.

"OH MY GOD you are SO DEAD you UNBELIEVABLE CU—"

She closed the twinned portals, unplugged the alarm, shut her eyes, yawned, and nestled back into her pillows. Only to find herself wide awake a moment later. Wide awake and cursing herself.

The casino.

The empty, unguarded casino.

The empty, unguarded casino that, last time Mollie had seen it, was filled with seven metric shit-tons of money. Cash money. Fucking snowdrifts of currency.

God damn it. Maybe she was just a stupid hick from potato country after all.

"You liked Cesar okay?" Michelle asked. She and Adesina were flopped on the sofa. Episode 13 of the *All Ocelots* TV show was cued up on the DVR and ready to go. Adesina had Misty Mouse clutched in her claw.

"I think he's very nice. And not just because he brought me the toy."

"But that didn't hurt," Michelle laughed.

"Well, no. But he really listened to us and he helped with the dishes."

"Yeah," Michelle said, turning on the show. "He is nice. And gets big points for helping clean up." On the TV, the Cherry Witch was pursuing some nefarious plan to take over the *Ocelot 9* forest. Every week there was a nefarious plan. It was kind of comforting.

Michelle glanced down at Adesina curled up beside her and saw she'd fallen asleep. She picked her up and carried her to bed. After she tucked the pink sheets around her daughter, she turned on the nightlight. Even in the half-light, the stars she'd painted on the ceiling in glow-in-the-dark paint lit up.

She kissed Adesina on the forehead, then slipped out of the room.

This was the time of night that Michelle didn't like. With Adesina in bed, she was alone. And when she was alone, her thoughts turned to Joey. And that was a complicated mess. Not just because of the sex—which was alternately tender and horribly violent—but because Joey was broken in specific ways and, no matter how hard she loved her, Michelle couldn't fix that.

She pulled Skype up on her tablet. A list of contacts appeared, Joey's name at the top. Michelle's finger hovered over her name a few times, debating whether or not to call. Then she tapped the screen.

To her surprise, Joey answered on the second ring.

"Hey, Bubbles," Joey said. Her silky Creole voice made Michelle miss her more. "Adesina asleep?"

"Yeah," Michelle replied, running a hand through her hair. "How'd you know?"

Joey laughed. "The only time you call now is when the niblet is in bed."

"What are you doing at home? I would have thought you were out fleecing the tourists." This was better. Giving Joey a hard time was better than trying to really talk to her.

"Fuck you, Michelle," Joey snapped. "I don't tell you how to run your life. You're still working for those Committee dickweeds." A couple of zombies appeared behind Joey.

Pretty standard Joey stuff, Michelle thought. *Get pissed. Get zombies.* This was familiar territory. She lay back on the couch, propping her head up on a pillow. She folded the tablet cover into its standing position, then put it on her chest.

"They do a lot of good, Joey," Michelle said defensively. "I wouldn't have Adesina without them."

Joey's expression softened. "You got a point. Don't suppose the two of you can come down for a visit? It's been a long fucking time."

Oh, yes, it had been a long time. Michelle felt a stab of desire shoot through her. But instead of saying what she wanted, she said, "I don't know, Adesina's in summer school and I'm doing a bunch of work for this L'Oreal thing."

"Oh, fuck that shit," Joey said angrily. "You could get out of that if you wanted to. A week. Are you really saying the Amazing Bubbles can't get a week off? That's some fucking bullshit."

She was right, of course, Michelle could probably get the time off, but she was scared. Scared of how much she wanted Joey. And how that usually turned out.

"It's not . . ." she began, and then Adesina's scream drove everything else from her mind. Michelle jumped up from the couch, her tablet hitting the floor with a thunk. Long ago, she'd discovered that that scream was the most terrifying sound in the world. Michelle ran to Adesina's room, slamming her foot and hip into the doorjamb. She didn't feel the pain, just absorbed it into her body.

Adesina was tangled up in her pink floral sheets, moaning, with tears running down her cheeks. "Adesina," Michelle said, giving her a little shake. "Baby, please wake up." But her daughter continued to scream. Michelle pulled her close and started running her hands across Adesina's wings. That had always worked in the past to calm her down, but the only thing it did now was turn the screams into a horrible low guttural moan.

"Adesina!" she said frantically. She smoothed the cornrows out of Adesina's face. "Adesina, it's just a dream. It's just a dream. Wake up! Baby, *wake up!*"

But Adesina wouldn't open her eyes. She ground her teeth, and the horrible growling grew louder.

"Jesus!" Michelle gathered Adesina even tighter to her chest, but it didn't help. That awful sound couldn't be coming from her daughter. A cold sweat broke out across Michelle's back. "Jesus! Baby, please, wake up!"

"They're coming," Adesina said in a thick, guttural voice. Her eyelids snapped open, but her eyes were rolled back and the only thing visible was the sclera.

Then she blinked. Her brown eyes stared up, and Michelle could see the fear there. Adesina pressed her face into Michelle's chest and put her arms as far around Michelle as she could.

My God, Michelle thought. She felt sick to her stomach. *It's finally happened. All that shit that went down in the PPA has finally caught up to her. The psychologist said it would.*

Her little girl was reliving that nightmare. Being taken by those soldiers from her parents. The charnel pit. All the dead children. Even Michelle had had more than a few nightmares about that.

"It's okay," she said, rocking Adesina. "You're home. We're safe here. Nothing can happen to you here."

But Adesina didn't answer, just kept crying and burying her head in Michelle's chest.

Michelle didn't know what to do. She could blow shit up. She could make it rain bouncy bubbles. She could absorb the blast of a nuclear bomb. But she didn't know how to keep night terrors away from her daughter.

She hadn't felt frightened or helpless since her card had turned. Until now.

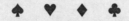

TUESDAY

THEY HADN'T MADE IT far. Once they were in the hills Baba Yaga tapped the driver on the shoulder, and nodded toward a pull-off into a stand of trees. For the first time the old woman had looked not just old, but frail as well. It was now full dark and the plan was made clear when the guard gave Baba Yaga his coat and she lay down in the backseat.

Franny wasn't sorry they'd stopped to rest. The wounds in his side and shoulder were hurting, and despite being cold and hungry he managed to sleep. He only awoke when a door was slammed. Morning mist crept along the ground and through the trees and reflected back the light from a small campfire. The guard had a couple of fish on sticks over the flames. The smell of the charing skin was maddeningly delicious.

Franny moved and hissed in pain. Whatever painkillers he'd been given at the hospital had worn off. He was stiff from sleeping in the van, and the bullet wounds were grinding points of agony. He finally climbed out of the van, and rubbed at his arms to try and warm up. Baba Yaga was huddled by the fire. He joined her.

"Can you point me toward where those guys came from?" he asked, pointing at the fish. "I'd like to wash up."

She indicated the direction with a jerk of her chin. Franny walked off and found the stream a short distance away. The water was bracing as he splashed his face feeling the rasp of thick stubble against his palms. A day or two more of this and he was going to look like the homeless guys in New York—bloody, dirty, and dressed in ill-fitting mismatched clothes. He paused to unbutton his shirt and inspect the bandage on his side. It was dark red with blood and some had trickled down his side. He sluiced off

the blood, unzipped, and relieved himself against a nearby tree. He returned to the campfire.

Stache offered him half a fish. He accepted it with a nod of thanks.
Baba Yaga was picking at the other half. Stache had a whole fish to himself. Franny supposed that was fair; he was a big guy topping Franny by
four inches and Franny was damn near six feet tall.

He studied the old woman from beneath his lashes, but she noticed.
"What? What do you want, boy?"

"I want you to level with me. I think you know a lot more about what's
happening than you're letting on."

"I do."

"So tell me."

"Why?"

"Because . . . because that way if only one of us makes it the word will
get out about . . . well, about whatever it is that's happening."

She gave him one of her bleak smiles that had nothing to do with
amusement or joy. "And if I tell you you drop me flat. Why be slowed down
by the old woman? That's what you would think. No, this way you will be
careful to keep me safe, and get me to people who might be able to stop
what is coming."

"And maybe you're just bullshitting, and you have no more idea than I
do what's going on." He measured stares with her.

Finally she gave a sharp nod as if she had resolved an internal question. "What did you feel?" she asked. "In the hospital."

"I told you."

"No, you told me what you *saw*. What did you *feel*?"

His appetite gone, Franny set aside his food. He didn't want to remember. Didn't want to answer. He realized he was going to have to give something to get something. He said, "Rage. Against . . . so many people. If
any of them had been in front of me I would have—" He broke off, stood,
and walked away. He looked back over his shoulder at Baba Yaga. "I'm not
that person. At least I don't think I am. I pray I'm not."

"Are you religious, boy?"

"I'm a Catholic."

"Not what I asked."

"Okay, yeah, I suppose I am."

"Then I will tell you this much. Hell is about to come to Earth."

She stood and walked to the car. It was clear the conversation was over.

The Angel awoke, unmoving. Only her eyelids fluttered open as she lay on the narrow hotel bed and stared at the man lying next to her. She knew from past experience that if she even twitched he'd awake instantly and she sometimes liked to watch him sleep for a bit. It was the only time his face was in repose, the only time his tense body was relaxed.

The sun had risen and enough light leaked through the partially drawn curtains in the Holiday Inn Express that a soft light illuminated Ray's harsh features and hard-ridged musculature. He lay flat on his back, his head nestled in his pillow, his mouth slightly open, a thin line of drool running down to his jawline. She smiled at his adorable appearance.

Sometime in the night he'd thrown off most of the rumpled sheet so that it only partially covered the hip and leg nestling against her, but still enfolded her curves. He was always hot, his skin and flesh palpably warm to her touch. It was part of his ace metabolism. Her eyes drank in his nakedness, still marveling at the fierce beauty of it. She'd never felt ashamed at the feelings it aroused in her, not even when they were new, unwed lovers, despite the lessons her mother had tried to beat into her.

His scars somehow added to the attraction she felt. They spoke to her of the price he'd paid over the years. Of course over the years most had vanished, faded away because of his extraordinary healing powers. Some recently acquired ones still lingered, longer than they used to. That worried her. Ray hadn't slowed down over the years she'd known him, but his ability to heal had.

But the long scar, the one that ran from his sternum to his groin, was still an angry red line stitched into his pale skin, straight and sharp as a razor cut. When they were new lovers it had taken her months to gather the courage to ask him about it, but he'd only laughed when she'd brought it up one night while they were in bed.

"That? I got that one on stage at the Democratic National Convention, back in 1990. That twisted little Nazi fuck Mackie Messer took off most of the fingers of my right hand and gutted me like a fish live on national TV. He could vibrate his hands like buzz saws," Ray had explained. He'd fallen silent for a moment, remembering. "Not my best moment, but no one knew who the hell he was and what he could do, least of all me. But, see?" He'd held his hand out for her inspection. "They all grew back and work just fine." He'd illustrated by caressing her breasts, teasing her nipples so that she'd shivered.

"Did you kill him?"

"Nah. I was too busy holding my guts inside me." His eyes had turned dark for a moment, but his hand never missed a stroke. "I was in the hospital for like eight goddamned months and that goddamned Senator Hartmann whose life I'd just saved never even sent me a get-well card. But he got his, eventually."

"Don't blaspheme," the Angel had moaned, and suddenly concerned with other matters, Ray never told her exactly what it was the senator had gotten. Later she'd looked him up in the SCARE archives and what he had gotten had been pretty bad indeed.

Back in the present, she smiled down at him. She had her own scars, some visible, some not, but the worst of her visible ones was the one that crawled over her flat stomach like a snake. Ray had never asked her about it.

The Angel suddenly realized that Ray's left eye was open and squinting up at her.

"How'd you know that I was awake?" she asked him.

"You're breathing harder," Ray told her.

Her smile broadened. "We have a busy day ahead of us."

"Just another day of saving the world."

"Do we have time, do you think . . ."

He grabbed her, pulled her on top of him.

"I'll always have time for you, baby."

This was, the Angel thought, her most favorite part of the day.

Barbara shook her head, scanning the pages before her. Under her feet, the floor of the UN jet throbbed, and the faint roaring of the jets penetrated even the soundproofed meeting room where she, Klaus, and Jayewardene sat, with stacks of flimsy printouts in front of them. The rest of the Committee aces were ensconced in the main passenger cabin, or perhaps mingling with the press crew at the rear of the plane. The Secretary-General was poring over his stack; Lohengrin had barely glanced at his. Barbara thumbed through hers quickly, looking for the ones that Ink, Barbara's assistant, had marked at the top with an asterisk.

Too many requests for intervention. It wears on all of us, and especially

Klaus. Barbara knew that Klaus was feeling overwhelmed by the red tape, the bureaucracy, the rules and regulations that were slowly strangling the Committee as it become more firmly enmeshed in the UN's structure.

The stack of reports had a bewildering array of global issues: the continuing eruptions of the volcano Eyjafjallajökull, which were disrupting air travel throughout Europe (no asterisk on that one); Barbara wondered what in the hell anyone thought the UN or the Committee aces could do about a volcanic eruption, or if they'd act even if they could; fighting in Dili, the capital of East Timor, between jokers and the police over promised health care reforms (an asterisk from Ink on this one, with the terse note *Could become an issue*); riots in Talas (that one prominently asterisked with the note *Got more on this at the office*); more Somalia piracy, but no asterisk; Kim Jong-un's threats to test a wild card bomb in order to create aces for North Korea, which had never had a significant outbreak of the virus (that one asterisked, with a note underneath stating *Still no reports of the DPRK having the virus, or labs capable of growing large quantities of it*).

"What about this Talas report?" Barbara asked Jayewardene. Klaus started at her comment and started to glance down at his own reports. "That's Kazakhstan, right? Not the one in Kyrgyzstan or Turkey, but the old Silk Road area? Ink seems concerned about it—do your people have more, or do you have a feeling about it?"

"Nothing more from my sources," Jayewardene answered. "But . . ." He gave a shrug of thin shoulders. "I don't like reading this . . ." Barbara raised an eyebrow, glancing at Klaus. Klaus just shrugged, however.

"I don't know," he said. "I see Ink's marked it, but there're so many places that seem worse off and more in need of attention. The South Korean stuff—maybe it's time we showed the DPRK where they really belong in the global scale of things."

"Sending aces to the DPRK would just make them think they're more important than they really are," Barbara responded as Jayewardene nodded. They all felt the jet banking, and Barbara's ears popped as the cabin pressure dropped slightly. Klaus yawned, whether to clear his own ears or not, Barbara couldn't tell.

"I suppose," he said, pushing his chair away from the table. "It doesn't matter. We'll be wheels down in just a few hours, and I don't know about you two, but everything I see here can wait until we're back in New York at the office. I'm going to see if I can grab something to eat, then try to get some sleep before we're back. Barbara?"

She shook her head. "I want to give Ink a call and see if any new reports have come in since she printed out these."

"More paper . . ." Klaus gave another shrug, shaking his head. "Whatever you want," he said. "We'll talk about what's next later, then."

He nodded to Jayewardene, and left the room. As the door closed behind him, Barbara turned to find Jayewardene's dark brown eyes on her. "Everything is good with you? And with Klaus?"

"Sure," Barbara told him. "Why wouldn't it be?"

"Just concerned. Klaus looks . . . tired."

"He is," Barbara told the Secretary-General. "We didn't get much sleep the last few nights, that's all."

Jayewardene lifted his chin. Barbara smiled at him disarmingly. She wondered whether he'd glimpsed something, or whether someone in the office—Ink, perhaps, she wondered; after all, she'd worked with him—had told him that Klaus was becoming more disengaged from the daily workings of the Committee, that he sometimes seemed overwhelmed, that he was only his old self when he was actively engaged out in the field, that Barbara herself was making more and more of the decisions for the Committee.

He lost an eye, and he lost friends that he'd had for years. She worried about depression and PTSD, but Klaus shut her out anytime she suggested that, or hinted that it wouldn't hurt him to talk to someone if he needed to. She certainly wasn't going to tell him that it was all putting an increasing strain on their relationship.

"He's fine," Barbara told Jayewardene. "We both are."

The Angel and Billy Ray scooted up the front steps of the Jokertown precinct—locally known as Fort Freak—and slipped inside through one of the double wooden doors held open politely by a blue-uniformed patrolman. She'd never been inside the precinct before so she stopped for a moment to glance around and get her bearings.

Having worked for a number of years for SCARE, she was used to something less than luxurious surroundings. But this . . . If SCARE was the redheaded stepchild of federal law enforcement, then Fort Freak was clearly that child's illegitimate offspring.

Though tidy, the reception area looked as if it had last been renovated during the depths of the Depression. The Angel could readily picture a kicking and screaming James Cagney being dragged through it by a couple of uniforms while shouting, "I'm gonna get you coppers!"

The floor, though clean enough, was worn linoleum tile that had clearly seen better decades. The wooden furniture—benches set against the faded walls, the handrails on the steps leading up to higher floors, the large desk that dominated the reception area's rear wall—were all battle-scarred by cigarette burns, knife blades, and what looked like the occasional badly patched bullet hole. Ceiling lights and desk lamps were translucent glass bulbs that the Angel imagined were once lit by flickering gas flames.

The air was a dull mixture of sweat, long unwashed clothing, booze, vomit, harsh antiseptic, the not-quite-human ichor that flowed through the veins of some of the local citizens, and the desperation and fatalism that tore at their souls. It seemed to settle into her lungs like swamp fog blowing off a chemical waste dump.

She'd never imagined that someplace that could make her long for her sterile little cubical office down the hall from Fish and Game existed, but this was it.

Billy Ray stopped, turned, and looked at her, impatience on his face. His expression changed when he saw the look on hers. He grinned crookedly.

"Makes our little slice of reality look good, don't it?"

She smiled weakly.

"Come on. The sooner we get this done, the sooner we can get out of this dump."

She hurried to his side. The wide-open reception foyer buzzed with floor traffic, uniforms escorting criminals, obvious detectives and probably some not so obvious, on their important business, helpless and hopeless civilians wandering about with dazed looks in their eyes, all flavored with that special Jokertown aroma. Almost all the civilians were jokers, and more than a few of the cops, including the joker with sergeant stripes on his blue blouse. Enfolding bat wings depended from shoulders, as he sat high in judgment behind the elevated reception desk. He looked down speculatively, his eyes going back and forth between them, but straying, the Angel noted, more often to her rather than her husband.

"What can I do for you, Mr. Ray?" he asked.

Ray smiled, pleased, the Angel knew, at being recognized.

"Sergeant?"

"Taylor," the desk man supplied, after Ray paused for a moment.

Ray nodded. "Taylor. We need to see the top officer on duty. Captain Maseryk?" The name was a question.

Taylor shook his head, his wings rustling slightly as he moved. The Angel wondered if his nickname around the shop was Bat Man.

"Captain Mendelberg, she's—"

"Busy," a voice supplied from behind them.

The Angel turned. It was the female detective who'd responded to the call at Norwood's hotel room. Razor Joan barely acknowledged the Angel with a flicker of her cold eyes. Instead, she focused on Ray.

"So this is the famous Billy Ray," she said speculatively, her eyes gliding over him, the Angel thought, as if he were a particularly tasty-looking T-bone on display in a butcher's shop window.

"Billy," the Angel said. "This is Detective First Class Lonnegan. She and Stevens responded yesterday to the situation at Jamal's hotel room," the Angel told him. She and the detective exchanged brief nods and glances.

"I see," Ray said. He frowned, as if he didn't. Really. "Any further developments?"

Razor Joan looked up at Sergeant Taylor, who suddenly looked down and found something very interesting in the papers that had been spread before him upon his desk. He picked up a pen and started to write furiously. She looked back at Ray and her expression changed, becoming noncommittal without softening.

"We should find someplace rather more private," she said, "to discuss this."

"How about the captain's office?" Ray asked. "Who's on day duty? Maseryk or Mendelberg?"

"Mendelberg," Lonnegan said. "But—"

"But what?" Ray asked. His tone had grown colder, his expression tauter during the brief exchange. The Angel could read the slight signs, see the tension in face and eyes and even the way he held himself. It had quickly turned into a contest between him and Lonnegan.

"You may have heard that we had some excitement here yesterday," the cop said.

"Yeah. I heard it rained jokers inside the precinct."

"That's one way of putting it. Since then, Mendelberg has been—" She paused slightly, as if searching for the proper word. The one she chose sounded oddly neutral to the Angel. "—occupied by the problem."

"I'll bet," Ray said. "Well, we've come to see her about this little problem. And others."

Lonnegan continued to stare at Ray, then she slowly nodded. "Yes," she finally said. "The captain's office. That might just be the place. Come right this way, Mr. Ray—"

"Billy," Ray said brusquely. The tautness of his expression, the Angel noticed, had gone down from eleven back to ten.

Lonnegan nodded approvingly. "Billy." She glanced at the Angel. "Bathsheeba—come this way."

She stepped aside as she gestured toward a corridor that led apparently into the core of the ancient precinct. Not to be outdone, Ray paused, unbent ever so slightly.

"After you, ladies," he said, and together they went down the hallway, abreast, Ray between the Angel and Lonnegan while the sergeant still studiously pushed papers around the surface of his battered old desk.

Five minutes with Ffodor's webcam roulette software and the wireless connection from a coffee shop in Taos gave Mollie a new doorway site. She chose a garden terrace behind a hedge on the campus of an engineering college in Chandigarh, India. It was sixteen hundred miles from Talas— just barely enough from her point of view. But it was random, a place she'd never visited before, and somewhere she'd probably never revisit. She wasn't about to scout the casino from within one of her own bolt-holes. After all, others had probably entertained similar thoughts about the place by now. And, on the off chance the chaos surrounding her last visit hadn't culminated in a permanent change of ownership, she wasn't giving anyone a chance to track her. Baba Yaga was bad fucking news. So was her pal, the drooling vegetable in the wheelchair—the guy looked harmless, but something about him gave Mollie the screaming clownies.

She paused, chewing the last bite of a cloying lemon bar. *Do I really want to rob that witch a second time?*

All it took was a little bit of bad luck to turn something simple into something rotten. The residual Taser ache in her chest served a useful reminder. Good. It would keep her alert.

Hell yes I do. She turned my life into shit. If not for Baba Yaga, I never would have come near that sick fight club shit in a million years. And Ffodor . . .

Mollie cleared her thoughts with an angry shake of her head. It rattled her table; other patrons glanced at her. She glared back at them until they became uncomfortable. Then she locked the real-time image on her tablet. A text banner flashed across the screen:

Be smart. Be safe. Be quick.

She gasped.

Ffodor, taking care of her even now. He had written the webcam software for her. It was yet another thing she never would have considered on her own, a simple idea that somehow made her ace that much better. She'd forgotten that he added a reminder . . . Her face turned hot, warmed by the blush of embarrassment when she remembered the misadventure in São Paulo that had prompted him to add the gentle reminder. The embarrassment turned to shame.

And then she couldn't see the screen anymore. She blew her nose on a paper napkin. It smelled like overly strong coffee and the chocolate syrup from her mocha, but for a moment she could almost smell the scent of weird Hungarian cigarettes, as though somebody had snuffed one just before she entered the room.

God damn it.

Mollie wiped her eyes, glad she hadn't bothered with makeup before getting a start on the day. She studied the image on the laptop until she could easily picture the secluded spot on the Indian campus with eyes closed. Then she scooted her chair back, stood, and went to the ladies' room. It was empty. She went into a stall. Somebody had used a black Magic Marker to draw an arrow pointing to the dispenser of tissue-paper toilet seat covers; above this they had scrawled in block letters, FREE! AUTHENTIC TAOS COWBOY HATS! Alongside this somebody had printed, in a different hand and ink, FUCK YOU, CHOLO.

Mollie opened a doorway in the back of the bathroom stall door. Its twin opened half a world away. A warm breeze and the scent of hibiscus wafted into the bathroom. She stepped from New Mexico to Punjab.

The hedge kept her in shadows. That was good, too—it meant her doorway into the casino wouldn't shine like a beacon if the place was dark. Footsteps, and a pair of voices laughing in a language she didn't understand, approached from the other side of the hedge. They passed. She waited for a moment to convince herself her arrival had gone unnoticed. Then, very carefully, she created a new doorway in the terrace. This was much smaller than the one in the bathroom, though, more porthole than portal. Its twin opened in the ceiling of a casino in Talas, Kazakhstan.

It showed her rows of overturned slot machines and stools, illuminated by the erratic flickering of damaged fluorescents. Some of the machines had been smashed until they spewed out coins. A rhythmic metallic crunching and jingling told her somebody was nearby. Mollie leaned left and right, peeking around the edges of the portal, until she glimpsed one of Baba Yaga's thugs and two of her "hostesses" scooping the loose money into pillowcases. The hookers had to keep pausing to pull up their tops lest they'd spill right out of their clothes when they bent over to scoop up more change.

Petty cash. Not worth it if Mollie could find a better score. Ffodor had taught her to appreciate the trade-off between time spent and reward gained.

She moved the Talas end of her transdimensional doorway to another corner of the casino. This time its opening favored her with the stench of rotting food. Mollie glimpsed an overturned buffet table, dented steam trays (one looked like it had stopped a bullet), and snowdrifts of slimy black caviar on the floor. She also saw plenty of smashed and battered furniture including a leather couch stippled with bullet holes.

There were bodies, too. Including—

Mollie gasped. Something sour crept up her throat. She coughed twice, trying to force it down.

Jamal Norwood lay strewn among the wreckage, half his head caved in from a monstrous punch. One of his eyes was . . . She'd bolted the second she saw him go down. Put a continent and more between herself and Jamal's killer. Fuck. He'd been pretty nice to her for a Fed, especially given the attitude she'd shown him. He sure as hell deserved better than to rot abandoned and forgotten in this shithole at the ass-end of the world.

Mollie swallowed down sour gorge. This was a dangerous train of thought. None of this was her fault. None of it.

Her third field of view looked over the gaming floor. This had attracted most of the looters, and these guys actually knew what they were doing. Organized bands of mobsters armed with automatics and crowbars worked down the aisles between the tables. She recognized some of them as Baba Yaga's thugs. They moved in teams from one table to the next. When Franny and Jamal had started evacuating the jokers and the place erupted into pandemonium, the gamblers had abandoned everything as the bullets

flew. Unfinished drinks, canapés, even their chips. Those gamblers who
had run out of chips had tossed watches, rings, earrings, and other collateral into the mix. The looters took everything they could find. Some of
the tables had cash boxes fastened underneath. But it seemed to be slim
pickings, though, since most of the money circulating on the gambling
floor did so in the form of chips. But that didn't stop the goons from emptying the pockets, purses, and billfolds of every dead gambler they found.
Or making a badly wounded gambler a dead gambler. They even—Jesus—
they even checked the mouths of the dead for gold fillings. Mollie only
had to watch one example of postmortem dentistry (this using a claw
hammer) to know she wanted to stay way the hell away from those sick
fuckers. She closed her viewing portal before somebody saw her.

Her fourth peephole opened on a dark corridor closer to the hostesses'
"lounge." It was quieter here. She sighed; the tension went out of her shoulders. But then something squeaked and she slammed the portal shut. Several long moments passed while she knelt alongside the terrace, panting like
an asthmatic, before she realized it had probably been a mouse. A mouse,
and not the squeak of a wheelchair. Of course not.

A fifth angle, chosen to show her the teller cages, greeted her with the
deafening screech of a saw blade on metal and an incandescent fountain
of orange sparks. It scared the shit out of her. Mollie flinched, eliminating
the portals. She waited again in case the sound of power tools in Kazakhstan drew attention to her hiding spot behind the hedge in India. When
nobody came running across the campus to investigate, she reopened the
twinned doorways, but this time even smaller.

Four goons, more of Baba Yaga's hired muscle turned entrepreneurial
spirits in the burgeoning field of abandoned casino wealth redistribution,
were trying to cut their way into the abandoned teller cages. The tellers
turned cash into chips and vice versa; the casino's daily gambling take
hadn't been rotated into the vault when everything went to hell. So the
money was just sitting there, unclaimed. Apparently the thugs couldn't
get the keys, or didn't know where they were stored. Or, more likely, they
didn't want to risk breaking into Baba Yaga's private rooms to look for the
key in the first place. Mollie didn't blame them.

She might have waltzed through a portal inside the cage. But the thugs
would see her, and they'd get royally pissed off when they saw her emptying the money drawers. Money they'd already decided was rightfully theirs.
For one thing, these guys were armed up to the eyebrows. For another, and

judging from the way the steel mesh rattled when they kicked it, it wouldn't be long before they made it inside. And she did not want to be inside the teller cages when those hormone cases broke through, not for a second. She needed to get rid of those assholes.

Actually, she could solve two problems at once. And it was a fucking awesome way to clear the obstacle, if she did say so herself.

Be smart. Be safe. Be quick.

Well, two out of three.

New portals. She stepped from Chandigarh to New York City. The cops at Fort Freak were too busy, and her entrance too quiet, for anybody to notice right away when she stepped into a corner of the precinct house. The casino evacuation had sent everything into chaos that hadn't subsided a day later. She gathered they were also trying to figure out where the hell their colleague Franny Black had gone. He wasn't among the casino dead, though, so he'd get in touch with them soon enough. It wasn't her problem. But she figured the cops would have Jamal's family notified and his remains treated properly. So she envisioned the spot in Talas where poor Jamal lay, and opened a doorway under his body. She gently deposited the deceased agent just outside the door to the captain's office.

The atmosphere in the precinct went from vigorous turmoil to undistilled mayhem. Which conveniently kept the cops distracted. She tried to be quick so they wouldn't notice her when she stepped from the precinct house to the teller cages in the casino. But the screech of the power saw gave up the game. The cops noticed her departure at the same moment Baba Yaga's goons saw her enter the cage.

People on two continents shouted at her simultaneously. Nobody looked happy to see her. Well, fuck 'em: she was accustomed to that. And about to get much more unhappy, all of them.

Mollie envisioned the ceiling of the police station halfway around the world, where she'd been an instant earlier. She put a portal roughly over the middle of the cops' desks. Then, as fast as she could manage, she opened a succession of portals under the thugs' feet.

Fwump, fwump, fwump, fwump.

They fell through the casino floor in rapid succession, plummeting through the ceiling in New York to crash into desks, cops, and each other. The tumbling power saw smashed a coffeemaker, sending up a black geyser. Peering down through the final hole, Mollie got an overhead view as one of the thugs tried to pull his gun only to get tackled by a big furry guy

who looked like something from a children's book. The remaining goons
went down under a scrum of uniformed patrol officers, including one who
looked like she was half racing hound, and some ass-ugly bug-eyed motherfucker. The shouting drew the captain (Mendelberg, according to the
door) from her office.

Mollie closed the transdimensional doorways. It left her conveniently
alone with the cash drawers, free to empty them at her leisure. She could
hear people elsewhere in the casino, now that the power saw had been
silenced. But the hookers were unlikely to bother her.

The drawers were locked. So she created an opening in the wall and
reached through to her parents' barn in Idaho, where she snagged a crowbar. Within moments tens of thousands of Kazakh tenge and a random
assortment of other currencies fluttered onto her bed in North Dakota. It
looked like mounds of Monopoly money. Less than five minutes was all
she needed to empty the casino of its last day's take. She didn't know how
much it was worth in real money. Maybe not as much as it looked. The
exchange rate probably sucked diseased donkey balls.

What the hell, she thought. She went back to the slot machines. She
left the thug and hookers to their pillowcases, but there were still dozens
of machines that hadn't yet been broken open. Mollie opened another
opening to her family barn and dropped the slot machines through one by
one. A whiff of manure entered the casino. Turned out a fully-laden slot
machine made a racket to wake the dead when it crashed onto the hard-
packed dirt floor of a barn. It frightened the cows, too. They started lowing.
Dad and Brent came to investigate the noise while she was working on the
fourth slot machine.

Her dad took all of two seconds to examine the mess in the barn. He
shouted at the hole in space. "Mollie! What in the hell are you doing?
You're scaring the cows, for Christ's sake."

"Hi, Daddy. You wanna round up the boys and get to work? Those slot
machines are hard to open, but they're full of cash."

Brent squinted at the Cyrillic script on the battered machines. "Uh,
where did these things come from?"

Mollie said, "No place you've ever heard of, dumbass."

"Oh, yeah? Who are you trying to rob this time? Who you gonna get
killed this time? I don't want to get stabbed again, you know."

"Hey! Screw you—"

"SHUT UP! Both of you," said their father. He licked his lips. "Brent, go fetch your brothers. Mollie, I see another row of machines behind you that ain't been touched yet, so keep at it."

It wasn't *We love you,* it wasn't *We miss you,* it wasn't even *Why don't you come home and help out on the farm for a while.* Not that she would ever go back to the farm. But it would be nice to know she was welcome. That she had a home to return to, if she wanted it. She didn't. But still.

Gazing into the barn, she glimpsed a length of coiled hose. It gave her an idea. "Hey, Daddy? Do you still have those hydraulic tools you bought at auction?" A couple of years before her card had turned, Mollie's father had scooped up a lot of machinery in an estate sale.

"Yeah, it's around. Why?"

Because slot machines were petty cash. But real wealth could be found in safes and fireboxes. And she knew where she could find a few. "I think I'll need them. I'm gonna try to snag a safe or two."

The squad room was like many others the Angel had seen in pursuit of her duties. Smaller and shabbier than most and also not as active. The Angel could sense that something was going on and as she exchanged glances with Billy, she knew that he realized it as well.

This was not a happy place. One or two of the cops were engaged in processing possible felons or were desultorily picking away at their computer keyboards with a couple of fingers. One, a big furry guy frowning with concentration who looked like a cross between an escaped Muppet and a child's nightmare, used only one finger at a time from his big, clawed paws and even so, in the brief look that Angel got, seemed to spend a lot of time backspacing and retyping.

This being the Jokertown precinct, there were other unusual-looking cops. But they weren't working. They were gathered in twos and threes in various corners of the usually busy room and engaged in quiet, almost ominous conversations. Most looked up at the four as they passed through.

Clearly, Lonnegan felt it, too. She stopped at the door to the corridor that led to the inner offices and turned back to the squad room with a frown.

"Slow crime day, people?" she asked. She continued to watch as the small groups broke up and people headed back to their desks, the various file cabinets standing against the dull-painted walls, or the coffeemaker.

A few donuts were left in the open boxes on the adjacent table. The Angel felt like she could use half a dozen.

The inner corridor was furnished with vending machines and a few scarred benches. It was in better shape than the outer chambers. It led to a small number of private offices, two of which had names on them. Joan led them to the office labeled CAPTAIN CHAVVAH MENDELBERG and knocked smartly. They entered at the sound of a muffled "Come in." Stevens and Lonnegan stood near the desk.

The Angel was a little surprised to see that the neat little office was cleaner, brighter, and had clearly been recently renovated with new and tasteful furniture and accoutrements, like the attractive carpet on the floor. Handmade and foreign, the Angel thought. She didn't know if that made it more, or less, expensive, but she was inclined to think the former. Captain Mendelberg was behind a neatly kept and recently refinished desk, nice-looking but nothing out of the ordinary, leafing through a report file. She was a young woman, maybe her mid-thirties, the Angel judged, and smart and driven to have already obtained such a high rank in the police force. She'd been touched by the wild card. Her skin was a not unattractive shade of olive, but nothing you'd want for a complexion, and her ears were prominent and frilly, as if she had special-effect alien ears for some kind of science fiction movie. They moved in a disturbing manner, seemingly independent of each other and maybe without control by their owner.

"Well." She set her papers down and looked up. Her expression was more prim than neutral, the Angel thought, and she was more than annoyed at their presence but hadn't entirely decided how to respond. "To what do I owe the honor of a visit by federal agents, Mr. Ray?"

"Kidnapping across state lines," Ray replied, pleasantly enough.

Mendelberg frowned. "I don't undertand."

"Kazakhstan is not on Long Island, Captain," Ray informed her pleasantly, and her olive complexion deepened.

"I'm missing an agent, Captain," Ray said with a degree of calmness that meant he was getting ready to blow. "He took off for Kazakhstan with one of your boys. Neither of them is back, but I did hear that a boatload of jokers ended up here last night—"

Mendelberg's eyes snapped upon Stevens and Lonnegan, standing together. Her mouth clicked shut and she said coldly, "That incident is still under investigation."

Ray opened his mouth to say something angry and, probably, the Angel thought, regrettable, but she grabbed his arm and hissed, "Listen!"

There were sounds coming from the squad room. Strange, mixed sounds of heavy objects hitting the floor, raised voices, barely discernible, some possibly not shouting in English, and then, finally, gunfire.

"What the hell?" Ray asked, whirled, and headed for the door.

But Stevens was closest. He threw it open and rushed out into the corridor, but before he could take more than a step, he tripped over something in the doorway and fell flat in the hall. The Angel, right behind Ray, looked over her husband's shoulder, an expression of horror on her face.

"Jamal!" the Angel cried out.

"I'm afraid so," Ray said. "What the hell is going on here?"

Jamal Norwood's battered corpse had been laid out before the door to the captain's office. There was no doubt that he was dead. His face had been smashed by either some object or a brutally powerful fist and one eye was hanging from its broken socket. The other was staring blankly. Ray hunkered down before the body, put his fingers on Norwood's cheek as Lonnegan and Mendelberg joined them at the doorway. Stevens had scuttled back to his feet and was looking at Norwood's corpse in horror.

"Sorry—didn't see him, not at all—"

His voice stumbled to a halt as Ray looked around.

"He's cold. Been dead for a while."

His words were punctuated by gunshots. Louder now that they were out in the hall, and much more numerous.

"Nothing we can do for him," Ray clipped.

He stepped over the body into the hall.

"Come on," he said, and went down the hall. The Angel and Lonnegan on his heels, Stevens right behind.

It took only moments to reach the chaotic squad room. The Angel blinked. It couldn't have been any different than it'd been the moment they'd left it. Armed thugs were squared off with knots of cops. Another suddenly fell from the ceiling and crashed onto facing desks, feetfirst. He staggered, dropping a bag, and coins fell tinkling to the floor, scattering everywhere. The newcomer rose reaching for a gun and before he knew it Billy Ray was on him. He had five inches and fifty pounds on Ray, but it did him no good. Ray took care of him while the Angel looked to the ceiling. There was a hole in it, as round and smooth as if it had been bored out by a corkscrew, and a head was looking down at the chaotic scene below.

Tesseract! The name flashed into the Angel's mind. The *American Hero* ace who had already racked up an unsavory reputation as a thief, but had never yet been caught red-handed or even arrested. Had she killed Jamal?

The Angel ran forward three steps and called her wings to her and surged up into the sky, but the startled young ace snapped shut the portal before the Angel could reach her. Frustrated, the Angel did a snap roll and caught one of the gunmen from behind. He screamed as she lifted him up from the floor and threw him hard against a wall. Plaster cracked and rained down upon the donuts sitting naked in their boxes. A sharp burst of gunfire destroyed the coffeemaker and hot liquid spewed over that quarter of the room, sending combatants scurrying for safety from the boiling coffee. An scruffy-looking one-eared tomcat sat under a nearby desk and yowled, his tail blown up to the size of a bathroom brush.

The seven-foot-tall Muppet with the wolf snout and bull horns grabbed the last of the interlopers who was still on his feet and plucked his gun away from him with one hand while holding him up high with the other. He kicked uselessly like a boy throwing a temper tantrum.

"QUIET," the beast roared. Everyone took his advice.

Billy Ray held his foe by a tight grip on his tie and glared him into utter complacency. He looked around the room where most were still shakily settling down. Some glared up at the ceiling, weapons out and waiting, but neither thugs nor money fell from the ceiling to join them.

"You look like crap."

"Thanks," Michelle said, opening the door wider. Mrs. Klein from across the hall stepped into the apartment.

"How's the kiddo?"

"Not good," Michelle replied softly. She went into the kitchen and poured a cup of coffee for Mrs. Klein. Cream, no sugar.

"Thanks for coming over," Michelle said, handing the cup to Mrs. Klein. "She had a bad night and I have Committee stuff to catch up on. I'd rather not leave her, but I think she's going to be okay for now." She rubbed her gritty eyes. "When we got back from the PPA, the psychologists warned me that she might have a delayed reaction from all the stuff that happened there. I guess it finally caught up with her. I made an appointment to take her to see the doctor tomorrow." She glanced over her shoulder. Adesina was still wrapped up in her pale blue blanket and curled into a ball on the sofa. She was asleep at last.

"I'll make sure she's okay. And you know I never mind looking after her. She's a sweet girl." Mrs. Klein took a sip of her coffee. "And you still make lousy coffee, Michelle." She put her cup on the dining-room table.

"Oh, hell," Michelle said. "I just remembered I forgot to call Joey back after Adesina's bad dream."

"You'll never keep a girlfriend that way," Mrs. Klein said, giving Michelle a smile.

"She's not my girlfriend," Michelle replied. She could feel her cheeks getting warm. "We've already talked about this."

Mrs. Klein shrugged her shoulders. "Well, I like her. And I think you like her plenty, too. But what do I know. I'm just the old lady who lives across the hall . . ."

Mrs. Klein was giving Michelle her usual hard time, though more kindly than usual. Michelle thought seriously about hugging her, but decided that would be awkward. Mrs. Klein was many things. But a hugger wasn't one of them.

"What the hell is going on?" Ray asked.

He and the Angel were in Mendelberg's office, which was as good a place to be as any in the precinct. Lonnegan was actually sitting at Mendelberg's desk, her feet up on it, looking pensive. The Angel was in one of the overstuffed chairs before it. Both were watching Ray pace around the room. "Norwood," he said. "Dead."

His body had been removed, Stevens detailed to take care of it.

"I've been afraid that might have happened," the Angel admitted.

"The thought of dying is always somewhere deep within us," Ray said. "You can't let it out. Can't dwell on it. But Norwood—"

"Do you think this Tesseract was somehow responsible?"

The Angel shook her head. "She's more sneak thief than murderer. But how did it end up at Mendelberg's door? Did she put it there?"

Lonnegan shrugged. "Got me."

"Where's this Francis Black?" Ray asked suddenly.

Lonnegan shrugged again. "Got me. What's he got to do with this?"

"Fits with what Stevens told us last night," the Angel said.

Ray took over the story. "Stevens said Black and Norwood had peeled back some of the layers of this rotten onion. They knew that the Russian mob was yanking jokers off the street and using this teleporter to bring them to some foreign casino where the owner, an ex-KGB agent with the lovely Russian name of Baba Yaga, made them fight like gladiators. And this shitbag Michael Berman made and sold videos of the fights."

"Berman . . ." Lonnegan said thoughtfully, then snapped her fingers. "He was brought in the other day. Made bail, though. And that Mollie kid—she was a production assistant for his skuzzy production company."

Ray nodded. "Which matches the info we picked out off Norwood's computer." He looked at Lonnegan. "What happened after the jokers started arriving?"

"There was complete chaos," Lonnegan said. "Some babbled crazy stories—which might not have been crazy after all. Father Squid dead—"

Ray and the Angel exchanged glances.

"Father Squid—" His expression suddenly went slack.

"The soul of Jokertown," the Angel whispered.

Lonnegan nodded. "Nobody believed it, but the rumor swept the precinct. And now . . ."

"And now," Ray said, "it feels true, in my gut."

"I know, right?" Lonnegan said. "He was just . . . always been here. Always quiet, gentle, but a rock of strength the whole community could shelter against. Nothing could stop him. Nothing could bring him down. He helped hundreds—hell, thousands—of jokers." She paused, briefly. "Hell, you didn't have to be a joker." The Angel was astonished to see tears form in the cop's eyes.

"What else did they say?" the Angel asked quickly.

Lonnegan took a deep breath. "Death matches took place in some club or something—obviously this casino. That kid who calls himself the Infamous Black Tongue was one of the captives. Mendelberg," Lonnegan said in a flat, affectless voice, "immediately clamped down on it. Shut them all up and marched them all off into protective custody in the old holding cells. She slapped a guard on them, wouldn't let anyone near."

"I'm not a lawyer," the Angel said, "but she can't do that."

"She did."

The Angel could see the tautness in Ray's body suddenly disappear, just like that. "Mendelberg ran the investigation—or rather noninvestigation—on those joker kidnapping cases and as far as I can see, she did more to discourage investigation than encourage it."

"Are you saying she covered it up?" Lonnegan asked. "That's some serious shit."

"Thing is," Ray said, "we just don't know. Apparently the only one in the precinct who felt strongly enough about it to buck her was Detective Black. We had our suspicions"—he glanced at the Angel—"but we knew that Black had to get solid dope on her if we had a hope in hell in making anything stick—"

"And then he blew it all up in our faces," Lonnegan said. "That snot-nosed, jumped-up patrolman who got his detective badge way too early."

"Favors?" Ray asked.

Lonnegan shrugged. "No one knows for sure. He's not particularly popular around the station. He never really talks about it, but his dad was once the captain here—"

"John Francis X. Black," Ray exclaimed. "Found dead in his office under mysterious circumstances on Wild Card Day 1986, wasn't it?"

"Right."

Ray whistled lowly. "Chri—ah, cripes. Talk about the good old days. I was here for that shit. Aces murdered. The Great And Powerful Turtle sunk in the East River. Aces High demolished. Armageddon threatened. Old dude found stuck halfway through a brick wall." He shook his head. "No wonder the death of a police captain almost went unnoticed."

"Water under the bridge," Lonnegan said. "We've got our own problems to worry about. Our own missing captain to find."

"Well," Ray said, "all the signs point in the same direction, no?"

The others sighed, shook their heads with weariness, or rubbed tired eyes. It was Lonnegan who said it aloud.

"The Russian Mafia."

Ray smiled, almost happily.

"So what more do we know about Talas, Ink?" she asked her aide.

Ink, wearing her usual short-sleeved blouse and Dockers, shook her head and ran her fingers through spikes of black hair. Ink was Korean, though she'd been raised as an adopted child in the States, and as usual, her skin was liberally covered with the tattoos that had given the woman her sobriquet. The wild card had given her the ability to control the appearance of those tattoos with exceptional detail and versatility. Today, the tattoos were echoing the reports she was handling, with text slowly scrolling down her arms like a fleshy marquee.

Ink had been with the Committee for only a few months now, and Barbara already wondered how she'd managed before. Ink had also become a semi-confidante for Barbara; there was something about the young woman: a carefully concealed vulnerability that drew Barbara to her.

"I can't tell you, Mizz B." Barbara had quickly given up any hope of convincing Ink to call her "ma'am" or "Ms. Baden," as did most of the staff. Ink's competence as Barbara's chief of staff more than made up for her casual attitude. "I've called the people who sent in the last three reports, and I'm sure they all *believe* they're telling me the truth, but they're also all telling me different and contradictory things: food riots, some kind of student uprising, an attempted military coup. I don't think anyone knows what's actually going on. But it's clear enough that there's *something* awry in Kazakhstan, and specifically around Talas. Whatever the trouble is, it is growing. Fast."

"I want you to call the U.S. Embassy in Bishkek," Barbara told the woman. "Tell them we've gotten troubling reports out of Talas and we need to know what the problem is there ASAP. They have to have good contacts on the ground there. Keep forwarding any new reports to my phone, especially when you can verify the truth of them."

"I'll do that. But I'm worried. Things are getting worse there, not better, and the contradictions in the reports . . ." Ink pressed her lips together. "Somehow, those worry me even more than what I'm hearing."

"I agree. I think we need people on the ground ourselves to tell us. I'm going to see Klaus now and try to convince him that we need to get boots on the ground there."

Ink nodded once to Barbara, ran fingers through her hair once more, and left the office, the tattoos on her arm losing the appearance of text and shifting to abstract, Escher-like patterns. Barbara gathered up the papers in front of her, put them in a folder, and went down the hall to Klaus's office. She nodded to his secretary, who waved her on.

"Hold his calls," Barbara said as she passed. Then, as she entered the office: "Klaus . . ."

He looked up from something he was reading; it looked to be one of the reports she was holding as well. Behind him, through the office windows, she could see the skyscrapers of Manhattan. "That the stuff about Talas?" she asked.

"Ya." His German accent, even after years in the States, was still strong. "Jayewardene sent this to me. Said it was something to watch." *Sumting to vawtch.* "I'd agree with him. Your Ink has sent you the same material?"

"She has, and I believe it's more than just something to watch," she told him. "We're not getting good Intel from anyone there, and we're not *going* to get it until we can see what's happening for ourselves. I think we need to go in now. Today, if possible. Half of Talas is no longer in communication with the world, and all these reports of bloodshed and violence . . ."

"Ah." He leaned back in the chair. "You know how much I value your counsel, my dear." He said it languidly, shaking his head so that his blond hair moved around his cheeks and brushed his eye patch. A hesitant smile lurked on his lips; she knew that expression—she'd seen it often enough over the years. *Go ahead and tell me whatever it is you want, but I've already made up my mind and you're wasting your time.* That's what that face meant.

Normally, it didn't bother her. No couple had a perfect relationship, and certainly not them. She had her own quirks that she was certain bothered Klaus, though he rarely complained. She knew she could be *too* diplomatic at times, that she sometimes spoke too formally, that people often came away from her thinking her distant, aloof, and cold . . . and that sometimes that perception was probably correct. It didn't bother her that Klaus's opinion had more weight than hers with the others of the Committee and those in the UN, that it was the image of Lohengrin that came to mind whenever someone mentioned the Committee. He *was* the leader, the head, the face of the Committee.

But lately . . . She worried about Klaus, about the discomfiture she felt in him. He was only energized when he was out in the field *doing* something. When he was here, he was just mostly burned out and tired, and his decisions . . .

You know how much I value your counsel . . .

"But?" she interrupted, and the edge on the word vanquished Klaus's smile. "You don't think this important enough? Klaus, I'm worried that if we wait on this one that it's going to escalate out of control."

His sigh was audible. "Right now, it's a local problem only. Not something for the Committee to become involved with. Ya, we need to stay on top of Talas and be ready to move if it continues to escalate or if it threatens stability in the region, but there is actual ongoing rioting in East Timor. *That's* where I feel we should be going, as quickly as we can."

Because there he could just lose himself in action. Barbara sighed. "Love, in Talas, half a city is in chaos and no one knows why, and it *is* spreading, by all accounts. I'd say that stability there has *already* been affected."

"Babs . . ." She hated that nickname, but had never been able to get Klaus to stop using it. Klaus gave another sigh. "Are you angry with me? What have I done?"

The change in subject annoyed her, all the more because it felt as if he were deliberately poking a finger into a new wound. "I'm not angry with you, Klaus. Not at all. This isn't about us, Klaus. I really feel it's a mistake to ignore Talas. Let the Secretary-General deal with East Timor," she answered.

He stared at her, and she held his gaze. Finally, he looked down at the report in front of him and shook his head. "I understand why you're worried and I appreciate your concerns, but I don't see a reason yet to go to Jayewardene and request that he allow the Committee to become involved."

"Half a city's already out of communication, Klaus. And the problem has grown over the last few days. What more of an excuse do we need?"

"I know. I understand. But it's still a local issue for the moment. The entire country of East Timor is in jeopardy with the riots there. The government could fall."

"Everything I've seen and everything Ink's given me says the locals aren't capable of dealing with Talas, and that they don't have a grasp on what's really happening there."

"Then when that becomes more apparent, we discuss it again. For now, I say we should plan on going to East Timor. At the very least, let's send a team there."

And I'll be leading them. She knew that would be the case without his adding the phrase. She also heard the finality in his voice. "All right," she said. "I'll have Ink copy you with her reports and comments. But I think waiting on Talas is the wrong strategy."

Klaus nodded. "I hear you," he said. "And I'll take the responsibility." Barbara nodded at that and turned to go. "Babs," he said behind her, and she stopped with a sigh. "We should talk. Tonight. Not about Talas. About us."

"We will," she told him. She smiled at him. "I'm not angry with you, Klaus, I love you—that's never changed. But I *am* worried about you. We'll talk."

"You look like crap," Ink said as Michelle got off the elevator on the Committee floor. She said it with a little too much pleasure.

"So I've been told," Michelle replied with a sigh. "Adesina had a bad night and I didn't get any sleep."

Juliet immediately stopped looking pleased about Michelle's crappy appearance. "What's wrong?" she asked. Bright red tattoos started swirling on Ink's face. Even though Michelle had screwed things up with Juliet—by sleeping with Joey, which had not been her finest moment—Juliet was still part of Michelle's life.

After Michelle had adopted Adesina, Juliet had become a de facto aunt. Recently, Michelle had convinced Babel to take Juliet on as her assistant. Not only because she knew Juliet would be great at it—hell, Ink had put up with Billy Ray at SCARE for three years—but because she and Adesina could see Ink more often if she was living in New York.

"I think everything she went through in the PPA is finally catching up," Michelle said. There was a tremor in her voice. *Do not cry,* she thought. *This is no place for that.* "It may be PTSD. I'm not sure. All she said was, 'They're coming,' which has to be about the soldiers. Or maybe about the doctors at the camp."

"Good grief, then why are you here?" Ink gave Michelle an impressive glare, and her voice rose. "Who the hell did you leave her with? Why did you leave her?"

Michelle put up her hands. "Hey," she said sharply. "Mrs. Klein is with her, and I made an appointment for her to see someone tomorrow." She really didn't like explaining herself. She wasn't a shitty mother. At least she hoped she wasn't. "I'm going to tell Lohengrin I need to take some time off. Which will thrill him to no end. But please, give me more of a hard time. You know how much I enjoy that."

A soft voice floated to them. "Girls." It was Margaret. "I think you can take this somewhere else or down a notch."

Michelle looked around the austere lobby—everyone was staring at them: secretaries, the mail boy, and what looked like a couple of visitors. Awkward. *So much for a professional demeanor,* she thought. Then Michelle saw Aero and Earth Witch standing with a couple of people she didn't know. One was a joker about her age. His face was a jigsaw pattern of flesh. Brown skin abutted ruddy white and all the subtle tints in between were present in patches on his face, neck, and hands. Michelle assumed his entire body was the same. She didn't remember getting a brief on him.

She learned later his name was Tiago Gonçalves—code name Recycler— and that he was from Rio de Janeiro. His power allowed him to assemble trash into a protective barrier.

Standing alongside Recycler was the Australian ace, Tinker. Tinker had come on board after the Committee was well established. And while his power was certainly handy (he could make any kind of gadget he wanted out of materials at hand) Michelle had discovered on more than one mission that he hated following orders. He didn't understand doing what was best for the mission even if you didn't like it.

There was one other person in the group. Michelle assumed he was Marcel Orie from the information in her brief. He was much taller than Michelle. His hair was salt-and-pepper-colored, and he wore round wire-rimmed glasses that gave him a professorial air. The expression on his face said he'd rather be anywhere but in the lobby of the Committee offices. According to the dossier on him, he could control lightning bolts, and his code name was Doktor Omweer. Michelle thought he would come in handy when she needed some bubbling fat.

Ana crossed the lobby and gave Michelle a hug.

"You do look like crap," she said, but she was smiling. "I'm sorry Adesina had a rough night. Is there anything I can do?"

"No, but you're sweet to ask," Michelle replied in a low voice as she hugged Earth Witch back. "You giving the new additions the nickel tour? Doktor Omweer looks like a treat."

Ana tried to stifle a laugh and ended up snorting instead. "I'm afraid none of us are worthy to hold his jacket. I'd offer to let you meet them, but I doubt he would deign to talk to you, you know, because you're a model and all."

Michelle shrugged. She didn't have a great formal education, but she wasn't stupid either. If Orie thought she was beneath him because of that, well, he was a snob. And all the education in the world didn't mean jackshit out in the field.

She nodded toward Aero. At least there was one new ace she liked. "I already know Cesar. He had dinner at my place last night."

"He asked me what the kiddo would like," Ink interjected. "Did he get her something?"

Michelle nodded. "Nice *Ocelot 9* toy," she said with a slight smile. She looked at Juliet still smiling. "Ink was a good auntie telling him what to get. Adesina was thrilled."

"You should meet Tiago," Ana said. "He's a great kid."

"I'd be happy to," Michelle said as she let a tiny bubble appear in her hand, then let it float up to the ceiling. She pulled off her baseball cap and her long, platinum hair cascaded over her shoulders. Then she shoved the cap into the outside pocket of her bag. "I guess I can say hello, but I'm supposed to see Babel and Lohengrin now. I'll do that first, then meet him afterward, if that works for you."

Ana nodded. "Sure. They're not going anywhere just yet. Barbara and Klaus are in the main conference room. We're going to need more space soon—they turned the small conference room into overflow for tactical support."

"You know," Michelle said with no small amount of resentment in her voice, "this place is getting too big."

Marcus thought, *Man, it feels good to have a ball in my hands!*

He wove through the kids, all coils and motion. He dribbled around them, sometimes over their heads, bouncing the ball with satisfying force on the packed dirt of the village court. He twisted a three-sixty to avoid a tall youth with unnaturally long arms. He faked another boy so decisively that he tripped and went down, laughing. He rose up into a two-handed monster dunk, powered by the long muscles of his tail. At the last minute he remembered not to hang on the rim, frail and rickety as it was. Still, the kids playing and the others watching loved it. So did he.

Spinning the worn ball on his upraised finger amid the kids' rapid Kazakh banter and high fives, Marcus couldn't believe how good he felt. What a difference a day makes! Bullet-riddled and desperate one day. Fit as a fiddle and surrounded by new friends the next. The Handsmith must've known what he was doing. He'd fished out all the bullets in Marcus's tail. He'd dropped the deformed chunks of metal into a tin bowl with wet, audible thwacks. Each of those sounds pulled him a little ways back toward the living. But even that couldn't explain how he felt. Only Nurassyl did.

He looked to where the boy stood at the edge of the makeshift basketball court. He swayed with excitement, grinning. "Slam dunk!" he called, the only words of English he seemed to know. His tentacled hands clapped

together. Those hands. The boy's touch had both eased Marcus's pain
and healed him. His wounds had closed almost as soon as the operation
stopped. The skin knit over them. He couldn't even find the bullet holes
in his scales. He'd slept like a rock through the night. When he woke he felt
as good as new. It didn't seem right that the nat world would only see deformity in the little boy, only the joker that made him different from them.
As far as Marcus was concerned, the boy was an ace. He'd told him as
much, which had caused the boy to flush red all across his gelatinous skin.

He's just a kid, Marcus thought, *but I owe him my life*. He wasn't sure
how to repay such a debt.

For that matter, he owed a debt to the entire village. They'd welcomed
him when he was down and out. No questions asked. Not one of them
spoke more than a few words of English, but even without Olena translating Marcus found communicating with them easier than he would've
imagined. They were all smiles and good humor and questions. Yes, he
lived in New York City. Yes, he'd seen the White House. No, he didn't know
Michael Jordan. Or Michael Jackson. Or Beyonce. Yes, America did have a
high incarceration rate for a Western country. It was amazing just how
much you could convey through pantomime. When they learned of his
name, they'd called for him to demonstrate what his tongue could do.
Marcus obliged them. He didn't mind. It was kinda fun to use his tongue
for amusement for once.

As the children called for another game, Marcus caught sight of Olena
emerging from a villager's cottage. She spoke a few moments with an old
woman whose face was marred by large pits that shifted and changed shape
and size. Olena embraced her, saying something Marcus couldn't hear.
That was another thing that kept amazing him. Olena treated the jokers
in the village with respect and empathy, without any sign of the revulsion
most nats betrayed at seeing jokers.

Leaving the woman at her door, Olena jogged onto the court and
grabbed Marcus by the wrist. She said something in Russian to the pro-
testing joker youths and then pulled him away.

Remembering he had the basketball, Marcus hooked it one-handed over
his head, sending it back to the kids on the court. Right after he did it he
wished he hadn't. The motion reminded him of the last time he'd seen
somebody do that. Father Squid. Back in New York on the night they got
snatched and transported here. So much had happened since that night.
He knew that at some point, when he was home again, he was going to

have to face it all. He hated it that he'd left Father Squid—shaped like a prayer bench now—back in the casino. He should've found some way to take him home to Jokertown.

The village wasn't much more than a cluster of houses around a single main road. A few minutes' walk and they were out of it. The view down the valley stretched out before them, all the way toward Talas. The road they'd driven out on, before turning off toward the village, drew a pale line into the distance. A line of tiny cars and trucks inched along it.

"You are really feeling better?" Olena asked.

"I feel great. Yesterday I thought I was done for. Today I'm healed. And we're free. We got away! Baba Yaga can't do anything to us anymore. Let's just go. We have the truck. Let's drive someplace—"

"Marcus, face reality." She counted the hurdles that faced them on her fingers. "We have no papers. No passports. No money. Baba Yaga's people would kill us both if they found us. Kazakh police; surely they look for you, for me too, for anyone involved in the casino. American embassy? I wouldn't want to go to them. We can't cross border checkpoint. We can't—"

"Stop!" Marcus snapped. "Stop saying what we can't do."

She gazed at him with her too-blue eyes, looking sadder than he had ever seen her before. "I do not like these things, but we can't ignore them."

Marcus didn't immediately respond. She was right, of course. What did he know of passports and borders and money in a place like this? If Father Squid were here he'd know how to handle this. But he wasn't. "Is there anyone you can ask for help?"

"If things were not as they are I could've asked my father. But if he was a different man none of this would have happened." Olena sighed and let her gaze drift down the valley again. "You never asked why I was in Baba Yaga's casino. There is a reason. You should know it. It is because of my father. His name is Vasel Davydenko. He is gangster."

"Like a rapper?"

"Not gangster rapper! Organized criminal. Ukrainian Mafia. Like Tony from *Sopranos*, if he was Ukrainian and wore Armani suits and traveled in jets and helicopters and dealt in nuclear weapons. For a time he worked for Baba Yaga. I can't even tell you all the things he's done."

A burst of voices made them both turn. The gang of kids from the village was coming toward them, buzzing around the Handsmith and his son, who could only progress at his slow slide.

"Were you . . . involved in any of it?" Marcus asked, knowing they'd soon be surrounded.

Olena shook her head. "Not me. When she was alive, my mother kept me away from it as much as she could. It was her deal with my father. He could use her family business as a front—launder money, use their warehouses—so long as I was kept away from it. She was no saint, my mother, but she wanted better things for me. She died a few years ago."

"Oh . . . I'm sorry."

She touched his hand. "You know why I speak English? I went to private boarding school. Switzerland. My parents thought I was safe there with politicians' and millionaires' daughters. Even royalty." She looked down the valley. "I was going to go to university in France. I should be there now."

Marcus swallowed. Boarding school. Millionaires. Switzerland. France. He suddenly felt completely out of his league. Again. In new ways. It was hard to twin all that with her life in slinky dresses serving joker gladiators, but she'd never really seemed to belong there either. "What happened?"

"My father made mistake. Stupid one. He got big ideas and went against Baba Yaga. He tried to kill her off. He tossed a coin, so to speak, but it didn't fall the way he wanted. She lived; he ran for his life. Baba Yaga couldn't capture him, so she captured me instead. Idea was to lure my father in to save me. If he surrendered Baba Yaga would let me go. It should work, see? My father has no other family. Only me, daughter. What father wouldn't give his life to save his daughter's?" She let the question sit a half beat, and then answered it. "Mine. He didn't surrender. That's why Baba Yaga gave me to the gladiators. To shame and punish him. You know the rest."

The villagers were getting closer. Marcus slipped his arm around Olena and dropped his voice. "How could he do that?"

"No matter how hard you try," Olena said, "the bull will never give you milk."

"Huh?"

"Ukrainian proverb. Means that my father is who he is. He cares most about himself, his pride, his life. I knew that. Now Baba Yaga knows it, too."

Before the villagers reached them, Marcus said, "So we're on our own. Big deal. Tomorrow let's drive as far as we can. If we run out of gas, fuck it. We'll walk. Or . . . slither, in my case. We'll get out of Kazakhstan, and we'll do what we have to do to get money. We'll find a way out. You hear me? I'm not giving up."

A moment later, the villagers arrived. Olena leaned down, smiling now, and fell into her rapid Russian. The kids clamored over each other, competing to answer whatever she'd asked them.

The Handsmith placed a burlap-covered arm on Marcus's shoulder. Looking into the distance, his face grew troubled. He said something. Olena looked up and followed his gaze down the valley.

"What's wrong?" Marcus asked.

"All the cars and trucks on the road," Olena said. "He doesn't like the look of it. There are too many. Something must be wrong in Talas."

Marcus said, "Tell him not to worry about it. I'll go down and take a look. See what I can find out."

Michelle pushed open the door to the conference room. ". . . there's something going on in Talas," said Babel. She sounded vexed. "It's unclear *what* that is. I say we send in someone to have eyes on. Find out exactly what's happening there."

"I don't care," Klaus replied. "I want to go to East Timor. We know there's something wrong there. And I say we send a team with me leading it."

Then Klaus glanced up, saw Michelle, and gave her a bright smile.

"Bubbles," he said with just a hint of boss dude in his voice. "About time you showed up."

Michelle smiled back, but his tone annoyed her. Klaus had become I'm-the-leader-now guy in the last year or so. Someone had to do it, of course, and admittedly, she sure as hell didn't want to. She'd led enough missions to know that. But still, it was tough to take him being boss when they were both founding members of the Committee. *And maybe it's also because you're a huge control freak. And you're obviously irritable as hell today.*

"Hey, Klaus. Hey, Barbara," Michelle said. Though Babel and Michelle weren't close, they had a mutual respect for each other's abilities. Michelle looked back at Klaus. "I was here yesterday, and everyone was gone except that new kid—Aero," she replied defensively. "I fed him, filled him in on procedure, and made him feel at home."

Klaus held up his hands. In his thick German accent he said, "Cesar was very complimentary about your help. We just could have used you earlier."

"I know," she replied, feeling a little guilty for sounding defensive. Klaus and Barbara had a lot on their plates. Since she'd gone part-time, Michelle had tried to take short-term missions so she could stay at home with her daughter. "I had a scary, rough night with Adesina."

"Poor little thing!" Klaus exclaimed. He'd met Adesina before and they'd gotten along famously. When it came to kids, Klaus was a soft touch. "No wonder you look so tired."

"I'm so sorry she's having problems, Michelle," Barbara said, tugging at the bottom of her perfectly tailored jacket. "But I'd like to send you to Talas."

"I'd rather she come with me to East Timor," Klaus interjected. "I think she'd be more valuable there."

A look of annoyance slid across Babel's face. It was quickly replaced by a neutral expression. "Sending Michelle to Talas makes more sense. She's run missions and is good at handling the media. And, *she* doesn't go off half cocked because she's spoiling for a fight."

Michelle dropped her purse on the large African mahogany table, then sat down in one of the leather chairs. "I don't think I can go to either place right now," she said. She toyed with the tassel on the zipper pull of her bag. "You don't know what it was like last night. It was horrible."

Babel sat down next to Michelle. She was impeccably attired: perfectly tailored navy suit—not too sexy—heavy silk blouse, mid-heel pumps. It spoke volumes about her position, and Michelle liked that. Though Klaus was the ostensible head of the Committee now, Michelle knew that behind the scenes it was Barbara keeping everything running.

"Look, I know it's scary when your child is upset, but we really need you to head up that team," Barbara said. Michelle knew Babel was being understanding, but she also knew that for Babel, Committee business would always come first.

"I'm sorry," Michelle said. "But I just can't right now. You've got plenty of other aces you can send, including the new ones."

"We can make it a short trip," Babel said. "Just figure out what's going on, report back, and you're home. In and out."

"It's never a short trip," Michelle said with a sigh. She wished she'd just called this one in instead of coming down to the office, but she'd promised to do the whole meet-and-greet thing. Coming onboard the Committee could be daunting. "I just can't go right now," she said. "I promised to meet the new aces. When we're done talking, I'll do just that. I'll do the whole welcome-to-the-team thing, but I'm out for any assignments right now."

She stood and grabbed her bag. "You'll find someone else. You're up to your neck in aces. Hell, send the 'B' team to East Timor and the 'A' team to Talas. You both get what you want."

Both Babel and Lohengrin gave her sour looks. For a moment, she felt a stab of guilt, but it was quickly replaced with concern for her daughter. As far as Michelle was concerned, everything else was bullshit.

Late that afternoon Franny had taken a turn behind the wheel. The roads had become narrower, more pocked with potholes, and finally had turned into dirt tracks weaving through the hills and forests. Baba Yaga checked her phone and issued instructions. She finally did break down and tell Franny where they were headed—a city called Shymkent. Apparently there was an international airport there, too.

It was a little over a hundred miles away, and they weren't making very good time since the old bitch seemed determined to take them there via cow paths: Franny grazed his head against the roof of the van, and felt the stitches in his side pull again as they bounced over a particularly rough spot. The waistband of his jeans was deeply stained by the blood that slowly leaked from his bullet wound.

"Why are we doing this backwoods tour now? We're far enough away from Talas for you to avoid both the cops and your competitors. Why don't we go back to the highway and make some time?" he complained.

She looked up from her phone. "We're in a van with American license plates. They'll notice."

"We'd be doing sixty, seventy miles an hour. Nobody would notice."

"The fools in Astana are sending in the military. There will be enough paranoia even before they are affected by—" She broke off abruptly. "Point is we'll be stopped. We cannot permit that."

"Because you haven't managed to buy off enough cops and politicians in the capital to protect you?"

"That's not my worry."

"You really think some mob bosses in Talas can roadblock a highway?"

"Not them. They are nothing. No, my former employer."

"I have a hard time picturing you working for anybody. So who is it?"

"Figure it out, boy, you have more than enough information."

Franny thought back over the investigation that had brought him to Kazakhstan. The former KGB agents who had been blown to kingdom come in New Jersey. The garroting of a cameraman who'd made the mistake of recording and selling DVDs of the joker fight club. Baba Yaga's proficiency with a firearm, and ability at defensive driving.

"Christ, you were a spy. KGB, right? Those guys in New Jersey were guys you knew back in the day. You were recruiting from the old sandbox."

"So, you are not a dunce. Good to know. Yes, a number of my associates had fallen on hard times. It was a tough adjustment to the Capitalist Paradise. I found it easy to hire them, and between us we knew enough secrets to keep us safe."

"So why is the KGB all butt hurt?"

"I took something from them when I left. I didn't trust them to keep it safe." She fell silent and he glanced at her in the rearview mirror. She looked sad, an emotion he'd never thought to see on that ancient face. "I never thought I would get old. That he would get old. When you're young you never do . . ."

Franny lost the thread because a flash of color among the trees caught his eye. Yellow and red and black. Franny jammed on the brakes, drawing an expletive from Stache and a hiss from the old lady as she clutched at the front seat.

He threw open the door and jumped out, running toward that writhing mass of coils. "Marcus! IBT!" The young man stopped and stared in shock at Franny.

Behind him he heard Baba Yaga scream out, "*Nyet!* Stupid boy! Drive, drive!"

Franny realized that command was meant for Stache not him. They were going to leave him. Marcus's expression changed from one of surprise to one of wild rage. Franny panicked and started to turn back toward the van when he was knocked to the ground as IBT shot past him. It was a rapidly flexing coil that had hit him behind the knees. Franny hit on his bad shoulder and screamed in pain.

"You bitch! You fucking bitch! Why can't you stay dead?" Marcus, screaming out the words.

"Marcus! No!" Franny shouted. In desperation he tackled the final few feet of IBT's snake body, trying to slow him down.

"Get the hell off me!"

"Wait! Listen!"

Franny could feel the powerful muscles in IBT's snake body flexing and thrashing against his chest and belly. It was like riding a bucking horse with nothing to grip. His hold was slipping because of the agony in his side.

Stache was trying to climb over the center console and into the driver's seat while drawing his gun. IBT's tongue shot out, and slapped across the man's face. He screamed, convulsed, and collapsed as the poison did its work. Baba Yaga leapt out of the backseat. Her mouth was working, wrinkles becoming deep crevasses around her lips as she worked up a mouthful of spit.

"Watch out!" Franny yelled, but Marcus seemed to know the danger.

He shot off to the right, and gave a hard jerk of his tail to take it out of harm's way. The violent move shook Franny loose and he went rolling across the dirt and pine needles. The wound in his side was screaming, and he felt nauseated and light-headed. He rolled onto his knees, and drew the pistol he was carrying just as Marcus lashed out with the tip of his tail, and knocked Baba Yaga into the side of the van. The old woman slid down, unconscious or worse. Marcus spun, his tongue lashing out.

"Fuck!" Franny yelled and fired a shot into the ground between Marcus and Baba Yaga.

The young man reared back, and his tongue missed Baba Yaga's body, but hit her on the left hand. She began to jerk and convulse. IBT, his torso supported on the coils, gave Franny a look of confusion and betrayal. Franny pushed his advantage.

"Back off," Franny snapped. He watched Marcus's mouth work, and the tip of his tongue appeared. "You want to bet your tongue is faster than a bullet?"

Franny scrambled over to Baba Yaga's side, and checked the pulse in her neck. It was thread-like and jumping, but she was still alive. There was a spreading bruise on her forehead and her hand was blackening.

"You . . . you're protecting her? Why?" IBT's head drooped and he added thickly, "She killed Father Squid." Marcus suddenly sounded very lost, young, and forlorn.

Franny collapsed until he was sitting on the ground and he slowly lowered his gun. Memories of mass at the church of Jesus Christ Joker, and Father Squid's deep resonant voice as he raised the host, or delivered his sermons. The joker priest had ministered to Jokertown for more years than Franny had been alive. Franny's father had known the man. "How? What happened?"

"*She.*" Marcus's dark eyes flicked toward the crumpled woman. "Told me if I won my last fight I'd go free, then I realized it was Father *Squid* I had to fight. He offered to let me kill him, but I couldn't do it. I just couldn't. She spit at me, but Father Squid pushed me aside. He saved me and died."

"How did she change him?"

"So you know what she can do?"

"Yeah, I saw it in action." Franny repressed a shudder. Marcus didn't even try.

"She turned him into a prayer bench." The fury was back. "Guess she thought that was funny. Now tell me she doesn't deserve to die?"

Franny hesitated. He could tell Marcus about Baba Yaga's hints that she knew some great and terrible secret, but why would the joker believe him? Franny wasn't all that certain *he* believed the old woman, and he had experienced the feelings of horror and rage in the hospital.

He could wax eloquent about how he would see to it she faced justice and that just killing her where she lay was unworthy of Marcus and the wrong thing to do. And run the risk that IBT wouldn't give a shit. Besides that was the kind of pious crap that Marcus had probably been hearing from people like Franny his entire life, and the young man had been acting as the guardian or vigilante of Jokertown for the past year.

Neither was a risk he dared take. There was only one choice. He lied.

"Well, you've done it."

"She's dead?"

"Dying. She was in tough shape at the hospital. This has done it." The choice Franny had made also meant that he couldn't offer to get the kid out of here. Marcus was going to have to be sacrificed to the possibility that Baba Yaga actually *did* know something. "You better get out of here. There are people after you, and they're not real sympathetic."

"Are you sure she's gonna die? I poisoned the shit out of her and she lived."

"Jesus, Marcus, she's also like a hundred years old."

"Yeah, and she's an ace—"

"Look, maybe she could neutralize your poison, but inertia's a bitch. You slammed her into a goddamn car."

For a few more heartbeats it hung in the balance. Franny held his breath and then Marcus gave a tense nod and slithered away, vanishing among the trees. Franny sighed and pressed a hand against his side, grateful that the kid hadn't thought to ask Franny what the hell *he* was doing with Baba Yaga.

The old woman's cell phone lay on the ground near her. Franny grabbed it up, but found the screen cracked, and it wouldn't respond no matter what he tried. Frustrated, he threw it hard against the side of the van.

He knelt beside Baba Yaga and tried to think past the pain, exhaustion, and confusion. It was poison. Should he try to suck it from the wound like he'd read in those old western novels his father had loved? Franny had read them to try and feel closer to the man he'd never known. He pushed aside thoughts of home, his mother, and decided not to make the attempt. He had no idea the power of IBT's poison. He might incapacitate himself. He decided to tourniquet the arm to try to keep the poison from spreading.

He ripped the sleeve off her dress, wrestled Stache out of the driver's seat, and using a stick and the dead man's tie he applied a tourniquet to the upper arm. He then lifted Baba Yaga in his arms, laid her on the backseat of the van, and secured her as best he could with the seat belts.

"Don't die," he ordered.

He started driving, picking roads that were heading east and north. Baba Yaga wasn't able to object now and he was going to find the damn highway.

Squirming back up toward the village, Marcus's heart banged in his chest, and not just from the effort of climbing through the rocky terrain. Seeing the old lady again had set it racing; knowing that she was dead kept it that way.

Dead. He hadn't been sure after he'd poisoned her. Now he could be. The news elated him. He was free of her. A life with Olena was really possible now. But Marcus's emotions were never as black and white as he wished they were. He couldn't shake a certain amount of shame at the way he killed her. It had been so easy in the end, just a slap of his tail. For all her evilness, Baba Yaga really was just a frail old lady. For all he knew she was someone's grandmother.

"If she was," he mumbled, bitterly, "they should thank me for taking her out."

He worked his way up a ravine, preferring to stay away from the road, even the quiet one up to the village. The sign at the intersection, he'd learned, identified it as a joker village. Not a place refugees were likely to head. Still, he didn't want any other chance encounters like the one with the cop and Baba Yaga.

He hadn't found out exactly what was going on in the city, but he knew that people—rich and poor, ace and nat alike—were fleeing Talas. The desperate unease he'd seen yesterday morning had only increased. Now the people looked downright crazed. From the trucks piled high with stuff it was pretty clear there was looting going on. He planned on warning the village, maybe setting up a watch and barricading the road. They had Olena's Glock. Maybe they could scrape up more weapons. Anyone coming to mess with the village would find them ready and waiting. A joker militia.

Coming up out of the ravine, he got a clear view back down the valley. "What the fuck is that?" he asked.

A helicopter. It cut across the valley from the northeast, heading toward the highway. He wasn't sure why, but from first sighting Marcus didn't like the aggressive, military shape of the aircraft. It paused above the highway at the spot where the smaller road cut away toward the village. It hovered there, like a wasp over a procession of ants. It rotated, leaned forward, and started up the village road.

Marcus *really* didn't like that. He picked up the pace of his slither, weaving through scrubby trees and around rocks. He squirmed for all he was worth, catching glimpses of the helicopter when he could. He lost sight of it as he came into the village. Whip fast, he carved through the cramped alleyways between houses and burst out onto the main street just as the helicopter roared into view. Marcus shouted an alarm. He grabbed two kids who were playing in the street and deposited them on their doorstep, and then he turned and rose up on his coils to face the oncoming helicopter. It flew right over him, a menacing shape that pummeled him with the downdraft of air from the rotors, sending dust and debris swirling. It traveled the length of the village, turned and circled back, slowly passing down the main street. Looking up, Marcus saw the pilots' helmeted, goggled faces staring down at him. Insects, all right. He waved his arms, as if shooing them away.

It didn't do any good. The helicopter touched down at the edge of the village, landing right in the middle of the street. Marcus had never been this close to one before. It was loud, that was for sure. And this one looked high-tech like nothing he'd seen flying over Jokertown. Sleek, with tinted windows along the main cabin and a blur of whirling rotors that hardly looked wide enough to lift it. The tail propeller spun inside a ring that housed it, looking like a tricked-out hubcap spinner. The engines half cut, and the rotors began to slow. Before they stopped, the doors on both sides of the main cabin popped open. Figures emerged. Before he could properly see them through the dust, Marcus shouted, "Back the way you came, motherfuckers! You hear me? You're not welcome here. Turn the fuck around and go."

A six-pack of heavies took up points around the aircraft. They wore military fatigues, had close-cropped haircuts, and hefted machine guns to complete the look. Other figures emerged, a handful of men in suits. A hulk of a man with wide, massively muscled shoulders that were barely contained in his black suit. The moment he was out of the helicopter and standing, it looked impossible that he'd ever fit in it. He slipped on a pair of dark sunglasses and looked around, disinterested, hardly seeming to notice the enormous snake-man standing just a few feet away.

The rotors slowed to a halt and the dust cleared, a tall man with steely grey hair that he'd combed back from his forehead disembarked. He took Marcus in with cold blue eyes. Amusement lifted the corners of his lips. He said something in what Marcus assumed was Russian. The big man responded, chuckling as he did so. The helicopter's engine cut off.

"Fuck you, too," Marcus said in the sudden silence.

The grey-haired man grimaced. He said, in accented English, "I did not say, 'Fuck you.' I said, 'They sent a black mamba to welcome us.'"

"Whatever," Marcus said. "The 'fuck you' stands."

Stepping closer, the grey-haired man said, "I know you. You fought in Baba Yaga's arena. You are a killer of jokers. That is not my business, as I am no joker. But with me you do not fuck, understand?"

Before he could answer, Olena arrived at a run. She skidded into the road between them, a few jokers following her. She spoke a mile a minute, a barrage of Russian or Ukrainian words that she spat like bullets at the grey-haired man. For a time, Marcus could only stare, not understanding a thing. Olena must've noticed. She switched to English.

"You!" she hissed at the man. "What are you doing here?"

The man pulled a coin from his jacket pocket and knuckle-rolled it. The coin flipped over and over as it passed from finger to finger. He began to answer in Russian or Ukrainian. Marcus couldn't tell the difference. Olena cut him off, "Speak English! You sent me to learn it, didn't you? Spent all that money. Speak English!"

Vasel shrugged. Taking in Olena's native clothing with something like disdain, he asked, "Precious daughter, what are you wearing? And is that any way to greet your papa?"

"Papa?" Marcus gasped.

"You're not my papa!" She made a fist with her thumb protruding between her middle and index finger. Marcus almost shouted for her to not hit him with that. She'd break her thumb. But she just waved it in a gesture that included all of the new arrivals.

Vasel shook his head disapprovingly. The coin still flipped from knuckle to knuckle. "You've become such a rude girl. I don't hold it against you. You've had a hard time, I know. I will make it right with you."

The big man paced with the mallets that were his fist swinging in warning. He scowled at the arriving villagers, who'd begun to cluster around them. No one came too close.

"You can't make anything right," Olena said. "You let Baba Yaga have me!"

"Everything I did was for you."

"Liar! How did you find us?"

"A father should always know where his daughter is," Vasel said. When that clearly didn't satisfy Olena, he added, "Tracking chip."

"What?"

"It was for your own good. Remember when you ran away from school with that boy? What was he, Algerian?"

"French," Olena corrected. "He was born and raised in Paris!"

"Algerian first. Algerian always." He glanced at Marcus. "At least he wasn't as black as this mamba. That little adventure cost me headaches, money, resources to find you. We drugged you on the flight back home, yes? That day and many after. Was not just to keep you quiet, though. Also, for you to recover from a little operation. Tracking chip. I had them place it under that tattoo you so foolishly had just gotten." He pointed at the spot on his own lower back. "Who would've thought my daughter would become tramp?"

Olena's face shifted through a series of emotions. Bewilderment. Disbelief. Shock. After all these, she settled on anger. An anger that could only be fully expressed in a torrent of words in her native tongue.

"I thought you wanted to speak English?" Vasel said.

She did, mid-sentence. "—a chip in me as if I'm a dog? That's what you did? I hate you! Hate you!" She spat on him. It was a vicious motion, full of loathing, but it only left a few flecks of spittle on his crisp suit.

Vasel seemed unperturbed. "With the chip I always knew where you were. Always, I had people spying on Baba Yaga, waiting for the moment to take her out, and to rescue you."

"Rescue me? You gave me to her!"

"You are alive, yes? And now you are free. When our informant told us that the shit had hit the fan in the casino, I was on my way to Baikonur. Lucky timing. I dropped what I was doing and came to find you. I should be in Talas now, taking advantage of the moment, but I came first for you. I get this thanks for it."

Olena shook her head slowly, contempt mixing with disbelief. "You didn't come here out of love for your 'precious daughter.' You want the company. You want my shares. You can do nothing without my permission."

"I can do many things without your permission, daughter."

Olena looked to Marcus. "Every legitimate part of my family's fortune came from my mother's family. When she died, Vasel Davydenko had surprise waiting. Her assets all came to me. As long as I'm alive, he's locked out of the board. Unless I say otherwise. If I die"—she grinned and turned a withering look back on her father—"he doesn't know what might happen then. I may just give everything away in my will."

Marcus tried not to looked too stupefied by the casual mention of "my family's fortune." One of these days, he really needed to figure out who and what this girl was.

Vasel pulled a handkerchief from his breast pocket and began to calmly clean the spittle from his suit. He glanced at Marcus, and then seemed to notice the growing assortment of jokers gathering around them. "That's enough talking like this. Get in the helicopter. I'll explain everything to you. Before long, you will love your father again." Vasel gestured to the big guy. "Andrii." He moved toward Olena.

Marcus, who had watched the interaction dumbly, surged forward. Andrii rolled his massive shoulders threateningly, but it was a small motion from Vasel that seemed to terrify Olena. She threw herself between him and Vasel, who hadn't done anything more than pluck his coin between two fingers as if he was about to throw it. "No! Don't kill him! If you kill him, you kill me."

Vasel studied her, amused. He motioned for the bodyguard to withdraw. "You must be joking with me. What is this black snake-man to you?"

Olena looked into Marcus's eyes when she answered. "He is my lover."

The gangster's one-word response was in Ukrainian, but it hardly needed translation.

Michelle let herself into the apartment. She'd gotten a late start in the morning, and by the time she'd dealt with all the Committee bullshit in the afternoon, traffic was turning into a bitch. She'd stopped and bought a pizza from Bruno's for an early supper. It may not have been a healthy dinner, but it was Adesina's favorite meal.

Mrs. Klein and Adesina were on the sofa watching TV. They both smiled at her.

"You got pizza for dinner," Adesina said, but her voice lacked its usual pizza enthusiasm. She was huddled down into her blue blanket, her wings folded tight across her back.

"Get enough for all of us?" Mrs. Klein asked as she stood up. "You went to Bruno's. They have great pies. And I see you got a large."

Michelle put the pizza on the dining-room table, then went and sat down next to Adesina.

"You feeling any better, pumpkin?" she asked. There were circles under Adesina's eyes and she looked exhausted.

How can I fix this? Michelle thought. A new flutter of fear bloomed in her chest. *I have to fix this.* She couldn't bear to see her daughter looking so frail and frightened.

"You look like you could use some dinner, pumpkin. I got your favorite—mushrooms and black olives."

A wan smile crossed Adesina's face. It looked like everything was a huge effort for her. *There has to be a way to stop this,* Michelle thought.

"I'm not hungry now," Adesina said, her voice getting softer as she spoke. "Maybe later?"

"But it's going to get cold and you hate cold pizza." Right now she just wanted to get calories into her daughter. She'd try for Mother of the Year later.

Mrs. Klein slid a couple of slices onto a paper napkin. "I'm going to head across the hall. If you need me, you know where I am. Adesina, feel better, bubbeleh. I'll bring you some cookies from De Roberti's Caffé tomorrow. The anise ones you like."

But even the promise of cookies didn't make Adesina look happy. Michelle and Mrs. Klein exchanged concerned looks. There was a new, stronger flutter of anxiety in Michelle's chest.

"I'll check in tomorrow," Mrs. Klein said, then took a sniff of the slices. "This smells yummy, even with those mushrooms and olives."

After Mrs. Klein shut the door, Michelle snuggled closer to Adesina. "How was your day? Did you get any sleep?"

Adesina shook her head and burrowed down into her blanket. "Not much," she replied. "I don't want to go to sleep again. There are things . . ."

"You know that you never have to worry about anyone taking you away again," Michelle said earnestly. "There are no soldiers here—no one who will ever hurt you again. You *know* I can keep you safe."

Adesina gave a slight nod, and Michelle knew that Adesina didn't believe her. And that felt like a kick in the stomach. Keeping her daughter safe was her job.

"But you know there are no soldiers here, right?"

Adesina nodded again. "I'm not afraid of the soldiers, Mommy."

"Then what is it? You've never been afraid of your dreams before. And you've been good about keeping out of other people's dreams."

Michelle worried about Adesina's ability to slide into dreams and how she could control them. It was a powerful enough capability that Michelle had tried to limit Adesina's use of it.

But Michelle had made an exception with Hoodoo Mama. Adesina had walled herself away in part of the dream world while Michelle helped Joey confront the event that caused her card to turn. Watching Joey get raped as a child was something that would haunt Michelle for the rest of her life.

Despite having Adesina protect herself, it had been a profoundly selfish and dangerous thing to ask of her daughter.

"If it isn't what happened to you with the soldiers, then whose dreams are they?" Michelle asked. She didn't like the sound of Adesina's voice at all. A dark undertone that didn't belong to her little girl.

"No one's," her daughter answered. Her eyes began to well up with tears. "I'm not in anyone's dreams. I'm in mine, but there's something coming. Something bad." She shuddered, and Michelle held her tight.

"Oh, pumpkin, everyone has bad dreams. They can seem very real. You know the difference between real real and dream real, don't you?"

"It isn't like that," Adesina said as she pulled away from Michelle's arms and looked up at her. "This was a real place. And there were real monsters."

The only real monsters since the virus had hit were people using the wild card as a weapon like they had on Adesina. Mark Meadows had been a monster. She was about to tell Adesina this, but three loud knocks on the front door rattled the door.

"What the hell," Michelle said, getting up from the couch. Instinctively, a bubble formed in her hand. Three more knocks, and Michelle crossed the distance to the door in a flash. Another knock, and she flung the door open.

Standing in the hall was Hoodoo Mama.

"Joey!" Michelle exclaimed, the bubble popping in her hand. Then her eyes narrowed. "What the hell are you doing here?"

Joey walked into the apartment, pushing Michelle aside. "Where's my girl?" she asked. Usually, she'd have some kind of zombie—Joey had taken to calling them toe tags—trailing behind, but today was an exception. Michelle closed the door, then followed her through the dining area into the living room. Adesina smiled a real smile, and Michelle felt a surge of happiness.

"Aunt Joey," Adesina said, though her voice was weak. "Momma didn't say you were coming."

"She didn't know, niblet," Joey replied. She gave Michelle a withering glance. "We were talkin' last night, and she heard you havin' a bad dream, and she didn't come back and tell me if you were okay or not."

"I guess I forgot." Michelle knew Joey was pissed. She was happy to have Joey here, pissed or not.

Joey gave her an I'm-dismissing-your-lame-ass-excuse gesture, then went and sat next to Adesina. Michelle followed and sat on the other side of her daughter. "You didn't have to come all this way," Michelle said. "I know you're busy taking advantage of the marks. You could have called."

Joey snorted. "I did call. You never answered. And you always assume the worst, Bubbles. I don't just fleece the marks. I've been takin' care of other business."

Michelle knew exactly what other business Joey was talking about. There was a rough justice Joey meted out on people who hurt children in any way. It was swift and brutal, and Michelle found she never could be angry with her for this. *Screw a system that protects those kinds of predators,* she thought. Michelle tried to work for a larger good, but secretly she was glad Joey did what she did.

"So what's got you all tied into knots, niblet?" Joey asked. There was concern and softness about the question. Joey was rarely gentle like this. Joey was brutal and angry most of the time.

"Nothing's going on," Adesina said, putting her head on Joey's lap. "But I'm glad you're here. Mommy misses you."

"You want some pizza?" Michelle asked. It was time to change the subject. She and Joey had already flogged that dead horse. "It's from that place you like."

"Does it have olives and mushrooms? Because you know that's disgusting."

Adesina giggled. "I'm weird that way."

A surge of happiness rolled through Michelle. If Adesina could laugh, everything would be okay. Sure, those nightmares were bad, but they could get through it with some help. And Joey was here. Adesina loved Joey.

It was just a bad day. That was all.

Just one bad day.

Andrii leaned his bulk against the side of the helicopter. He stared at Marcus. He'd been doing that the whole time Olena and her father had been inside the aircraft, talking. It hadn't been long, but the seconds dragged by, and Andrii's sunglass-shaded eyes just stared and stared at him. Or seemed to, at least.

The helicopter door opened. Olena stepped out. Vasel began to climb out after her, but Olena had grabbed Marcus by the hand and led him away before the gangster touched earth.

At the edge of the village, Olena embraced Marcus. She kissed him, smeared the tears from her eyes onto his cheeks. "You all right?" he asked, looking back at the watching gangsters. "You want me to beat on them?"

She shook her head. Still planting kisses on him, she said, "You can't beat my father. He's an ace, Marcus. He is like Baba Yaga. She spits and you are dead. He flicks his coin and . . . that's the end. Believe me, Marcus, you do not want to fight with my father. He doesn't miss."

Throat suddenly dry, Marcus said, "Right. I stay on his good side, then?"

"He has no good side. He is a bull, remember?"

Vasel shouted Olena's name and said something in Ukrainian.

"What the fuck does he want, anyway?"

Olena pulled back a little, straightening. She cleared her throat. "I am going with them." She spoke over his immediate protests. "I *have* to! There is no choice."

"What? Are you forgiving him?"

"I will never forgive him, but . . . he's my papa. I sat there listening to him, hating him, and yet knowing his voice from since I was a girl. You won't understand. Anyway, if I don't leave you he will kill you." Marcus tightened his grip on her shoulders. "Believe me, he will. But if I go he will give you money. Make a phone call. Nobody will stop you from leaving. Fly home to New York, Marcus. If you love me, live. Get away from here, from Baba Yaga and all of this."

Marcus grunted. "Baba Yaga is dead."

Olena tensed. "You don't know—"

"I do. I didn't get a chance to tell you. When I was out I saw her. I took her out. Dead."

"Are you sure?"

"One of the Jokertown cops was with her. He felt her pulse and confirmed it. She's dead, Olena. Go with your dad if you want, but don't say it's because of her."

Olena was silent for a moment, and then said, "That changes everything."

A few minutes—and increasingly annoyed shouts—later, Marcus and Olena rejoined the gangsters.

"There's a change of plans," Olena said.

"No change of plans," Vasel said. The coin danced on his fingers.

"Baba Yaga is dead," she went on. "Marcus killed her. Police confirmed it."

The coin stopped, pinched between two fingers. "I've heard nothing of this."

"Not Kazakh police. American. One of those that brought down the casino. She's dead, Papa. That means everything is changed. When we talked you asked me questions. Had I been in Baba Yaga's office? Could I describe how to get to it? There's something in there that you want. Something that you know looters won't even notice. Marcus and I know the place from the inside. We can get whatever it is you want. In exchange, you let us go. Me and him together." She crossed her arms. "See? Change of plans."

At least Secretary-General Jayewardene agreed with her. He flatly refused to allow Lohengrin to leave the city for East Timor, or to send any of the Committee aces there at all. That made Klaus petulant. "That *scheiss korinthenkacker* would rather have me sit on my ass at a desk than be out there where I can actually be doing something worthwhile," he complained to Barbara as they undressed in their apartment late that night.

"I know," she told him soothingly. She could see the scars on his body: so many of them. Too many. She bit her lower lip as she slipped on her nightgown. The truth was that Jayewardene had nixed the East Timor mission at Barbara's insistence, but that was nothing she wanted to admit to Klaus. She and Jayewardene had had a long discussion after she and Klaus had met with Michelle about East Timor, about Talas, about Klaus. "I understand how you feel, love, but I'm sure Jayewardene has good reasons. The situation in Talas . . ."

Klaus gave a derisive huff at that. "We'll wait too long on that, as well," he said. He stared at her with his single eye. "You agree with him?"

She shrugged, sitting on the edge of the bed. "I think that Talas is potentially something important, yes. I don't necessarily agree with him that we should be waiting another day for more information."

Klaus sniffed again. *"There,"* he said, "I agree with you." The faint trace of a smile touched his lips, then vanished again. He reached for the light on a nightstand next to the bed and switched it off. In the darkness, she felt the bed move as he slid under the covers. "Are we good?" *Are ve gut?* "You and I, I mean."

Barbara slid over and pressed against the side of his body. She stroked his chest, feeling the ridges of the old scars. "Yes," she told him, kissing his neck. "We're good. But I worry about you. It feels . . ." She hesitated, not certain how much she wanted to say. "It feels to me like you're not happy anymore: with the Committee, with all that happened to you since you joined."

"It's all changed. It's not like it was when I started this."

"I know. And I know you hate all the red tape around everything, and the reports and the meetings, and all that—all the things that I end up handling. Which I don't mind," she hastened to add.

"And which you do exceedingly well. Without you, there would *be* no Committee anymore. So do you think I'm not happy with *you?*" he asked.

Her fingers stopped moving on his chest. "Sometimes," she admitted. "Yes."

He turned to her with that, one arm sliding under her and the other around. "You shouldn't think that. Ever."

"But I do, every once in a while. You want to be out there being Lohengrin and saving the world and I understand that, but sometimes the right thing isn't just to rush in blindly, it's to wait and to negotiate . . ." His mouth covered hers, stopping the words. She resisted, wanting to continue the discussion, but there was also the desire to just be with him, to drown all the fears and uncertainties in just being with him. She brought her arms around his neck, pulling him to her. His hands pulled at the hem of nightgown and she lifted her hips to help him.

And for a time after that, there were no words at all.

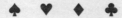

"She asleep?" Joey asked, stretching out on the couch. Michelle liked seeing her there.

"Yeah. I had to leave the light on again, but after a while she drifted off. I think she'll sleep. She's been up since last night."

Joey kicked off her shoes, then shook her head. "That's some fucked-up shit, Bubbles. I guess things really are starting to catch up with her. Those fuckers in the PPA—if I could've, I woulda killed them twice."

Michelle lifted Joey's legs up, sat down next to her, then put Joey's legs down in her lap and began rubbing them. Something inside Michelle uncoiled. It was a rare moment when they were just together with nothing terrible coming at them from all sides. No leopard men, no Tom Weathers, no secret organizations trying to steal their powers, no assholes causing chaos just because they could. And it was precious to her.

"That feels awfully good," Joey purred. Michelle knew what kind of mood Joey was in when she used that tone of voice. A quiver ran through

Michelle. There hadn't been a lot of times they'd had sex, but Michelle remembered all of them in great detail. And she wanted more.

But how could she be thinking about screwing Joey after the night Adesina had had? It felt like she was being a terrible mother.

"You know, fucking doesn't make you a shitty mother."

"Get out of my head," Michelle said with a weak laugh. She shoved Joey's legs off her lap. "She's just in the other room."

Joey sat up and slid closer to Michelle. "You want to. I know you do. And she's going to be okay. I promise. We won't ever let anything happen to her." Then she reached out and caressed Michelle's breast. The nipple stiffened and Michelle gave a little gasp. It had been a long time since anyone had touched her.

Then Joey pinched the nipple hard, and Michelle felt herself getting wet. She would never have admitted it to anyone, but when Joey got rough it excited her.

"C'mon," Joey said, standing and holding out her hand. Michelle took it and let Joey lead her into the bedroom, and then closed the door behind them.

Joey pushed Michelle onto the bed and slid her hand up Michelle's leg. Michelle felt another wave of desire, then guilt.

"We shouldn't," she said weakly. But it felt so good and it had been so very, very long. "Adesina's in the other room."

Joey lifted Michelle's T-shirt and began licking her stomach, slowly teasing upward with her tongue until she got to Michelle's breasts where she lingered, alternately stroking and slapping the nipples.

Michelle was trembling, and she felt an electric shock slide through her. Something had been lurking inside her and she didn't want to face it. Didn't want to deal with the need.

"I want you and I can tell you want me." She clenched her legs tightly and rolled them both on their side, and then yanked Michelle's sweatpants down. Michelle was afraid of Joey. Afraid of how Joey made her feel. And afraid that this had been what she'd wanted for a very long time. And then she was dizzy.

"You're human. We all got shit we need," Joey said, kissing her softly. And then she began doing things to Michelle. Things that Juliet and Michelle had never done the entire time they'd been together. Joey brought her so close and then let Michelle hover just below the edge.

And then, Michelle was falling and something broke open inside her. While she was still a bit hazy, Joey said softly, "The world is a shitty fucking place and sometimes you need to be selfish."

Michelle grabbed Joey, rolled her over, and began kissing her and yanking Joey's clothes off as fast as she could. For this moment, she was selfish. And she knew that this was what she'd needed for a long, long time.

Mollie left her dad and older brothers—Brent, Jim, Mick, and Troy—banging away at two dozen Kazakh slot machines while she crept deeper into the casino in search of more loot. The goons' attempt to break into the teller drawers had made her less skittish: Baba Yaga's people had been hired to make sure nobody tried to steal from that terrible old witch, and nobody in their right mind would dare betray her while the hag was still around. Probably, then, she'd gotten plugged during the fight in the casino while the jokers escaped. And good fucking riddance.

So Mollie figured she was free to explore. Others were doing the same. Some looters kept their distance from one another, but others had apparently decided it was easier to let others do the hard work and then kill them.

Some were in it for money. Others for the wonton joy of destruction, from the sound of it. The casino echoed with crashes, bangs, random pops of gunfire, and drunken laughter. More than one lost soul wandering through the abandoned casino carried a bottle; they'd probably raided the bar first thing.

Jamal's wasn't the only body. Others had been beaten, or shot, or stabbed, or pulled apart during the chaos of the jokers' escape. Some of the dead were the joker gladiators themselves, probably cut down during the attempt to escape. One guy lay beside the overturned buffet trays. He had to be well over seven feet tall; his skin looked like armor. It was the guy who'd killed Jamal, no mistaking him, but the bloody hole in the side of his head made it look like he'd tried to clean the wax from his ears with an auger bit. He'd been full of murderous intent, and almost gleeful about it, when he pulverized Jamal's head. The flickering lights glinted from a sheen of oil on his horns.

Horns. Oh, shit. She remembered this guy. It seemed like a million years ago. He'd looked so badass, but she could have sworn he sounded like a little kid. He'd actually cried in the van, whimpering something about his ailing mother, pleading with them not to take him away and leave her alone . . . But they did, and then he became a murderer, and then he was murdered. She wondered if he really did have an ill mother, and whether—

NO. *It's not my fault. None of this is my fault. They forced me to do this, Baba Yaga and Berman. This blood is on their hands. Not mine. I'm as much a victim as the gladiators were.*

Mollie might have been a criminal, but she knew right from wrong. And the forced death matches, well, that was some sick twisted shit. She'd witnessed part of one match and from then on had made a point of never seeing another.

She shook her head, hard, as though she could shake away an unpleasant memory. But it clung to her like a cobweb. Sometimes it felt like a miracle she could move at all, dragging along so many sticky memories as she did.

Anyway. If she hadn't skedaddled when she had, the big guy would have done in her and Franny, too. She'd probably be dead right now if she hadn't picked the lock on the cuffs that baby-faced Boy Scout had used to chain himself to her. She'd done him a favor, too. If he'd thought about it for half a second he'd have to realize she'd made it a lot easier for him to defend himself. And since she hadn't found his body next to Jamal's, he probably made it out of the casino. So, really, Franny was lucky Mollie got away from him when she did. She hoped he saw it her way.

"Michael fucking Berman. Franny fucking Black," she muttered to herself while crawling under a roulette table to wrench out the cash box. "Noel fucking Matthews. Baba fucking Yaga." So preoccupied was she, muttering the names of those who'd made her life such a piss parade, that she didn't hear the crunch of footsteps on broken glass. But then she caught a whiff of the medicinal stink of cough medicine. She scurried from under the table on all fours, to find an oily joker standing over her. She banged her head trying to scramble to her feet.

"SHIT!" she yelled, rubbing her scalp. "You scared the piss out of me."

The joker cocked his head and stared at her. The flickering half-light lent a peculiar sheen to his greasy skin. He was backlit, making it hard to see his face, but she'd recognize the smell anywhere. It made her woozy. She leaned against the table to steady herself while her heart stopped trying to chisel through her breastbone. She knew Vaporlock; they'd worked together, doing snatches for the fight club. They weren't besties, but they'd talked a little, enough to know he wasn't keen on the cage matches. And that he found the drooler in the wheelchair creepy as fuck, too. So they shared a couple things in common.

"I guess we both had the same idea. I take it you-know-who isn't around?"

The instant the words came out of her mouth she realized she had just kicked herself in the molars. Vaporlock hadn't returned to the casino as she had—he must have been here when the shit went down and got left behind. *Oops.*

She didn't need to see his face to know he wasn't all that happy about it. There was a tension in his body language, like a tightly coiled spring. He stepped closer. A wave of medicinal miasma crashed over her. Mollie's head spun. She tried to retreat but bumped against the roulette table. "Back off, hey?"

He didn't. The funk threatened to suffocate her. Mollie created a new pair of portals. One hovered in the air to her left; its flipside opened on an observation deck overlooking the Atlantic Coast of Nova Scotia. A stiff sea breeze gusted through the casino, blowing cocktail napkins and loose currency past Mollie's feet like autumn leaves.

The smell didn't dissipate. Vaporlock reached for her, stepping into the light to do so. Mollie gasped.

Dried blood caked his fingernails, but it was still wet where it coated his hands up to the wrists. His mouth, too. Oh, God, flakes of blackened blood peppered the grease around his lips and coated his teeth like he was some kind of goth-vampire wannabe. But Mollie knew it wasn't makeup. He'd done somebody, done them messy, and very recently.

"Oh, Jesus. What . . . what have you done?"

He lunged. She tried to sidestep through the portal but the wooziness turned her legs to jelly. She stumbled. They went down in a heap. The portal disappeared. The wind died. Vaporlock crawled atop her. She held her breath. He took a fistful of her hair and slammed her head against the floor. The blow caused her to inhale; she got a lungful of fumes. The room spun. She felt herself sliding into darkness. He pulled her head back for another bash. *Soft, soft, make the floor something soft*—Blacking out, she struggled to envision one last portal pair. They splashed down in the People's Paradise of Africa, or whatever it was called these days.

The last time she'd created a portal on this spot, it had opened on a yacht. The boat was long gone, though, so they both went into the drink. The plunge caught Vaporlock by surprise. He released her and kicked to the surface. Her burning lungs forced her to surface, too. She took a deep breath; it still made her head spin again. The crazy motherfucker was still too close. He treaded water a few feet away, spluttering as though he'd swallowed a mouthful. *Good. I hope some fucked-up parasite lays eggs in your esophagus, you shitbag.*

Mollie opened a return portal. A deluge flushed her back to the gaming floor in Talas. She staggered to her feet amid flapping fish and a smattering of dockside jetsam. The carpet squelched underfoot. The momentary gust of African humidity carried a mélange of outboard fuel and cold medicine. Mollie rolled her eyes. Like a draining bathtub, the portal had sucked Vaporlock back, too. She'd meant to leave him with the crocodiles.

She scanned the room for something hefty. She settled on a ten-foot leather sofa in the corner. She dropped it on Vaporlock's head as he staggered to his feet. He made an *oof* sound but didn't get up.

Voices and footsteps approached; the splash had made a ruckus. Mollie stepped into her Bismarck apartment. There she changed out of her sodden clothing and leaned against the bathroom counter until she stopped shaking. She might have caved his head in. She was okay with that, all things considered. But what the hell had come over him in the first place? It's like he was somebody else entirely.

She plucked a beer bottle from the refrigerator in Idaho. Downed it. Wiped the back of her hand across her mouth. She waited for the burp, then returned to Talas.

Mollie emerged on a catwalk that opened on a series of cheaply furnished bedrooms. She didn't bother looting the hookers' quarters; Baba Yaga wouldn't have allowed them to keep anything of value. But Mollie wouldn't have wanted to touch anything in those rooms without disinfecting it with a blowtorch first. The last thing she needed was to contract some mutant hybrid of gonorrhea and the Andromeda Strain while swiping paste gems from a call girl's bedside table.

Mollie hadn't always known how to tell the difference between real and fake jewelry. Thanks, Ffodor.

But if anybody in this shithole had real jewelry, it was the queen bitch herself. Mollie'd had an "audience" with the old witch; the memory was traumatic enough that she could still picture the scene. She opened a gateway into Baba Yaga's quarters without trouble. A few minutes of watching and listening convinced her the coast was clear. It was hard to case the apartment without looking at the furniture, but she tried.

She swallowed her revulsion long enough to tear the bedding from Baba Yaga's bed and, like the hookers she'd seen earlier, turn a pillowcase into a makeshift swag bag. Baba Yaga owned enough jewelry to fill the damn thing—Mollie had glimpsed diamonds, sapphires, pearls, rings, pendants, and more during her one and only visit. She'd cased the place even while Baba Yaga fulminated at them; she couldn't help it. Ffodor had trained her too well. And then he—

Nope. Nope. Not my fault.

The earring stands on the vanity, where before they sparkled like little bonsai trees fruiting with gems, were bare. Mollie tiptoed across the room and peeked into the open drawers; they contained several velvet-covered jewelry cases. But these, too, were empty. She even knelt on the carpet and felt around the edges of the vanity, assuming *something* must have fallen free during the snatch. Not a crumb. Some gutsy SOB had already cleaned Baba Yaga out and did a thorough job of it.

"God damn it," she muttered. It was never easy. Why was it never easy? Jewels are easy to carry, easy to hide, easy to fence. So of course there'd be none left for her. No, she had to deal with the hard stuff.

So she gave up on the small stuff and searched the rooms for lockboxes and safes. Ffodor had taught her how to look for what she'd come to think of as "rich people" hiding places. And, sure enough, she found one safe embedded in the back of the walk-in closet, and a second in the floor under the bed. Mollie called through the portal to Idaho to let her dad and brothers know she needed a hydraulic cutter to get the safe out of the wall. They'd have to run the lines through the portal, but she could do the work herself. She'd grown up on a farm; she could use tools.

She was waiting on her dad to hand her the cutter when, purely by accident, her gaze touched some pieces from the Russian mobster woman's furniture collection. Vanities, divans, chaise longues tables, lamps, armoires.

Chairs.

Before she knew it, Mollie was slumped against the wall, hands on her knees, tears dripping into the carpet.

"I'm sorry," she wept. "Oh, God, I'm so sorry."

We weren't smart enough, we weren't quick enough. It was never safe. But she'd insisted. And now Ffodor . . .

"Mollie? What the hell is going on over there? You having some sort of woman trouble?"

Quickly, she blew her nose on an antimacassar and wiped the back of her hand across her eyes.

"No, Daddy. It's fine. You got that cutter for me?"

A steel bit, several coils of yellow rubber tubing, and a pair of safety goggles flew through the portal from the Idaho barn to land on a Persian rug. The chug-chug-chug of a hydraulic compressor wafted the sickly sweet scent of machine lubricant into air already thick with cow manure and Baba Yaga's designer perfumes.

Mollie lugged the tool into the closet. She donned the goggles, braced herself against the door frame, pressed the bit to the wall, and pulled the release. The bit chewed through the drywall like it was wet toilet paper. But when she hit the first stud, the chugging became a rattle and the faint smell of lubricant suddenly became overpowering.

"Whoa, whoa, whoa! Stop. Mollie, stop!"

She killed the cutter and returned to the portal. The hose had ruptured, spewing hydraulic fluid everywhere. Dad and Brent were dripping with it. Wisps of smoke wafted from the compressor; it smelled like ozone and melted plastic.

Mollie swore again. They'd probably blame her for this, too.

A cool breeze slid across Michelle's body. Next to her, Joey was asleep, tangled up in the sheets, snoring softly. She wanted Joey again, but was loath to wake her up. It wasn't often Joey looked relaxed. Her normal state was a feral wariness. Michelle liked seeing her face in repose occasionally.

The usual evening street noises floated up. Someone was yelling at someone else about random bullshit. Cabs and cars were honking impatiently, and the farty sound of buses braking was comforting. Michelle slid from the bed, making sure not to wake Joey. She slipped on a robe and walked down the hall to Adesina's room. There was a slice of pale light spilling from the partially open door. She pushed the door open a little wider, then stepped inside.

The room faced the apartment complex courtyard that dampened most of the street noise. It was quiet here compared to the rest of the apartment. Michelle loved this room. When she looked for a place for the two of them to stay, this room was what sold her. She could see Adesina living in this room.

Normally, Adesina had an odd little wheeze when she slept. But Michelle didn't hear it now. Cold sliced into her.

"Adesina," she whispered. "Baby?"

Nothing moved under the covers.

She stepped closer to the bed. "Baby . . ." There was no response. Michelle snapped on the bedside light, pulled the covers back, then jerked away from what she saw.

In the center of the bed, Adesina was building a cocoon. The lower half of her body was already encased in the fine opaque filament.

"Baby, oh, God, no." Michelle reached out to touch her, and Adesina's eyes snapped open. They were black and shiny—not her usual brown—and showed no recognition of Michelle. They were lifeless and inhuman. Michelle recoiled. All the while, Adesina's mouth kept extruding the silky thread wrapping around her. Adesina's legs manipulated the filament, helping to snug herself in the cocoon.

"What the fuck is going on?"

Michelle heard Joey, but it was as if she were a long way away.

"Michelle, fuck me, what's happening to the niblet?"

Michelle shook her head. This was what Adesina had done when she had been injected with the wild card virus. At the time, the trauma had been so great that she had wrapped herself away from the world in order to survive. So whatever was happening to her daughter now, it was bad enough that she was responding in the same way.

Michelle reached out to touch her daughter, but Joey stopped her. "Don't," she hissed. "You don't know what touching her might do."

Michelle yanked her arm away. "She's my baby!"

But she didn't know what to do. She was helpless. And no matter how much she wanted to do something—anything—she couldn't help her child.

WEDNESDAY

ALL THROUGH THE NIGHT, Michelle watched in mute horror as Adesina encased herself. By morning, there was a cocoon the size of a basketball in the middle of Adesina's bed.

"What should I do?" she asked Joey. She'd lost count of how many times she'd asked it in the course of the night.

"I don't know," Joey replied, as she had every time Michelle had asked.

Michelle was sitting on the edge of Adesina's bed, her hand lightly resting on the cocoon. It felt like rough woven canvas. She'd let Adesina finish building the pupa before touching it. And Joey had helped. Joey had held her hand all night and kept her from going crazy with fear.

But she needed to do *something*. It was past time for sitting on her ass. She didn't know what had triggered this. She'd thought it was PTSD from the horrors of Adesina's life in the PPA. But Adesina had insisted that wasn't the case—that there was something else walking through her dreams. Something horrible enough to send her into what amounted to a coma. And what would she be when she came out of it?

Then there was the question Michelle didn't want answered: would she ever come out of it?

"C'mon," Joey said. "Let's get the fuck out of here for a while." Michelle let herself be pulled from the room.

In the living room, the TV was on, but the sound was turned off. A jittery video of a city with a yellowish-green haze hanging over it was on the screen. The city squatted on a broad plain ringed by mountains. The banner under the image identified the city as Talas in Kazakhstan. The film was replaced by talking heads and Michelle turned away.

"Here are our options, Michelle," Joey said, holding up one finger. "We can wait this thing out and see what happens. Maybe she comes out of this on her own like she did before."

Joey went into the kitchen. Michelle followed and stood in the doorway as Joey began making coffee. "Two, we call in some help. I dunno who the fuck we call, though. Some doctor? Maybe a joker doctor who might know how to deal with this."

"I already called a doctor to come by today, but that was before this. And what exactly could the doctor do?" Michelle asked. She opened the refrigerator, took out the cream, and set it on the dining-room table. "Tell me my daughter is encased in a cocoon? Pretty sure that's self-evident."

Joey lit the burner under the coffeepot, then looked at Michelle with serious eyes.

"Or we can try to go in there with her. You know, like last time. Maybe she'd be able to let us in."

"No," Michelle said, holding up her hands. "We talked about this. There's too much adult stuff rattling around in our heads she doesn't need to be exposed to. We made sure she couldn't get to those parts last time, but now, who knows just how bad things are for her in there—and if she could control things the way she did before."

"We could call Wally," Michelle said, thinking out loud. "He dealt with all kinds of issues when he brought Ghost back. Maybe he'll know someone who can help. Someone in Jokertown."

Joey shrugged. "You know plenty of people there," she said, turning up the burner under the coffee. "And if you thought any of them could help, you'd be on the phone to them right now."

Michelle sat down at the table and traced the wood grain with her finger. A few minutes later, Joey set a cup of coffee in front of her. She sipped it, and though normally she loved Joey's coffee, today it tasted like nothing at all.

She couldn't just sit here. It wasn't in her nature. She pulled her phone out of the pocket of her robe. One button push was all she needed.

"Hey, Wally. It's Michelle. Can you come by my apartment after you drop Ghost off at school? There's something I need to show you."

They reached Shymkent in the cold hours of Wednesday morning. Franny had been forced to stop more than he wanted to allow troop conveys to rumble past. He'd stopped twice more when he became alarmed by Baba Yaga's moans and the streaks of black that were spreading like tentacles up her arm. One time he managed to get a bit of water down her throat and she had cried out what sounded like a name, *Tolenka*, and clutched at Franny's shirt. More alarming were the few tears that ran into the wrinkles on her sunken cheeks. She didn't seem like the kind of broad who would cry about anything.

During the drive Franny had tried to plan. He would have to find a pilot with flexible ethics, and hire a private jet. He hoped that satchel held enough to do the job. On the outskirts of the city he debated—hospital or hotel or just park the car at the airport and wait for morning? He glanced back at Baba Yaga. Her skin was waxy, yellow, and drool ran from the corner of her mouth. If possible she looked worse than she had only a few hours before. He had to find medical help, but if he went to a hospital there were going to be awkward questions. He was also low on gas, and when he spotted an all-night truck stop he pulled in to refill the tank.

As he climbed out of the van there was a sound like a giant chewing rocks and out of the darkness came a link of tanks grinding their way down the street. First troops and now tanks. Things were clearly escalating, but what? Once more he thought about Mollie. She could have taken him anywhere and it would probably be better than this shit. He shook it off and went inside to pay.

The man behind the counter had a five o'clock shadow that almost rivaled Franny's and soul-empty eyes. Those blank eyes did flick down toward the bloodstains on his shirt and the waistband of his trousers, but no comment was made. Franny didn't speak, just jerked his head toward the van and the gas pump and laid money on the counter. The man was equally silent, just turned on the pump.

As they drove away Franny had a feeling he had overpaid by a lot, but since he had no idea about Kazakh money he let it go. He realized he was exhausted and ravenous. The last food he'd eaten had been half a fish yesterday morning. Sitting in the van didn't look like a good option for either of them, and from a hotel maybe he could try to find a doctor. It would also be good to take a shower, eat some food, and maybe at some point he'd get to sleep. Assuming he could with the grinding agony in his side and shoulder. Maybe that hypothetical doctor could get him some painkillers.

He picked a run-down-looking hotel with a lot of trucks parked in front of weathered doors. He buttoned the tux jacket to hide the blood that now formed a Rorschach test on his shirt. There was a heavyset woman with bottle-blond hair behind the desk, a cigarette hung from her lower lip as if affixed there with glue. She was staring at an old-style tube TV that sat on the counter. The images showed mobs in the street, police in riot gear, bricks and stones and Molotov cocktails being thrown. Occasionally the picture would cut back to an older man in a suit behind the ubiquitous news desk. He and his female counterpart sounded serious, but Franny had no idea what they were saying. Then he recognized that equestrian statue. The riots were occurring in Talas. At first his reaction was indifference—*couldn't happen to a nicer shithole*. Then he remembered the fear and the gnawing rage he'd felt in that hospital, Baba Yaga's ominous warnings, and he felt a lot less dismissive.

The clerk continued to ignore him and watch the television. This time he was going to have to speak.

"Uh, hi. Need a room. Two beds." He should have left it at that, but he found himself adding, "I'm an American. Came to visit my grandma. We got lost that's why we're so late—"

"Don't care," the woman said. "Four thousand five hundred tenge."

"Uh, wow, okay."

"You got dollars?"

"Yeah."

"I'll take twenty-five of those instead."

"Okay."

Franny returned to the van and pulled out a bundled stack. Everything in the bag were hundreds. "Well crap." He folded a bill between his fingers and thought; made up his mind. Returning to the lobby he held the bill so the woman could see the denomination.

"How about this. I need a clean shirt and pants, socks and underwear, a razor and shaving soap, some pain pills and antibiotic ointment and bandages. Oh, and something to eat. I get that from you and you get this hundred to cover the cost and another hundred when you deliver."

The woman shifted the cigarette to the other side of her mouth. "Deal." She slid a key across the desk to him.

"Don't call the cops."

"You think I'm an idiot? They would just take the money from me."

Franny nodded, swept up the key, and left. Parking in front of the room he unlocked the door and left it standing open while he went back for Baba Yaga. She weighed next to nothing, but it was still almost too much for his shoulder and side. By the time he carried her through the door his legs were shaking and tears of pain were rolling down his cheeks. He collapsed onto his knees and dropped the old lady. She gave a moan, and a babble of Russian. Her eyes rolled back and Franny panicked.

"Oh, shit, oh, shit, oh shit, don't die."

He checked her pulse. Nothing. He had taken CPR as part of his training for the NYPD. He leaned down ready to start CPR, then jerked away from that slack mouth wet with drool. Did she have to be conscious to use her power? Or would her spit kill him? He decided not to find out. He started chest compressions and felt a rib break beneath his clasped hands. The old woman gave a gasping breath.

Shaking in reaction Franny gritted his teeth and lifted her onto the bed. He returned to the van for the satchel, then sank down onto the other bed. He pulled the pistol out of his waistband and set it next to him.

A knock at the door jerked him from a sleep he hadn't intended to take. He yelled as the sudden clenching of his muscles tore at the wound in his side. He groped and found the pistol. Clutching it tightly he tottered to the door, and looked through the peephole. It was the woman from the front desk. He opened the door. She carried a paper bag that sported a spreading grease stain on the bottom, and was filling the room with both strong and tempting odors. She also had a bag of clothing and toiletries and the requested medicine.

"Thanks," Franny said, and he handed over the second hundred. He hesitated then said, "Wait." He went to the bed and pulled out another two hundred dollars.

The woman was staring blank-eyed at Baba Yaga unconscious on the bed in her absurd evening gown.

"Your grandma don't look so good. You don't look so good."

"Yeah. We need a doctor. One with your discretion."

"What? What is this dis . . . dis—"

"Somebody who won't talk."

"I don't know any doctors." Franny closed his eyes and swayed. Hopelessness washed over him. "But I know a vet," she added.

"I'll take anything." He handed her the money.

She left and he opened the bag. The food proved to be meat wrapped in soft pastry. It was like lamb, but much stronger. He guessed it was mutton. He didn't care. It was delicious. He left one of the pastries for Baba Yaga assuming she ever recovered enough to eat, and hit the shower.

The tile was cracked underfoot and the wallpaper in one corner of the bathroom had pulled loose to reveal mold growing beneath it. The hot water eased the tension in his back and shoulders, but stung both bullet wounds. The purloined dress shoes had rubbed blisters on both his heels so that was another source of pain.

The bandage on his side was filthy. He gritted his teeth and ripped it off, figuring no covering was better than risking infection. The wound was gaping open where the stitches had ripped loose. Franny dabbed the strong-smelling ointment onto his bullet wounds, gasped at the pain, and stuck on clean bandages. He then wrapped a tissue-thin towel around his waist and stood over the stained sink to shave. It felt good to scrape away three days of beard.

Slipping back into the bedroom he paused at Baba Yaga's side. Her breathing was labored but at least he had her breathing again.

He lifted her arm to check her pulse and she woke. She stared up at him, her eyes cloudy. She seemed scared as well as confused. "Tolenka?" she whispered.

"No, Frank. Would you like to eat something? It's a bit cold, but—" She shook her head and moaned.

Her lips were dry and cracked and she ran her tongue constantly across them. He went into the bathroom and filled a plastic cup with water. He held her while she took a few small sips. It seemed to revive her somewhat. She seemed to actually see him.

"You shaved," she said faintly.

He rubbed a hand across his chin. "Yeah." He suddenly realized he was still wearing just a towel. The old woman seemed to read his thoughts, and gave him that grim smile, though it seemed more like a grimace. "You're not hard to look at, boy."

"Thanks, I guess. Do you want to try and eat?"

She shook her head. "Too sick. Like fire in the veins." Her voice was threadlike, fading. He barely heard her add, "Maybe better . . . to die . . . now. Not wait . . . for . . ." She slid once more into unconsciousness.

Franny changed into the clean clothes the woman had brought. Fatigue dragged at every muscle and his eyes felt like they'd been washed with sand. He settled in a sagging chair to wait, pistol in his lap. He checked to make sure he didn't have a round in the chamber in case he fell asleep again and dropped the damn thing but the grinding pain from the gunshot wounds kept him awake. Almost two hours later the woman returned with a short, fireplug-shaped man with pronounced epicanthic folds and iron-grey hair.

"Someone is hurt," he said. He spoke English with a decided British accent.

Franny nodded. "My, my grandmother. She's . . . poisoned. A snake. I think she may have a broken shoulder, too."

"Big snake," the vet said.

"You don't know the half of it."

"Let's look." He moved to Baba Yaga's side and studied her left hand where IBT's tongue had given her a glancing blow. It was horribly swollen, blackened with red streaks sweeping up the arm toward Franny's makeshift tourniquet. The vet drew in a hissing breath between his teeth. "This is bad. How long ago did you apply the tourniquet?"

Franny rubbed at his forehead. "I don't know. Twelve, fourteen hours?"

"The circulation's been cut off for too long. The arm needs to come off."

"Shit." Franny ran an agitated hand through his hair. "I didn't know what else to do."

"It was the right thing. Old lady like this, the poison would certainly have killed her."

"How many questions are there going to be at a hospital?" Franny asked.

"A lot. I can do this. I amputate legs off cats and dogs, but we have to go to my office."

"How much?" Franny asked.

"Five thousand—American."

"Could she survive to get to New York?"

"Probably not."

"Will she survive the surgery?"

"Maybe."

"Not a lot of certainty either way."

"She's got a better chance if we get the arm off. I'm going to need help. Are you squeamish?"

"I've watched autopsies," Franny answered.

"Then you'll probably do."

It took a day to fix the hydraulic cutter. Mollie kept a periodic eye on Baba Yaga's apartment in the casino. Nobody showed up, though, so after Dad and Brent managed to clean spilled lubricant from the compressor valves and replace the shorted wiring, they were ready to try again.

As Mollie'd expected, the safe was welded to beams inside the closet walls. But the cutter, designed for chewing through broken farm equipment, made short work of the studs. Mollie had managed to get the safe half pried out of the wall when the shrieking started.

The cutter was so loud that at first she thought it was her imagination. Then she heard it again, so she momentarily switched off the cutter in order to listen. She leaned out of the closet, cocked her head toward the portal to Idaho.

She called, "Everything okay back there?"

Brent said, "You done yet? Why are you stopping?"

Mollie shrugged. *Weird.*

But just as she was about to return her attention to the half-extricated safe, she heard it again. And this time she heard it clearly. This was more than shrieking; it was an almost inhuman wailing, coming from outside the casino. Something about the noise triggered some remnant of the hindbrain that evolution had forgotten to remove from modern humans: she jolted with a physically painful urge to flee, and the nape of her neck broke out in tingling gooseflesh. She dropped the cutter and went to the bedroom window.

Given what she knew of the casino and the people who ran it, not to mention the people it catered to, she'd half expected to find a demilitarized zone outside the window. Her mental picture of Talas was of a place that could have been featured for a cover story in *Shitholes of the World* magazine. But in fact Baba Yaga's apartments overlooked a scene that might have been anywhere in Europe. Folks on the street weren't dressed any worse than they might have been in New York, or Perth, or Johannesburg. The streets—clean, leafy boulevards—featured fountains, pedestrian arcades, and an impressive investment in public art. She saw cafés, tram stops, people strolling hand in hand or pushing strollers. Oil money at work, Mollie realized. Maybe the local oligarchs preferred not to live in a shithole. Even the mountains in the far distance were rather picturesque. It didn't seem so awful.

Except for the guy sitting outside a sidewalk café near the end of the
street, shrieking like a monkey with its arms stuck in a garbage disposal
while he repeatedly rammed the neck of a broken water bottle into his own
eye socket. Bloody debris rained over his and neighboring tables.

Nobody tried to help him. Nobody tried to stop him.

"What the *fuck*?" she gasped.

In fact—

Mollie emptied her stomach. Half-digested chunks of bacon and egg
spewed across the window sash. Runnels of yellow chyme trickled down
the wall. She staggered, caught her balance on a divan, realized the divan
had probably been a person once, nearly choked on a second wave of stomach acid, and stumbled against the wall.

Fuck Talas. She'd thought the joker fight club was the sickest shit she'd
ever seen, but compared to the self-inflicted carnage on the street it was
downright tame. What the fuck kind of messed-up shit was that? To hell
with Bumfuckistan. She'd take Baba Yaga's money and get way the hell
away from here.

The shrieking hadn't stopped by the time she wiped the worst of the
taste from her mouth. If anything . . . the hair on Mollie's nape tried to
stand on end again . . . it was stronger now, a chorus rather than the
lamentations of a lone viciously suicidal nut job.

She chanced another peek. The streetlights went out a few seconds later,
but not before she saw the entire café going mad. The first guy was now
trying to—*oh, Jesus*—

Mollie's stomach rebelled again. She doubled over, dry heaving.

—he was clawing at his mangled eye sockets, trying to scoop the gore
into his mouth. While others slashed each other with silverware, teeth,
even their own fingers. In seconds the street scene had gone from something normal to a fucking massacre. She'd glimpsed an Audi running back
and forth over the same pedestrian, spinning tires spraying viscera to rain
on passersby who were too busy trying to chew each other's faces off like
starving rats to care. In the residual glow of the casino marquee, a young
woman pushing a stroller stopped, lifted the child overhead—

(Mollie pounded on the window. "Jesus Christ! Stop! STOP!" But nobody could hear her.)

—and slammed the mewling baby on the ornamental points of the
wrought-iron fence around the café. Passersby hurled themselves at the
impaled newborn, like a psycho cannibal rugby scrum, and in the instant

before the casino marquee blinked out all Mollie could see of the murdered child were gobbets of flesh fountaining from the center of the pack.
Mollie screamed until her knees gave out.

She crawled away from the window, dry heaving, tasting bile. *I'm safe,
I'm safe, I'm safe,* she reminded herself. *Those fucked-up motherfuckers can't
get in. Baba Yaga's quarters are locked from outside. If those psychopaths outside try to break into the casino they'll first have to deal with everybody else
trying to rob this place.* The mobsters had automatic weapons; they'd mow
down the psycho cannibal flashmob before it got halfway across the lobby.
*And I can be gone in half a second. I'm safe. I'm not in any danger. I'm safe. A
few more minutes and I never have to come back.*

This she promised herself. *The world is a big place*—more wisdom from
Ffodor, that—*and even I haven't seen it all. So Talas and its zombie flashmobs
can fuck themselves all the way to hell and back.*

Money. Get the money. Mollie returned to the safe. Her body went on
autopilot while she finished cutting it from the wall. She didn't see her
work, only a man slavering over the remnants of his own ruined eyes while
a mother slammed her baby—

*No. NO. Don't think about it. Don't think about any of it. I'm safe. Don't
think about the baby. Don't think about that chair in the corner. Don't think
about Ffodor. Don't remember the iron fenceposts sticking through—*

NO! Don't think about any *of that shit.*

Mollie heaved on the cutter. Baba Yaga's safe crashed to the floor amid
crumbled drywall and fragments of hot steel. She was just about to drop
it through the portal to Idaho when the shrieking started anew. And much
closer.

The skin all over Mollie's body prickled with gooseflesh. A sheen of cold
sweat instantly dampened her forehead, armpits, under her breasts, and
even the top of her ass crack. Her hands shook so violently she flung the
cutter aside.

"Fuck fuck fuck oh fuck—"

Sporadic bursts of automatic gunfire punctuated the screaming.
More gunfire. More screeching. An unintelligible chorus of screams. No
language, just mindless expression of some raw red emotion that Mollie
couldn't hope to identify. The corridors echoed with incoherent rage.

The shriekers had forced their way inside the casino.

Marcus couldn't tell which thing he hated most about being in the heli-copter: the noise, which was enormous even with the sound-blocking ear-phones clamped over his head; or the vibrations, which made his scales tremble; or the motion of the thing, its weird, unnatural tilts and curves, changes in height that made his stomach lurch; or the frightening speed the land scrolled by beneath them; or the fact that his coils were jammed into the small cabin so tightly that he pressed against the legs of everyone in the group; or the eyes on him, staring, cold as a Ukrainian winter, Va-sel the most frigid of all. He even hated the daunting array of dials and buttons and colorful electronic displays he could glimpse between the pi-lots in the cockpit. All those gadgets mattered, and he couldn't make a bit of sense of them. *Snakes,* he thought, *weren't meant to fly.*

Marcus had been all for driving back in the truck, but Vasel nixed that idea. It would take too long, especially fighting all the traffic fleeing Talas.

"I have a helicopter for a reason," he'd said.

Marcus knew what it was; to scare him shitless.

Olena, sitting beside him, said, "Look, there are even more cars on the road now. Trucks. Buses. Donkeys. Carts. People on foot. Everything."

Her voice came to Marcus not from her lips, but through the earphones. It was intimate, but strangely disembodied. He didn't look, afraid he'd hurl if he did. "I'll take your word for it," he managed. "Am I the only one who thinks this is all a bad idea?"

Vasel answered with a sarcastic-sounding dribble of incomprehensible words.

"English, Papa," Olena said.

Vasel sat across from them, staring at Marcus with undisguised dis-dain. He spoke, his lips moving and his voice appearing at Marcus's ears. So much for the intimacy. "You are afraid. Blacks are not brave when it matters, are they?"

Well fuck you very much, Marcus thought. He said, "You don't know anything about me."

"I know enough. I know that my daughter will tire of you soon. Jungle fever. It always breaks before long."

Olena said something that must have been a Ukrainian curse. She reached across and punched her father in the shoulder with a small, tight fist. It probably hurt, but the man's face didn't register the blow. The guards and soldiers smiled, reminding Marcus that they too could hear everything being said. He tried to change the subject. "Have you considered that anything valuable in the casino is gone by now? Place has been crazy for days now."

"Looters want money, guns, jewels, electronics," Vasel said. "Trinkets. Those things don't interest me."

"What does?"

"That is need to know only." Vasel smiled. "You don't need to know, do you?"

Marcus *wished* he didn't need to know. He wished he wasn't here, and that whatever future he was to have with Olena didn't hinge on whatever it was this mission was about. He also felt uneasy about leaving the villagers alone. Just a couple days with them, but already they seemed like family. Leaving them didn't sit right with him. He hoped that whatever was driving people from Talas wouldn't touch them, especially Nurassyl.

One of the soldiers at a window said something. The others craned toward the windows to see whatever he was talking about. Marcus didn't. For a time they chattered in Ukrainian. When she could, Olena explained. "The army has the road blockaded. It looks like they're not letting anyone else leave the city. Not just the road. They have a whole perimeter set up, tanks and armored vehicles patrolling it."

"They're not letting people in?" Marcus asked. "But we're going anyway? Great."

"I can see Talas," Olena said. "We'll be there in a few minutes."

That's one thing the helicopter had going for it. The flight was going to be mercifully short. They could get in fast, which also meant they could get out fast. That, Marcus told himself, was what this was all about. Vasel could have whatever it was he wanted, and he and Olena might just get out of here together. Just a few more hours of this crap and—

The engines sputtered, a quick staccato barrage of sound and silence as the helicopter lurched to one side, corrected, and then tilted too far the other way. Marcus clutched Olena's hand, and she his. "Oh, please don't . . ."

The returned roar of the engines drowned out his voice, a sweet sound if ever he'd heard one.

It didn't last. The pilot had just begun to say something when the engines cut out again, taking the pilot's voice with them. For a few stunned seconds everyone shared the horror of the sudden, enormous quiet. Then the bottom fell out. The helicopter dipped forward and hurtled into a dive.

Looking out the window, Marcus could see the rotors spinning, but not like before. They were going down. He looked at Olena. She stared right back at him. Beautiful. Terrified. Her face white like it had never been before. He said, "We'll be okay. We'll be okay."

She said something back, but he couldn't hear her.

The helicopter banked sickeningly to one side, and then jerked back the other way, spinning so fast the motion yanked everyone's heads around. One of the soldiers vomited. Vasel was shouting, tapping on his earphones, turning and trying to speak directly to the pilots. They were frantically at work, one of them with an iron grip on what looked like a giant joystick, the other with hands flying over the dials and knobs and displays. They had all gone dark.

Marcus glimpsed the earth, seething up toward them as they dropped. He ripped off his earphones, and slipped Olena's off her head as well. She said, "Marcus, I—" And he said, "Olena, I—"

The nose of the helicopter suddenly rose, the back end dropping, making the whole world tilt. They were going to crash. Marcus knew it. He so wanted to get the words he wanted to say out of his mouth, but they'd vanished. He still tried again, "Olena—"

The helicopter leveled, and landed hard. It bounced into the air again, but came down a moment later and steadied. Marcus stared into Olena's face, breathing hard, only slowly letting himself believe they'd actually landed. "Olena—"

This time he got cut off by the sudden jostling of the soldiers and the bodyguards as they ripped their seat belts off, lunged for the door, and jostled their way out of it. Vasel, looking mildly annoyed, sat still until they were out. He watched Marcus. He slowly took off his earphones and said, "Exciting times, yes?" He exited the helicopter.

Olena and Marcus followed him. Marcus slid/tumbled out of the helicopter. Gasping, he slithered away some distance before turning back and staring, heart still pounding, at the helicopter. The rotors whirred slowly to a halt as the others, bent beneath them, visibly shaken, talked fast and gesticulated.

"Damn," Marcus said. He knew now which part of being in a helicopter he hated most. The emergency landing part.

The clinic was in a run-down storefront. Franny had given the desk clerk another two hundred dollars. The vet carried Baba Yaga to the van while Franny carried the satchel and the guns. The vet didn't remark on the pistol in his waistband or the Uzi.

Once at the office the vet had told Franny to pull into the alley and wait. It was hot in the van, but if he rolled down the windows an effluvia of rotting garbage from the dumpsters wafted in and had his stomach rebelling. A few minutes later the vet emerged through a back door, and motioned to Franny. Grunting with pain he carried Baba Yaga into the office.

"I sent the receptionist home. Closed the office. We won't be disturbed."

There was a steel table in the middle of the back room surrounded by cages. A few of them contained unhappy occupants either mewing piteously or barking frenziedly. In one of them an iguana stared unblinking at Franny. The flat eye reminded him of Baba Yaga's gaze. With a nod the vet indicated that Franny should place Baba Yaga on the cold metal surface.

The vet tossed him a green gown, mask, and gloves. The man, who was loading up a tray with various instruments and a stack of gauze squares, noticed the efficient way Franny pulled on the gloves. "You're not a doctor or you wouldn't need me and you mentioned autopsies. Policeman?"

"Yeah." Franny thrust out his hand. "I'm Francis Bla—"

"No names. It's better that way." An IV was inserted. "Okay. We begin. If you faint I will step over you and go on. But if you faint she will probably die because I do need your help."

"I won't faint."

"We need to expose the arm," the vet ordered and returned to laying instruments on a tray.

Which left Franny to undress the old woman. He pulled her to a sitting position, and unzipped the dress. He pulled it down to reveal a wrinkled, age-spotted chest, an incongruous pink lace bra, and a medal hanging on a chain around her neck. It was a single gold star suspended beneath a red ribbon. On the back was a portrait of a handsome man in the oversaturated colors that typified Soviet era art.

The vet nudged Franny with an elbow and handed him a stack of gauze pads. "Be ready to blot."

He took a scalpel and cut through the skin about three inches above the woman's elbow. Oddly he cut on a vertical line before turning the blade. Franny was blotting and throwing blood-soaked squares onto the floor. When the vet was done cutting there was a large flap of skin hanging loose.

"Give me that kelly clamp," the vet ordered and indicated the instrument with a jerk of his chin. Franny handed it over and the vet clamped off an artery that had been pumping small gouts of blood.

Next the vet fired up a small saw. The piercing whine filled the room and set the dogs to howling. That noise and the flash of white bone among the blood and viscera had the mutton pastry knocking at the back of Franny's throat. He swallowed hard. Bone dust dusted the angry red edges of the wound and filled the air with a smell like burning hair as the saw gnawed through the arm. Baba Yaga's arm fell with a dull thud onto the table.

"Almost done. You're doing good."

Franny nodded and continued to hold and hand as instructed while the vet folded the flap of skin over the stump and sutured it closed. Antiseptic was smeared across the stump and a bandage applied. He finished with a couple of injections.

"Antibiotics and painkiller," he explained. "Now it's up to how you care for her and her own resilience. But you need to leave so I can reopen."

"I need some pain meds and could you look at this wound in my side?" Franny asked as he took off his shirt. "I think the stitches have torn loose."

The vet ripped away the bandage, sucked at his teeth, and glanced up at Franny from beneath his brows. "That's a bullet wound. As is that one." He nodded toward his shoulder.

"I take it that's going to make some kind of difference," Franny said.

"Yes. It means I want more money. I want ten thousand."

"We agreed on five."

"That was before . . ." He gestured at Franny's wounds. "Bullets."

"Okay."

The vet turned away and prepared an injection. Franny got into the satchel. Ten grand wiped out the stash of dollars. He noticed the vet craning to see what was in the bag. Franny realized that he had no idea what was in that syringe. He drew the pistol out of his waistband. He held the gun in one hand and the stack of wrapped bills in the other.

"It's just lidocaine to numb the area," the man said, but Franny hadn't missed the flicker of anger in his dark eyes.

"No. Not shots."

The vet carefully set aside the syringe. "All right, but it's going to hurt."

"I wouldn't count on me passing out," Franny said.

The vet worked quickly and none too gently to clean the wounds and stitch the hole in Franny side. There was one moment when Franny wondered if he could hang on and he realized the whimpering sounds were coming from him and not one of the dogs in the cages. Eventually it was done. Fresh bandages were in place and the vet thrust a bottle into Franny's hands. He looked at the label and inwardly cursed because of course it wasn't in English. The Cyrillic letters seemed to do a mocking dance.

"What the fuck is it?"

"Tramadol."

Franny recognized the name. It had been given to their Lab Lady when she'd been hit by a car. "Reassure me that you wouldn't lie to me, Doc."

"Not when you have a gun . . . and I don't have my money," the vet said pointedly.

"Okay." Franny tossed over the stack of bills. He picked up Baba Yaga and backed toward the door. "No calls to the police, right?"

"Of course not. They'd just take the money from me."

"Nice police force you've got here," Franny grunted, and he stepped back into the alley.

The casino reverberated with shrieks, gunfire, and a rhythmic thumping, like the sound track to a madman's nightmare. Mollie shivered in the corner of Baba Yaga's closet, knees to her chest. The harder she tried to block out the images from the street the deeper they etched themselves into her eyelids.

The thumping grew louder. More than just a thumping, it resolved into a *fwump-fwump-fwump-fwump* that shook the building like the world's most obnoxious car stereo. Helicopters, she realized. She hadn't recognized the noise because she'd never been so close to one before. And these were *really* close. Landing on the street close.

Thank God. Thank God. Somebody's coming to restore some order. Did they have something like a National Guard in Kazakhstan?

Mollie hauled herself upright. She'd been curled in the corner a good while; her ass was numb. She went to the window, taking extra care to not look anywhere near the café and the wrought-iron fence with the—

No. No. It's over now.

Sure enough, there was a helicopter in the wide intersection just down the street, blades pinwheeling to a stop. But it didn't look military. It didn't look official at all. Nor did the neckless thugs pouring out of it with submachine guns clutched to their chests. She'd seen enough mobsters hanging around the casino to recognize the type.

They were not the type to content themselves with petty cash. They knew what was what; they'd be coming for the vault, and the safes. Mollie reached through a hole in space to check the locks on Baba Yaga's door. All solid, all secure.

She was about to turn back to the closet when movement caught her eye. Crouching in the window, she peered down toward the street just outside the entrance. She glimpsed the tail end of an enormous snake slithering under the marquee. She recognized the markings. Marcus something. He was one of the pit fighters, and a real badass, too.

Was he here to help, or had he joined up with the psycho cannibal flashmob, as Vaporlock had done?

She didn't want to find out. The greasy guy had nearly done her in. She'd have no chance against the snake guy if he decided to throw a couple coils around her.

The pilots could explain what happened, but not why. The engines failed, that was obvious. The electronics went out, too. But they couldn't find any reason for it. Everything had been fine before the failure, all the gauges reading as they should, plenty of fuel left. They also couldn't explain why nothing they tried could get the helicopter started again. They worked at it, but it was dead. A useless hunk of metal.

The landing itself, it turned out, was a textbook autorotation maneuver, whatever that meant. Vasel shrugged it off as standard procedure in the event of engine failure. Marcus kinda wanted to give the pilots high-fives and backslaps, but he kept control of his enthusiasm. There wasn't time for it, really, as Vasel kept them on task. They were near enough to the city to approach it on foot. They left the pilots to get the helicopter working again, and the rest of them set off.

Sliding down the debris-cluttered road, Marcus took in the city as they approached it. The sun was high in a cloudless sky. It should have lit the scene with midday clarity. It didn't. It was as if the daylight evaporated as it fell, leaving the city looking not exactly dark, but somehow unlit. Dead or undead or something he couldn't put his finger on. A pall hung over it that just shouldn't have been there. Smog? Maybe, but it looked weird.

"Where's the casino?" Vasel asked them. "Quickest way."

Olena took the lead. The armed guards formed a protective circle that Marcus was glad to have around them. They wore half-full packs, weighted with ammunition. There were still people around, ones who weren't fleeing the place. From a distance Marcus had taken comfort in that. If not everyone was flipping out maybe things weren't really so bad. But once inside the city limits that tenuous reassurance vanished. Yes, there were people still in the streets, but they weren't acting normal.

One man stood on a street corner. He looked to be nibbling on a troublesome fingernail, oblivious to the armed group passing by. It wasn't until Marcus noticed the blood dribbling down his chin and the front of his shirt that he realized the man was eating his own fingers—literally *eating* them—pulling on the flesh and gnawing at the bone.

"Did you see that?" he asked Olena. "Something's not right here. I mean *really* not right. You feel it?"

"Feel what?" Olena asked.

Marcus couldn't answer. He hadn't known there was an *it* until he asked the question. At first he thought it was irritation at being dragged on this mission. Then it was worry over the chaos, and then horror at what Vasel had done to the soldier. All of that was true, but there was something else growing on him as well. He couldn't name it, though, and that annoyed him. "You said your dad's an ace, right? What's his power? Something good, I hope."

"No," Olena said, with a curt tone that closed the topic, "is nothing good."

A little farther on an army truck sat in the center of an intersection. A gunner slumped against a machine gun mounted in the truck bed. Vasel motioned for the guards to keep their weapons hidden. They approached cautiously. The street and sidewalks were cluttered with objects that at first Marcus couldn't make out. When his tail bumped against something soft he looked down. A mangled half face looked up at him. He surged back, crying out. A dead body. That's what lay in pooling blood all around the truck. Bodies, all of them torn apart, mangled and in unnatural positions.

The gunner must've heard Marcus's cry. Looking at them, he began to howl like a wolf. He yanked the gun around and began strafing them. His aim was high and wild, mostly splintering the plaster wall behind them. At least one bullet found its target, though. It all but exploded the head of one of the guards. They all scrambled, hit the ground, dodged behind parked cars. A few of the guards returned fire. They missed. Vasel didn't.

The gangster stepped out in front of them, cool as you please. He snapped his fingers and sent his coin toward the gunner. It flipped over and over in the air in a strange slow motion. Marcus's eyes followed it, transfixed. It was beautiful the way it twinkled. If he was nearer he would've reached out and caught it. Luckily, he didn't.

The soldier did, though. He relinquished his grip on the machine gun long enough to swat at the coin. It hit his palm and stuck to it. The expression on the man's face changed from senseless rage to instant terror. He stared, wide-eyed, at his palm and tried desperately to shake the coin free. His mouth fell open as if to scream, but he got out nothing more than a guttural, trembling wail. His veins and arteries went black beneath his skin. He looked at Vasel, pleading, and then around at others. He threw back his head, sputtering. And then his body fell apart. Skin and tissue sloughed off his bones. His internals slipped down around his waist and then burst through the skin. And then he crumpled, becoming a pile of stinking meat and bone, blood and faces.

Vasel lifted his hand and the coin flew back and slapped against his palm. A second later, he had it dancing on his fingers where every eye could see it. He looked at Marcus, a bemused expression on his face. "See?" he asked. "Heads or tails. It doesn't matter. Either way, I win; they lose."

As he strolled away, Olena muttered, "I told you. His power is nothing good." She pulled him close, her face near to his and deadly serious. "Marcus, never catch his coin. Promise me. If he throws it, look away. Swear that you will look away."

Marcus did. She kissed him for it and pulled him into motion. The swearing was an automatic response on his part. The reality that his girl-friend's father could turn him into a steaming pile of mush with the toss of that coin was a bit too much to process.

Olena said something in a tone ominous enough to cut his thoughts off. "Why are they looking at us like that?"

They were a family of five that had just come around a corner and stood staring at the group. A father and a mother, three kids of various ages, the youngest perhaps five or six. To an armed group of thugs the family should've posed no danger. Yet the way they stared . . . The way the father's lips pulled back and his teeth clattered against each other . . . The way they crouched and held their hands curled before them, their fingers abnormally long . . . They started toward them at a run. They came on like animals, like they wanted to rip them limb from limb and devour them.

The guards opened fire. The family ran right into it. Their bodies twisted and jerked as the barrage of bullets ripped them to pieces, kicking out plumes of blood. The guards kept firing even after they'd all gone down. They sent rounds into the bodies, making them quiver from the impacts. Vasel had to yell and smack them to get them to stop.

Marcus wanted to look away from the corpses, but he couldn't help but slide a bit closer. Their fingers really were longer than normal. They were multi-jointed, twisted things that even in death seemed clenched in a rictus of pain.

"Jokers," Andrii said, disgustedly. So he knew at least one word in English.

Vasel pressed his coin against his cheek as he nudged a corpse with the toe of his pointy shoes. "Black mamba, are these your kind?"

"My kind?" Marcus asked, letting a savage edge sharpen his words. "Jokers."

"Look, I had nothing to do with them! I don't know what they were."

"Papa, let's get out of here," Olena said. "Something is very bad here."

Vasel ignored her. He straightened. Looking at Marcus, he concluded, "They are jokers. Deformed like this—what else could they be? This is their night of revenge. Are you with them, or with us?"

"I'm with her," Marcus said.

"I don't know about that." Vasel's coin was in his hand again, sliding like a living, acrobatic thing over his fingers. "Maybe I'm through with—"

"Papa!" Olena snapped. "You know my promise."

Vasel thought a moment. Then he shrugged. The coin disappeared. He said, "I must love my daughter very much, see? Even now I'm proving it."

Now that he was back in civilization Franny realized he could buy a prepaid cell phone and get in touch with the precinct. It wasn't hard to locate a large shopping center called MEGA. As he drove into the parking lot he spotted a new, upscale hotel that actually looked like a hotel, and he wished he'd driven a little farther into the city proper last night and found the first-world hotel. They probably would have had room service and no mold. On the downside they probably wouldn't have had such a compliant desk clerk.

He pulled into a space in the parking garage, grabbed money out of the Big Bag O'Cash and Jewels. He figured the old lady wouldn't come out of the anesthesia while he nipped inside. Within minutes he was back in the van.

He pulled out so he would have better reception, found some street parking, and turned off the van. Overhead five helicopters beat their way across the sky, and contrails crossed the sky like spiderwebs. Franny dialed the number for Fort Freak.

"Fifth Precinct," the receptionist sang out.

"This is Detective Francis Black, put me through to the duty captain."

"One moment."

"Mendelberg."

He wasn't happy to hear the voice of the joker captain. They had butted heads more than a few times during his investigations of the missing jokers, but she was the one on duty so he'd make the best of it.

"Captain, it's Francis Black."

"Still enjoying your all-expenses-paid trip to fucking Kazakhstan, Black? You need to get your ass back to New York and help us straighten out this clusterfuck."

"Great. Can you wire me money, identification? Contact the authorities here in Shymkent to clear us and get us on a plane."

"Who is this us, Kemosabe?"

He wondered if Kemosabe was some Jokertown reference that he hadn't heard, but let it go. "Baba Yaga. I've got her under arrest . . . well sort of. I want her back in New York. She says she has information 'cause there is some really weird shit going down over here—"

"Yeah, that's why you need to get the fuck out of there. People are saying it's a new wild card outbreak or maybe some kind of toxic spill. Look, you've got no jurisdiction over there. She's Kazakhstan's problem. Leave her."

"It's our people she brutalized. She needs to face justice in New York. And if I leave her here she'll die. She's been hurt—"

"Let her die. From what the jokers have told us it's what she deserves."

"No."

"You have zero authority to arrest or extradite anybody, and you are *so* on the bubble, Black. If you don't want your ass fired—"

"I want to talk to Maseryk—"

There was an abrupt click and the line went dead. Franny called back to the precinct.

"This is Black again. I got disconnected."

"Hold the line." A few seconds later the receptionist was back. "Captain Mendelberg is in a meeting and can't be disturbed."

"What the hell? I was just talking to her."

"She can't take the call. You can try again later."

"Then get me Maseryk."

"He won't be in until tomorrow. Sorry. I'll give Captain Mendelberg the message." The receptionist hung up.

Maybe Mendelberg was on the phone to SCARE? Or trying to arrange for them to get back to the States. Should he wait? But there was something off about the situation. In the backseat Baba Yaga stirred and cried out in pain.

Franny slewed around though it hurt like the blazes. "It's okay. It's okay. You're safe."

"Where?"

"Shymkent."

"Good. Must get farther . . ." She looked down at the sleeve of her dress falling empty onto the seat next to her. "My arm."

"I'm sorry. It was killing you."

She just nodded. Franny wasn't sure she fully understood. Or maybe she was just that cold. "We must go, boy . . . now . . . before it reaches us . . ." Her voice trailed away.

"Before *what* reaches us?"

"Madness and death."

"That tells me nothing."

"Get us far . . . away from here, boy. So we can live . . . for a little while longer."

Barbara walked into the conference room to find it ablaze with flat screens, each one set to a different news channel and all of them with the sound muted. The conference table was piled with paper: news reports compiled

by Ink, Barbara assumed. Secretary-General Jayewardene was seated before one pile, reading studiously. At another was Klaus, though he wasn't
reading; he was watching the flat screen across the table, where Wolf Blitzer
was standing in front of a satellite map of Kazakhstan, zooming in on the
city of Talas. As Blitzer's mouth moved silently (a small blessing, in Barbara's opinion) the display toggled back and forth between two satellite
images, one dated a month earlier with the buildings intact on a sunny day,
and another dated the day before, which showed only a circular darkness
around the city, with ominous plumes of smoke curling out from the edges
like black tentacles.

"Ah, Ms. Baden," Jayewardene said. "I've been looking at the excellent
reports that Ink has sent us." He tapped the pages in front of him with a
thin finger. "This is . . . interesting. And troubling."

"Yes, and once again we're wasting time talking about it when we
should already be moving," Klaus said before Barbara could respond. She
ignored the comment and slid into her own chair, addressing Jayewardene.

"I read most of the reports in the car on the way here," she said. "Ink
sent them to my phone. Anything new?"

Jayewardene waved a hand at the screens around them. "No one knows
anything for certain," he said, "which is why it would be a mistake to send
anyone to Talas now." That was directed to Klaus, whose lips twisted into a
scowl. He slumped back in his seat. "In any case," Jayewardene continued,
"we would have to have authorization from President Karimov before we
could send anyone into that country. I've reached out to Temir Bondarenko, their UN representative; we should hear from him later today. Then
we can decide."

"Ink's updated me on what the news channels have been saying," Barbara said, glancing up at the screens again. On MSNBC, Chris Matthews
was listening to one of three "expert" talking heads on the screen with
him. On Fox, a scroll bar across the bottom asked the question *Kazakh
Spring? Putin denies Russian involvement.* "I've heard everything from this
being Russia trying to undermine President Karimov's government, to a
toxic spill in the Talas River, to a new wild card virus outbreak. Everyone
is contradicting everyone else. I haven't been able to get anything solid
and verifiable."

"Which is why we need to get aces on the ground there," Klaus grunted.
"Why can't anyone see that?" His single ice-blue eye tracked from Jayewardene to Barbara. "You stopped me from going to East Timor because

you were worried that Talas was going to blow up. Well, it looks to me like it has. So let me put together a team. Bubbles might be out for the moment, but I could get Aero, Brave Hawk, and Tinker to go with me—"

Barbara saw Jayewardene shaking his head before Klaus had finished talking. "Not without President Karimov's blessing," he said. "We don't want this to become an international incident on top of everything else."

"So we sit here with our thumbs up our—" Klaus stopped, his mouth snapping shut audibly.

"I know you want to help, Klaus. I know," Barbara said. "But the Secretary-General's right. The Committee's SST can reach Talas in six hours with one refueling stop. Even with needing to get equipment and supplies on board, we could put a team on the ground in less than twelve hours. But we need permission, and we need to have a better idea of what we're sending people into, for their own safety. For that matter, who do we send? If this is all due to a toxic spill of some sort, for instance, Talas needs hazmat teams, not aces. If it's a disease outbreak, then UN needs to send doctors and nurses and medicines, and we should be coordinating with the Red Cross. We can't all just hop on a plane and go to Egypt." Lohengrin exhaled, a snakelike hiss, at that reference to the past. Barbara spread her hands wide over the papers. On the screen above Lohengrin, MSNBC was now showing a clip of two Kazakh jokers being interviewed a few days before.

"Then let me know when you have your permission and when you've actually decided something," Klaus said, and Barbara could hear the undercurrent of rage and frustration in his voice. He pushed away from the desk, scattering papers. He picked up one of the sheets between forefinger and thumb and waved it toward Jayewardene and Barbara both.

"You can't fight a war with paper, no matter how hard you try," he said, his German accent more pronounced than usual, and left the room.

The light was weird. It was jaundiced and foul and he couldn't see well in it. It wasn't exactly night, but no day had ever felt like this. Mist oozed up from the ground. It rippled and morphed in the air, changing the shape of things seen through it. Through it the casino didn't look much like it did when Marcus had glimpsed it on the night of the breakout. He recognized it, sure. There was the awning over the opening. There was the big blocky sign with the weird letters, and the flash entrance and the big plate-glass sliding doors through which the high rollers had been fighting to escape. But nothing looked right. The building sat like a malignant creature, as if its windows were eyes and it was only pretending not to be staring at the approaching group. He couldn't shake the feeling that the building and everything around it shifted when his eyes weren't directly on it—a slithery motion that he could never truly catch, that snapped to stillness each time he looked.

Marcus was sure there was more to all this than some weird outbreak of violence. There was something in the air. He could smell it. He could feel it on his skin, something oily about it. It reminded him of the arena. It was the smell of the maddening, murderous fury that he'd felt there. That had been one thing in that small space, for amusement and controlled by Baba Yaga thugs, but what would happen if there was nothing to control it? If that horror had no bounds? If it didn't fade when a fight was called?

Under the awning, Vasel pointed a finger at one of the thugs and spoke Ukrainian. He glanced at Marcus and deigned to speak English. "You stay here with him. Nobody comes in this door."

Marcus started to protest, but Olena shook her head. "We will be quick," she said. "I know the way. Five minutes only and we'll be back."

Watching the others vanish into the mouth of the casino, Marcus couldn't help feeling they were being swallowed. The casino was a living beast. It always had been. *Why the fuck am I letting her go?* It seemed the worst thing ever. The stupidity of it clenched a fist around his heart and left him gasping. He whispered, "Fuck. Fuck. Fuck!" He would've yelled it but he was afraid to. Afraid of what might hear him.

The thug yanked him around by the elbow. He hissed something. The words were incomprehensible gibberish. The guy looked jittery, his eyes jumping about and his cheeks twitching. "Hey, you all right?" Marcus asked. Of course, the guy couldn't understand him and didn't answer.

Marcus shook his head to clear it. He took in the grassy oval in front of the casino and the streets that circled it and the buildings beyond. Figures moved, but most of them were far enough away that he couldn't see them clearly. That was for the best. One man looked to be dragging a corpse behind him as he limped forward, leaving a dark smear as he went. Something scrambled up the side of a building in the distance, a dark shape that moved from window to window until it found one it liked. It smashed the glass and disappeared inside. A scream cut the air. From inside the room with the smashed window? Marcus wasn't sure, but he wondered what was happening in there. He had a notion that the scrabbling creature was killing. Eating. He swallowed, wishing he could see. Maybe it was fucking and eating and killing at the same time. He counted the stories to the smashed window and how many rows over from the edge of the building. He could go there and look and maybe he could fuck and eat and—

Marcus pushed the thoughts away, shocked at himself. *What the fuck? Why would you even think that?* Instead, he pulled up Olena's face. The one he knew, not the flip side that he now feared was behind it. He wondered how he could've forgotten her for even a second. Her face, and with it he remembered what they were doing and why and what could be after they escaped this place. That's what they were going to do. Not join in the horror, but escape it. He tried desperately to hold on to that.

Cool the fuck down, Marcus. Five minutes. Five minutes and we'll get out of here.

The only problem was that he doubted they had five minutes. His skin itched. Adrenaline coursed through him, screaming at him, ripping at every fiber of his being, telling him to flee. To fucking flee right now. There was the guard, but he could kill that fucker in an instant. Smack him with his tongue and pick up his Uzi or whatever the fuck it was and squirm. Anyone got in his way he'd shoot them to pieces. He could see it in his mind, bodies jerking, limbs twirling away, heads exploding. He'd kill every crazy fucking thing in here.

Marcus looked at him, mouth awash with the glorious tang of poison. He didn't strike.

The man's small eyes were pinned to something in the distance, so intense in their fear that Marcus forgot his sudden murderous anger. He turned. Something large was moving on a street adjacent to the green space in front of the casino. He couldn't see it yet, just the shadow of it cast huge against the buildings. Slow moving, many limbed. Massive.

"No," Marcus said. Whatever was about to step into view . . . No. He didn't want to see it. He didn't want it to exist. No, it shouldn't and hadn't and couldn't exist. Just no.

The creature had many legs. Tall, spindly things, jointed like a spider's. But it didn't move like a spider. It progressed forward slowly, both deliberate and meandering at the same time, like some prehistoric giant grazing. Its bulbous body looked, from a distance, to be spotted with blotchy stains. Above it a massive, tentacle-like head. Marcus knew it was a head by the way it moved, turning this way and that as if it were looking around. It had no eyes that he could make out, but still he was sure it could see. No mouth or ears, but he knew it was a head.

"Are you seeing this?" Marcus asked.

The thug didn't say anything. Of course he wouldn't, but yeah he was seeing it.

Marcus knew without any lingering doubt that this was no crazy night of bizarre jokers let loose on Talas. He'd suspected that for some time, but seeing this thing . . . Seeing this he knew in every molecule of his body that it wasn't of this earth. It was *other*, and not even other like jokers were other. Something else. Much worse.

Once in the clear, Marcus realized what the creature was doing. Though it walked with what looked like randomness, it wasn't without purpose. Its legs swiped out at anyone near enough to reach. It shoved the people—creatures, jokers, monster, whatever—into its pocked body. What he thought were blotches were cell-like divots. Once jammed in there, the people thrashed and fought, but they were stuck. And soon they grew still. The creature passed over dead bodies, ignoring them, snatching only the living.

"It's grazing," Marcus said.

As if words were all he was waiting for, the thug lost it. Letting out a scream, he ran forward, Uzi blazing as he did so. He shot wildly: at the body, the legs, up at the head that turned and studied him with more disinterest than alarm. He nearly got under the monster. He tilted his weapon to unload into its underbelly. That's when one of the legs lifted. It swiped around in a motion that started slow but morphed into deceptive speed. It snatched the man up and shoved him, still screaming and firing, into one of the pits in its undercarriage.

The amorphous head turned toward Marcus, who had slithered forward when the man attacked. The creature eased its bulk toward him, like an ocean liner making a slow turn. Marcus drew back into the casino's entryway. He hid in the shadows, pushing his tail back into the farther dark. He waited, trying to keep his breathing from rasping too loudly. He couldn't. The great underbelly of the thing grew closer, but he couldn't see the head anymore. He could feel the weight of its steps making the ground tremble. He could've squirmed farther in, but he was transfixed.

The creature shifted again. It turned and showed him its side and moved on, legs taking their slow, ghastly steps.

There were so many cells, pits like smallpox scars, each the perfect size for whatever had been shoved inside it. Each pit pulsed and relaxed, squeezed its inhabitant and then let go. Each time the people inside died a little more. One after another emaciated faces slid by Marcus. Skin shrunken to skulls. Cavernous eyes and bulging cheekbones, bare skulls as hair sloughed away. Some of them looked at him. That was the worse part. They were so desolate. Faces of people who knew the truth of the world and had been shattered by it. Marcus had seen faces like that before. Black and white images that he couldn't place. But yes, he had seen them. He tried to remember where.

Ray and Angel met Lonnegan and Stevens, as arranged, on the lowest step leading up to Fort Freak's main entrance, away from the trickle of traffic entering and leaving the precinct house so that they couldn't be overheard if they spoke quietly. Which they did.

"What's the latest?" he asked Lonnegan.

The detective shrugged. "They're interrogating the thugs who fell from the ceiling. But they're just dumbfucks with guns who were looting the casino. And their story is . . . confused. At best." She paused. "And Norwood."

"We got in touch with the family," the Angel said. "They're coming in to claim possession of the body."

Lonnegan nodded. "At least they have that."

"At least," the Angel agreed. "Others—Father Squid—who knows who else?—are still missing."

"The jokers are telling their stories," Stevens said.

"Who ordered them held incommunicado?" Ray asked.

Lonnegan and Stevens exchanged glances.

"Mendelberg," Stevens said.

"Why?" Ray asked loud enough to draw a glance from a passing cop.

"We don't know. Maseryk's pissed," Stevens said. He looked worried. "I hope he's not in on—"

He shut his mouth, suddenly.

"On what?" Ray asked, his voice suddenly smooth as silk.

Lonnegan and Stevens exchanged glances again.

"Whatever the hell that's been going on in the precinct," Lonnegan said frankly. "Mendelberg is gone. Took off mid-shift. No one knows why."

Ray nodded. "Someone call her residence?"

"Several someones," Lonnegan said, "including Maseryk. He wants me to check out her residence."

"That's a start," Ray said. "Why don't you take Angel with you?" He turned an eye, suddenly frowning. "I'll take the kid here and he can introduce me to the intricacies of the precinct house. There's some stuff I'd like to check up on. Some interrogations I'd like to observe."

"Uh," Stevens said.

Lonnegan nodded judiciously. "Good idea."

"What about Maseryk?" Stevens asked.

"You let me worry about Maseryk," Ray said. He turned to the Angel. "Be careful," he said. "Now we got teleporters involved, Kazakh gunmen, and God alone knows what the fuck else will turn up next."

"You too," the Angel said. She wanted to kiss him, even briefly, and she knew Billy knew it, but he smiled his somewhat crooked smile, and gripped her hand, warmly, briefly.

He looked to Lonnegan, nodded, and said crisply, "Good luck." She nodded back and he turned and took the steps at a methodical jog, Stevens following in his wake.

"Come on," Joan said to the Angel. She gestured with her head in the direction opposite to the one the boys had gone. "Let's go get my car."

"And then?" the Angel asked, falling in step. They were of a height, the Angel fractionally taller, and they matched strides, walking fast.

"We find Mendelberg."

"If she's really not at home?"

"We hope we don't find her body."

The Angel had to agree. They walked on, reaching a busier street and getting glances and the occasional catcall from the cheekier onlookers and passersby, as was not uncommon in the city, not even Jokertown.

"A girl hanging out with you could get a complex pretty quickly," Razor Joan commented.

The Angel glanced at her, looked away. "You're very pretty yourself."

Lonnegan unself-consciously ran a hand through her long blond hair. "I do all right," she said. "But you look like a young Sophia Loren, Jesus Christ, look at you—"

"Don't—" the Angel began automatically, then cut herself off. She wasn't sure why. It was hard for her, talking like this with another woman.

"Don't what?" Lonnegan asked. Her expression was quizzical, almost innocently.

"Don't blaspheme," the Angel said. She could feel herself blushing. "I—" She paused. She couldn't say, I'm sorry. "I grew up in a very religious home."

Lonnegan snorted, not in an unfriendly manner. "So did I. And look how I turned out. I drink and I smoke pot—it's true what they say; cops get the best weed—and I fornicate and I take the pill and I kill people."

"So do I," the Angel said. "Except for the drinking. The pot smoking. And taking the pill."

"Well," Razor Joan said, "I admit that I'm not big on the drinking part, but if you're a cop and you want to have a good relationship with your co-workers, you have to drink some. Pot on the other hand—it really makes for some incredible sex."

The Angel had never talked about this before, but somehow the words came. "Billy and I already have that. I'm not sure I could handle it if it was even more incredible."

Razor Joan laughed, again, in not an unkind manner. "Why you sweet little Southern thing, you! Well, not so little, obviously." She paused, then asked wickedly, "I noticed you didn't deny the fornication part."

"Well . . . It was a sudden thing when we met. After all, the apocalypse was just around the corner and I had never . . ."

"The Apocalypse? Good Lord! Uh—no blasphemy intended. We do have to sit down sometime and talk. Well—I suppose that's as good a reason as any to lose your virginity . . . although that Apocalypse never did happen, did it?"

"Of course not," the Angel said. "We stopped it."

"We *do* have to sit down and talk some time," Lonnegan muttered. "So, not to pry—well, screw it, I am prying. Isn't it kind of dangerous, you and the mister trying for a baby?"

"Huh?" The Angel was nonplussed.

"Well, you didn't cop to using birth control and you know what is most likely to happen when two aces have children."

"Oh." It was a fact of life for the Angel that she'd lived with for so long that she hardly ever thought of it. And yes, she did know what happened, usually, when aces had children. Genetic laws were such that the odds were that it would die a horrible death. There was a slight chance that it would live as a terribly deformed joker. The possibility that it would draw an ace from the deck of the wild card was infinitesimally small. But still, the Angel had met John Fortune, the son of two aces, who'd been a good boy who turned into a courageous man, so there was always hope. If it were possible that she could bear children.

"Doesn't apply," she told Lonnegan. But she wasn't yet ready to delve deeply into her personal life with a stranger. "I'm sterile."

Lonnegan realized she'd struck a nerve. "Oh, honey, I'm sorry." The Angel saw her flustered for the first time. "They have treatments now—"

The Angel shook her head. "Not a chance." She stopped. A delicious aroma was wafting down the avenue. She realized that she hadn't eaten for hours, as did her stomach, which grumbled audibly and angrily. She knew that she needed refueling. She stopped, pointed to the hot dog cart parked by the curb, a dozen feet ahead of them.

"Hungry?" she asked Razor Joan, who was still observing her closely, as if trying to unravel an enigma.

"Sure. I could use something before we head off for Brighton Beach."

The Angel nodded and turned to the joker vendor who wore a white, puffy chef's hat and a less than spotless white apron.

"What can I get you ladies?" He had a spatula in one hand, a can of soda in the other, an open bun in his third, and a squeeze bottle of mustard in the one that grew out of his chest. The smell of onions and peppers popping on the grill drew a rush of saliva to the Angel's mouth. They'd rushed off to the meeting without getting a bite of breakfast.

"Six brats with the works—onions, peppers, and sauerkraut—and three Dr Peppers." The Angel turned to Lonnegan. "What do you want?"

Lonnegan laughed in sheer disbelief. "I'll have two dogs with sauerkraut and mustard." She laughed again. "Some of us have to keep an eye on our figures."

"Mollie!" Dad's voice floated through the portal to Idaho. "Jesus Christ, what the hell are you waiting for?"

I'm safe, she reminded herself. *I'm smart, I'm safe, I'm quick. Smart enough not to venture outside these locked quarters, safe behind a locked door, quick enough to get away if anybody tries to break in. I'm okay. They can't get me.*

She returned to the closet. "Heads up!" she called. She pushed the liberated safe through to Idaho. It crashed to the floor of the barn to smash against a pair of mangled slot machines. Dad and Brent hauled the safe aside and went to work with more hydraulic tools while the other boys kept pounding on the pile of slot machines. Judging from the mounds of coins it appeared they'd gotten the hang of opening them.

Mollie dragged Baba Yaga's bed aside. Then she moved the portal so the lines for the hydraulic cutter could reach the safe in the floor. The whine of the cutting tool helped to drown out the screaming and shooting and murdering of the pitched battle from elsewhere inside the casino. It would be over quickly; how could an unarmed homicidal cannibal flashmob hope to overpower angry Ukrainian and Kazakh mobsters armed to the teeth with automatics?

She tried to focus on extricating the safe. But all she could see was the baby, its head impaled on an iron fence post, passersby tearing viciously at each other in the scramble to consume the twitching infant . . . Why WHY *WHY* the fuck would people do that? What the hell had happened out there? It made her so goddamned angry she boiled over with an empowering rage that made her invincible. It was sick and wrong and she needed to make those motherfuckers understand . . . Maybe she'd smash their faces against metal spikes and see how they liked it . . . They'd cry for mercy and repent when it was *her* teeth in their throats, *her* fingers gouging their eyes . . .

The cutting tool died out. So did the lights. It was as though the creeping blackout on the street had oozed into the casino to play havoc with the power here, too.

Distracted by her own swelling sense of rage, and the nightmare vision playing on endless loop inside her mind's eye, and half deaf from the residual whine of the hydraulics, she didn't hear the footsteps. She didn't realize she wasn't alone until a double loop of hydraulic lines and electrical cables snapped tight against her throat. She dropped the cutter, fingers scrabbling at the bands of plastic and rubber pinching off her windpipe.

"Cunt! You fucking cunt!"

Spittle misted the side of her face as Brent screamed in her ear. He hauled on the cables hard enough to physically yank her off her feet. Flecks

of more spittle pattered against her neck while he screamed at her, while
her fingers clawed ineffectually at the cables around her throat, while her
lungs burned, while her dangling feet kicked wildly for purchase.

A red veil fell over the contracting world. Baba Yaga's bedroom and all
of her furniture—her enemies, her victims—retreated to the end of a narrow tunnel. Mollie flailed, squirmed, kicked, but Brent was too big, too
strong, too enraged. The cables cut into her neck. Just before the lights
went out, a voice whispered to her from the past, from vastly better days:
Be smart.

Mollie created a doorway to Idaho under Brent's feet. Together they fell
from Talas to the family barn. The impact jarred him hard enough to
loosen his grip. She rolled away through dirt and straw, unwrapping the
cables around her throat. Mollie sucked down air with explosive gasps. The
red veil over the world receded, leaving a pounding headache and incandescent rage in its wake.

That motherfucker. First he booby-trapped the refrigerator with a
mousetrap, then he fucking tried to strangle her while she was in the
middle of trying to make them all rich. She'd slash him open, and strangle
him with his own intestines, she had no choice he was infected with a
madness that only she could see a festering boil filled with pus that could
only be cleansed tying it off with his own entrails and pulling tightly to
rupture the cyst and then she would consume the madness before it rein-
fected the others consume it transform it spit it out reborn reformed re-
purposed they didn't understand she had to show them but Jim and Troy
were too busy smashing at each other with crowbars to hear the truth of
her revelation and she couldn't find a blade for opening Brent's stomach
but there were knives in the kitchen blades for cleansing toward the house
she went but Dad was in her way Dad looming over her with a pitchfork
and he had the infection too and she had to cleanse him but he lunged at
her she leapt aside and then the screaming started again as the tines went
through Brent's stomach because Dad knew the only cure was to be found
in her brother's innards so he twisted the fork and Brent screamed again
but Dad was doing it wrong and he'd never cure his own sickness this way
so she folded space and then the pitchfork tines went through a hole in
Brent into Dad's own gut and he screamed and dropped the pitchfork as
the red sickness seeped out of him but the thing wearing Troy's skin planted
another crowbar blow to Jim's face and she had to cure him too but now
Dad held the pitchfork handle like a staff and he swung it at her head

cracking against her temple swinging bashing kicking at her smashing at Mollie breaking her concentration—

The portal to Talas blinked shut. And just like that, the rage and madness left her. She could see and think clearly again. Apparently so could her family, because now the barn echoed with the horrified screaming of the confused, horrified, viciously wounded Steunenberg clan.

What the . . .

How did . . .

Jesus fucking Christ . . .

They'd turned into a lunatic psycho-cannibal flashmob just like the one she witnessed on the streets outside the casino. In fact she'd tried to—

Oh, holy fuck. She had actually intended to pull out Brent's intestines and use them to "cure" him of his evil. She'd actually *believed* that made sense, *understood* it would work, *knew* it was the right thing to do.

It hurt, the dry heaving. Her stomach gave up nothing but a few drops of bile. Her throat stung, burned raw by acid and shame and *fuckfuckfuckingshitwhatthehellwasthat*. The others were emptying their stomachs, too.

Screw Talas. She was never, EVER going back. It was a fucking lunatic asylum hellhole, and she wanted no part of it. Somebody must have decided to use it as a testing ground for chemical warfare or something. To see what happened when you doused an entire city with something that turned people into psychopaths. Yeah. That was probably it. Well, to hell with the second safe. They'd taken as much as they could from Baba Yaga, so Mollie had no absolutely no reason whatsoever to return. Good.

Except: the chair.

The lone Louis XIV chair standing incongruously among a dozen other pieces of furniture, no two of the same style. Lost and abandoned in a city full of psychotic madmen. They'd break into Baba Yaga's quarters eventually. Would they smash to flinders everything they found in the insane scramble to destroy one another as fiendishly as possible?

She couldn't leave it vulnerable like that. It was already going to be hard to face herself in the mirror every day in the aftermath of whatever had come over her and her siblings. But if she left Ffodor there, inside that horrifying maelstrom of sickness and madness . . .

Mollie reopened the portal to Talas.

Writhing on the floor, her father cried, "Mollie, no!"

Mollie leapt back into Baba Yaga's quarters. Somebody was just outside, shouting in Russian and kicking the door to the apartment. The locks looked ready to fail. The door frame had cracks in it.

The chair was heavy, but she could lug it. She couldn't bear to damage it by dropping it through a hole to slam into the barn floor like the slot machines, so instead she pushed it through an opening in space between Kazakhstan and Idaho, then closed—come ON, *close* you son of a bitch—the doorways again. It took a few seconds, but by the time she broke the connection to Talas, Troy was already hefting the crowbar again and leering through his unrecognizable toothless ground-hamburger face. He dropped the crowbar and started keening again. But it wasn't mindless screaming anymore. The wounded Steunenbergs raised their voices in a chorus of despair.

The Louis XIV chair couldn't have been more out of place amid the dirt, hay, and cow shit of the family barn. But Mollie dragged it into the corner of the cleanest stall, curled up in it, and cried herself asleep.

There were military police and barricades at the entrance to the Shymkent International Airport. Franny, trapped in a line of cars, watched as car after car came to a stop, had a conversation, executed a U-turn, and left. While he was waiting a military jet came screaming in overhead heading for a landing.

Eventually it was their turn. A guard leaned in the window and peered at Franny and at Baba Yaga. Franny stiffened until his muscles felt like they were going to crack. The man said something, and Franny shook his head.

"English?" he said hopefully. The guard shook his head.

He repeated what he had said before in more emphatic tones and hand gestures that seemed to indicate no entrance.

There was the sound of a car door slamming. A woman walked up, mid-forties, very chic, spoke to the guard and then turned to Franny.

"I heard you say you were English." She spoke English with a pronounced Italian accent.

"Uh . . . American actually, but I don't speak the lingo here."

"The airport has been taken by the military. All commercial flights have left or they are grounded. They are saying to check back tomorrow."

"All commercial flights. Are there private planes? Are they flying?

Could you ask for me? My grandmother is really sick. We came here so she could show me home and she got blood poisoning. We need to get back to Manhattan—" Franny clamped his jaw shut to stop the nervous, exhausted babble.

"I will ask. Poor lady. She looks very bad."

There was more conversation. In the line behind them someone began blowing his horn. The woman turned back to him. "There are a few private planes still here, but he says it's not permitted to enter the airport grounds. I am sorry."

"Well, thanks for your help." She returned to her car. Franny executed the U-turn and drove away. He then set out driving around the perimeter of the airport. Somewhere there was going to be another gate for deliveries. And perhaps a persuadable/bribable guard.

The Angel had never been to Brighton Beach before. It had an aura of middle-class respectability about it, but the Angel knew that that was a bit of a lie. Still, it was largely quiet and homey-looking, especially the old but well-tended apartment building where Captain Mendelberg had a first-floor, two-bedroom apartment.

Miraculously, there was a parking space available right across the street from it, where Lonnegan expertly maneuvered her car. They got out and sauntered across the street, and pushed the doorbell once and nearly instantaneously an old and pleasantly plump woman in a long flowered dress, sensible shoes, thick stockings of some artificial material that wasn't nylon, and a babushka opened the door.

"Yes?" she asked pleasantly, with a pleasant smile.

Lonnegan showed her her badge.

"Is Chavvah Mendelberg in?" Lonnegan asked. "We work with her, but she didn't show up this morning and we haven't been able to get in touch with her. We're concerned."

The sight of Lonnegan's badge, the Angel thought, had caused the expression on the apple-cheeked old lady to become withdrawn, ever so slightly.

"Why, Chavveh hasn't lived here for months."

Joan looked at her blankly. "For months?"

"Why, yes."

Joan looked at the Angel, frowning, then turned back to the old lady. "You're *sure?*"

Her eyes suddenly turned hard. "I'm the landlady, ain't I?"

Before she could agree, the door closed suddenly, loudly, in her face.

They looked at each other again.

"What now?" the Angel asked.

"Well," Joan said thoughtfully, "there's always Uncle Ivan."

The day had gone entirely to hell after the morning conference with Jayewardene. Klaus had left the office before she could talk to him, not returning until an hour ago and not answering the text she'd sent him; she wasn't sure where he'd gone or why, and she'd been too busy to find out. Ink had been passing reports to Barbara all morning, and all of them were depressing. Accompanied by Ink, she went into the afternoon staff briefing feeling harried and stressed.

This should have been Lohengrin's meeting, but he'd finally sent a text message that she should run the briefing, that he'd be there but hadn't been able to prepare. That told her more than any words about Lohengrin's attitude.

They all looked up at her as she entered the room. She tried to smile at Klaus, but his face was frozen with an expression she couldn't quite decipher. Michelle—Bubbles—wasn't present but several minor aces were: Aero, the Spanish air-manipulating ace; Doktor Omweer, the first significant ace from the Netherlands; Wilma Mankiller, the Canadian strongwoman; Snow Blind, another Canadian ace with the ability to temporarily blind people; along with two of the aces who had been to Peru with them—Brave Hawk and Tinker. Barbara sat at the head of the table next to Klaus; Ink took the chair on the other side of her, an iPad sitting in front of her to call up reports, photos, and videos as Barbara needed. "Secretary-General Jayewardene wanted to be here but he's meeting right now with Representative Temir Bondarenko of Kazakhstan at the UN. I hope he'll have news for us later."

"What *is* going on there?" Tinker asked, his muscular arms flexing as he shifted in his seat. Barbara shook her head.

"We're still not certain." She didn't dare glance over to Klaus. "Hopefully Mr. Bondarenko has better information he can relay to us. Right now, it's apparent we have a crisis there that seems to be getting increasingly worse and widespread every few hours, but exactly what's causing it . . ." She shrugged. "And there's more critical news that I've just received in the last few hours." Ink had told her that Klaus hadn't yet been given the report; she heard his chair turn to look at her. "I hate having to relay this news, which I know is going to pain many of you here, myself not least of all. General Ramos has been assassinated in Peru, apparently poisoned. The New Shining Path, and especially Curare, are suspected."

The flat screen on the wall erupted with photographs: General Ramos, Curare, Cocomama, then a sequence of pictures and videos of street fighting between rock-throwing mobs and armed police. "There have been incidents in Lima, in Iquitos, in Trujillo," Barbara continued as the aces watched the screens. "At Machu Picchu, a group of tourists was assaulted and robbed by a suspected New Shining Path group; some of the injuries were severe." Barbara couldn't hold back the sigh that escaped her. "A bare two days after having signed a peace accord, and it looks like everything we accomplished there is already falling apart. We may end up having to go back. The Secretary-General's office has already had overtures from President Fujimori's office."

Klaus's fist came down hard on the table, startling Barbara. "Paper doesn't solve anything," he muttered. "Signatures and empty words. That's all they are."

Everyone stared at him. Klaus slumped back in his seat, shaking his head but saying nothing more. He waved a hand toward Barbara, who took a deep breath, glancing past Klaus to the window to where the East River glistened in sunlight with the tourist boats plowing its brown water, as if nothing at all was happening out in the world. "On yet another front, I've talked to the various embassies in East Timor, and with President Ramos-Horta. They all seem to feel that things are calmer there today, and the Secretary-General agrees with me that for right now, sending one of our teams in would be premature. Talas is where our attention needs to be for the moment."

"Then what about sending in an advance team to scout things out and report back directly to the Secretary-General, Lohengrin, and you?" Doktor Omweer asked, his words touched with a strong Dutch accent.

"Are you volunteering, Doktor?" Barbara asked, and the man's eyes widened.

"I? If that is your wish, I certainly would do so. After all, there was a reason I was chosen to control the power of lightning. No one else could—"

"Yes," Barbara interrupted before the man could go on—as they all knew he would. She heard a quiet snort of laughter from Ink, who openly referred to the ace as "Herr Doktor Earworm" for his tendency to ramble on and on about himself. "At this point no decisions have been made, but an advance team is something that the Secretary-General and I have already kicked around." Klaus glanced sharply at her with that. "If we decide to go that way, I'll certainly remember your offer. But right now . . . Let's look at the information we *do* have, sketchy as it may be."

Barbara nodded to Ink. The window shades closed, hiding the view of the East River, the room lights dimmed, and grainy and dark videos began to play on the screens around the room. Dozens of people—men, women, children—ran screaming across a wide boulevard from what looked like a cloud of rolling darkness that pursued them; those who fell in the rush were simply trampled. In the light of a streetlamp in the middle of a square, a crowd appeared to have set upon itself, with people striking each other chaotically. A joker, wearing only the remnants of torn and bloodied clothing, ran clumsily toward the camera, her left side visibly larger and more muscular than her right; in her left arm, she brandished what looked to be someone's lower leg. She stopped a few feet from the lens and took a bite from the leg's calf, glaring at the camera in freeze-frame.

"We'll start with this," Barbara began.

I have to be dreaming, Marcus told himself, pleaded with himself. *Please just be a dream. That's all. The longest, most fucked-up nightmare the world has ever known. Please, let me wake up.*

The one good thing about nightmares, he'd always thought, was that when they got bad enough and presented horrors too enormous to face, he'd wake up. The unthinkable—being unthinkable—would drive him out of the subconscious and back to reality. He'd find himself gasping, tangled in sweat-stained sheets, eyes casting about the dark corners of his room, and relief would wash over him like a narcotic. God how he wished that would happen now.

It didn't, and the faces of the trapped ones still haunted Marcus when

Olena ran through the casino lobby. She raced for the door, and was nearly through it before Marcus called to her and slid out of the shadows. She spun, her face white-pale even in the murky light. She looked terrified. She stepped back from him, stumbling over debris on the floor. "No!" she yelled. "No!"

"Olena," he pleaded, "it's just me. It's Marcus." He nearly said that he wasn't a monster, but considering the things he had thought, and the moments he'd forgotten her, and the fear behind it that he was only a stray thought or two from doing vile, vile things . . . He just said, hoping it was true, "It's me. It's me that loves you."

To his relief, her face flashed with recognition. She ran toward him, smashed into his chest, and squeezed him. Nothing had ever felt better. But it was over in a heartbeat. She fell back, her face going hard. She grabbed his hand and pulled him toward the door. "We have to go."

"Do they have the stuff your dad wanted?"

"Doesn't matter."

"But . . ." Marcus peered back into the casino, looking for signs of the others. "What about your dad?"

Olena breathed a moment, clearly controlling her frustration with him. "There was something in there. A thing that . . . that . . . that just shouldn't be. A mouth."

"A mouth? Olena tell me!"

She looked annoyed, gritted her teeth, but she spoke in a fast whisper. "We got to Baba Yaga's offices quickly. It was dark and our flashlights didn't work and there was no electricity. But we used lighters and found the room. Andrii made a fire in a trash bucket and we went to work. I thought we were really going to get away with it. And then something blew out the fire. Just like that it was gone. Something began moving around us, making a sound like . . ." She opened her mouth and, hissing out a long breath, trilled her tongue in a staccato rhythm. "It was language, but not of this world. It was the tongue of Lucifer. That's what it was. We could see nothing. We couldn't see it at all, but the way it talked and laughed . . . We knew it could see us fine. It kept moving. And then, just before it struck, its body lit up. A great, awful mouth. Rows of teeth. Just a mouth and two legs. The light lasted just long enough for its jaws to close on Andrii's head. Then it went dark. Darker than before. That's when I ran. The others . . . I don't know. There. You know. Let's go now."

He didn't argue with her, and he decided not to tell her about the things he'd seen. "You still have your gun?"

It was a stupid question. She had it out and held in a two-handed grip. She answered, "What does it look like?"

Not only did she have it, she used it. As they ran, hoping they were moving toward the edge of the city, they passed one monstrosity after another. Some ignored them; others came for them. Olena clipped the knee of a girl with screaming mouths on both her cheeks. It didn't stop her screaming, but she could only scrabble after them, dragging herself with thin arms. After that, Olena shot a man through the heart when he came at them. Literally, through the heart. The organ was on the outside of his chest, beating. It popped like a blood-filled balloon. And then there was a drooling, big-mouthed monster of a thing. It was something like a gargoyle, but like the underworld version of one. Stalactite-like protrusions hung from its flesh, dangling when it moved. It had eyes, though it didn't seem capable of opening them. They moved beneath the cream-colored skin of its eyelids. It turned toward them, nostrils flaring. But it didn't move. Marcus thought they could go around it. Olena had a different opinion. She slammed one shot right into its forehead, exploding the back of its head in a spray of muck.

When Marcus looked at her, she said, by way of explanation, "What? You saw it. It was sniffing. Sniffing!" She punctuated this by stomping on the shattered skull until she slipped.

We really, really needed to get out of the city, Marcus thought.

He spotted the grazing thing in the distance and pulled Olena back from the road leading toward it. "Not that way. Don't go near that."

They cut across the street and veered off on a diagonal that led to one of the bridges over the river. As they ran for the bridge a figure rose up out of the river, rubbing his chest and arms like he was washing. He was tall, twenty feet or so. Scrawny, with bulging knees. Butt naked. It was this particular part of his anatomy that was most prominently projected toward them. His head and hands were outsized even for his tall frame. But it was the way his skin glistened that drew Marcus's recognition. Beneath the river water the muck he was trying to wash clean clung to him. His efforts only smeared it across his flesh.

When the scent of him hit Marcus he couldn't help but gasp, "Vapor-lock?"

"You know that thing?" Olena asked.

"Yes."

"Then he's a joker."

"He was. But he wasn't like this before. He's changed."

The figure turned and looked over his shoulder, his back twisting at an unnatural angle. His face was a distorted version of what it had been: his nose beak-like, his eyes tiny and deepset. He locked on Marcus. Recognition. And then he was clambering up the riverbank and running toward them. His large feet smacked the pavement. He ran teetering, legs seeming close to buckling with each stride, but he came on fast. His hands raked his chest, cupping up gallons of the potent muck that splashed away as he ran. He gabbled unintelligibly and looked like an excited, tottering child. For a moment Marcus thought it was boyish excitement that twisted his features. But as he got closer he knew it couldn't be that.

Olena's gun popped severals times in mechanical procession. Vaporlock flinched at each impact. But bullets weren't going to stop him. His expression went ugly. He came on even faster. Marcus surged forward, his tail a weaving curl of straining muscle. He rose up, leaned forward, and slammed into the joker's abdomen with all the force he had. His JV football coach would've been proud. He felt the air go out of him as the joker's body caved around his shoulder. Then they were down in a writhing mass of long limbs and scales and Vaporub. Marcus punched and clawed at him, but his punches slipped away and he couldn't keep hold of him. The smell was so overpowering that he tried not to breathe.

He broke free. He twisted away and circled with serpentine grace and power. Vaporlock rose awkwardly to his feet. Marcus tagged him with his tongue. It was a solid shot, hitting him at the protrusion of his Adam's apple. The joker grasped at his neck. His face turned a shade of blue. But it was the impact that hurt him; not the poison. To the fists, then. Marcus swung for his head. Vaporlock dodged. It was an awkward dodge, more like a stumble than a planned move, but it worked. By the time Marcus had his torso back above his coils, Vaporlock was throwing handfuls of muck at him. Marcus knew what would happen if any of them hit his face full end. End of story. He writhed like a mad dancer, his head bobbing and weaving. He kept his face clear of all but a few droplets, but his torso took hits. His tail.

The adrenaline was scorching through him with such intensity that it took him a moment to notice the way his flesh stung where the muck stuck to it. Not only was it overpoweringly pungent, it burned like acid. He tried to wipe it away. It only spread all the more. He was smoking, the vapor clouding his vision and making him cough. He knew he had to end this fast, by whatever means necessary.

He surged in, his tail whipping up in a sidewinder motion. He feinted a punch. When Vaporlock pulled back, he swiped his legs out from under him with his tail. The joker's big feet went up into the air as he came down hard on his back. Marcus coiled around him, being careful to keep his torso and face as far away as possible. And then he squeezed with every muscle in his tail. Vaporlock struggled. He gurgled and wrenched his head around. The serpent in Marcus loved the feel of it. A body struggling, trapped within the coiled vise of his muscles. He squeezed, hoping to feel bone crack and organs burst. He squeezed.

The joker wasn't an easy kill, though. As moments passed, the heat on Marcus's scales increased. He could smell them burning. Bitter smoke stung his eyes. He had Vaporlock in the death grip, but the touch of him was eating through his scales. It grew more and more painful frighteningly fast. Suffocation was going to take too long. Marcus writhed into a different position without loosening his grip. He grabbed for Vaporlock's head. It was hard to get a grip on it as he twisted and fought, teeth gnashing. When he finally had him with a white-knuckled grip on both his ears, Marcus began smashing his face on the pavement. He cried out in pain and desperation and fury. Smashing. Smashing. Smashing until the man's face caved in, skull broken and oozing new liquids. Disgusted, Marcus released him and squirmed away from his touch.

Olena ran toward him, but pulled up short. "Marcus, you're burning!"

His scales sizzled and smoked. Some of them began to fall away, revealing the naked, blistering skin underneath. Marcus cast around for something to help him. He went over the railing of the bridge in an arch, hitting the river as he twisted onto his back. For a moment he squirmed in the water, bumping boulders as the current flushed him under the bridge. The touch of the water was beautifully cooling. He rubbed at his scorched flesh, hard, feeling it flake away and leave the raw skin underneath. He was out of the river as quickly as he could, driving himself through the pain and back to Olena. She had already attracted the attention of a naked, aroused man who was lumbering toward her on legs that buckled and hyperextended, barely seeming to keep him upright. The only thing steady about him was his erection, which directed him unerringly toward Olena. She didn't even see him, so intent was she on Marcus.

Marcus swept around her and punched the guy, sending him spinning. He grabbed Olena's hand. Holding it tight, he turned and found the mountain they'd sighted on before. "There's our mountain," he said. "Come on."

"That's her?" Wally asked, a shocked expression creasing his metallic face. "I mean, you told me about how you found her, but, but I never thought . . ."

"I was hoping you might know someone," Michelle said with a thread of panic in her voice. "Because of Ghost."

Wally shook his head. "I don't think the doctor I used would help. She's a psychologist who deals with joker kids and trauma. But she'd have to talk to Adesina. And I don't see how she could."

They went into the living room. Joey was watching the TV with the sound turned down low. The same film of Talas was playing, but now there were drone photographs of the city. These showed a thick cloud almost completely obscuring the buildings below. And then a banner saying "Breaking Footage" appeared below shaky video of people running out of the fog. Most of them looked terrified, but some, well, Michelle knew what jokers looked like. *Yet another PPA situation,* she thought. *And more people will suffer.* She tried hard not to care, but she didn't succeed.

The scene cut to a man dressed in military garb standing in front of a group of soldiers. Even with the sound off, Michelle could tell he was doing a PR spin on the situation.

And that was where they wanted her to go. Well, whatever was happening, Babel and Lohengrin could handle it without her. But despite everything going on with Adesina, she couldn't just ignore that something wrong was happening in Talas. Something messy and bad.

"Got any ideas how to help the niblet, Wally?" Joey asked, snapping Michelle back.

Wally shook his head and eased his weight onto the sofa. It gave a groan as he sat. He looked at the TV and said, "Have you been watching this? It's very strange."

Michelle glanced back as the camera panned across a broad swath of land and came to rest on the city in the distance. The puke-green miasma was obscuring much of the city now.

Michelle's phone rang. She looked at it and saw Babel's name on the screen. *Shit*, she thought. For a moment, she considered letting it go to voice mail, but she picked up.

"Michelle here," she said.

There was a brief pause, then Barbara began talking. "Have you been watching the news?" she asked.

"Sort of," Michelle replied. "I have bigger things on my plate. As you know."

"It's not bigger than this," Barbara snapped. "I'm not sure exactly what's happening—that's why we need you there—but whatever it is, it can't be good."

A bubble began forming in Michelle's free hand. It quivered there with a promise of destruction or beauty. She'd been Johnny-on-the-spot for the Committee since joining. It was only when she had adopted Adesina that she'd backed off some of her duties. She popped the bubble, absorbing its energy.

"I can't go. I told you yesterday."

"Michelle, don't make me beg." There was a thread of real anxiety in her voice.

"Jesus," Michelle replied with exasperation. She rubbed her forehead with her index finger. "I'm not pulling some power play here. I just can't leave. I'm not sure how much clearer I can make this." And then she disconnected the call.

Enough was enough.

"They really on you?" Wally asked. The sofa gave a little groan as he shifted his weight.

"That place," she said, pointing at the TV. "They want me to go there. To Talas. Help with some mission, as usual."

Joey looked at the TV. "Looks like some weird shit is going down," she said. And Michelle was surprised that she wore a concerned expression on her face. Normally, big world events didn't interest Joey much. "Whatever it is, some asshole is behind it. Might even be some wild card thing." Her mouth twisted into an angry line.

"I hope not," Wally said. He looked at the TV, and Michelle could see he was getting more upset. They'd all three been in the PPA together—and it had ended especially badly for Wally. Joey had almost died—as had Michelle. But it was losing Jerusha that had marked him. After Gardener's death Wally was never the same.

And then Michelle flashed on the moment that Mummy—a child ace whose power allowed her to suck the water from her victim's body—had latched on to her arm. Michelle had felt herself desiccating with every moment. First, her mouth had gone dry. Then her arms had withered. Then her skin had tightened on her body. She had warned Mummy to stop. Warned her that only one of them would be walking away. And still the girl had kept her hand clamped around Michelle's wrist.

Then Michelle had killed Mummy.

Killed a child whose only crime was being injected with the wild card virus. But as Michelle had looked into Mummy's eyes and told her to stop, she'd seen nothing there. Nothing human anymore. Either the wild card virus had done it, or the training from the PPA had. It didn't matter now, though, because Michelle had to live with the fact she'd killed a child.

We make terrible choices, Michelle thought. *Terrible choices when we use our powers.*

"You okay, Michelle?" Wally asked, pulling her back to the present.

Michelle blinked and gave a little start. "Yeah," she said, rubbing her arm absentmindedly. "Yeah, just fine."

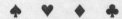

The first portal pair Mollie ever created was just about the size of a baseball. Which in retrospect wasn't all that surprising, given that her card turned on a late spring evening like so many others at the Steunenberg farm: with the boys doing some batting practice behind the barn and deliberately aiming for her head. After that it took a while before she felt confident enough to make a portal large enough to step through. So much of her early practice had involved going into town the old-fashioned way, in Mom's minivan, and trying to shoplift or swipe cash from open registers. Sometimes one or two of the boys came along to serve as distractions. But back in those very early days Mollie lacked the nerve to be quick and decisive while the boys lacked subtlety (which they still did, and always would). So Mollie Steunenberg's ace became a notorious source of aggravation (and no small amount of amusement) for Coeur d'Alene's finest.

Which might be why, in the aftermath of the chaos that erupted when Mollie folded space between the barn and Kootenai Emergency Health Center in downtown CdA, the cop on duty at the hospital didn't believe a single thing she said. It wasn't the best lying she'd ever done. In fact, it was pretty much the worst. Mollie was exhausted as hell, still recovering from her rage-fugue, and so traumatized by what she'd seen and done in the barn she could barely stand much less spin a tale. But the cop started pelting her with questions even while a parade of stretchers went squeak-squeak-squeaking through the hole in space, trailing hay, manure, and shouted medical jargon.

She vaguely recognized the cop from her early days trying to swipe caramel bars and petty cash from the Walgreens. He touched her gently on the shoulder and pulled her aside to make way for the medics.

"Okay. Can you tell me what happened?"

(On the other side of the portal, the first EMT on the scene gasped even as she rushed to stabilize the injured. "Jesus. What the *fuck* happened here?")

Mollie cleared her throat. It hurt like somebody had tried to cut her head off with a shoelace.

She spoke with a rasp. "Well, see, we—"

The cop bent forward, staring at her neck. She caught her own reflection in a windowpane; she had vicious purple wheals around her throat. She'd have to hide them under a scarf until they healed.

"Good God. Who did that to you?"

"What?" she rasped. "No, no, this was an accident—"

The welts from the blows she'd taken to the head were easily hidden under her hair; thank God Dad hadn't managed to hit her in the face or blacken her eyes.

("We have two Caucasian males, ages unidentifiable, extreme facial and cranial trauma!" First came the stretchers with Jim and Troy, who had beaten each other's faces into unrecognizable pulp. Mollie wondered if the EMTs noticed the bloody crowbars, or the teeth scattered across the barn floor like hailstones. *Ages unidentifiable.* Mollie coughed wetly and tasted warm vomit.)

The cop said, "What kind of accident?"

"Um, we were working on some, uh . . ." She shook her head, but nothing could clear her muddled thoughts. "See, our dad got some hydraulic equipment at auction a few years ago. From an estate sale, back when Mr. Geitzen died of that heart attack and his wife gave up and sold their land to Monsanto. His second wife, I think. Dad figured—"

The cop gestured at her neck and the barn on the other side of the portal.

Oh, shit, she realized. *If he looks he's going to see the slot machines.* She inched back, around the side of the hole in space, so that if he stood near to question her he wouldn't be able to see through the portal. But what the hell was she going to do about the EMTs? Just hope they were too busy saving lives to notice a pile of stolen casino equipment? *Shit, shit, shit.*

"Okay. So this was a machinery accident?"

"Yeah. Uh, yeah. The machinery. It was hydraulic, see."

("—male with multiple deep abdominal punctures!" That was Brent's stretcher. Mollie shouted at the scrum of nurses and doctors sprinting past. "He got a dirty pitchfork in the gut! He could have tetanus!")

"Pitchfork?" The cop squinted at Brent's stretcher, already receding down the corridor, then frowned at her. "I thought you said something about machinery?"

"Oh, yeah, it was. Both, I mean. See, the hydraulic line, it, um, there was a really big pressure surge and when it blew it sent a pitchfork, um, across the barn."

("—multiple compound fractures to the arm, possible dislocated shoulder—" Mick screamed like the madmen of Talas every time his stretcher hit a bump. His shattered arm had more kinks in it than a carpenter's rule.)

The cop blinked. "Jesus. What happened to him?"

"Oh. Uh, Mick was standing too close and when the compressor came apart it tossed him higher than the hay loft. He came down really hard. People think dirt floors are soft, but they're not, you know, not when they're hard-packed by people and cows and equipment coming and going all the time."

"Sure."

("—White male, early fifties, multiple deep punctures to the abdomen, massive internal bleeding—"

"That's my dad," she shouted. "Check him for tetanus, too!")

"Another pitchfork injury?" The cop cocked his head a little bit, squinting at her as though trying to read fine print tattooed under her eyes.

"Yes. I mean, no. I mean, yes, but it wasn't another pitchfork. It was the, uh, the same one."

"The *same* pitchfork got your brother *and* your dad in the gut?"

"Yeah. The tines went right through Brent and got Dad, too." At least that was mostly true. The cop grunted and shifted his pose, clearly a little squicked out by the mental image of a dirty, rusty, manure-flecked pitchfork going straight through somebody's stomach and poking out his back—

Mollie doubled over. Panted. Fought to swallow down the gorge before it splattered all over her shoes.

At least some of the sympathy had returned to the cop's gaze when she levered herself upright again. But it winked out like a snuffed candle when, just before Dad's medical scrum turned the corner, an ER nurse shouted plain as fucking day: "—*multiple bite wounds and a severed ear!*"

The puke surged up her throat so violently it actually jetted from her nostrils as well as her mouth. It splattered across a row of chairs in the clinic entryway and the backsplash stippled the cop, whose quick reflexes had saved him from the worst of it.

Kneeling on all fours on the hospital floor, Mollie couldn't remember if she was the one to have bitten Dad's ear off, and if so, if she had swallowed it. Watching the last streamers of puke and spittle trailing from her lips, she wondered if they'd find Dad's ear in the contents of her stomach. The thought made her stomach convulse again; she tasted bile. How would they ever be able to look at Dad and his lopsided head without remembering how they'd temporarily become mindless eaters of their own kin?

An orderly put Mollie in a wheelchair, wiped her face, and wheeled her out of the way while others started the tricky task of disinfecting the whole damn waiting room. The cop knelt beside her chair. He ran a hand through his hair. "Did I just hear something about bite marks?"

Three gold bracelets and a Krugerrand had gotten them past the guard at a back gate. They were in an area with hangars and warehouses and relatively far from the activity going on closer to the terminal and the main runways. Franny hoped they would be overlooked.

He also had a feeling chartering a plane to get them back to the States was going to cost a hell of a lot more than the baubles he'd traded. That's why he'd parked next to a hangar and was making a careful inspection of the contents of the satchel. In addition to the stack of passports and the bundle of cassette tapes there was a heavy emerald and gold necklace, a diamond and pearl choker—he found himself wondering how Abby would look in the choker and nothing else—a tangle of diamond tennis bracelets. There were rings with multi-carat gemstones. A velvet pouch held an array of loose gems. They threw prismatic fire in the sunlight.

"I wore that . . . at an embassy ball." Her voice was harsh. Franny realized he was still clutching the pearl and diamond choker. "I was beautiful. He thought so. Thirsty," Baba Yaga finished and she sounded old and scared.

"I'll try to find you some water. I've gotta leave you for a while. Look for a pilot and plane. Will you be okay?"

Her response was mumbled and the words seemed garbled. Franny had to take it for assent. He put the pouch of gems in one pocket and the emerald necklace in the other, secured the pistol in the small of his back, and headed out.

Many of the hangar doors were closed. He spotted one with the doors open. A woman sat on a bench out front smoking a cigarette. As he drew closer he saw she was younger than he'd first thought, and attractive in a leggy, outdoorsy sort of way. Long brown hair was secured in a ponytail and she had a tattoo of teardrops that began at the side of her left eye and down onto her cheek. He smiled and walked forward.

"Hi, you speak English?"

"A little." She held up her thumb and forefinger about half an inch apart. She had an accent he couldn't identify.

"Is that your plane?" He nodded toward the plane in the hangar. It was a dull white and stained in places. It also didn't look like it could cross the Atlantic, but maybe it could get them to a city with an airport that was open.

"Yes."

"Could I charter it?" The woman frowned. "Hire it. Have you fly me somewhere." He made a swooping gesture toward the sky.

"Sure. Yeah."

"Great. Look I don't have money—" There was a sharp frown at that. "But I've got these," he hurried to add as he pulled out the pouch of gemstones.

The woman's brown eyes lit up at the sparkle. "That will do nice."

She ground out her cigarette in a bucket of sand, stood, and sauntered over to him. Her white blouse was unbuttoned enough that he could see the swell of her tanned breasts. She was obviously a fan of sunbathing topless and Franny felt a reaction. She smelled of soap and cigarettes and rose perfume.

"Where you want to go?"

"Someplace with an international airport. Could you get us to . . .

uh . . ." Franny thought about the maps he'd studied before he and Jamal
had started on this mad journey to rescue the jokers. He considered Russia
but given Baba Yaga's concerns about the KGB, or whatever it was called
today, he decided against that destination. "Ukraine or Turkey?"

"Sure. Have to file flight plan. Give me jewels and I'll go do that."

"Let me think about that. Uh . . . no. You go file the flight plan, you'll
get the jewels when we land."

Perhaps it was the fact she was a pretty woman. Or that he was past
the point of exhaustion. Or the pain pills he'd swallowed, but he missed
the signal, the warning in her eyes and body so the toe of her cute ankle
boot took him right in the nuts. Screaming, he doubled over, clutching
his abused balls as agonizing pain shot straight through the top of his head.
Vomit filled his mouth and he fell onto his knees.

The pouch fell out of his hand, jewels glittering like multicolored rain
drops cascaded out and went dancing across the tarmac. The woman went
scrabbling after them. Franny wanted to grope for his pistol but couldn't
make his hands release his throbbing balls. *The emeralds, shit!* If she
searched him they'd be gone, too. Groaning, he reached back, grabbed the
pistol grip, and pulled it free.

The woman paused, hand in her pocket where she'd thrust a handful
of gems, saw the gun. Her face twisted with fury and she didn't look so
pretty any longer. She spat out something that sounded like curse words
and bolted like a greyhound hearing the starting gates slam open.

Groaning, Franny climbed to his feet. There were a few gems glittering
on the ground. Moving like he was as old as Baba Yaga he tottered around
and picked them up. Of the woman there was no sign. He just hoped she
wouldn't go and alert the soldiers. If the military was as corrupt as the
cops he was probably safe.

One thing the experience had taught him—he wasn't going to be able
to negotiate a deal then go back and get Baba Yaga. He needed her with
him while he found a pilot so they could leave right away. He returned to
the van for the old lady. She was conscious, but barely.

"This is proving harder than expected. I need to take you with me and
you're going to have to walk at some point because I need my hand free
for the gun. Can you manage?" She grimaced but nodded. He slipped the
satchel strap over his good shoulder, clasped the emerald necklace around
her throat, and picked her up.

With Baba Yaga in his arms he moved on through the buildings, heat rising off the tarmac, sweat trickling down his back and sides and into his sideburns.

"The black. Did you . . . kill . . . him?" Her voice was threadlike.

"No," Franny snapped. "He told me what you did. To Father Squid." He discovered that rage had a taste and Baba Yaga cried out as his arms tightened around her. He fought for calm.

"The priest . . . was noble . . . always makes you stupid . . ." Her voice trailed away.

He wanted to tear into her. Tell her about Father Squid. His place in Jokertown, his kindness, his decency, his basic goodness. Instead he muttered, "You're a goddamn monster."

"No, boy, the monsters are coming."

Another open hangar beckoned. He approached with a lot more caution this time. There was a man inside, older with Asian features. He was actually prepping the plane. This plane sported not only stains but places where the paint had chipped and rust had taken hold. The glass over the cockpit was pitted in places.

"Fucking *Millennium Falcon*," Franny muttered. "Well as long as it can outrun the Takisians or whatever the fuck we're running from in Talas . . ." He set Baba Yaga on her feet and kept his left arm around her. He figured his wounded shoulder could handle her weight better than the recoil if he should have to fire the gun.

The man had stopped, clipboard in hand, pen poised to write, and was staring at the gun. The sight of one did tend to focus the mind, Franny thought.

"My grandmother's hurt." A spasm ran through Baba Yaga's frame when he said grandmother. He ignored her and went on. "We need a way out of here. You fly us and you can have her necklace." The man's eyes were blinking rapidly and he didn't respond. "Oh fuck, you didn't understand a word I just said, did you?"

Baba Yaga started speaking. Her hand went up and touched the necklace. The man's eyes flicked to the emeralds, but almost immediately went back to the gun. He answered her. Franny understood one word—*Tehran*. Great, not at all the direction he wanted to be heading.

There was more talk. Despite the weakness of her voice there was something in Baba Yaga's tone that had the hair on the back of Franny's neck standing up. The man seemed to feel it too because he nodded, then gestured to the plane.

"Get me aboard, but make him come with us. Then watch him during the final check. I told him you would kill him if he tried anything."

"Interesting negotiating tactic."

"Worked better than yours," she grunted, and she slapped her hand against his crotch. Despite the fact it was a feather's touch Franny sucked in a sharp breath. "I've kicked enough men in the balls to know the signs."

The shit plane wasn't very fast either. It took over three hours to reach Tehran. Franny had spent the entire time standing in the cockpit with the gun trained on the pilot to make certain he didn't radio anybody. His legs were aching and shivering, his back hurt, his balls throbbed, his head was pounding, and his gunshot wounds were burning. On the upside all the various pains were keeping him awake.

The pilot looked up at Franny, said something, and gestured at the radio. He made a helpless gesture and shrugged. Glancing back over his shoulder to where Baba Yaga huddled among the crates he yelled, "Hey, Baba Yaga. The guy's gotta call the tower now. Or at least I think that's what he's saying. I need you."

"Help me, boy."

Franny moved to her, hauled her up, and supported her into the cockpit. She and the pilot gabbled at each other. He unlimbered the radio and made the call. A lot of numbers and letters were exchanged. Oddly the codes were exchanged in English. Then Baba Yaga took over the radio and in a completely different language started talking to the ground.

"You speak Arabic, too?" Franny asked.

She gave him a disgusted look. "It's Farsi. And no wonder you Americans mess up everything when you go out into the world."

At one point she looked back at Franny and ordered, "Bring the passports." He brought her the stack and she fanned them out on the instrument panel. Most were for her. The others showed pictures of B.O., Baldy, and Stache.

"Unfortunately I don't look anything like your goons."

"Won't matter." She handed him B.O.'s passport. "They will have something to stamp. Bureaucracy will be served." She gave the radio back to the pilot and slumped in the copilot's chair overcome by just the effort of talking. Her eyes closed and her breathing was sonorous.

A few minutes later they were on the ground and rolling to a stop.

"Okay, let's get out of here," Franny said.

"No. We wait," she ordered.

Franny had spent enough time in her presence to know when she had that tone no explanation was coming. Trucks arrived to start off-loading the cargo. Men in uniforms arrived, customs officers Franny assumed. They checked the bill of lading, gave a glance at the passports. Left. The unloading continued. Franny sank down on the floor of the cargo bay with his back against the curving side of the plane. About thirty minutes later a man in a tailored Western-style suit arrived. He and Baba Yaga had another conversation in what Franny now knew was Farsi.

She motioned to Franny and indicated he should remove the necklace and give it to the pilot. He did. She then took the cassette tapes out of the satchel and handed it and their remaining funds to the man in the suit. He picked up Baba Yaga and carried her off the plane. Franny scrambled after them. He wouldn't put it past the old bitch to leave him even after all this.

"Fairuza tells me the air space over Kazakhstan has been closed. We are lucky, boy. We are riding the wings of the storm."

"Yeah, real lucky," Franny grunted as the stitches in his side pulled.

When they came around the freight plane there was a sleek, modern jet waiting on the runway with the steps down and the engines starting. There was a big man in a white coat climbing aboard. A stethoscope hung out of one pocket of the coat. Despite these medical trappings the man was far more reminiscent of the late (unlamented) Stache, B.O., and Baldy. Apparently Baba Yaga was done relying on Franny.

The man in the suit carried Baba Yaga into the plane. Franny followed and gaped at the elegance of the interior. There was a final conversation between the man and Baba Yaga and he left. The doors were closed and they began to taxi down the runway. Baba Yaga reclined in a wide leather seat, clutching the tapes to her withered bosom with her one remaining hand.

Franny scrambled into a seat and hooked the belt. "How . . . how?"

She opened her eyes and pierced him with one of her cutting looks. "A few favors. A little blackmail. And money. Lots of money. It is a power greater than all your aces."

The mansion was set back from the double-gated entrance at the end of an impressively long, slightly loopy gravel driveway. The rococo wrought-iron gates were impressively tall and so thick that the Angel figured they'd be a worthy test of her strength. A call box was set in the stone part of the wall that swept out beyond the limits of their sight, right and left both and finally dwindled away in the distance. The call box was, the Angel suspected, just out of reach. And she was right. Lonnegan had to unbuckle her seat belt, open the car door, and lean as far as she could through her down-turned window to press the buzzer.

She leaned back to a more comfortable position, static cackled on the air, and a male voice said something in Russian.

"You're in America now, Jack," said the cop. "Speak English."

"But of course, madam. Who may I say is calling?"

"Detective Joan Lonnegan."

"Ah." A pause. "Aren't you somewhat off your beat?"

"Not so far that I can't drag your ass to jail if you keep annoying me."

"Very well. I shall see if the master is in."

They waited perhaps forty-five seconds, then the metal gates slowly creaked open.

"Into the bear's den," Lonnegan muttered.

"Is this really wise?" the Angel said, watching the stone monstrosity loom larger and larger as they approached.

"Well," Lonnegan considered, "Ivan Grekor may be the biggest Russian asshole in this city, but even he hasn't taken to slaughtering NYPD detectives and SCARE agents out of hand. Yet. Besides, the boys know where we are."

"Comforting."

It was a slow, crunchy drive down the looping driveway over the crushed gravel. By the time they'd arrived a reception committee was waiting for them before the front entrance, which was raised five stone steps up off the ground. The Angel was no architectural expert, but it looked as if the stairway leading up to the entrance, the columns flanking it, and the front facade surrounding it, seemed to be marble. In what style she couldn't venture a guess. But it was very ornate.

"Detective Lonnegan." A handsome old geezer with a head of beautiful silver hair leaned down and looked into the car. He was dressed either as a butler or an ambassador, the Angel was unsure which. She decided to go with butler, mainly because he had an English accent. "Ah," he said when he spied her. "And whom else shall I be introducing to the master?"

"This is Ms. Fox, SCARE operative, also known as the Midnight Angel."

"Delighted." He seemed as if he actually were, and held out an unnecessary helping hand to first aid Lonnegan and then, after scurrying around the hood, the Angel exit the car. They both stopped to look at the man who waited behind the butler. He wore a badly cut suit, dark sunglasses, and either was one of those guys who had to shave twice a day or had decided to skip a couple of days. He held out his hand for the car keys.

Lonnegan shook her head. "Uh-uh. I've busted too many of you guys for running hot car rings, and I'm very attached to my ride." It was a slightly worse for the wear maroon Toyota Corolla of uncertain vintage.

The butler looked up at the sky with a long put-upon expression on his handsomely lined face.

"As you wish, madam."

They followed him up the stairs, into the mansion, for a long walk down beautifully carpeted hallways and rooms, the hood following close behind.

The inside was as stylistically jumbled as the outside, and extravagantly decorated. At one point as they passed a statue in a shadowy nook, Lonnegan leaned over and whispered to the Angel, "Isn't that statue in the Louvre?"

"I hope so," she replied.

Just as the Angel was feeling totally overwhelmed and helplessly lost, they entered a room that seemed large enough to host football games. The windows in the rear wall were covered by thick drapes and it was almost totally dark, making it hard to discern the nature of the certainly ostentatious furnishings. Somewhere, perhaps fifty feet away in the gloom, was a small gleaming lamp sitting on a large desk that had an equally oversized overstuffed chair behind it.

Without missing a beat the butler pulled out a flashlight and, like a movie usher, led them down a luxuriously thick carpet toward the desk.

As they got closer the Angel realized that the desk was probably older than America and that the lurking hulks set on either side of it were also overstuffed chairs, but not as large nor as padded as the one behind it, where sat Ivan Grekor, aka Ivan the Terrible, the head of the Russian mob in New York City.

"Forgive the overwhelming size of what I like to call my office. Ha-ha." Grekor didn't actually laugh. He simply said ha-ha. "I dislike being ostentatious." *Sure you do*, the Angel thought. "But I like to be among my things even more. Ha-ha."

He was small, though the embroidered smoking jacket he wore made his size difficult to assess. His head was finely, almost delicately featured, though lined with age, particularly around the eyes and mouth. His white hair was clipped short. His thick white mustache was too big for his face. His eyes, the Angel thought, were the deadest eyes she had ever seen in a human face. She'd seen shark eyes that were friendlier, as she recalled, even when the shark was trying to eat her.

"Please sit." The mob boss indicated the chairs placed before his desk.

"Sorry to call without notice," Lonnegan said.

Grekor waved her apology away. "Is nothing. I'm very busy. Business." As he spoke he closed the big old-fashioned ledger that had been open before him. "But I always have time for the ladies. Now, of course I recognize the famous and beautiful Razor Joan Lonnegan." He turned to the Angel and speared her with his black gaze. "But who is this ravishing creature?"

"This is Ms. Fox," Lonnegan said dryly. "AKA the Midnight Angel. She's a SCARE operative."

"Oooh. A Fed. Ha-ha." Grekor lifted his hands in mock alarm, but no sign of humor touched his expression. "I know, lovely lady, that the Federals pay so poorly. I'm sure that we could find you a position in my organization, perhaps on my personal staff, that would be much less onerous and would pay so much more."

The Angel could hardly believe her ears. "I don't think my husband would approve," she said.

"Your husband?"

"Billy Ray."

"Ah." For the first time something touched Grekor's eyes, but whatever emotion it was, it fled so quickly that the Angel couldn't identify it. She hoped it was fear. "Well, a man must try. Ha-ha." He turned his attention back to Lonnegan. "The most beautiful ones are always taken, *nyet?*" He sighed, shrugged padded shoulders. "Well, what can I do for you ladies?"

"Right," Lonnegan said. "Well, Mr. Grekor, we're looking for someone whom you may have seen recently. Captain Chavvah Mendelberg."

"Mendelberg," he said, thoughtfully.

"Yes. Of the Jokertown precinct."

"Oh!" Grekor said. "Yes! With the red eyes and fishy ears. Yes, of course. What makes you think I have seen her recently?"

"Because she's been working for you," the Angel said.

"Many people work for me, dear lady."

"How many of them are police captains?"

The mob boss spread his hands. "You might be surprised. Ha-ha." He looked thoughtful. Except for his eyes. "But, as it happened, we did have a consultation earlier this evening."

Lonnegan and the Angel exchanged quick glances.

"And?" Lonnegan asked.

"I told her that I could not help her, as much as I wanted to. I suggested a trip may be in order. She has, you know, dual citizenship with the United States and Israel." He checked the understatedly elegant gold watch on his left wrist. "I believe you have just enough time to intercept the evening flight out of Newark. If you hurry. Ha-ha."

"We'd like to take her quietly," Lonnegan said, "like, at her apartment. But she seems to have moved out."

"Oh? Don't you know?" Grekor said innocently. "She moved some time ago. It seems that she came into money. Someway. Somehow. Ha-ha."

The Angel's eyes narrowed as she and Joan exchanged glances, then looked back at Grekor.

"And you know this new address?" the Angel asked in as light a tone as possible.

"Of course," the crime lord answered, and told them.

"Why are you telling us this?" the Angel asked.

Grekor flipped a languid hand. "Because I like you, I do you a favor. Maybe someday you do me a favor, *nyet?*"

The Angel stood. "It'd be my pleasure to appear as a character witness at your upcoming trial."

"First, you have to catch me."

"That will be *my* pleasure," Lonnegan said. She stood and both turned to go.

"Dear ladies," Grekor said. They stopped and looked back. "Be careful. You are not the only ones on the captain's trail this night."

The two women looked at each other, turned, and walked rapidly away, both reaching for their cell phones.

"I think he liked you," Lonnegan said.

The Angel shivered. "I feel like I need a shower."

"'The very beautiful ones are always taken, *nyet?*'" Lonnegan mimicked. "He deserved a shot to the nuts for that one alone."

The Angel laughed, for the first time in days. Lonnegan joined in.

"No, but, seriously." She paused, snickered again. "Seriously. Why'd he cough up that information so easily?"

Lonnegan took a turn sharp enough to squeal the Corolla's tires. They were in a hurry. "Well, first, he didn't really tell us very much, but I guess he did at least confirm our suspicions. Second, I believe he wants us to take out his garbage."

"And that cryptic warning at the end?"

"I do believe that he has two bags of garbage to dump."

"That could be."

They drove on in a silence broken only when Lonnegan's cell phone beeped a dramatic ringtone. It took the Angel a moment to realize that it was the theme from *Dragnet*, which she fondly remembered watching in reruns as a child. It had followed *Emergency* in the afternoon, another show she'd loved. She'd had something of a crush on Randolph Mantooth.

Lonnegan fished the phone out of her shirt pocket and flipped it over to the Angel, who almost bungled the catch.

"Answer it," Lonnegan told her. "I better keep both hands on the steering wheel or we're going to make some citizen very unhappy by sideswiping their vehicle."

"Hello," the Angel said.

"Joan?" It took the Angel a moment to recognize the voice. It was Michael Stevens. Joan had checked in with him and Billy when they'd left the crime lord's ostentatious mansion for a quick report. He'd reported that Mendelberg was still missing and when Joan had told him that she might be fleeing to Israel, he'd offered to check with the airlines.

"Stevens," she said crisply. "It's Bathsheeba." There was a moment of silence. "The Midnight Angel."

"Oh. Bathsheeba. Hi."

"Did you call the airport?" she prompted.

"Yes. No Mendelberg ticketed on the El Al flight. A couple of last-minute passengers, though, two of 'em female."

"She was probably ready to run," the Angel said. "Probably on a fake passport."

"Right. We're having the gate staked out by plainclothesmen from Jersey in case she manages to slip away from us."

"Excellent," the Angel said, relaying the news to Lonnegan, who was making impatient gestures.

"Excellent," she concurred. "What's going on at HQ?"

"What's happening at the precinct?" the Angel asked.

"My God!" Stevens proclaimed. The Angel let it pass. "You should have seen it! Ray blew into the building like a freaking tornado. I think he shook dust off the ceiling and walls that'd been there since the thirties. Everyone just stood there, dumbfounded. We thought Ray and Maseryk were going to go at each other, but the captain started to listen when he realized that Mendelberg might have been involved in a cover-up. The jokers being held for illegal entry were being questioned and for the first time their stories got spread around and Maseryk was so mad he, well, nobody had ever seen him like that. Everyone else was pissed off, too. Maseryk has a dozen and a half cops taking detailed statements from the jokers right now, and he's rounded up a carload to head right off to Mendelberg's apartment. Me—I left a while ago. I'm almost there now—"

"She's moved. She has a new apartment, but kept the old one for a dummy address," the Angel told him.

"Crap!" Stevens said. "Where—" The Angel repeated the address that Grekor had given them. "That's not too bad—I'll have to reroute the others."

"Be careful," the agent warned. "If you get there first just keep watch as best you can. Make sure she doesn't get away. Grekor may have sent a hitter after her. Wait for us to get there before you go in."

"Will do."

"Well?" Lonnegan kept saying. The Angel held her off with an outthrust palm, then finally gave Lonnegan the abridged version after Stevens signed off. "They freed the jokers. The only question is who gets to Mendelberg's first—Stevens, us, or a car full of angry cops from the precinct."

Lonnegan looked grimly out the window.

"It's going to be us."

She slammed the car into a higher gear.

"Don't look at them," Marcus said. "Don't make eye contact. Just look up at the mountain."

They were still in the city, moving fast, as they had been for what seemed like hours. Olena answered him in Ukrainian. She'd been doing that more often recently, slipping into her native tongue and holding frantic conversations with herself. She wanted to shoot at everything, her eyes large and frantic in a way that took all of her beauty and twisted it. Marcus knew she was on the verge of losing it, of going batshit crazy like the rest of the city. He might've, too, if the need to save Olena hadn't been there to hold on to.

He squeezed her hand. "Listen to me! Just look up at the mountain. Are you looking at it?"

"It's not there anymore," Olena said. "There's too much fog to see it. Marcus, they're hunting us."

Marcus didn't look up to confirm or deny her claim about the mountain. And, yes, fuck, they were being hunted, shadowed from behind and off to both sides by a pack of canine shapes that moved behind blurring ripples of the miasma. Contrary to what he was telling her, he didn't take his eyes too far away from the creatures. Their elongated shapes loped like no dogs he'd ever seen before. Their dimensions were all wrong, sizes hard to judge. There were things not right with them that he couldn't quite make out in the murky light. They communicated with each other in a barking chatter akin to language. They got louder and more urgent all the time. And they were getting closer. Bolder. Hungrier.

He didn't know how much time had passed since he'd killed Vaporlock, but it felt like hours and hours, like that fight was some distant memory pushed far away by the horrors of a deranged city filled with monsters, human and otherwise. Bursts of gunfire. Shouts. Explosions. Whole swaths of the city in flames. Madness everywhere he looked. Hiding in the shadows of an alley, they'd watched a mob pass just in front of them, men and women carrying saws, butcher's knives, axes, walking with severed heads gripped by the hair and dripping blood. They'd found something writhing toward a dead body in a roundabout. It looked, at first, like an enormous grub, something dug out of the rich mulch of a garden. Pale. Soft-bodied. Squirming. It had no face at all, but it did have circular rows of teeth that gnawed the hands from the body. Only the hands. When it was done, it rose unsteadily. It stood upright and became a teetering grub-like cone that waddled away in a grotesque semblance of the human being it had once been. After that, they'd stumbled across a group of children with their faces buried in a dead woman's opened belly, eating like animals. The children looked up at Marcus and Olena. Their faces were wrong, not just because they were splattered in blood, wronger than that, their features warped as if their flesh was hot wax melting away from their skulls. Olena put bullets through them that blew the backs of their heads off. She shot and shot until the gun only clicked when she pulled the trigger.

So here they were, out of ammo, hunted by dog-things and still in this godforsaken city.

"We're almost out of this," Marcus said. "Look at me, Olena. We're going to be okay. Just a little farther. We'll reach the soldiers and we'll be safe then. Okay? We'll get the fuck away and let the army deal with this shit."

Olena's eyes caught on something. "No," she said. "No, no . . ."

One of the dog-things stepped into view, closer than ever before, moving on its overlong legs. Where a canine face should've been was a decidedly human visage. A man's eyes and nose and mouth. Lips drew back from human teeth as the creature snarled. Its cheeks quivered, and its nose scented the air.

Olena said, "Its face . . . Its face is . . ." Instead of finishing the sentence, she screamed.

Marcus whirled at a sound behind them. Another of the creatures, this one with a woman's face, chattered behind them. He grabbed the Glock from Olena and waved it. The person inside the beast must've recognized the danger of the weapon. It paced, looking frustrated. Eager. Others of its kind emerged, each of them just as horrible.

Marcus scanned the scene. Cluttered street, storefronts with shattered windows, a car with a fractured window . . . That would have to do. He pulled Olena toward the car. He yanked the old-style handle of the backseat several times before it opened. He stuffed Olena inside and slammed the door. She looked at him, confused, scared. Her hands banged against the glass. And then she stopped. Her eyes widened as she took in something behind him.

He turned just as the first of the dog-men leapt at him. He punched it, clocking it good on the chin. He spun with the motion, his long serpentine length squirming with him. All the dog-men converged, snarling, rabid, their faces bestial, teeth bared and snapping. From then it was a full brawl. Marcus punched with both fists, his torso tilting and swerving and dodging from atop the coiled muscle of his tail. He swiped one dog out at the legs. Grabbed another by the neck and pounded its face with his other fist. He slapped his palm to the forehead of one that tried to bite him. He tagged it with his venom-soaked tongue. One down. He tried to count the rest, but everything was a blur. His veins pumped with murderous fury. If he let them, they'd eat him. They'd eat Olena. He wouldn't allow that, so he fought like he'd never fought before. Fists flying. Torso twisting. Tail a thick whip. His tongue shot out again and again, wet with venom.

But he needed to hit bare skin for it to work, and that was limited to their faces. A small target, with a ravening mouth as part of it. The dog-men tore at him with their paws. They raked his scales and carved trenches in his flesh. As much as he spun, there was always one he couldn't see, biting his back. Arm. Clamping down on his shoulder. One of them bit down on his wrist and savaged the skin there as it yanked its head from side to side. He couldn't shake it off. Another one got a grip on his shoulder. Others pressed down on him, gradually overpowering him.

Going down under the weight of them, his eyes found Olena. Her face pressed against the glass, anguished, distorted. He couldn't let her watch him die. He couldn't leave her in this nightmare. He couldn't. He wouldn't.

He grabbed the furred head of the creature chewing on his arm. Clenched in his fist, he held it steady. His tongue snapped out and hit it on the bridge of the nose, splashing venom into both eyes. It released his arm and Marcus shoved it into the several others. He carried the motion into a squirming roll. He rose up on his tail, lifting the dog-man that chewed on his shoulder and dug into his back. The others clawed at him, barking, yapping, spitting foam. He rose as high as he could, and then arched. He threw himself forward and dropped so fast that the creature on his back flipped over. He slammed it down on the hood of the car and heard its spine break. It yelped in pain. It released his shoulder. Marcus grabbed it and hurled it at the others. They darted out of the way, regrouped, and converged on him.

He didn't know what else he had in him. He slithered back to the car, ready to fight them all as best he could. If it was the last thing he did, he'd die here, with Olena behind him, fighting for her. For a moment that seemed exactly like what was about to happen. The dog-men came toward him, human heads low, growling, smelling his weakness. There were too many. He didn't have the venom for all them. He tried to pick one to hit. He focused on one and was about to tag it, when it turned. Others did, too. One by one, they all rounded on the spine-broke dog-man. Their growls faded, and in its place the spine-broke creature's suffering grew. It was whining, mewling, chattering in some almost human language. The upper part of its body scrabbled to rise, but the lower portion was as limp as a corpse. The pack gathered round it. Curious. Sniffing it. Fascinated, seemingly, by its suffering. They inhaled it, breathing deep, mouths dripping saliva.

And then they attacked.

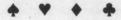

Klaus, Jayewardene, and Barbara watched the raw live feed from Al Jazeera that the Secretary-General had secured for them. The camera work was jerky and wild as the cameraman and Darren Cole, Al Jazeera's journalist, made their way toward the waiting Kazakh general. "How about shooting the interview from over there?" they heard Cole say to the cameraman. He pointed toward where a jeep was parked. "That'll put the barricades right in the background and the bodies right behind us." The camera feed steadied as the operator stopped, then zoomed in tight on General Ospanov's grim face. Behind the man, they could see the rolls of razor wire that formed a barricade across the main road out from Talas. Behind, the outskirts of the city were in flame, and bodies lay in grotesque poses across the pavement between, around, and inside the cars scattered crazily there, bullet holes prominent in the windshields and along the sides. Several of the cars were merely burnt-out hulks.

"Okay, Shahid," Cole said, and the camera zoomed back to show Cole with a foam-wrapped microphone tilted toward General Ospanov. "General Ospanov, we appreciate you taking the time to speak to Al Jazeera about the dire situation here in Talas, where it seems that the chaos continues to spread uncontroll—"

"No," the general interrupted loudly. "It is not spreading," he said in thickly accented English. "We have contained the problems here, and have taken firm control. There is still difficulties in Talas, yes, but spreading? No. That we will not allow. Nothing passes here."

Barbara heard Klaus's audible scoff at that statement. *"So 'ne Scheisse!"* Babel shook her head at the vulgarity, glancing over at Jayewardene, who continued to calmly watch the video.

In the camera, Cole's attention had shifted past the general, continuing to talk about how things were under control, to the road beyond the barrier. The camera operator noticed, and the picture went briefly out of focus as the lens swiveled and zoomed in again. Blurry figures resolved into uniformed, armed men moving among the bodies. They were stooping down as they moved among the bodies.

"What are those soldiers doing?" Barbara asked aloud, a moment before the camera zoomed in yet closer and they all realized the answer. At the same moment, Cole's shocked voice overrode the general's commentary. "My God, General, your men . . . Are they . . . are they *eating* those bodies?"

The camera pulled back again, displaying the naked shock on Cole's face and the smile that pulled at General Ospanov's lips as he unholstered the pistol on his belt, pointed it directly in Cole's face, and pulled the trigger.

The report of the gun was accompanied by a spray of blood, brain matter, and bits of skull from the back of Cole's head. The reporter seemed to stand for a breath, then collapsed. They saw the general look toward the camera, and the video spun crazily as the operator evidently began running. There was another sharp report, then another, followed by a sickening thud and darkness. The camera feed went abruptly to static.

The three sat for a moment in stunned silence. Then Klaus stood, his face flushed red and angry. "I don't care what anyone says. We are going there. We are going there *now*."

"The Kazakh government hasn't—" Jayewardene began, and Klaus cut off his objection with a wave of his hand. His single eye glared at both of them.

"Barbara was right all along." Klaus nodded to her, and she managed a thin smile in return. "This is where we are needed, and after seeing this, I don't give a fucking damn about waiting for permission from the government. We are going."

Jayewardene was shaking his head, but said nothing. "Babs," Klaus continued, "you make sure the Concorde's fueled and loaded with the satellite phones, provisions, and other equipment we're going to need. I want it ready to leave in an hour. We'll also need Earth Witch and Michelle, if we can get her; I'll call them. Maybe Tinker and Brave Hawk, too, and anyone else you think would be useful; have Ink get hold of them. In the meantime, I'll go to the apartment and pack our things."

She could hear the old excitement in his voice. His remaining eye sparkled with intensity, and she could nearly feel the energy pulsing from him. *Yes, this is the way it should be with him . . .*

"Barbara can't go with you." That was Jayewardene. His bald statement punctured the energy in the room.

"I need her," Klaus said, glaring at the Secretary-General with an ice-blue eye as cold as ghost steel. Jayewardene sat placidly at the table, with what was almost a smile on his face. Barbara had also turned to look at him quizzically. "You can't be serious," Klaus railed. "What about the language problem? I need Babel there to make sure everyone understands each other, or to make sure that they don't, if it comes to that. I—we—need her: to coordinate negotiations or just to talk to people on the ground there. She's essential."

Jayewardene shook his bald head. "Where she is needed more is *here*—to coordinate everything with the UN. I need someone who knows the Committee and its strengths, someone who will be in charge, who will be the general coordinating everything. Here. That's where a general should be, *not* on the front lines. I need Barbara here . . . and so do you, Klaus. I *know* this." He put quiet emphasis on the word.

"But Klaus is right," Barbara said. "The language issue . . ."

"There are translators who can do that for the team," Jayewardene said. "But there is no one else *here* who can do the rest of what is needed—here in New York. We have strategies to talk about and new reports to examine. Klaus, I agree with you. We can no longer wait. You have the decision you wanted, but we have much planning to do before we get there. Right now, Barbara, you're more valuable in New York, where you can interface with me and the authorities we're still in touch with in Kazakhstan, where you can make certain that everyone stays informed and in the loop, and where you can send Klaus whatever additional help he might need."

"Ink can do all that for you, Secretary-General," Barbara insisted. She wanted to scream, wanted to yell, wanted to shatter the placid calm on Jayewardene's face even as she knew he was right. It was nothing she would admit, not to either of them, but the decision *felt* right, even though the thought of Klaus going into this uncertain hell without her threatened to tear her apart. She forced herself to keep her face calm, all the emotion dampened and held down.

She noticed that Klaus had stopped arguing, silently watching the two of them.

"Ink isn't anywhere near as experienced or as effective as you are," Jayewardene persisted, as she expected. "While I agree that she has much potential, she's still learning the Committee, the personalities that are involved, and how you function within the organizations to which the Committee reports and with which it's associated. You know those things intimately, and you're used to dealing with all the rules and regulations and still getting what you want. That's your strength and your value, even more than your ace ability. From these reports, it doesn't seem that negotiation and understanding are what we'll be needing. I've made my decision here, and it's the one that *has* to be made," he told her. "You know that too, I think. Talas . . ." His voice trailed off at the name, and he glanced at the video screens around the room. "This is like nothing we have faced before, and therefore we can't react to it as we have in the past."

He's right. He's right, one part of her mind insisted, but the other still screamed in terror and fear. *I need to be with him, especially now. He needs me . . . and I need him. I can't lose him.*

She waited. Klaus still said nothing, carefully looking away from both of them. Barbara nodded once, tightening her lips against the press of emotions. She wanted Klaus to insist that she must go. She could see that he was already impatient to be in motion, to be streaking toward the action, wrapped in ghost steel and certainty. But he still didn't speak, didn't give her a clue as to what he might want her to say.

"Fine. I'll stay," she told them, though her gaze was now entirely on Klaus. She imagined him stopping her, shaking his head and insisting that this decision was wrong. But nothing changed in his face or his eye, and she released an unheard sigh. "I'll get things under way with transportation, Klaus. Make the calls you need to make, and get yourself ready. I'll take care of the rest."

"I can see the soldiers," Marcus said. He held Olena by the wrist, leading her through the rugged terrain outside of Talas. The landscape was barren and scrubby, sinister under the roiling light. He kept them moving toward where he thought their mountain landmark was. The main road was off to his left. He could see the vehicles clogging it, and the river of humanity flowing around them. He liked having the road near, but wanted to avoid people—and other things—as long as he could. "We're almost there, Olena. Just a little farther. I can see them. I really can."

It was true. When he rose up as high as he could on his tail, he could make out the silhouettes of the tanks and barricades and the men who manned them. Not far now, so he kept talking. He felt like he had to, like it was the only way to keep her with him. Since he'd pulled her out of the car and slipped away as the dog-men devoured one of their own, it had grown increasingly hard to keep her calm. They'd found her father's helicopter soon after, but one of the pilots was dead and the other was nowhere to be seen. Olena had started calling for them, running in circles around the aircraft shouting in Ukrainian. It took Marcus several minutes to convince her they'd just have to keep moving. On foot and tail instead of in the air.

Each time he ran out of encouraging things to say, her eyes became jittery things that looked like they wanted to leap from their sockets. He knew that she was seeing and thinking horrible things. Things that were there and maybe also things that weren't anyplace but in her mind. Once, she'd panicked so intensely that she fought to get away from him. She'd scratched at his face, seeming, for a few frantic moments, not to recognize him at all. He was crying by the time he got her back, begging her to see that it was just him. Just Marcus.

God, we have to get to the soldiers, he thought. Maybe they had doctors there that could treat her. He clung to the thought, voiced it out loud, making himself sound sure of it. Everything, he told her, would be all right soon.

As if to confirm this, a sleek jet appeared out of nowhere, announced by a boom that Marcus felt through his tail. The jet roared by overhead, straight toward Talas. It looked like a glistening savior, a thing of technology and reason. It was, Marcus thought, the outside world taking notice of whatever was going on here. "Look," he said, placing one arm around Olena and pointing with the other, "help is coming. People know what's going on here. I bet they'll send aces to deal with all this." He squeezed her, thrilled to see a glimmer of hope return to her face as her eyes followed the jet's progress. "The worst of this is . . ."

Olena inhaled a sudden breath. Marcus looked back toward the city. The jet's nose dipped. Its high-tech power seemed to wilt. It rolled, banked, and then slammed into the upper floors of an apartment building at the edge of the city. It exploded into a ball of fire and smoke and whirling debris.

"Fuck. Fuck . . ." Marcus exhaled the word several times before he remembered Olena. For her, he tried to regain his certainty. "Come on. Let's get to the soldiers. We reach them and we're safe."

A few minutes later, he learned the truth. He'd been hearing sporadic gunfire since they first entered Talas. It had become background noise. But as they neared the cordon and he angled them closer to the road to join the others fleeing, the staccato bursts increased in frequency and volume. Marcus couldn't see what was happening until he came up over a rise and got his first good view of the cordon. It wasn't the scene he'd hoped for.

The soldiers were shooting, but not to defend the refugees. They were firing right into them. Bodies littered the highway. The place was in chaos. People running for cover. Others pleading with the soldiers, approaching with their hands held high, only to be shot down where they stood. Some cut away from the road and tried desperately to climb through the barbed wire and over the barricades. Many hung caught in the barbed wire, macabre, bloody rag dolls. Marcus remembered the soldier in the tank in Talas. Why had he ever thought these ones would be any different? He knew. He'd thought it because he had to. Needed to. Wanted to.

Things whizzed through the air above them. A moment later he heard the machine-gun reports that trailed the bullets. He ducked, pulling Olena down. Soldiers along the barricade nearest them had opened fire. Pressed to the ground, exposed, Marcus cast around for someplace to hide. Back down the ravine, he thought. That would take them out of the line of sight.

He'd just started to try and explain this to Olena when a blast of tank fire stopped him. *A tank? They're shooting at us with a tank? What the fuck?* The machine-gun barrage increased as more soldiers turned their guns toward them and other tanks maneuvered to fire. That's when Marcus realized they weren't aiming at him and Olena. They were shooting at something beyond them. As soon as he understood that, he felt it, that something enormous was approaching from the city. He heard the impact of its steps on the ground, crushing plants, snapping things. He felt tremors through his tail. Just like back in Talas, when . . .

He snapped around and looked back toward Talas. There it was, the harvesting monster he'd seen from the casino. It was huge, bigger than before, prehistoric in its dimensions, with more grotesquely long legs than before. Its body had swelled, widened, stretched taller and pocked with even more of those horrible cells. Above it all that sightless, earless, mouthless, amorphous thing that was the creature's head swayed and wobbled in a strange slow motion. But the creature wasn't slow. Those long legs moved it forward with deceptive speed. Forward, right toward Marcus and Olena.

Olena began babbling. Her voice was so fast and high-pitched that it didn't seem right, the sounds harsh and incoherent and not really like language at all. Her eyes were at their crazed worst. She squirmed out of Marcus's embrace and got to her feet. She looked at the approaching monstrosity, and she screamed. Marcus lunged toward her. He grabbed her and tried to get her to focus on him, but she had eyes only for the monster. Her face, which had always been so beautiful, became a desolate horror that he could barely recognize.

The harvester headed straight toward them, nearer every second. If Marcus couldn't still her, one of those reaping arms would grab them both and . . . He pleaded with her, tried to cover her mouth, to hold her still. But she was a writhing fury, completely frantic. She scratched and tore at him. She bared her teeth, lunged, and sunk her teeth into his shoulder. He released her, staring in horror at her blood-splattered face. Behind her, the harvester came on, massive, almost upon them.

Marcus did the only thing he could think of. Quick as he thought it, his tongue shot out and thwacked wetly on Olena's neck. Poison. Delivered to skin. As she dropped, he swept forward and caught her. He cradled her limp body tight to his chest and squirmed toward the cordon beneath an onslaught of bullets and mortar fire directed past him at the looming monster. Marcus surged over the barricade. He fixed his eyes forward and slithered with everything he had. There was only one place he could go now. Only one person who might be able to save the woman he loved more than he would ever have thought possible.

The Angel stood before the door to Mendelberg's apartment, thinking, *I've been in this spot before.*

She and Lonnegan had beaten the precinct cops to the apartment, but not Stevens. The three-story building that housed it was part of a row of old brownstones, close to the river in a nondescript, middle-class area, decent but certainly not extravagant. Mendelberg's apartment was on the center floor. Stevens was waiting for them when they arrived, lurking by the big potted plant adjacent to the elevator door.

"Been here long?" Lonnegan asked.

"Two minutes," Stevens said. "No sign of Mendelberg."

They all peered at the door on the left end of the corridor.

"Sure that's it?" the Angel asked.

"2A," Lonnegan affirmed.

"You better be right."

The corridor walls were a faded green. The carpet was on the edge of being threadbare. As they stood in front of the door the Angel was in the lead. The cops had drawn their guns. The Angel glanced back and nodded. Lonnegan and Stevens took a step backward as she called up her sword. They were close enough to feel the heat from its flame on their faces. The Angel kicked the door near the knob, and it slammed straight back into the room, torn off its hinges. The mechanism of the lock and bolt dangled from the frame.

The Angel led the way inside, scanning right and left. Lonnegan and Stevens followed, splitting left and right behind her.

It was a rather nice room. The carpet was deep pile plush, the walls a tasteful shade of deep, restful green, with half a dozen nice oil paintings and a cabinet of expensive-looking jade curios against one wall. The furniture, too, looked expensive though the Angel couldn't say where or when it had been made. Unfortunately, the flying door had smashed one spindly-legged little table and shattered the once-elegant vase that had stood upon it.

Before anyone could say anything, Mendelberg suddenly appeared in an open doorway that led deeper into the apartment, feet spread, an automatic held up before her in a two-handed shooter's grip. Her expression was grim, her scarlet eyes burned like bonfires in hell.

"You bitches broke my Ming!" she spat.

"Hey!" Stevens said.

"Shut up!"

The Angel was marginally closest to her. Mendelberg's pistol was aimed more at her than anyone else.

"Good evening, Captain," Lonnegan said. "We heard you weren't feeling well so we decided to stop by and see how you were doing."

Mendelberg hissed, her weird ears fluttering like fish fins caught in a swirling current. Her pistol shifted, fractionally, and focused on the female cop.

"I always hated you, Lonnegan," the captain said. "Always so cocky, so sure. Always acting like the queen of the precinct.'

Lonnegan smiled easily. "That's good to know," she said. "I'd hate to think that a shit-stain like you liked me."

"Your nat feelings hurt, Lonnegan?"

"The only thing that hurts is my knowledge of all the pain you've caused, all the suffering and death. And for what? Grekor's filthy money?"

"Do you think this stuff pays for itself?" Mendelberg asked, gesturing around her with the pistol. "This is nothing, *nothing*, compared to what my family had before the Nazis stole it all. And then they came to America. To *Manhattan*, just in time to be born from their twisted genes."

"Sad story," Lonnegan said laconically.

"Sad? You don't know sad, *shiksa*. I was born in Jokertown. I lived in the filth and among everyday horrors that could freeze your liquor-diluted Irish blood. I worked my ass off to get out of that place. Graduated magna cum laude from Columbia. Finished number one in my class in the Police Academy. And for what? Finally when I made captain, where did they send me? Back to that hellhole I worked so hard to escape. Back to the crapsack precinct, Fort Freak." Mendelberg shrugged. "So I took the Russian's money. Why not? It was as good as the city's. Better, because it was tax free."

"Jokers died because of what you did," the Angel said.

"Jokers die every day."

"Father Squid died," Lonnegan murmured.

"A priest of a false, bastard religion."

"Jamal Norwood died," the Angel said.

"A shitty actor and jumped-up government stooge." Mendelberg shook her head. "I was almost there," she said quietly. "I had almost saved up enough . . ."

"For what?" Lonnegan asked.

"For what?" Mendelberg's voice rose to a near shriek. "To fix these." She turned her head so that her audience could see her filmy ears straight on. "To become human!"

"Goddamn," Lonnegan said. The Angel couldn't find it within herself to rebuke her as comprehension struck them all. "You betrayed your people and your honor because you wanted plastic surgery?"

"*I deserve it!*" Mendelberg screamed, and the ghost rose right out of the floor before her.

The Angel recognized him immediately. It was the gunman who'd escaped from Jamal's hotel room by slipping away through the floor. He was a plump five-foot-six or so, with fat cheeks, protruding watery blue eyes, and clothes that looked like they came from a parody movie about the disco era. He wore a glittering puce—she guessed—shirt of some hideous synthetic material that clung disturbingly to his rotund figure, tight pants, ditto, and shiny black patent leather half boots. He looked pissed, and drunk, which was a bad combination. He stared at Mendelberg, one of his guns pointing at her, while he tried to cover the Angel and the others with a second.

"Son of a bitch!" Mendelberg screeched, and opened fire.

Bullets flew like angry wasps, right through his chest and torso while Angel, Lonnegan, and Stevens ducked for cover. Mendelberg emptied her magazine, to no avail. The hit man, as he tried to cover everyone, spotted and recognized the Angel for the first time.

"You killed my Andrei!" he shrieked in a voice that was so heavily accented that he sounded like Boris Badonov from the old Rocky and Bullwinkle cartoons that she loved when she was a child.

"No I didn't," the Angel said as calmly as she could. She would have been more afraid if she hadn't noticed that she could sort of see through his guns, much like you could sort of see through his body. She hoped Lonnegan and Stevens had noticed the same thing.

"You lie." His hand was not exactly steady and his words were somewhat slurred. At least she thought they were, and not just oddly accented.

"She's telling the truth," Lonnegan said.

"Shut up, you unnatural creature!" the Russian hit man ordered, his attention and his gun wavering between the two women.

"What?" Lonnegan said, baffled.

"Woman police!" he exclaimed. "Is unnaturall Here or In Mother Russia. No woman tells me what I can do! I spit upon you useless creatures."

Lonnegan groaned. The man was stark mad, the Angel thought. Mad, drunk, and as dangerous as hell was real.

"I am telling the truth," she said, trying again. "He's in the hospital."

"You put my Andrei in the hospital!" he cried, revising his accusation. "Which one? I will go to him!"

"Hey!" Lonnegan barked. "Over here, Rasputin."

The Russian veered crookedly, focusing on her. Stevens was crouched on the floor, hand clapped to his upper right arm. One of Mendelberg's wild shots had clipped him. He was grimacing, but was much more cogent than Mendelberg, who stood in place, wide-eyed and chest heaving, still pulling the trigger, which was clicking away uselessly.

"Look at me," Lonnegan ordered. "Your pal is safe and sound. We can take you to him."

The hit man tried to spit, but nothing materialized out of his only somewhat substantial mouth.

"Useless, unnatural woman." He leaned toward Lonnegan, now floating an inch or two off the floor. "This goddamned country is full of them."

"You drop your guns," Lonnegan said, "and we'll take you to Andrei."

A crafty gleam came into his bulging eyes. "Of course."

"You try to trick us," Lonnegan warned, "and you'll never see Andrei again. I'll track your ass down and make sure you spend the rest of your life in some Siberian ice cave."

"Nothing can hold me." He drifted toward Lonnegan like a drunken ghost, the gun in his right hand, still insubstantial, pointing right at her. "But first, before I go see my beloved Andrei, I kill the bitch who put him in the hospital."

He whirled, solidifying his body and his weapons, but Lonnegan had kept his attention long enough for the Angel, as silent as a ghost herself, to release her sword and drift across the thick carpet until she was close enough to grab his wrists. She forced one arm up and one down. The hit man yelped and squeezed off two shots, one into the ceiling and one into the floor. Both fortunately flew off harmlessly, startling but missing those in the apartments above and below Mendelberg's.

She twisted his wrists. Two cracks came simultaneously. The Russian howled and dropped both weapons. She head-butted the Russian into oblivion before he could focus to fade out. She looked at Lonnegan and nodded. The cop nodded back.

Mendelberg made a strangled noise and collapsed to the carpet in the open doorway where she stood. Her body was shaking all over and the Angel could see frothy bubbles running down the side of her chin.

"She's having a seizure," the Angel cried, and rushed to the captain's side. As gently as she could, she pushed her gauntleted hand between Mendelberg's jaws. Lonnegan joined her, holding her neck so that she couldn't bash her head. Fortunately, the thick carpeting had so far prevented any serious damage. Her heels tattooed the floor.

There was a commotion in the open doorway. Maseryk burst into the apartment, glaring, pistol out.

"Freeze!" he shouted, and looked around uncomprehendingly.

Ray strolled into the room, accompanied by a gaggle of other cops.

"How's it going, Angel?" he asked.

"Fine, Billy. Just fine."

"Of course it is," he said. He glanced around.

"Hey," said Michael Stevens, "I'm bleeding over here."

Nothing had been resolved by the time Wally left to pick up Ghost, and Joey headed out to pick up dinner. And no doubt to pick up a couple of toe tags as well.

Michelle looked at her phone. There were eleven messages—from Klaus, from Barbara, and even one from Juliet. She went into Adesina's room. There was something obscene about that cocoon sitting on the bed, surrounded by the normal things found in a child's bedroom. The bed adorned with pink floral sheets and stuffed animals. Posters of ocelots on the wall and even one of Joker Plague. Michelle had introduced Adesina to Drummer Boy once, and Adesina had liked him, but he was too old for her to have a crush on. Michelle couldn't figure out why the poster was there, but sometimes she just didn't understand her daughter.

There was a knock at the front door, and Michelle went to answer it.

Jayewardene stood in the hallway, the hall light shining on his bald head.

She stared down at him, bewildered that the UN Secretary-General was standing on her doorstep.

"Are you going to invite me in?" he asked. He said it lightly, but Michelle could tell he was vexed. Manners were important to him. Right now, she really didn't care about his desire for protocol.

"I don't know," she replied tersely. "Depends on why you're here. Actually, you know, I don't care why you're here." She started to close the door.

He stepped into the doorway. "I am here about the Talas mission."

Michelle shook her head. "This is insane," she said. "I told Barbara and Klaus—I don't know how many times—I can't go."

"Michelle, I understand, you're worried about your daughter, but sometimes there are things that are bigger than the small realm of our personal lives. This is one of those times."

Michelle cocked her head to one side and gave him her very best are-you-fucking-kidding-me look. "This is my family," she said hotly. "Nothing takes precedence over that." Then she pointed at the TV. The sound was still off, but the coverage of Talas was playing. "No one knows anything about what's going on there! This could be some random bullshit. Or yet another PPA situation. You know how to handle those. You can do that without me."

"Invite me in, Michelle," he said. "I can't stay out here. I don't have any security with me."

Michelle stepped back to let him in. "Whose goddamn fault is that, Jayewardene?" Normally, she would have done the polite thing and invited him into the living room and made her shitty tea and served some cookies on her cracked and mismatched plates. But this wasn't normal and she'd had it with everything Committee related.

"We need you, Michelle," he said earnestly. "You've had experience with this sort of fieldwork. You can lead and you can follow orders. You're a team player and we need you to help with the new recruits we're sending along."

"Oh, God, you can get any number of other aces to help." She was utterly exasperated. "You know what, let me show you why I can't leave."

She turned and left him at the front door, not bothering to see if he was following her. Once he saw Adesina's condition, he would stop bugging her about this stupid mission.

"This is what my daughter did to herself, Jayewardene," she said, pointing at the cocoon in the bed. "I thought it was PTSD, but now I have no idea what caused it. I don't know when she'll come out of it. I don't even know what she'll be when she comes out of it. Can you tell me I should leave my baby alone right now?"

Jayewardene stood in the doorway. The corners of his mouth were turned down and his brow was furrowed. Then he looked at her with such compassion Michelle almost burst out crying. That wasn't what she expected from herself or from him. "I'm very sorry, Michelle," he said softly. "It must be awful to see her like this."

And then she was crying. She wiped the tears away with the back of her hand. "I just can't believe you want me to go!"

Jayewardene gave a heavy sigh. "I wish it hadn't come to this."

"Come to what?" she asked. Her nose was running, and she grabbed a tissue from the box on the nightstand.

"I've seen you there," he said. There was a heaviness in his voice.

"Well, what the hell does that mean?"

"It means I have a wild card, too."

Michelle looked at him blankly. There had never been the slightest hint that Jayewardene had a wild card. "And what does yours do?" she demanded. "You're obviously not a joker, unless you're hiding some kind of prehensile tail under that suit."

"I'm a precog," he said. It sounded as if it was a relief for him to tell her. "I see glimpses of the future. And Michelle, my visions are always right."

"I suppose you're going to tell me you had a vision of me in Talas."

"Yes," he said. "But more importantly, your daughter was in my vision, too. The only way you can save her is to go."

"Oh, bullshit," Michelle said. She brushed past him as she stalked out of Adesina's room. "I can't believe you're telling me this. This is a new low even for the Committee."

"Michelle!"

She stopped. He'd never used that tone of voice with her before. She hadn't even known he possessed such an angry and commanding timbre.

"Do you think I would reveal my power unless it was absolutely necessary? Do you understand the implications should this become public knowledge? Only a handful of people know about my ability. And now you are one of them. Do you think I do this lightly?"

She was taken aback. She'd been so caught up in her own indignation she hadn't really considered what his wild card meant. In his position he would be considered dangerous. Knowing the future was incredibly powerful—even if it was as he described, just bits and pieces, but always right. And how many people would like to get their hands on that ability? How many others would kill him to prevent what might be revealed by his power?

But he'd offered her some hope. She could go to Talas and maybe help Adesina. It was something she could *do*. Just then, there was a knock on the door.

Michelle went and answered it. Joey was back with groceries. Two zombie dogs were with her, both large mutts. They seemed pretty fresh— hadn't begun to smell yet.

"We have company," Michelle said as she let Joey and the dogs in. Joey put the bags on the table and walked into the living room.

"Jayewardene," she said. "This is pretty fucking weird."

"Hello, Miss Hebert," he said. "It's so very nice to see you again. I trust your visit has been pleasant."

Joey snorted. Formal politeness never impressed her. "Jayewardene. I guess y'all decided to send in the really fucking big guns."

"Indeed I did," he replied. He looked back at Michelle. "What do you say? Will you help us? Will you help your daughter?"

The zombie dogs lay down on the floor and stared up at Michelle. Joey stared at her for a long moment, too. "What the fuck is all this about? What did he say?"

Michelle looked away for a moment, then looked back at Joey. "I can't tell you how, but he says the only way to help Adesina is for me to go to Talas."

"That sounds like an incredible amount of bullshit," Joey spat. She jerked her thumb at Jayewardene. "Why would you believe anything those fuckers say?"

Michelle exchanged a long look with Jayewardene. His expression was closed, and she knew he was waiting for her to make a decision.

"Joey," she said, turning away from Jayewardene. Her voice was low and urgent. "I need you to trust me. Really trust me. You know I'd never leave Adesina unless I thought I could help her."

"What did he tell you?" Joey demanded. She had a stubborn expression on her face that Michelle knew all too well. "Tell me!"

Michelle ran her hands through her hair. "I told you already," she said more forcefully. "I can't tell you. You know I would if I could. Please, please trust me."

Joey glared at Jayewardene. "I don't know what the fuck you said, and my girl wouldn't leave if she didn't think it would help. But I've got my eye on you. You know the dead are everywhere."

"Miss Hebert, I respect you and your power more than you know," he said with a slight bow. "And please know that were this not imperative, I would not be asking it of Miss Pond."

Joey snorted. "Oh, you are one slick motherfucker, Jayewardene." She sighed and took Michelle's hand. "I can stay and take care of the niblet. And just so you know, I've never seen you do anything but what you thought was fucking righteous."

A surge of relief went through Michelle. She knew Joey would protect Adesina with her life. "Thank you," she replied, squeezing Joey's hand. "And I'm going to call Wally and see if he can help out, too."

"I can do it by myself," Joey said. The dogs hopped to their feet. "You know I can."

"Good grief, of course, I know it. But it never hurts to have someone else just in case."

Joey petted one of the dogs. Michelle tried not to be completely squicked out by it. "Yeah, Wally's a good person."

"Then it's settled," Jayewardene said. "How soon can you be ready?"

"I have a bug-out bag in the closet," she replied with a shrug. "Started one right after my first mission for the Committee." She went to the hall closet and pulled out a regulation military duffel bag. Inside she had clothes, some rations, water, a first-aid kit, and a solar battery charger for her phone. There were some odds and ends in there, too. Leftovers from previous missions.

She dropped the bag and went to Adesina's room. She kissed the top of the cocoon, and tears welled up in her eyes. "I'll be back soon, baby," she whispered. "Aunt Joey's gonna take good care of you."

Joey was standing in the doorway when she looked up. Then Joey was in her arms kissing her. It was surprisingly tender.

"Don't be a fucking idiot out there," Joey said when they broke apart. "I need you back in one piece."

Michelle laughed in spite of herself. "What are the odds I'm not coming back in one piece? It's like you don't know me."

Joey took Michelle's head in her hands and held it still. "I'm not kidding," she said earnestly. "I need you."

"I need you, too."

"Now get the fuck out of here and go save your daughter."

The Angel and Billy Ray found an empty lounge down the corridor from the conference room. They looked out the large picture window upon New York City, spread before them in the darkness, glittering like the stars strewn across the sky.

"Been a long day," Ray said.

The Angel put an arm around his waist, laid her head on his shoulder. "We did good today," she said.

"Yeah." He inclined his head to touch hers.

"What's wrong?" the Angel asked.

Uncharacteristically, Ray sighed. He was in a mood that the Angel had rarely seen in the years they'd been together.

"I don't like this," Ray said. "You know I want to go with you, but the agency ain't going to run itself. I can't pick up and go when I want to anymore. Not that I really want to this time around."

The serious tone in his voice disturbed her. "Why not?"

"I've been everywhere—including that freaking alien dimension back when we first met—and I've seen lots of weird shit go down. Thought I'd seen damn near everything, but now, I'm not so sure." He turned to face her and put his hands on her narrow waist. She entwined hers and rested them on the back of his neck. His intense green eyes, almost on a level with her own, were shadowed with an uncertainty that the Angel had never seen before. "It smells bad to me. You're going into a totally uncertain situation and I ain't too sure that Sir Galahad is the guy who should be leading you into this particular crapsack. But what can I do?"

"Don't worry, Billy. The Lord will watch over me."

"He damned well better," Ray said, "and I'll be waiting in the wings in case he fucks up. You just call me and I'll be there. Screw SCARE."

"Billy," she whispered. She put a gloved finger against his lips. "Don't blaspheme."

Then they were kissing, pressed hard against each other, holding each other tighter than normal people could. It was, the Angel thought, simply heaven. She wanted this moment to last forever.

"Get a room, you two."

They broke off the kiss and turned their heads, Billy wearing the scowl that meant he was really annoyed. Bubbles was standing in the open entrance to the lounge. She was beautiful, the Angel thought, taller than her and slim as, well, a model. Graceful and elfin, like all those lovely blondes in Peter Jackson's *Lord of the Rings* movies.

"I always seem to be interrupting you two, don't I?"

"You don't have to enjoy it so much," Ray growled.

Bubbles wiped the little smile off her face. "Sorry guys. I don't, really. Klaus sent me to find you, Sheeba. We're heading out to the airport." She turned to go, stopped, and looked again at them, the grin back on her lips. "I guess you have time to say good-bye one more time."

She turned and walked away.

"Not the way I'd like to," Ray said in a low voice.

"I know what you mean."

He put his arms around her waist again. "I've been thinking," he said, carefully. "When you get back. Maybe we should change it up a little."

"Change?" she said.

"I'm getting tired, Angel. I've saved the world I don't know how many damned times, and, fuck, it just needs saving again by the next weekend. How much is enough?"

"Maybe you need a vacation."

"Yeah, a long vacation."

"How about in beautiful, sunny downtown Talas?"

She was gratified at the smile that lifted his craggy, slightly mismatched features. "Maybe," he said.

"Good-bye, darling."

She kissed him again, a quick kiss this time because she didn't think she could just walk away from another long one.

He let her go. She turned and walked away. She looked back as she left the lounge. He was still watching her. He lifted a hand and she blew him a kiss and then went down a branch of the corridor and was gone from his sight.

The tarmac stretched out into darkness from the yawning, huge mouth of the hangar, the lamps lining the taxiway blurred in fog. The eastern horizon was lightening as dawn approached. Around the Committee's private Concorde, workers were loading the last of the equipment and supplies. The Committee team, with the exception of Klaus, was already on board. The pilots could be seen in the cockpit, making last-minute checks.

Klaus, with Secretary-General Jayewardene and Barbara flanking him, stared into the early morning fog. Barbara thought he was already imagining himself in Talas, already deciding what needed to be done there—he certainly was no longer fully present here. One of the ground crew came up to them. "We're ready, sir. You need to be on board before they can start the engines."

Klaus nodded. Barbara clutched at his arm, turning him. "Be careful," she told him. "Let me know if you need anything, and I'll get it to you. But . . ." She sighed. "Please be careful."

He smiled at her, the lines of his face crinkling with the gesture. "I will," he told her. "We'll stay in close touch; you get things moving here, and we'll take care of Talas."

Barbara clutched his arm tighter. Behind Klaus, she saw Jayewardene step politely back a few steps and engage the ground crew leader. "Klaus, I don't like this. I agree that I should stay here, that this is where I'm needed more, but I don't like it."

His hand stroked her cheek, and she leaned her head over to trap his fingers against her shoulder. "I don't like it either. But I'll be back soon."

She wished she could be certain of that, but her stomach was roiling in protest. She lifted up on toes and brought her lips to his. The kiss began as gentle and quick, but she found herself pressing more tightly against him, and the kiss became more urgent and desperate. Her eyes were tearing and when she blinked, twin streaks of wet rolled down her face. *"Mein Liebling,"* he whispered, pulling back from her. "Don't worry."

Barbara brought her heels down to the tarmac. She wiped at the betraying moisture on her face, sniffing. "I'm not. I'm sorry . . ."

Klaus shook his head. "Don't apologize." He bent his head down and kissed her forehead this time. "This will be over soon. I promise you. You . . . you are better at what's required here than I am. Me . . . I'm better at what will need to be done there. It's why we are a good pair, *nein?* A good team."

She laughed, once. "Then go do it," she told him. She took his hand, pressing it with hers, then let it drop. Klaus nodded. Taking a long breath, he glanced at Jayewardene. "Secretary-General," he said. "We'll handle this."

"I have every confidence in that," Jayewardene answered. And with that, Klaus strode toward the stairs leading up into the plane. He moved quickly up them, two at a time. At the top, he waved back at them once, then entered the plane. The ground crew pushed away the stairs; someone inside the plane shut the door, and the turbojet engines began their slow whine as they warmed up. A wash of hot air blasted Barbara and Jayewardene as the jet slowly turned and began to taxi toward the runways.

"He will be safe," Barbara heard Jayewardene say against the roar of the engines. "We will do what we have to do here to ensure that."

"Yes, we will," Barbara told him. "We will."

"Hey, Sheeba," Michelle said as the Angel slid into the seat next to her. The plane was almost ready to depart. "That was some impressive canoodling you and Ray were up to back at HQ."

The Midnight Angel rolled her eyes. Michelle gave her a teasing smile, but would never admit that she was a little jealous—hell, a lot jealous—of their relationship.

Though Michelle and Billy Ray would always have a thread of tension in their interactions, she did admire how much he loved the Angel—and how willing he was to display it.

"I'm not sure about this group," Michelle said, glancing around the plane. Bugsy, Earth Witch, Lohengrin, Tinker, and the Lama she'd done missions with before and she knew what their strengths and weaknesses were. But the new kids—Doktor Omweer, Aero, and Recycler—were unknown elements. She liked Aero. But just as Ana had said, Omweer was a boring jerk. He had barely deigned to say hello to her. Recycler seemed like a decent guy.

"Where's Klaus?" Sheeba asked.

"He's in the back talking to Babel on the satellite com-link. I'm not sure what else they have to talk about at this point."

There was a knowing smile on Sheeba's face. It took Michelle a moment before she realized what that expression meant. "Oh," she said. "Klaus whispering sweet nothings while on a mission? Sure doesn't seem like him." The Angel shrugged.

"How's your little girl?" Sheeba asked politely. Michelle felt a stab in her chest. She still wasn't sure she was doing the right thing.

"Not good," Michelle replied. Then she explained what had happened to Adesina.

The Angel frowned. "I can't believe you'd leave her," she said.

"Trust me, it wasn't my first choice," Michelle replied with a sigh. "But Joey is with her. And Wally agreed to help out, too. I think she's in good hands."

The Angel's eyes grew round, and she looked at Michelle with disbelief. "You left her with that . . . that savage."

"Hey!" Michelle snapped back. "Hoodoo Mama is not a savage. She just swears a lot." She could feel a small bubble forming in her hand. "There are only a couple of people I trust with my daughter, and she's one of them. She'd do anything to protect her."

"I'm sorry," the Angel said, though she still sounded dubious. "I don't know her, and most of what I know, I know from other people. I was unfair and un-Christian."

The bubble floated up to the ceiling and popped. "It's okay," Michelle replied, relieved that things hadn't escalated into a fight about parenting. She liked Sheeba and hated the idea that she might think of Michelle as a bad mother.

Just then, the pilot came out of the cockpit. "Hello, folks, I'm Captain Brown and I'll be getting you to Talas today. Our flight time should be roughly three and a half hours. Time to strap in."

Once they were aloft, Michelle got up to see how the other team members were doing. Aero, Earth Witch, and Bugsy were clustered around the galley.

"A little early in the trip to be drinking," Michelle said. Bugsy opened a beer, then handed it to her. She took a swig. It was hoppy, cold, and just what she needed.

"I dunno," Bugsy said with a shrug. "Pretty much all of these missions could be better with booze. And lots of it."

"You got that right," Ana said. She gave Michelle a conspiratorial grin, then drank half her bottle in one long pull.

"You might want to slow down on that," Aero interjected. "We're flying supersonic, and that means the alcohol is going to hit you hard and fast." Then he gave Michelle a wink.

"God, I hope so," Michelle replied, and Ana nodded to show her support. They'd been together on enough assignments that Michelle knew one beer would be it for both of them. Neither of them would risk the mission.

Recycler and Tinker made their way to the bar. Omweer stayed in his seat and gave them a withering look over his glasses. Then he went back to reading his journal. *What a peach,* Michelle thought.

"Give me one of those," Tinker said. He was dressed in his usual beach-bum attire. Puka shells, raggedy blue jeans, and a button-up denim shirt opened enough to show off his tan and his sun-bleached chest hair. "Not bad," he said, taking a chug. "Got anything to eat?"

Ana turned and pulled out the galley's metal drawer. "Looks like sandwiches." She took the drawer all the way out and put it across two of the seats. "Help yourselves, folks."

Everyone grabbed a sandwich and went back to their seats to eat. Michelle grabbed two sandwiches, one for her and one for Sheeba.

"Here you go," she said as she sat down. "I hope you don't mind roast beef."

The Angel smiled. "Not at all. Thanks for thinking of me."

"We've gotta think of everyone now," Michelle said. "The only way we get the mission done is by having everyone's back. And remembering why we're here. But this isn't anything new for you."

"And this is why you left your little girl?" the Angel asked.

Michelle toyed with the wrapping on her sandwich. "She's the only reason I'm going." The thought made her feel as if she were being punched in the heart, and she got up to go grab a tissue. On her way back from the bathroom, she saw Recycler sitting by himself.

"Hey there, Tiago," she said with a smile. "How're you doing?"

He gave her a wan smile. She liked his face despite the mash-up of colors. A far as jokers went, she'd seen far worse.

"I read in your dossier that you were recruited off *Heróis Brazil*," she said. "Have you ever been in real combat before?"

A bitter smile appeared on his face. "I lived in the slums of Rio de Janeiro. My card turned and I figured out what my ace power was when I got caught in the middle of a shoot-out between the curinga and Colombian gangs. I turned myself into a fortress of trash, and stopped them from killing a whole crowd of people," he said proudly. "I only went on the show because I was going to go to jail for kicking their asses."

"Good," she said. "Then I can rely on you not to lose your head in a fight."

He took a bite of his sandwich. There were two more on the tray in front of him. She saw the edge of one peeking out from his backpack. He was skinny as a rail. Either his metabolism was amazing, or he wasn't used to having food available.

"I just want people to know that curingas aren't freaks," he said, leaning forward. There was a blaze of pride in his mismatched eyes. "That we can be *heróis*, too. That we can have ace powers. You don't know what it's like to be a curinga."

Michelle sank back into the seat across from his. "No," she replied softly. "But my daughter is a joker and I don't think she's a freak."

He looked a little chagrined. "My apologies," he said. "I forgot about your daughter. A pretty ace like you—you must have everything—why would you adopt a joker?"

"Because she needed me," Michelle said. Those damn tears began welling up again. "And I needed her."

"I can take orders," he said abruptly. "I can be part of the team."

She ducked her head for a moment to get the tears under control. Then she looked up at him. "I think you're going to be fine," she said. "I think we're lucky to have you."

She got up and walked back to her seat. Sheeba was reading the brief they'd all gotten about Talas. It was a thin folder.

The Angel looked up at her with luminous eyes. Sheeba was beautiful, but Michelle had never been sexually tempted by her. It wasn't just because Sheeba wasn't interested in women, but Joey tended to be on her mind when those feelings arose.

"Not much to go on," Michelle said, pointing at the folder. "This is just about the least information we've had going into an assignment."

The Angel nodded. "I don't like it at all—too many ways for everything to go wrong. And half of the members of this team have never worked together before."

"True enough," Michelle replied. She glanced over at Doktor Omweer and sighed. There was no way around it. She had to talk to him. "I'll be right back."

Marcel looked up as she approached his seat. He was sitting alone and seemed perfectly happy with that. A frown slid across his face as she sat down opposite him.

"I'm sorry to disturb you," Michelle said. The only reason she was sorry was because she didn't want to talk to him. Sometimes she did feel embarrassed that she didn't have any substantive education—despite child labor laws that were supposed to ensure that. Omweer just intensified that feeling. "Look, Dr. Orie, I know you think I'm an idiot and you have contempt for what I do for a living, but I've seen far more combat than you have and as far as this mission is concerned, you're low man on the totem pole."

She knew this was a certain amount of dick waving, but she needed him to respect her enough that he would follow her orders should anything happen to Klaus.

He gave her a patronizing smile. "My dear girl, of course I understand the hierarchy. Most sincerely, I would rather be anywhere than on this mission. I have real work to do, and it is only my sense of duty to my country that keeps me here."

He stopped talking. Michelle assumed their conversation was finished. Thank God.

"You can't help your wretched upbringing," he continued. "We can't all succeed in academia."

Michelle felt herself blushing. Then her embarrassment was replaced with anger. She gave him an icy smile. "Marcel, I don't give a shit what you think of my 'wretched upbringing.' We can't all be smug, overeducated assholes. Do your lightning thing, don't get dead, and don't get anyone else dead. It's pretty straightforward."

He opened his mouth as if to say something else, but she narrowed her eyes and gave him her best killing look. His mouth snapped shut, and he picked up his journal and began reading again.

Michelle went back to her seat with Sheeba. "I really hate that guy," she said in a low voice.

The Angel laughed. "Get in line," she chortled. "At least you didn't get him started on mathematics and statistics. Talk about a bore."

"Oh, there's no chance he'll go on about anything like that with me. I'm a simple girl with a simple mind, far too stupid to be engaged in such a conversation." When Michelle thought about it, she was actually quite pleased he thought she was an idiot.

The plane was climbing to its final altitude. When it went supersonic, it felt like someone was gently pushing her in the back. The clouds thinned out and then vanished altogether. They were at the edge of the atmosphere now. The sky was littered with stars, and the moon was a bright, silver disc.

She stared out the window, looking into the vastness before her. It made her feel small. And much to her surprise, that didn't bother her at all.

Franny stood in the bathroom on the Gulf Stream V. Unlike the coffin-like space on a commercial plane this washroom actually had a narrow shower along with the sink and toilet. He lifted the real cloth towel out of the sink, and wrung it out. The whine and rumble of the jet engines was a soporific. He had managed to grab a little sleep before Baba Yaga's moans had pulled him awake, and the nurse, using a lot of gestures and repeated single words, had given him this task.

There had also been an unwelcome discovery when he awoke. The pistol he'd been carrying since Talas and the burner phone he'd purchased in Shymkent were both gone. He was beginning to get a bad feeling that the roles had reversed and that Baba Yaga was no longer his prisoner. Rather he was hers.

He made his way back to Baba Yaga. The seat was reclined as far as it would go. The male nurse was checking the pulse in her remaining wrist. Franny laid the wet, cool cloth on Baba Yaga's forehead. She gasped, tried to sit up, and cried out in pain.

He eased her back down. "Hey, it's okay."

"Where are we?"

"Somewhere over the pole. I think."

"Good. Good," she sighed. She stared at him. It was like being studied by an ancient dinosaur. "What is your name, boy?"

"Francis Black."

"Francis." She drew it out as if rolling it across her tongue, tasting the name.

"Only my mother calls me Francis and only when she's mad."

"So what do they call you?"

"Frank, but the people I work with call me Franny."

"A girl's name."

"Yeah, cops. They like to think they're funny. They're not."

He lifted the nearly dry towel from her forehead, went back to the bathroom, and soaked it with cold water again. The nurse was switching out an IV bag. When he returned he asked, "So, what's your name?"

"You know my name."

"I've heard the legend of Baba Yaga. It's a handle like Curveball or The Turtle."

"And you don't think it fits?" she asked, and the wrinkled lips quirked, the briefest flicker of a smile.

"A creepy, scary old woman who eats children and decorates with skulls . . ." Franny pretended to consider. "Nah, don't see the similarities at all."

She responded to his ironic tone with another wintery smile. "Watch yourself, boy."

"I thought I had graduated to Frank now."

That seemed to amuse her and she gave a chuckle that quickly became a paroxysm of coughs that shook the thin body. She moaned and tried to guard the broken shoulder and the stump of her arm. Franny knew she was a monster who had kidnapped jokers, forced people to fight to the death for pleasure and profit, but she was also a suffering old woman. He held her close, trying to steady the bones in her shoulder while the nurse held the stump of her arm to keep it still.

Eventually the spasm passed, and he laid her back down. She was panting in pain, and sweat slicked her face. He wiped it away with the towel and went to get her a cup of water. The withered lips closed on the edge of the cup as he held her against his shoulder, and guided the cup to her lips. After a few sips she nodded and he put her down again.

"My name is Mariamna. Mariamna Solovyova."

THURSDAY

MOLLIE STAYED AT THE hospital all night. She stayed, numb, until somebody (the cop? a doctor? she barely remembered the conversation) convinced her that Dad, Brent, Mick, Troy, and Jim had been stabilized after their first rounds of emergency surgery. Or, at least, that they weren't in immediate danger of dying from their wounds the second she opened a portal in space leading back to the farm. Which was about all the reassurance on offer; Jim and Troy wouldn't come out of emergency surgery for hours. The doctors were still in triage mode; saving the remains of the brothers' faces had never been an option.

There were physical injuries and there were mental wounds. Dad and the boys would have a crippling case of both. Mollie wore one around her neck and another in the images that snaked through the dark spaces of her mind every time she closed her eyes.

She stepped from a hospital stairwell into the barn. Staring at the pile of blood-spattered loose change from the slot machines, she realized her mistake. She didn't want to be here. She wanted to be anywhere but here. She wanted to steal some food from the fridge and go to her Bismarck bolt-hole. She entered the farmhouse the regular way, through the kitchen door. And was immediately enveloped with a warm buttery, creamy, beefy aroma: Mom was cooking a big pot of stroganoff.

Oh, shit. Mom, thought Mollie. She'd never thought to go get Mom, or warn her that half the family was in the hospital with grievous injuries. The kitchen door banged shut behind her before she could catch it. Mom came into the kitchen a second later, as though summoned by the racket.

She still wore her apron, and carried a dish towel draped over one shoulder.

From the other room came the sound of a TV rapidly flipping through the channels. The younger boys—Adam, Michael, Jeff—hated *Wheel of Fortune* and always changed the channel when Mom and Dad were out of the room. They must have come home from school while Mollie was at the hospital. Rural bus routes sometimes got them home an hour or more after school let out.

Mom said, "You all almost done out there? Whatever stupid scheme you got going now, it's taking your father and the older boys away from their chores. You come and go as you please, dropping in when it's convenient, or when you're hungry, or when you have laundry you don't feel like doing yourself, but you forget this is a farm with work to be done."

Who would do the work now? How long would they be in the hospital? Even after they're discharged, even if they eventually heal, it'll take a long time before . . .

"Mollie!" Mom snapped her fingers at Mollie. Drying her hands on the dish towel, she said, "I asked you a question. How much longer are you gonna be wasting everyone's time in the barn?"

"There's been . . . Mom, something happened. Something bad."

She started to explain but realized she couldn't. That she didn't know how to explain what happened because she didn't understand it. Didn't even want to think about it. She managed to say, "They're in the hospital."

Mom dropped the towel. "Who?"

"All of them."

"I didn't know what else to do," Marcus said, for about the hundredth time. "I just didn't know . . ." He carried Olena's unconscious body pressed to his chest. Face flushed and sweaty, his breathing came hard. His arms quivered with fatigue, but he kept moving. His one goal the only thing driving him.

The hours since he broke through the barricade had been one long misery of motion and worry. He dodged soldiers and troop transports heading toward Talas, and refugees fleeing the city in vehicles and on foot. He darted for cover as helicopters flew in low, thrumming their way toward Talas, and squirmed even faster when fighter jets appeared, always instantly there, announcing themselves with an earsplitting roar.

All the while he kept checking Olena. For a time she had been feverish. She had bouts of trembling, and would occasionally mumble something. Later she went deathly still and got cooler to the touch. Her breathing became so faint Marcus feared time and again that she'd died. That he'd killed her. If that turned out to be true, he wouldn't be able to live with himself. He'd go to Talas and give in to the madness. Part of him wanted to do that even now. First, though, he had to try the one thing he thought might save her.

It wasn't until he cut away from the highway and up the valley toward the village that the last sounds of the chaos truly fell away. By the time he dragged himself down the main street of the village under the lightening sky of dawn, the world seemed almost normal. Quiet. Tranquil. The dusty street was empty, breath held. He slid down it, Olena so very limp and cool against him. He set her down on the street in front of the Handsmith's house. He hated the way her head lolled, the way her arms and legs flopped. He told himself that she wasn't dead. Not yet. Not yet.

He slithered away to pound on the Handsmith's door. "Jyrgal! Jyrgal! It's Marcus. Please help me!" He kept up his pounding on the frail door until it opened. Jyrgal looked warily out at him, wearing only a long nightshirt. The amorphous stubs of his hands were uncovered, writhing. His wife stood behind him, looking frightened.

"Olena's dying," Marcus said. "She's cold and barely breathing. She needs Nurassyl."

The man stared at him, perplexed and, of course, not understanding his English. Marcus grasped him by the arms. He pulled him through the doorway and pointed at Olena. Jyrgal said something under his breath and rushed to her. He knelt beside her, checked her pulse, her forehead. He looked back up at Marcus. He wanted, Marcus knew, to understand what was wrong with her. Even if they spoke the same language, what could Marcus say? That he'd poisoned her to save her? And how could he convey what he'd been trying to save her from? He couldn't explain anything, so he just pleaded, "Please. Bring Nurassyl. Please . . ."

The Handsmith glanced back toward his house, taking everyone's eyes with him. Aliya stood in the doorway, Nurassyl half hidden behind her, pressed tight to her hip, his large eyes wide with concern. Marcus called gently to the joker boy. "Nurassyl, please come. She needs you." The boy stared at him, his mouth an oval as round as his eyes. Marcus pointed at his tentacled hands. He mimed his healing touch. He pointed to his own cuts and burns, touching them, and then pointed to Olena. "But not me," he said. "Her. Heal her." He didn't know how to act that part out, so he gestured toward her, beseeching, letting the unconscious evidence of her speak for him.

After a confirming nod from his father, the boy slid forward on his many tentacled base. When he bent over Olena his eyes grew attentive instead of fearful. He pulled his hands away from his chest, tentacles squirming. He touched one hand to her neck, at exactly the place Marcus had tongue-tagged her. The other he eased across her forehead, down across her nose and mouth. The tentacles expanded to cover her face entirely. Marcus almost cried out, afraid that she wouldn't be able to breathe. He stopped himself, though. As strange as it was to watch, this was what he'd brought her here for. Nurassyl, the boy who he'd named an ace. He knew what that healing touch felt like, he just hoped it would be enough to save her.

The nurse was busy in the plane's galley heating soup for Baba Yaga. Franny had slept for a few hours and awakened ravenous. He made a sandwich of cheese and hummus and dreamed about getting home and having a cheeseburger and a beer. There was a well-stocked bar on the plane, but he resisted. He needed to keep his wits about him, and he didn't think a combo of bourbon and pain pills would help him do that. He returned to Baba Yaga and settled in the seat across from her.

"We need to start making some plans."

"The plan is that you take messages from me to people who can actually accomplish things," she snapped.

He held on to the fraying ends of his temper. "Okay, fine, but I've got to be able to tell them something other than a criminal needs to talk to you." He decided to test his premise. "Besides, which, I've arrested you," he added. "You can tell them yourself."

She laughed and it was surprisingly robust like the harsh cry of a crow. "You've arrested me? You would be adorable if you weren't so foolish. My plane, my people. I could have you beaten senseless or tossed out if it pleased me to do so."

Franny glanced down the length of the plane to where the nurse stared with cold eyes at him. The nurse had four inches and probably eighty pounds on him. Franny *might* have been able to take him if he wasn't wounded and exhausted. In his current condition he didn't have a prayer.

"Okay. I see your point. Still doesn't obviate mine. I need to know what is happening."

"Something is entering the world, and it will not be kind to our reality. It will bring horrors, madness, and change. Can humans survive?" She fell silent, then gave a tiny head shake. "Doubtful."

"More hints and no specifics. Fucking give me something!"

She bowed her head. He could see the line of white between scalp and the bright red where her hair was growing out. "I will tell you a little story. Once I was young." She shot him a bleak smile. "Yes, it's true . . . and beautiful. My companion and partner was a hero of the Motherland, handsome, brave, fearless." Her hand went unconsciously to her breast and that medal. "He had a great power that he used in service of the revolution. He was known as Hellraiser, but I knew him as Tolenka."

"Okay, great. This is relevant how?"

"You met him or his body in that hospital room in Talas."

"That joker?"

"He was not a joker. He was an ace. What is in him has twisted and deformed him," she said.

"What is in him," Franny repeated with a growing sense of dread.

Baba Yaga looked up. "A creature too powerful, too fearsome to be banished." The flow of words stopped and she gazed at memories. "All we could do was hold it at bay."

The nurse arrived carrying a steaming bowl of soup. Baba Yaga waved Franny away.

It was a clusterfuck.

There was no other way to describe the conglomeration of military, medical, and media clumped together outside the fog-enshrouded city of Talas. Michelle closed her eyes and rubbed her forehead with her index finger. Even by normal FUBAR standards, this was a corker.

As they pulled up in the armored Hummer, Michelle saw that the Kazakh army was dominating the area. There were khaki military tents set up, but they seemed to have been placed haphazardly. Michelle saw pairs of guards walking the perimeter.

About seventy-five meters from the military camp was the Red Crescent encampment. Like the military setup, there were tents erected, but the pattern to them was even more haphazard than the military one—as if they had gone up fast. There were people in yellow hazmat suits removing patients from ambulances. Michelle saw that most of the people on stretchers had drawn a Black Queen and some appeared to be jokers. A handful looked like nats, but they were crying or babbling incoherently as they were carried off. A frantic hum was in the air.

A phalanx of media was set up behind an orange honeycomb-plastic barrier. The stretchy webbing was doing little to stop the TV crews from encroaching on the buffer between them and the people doing the real work inside the Red Crescent compound.

Just inside the barrier, a woman—Michelle assumed it was one of the Red Crescent doctors—was talking to a reporter from MSNBC. The doctor had her hazmat helmet cradled in her right arm. Michelle couldn't hear what was being said, but from the expression on the doctor's face, she wanted nothing more than to end the interview.

"Jesus," Bugsy said as he began taking video footage with his camera that Michelle knew he would post on his blog later. "They sure know how to put on a show."

"I get the feeling this wasn't exactly planned," Michelle replied. She knew all too well how difficult it was to control the media once they got hold of something juicy. "And please don't be quite so obvious about the filming. I know you want the inside story, but don't be an asshole about getting it."

Bugsy looked hurt. "Okay, maybe I'm an asshole sometimes, but I'm here to help the Committee, so lay off." A couple of wasps detached from his hand and landed on Michelle. She brushed them away impatiently.

"As long as you do what Lohengrin needs you to do, we're good," she replied. "But the mission comes first. The rest of us—" She pointed at the other aces who were grouped by the Hummer. "We're here for one reason—and we can't afford anyone screwing that up."

The Angel and Ana came over to them. "This is nothing but a huge mess," Ana said. She shoved up the sleeves of her denim shirt then glanced around. "Does it look like the army tents have been moved recently?"

The Angel and Michelle turned and looked back toward Talas. There was a large area with flattened grass and dirt roads winding to nowhere. It was about 250 meters from where the military camp was now.

"I think you're right," Michelle said. The Angel nodded in agreement. "And the fog is covering part of that area."

"Have you called Barbara yet and told her what's going on?" Sheeba asked Michelle. She sounded cool and regal like she always did.

"I thought Klaus would be doing that," Michelle replied, pulling her phone out of her pocket. It was Committee standard issue and would work just about anywhere. "But you know, it might be helpful for her to hear what's going on from a different point of view."

A uniformed private hurried up and snapped a salute at Klaus, who was standing a few meters away. "Mr. Hausser, sir," he said hurriedly in heavily accented English. "I have orders to bring you and the other Committee members to General Nabiyev for a briefing on the situation."

Michelle looked around again. Yep, there was no doubt about it. The situation was a clusterfuck. While the others followed Klaus, she stayed behind to call Barbara. It went directly to Babel's phone. Michelle was prepared to tell Babel everything she'd seen, but instead of Barbara, Ink picked up.

"Director Baden's line."

"You know it's me, Juliet," Michelle said with some irritation. "There's caller ID on this phone."

"I'm waiting."

"Jesus, 'Rooster in the henhouse,'" Michelle said, giving the pass phrase. "I cannot believe you."

"Oh, c'mon, Michelle," Juliet said impatiently. "You know procedure. Let me get Barbara."

Michelle waited for a moment, then Babel came on the line.

"Michelle, I didn't expect to hear from anyone so soon. Did Klaus tell you to call?" There was a faint anxiousness in her voice.

Michelle looked around to see if anyone could hear her, then walked closer to the Hummer, just to be sure. "Things are pretty confused here," she replied. She pulled her cap even lower over her forehead. Though the other aces were pretty well known and it was possible they'd been recognized by the press, Michelle was much more high-profile. It might set off a frenzy if the press knew the Committee had taken an interest in Talas.

"Klaus and the rest of the team have gone to talk to General Nabiyev.

I'll keep in touch with you as much as possible. I figured you could use someone letting you know how things are going—and how Klaus is doing."

It sounded like Babel gave a tiny sigh of relief, and Michelle knew she'd done the right thing. If Joey had been in a similar situation, she'd want to know what was going on with her, too.

"Klaus is Klaus," Michelle said. "Taking control, doing his Klaus thing. I can't stay long or I'll be missed. I know it's not protocol, but I'm going to call Joey about Adesina."

"I'm giving special permission for that, Michelle," Babel said, her voice not altogether businesslike. "I know you didn't want to leave her, and I'd rather you know how she's doing than not. Just make the call quick."

"Thanks, Babs," Michelle said.

"Stop calling me that."

The connection was broken. Michelle immediately called Joey. The phone rang a couple of times, then Joey picked up.

"It's me," Michelle said hurriedly. "I only have a second. How's Adesina? Any change? I don't suppose you've had any dreams . . ."

"I'm sorry, Michelle. The niblet hasn't done anything. No visiting me in dreams. Just the same as when you left," Joey replied. "Wally came over with Ghost. There was no response."

"Oh," Michelle said in a small voice.

"You get there okay?"

"Yeah, but it's a mess here. I just hope we can figure out what's going on soon."

"Yeah, me, too." There was an odd tension in Joey's voice, but Michelle didn't have time to tease out what it was.

"Okay," Michelle said. "I'll call again soon as I can." Then she tapped the off button on her phone. The quick phone call to Joey wasn't nearly enough time. Even though nothing had changed, she wanted to talk to Joey about how much she hated being away from them both.

She started walking toward the general's tent. She hoped Nabiyev realized what kind of situation he had by the tail, but you never knew what you might get with military. Like most people, sometimes they were the best thing ever, and sometimes they were so clueless you despaired for the human race.

Fortunately, Nabiyev was the former. Michelle knew he was feeling the strain of being in charge of a rapidly deteriorating situation. There was a thin sheen of sweat on his forehead, and the collar of his shirt was damp despite the unseasonably cool weather.

"Thank you for coming on such short notice," Nabiyev began. He was tall and thin with a sallow complexion and eyes. "Things are getting worse, and we're still not certain what is happening. We can't discern the nature of the fog. And as you can tell by the drone photos, it's expanding. We've already moved back our forces once to avoid possible infection.

"We believe we have the source pinpointed." He jabbed a finger into the map on the table in front of him. It landed roughly in the center of the fog, and the ID marker read: NAZABBAYES MEMORIAL HOSPITAL.

Klaus looked at the map and back at Nabiyev. "Have you sent in any forces?" he asked.

"Of course we have," the general replied acerbically. "Do you really think I would allow this thing to escalate without taking some kind of action?" His eyes narrowed. "I realize you have your little band of aces here, but we have men brave enough to go in there without any powers. And we have an ace of our own!" He pointed across the room to a short, dark-haired, brown-eyed woman. Her nose was broad and flat. Michelle noticed that her freckled fawn-colored skin had a subtle golden glow to it.

"This is Inkar," he said with no small amount of pride. "She is our first ace. Show them your power!"

Inkar looked appalled and uncomfortable. "With all respect, sir. There is hardly enough room in here for all of us, much less me in my Tulpar form."

The general frowned, then nodded. "You must show them after we're done here." Inkar nodded, but Michelle could tell she wasn't happy being asked to put on a show.

"Yes, you have an ace," Klaus began. "But we can still help you . . ."

"Klaus wasn't judging your men, or your approach," Michelle interjected. Sometimes Klaus could be a little too direct. Barbara was a past master at smoothing those times out, and Michelle wished she were here. "We just need to know where everything stands at the moment. From the outside, things are very confusing."

That seemed to mollify Nabiyev, and when Michelle glanced over at Klaus, he didn't seem annoyed with the interruption. The last thing they needed was getting into a tangle with the military—or each other.

"We sent one platoon in," Nabiyev said with a heavy sigh. "Most of them didn't come back. And the few that did, well, you can see them in the infirmary. The injured civilians coming out are in the Red Crescent compound. And on top of everything else, we have every major media outlet camped just outside our position."

Klaus frowned. "Before we head out, we should get a better idea of what we're dealing with," he said. "Michelle and Ana, you go check on the civilians who've come out of the city and see if the doctors have any idea what's happening to them.

"Aero, you and Angel go talk to the soldiers who were in the zone. Maybe they'll have some insight into what's going on."

He motioned to the rest of the aces. "Doktor, Tinker, Recycler, get as close to the perimeter of the fog as you can. Get some more recent pictures and video."

There was a gleam in Klaus's eye. Michelle knew that expression. He got that look whenever he was about to jump into the fray.

Representative Temir Bondarenko of Kazakhstan was a thin, tall man, who looked as if he might break in half if he fell down. That impression was enhanced by the drawn and sallow face; Bondarenko looked as if he hadn't slept in days. Barbara figured that might actually be a correct assessment. Evidently, Ink felt the same way as she ushered the man into the meeting room where Barbara and Jayewardene were waiting. "Coffee?" she asked. The tattoos on her right arm swirled: a pot pouring dark liquid into a mug.

"Ah! Yes, please," Bondarenko answered. "I would . . . like." Barbara rose from her chair, as did Jayewardene. The man's handshake was firm but not overmuch so, and he sank quickly into the seat that Barbara offered him. His accent was strong, and it was obvious that his English was limited.

"Would you be more comfortable speaking in your own language?" Barbara asked. "I can make it so we can all understand each other."

Bondarenko nodded, and Babel closed her eyes momentarily, letting her wild card ability fill the room, encompassing all three of them. "I know your ability, Ms. Baden. Secretary-General Jayewardene has told me of it. Thank you." He clasped his hands together on the table. "This situation is awful," he said. "Nothing less. I appreciate having the opportunity to meet with you, and to hear that Lohengrin and other aces are already on their

way to help. I wish you to know that my country is grateful." He paused
as Ink entered with a tray holding a pot of coffee and three mugs. She set
it down near Bondarenko, shaking her head covertly to Barbara: *nothing
new from Lohengrin.* "And I am personally grateful as well," Bondarenko
finished.

"Your family is in Talas?" Barbara knew from Ink's background material that this was the case, and Bondarenko verified it with a quick nod as
he poured himself coffee.

"Yes," he said. "I've not heard from them in two days now. I hope they
left before . . ." He didn't finish the sentence. He took a sip of the coffee.
"Your aces will be there . . . ?"

"They've already landed. Thank you for arranging for them to land at
your airbase and having your people meet them. That will be a great help."

A nod. "I have photographs of Talas that you should already have in
both of your e-mails—aerial photos of Talas taken over the last two weeks.
It's possible by looking at the sequence to determine where this disturbance
began: in the hospital on Appasovoy Street in the city. You can see fog
spread out from there. That must be the center: that hospital. I am certain
that someone, or something, there has caused this."

Barbara glanced at Jayewardene. The Secretary-General said nothing,
but his lips pressed together tightly. "Thank you, Representative Bondarenko. That will be an immense help to all of us. I'll have Ink relay that
information to Lohengrin and the aces via satellite phone, along with the
photos."

"And I will let Brussels know so that the UN is aware as well," Jayewardene added. "As Ms. Baden said, this is excellent information. If there's
anything else that you find out . . ."

"Then I will tell you immediately," Bondarenko said. "That I promise.
This horror that has been unleashed on my country has to be stopped. Too
many, far too many, have already died." The sadness in his eyes, the exhaustion on his face, all pulled at Barbara.

"Representative," she said. "Your family. Do you have pictures of them?"

The trace of a smile slid across his face, and he pulled out his wallet,
sliding out a snapshot from a pocket there. Barbara looked at them: a
woman holding three children and smiling at the camera. She could see
Bondarenko's features echoed there, especially in the eldest, a daughter.
"You have a beautiful family," she told him. "And you must be terribly
worried about them."

His eyes shimmered at that, and he took a long breath. "Very much so," he said. "They'd gone back to visit family, then this thing happened. I don't know . . ." He stopped, giving Barbara a wan smile. He started to reach for the photo, but Barbara tapped a finger on it.

"May I have my assistant scan this? I want to send the photo to Lohengrin and the aces—that way, if they see your family, they can send word back here immediately."

Bondarenko blinked hard. "Yes," he said. "That is kind of you, Ms. Baden. Yes. Thank you."

She smiled at him. "There's no need for thanks," she told him. "We both want the same thing, Representative Bondarenko. We want this carnage ended, and we want those we love and care about back safely with us."

Olena was alive, that much was certain, but it was all they knew. She lay on her back on a low cot in one of the villagers' humble homes. Sleeping. Marcus sat beside her, his tail coiled and bulky in the small room. The verdict was still out on everything: if Nurassyl's power had overcome the poison, if she'd wake up, what she'd say if she did, and what the villagers were going to do with him. They let him be alone with her, but only after a lively debate, not a word of which he could follow. As far as he could understand, they were giving him the benefit of the doubt for the time being, waiting for Olena to recover so they could hear what she had to say.

Marcus wore an oversized sweater one of the jokers had given him to replace his tattered, blood- and filth-smeared shirt. Nurassyl had healed Marcus as well, much against his protests. Marcus had refused treatment at first, a sort of punishment to himself. But Nurassyl was insistent, in his quiet, gentle way.

Now, Marcus watched Olena breathe, following each slow rise and fall of her chest. He could almost see the air flowing in and out of her thin lips. She looked marvelously peaceful, but his mind reeled. She *looked* calm—and Nurassyl's power had obviously saved her from his poison—but had the boy been able to save her mind? Was she still Olena? If so, would she understand why he'd done what he did? Would she even wake up sane? For all he knew, she might still be that bloody-faced, raging, barely recognizable terror. And if she was all right, what then?

Jyrgal's wife, Aliya, made Marcus a pot of tea and set it on a table beside him, with some small, sweet-looking cakes. She was a quiet woman, a nat, it seemed like, slim and plain and, Marcus thought, perfectly lovely. Of course she was. Wife to Jyrgal and mother to Nurassyl; how could she not be a lovely person? Marcus was famished, but it was a dull hunger and he didn't yet want to feed it.

Alone after Aliya left, Marcus wondered if he should try praying. He hadn't done that since back in his old life, when he was still a nat and his family loved him—or claimed to. He let the only prayer he knew by heart start to form in his mind. *Our Father, who art in heaven, hallowed be thy name . . .* That's as far as he went with it. The words didn't feel right anymore. It was a prayer from his old life, and that had never felt farther away or completely unattainable. It was a life that had nothing to do with him anymore. Why pray to a god who allowed the things that happened last night? Who had allowed the wild card virus? Who never once proved that he gave a crap about the people he was supposed to have created in his image?

Marcus whispered, "Do you hate us so much?"

Father Squid would've said just the opposite. Marcus couldn't understand how the priest had managed to find God after all the misery he'd seen. He'd been able to pray, to believe, to love, even in the midst of Jokertown's squalor. He always said that God loved jokers most of all. Those challenged by the virus had a harder lot in life, but they'd be rewarded for it in heaven. Marcus thought that maybe he could pray to *that* God. He bent his head, closed his eyes, and started again.

"Dear God—God of jokers, I mean—I don't know if you've noticed me. If you have, you probably don't think much of me. I've done a lot of things I'm not proud of. But it's hard, being like me. People make it hard, you know? I try to do the right things. If you know everything, you know that. God, I just want one thing. Save Olena. I love her. I love her like I've never loved anybody. And she's a good person. You can see that, right? The world needs good people, right? And I don't mean *just* live. Let her be all right. If you do that, I'll do whatever you ask of me. I swear it. Whatever you ask, I'll do it. Just let me know what."

He paused, unsure what to say next. That was it, he guessed, and it felt just as hollow as he figured it would. He exhaled a weary breath, opened his eyes, and found Olena awake and watching him. He stared at her, pinned to the moment, unsure which Olena she was, not wanting to say or do the wrong thing.

"I didn't know you were religious," she said. "It's sweet of you to want to 'save' me, but that's not for me." She grinned suggestively. "I'm too much of a sinner."

Marcus still found it impossible to speak. She was awake. She was talking with him, smiling, joking even. So she wasn't insane, and she didn't hate him. She'd even said he was sweet. It was too much. He didn't have the words. So instead he kissed her. Softly at first, and then with more passion. She returned it, making sounds low in her throat. He loved the feel of her lips and her arms, her skin so soft and warm. Her hands slid under the sweater, moving over his torso as she pulled him closer, as hungry for him as he was for her. He was so flooded with relief and filled with desire that he didn't question the instant passion. He let it become everything, all the horrors forgotten. He squirmed on to the bed, twisting her with him so that she broke the kiss to laugh. She straddled him, legs wrapping around his smooth, scaled lower torso. He felt the pressure of an erection pressing against his scales, starting to emerge. It would have, except that she grinned and exclaimed, "You're crying!" She wiped tears that Marcus hadn't known were there from his cheek. "Silly boy. Why do you cry? You are being strange."

"I just can't believe you're all right."

She leaned in and kissed the moisture away from one cheek. Lips wet on his skin, she asked, "Why wouldn't I be?"

As aroused as he was, he put a hand to her chest and gently pushed her up so he could see her face. "With all the stuff we saw . . . The way things got so crazy . . . Olena, I'm sorry for what I did, but it was all I could think to do to save you. You were so close to . . ."

His words dribbled away as the expression on her face morphed from amusement to bewilderment, and then to something darker. She sat up and swiped her hair from her face, shoving it behind an ear. "What are you talking about?" She looked around the room, taking it in. "What did we see that was crazy? And where are we? I don't know this room."

Marcus asked, "What's the last thing you remember?"

"I . . ." The rest of the sentence got caught in the wrinkles of her forehead, or lost in the glazed look in her eyes. "I'm not sure. My father . . . did he come here?" Marcus nodded. "Yes, I remember that. We made a deal with him to go back to Talas. In the helicopter, we flew there." She stopped. Backtracked. "We flew toward there. We saw the soldiers and the city approaching." She fixed him with her blue eyes. "That's all. Did something happen? Did we crash?" And then, after a pause, "Why don't I remember?"

He chose to answer the third question instead of the ones that preceded it. "Nurassyl healed you. Maybe that meant taking away the memories of what happened."

"Healed me from what?" she asked. When he didn't answer immediately, she asked again, with an edge to her voice this time. "Marcus, healed me from what?" She stared at him, waiting, patient in her impatience.

Someone pulled aside the curtain that hung in the doorway. The Handsmith looked in. Seeing Olena, he grinned. He called something over his shoulder in Russian and then addressed Olena. She responded in kind. They fell into conversation. Her face grew graver as they talked. The Handsmith was calm, gentle as always, but there was a tension in him Marcus hadn't seen before.

Olena finally looked at her lover. "Jyrgal says that Nurassyl healed me from poison. From your poison, he thinks. He asked me if this was true, and for you to explain. Also, though, he wants to know what is happening in Talas. Something very strange, he says. He asked me about all these things, but I cannot answer. Only you can."

And just like that, the reprieve was over. It all crashed down on him again. All the things he'd seen. All the things he knew were still out there. With Olena back, he had a voice again. He knew he had to use it. He said, "Ask him to call the whole village together. I've things to say that everyone needs to hear."

One of the soldiers escorted Michelle and Ana to the Red Crescent command tent to meet Dr. Asil Bahar, the man in charge of the Red Crescent rescue effort.

He wore a lab coat over hospital scrubs. His dark hair was tied back into a short ponytail. There were several stacks of medical charts on his desk along with a couple of cell phones.

He made no bones about how busy his people were and how much he didn't appreciate being interrupted. "You do know we are independent from the military here? General Nabiyev has no authority over me. And I certainly have no obligation to the Committee. I don't have time to play tour guide." He had a beautiful upper-class British accent. Scorn dripped from it.

"I realize there's something extraordinary happening here," Michelle said, using her very best I'm-here-to-help voice. "If the Committee is going to go into Talas, we need to have *some* idea of what we're up against. We need to be prepared. We will do everything we can to make our visit as short as possible, but we need to know what you think is happening so we can decide what to do."

Bahar snorted and then gave a slightly hysterical laugh. "You want to know what you're up against, Miss Pond? Please, allow me to show you."

He turned and walked out of the tent without bothering to see if they were following. Ana gave Michelle a what-the-hell-was-that-all-about expression. Michelle shrugged, and then they followed Bahar out.

He led them past a row of medical tents to three others set apart. As they got closer, a wave of putrid air hit them. Ana gagged. Michelle knew that smell. It smelled like the charnel pit from which she'd pulled Adesina.

"Jesus," Ana said, lifting the hem of her denim shirt to cover her mouth and nose. "What the hell?"

Bahar smiled grimly, pulled disposable hospital masks out of his coat pocket, and handed one to each of them. Then he put one on himself. "We've been using these three tents for the ones who died from whatever is happening inside Talas. You won't need this mask for contagion, but it will help some with the smell. This is what has been coming out of Talas. Please come in and see."

Michelle and Ana hesitated, then put on their masks. Bahar stood holding the flap, obviously waiting for them to go in first. Michelle stepped through the opening. A narrow path ran through the center of the tent. Corpses were stacked up on tarps along the walls. In the bleak light from the overhead bulb, they saw the carnage coming from inside Talas.

Some of the bodies were no longer human. They were shapeless sacks of flesh with blood seeping out of mysterious orifices and what appeared to be bite marks and other kinds of wounds. One body, if you could call it that, stood out to Michelle. A small blob wearing OshKosh B'gosh overalls covered in blood and what looked like brain tissue. When she was a child, Michelle had been the face of the OshKosh B'gosh brand for girls. Gorge suddenly rose in her throat, and she barely made it out of the tent before ripping off her mask and spewing out the turkey sandwich she'd eaten on the plane.

She wiped her mouth on the back of her hand. Then she put her mask on and went back inside.

"You okay?" Ana asked. She was pale and her voice trembled. Michelle felt the same as Ana looked.

Michelle nodded. Dr. Bahar didn't speak. He just took a wet wipe from his pocket and handed it to her. She used it to clean off her hands.

"Is this how everyone looks when they come out?" Michelle asked. She could smell her own pukey breath, but it was better than the smell of putrefaction in the room.

"No, some of them come out almost normal. Most of them who come out alive are . . . well, let me show you."

They followed him to another hospital tent. This one was bigger than the tents with the corpses. "You won't need your masks in here," he said. "Far as we can tell, none of them are contagious. We've been isolating the patients as they come out of the zone. Once we're sure they're clear, we put them in tents like this."

Inside the tent, there were rows of cots. At the far end, a woman was examining one of the patients. She looked up and nodded at Bahar.

"Dr. Rahal," Bahar said, leading them to her. "These women are from the Committee. They're here to get an idea of what we know about what's happening in Talas. Dr. Rahal is our head epidemiologist."

Michelle extended her hand and Rahal gave her a quick dry handshake. Then she shook hands with Ana. Rahal was a dwarf, a little under four feet tall. Her grey hair was pulled back in a severe bun and, like Dr. Bahar, she wore a lab coat over scrubs.

Michelle glanced around the tent. Most of the people were nats. Many of them were strapped down to their beds with glazed expressions on their faces. One or two looked as if they were growing blood-filled masses on their faces. *Jokers?* Michelle wondered. Maybe this *was* another PPA—another wild card disaster.

"So are we dealing with a weaponized wild card virus?" Michelle asked. "Because it's happened before."

Rahal shook her head. "As far as I've been able to ascertain, no. This is nothing like what happened in Africa. Whatever is causing this, I think it's not the virus. Some of the other doctors disagree with me."

She gestured at the patients. "The less violent ones we've just sedated, but as you can tell, there are people who are too dangerous not to restrain."

"What about the ones who have . . . things growing on them?" Ana asked. There was a tremor in her voice and a drawn expression on her face. She jammed her hands into her black pants.

"No, they're not jokers," Rahal said. "I'm not certain what they are. From the tests, they appear to be human."

"Oh, God!" one of the female patients began to wail. "Oh, God, why have you forsaken me? I ate your flesh. I drank your blood. I did as you asked."

Chills broke out along Michelle's arms. The voice was cracked and filled with madness. Then the woman began grinding her teeth so hard Michelle was certain she was going to break them.

A nurse rushed into the tent. He had a carryall filled with syringes and vials.

"You're going to have to up the dosage of Valium to fifty milligrams three times a day," Bahar said. The nurse put the carryall down on a table at the opening to the tent. "And we're going to double the dose of Clozaril."

The nurse looked surprised, but did as he was told. Ana leaned over and whispered into Michelle's ear, "The Valium dose alone is enough to take down a horse. I have no idea what the Clozaril is for. Maybe something for psychosis?"

"Jesus," Michelle murmured. Then louder she said, "Dr. Rahal, do you have any idea what's wrong with these people? Any kind of guess?"

Rahal shook her head. "No. We've checked for everything we can think of. Chemical. Biological. As I said before, the wild card virus doesn't seem to be involved, but who knows? Until we have more information, I can't make any kind of definitive conclusion."

Then she gave a contemptuous smile. "One of my colleagues thinks it's mass hysteria. Make of that what you will."

Michelle thought about the tents with the corpses. And how those deformed bodies looked. And after her time in the PPA, there was one thing she knew for certain: what was happening here was for damn sure not mass hysteria.

"I think it's time to do more reconnaissance," Nabiyev was saying as Michelle and Ana came back into the command tent. "I have a unit chosen from my people. Who do you suggest from your group?"

Klaus turned toward the rest of the aces. "I think Bugsy and Lama are the best choices to help. Bugsy can send his wasps ahead, and Lama can astral-project, so he'll be safe back here at camp and can report on what's happening."

The Lama blanched. He was a notorious coward, and Michelle wished he wasn't on the mission at all. He wasn't a bad guy, but the last thing they needed in this situation was the Lama acting like a complete candy-ass.

"So, we've got a plan for reconnaissance," Klaus said, sounding pleased. He looked like he was fairly itching to be on the move. "What about after?" He tapped the map next to the pin indicating Nazabbayes Memorial Hospital.

"We'll need to go in and deal with whatever is happening in there depending on what the recon finds," the general said. He put his hands on his waist, then looked around the room at the Committee aces as if he was appraising their worthiness.

"I think we should send the troops in along with our aces," Klaus said, "after we get some information from Bugsy and Lama." He was fairly bouncing on his toes.

Michelle realized Klaus had changed since he'd lost his eye. His desire to lead the Committee had been replaced by the need to be in the field kicking ass. Michelle understood the impulse. She could be a blunt instrument herself.

The Angel liked exactly none of this. She felt awash on a sea of tension and fear that roiled off the city hunkered stolidly before them, presenting a blank yet somehow sullen face. The unnatural mist hid most of Talas, and what had attacked the troops milling about the camp like ants cut off from their colony. Some were dazed, some had been hurt and were being taken off to the Red Crescent tents clustered in a corner of the camp. All looked spooked. She doubted that any could provide useful intel, and that wasn't even considering the language barrier. She glanced at Bugsy, who was looking around with as little enthusiasm as she had.

"I don't suppose you speak Kazakh?" she asked.

He looked up, blankly, from the lens of his video camera and stopped filming.

"Or Russian?"

That elicited a shake of his head.

She sighed.

"I do," a soft voice said.

The Angel looked around to see a small, young girl, perhaps in her teens, looking at her and Bugsy. She had a broad, flat-featured face with a snub nose and small, warm brown eyes. She was maybe five two and was dressed in Western though conservative style, in pants, a long-sleeved shirt, and sturdy-looking work boots. Her skin had a slight golden sheen that marked her as apart from normal.

The Angel smiled at her. "Kazakh," she asked, "or Russian?"

"Both," she replied with a smile. Her teeth were even and white. "I am Inkar Omarov," she said, "and you are the famous aces Bugsy and Midnight Angel." She looked at Bugsy. "I read your blog."

Bugsy brightened. "Hey, what do you know, a fan, all the way out here."

The Angel spared him a brief frown.

"I have read about both of you in *ACES*." She smiled diffidently, shyly. "I, too, am an ace."

"Excellent," the Angel said with a smile. "We can use your help in questioning the soldiers. We have to find out what's happening in the center of Talas."

Inkar inclined her head. "Of course."

They spoke to over half a dozen troops, but elicited only a story of confusion and failure. The soldiers were respectful of Inkar—it seemed that she was well known among them and had a considerably highly regarded reputation among her conservative countrymen—but hard info was scarce among the mystified and still-frightened soldiers.

Lohengrin approached, wearing his ghost armor, his only concession to the heat the lack of a helmet. He was accompanied by Bubbles, almost elfin in her slim beauty, and Doktor Omweer, the tall, khaki-clad Dutch ace. Omweer towered over all, even Lohengrin. He was an imposing six foot seven and well regarded by his ability to call upon and control lightning, if not exactly well liked. He was a peculiarly studious and serious man who'd rather spend his time studying obtuse mathematics rather than gadding about the earth, saving it.

"Have you seen the Lama?" Lohengrin asked. "I want him and you, Bugsy, to go off on a scout."

Bugsy sighed. "Yeah, sure, a scout. Like I haven't done that before." He pursed his lips. "Last I saw him, he was snoozing in the back of an SUV."

Lohengrin looked annoyed. "Well, go wake him up and get to it. We're getting ready to go in, but we desperately need some kind of clue about what might be waiting for us."

By his calculations Franny figured they had to be getting close. Since he'd never in his life flown on a private plane he had no idea where they would land. Tomlin? Newark? The customs officers in Tehran might have been willing to accept the wrong passport, but that sure as hell wasn't going to work in the States.

Given the efficiency with which Baba Yaga had arranged for their flight he assumed she had something in mind, but he needed to know what. There was nothing he could do at thirty thousand feet. He'd have to wait until they landed and look for an opportunity to escape and take Baba Yaga with him.

The old lady had slept after she'd eaten her soup, but he needed more information. Especially if the daring escape with Baba Yaga in tow didn't work out. He returned to her.

"So we were at the point where you were holding something at bay." He raised his eyebrows inquiringly. "I'm trying to figure out how kidnapping and torturing jokers is relevant to any of this."

"You think I'm a monster—"

"Got it on one."

The insult bounced off her emotional armor. "There was a reason for the death and pain I inflicted on those jokers. Their suffering kept this thing under control. Before he was lost Tolenka advised me of what I must do." Her hand reached out and touched the stack of cassette tapes. "Over the years I refined and perfected the formula. Just enough blood and death to keep it sleeping. Too little and it would awaken. Too much and it would awaken." The wrinkled lids lifted and the grey ice pierced him. "Then *you* blundered in. The big hero. And now it is coming."

She fell silent. A line of ice traced its way down Franny's spine. He didn't doubt what she had said. What he had felt in that hospital room defied description or explanation.

"Why didn't you tell someone? Get help to find a solution other than murder?"

"Humans are stupid, frightened monkeys. Anyone I trusted would probably have done something foolish and unleashed this horror sooner. No, I did what I had to do."

He felt a strange stir of sympathy. "What a terrible choice. Killing a few to save millions, hell billions. That can't have been easy."

The look she bestowed on him was contemptuous. "No, it was very easy. I live on this world. All that I have worked to amass is here. I'd be a fool not to protect it."

The cold calculation of her response awakened a blaze of anger. Franny stepped back, felt his hands clenching into fists. "So you did all this because you keep your *stuff* here?" She just looked at him. "God, you are disgusting."

Her dry laughter followed him down the aisle of the plane. He went into the lavatory and sluiced water onto his face, allowed his racing heart to slow, waiting for the anger to leech out so he wouldn't try to slap that smirk off her face. Once he was calm Franny returned to her.

"So what do we do? How do we stop this?" he asked.

"There are things that must *not* be done, but I will tell only your great heroes, not my errand boy."

Franny returned to the bathroom. His fist shattered the mirror over the sink. It helped quell the rage, but not by much.

Marcus stood in the center of the street, surrounded by the entire village. They all listened as he laid out the whole unbelievable story. It fell to Olena to translate, which she did, her voice growing increasingly flatter and more distant as she went. Her eyes glazed and seemed reluctant to meet his. Marcus tried to keep himself to the basic facts, but it was hard. There was too much to say. Mostly, he tried to convince them to believe him, and to agree to flee the town and get as far away from Talas as possible.

"We have to get out of here," he said. "There's something horrible happening in Talas, and it's only getting worse, spreading. Let's plan, pack up, and go."

When he finished speaking, the villagers spoke among themselves. Olena didn't translate their deliberations.

Looking from face to face, he tried to read their reactions. He couldn't, but he did marvel that he had come to know them so well over just a few days, when he couldn't speak their language. Timur, with his head wrapped in a turban-like horn. Anara, with gill-like vents in her face, pretty not despite them, but because of them. She had served sweetened tea to the guys playing basketball just a couple days ago. Jyrgal, with his hands hidden within their burlap mittens. Nurassyl, to whom he owed both his and Olena's lives. Jokers, most of them, like him. That they had in common, no matter the barriers of language and culture. Behind whatever the virus had bestowed on them, they were just people. Mother and fathers, sons and daughters, friends and rivals. There were nats among them, people like Aliya. He wanted to save all of them from what he'd experienced in Talas.

After conferring with the others, Olena approached him. "So, what did they decide?" Marcus blurted. "Will they leave? We should go as—"

Olena cut in. "They are split. Some have heard enough and want to go. Others cannot believe your story. Timur and some of the other men are going down the valley, toward Talas—"

It was Marcus's turn to cut in. "No! They can't do that! They'll walk right into it!"

"You're asking them to abandon their homes, all because of some crazy story. If you'd blamed it on the Russians—said it was nuclear accident or something—that they'd have believed. But this? And all on your word? No, they have to see for themselves."

Marcus pressed a palm to his forehead, noticing for the first time that he had a pounding headache. He'd had it for a while, he realized. "None of what we saw was believable. I was there and I barely believe. Of all of it there's one thing I can't get out of my mind. It's the faces of the people stuck inside that monster. I knew that I had seen faces like that before. Now I remember where. In school they showed us old footage of the Holocaust. World War II, you know? Concentration camps. That's what those people looked like. That was the desolation in their eyes. Like they'd realized that there was a hell, and it was right here on earth." He sighed. "They'd believe you, if you remembered."

Olena's blue eyes came up, sad and beautiful. And challenging. "But I don't," she said, her voice edged with frustration. "According to you, I was crazy. You had to poison me, and Nurassyl had to take away my memories to save me. According to you my father is dead. My father, who has never been afraid of anything." She gestured angrily toward the villagers. "I'm just like them: nothing but your word to go on."

A fighter jet appeared up the valley. It roared past the village. There and gone in a moment. In the uneasy silence as its roar faded, Marcus asked, "But, you believe me, don't you?"

"I don't know what to believe," she said. He reached to hold her hand, but she flinched. She raised a palm to fend him off. Shaking her head, she said, "Give me room. I need to think. We all do."

Watching her walk down the village road, toward the down valley edge of town, Marcus said, "Shit."

It had been hours, and they still hadn't heard from Bugsy or the Lama. Some of Nabiyev's soldiers had staggered out of the gradually expanding miasma, but they were in no condition to do anything. Some of them looked as if acid had been thrown in their faces. They screamed and clawed at themselves until the army doctors managed to shoot them up with co-pious amounts of morphine.

And then there were the other men. One of them ran up to Michelle. "Can't you feel him?" he asked, grabbing both of her arms and holding on tight as his fingers dug into her flesh. Shockingly, it hurt. Nothing like this had hurt since her card had turned. She tried to yank out of his grasp, but his hold was unbreakable. His breath was hot and smelled like the corpse tent. It was as if he was already dead. "He's coming for us. He's com-ing for all of us. He wants . . . gnahd hsdnga kjdiuk . . ."

His hold loosened and Michelle jerked her arms away, staggering back-ward. His gibberish continued even as blood began to drip from his nose and ears. He coughed and spattered Michelle's face with blood. Ichor streamed down his chin onto his neck, and he collapsed.

Jesus, she thought, wiping her face with the back of her shaking hand. Nothing she could think of other than the wild card virus that would change people into monstrous creatures. But that didn't explain the ram-pant crazy.

"Come away from him," the Angel said, pulling at Michelle's arm. She was strong, and Michelle followed, surprised that the Angel could move her heavy-duty bubbling weight. "He's insane and probably dying. And the medic is already here."

The Angel released Michelle's arm when they reached the Hummer. There was a bottle of water lying in the front seat. Michelle grabbed it and rinsed off her face. Her hands were still shaking. He'd touched her and it had *hurt*.

Inkar was leaning against the Hummer. She had a stony expression on her face. Whatever was going on, she was pissed about it. *Better pissed than afraid,* Michelle thought. She thought about Adesina and how Jayewardene had insisted that the only way to keep her from dying was to come to Talas. He'd better be right.

The Lama was lying in the back of the Hummer next to Bugsy's empty clothes. His body was limp now that he'd gone into astral form. His hair was wet with sweat and his olive skin was paler than normal. Every so often, a terrible moan would escape him. *He's not even physically there,* Michelle thought. *How can he be so freaked out?*

A buzzing sound filled the air. As it grew louder, Michelle turned to see Bugsy's wasps coming out of the fog from Talas. But they weren't flying in their usual tight formation. They tumbled and collided until they finally reached Bugsy's clothes and slid in. They didn't quite fill the pants and shirt anymore. When he finally coalesced, Bugsy was much smaller than normal. It was as if he'd lost an enormous number of his wasps.

"What's happening?" Ana asked, her voice tight. She stared at Bugsy. Her eyes were wide, and her mouth was pulled into a tight line.

Bugsy giggled. His eyes were wild. Some of the wasps hadn't fully integrated, and he picked them off his body and began eating them delicately, one by one. He would titter and then eat a wasp.

Then, without warning, he exploded back into his wasp form and flew back in the direction of Talas.

"Jesus," Michelle said. Her voice trembled. "What the hell is going on in there?"

"You're certain of this information?" Lohengrin asked. His image stuttered through the Internet connection, though the voice was clear enough. Barbara nodded. From the viewscreens arrayed around here, other faces also reacted with some lag from their various distances: Secretary-General Jayewardene was in Barbara's office with her, but the others were elsewhere in the world: General Nabiyev, who replaced General Ospanov after his murder of the Al Jazeera reporters; President Karimov of Kazakhstan; U.S.

Secretary of State Obama in Washington; General Ruiz of NATO in Brussels . . .

"I've had Ink verify the timing of the satellite photos that Representative Bondarenko gave to us, Klaus," Barbara said. "The conclusion he drew appears to be absolutely correct—the hospital is the focal point. Whatever's caused this is coming from there, and still is. The fog, the disturbances: they're a nearly perfect and ever-widening circle, like a ripple in a pond—and the stone that caused the ripple is there in that hospital."

"All of us here are in agreement," Jayewardene responded. "We are ordering an attack on the hospital with the intention of wiping out whatever or whoever is causing this. General Nabiyev has ordered a tank division to be ready to enter the city. Drones have already proved useless within the affected area, and President Karimov has said—and we agree with him—that we can't just indiscriminately bomb the area because hundred or thousands of innocent citizens might die." Barbara saw Karimov's solemn, pudgy face nod a few seconds afterward.

"Klaus," Babel said. "We want you and the major aces there with you—maybe Bubbles, Earth Witch, Doktor Omweer, Aero, whomever you feel is best suited and willing—to accompany General Nabiyev's tanks, as an ace escort."

She hated saying that, and she hated the obvious eagerness in Klaus's face at the statement. At that moment she wanted nothing more than to *be* there with him, to be at his side rather than thousands of miles away. Fear dug fingers into her gut and twisted.

"Excellent," Klaus said after a brief delay, his smile broken in the erratic video feed. Behind him, she thought she glimpsed Michelle, Earth Witch, and the wings of Aero, with the fabric of a tent behind them. Through the tent's open flap, she could see a lowering sun nearing the horizon. "We'll be happy to do that. It's better than sitting here. Don't worry. We'll take care of whatever is behind this."

"Then it's settled," Jayewardene said. "We'll leave the details of the mission to you and General Nabiyev. I believe we're done here. Secretary Obama, if you'd please relay to President van Rennsaeler how much we appreciate her cooperation. Thank you all. I know everyone's busy, so I'll simply say how grateful I am for everyone's work, and we will all stay in touch. And with that, I'll leave all of you to your work." The screens, after similar statements, began to flicker out, one by one.

"Klaus," Barbara said quickly, hoping he'd hear her with the lag in distance before he broke the connection. "Stay with me, please . . ." Several seconds later, all the screens were blank except for his. Barbara glanced at Jayewardene, who nodded understandingly, and left the office. As the door closed behind him, Barbara realized she didn't know what to say, or rather had so much she wanted to say to Klaus that the clutter of the words stopped her voice.

He smiled at her. "I'll be fine," he told her, as if he understood her silence.

She summoned up an expression to match his own, which was more difficult to do than she thought it would be. They talked, with a few seconds' pause between each exchange. "You'd damn well better be."

"You don't need to worry about me."

"But I do. And I will until I know you're safe. If I were there—" She bit off the rest of what she was going to say. "I know. I'm needed here."

"You are. Look at what you've accomplished already for us." His hand waved, almost angrily, she thought. "You can navigate all the *scheisse* that they throw at us. I can't, at least not well. I just get angry. I'm best here."

"We're best together, my love."

He smiled again. "Yah," he answered. "And we will be again. Soon."

"You promise?"

"I swear it."

"I talked to Michelle earlier today. She said things were really confused there. Klaus, I can't help but be worried, especially stuck back here."

His smile dissolved. "We both know the risks, *mein Liebe*. This is what we were given our gifts to do."

"Just don't take any risks that you don't have to."

"I won't. I have a lot of incentive to come back, after all."

"I'll make it worth your effort, I promise," she told him. She kissed her own fingertip, then pressed it against Klaus's lips on the screen. A moment later he did the same, his fingertip against hers.

"I have to go," Klaus told her.

"I know. So do I."

"I love you." They said the words together despite the time lag, and the synchronicity made them both laugh.

She wasn't sure which one of them ended the connection first.

Mollie wanted to go anywhere else, but she had to take Mom back to the farm. Somebody who didn't know the woman might have thought her mom had spent all her energy losing her shit at the hospital while the doctor recited an extensive list of injuries and surgeries. But Mollie's mom was stronger than that. Strong enough to bitch Mollie out the moment they returned.

"What did you do to them?"

"Mom, I didn't do anything—"

"You didn't do ANYTHING? You didn't fill our barn with stolen slot machines from God-knows-where? You didn't convince your father and your brothers to go along with another one of your stupid ideas? You didn't try to cheat the man who *killed my Todd?*"

It always came back to that. It always came back to Noel and the Nshombos' gold and those awful few moments in the barn.

"He was my brother, too," said Mollie. Her voice was unrecognizable, hoarse and small, stomped flat by guilt and regret.

"Yeah, 'was.' He *was* my son. He died because of you. But that wasn't enough, was it? No, you gotta put your father and half your brothers in the hospital. You won't be happy until you kill this whole family, will you?"

"*I DIDN'T KILL TODD!* Stop carrying his coffin. Stop acting like I'm the one who shot him! It was my idea but Dad and the boys agreed to it. It was *their choice.*"

"They never should have listened to you. I'll make sure nobody in this family ever listens to you again."

Mollie pointed to the kitchen table. "You sat right there! You sat *right there* and listened to my suggestion and you agreed with everybody else that it was a terrific fucking idea to steal that gold! You're just as guilty of Todd's death as I am. Stop acting like it's all on me."

A trio of heads poked around the corner. The yelling had summoned the younger boys. Mom hadn't even waited to tell them their dad and brothers were in the hospital before rounding on Mollie.

"It is on you!" she cried. "It's all on you. If not for you none of this would have happened. It wouldn't have happened back then and it wouldn't have happened today."

Not fair. Maybe it was true. But it wasn't fair. She didn't know. How could she?

"How could I have known any of this would happen? How can you blame me for not knowing the future?"

Mom said, "I blame them. They should have known how stupid you are. They should have known your ideas are stupid and dangerous."

"No. They all made their own choices. You're just as guilty as I am. Have you ever asked yourself what might have happened if you'd actually weighed in with your own opinion for once?" Mollie paced. "No. You know what? This really is your fault. Because none of this would have happened if you hadn't convinced me to try out for that stupid game show in the first place!"

"You told us nothing could go wrong!" Veins bulged from Mom's forehead. "You told us it would be easy and that we'd all be rich!"

"Well, at least I tried. Instead of watching game shows all day and wishing somebody would wave a magic wand and make me rich without any effort, like you do."

The slap actually turned Mollie's head. The pain came an instant later, the hot sting where, she knew, her face already sported a pink handprint. A warm, salty breeze gusted into the kitchen from the portal to an Australian beach that opened in the kitchen wall.

Mom yelled, "Don't you go nowhere, Mollie Steunenberg! Don't you run away again and leave me with this. You stick around and take me back to the hospital in the morning."

The portal snapped shut. Mollie stomped out of the kitchen. En route to the spare linen closet for blankets and a pillow so she could sleep on the downstairs sofa, she barged past the three youngest Steunenberg boys.

"What did you do now to make Mom so mad?"

"Yeah, why is Mom crying?"

"Mollie, where's Dad and the others?"

"Fuck off, turdlet."

"Klaus? Is it true, the reports about Bugsy and Lama?"

The carrier line of the satellite phone hissed as she waited for Klaus's reply over the private and secure channel—she wished she could see his face, but this was nothing she wanted to leak out. The report that Ink had given her was frightening: Bugsy having lost a huge percentage of his wasps and eating the survivors, the Lama gone mad and spouting gibberish, then running back into the fog . . .

Klaus, I want you back here . . .

Klaus's voice was serious and curiously flat-sounding. "It's true. We think someone's weaponized the wild card virus."

Barbara forced herself to sound calm. "We think the same here. I've talked to CDC and to the UN doctors, and I've spoken with the Red Crescent people. They're sending full-face filter masks for you that should keep you from inhaling the virus. The worse part is that it appears the virus has been altered so that people who've already been infected—like Lama and Bugsy—can be infected again. Klaus, maybe going in isn't the best option. Maybe programming some cruise missiles to hit the hospital . . ."

She heard his protest beginning before she could finish. "Too much potential for collateral damage, and the drones we've already sent in get wonky. We wouldn't have any assurance that the same wouldn't happen with missiles. God knows where they'd actually come down. No, we have to go in ourselves, so we can control the situation." He paused for a second, but began speaking again before she could respond. "Babs, I sent them in. And I'm going to make sure that whoever did this pays for it. In full."

There was an undertone of pleasure in his statement. She could hear it even over the phone. *Being in action. Doing something, not sitting behind a desk, getting his hands dirty. That's what drives him . . . and some of the others, too.* She glanced at his photo on the desk—taken several years ago, before he lost his eye, before he'd lost the friends he'd once had. That Klaus smiled in a way she hadn't seen him smile for a long time. She wondered what his expression looked like now, at the thought of going into Talas, of gaining revenge for whoever had injured Bugsy and Lama. "I'm planning to split the group up into two teams as soon as we're inside the perimeter," he was saying. "Michelle will be with Aero and Earth Witch, doing some general scouting of the area and hopefully finding Lama. Angel, Inkar, and myself will be accompanying the tanks to the hospital and dealing with whatever's there."

"And everyone will be wearing the filter masks," Barbara said.

She heard him give a huff that might have been exasperation. "Everyone will be wearing the masks," he answered. "I need to get things moving on our end, Barbara. There isn't much time. Thanks for your help. Don't worry yourself. We'll be fine."

"I know you will," she told him, "but that won't stop me worrying."

"Understood," he said. "I love you."

"And I love you. So stay safe."

"I will," he told her, and with that, the connection was gone. Barbara placed the satellite phone in its cradle and leaned back in her chair. She stared at Klaus's picture for several breaths, then pressed the intercom button on the side of her computer monitor. "Juliet," she said to Ink, "let's get the conference room set up. I want to be able to watch all the video feeds from Talas."

Klaus tapped his finger on the map next to the pin indicating the hospital complex, then slid his finger down the main road leading to the military encampment.

"There's no reason to be subtle going in," he said. "We go in together, then split into two groups. The first group will be mine. We'll head up the main boulevard with a platoon of your men, General. We'll also take the tanks. Doktor Omweer, Angel, Tinker, and Inkar, you'll come with my group. Michelle, I want you to lead a second group. You, Earth Witch, Recycler, and Aero. Take a squad with you and a couple of Hummers. You're going after the last location we had for Bugsy before his transmitter went dead."

She nodded. "Once we get Bugsy, we'll rendezvous with you." She didn't want to say anything, but she thought the soldiers might slow the aces down. But she also knew that the Kazakh soldiers wanted their people out as much as the Committee people wanted theirs. They'd figure it out. Making things work was what she did.

Franny had been mulling possible escape plans. Unfortunately they all crumbled to ash the minute he walked down the steps of the plane. It wasn't Tomlin. It was a small airport that judging by the direction of the skyline of Manhattan was in fucking New Jersey. Also judging by the westering sun it was sometime in the afternoon. Franny realized he had no idea what day it was. Maybe Thursday?

There was also a welcoming committee. Seven large men in cheap suits with distinctive bulges beneath their arms. In the center was a dapper little man with milk-white hair and a ridiculously luxurious mustache. Franny recognized him from the NYPD files—Ivan Grekor, the most ruthless and efficient Russian mob boss in New York.

The wrinkles around Grekor's eyes deepened as he smiled at Baba Yaga. Opening his arms wide he called out in Russian. She replied in the same language. Franny heard his name float by. They were surrounded by the phalanx of guards and hustled into the small white terminal building. Franny saw a sign and realized they were at the Teterboro airport.

There were more Russian goons inside and support staff, TSA customs people, and a few well-dressed travelers huddled on the floor. One security guard was unconscious and bleeding. Franny couldn't control the impulse so he ran over and dropped to one knee next to the man, felt for a pulse.

"He won't die of it, young man," Grekor said, amusement lacing the words. He glanced at Baba Yaga. "Mariamna, you are picking them younger and younger."

Baba Yaga gave a crack of laughter at Franny's horrified look. "Oh, this one is not a toy for the bed, Ivan, just a tool for the hand."

Franny stood. "Trust me when I tell you that doesn't sound any less creepy."

Baba Yaga looked from Franny to the unconscious man and back again. "You see what happens when you try to be a hero? You understand what I am saying, yes?"

"Yeah, you're coming in loud and clear."

"Good."

"Mariamna, what do you wish to do now?" Grekor asked. "I worry for you. You are hurt."

She gave him that mirthless smile. "Yes. I need a hospital. Someplace we can control. From which I can direct events."

Grekor stroked the absurd mustache and frowned off into space. "The Jokertown Clinic. Not too large, not a lot of security and doctors that specialize in the wild card."

"Jokers," Baba Yaga said with disgust.

"And aces."

Franny felt a surge of hope. The clinic wasn't all that far from Fort Freak and help and he'd have a better chance escaping from the old bitch and her army of goons there.

The hospital called a few hours later. Mick had been the lucky one, escaping the carnage with just a few broken bones. Mollie opened a portal to the hospital in Coeur d'Alene the third time that day, and helped Mick back into the farmhouse.

They didn't speak to each other. They barely looked at one another, each barely acknowledging the other. To acknowledge each other was to accept as real the confusing and horrifying "incident" in the barn.

That's the word they used. Incident. As though that word were large enough to contain the mindless homicidal ragestorm that had swirled through the barn.

Families fought sometimes, sure. She and her brothers had blackened each other's eyes, even loosened a tooth here and there when they were younger. But even the most dysfunctional families in the world, the most fucked-up lowlife reality-TV hillbilly families from one of Berman's sleaziest productions never tried to *pull out each other's intestines*. And yet there in the Steunenberg barn she'd felt it was necessary . . .

Accepting its reality meant accepting they were all just half a heartbeat from murdering each other, from setting upon each other with extraordinary ferocity. To accept that an indescribable viciousness lurked inside each of them, and that it could break free without a moment's notice. It didn't make any fucking sense. And that was the most horrifying part of the whole thing—it *had* made sense when it was happening, like there was a logic that only Mollie could see . . .

She couldn't stand the feeling of being trapped inside her own skin. Of being trapped inside the person who had thought and done those things and had yearned to do still more. Mollie's ace made her very, very good at running away from trouble, but she couldn't run away from herself.

Too tired to endure the angry, accusing glances from Mick and Mom, Mollie went out to the barn. She hosed down everything, sluicing away the blood and the teeth and the gobbets of flesh. Then she used a cutting torch and the hydraulic jack to take out all her shame and frustration on Baba Yaga's safe.

Of course, the fucking thing was empty.

The loose change from the slot machines had to be changed into dollars before it was any use. The coinage was heavier than hell, too. Hundreds of pounds. But at least dealing with it was a simple mindless task that didn't require conversation. That struck Mollie just fine. Mick was too dinged up with painkillers and casts to do much work, but the younger boys sorted the foreign currency and separated the coins into luggable quantities. Mollie opened doorways in search of cities where she could change Kazakh tenge into real American dollars. It wasn't easy to find places; it was like she really had stolen Monopoly money. Half the places hadn't even heard of tenge. And when she did find currency exchanges familiar with the exotic monies of Bumfuckistan, the rate sucked out loud.

Scouting currency exchanges proved exhausting, far harder than it should have been. A regular day for Mollie had her traveling around the world twice before breakfast. This should have been a snap. Scouting the exchanges should have been the work of an hour, tops. But the doorways didn't want to cooperate. Sometimes they slipped away from her, closing before she intended, or taking an extra few seconds to open and close. Sometimes they didn't open where she wanted them to. Each time she fixated on the transdimensional weirdness to try to force the goddamned things to cooperate, she remembered the portal she'd opened *inside* Brent's body, Dad's pitchfork going straight through into himself . . . She'd never done that before. Never even contemplated opening a portal on somebody's person. It was as though her ace had become contaminated by that single action, and now she confronted a self-doubt she hadn't experienced since the first few days after her card turned.

What if she accidentally opened a doorway into the center of another homicidal cannibal ragestorm flashmob like the one in Talas? It had come without warning. How could she know it wouldn't happen again at the next location, or the next, or the next? It was difficult to open a door when the abject terror of what you might find on the other side had you pissing your pants.

She hit the sack on the farmhouse's downstairs sofa after changing every last coin from Talas. She fell asleep almost instantly, still in her clothes. It wasn't restful sleep. She woke up every hour or so, panting and damp with sweat from a nightmare that put her on that street in Talas, where she was a willing member of the crowd that hurled itself upon a twitching baby, or in the barn, striving to murder her family.

Lohengrin was fuming. It took five hours to get the tanks on the road when it should have taken, the Angel thought, fifteen, twenty minutes, tops. There were four tanks, an ace with each, along with a couple of platoons of Kazakhstan regular army. They looked professional and smart. All were well armed and wore night goggles. An advance squad melted fearlessly into the dark ruins ahead of the column, two others flanked right and left. Lohengrin was riding the lead tank, the Angel was on the second. Earth Witch walked alongside the third, while the tall, striking figure of Doktor Omweer stalked behind the fourth.

The Angel was appalled as she looked around the twisted, blackened landscape, cast in the eerie light of night-vision goggles. It was as if she were witnessing hell on earth, as if God himself, the perpetually angry Yahweh of the Old Testament who had so frightened her when she was a child, had reached out a vengeful hand and blasted the city of Talas.

The air stank of demons, or at least how she imagined demons stank. Maybe it was the eerie green mist that was everywhere, forming a thick carpet near the ground and casting tendrils and tentacles over the ruins through which they moved. It caressed her face with a strange, moist, greasy touch that made her screw up her face in distaste. It was like an unsavory miasma boiling off a nearby swamp. But there was no nearby swamp, no discernible origin for it.

An old memory struck the Angel. It was when she'd been working for ex-President Leo Barnett's Millennial Society and had rescued John Fortune from the Allhumbrados, met Billy Ray, and saved the world from the Apocalypse. At one point while running from the Enlightened Ones they'd called in an ace known as the Highwayman who could secretly transport people and/or contraband via what he called "shortcuts," which were actually paths through alternate dimensions. The smell of Talas reminded her of an odor they'd encountered in that alien dimension. She had no idea how that could be. But it gave her a queasy feeling she tried to thrust aside, knowing full well that she had to stay on the alert and discard all distracting thoughts. But like the very tendrils of the greenish mist itself, the notion seemed to creep over her at odd moments and caress her very brain, sending shivers she couldn't ignore down her spine.

They worked their way from the city outskirts to its interior, the only sounds the clanking from the metallic beasts that led the way, the rumblings like growls from their engines. In the lights of their bright lidless eyes she could see that the damage around them was increasing. Some buildings had been reduced to rubble, slowing the tanks as they made their way down deserted but debris-choked streets. The fog grew deeper, turning into a pall that hung in the air like filthy shrouds, unmoving in the hot, breeze-less sky, like the noxious fogs that choked nineteenth-century London often described in the historical romances she read. The stench also grew stronger.

The scattered soldiers, perhaps unconsciously, pulled closer to the dubious protection offered by the tanks. They suddenly stumbled to a halt as their engines died and their headlights went off. Simultaneously, ahead of them the sounds of automatic gunfire suddenly crashed through the night. Shrieks of pain and fear followed. The gunfire cut off as suddenly as it had begun.

Lohengrin, who'd been speaking lowly into his com unit, giving a running report on their progress, suddenly turned and shouted, "Angel!"

"Save my soul from evil, Lord," she murmured, not only to call her sword to her but also as a fervent prayer that she hoped would send her the grace she needed. Wings of feather and flame appeared on her back, lighting up the night around them. They reached higher than her head and their tips swept the ground and they were wide enough to enfold Billy to her in intimate moments when she was careful to keep the flames damped; she never felt their weight nor even was quite sure how they remained attached to her. In truth, like Peregrine's, the first winged ace, they weren't large enough to get and actually keep her airborne, but she never stopped to analyze her powers. She just accepted them on faith.

"Help the scouts," Lohengrin shouted. "If you can't—find the epicenter of this, this activity. Report back as soon as you can. We need the information! Everything's gone dark—even to infrared."

She nodded again, flapped once, twice, and rose slowly into the air. She attained a height of twenty feet and shot forward, arrowing ahead to where the scouts should be. She pulled the now useless night goggles off her face and tossed them away. The only light in the city was thrown off by the divine flames that ran on her wings. She thanked God that they lit her path, flickering in the dark like candles.

The Angel hovered, her wings barely flapping. She'd reached the position where the scouts should be. There wasn't much to see except the vista of awful destruction. She unholstered her cell phone and speed-dialed Lohengrin to report in, but was not hopeful that it would be working. It wasn't. It was dead as disco. What in the world was going on?

She hung in the air a moment, undecided. She looked around at the devastation and something caught her eye. It was a blot, a big, shining dot, glowing atop a partially destroyed building, which, despite the damage to it, was the tallest standing structure in the vicinity. She put the cell away and raised the binocs she carried in what Billy laughingly called her utility belt.

It was like . . . for a moment her brain froze and she couldn't decide what it was like, other than the most grotesque thing she'd ever seen, including the creatures she'd seen when she and Billy had braved the Highwayman's shortcut. It was bigger than she was. Its head and body were ratlike with phosphorescent fur, beady black eyes, and a pink, naked nose surrounded by bristles. It supported herself on too many legs, the Angel thought, white, bony, multiply-jointed and spindly legs that looked like gigantic crab legs, complete with clacking claws and armored with knobby spikes and sharp-looking spines. Its wings dwarfed its body. They were black and rubbery-looking, like bat's wings shot through with crinkled red veins and ending in long, clawed, graspy-looking skeletal hands. Its naked pink tail dangled down between its legs to the roof of the building on which it crouched. At least, the Angel thought it was its tail.

The binoculars brought it startlingly close. So close, in fact, that when it looked up at her and made eye contact she could see the glint of intelligence in its eyes, as well as the saliva that dripped in oozy ropes from between its far too many sharp, pointed teeth. It opened its mouth and in a loud, high-pitched, ear-hurting tone cried, "Squeeeeeeeeee!" and launched itself in the air.

It came right at her, fast.

Its body, the Angel realized, was at least twice the size of her own, its wingspan ten times hers. The thing between its legs was an angry red stinger that arched upward, thick greyish liquid glistening on its barbed tip.

Choking back a useless expletive, the Angel slung the binoculars around her neck and beat her wings hard, trying to gain altitude as quickly as she could. If this was to be a dogfight, she wanted the higher sky.

The stench of it reached her before it did. Naturally, its odor was a repulsive, mephitic stink wrapped in the sugary, rotten scent of overripe bananas. It was bigger than she was, probably stronger, and had a longer reach and more weapons. Her only hope might lie in her agility.

She could hear the clattering that came from the clawed tips of its legs, which were clacking like castanets. She turned and realized that she'd misjudged its speed and it smashed into her shoulder and a clawed leg tore her side. The force of the collision pushed them apart. It tried to grab her with its skeletal legs, but a desperate swipe of her sword sliced one cleanly off.

Its explosive chitter rattled angrily, as did the tip of its angry red tail. The Angel somersaulted helplessly away, thankfully missing the gooey substance it had flung at her. She folded her wings around her and snap-turned on a dime, slipped behind it streaking upward, sword first. She swiped at a great leathery expanse of wing, struck it glancingly and the blade bounced off its leathery surface. The beast tucked itself into a ball, flipped forward, and struck the Angel with its back. The blow buffeted her and knocked the wind out of her lungs. Gasping for breath, she lost her sword and control of her flight path.

So much for my superior agility, she thought as she spiraled downward.

The creature came out of the tuck position with its head pointed downward and snapped its wings open. The air filled them like sails and it rotated to soar right at her, still upside down, all three pairs of legs and six claws outspread and open to embrace her.

When she'd first acquired the ability to call up her flaming wings she was moderately capable in their use, but complicated stunts had been beyond her. It had been Billy's idea to call upon Peregrine and the aging though still glamorous ace had been unstinting with her time, experience, and the knowledge she'd accumulated over decades of flying, going back to her early days of fame as "the flying cheerleader." The Angel called upon that training, calmed her mind as the air returned to her lungs, and took a deep breath.

The monster was almost upon her, drooling as it smiled. She rotated her body away from the approaching bulk and banked sharply. She was, she realized, quicker than the beast. She had less mass to maneuver, and with her ace strength, more power to maneuver with. She wanted nothing to do with a face-to-face encounter with the thing. It could still outreach her and had too many weapons to bring to bear. Her first instinct to attack from behind had been correct. She'd just chosen the wrong target.

She went in without her sword and as the thing tried to follow her pulled a perfect Immelmann roll to end up behind it, positioning herself for another attack. She put on as much speed as possible and slammed into its back as it tried to swerve away. She grabbed handfuls of greasy-feeling fur to pull herself up to its neck, clamped her knees high up on its torso, and snaked a strong arm under its snapping jaws.

She gripped the arm encircling the monstrosity's neck with her other hand and yanked with all her strength, cutting off the outraged scream that erupted from the rat-bat's throat as well as any possibility of more air going down it. And then she hung on like grim death.

The skeletal hands at its wingtips couldn't reach her, nor could the claws on its legs. It shook its head from side to side, but the slavering jaws were useless. It darted and jinked like a burning moth, but nothing could break the Angel's death-grip. She kept squeezing and jerking and finally she felt something give under the awful pressure she was applying to the thing's throat, and with a final surge of strength she heard an audible crack and the monster's neck snapped.

She screamed in triumph but didn't let go until a moment later when she felt the thing's body sag like a rag doll. Its wings ceased to flap, the arc of its flight flattened, and they started to plummet to the ground. The Angel hung on for a final few moments, breathing deeply despite the creature's stench, and then she finally kicked away from the falling corpse and flapped her wings to hover momentarily while gathering strength from her almost depleted reserves. She watched it fall a couple of hundred feet. It made a satisfyingly loud sound when it struck the roof of a building far below, crashed through it, and disappeared from her sight.

She dallied for a moment, considering her next action. She already had the feeling that things weren't exactly going as Lohengrin and Babel had planned, but she also realized that the one thing they desperately needed to complete their mission was up-to-the-minute information on the situation on the ground. Turning back wouldn't get that information. Going forward, whatever other bizarre dangers she faced, might.

She decided to fly farther into the city and check out the spot that Lohengrin had said was the epicenter of all this strangeness. It might not be the smart thing to do, she thought, but it was the thing she had to do.

If she'd thought that the encampment was a mess, Talas was turning out to be a disaster. Their job was to extract Bugsy, but the conditions were getting worse. They'd had a general idea where Bugsy was—at least until his tracker had gone dead.

The fog continued to thicken the farther they went into the city. Michelle was already having trouble seeing the others through the hazmat mask, but Klaus and Barbara had insisted on everyone wearing one.

Not sure this is going to do me any good after the faceful of blood I took, she thought.

They were on foot now, having abandoned the Hummers a few klicks back. First, the radio had started going wonky, and then the navigation system had stopped working. Finally the power steering had gone out, and handling a Hummer without it was damn near impossible.

Maybe Klaus had been wrong about splitting up, but it was too late to worry about that now. It was too late for a lot of things.

The fog was thick here and made the buildings look hazy and insubstantial. She felt eyes staring at them from darkened windows. Appraising them. Hungering for them. It was the same for every building, the small stores, clothing shops, and restaurants. The stench of rotting food escaped the groceries they passed. The buildings around them were all possessed by whatever was residing here now.

Those malevolent eyes watched them. She tried not to think about how that felt like a spider was crawling across her flesh—or more like a thousand spiders.

The blocky modern apartments were the worst. There were faces in almost every window, deformed by whatever was happening here, though some looked as if they'd mutilated themselves. They stared down at the group with cold malice.

Michelle was tempted to bubble some of them, just to send a warning, but held herself in check. They were a small group and even though it was likely they could take on one building's occupants, Michelle didn't want the trouble of protecting the soldiers and fighting off who-knew-what.

The soldiers were becoming a major pain in her ass. And she wasn't even sure Aero, Recycler, and Earth Witch weren't going to drag her down, too. A surge of anger went through her. It was always like this. She wanted to do something *now*. Get rid of them all, so she could go in alone. It would be much easier that way.

The fog was slowing them down. Whatever was happening in Talas had caused wholesale chaos.

The streets had buckled as if a 6.0 earthquake had just happened. Cars were abandoned willy-nilly in the street. Some had ended up on the sidewalk, some halfway into the sides of buildings. Windows were smashed. Fires smoldered in the street. Clots of people ran shrieking through the mist. But when Michelle's group tried to catch up to them, they vanished as if they'd never been there. Blood and shit covered the street, and severed limbs were worming their way through both.

The group stopped and stared.

"How could this be a weaponized wild card attack?" Aero asked. And then he started gagging. After a moment, he managed to get control of himself. "If I believed in hell, this is what it would look like."

"I'm beginning to think we're in an upper level," Ana replied. "It's been getting worse the farther we go in."

"We should keep moving," Michelle said. She tried to keep a tremor out of her voice. What had they walked into?

They turned down a street that had been on the map as being the way to Bugsy's location. Bodies were tied to almost every streetlight, garbed in tattered and blood-soaked clothes. All of them had had their intestines ripped out and left to dangle. Then Michelle saw the knives in their hands. They had killed themselves, she realized. Bile rose in the back of her throat. Someone had tied them to the lampposts, and they ripped out their own intestines. Rictus grins were plastered on their faces.

"*Madre de Dios*," she heard Aero say as if he were very far away.

Mary won't help them or us, she thought. *I thought you weren't religious, you liar. Turning to a God that isn't there.*

She heard someone whimpering. She turned around to see who it was.

One of the Kazakh soldiers was trying to tear his hazmat mask off. She ran to him and grabbed his wrists. "Stop!" she cried. "You've got to keep your mask on!" *Idiot,* she thought with a stab of anger. *Why the hell am I stuck with all these fucking idiots?*

"He doesn't speak English, miss," one of the other soldiers said. "I can translate."

"And you are?" *Another pain in my ass.*

"Nurlan. He's Dasha."

It would be so easy to just kill you both, she thought. And for a tiny moment, that thought horrified her.

"Tell Dasha everything is fine," she said, though she didn't believe it for a moment. They hadn't been in the fog zone that long, and already the stupid behavior was starting. And that pissed her off to no end. The soft buzzing in her head was getting louder.

Nurlan spoke to Dasha. When Dasha answered, Nurlan got an odd expression on his face.

"He says the faceless god is coming."

Michelle was perplexed, then utterly exasperated. She'd *known* they would be a drag on the mission. "What does that mean?"

"I don't know," Nurlan said. He licked his lips nervously. "He's just babbling now."

"For fuck's sake," Michelle said. Her annoyance grew. And grew. Part of her realized she was overreacting, but she couldn't stop herself. She didn't *want* to stop this terrifying anger. And the buzzing grew louder.

"Oh, good grief, we don't have time for this bullshit. Look at those corpses. They're *real*. Some invisible whatever is bullshit. Talk him down. Do whatever you have to do to get him moving." Her gaze swept across the other soldiers. They appeared to be okay, but a couple of them did look a bit twitchy.

Just what I need, she thought bitterly. Babysitting some wet-behind-the-ears nats. Fabulous.

I could kill them, she thought. *I could kill them and make all this easier. They're nothing but a burden slowing me down. Just like Adesina.* A wave of nausea swept over her. *Oh, God, how could I think that? I'd never think that. She's my baby. My little girl.*

But she couldn't dwell on Adesina. Not now. There was something in Talas that needed to be done, or her baby would die. Jayewardene had been specific about it. She had to go to Talas or her daughter would die.

"Okay, people, we need to keep moving toward Bugsy's last location, and we're not doing that by standing around," she said. Her voice was tight with annoyance. Her anger felt like an itch she wanted to scratch, and it swept away her fear about Adesina. She felt the tingling of a bubble forming, but balled her hand tight and popped it.

Earth Witch and Aero flanked the soldiers, and Recycler took up the rear. Michelle was on point. She turned and started off again, not bothering to see if any of them were following.

With each step, the fog obscured more of their path. A cold drizzle began to fall. In the distance, she heard shouts and screams. Occasionally, there was gunfire. There was also a static squawk on her com. Klaus checking up on her, no doubt. Checking on her as if she were some rookie who didn't know what the hell she was doing. *Screw him,* she thought. *All the fucks I give about Klaus and his band of pussies. I've got a batch of useless nats to drag around.*

Up ahead, Michelle saw a blurry, vaguely human shape standing in the road. Then it began to change. Tentacles grew out of it, and it began slithering toward them.

Dasha's whimpering got louder. "For God's sake," Michelle snarled. "Get him to knock that off!" She turned around. Six of the soldiers looked fine, but the other four had horrified expressions on their faces. Then they bolted, heading back in the direction they'd come from.

"You've *got* to be kidding me!" Michelle snapped. "This is just a joker of some kind. Good Lord, you'd think they'd never seen a joker before."

There was a burst of gunfire. Aero screamed, "No!" as the soldiers who hadn't fled began firing at the ones who had. The fleeing soldiers collapsed. They didn't move.

Then they turned and opened fire on the joker who had advanced on the group.

The joker—for what else could it be—gave a hideous scream, and everyone cried out in pain. It felt as if someone had jabbed ice picks in her ears.

"I can't believe you killed them!" Aero exclaimed. His face was twisted into a mask of rage. The soldiers looked back at him.

"Why not?" Nurlan asked with a shrug. Sweat was running down his face, and the whites of his eyes were turning red. "They were deserting. They were running away from that." He pointed at the dead joker.

"You don't shoot someone in the back! Jesús Christo! You animals!" His voice deepened and took on a dangerous growl. Michelle saw him reach into his pocket and pull out one of the steel balls he used to create shrapnel with his air-manipulation power.

"Cesar! No!" she shouted. But part of her was perfectly fine with Aero killing the soldiers. Part of her wanted to help him do it.

"They're subhuman," he snarled. "They don't deserve to live."

"You don't get to be judge and jury," Ana shouted. Her face turned red. The cords in her neck bulged. "How would you like it if I judged you the same way?" She spat the words out.

The earth at Aero's feet suddenly bulged upward and encased him up to his neck. He couldn't move, much less release his weapon. But Michelle knew he didn't need his weapons to kill Ana.

"We're not them," Ana said. Her eyes were wild, and she was breathing heavily. "We're better than that."

Nurlan looked at Ana with a cold, indifferent expression on his face.

"Why are you better? That one"—he pointed at Michelle—"has killed before. I believe you have, too, Earth Witch. I don't know about Aero.

However, the slum dweller—" He jerked his thumb at Recycler. "He doesn't have the balls to do anything. Unless it's stabbing someone in the back."

Recycler immediately pulled more debris onto his already large trash armor. Broken tables and chairs sailed through smashed windows. Cardboard boxes ripped apart, then were reconfigured on his body. Stinking, rotting foliage flew toward him, leaving foul, ropy streams of water behind. As his armor grew, he uttered a single harsh laugh.

"You *cadela*," he said, fury twisting his voice. "Stupid asshole." He started toward the soldier. In an instant, the ground opened under him, and he dropped into the hole.

"When I get out of here, you're dead!" he yelled at Ana. "I'll tear your head off just to see the blood squirt from your neck, you whore." Ana shrugged and laughed. He began climbing out of the hole, but she just made it deeper.

One of the soldiers turned his rifle on Ana. Michelle grabbed her and turned around, shielding Ana's body from the flying bullets. *Just like Ana,* she thought sourly. *Always needing to be rescued. Useless. Not a man jack of them who deserves to be on this mission. It would be so easy . . .*

As the bullets hit, Michelle grew fatter. But today, the impacts hurt. She screamed in pain. "What the fuck?" she cried.

There was another hail of bullets, but they didn't hit Michelle. She released Ana and turned around to see the soldiers firing on each other. They giggled like children at a party, and one by one, they fell. The dead solders were unrecognizable now. Eyes hung from shattered sockets. The bullets had ripped off cheeks, exposing teeth and gums. Scalps flapped off skulls like bad toupees.

Only Nurlan remained standing. He turned toward her and Michelle saw blood dripping from his eyes.

He pulled off his hazmat mask. Then he removed his holstered Makarov PM and shot himself in the head.

Secretary-General Jayewardene sat at the conference table across from Barbara. At the front of the room, at the head of the table, screens were set up with a few live feeds: one from the lead tank in the Kazakh squad, another from the officer leading the Kazakh assault, and another—on the largest screen directly in front of Barbara—from a body cam attached to

Klaus. A screen to one side held General Nabiyev, so that the three of them could consult during the operation. Ink was in the office with Barbara. It was nearly five-thirty in New York; well after midnight in Kazakhstan. Headlamps from the tanks and accompanying vehicles swept over mostly empty streets, with abandoned cars on either side of the roadway, most of them pushed aside by dozers earlier. The image from Klaus's body cam was tinted heavily green; his camera had a night-vision lens. "We're getting close to the edge of the disturbance," she heard Klaus say. His voice was heavy with his breathing; in the night-vision view, his ghost steel armor looked emerald, and his sword gleamed like a CGI weapon in a science fiction movie. Ahead of them, the fog extended sickly green tendrils high above the roadway. The video was jumpy and unstable, moving with each of Klaus's strides. "Nothing's moving out there that we can see, though listen . . ." His voice went silent except for his breathing and the video stilled as Klaus stopped. Barbara could hear the sound of the tanks' motors and the metallic clanking of their treads on concrete, but, faintly, they also could hear screams in the distance, more than one, and at least one of the voices sounded entirely nonhuman. "Did you get that?" Klaus said a moment later, and the video jumped as he started walking again. "There's something going on not too far ahead." An electronic chirp followed: Klaus shifting to the private communications channel for the aces. "Aero—want to check it out? See what we're heading into before we split up?"

Another chirp, and a voice answered from a speaker set on the conference table, set to that private channel so she and Jayewardene could overhear their communications. "Sure, boss. Be right back . . ." and a moment later, they saw his form flit by overhead.

Then there was nothing but the static of the satellite relay for several seconds, then a click: "It's damn hard to see in this soup, and with this damn thing strapped to my head . . ." Aero's voice, muffled by his filter mask. There was a scraping sound, then. "God, it smells horrible, like dead things rotting everywhere. What the hell . . ." They heard a shriek, a banshee-like howling, then more cursing, and a scream that was all too human, followed by a sickening thud.

"Aero?" she heard Klaus say, then again, more urgently. "Aero?" Silence answered, and in the video feed, Klaus's body cam swayed wildly as he started to run. "Everyone! Let's go. Michelle and Ana, find Aero. Inkar, you're with me . . ."

Barbara's hands curled into involuntary fists on the table as she saw

Klaus racing ahead of the slow-moving tanks and into the puke-green haze. Inkar, in her Tulpar form, a golden winged horse, raced ahead of Lohengrin. The video quickly became nearly useless. She could see shapes looming in the gloom, some of the buildings and cars, but others moving. An antlered head . . . a waving, sucker-laced tentacle that Klaus's sword severed . . . a crowd of howling figures running . . .

On the video feed from the lead Kazakh tank, a *thing* came out of the fog: taller than a house, great spidered legs gouging the concrete of the roadway like gigantic pile drivers, its carapace above seeming to be composed of a dozen or more naked human bodies, writhing and wriggling like maggots inside a gelatinous sheath, their heads staring as one toward the tank, mouths open in screams of rage. Barbara could hear the creature, howling like a crazed mob, as the front two spider legs grabbed the turret of the tank, lifting and swinging it, sky and fog and ground spinning madly in the video, then that feed went dead.

The voices on the communications channel were equally chaotic, coming fast and on top of each other, so that Barbara could barely determine who was speaking and to whom; there were horrific sounds intermingled among the words. But what was oddly most terrifying was that someone started singing, and the voice was Klaus's.

". . . *Ein Jäger aus Kurpfalz* . . ."

". . . Aero, is that you? Aero, what the hell are you . . ."

". . . *der reitet durch den grünen Wald* . . ."

". . . I . . . I can't feel my hands . . ."

". . . *So komm ich weit umher* . . ."

". . . Who are you? Damn it, answer me or I swear . . ."

". . . *bis dass der Kuckuck 'Kuckuck' schreit* . . ."

". . . one little cut, two little cuts, three little cuts . . ."

". . . *Juja, Juja, gar lustig ist die Jägerei* . . ."

". . . Klaus? Where are you? . . . Oh Christ! Oh God no!"

". . . *allhier auf grüner Heid'* . . ."

". . . I'll kill you, you bastard. I'll kill you . . ."

On Klaus's screen, there was suddenly a lessening of the fog, and Barbara could see a child—a little girl in ragged, torn clothes, her dark hair scraggly and matted, her large eyes circled in bruised flesh. "Help me," she said in English, in a pitiful, weak voice. "Please help me."

". . . *allhier auf grüner Heid'.*" On the screen, she saw Klaus stop, his song ending. His armor-clad knee came into view: he'd knelt in front of her. "I have you, *kleines*," he said. "I can help you. Just come here. Come to me . . ." She saw Klaus's arm reach out to the child . . . and the child smiled, her mouth opening wide and wider still, impossibly, like a snake unhinging its jaw, and in the bloodred maw of the girl's mouth there were rows of needled teeth dripping a grey ichor. She lunged at Klaus, hissing, as the video feed tumbled into chaos and went dead.

Over the communications channel, she heard Klaus scream: a long wail of agony, and the sound pulled Barbara from her chair.

"Get them out of there!" Barbara shouted, at Jayewardene, at the flat screens, at General Nabiyev, and especially at the flickering, static-laden screen that had held Klaus. "Get them out! Klaus!"

She could feel Juliet's hand on her shoulder, pressing hard. "Klaus!" she shouted again. She was sobbing, not caring that Jayewardene and General Nabiyev could see. "Klaus, get out of there! Oh, God . . . I let him go there. I let him go there without me . . ." She sank back into her chair as Ink murmured unheard words, her arm around her, as Jayewardene asked General Nabiyev what was happening.

There was no answer beyond the static.

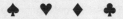

There had been armored limos waiting out front of Teterboro. Franny had hoped the caravan of Russian mobsters would be stopped, but Grekor was efficient. The people at Teterboro had been relieved of their cell phones, the landlines cut, and they'd been tied up. Eventually the lack of response from the tower would get someone's attention, but it was a quick trip into Manhattan and they had reached the clinic before that happened.

Franny had been handcuffed to a door handle in the limo and left with one guard while Grekor's goons entered the small hospital. Franny had jerked at the sound of gunfire, but it was only two shots. He prayed no one had been killed.

After some time had passed a thug arrived at the car, unlocked the cuffs, and dragged Franny into the clinic. He was taken to a room where Baba Yaga was ensconced in a hospital bed propped up by a mountain of pillows.

Dr. Finn was at her bedside, his hooves beating out a nervous tattoo on the floor. The joker's expression was mutinous and he kept throwing glares first at the man holding a gun on him and then at Baba Yaga. Grekor was seated in a chair looking very much at ease.

Finn reacted when Franny was pushed into the room. "Detective Black! Why are you . . . ? Do you know . . . ? Are you . . . ? Are you with these people?"

"Not willingly."

"I've been treating some of the kidnapped jokers. They said you rescued them."

"Yeah, I just didn't manage to rescue myself."

"Enough!" Baba Yaga snapped. "Time for you to do your job, errand boy. You will—"

Finn interrupted. "You have invaded my clinic, threatened my staff, locked up my security chief *after you shot at him*. You want medical care? Go find it someplace else. I won't do a damn thing for you."

Grekor looked over at one of his guards. "Start killing a patient every fifteen minutes."

Finn gaped at the man. Franny grabbed him by the upper arm. "They'll do it, Doc, trust me."

Baba Yaga fingered the sheet with her remaining hand and studied Finn. "I am certain there are other doctors here and I have always wanted a horse hair sofa," she mused. Her mouth began working.

"And *don't* piss her off," Franny added urgently.

"I know what she can do. The jokers told me." Finn had recovered his equilibrium. He approached the bed with mincing steps, placing each of his four hooves with elaborate care. "Yeah, you can kill me horribly, your thugs can shoot patients, but while we're treating you we can also kill you in a hundred different ways."

Baba Yaga leaned back, swallowed the accumulated spit, and studied Finn. "You're stupid brave. And what about your Hippocratic Oath, *Doctor*."

"It's flexible in your case. And I'm not so much brave as I have leverage. We have each other by the short hairs. You want care? Stop issuing threats." They stared at each other for a long time. It was a ludicrous sight. The ancient one-armed crone in the bed with her dual-colored hair, and the paunchy torso of a fifty-something man in a Hawaiian shirt and white coat set atop the body of a palomino pony. "So shall we call it a stalemate and move on?"

Baba Yaga cracked one of her wintery smiles and nodded. "All right."

She looked at Franny. "Go, bring me the Secretary-General of the UN and the head of the Committee. It is time they knew what they're facing."

"You've got a phone."

"You don't think I've tried?" she snapped. "They are all in a panic and no one will take my call."

Franny jerked a thumb at Grekor. "Send him. I'm going home." He turned and started for the door, only to hear the distinctive snick of rounds being chambered. He looked back at a phalanx of guns.

"No, you will go. Grekor is a known criminal. People think you are a hero. They don't know you are the hero who has destroyed the world. So why don't you go and try to undo some of the harm you have done? Also, I'll kill you if you don't," she added prosaically.

Dr. Finn was staring at him in confusion. All of Baba Yaga's taunts and accusations came crashing back: *"You're a fool, boy." ". . . you blundered in . . ." "You think you're a hero." ". . . destroyed the world. I hope it was worth it."*

"What?" Finn began.

"I've got to go."

Marcus paced out his agitation. He carved a long, sinuous oval on the dusty road. "We have to go," he whispered through gritted teeth. "Come on. Let's just go." He wasn't speaking to anybody but himself, and it wasn't the first time he'd said it. Now that Olena was safe, the only thing that mattered was getting out of here. Each passing minute of inactivity was torture, but time kept dragging on. Most of the villagers still talked among themselves in small groups. They cast uneasy glances at him, ones he couldn't read. A few had returned to homes, or gone off to do other things. Marcus wasn't sure he'd convinced anyone—even Olena—how much danger they were in.

A truck's engine rumbled to life. Timur, and the group of men he'd organized, climbed into the vehicle.

"Shit," Marcus said. He squirmed toward them. Palms held up, he cast his tail across the road, blocking it. "Don't go! You don't know what you're heading in to."

At first the men couldn't understand him. Both sides shouted at each other with increasing anger. Olena arrived and did her best to translate. Marcus said, "Tell them that when they get near the contagion the truck's engine will fail. It'll just die, and when it does it'll be too late for them to escape on foot." Olena spoke for him, but in answer Timur revved the truck's engine. He jolted forward a few feet, rocking it. Clearly, he had more faith in his engine than in Marcus's claims.

"You have to let them pass," Olena finally said.

"No."

"Yes, Marcus! They're free men and this is their village. They have the right to—"

She cut her words when a shout reached them. One of the village boys was hobbling up the main street, hard work with his deformed left leg. He shouted something over and over again.

"What's he saying?" Marcus asked.

Olena listened for longer than Marcus could stand, and then said, quietly, "Something is coming up the road."

Marcus caught the specificity of her wording. *Something.* Not someone. He said, "Tell Timur to wait a minute. Let's first see what this is. Tell him."

She did, and instead of driving away, the men climbed out of the vehicle and gathered at the edge of the village, looking down valley. It wasn't long before they saw it. A shape, pitch-black, appeared from around a turning in the dusty road, perhaps a hundred yards away. It was too wide and hunched to be human. Furred, bushy-looking. Whatever it was, it faced away from them, showing only its back, coming closer with a weaving diagonal gate. Marcus felt the familiar dread of the miasma drench him again. Just seeing this thing brought it back. It was talking. It was barely audible at first, a low whisper that, as soon as he heard it, Marcus wanted to listen to. *Needed* to listen to, the unintelligible sounds suddenly very important that he hear.

"What is it?" Olena asked.

"We should run." Marcus said it, and knew it to be true, but he didn't move. He couldn't help but stare at the approaching thing, listening to it. He wanted to grab Olena and slither away. He knew he should stir everyone into motion. In his mind he saw himself do that, felt himself forming the words and turning and yet . . . he stood stock-still, unable to move, waiting, and yet hating that he was waiting.

"Run," Olena said. "Yes, we should." But she didn't move either.

None of them did.

The thing kept backing toward them, moving in a crab-like sideways shuffle, first to one side, then cutting back the other way, getting closer all the time. In all the furred blackness of it, the thing that stood out were its eyes. Each time it angled toward them, one eye watched them. The left. Then right. Then the other again. Marcus could see the bulbous whites of them, and the tiny black dots at their center. They jerked and twitched, as feverish-looking as the thing's string of unintelligible whispers.

Then Marcus began to understand the whispers. He heard them in his own head. The language wasn't English, but he knew what the creature was saying. It was asking if he wanted to see its face. Over and over. Asking. Promising. Coming closer. "Do you want to see? Do you? Do you? Do you want to see my face? I'll show you. I'll show you now. Here I'll show you now."

It turned. And the face it showed them was monstrous. It was all face, his entire body a concave plate displaying a rabid, shifting, jiggling horror. The eyes danced with glee from behind a long snout that levered open. Inside, an endless abyss lined with row upon row of curving, fetid yellow teeth. Somehow, the thing still talked, even though his mouth gaped open, tongueless.

"I'm showing you. I'm showing. Look at me. Look at me. Look at me. Watch eat you now. Watch me—" The barrage of words stopped suddenly. The monster's eyes ceased their twitching. Instead they grew larger, making his pupils into pinholes on large white balls. The glee fell from it, replaced by terror. And then it dropped. All of it. The monster fell apart before their eyes, liquified. It splashed to the ground, a sack of organs and flesh and hair. And two eyes that slowly dissolved, terror in them until the last.

Behind the corpse, a man strode up the road toward them. Strong strides. Shoes that clipped against the road. Expensive, though tattered, suit. A cold face that Marcus knew. Vasel. His hand snapped out one side, and a shimmering coin flew from the monster's remains and slapped against the man's palm. He strode up to the steaming heap and jumped on it. He leapt and leapt, slamming his hard heels down on anything with form enough for him to squash, which wasn't much. He let out a string of what could only be Ukrainian curses. He was at it for some time, slipping occasionally, so furious in his work that the villagers had to jump back to keep from being splattered.

When there was nothing left worth stomping, the gangster looked up. Wild-eyed. Murderous, as if he was inviting any of the villagers to be next to feel his wrath. Nobody moved except for Vasel, the coin twirling from knuckle to knuckle, flashing.

"Papa?" Olena said, her voice small as a child's.

Vasel looked at her, noticing her for the first time. He stared, his eyes hard at first, but changing as recognition came slowly into them. He glanced at Marcus. Chin raised, he made a noise in his throat, as if to say it was all coming back to him. To Olena, he said, "Beloved Daughter." The words should have been pretty, but they weren't. "You left me to die. You left me to the mouth that lights up before it bites down. And the reaper. And eaters. And the things you can't see but can hear. So like you, daughter, to choose him over me. Always that way with you. Your mother over your father. Ukraine over Russia. A towel-head over me. This mamba over me. Listen; you even want his language more than your own."

"Papa," Olena began, but faltered.

"You should've waited for me! Who could protect you better than I?"

"I got her back here, didn't I?" Marcus said.

"I . . . I didn't choose anything. I was unconscious. I don't remember anything after the helicopter flight. Where are the others? The pilots and your—"

Vasel silenced her by grinning, a malicious, uneven smile devoid of anything like humor. "You don't remember? Lucky you. Better that way. Don't remember, and don't ask about the others. Pray that they are dead, all of them." He strode down the village street, first to an old car, then past it to a flatbed truck, calling out something in Russian.

Olena following him, with Marcus slithering just behind her. She peppered her father with more questions, switching into Ukrainian when he wouldn't answer. When Marcus asked what he was shouting, Olena said, "He wants the keys to a car. A truck. Anything."

"Where's he want to go?"

She asked him. First in Ukrainian. And then—when he looked at her—she repeated it in English.

Vasel pointed back toward the smeared remains of the creature he'd stomped to pulp. "Things worse than that are coming for us. The gates of hell have opened. I must close them. So I go to Baikonur." His eyes moved away from her and settled on the men standing near Timur's truck. He started toward the truck. "There I can end this. I'll send them back to hell, all of them."

"What's Baikonur?" Marcus asked once Vasel had engaged with the men by the truck.

"Soviet military facility."

"What's there?"

"Soldiers. Planes. Rockets. Missiles. Everything."

Marcus liked the sound of that. So long as they weren't directing all that weaponry at them, it might be the safest option they had. "Is it far?"

Wincing, Olena touched her fingers to her temples. "I don't know, Marcus. Yes. It's far."

"Far away from Talas . . ." Marcus chewed that over, latched on to it. "Olena, tell your father we'll get him to Baikonur. And then tell everyone else. We're all going."

"Let them go, Ana," Michelle said. "We need them now that the soldiers are all dead."

Recycler was still trying to climb out of his pit. And Aero, still trapped up to his neck in a muddy tube, looked at Ana—and Michelle knew he was thinking of exploding her lungs. It was what Michelle would have done in his position.

Ana glared at Michelle, but did as she asked. Aero's mud encasement dropped away. He was filthy up to his neck. Michelle saw him reaching into his pocket, and she sent a soft bubble that knocked him off balance.

"No blowing up Ana," Michelle said coldly. "We haven't finished the missions yet. You can kill her later."

"You bitch!" A wave of earth surged up and swatted Michelle across the street into the wall of a café. It left a Michelle-sized hole in the wall. She had plumped up, but the pain from the blow had almost knocked her out.

This is wrong, she thought angrily. *I don't hurt. I never hurt.* But she was scared, too. She didn't like what was happening. Not at all. *I don't like pain. No one likes it.* Something tickled the back of her mind. Something she had forgotten. But it slipped away. Then she felt a rage building in her. And it needed to go somewhere.

Another wave of dirt rose up, and Michelle blasted it with several bubbles. It exploded, spraying dirt that rained down on them all.

"He can kill me later? What all the fucks, Michelle," Ana said angrily.

The cold-hard indifference slipped from Michelle, and for a moment, her rage slid away as well. "I don't know why I said that," she muttered, holding her suddenly pounding head. The buzzing and pounding made her want to vomit. The combination was worse than any migraine. A migraine would have been a relief.

"I'm sorry, Ana," she said, then immediately regretted it. Why the fuck should she apologize to Ana? It was getting difficult to concentrate on anything other than her rage and the splitting headache. How the fuck was she supposed to find Bugsy with people this useless? Ana, Recycler, and Aero were getting in her way. She needed to get the mission done so she could save Adesina. *Even if Adesina is a freak of nature,* hissed something nasty in her mind.

She made her way out of the rubble of the store. As she did, she realized her hazmat mask had come off. She didn't retrieve it. Whatever it might have been protecting her from, it was too late to protect her now.

The mist had become thick and oily, and things were moving in it. Things she only occasionally caught out of the corner of her eye. They slid and dragged themselves through the destroyed streets with a wet slithering sound.

And now there were things whispering to her, too. She couldn't understand what they was saying, but they filled her with dread. She shook her head, but the voices persisted. Her head was going to explode if the pounding, the buzzing, and the whispering didn't stop.

"We need to go," she said thickly. "Leave the soldiers where they are."

"Jesus," Ana said. "What the hell is wrong with you?" The earth around her was rippling. "We can't just leave them. What'll Klaus say? It's a mess and he really doesn't like messes."

"I could clean it up," Recycler said with a laugh. "But I'd just as soon let those *pouco cadelas* rot in the street. People died and were left rotting all the time in Rio, so why should I care about them?"

Michelle blinked. Recycler didn't look like himself. He looked like Wally. If Wally had had something terrible happen to him. His skin was rusted through, and the muscles underneath looked like red raw ropes. He smiled, and Michelle shrank away from the madness there. She turned, and Ana wasn't Ana anymore either. A vile, pulsating cocoon lay on the ground covered in foul-smelling goo.

Adesina, Michelle thought. *Why are you here?*

Something grabbed her wrist. She looked down and saw Mummy's desiccated hand. It spun her around, and now she was looking into Mummy's inhuman eyes. The creature was saying something, but Michelle couldn't hear it. Her mouth went dry as Mummy's power began leeching the water from her body.

And then rage filled her. "I killed you once, you little bitch," Michelle snarled. "I'll kill you again if you don't let go."

Mummy released her hand, but Michelle suddenly didn't care. She grabbed Mummy's head with both hands. With a glorious release, she let two massive bubbles explode. Mummy's head collapsed into a spray of blood, pulverized bone, and grey matter. Michelle laughed as Mummy's body slid down to the ground. Then she peppered the body with marble-sized bubbles until it was nothing but a smear on the ground.

"Holy fuck," she heard Adesina say. "What have you done to Aero?"

It wasn't difficult to find the black spot. The Angel saw it from a mile away, darker than its surroundings, as if it was absorbing even the feeble star-light that illuminated the night and silent as the mouth of hell. She felt more and more fatigued as she approached it, not only physically, but mentally as well. *Was all this effort even worth it?* she wondered. *Why am I even here?* She was tired and desperately in need of rest and she missed Billy badly.

She hovered over the dome that had embraced a large, modern-looking four-story building, realizing that Satan was whispering in her ear, telling her that she should give up and forgo her duty. She should turn her head and fly away when all around her she could see destruction that had brought misery to thousands.

Destruction all around her . . . except for this one building.

It looked intact, at least outwardly, though the other structures around it had been hit particularly hard and mostly reduced to rubble. Across the street from the building covered by the darkness was a parking lot. There was some rubble within it, a few abandoned cars, and what looked like broken bodies strewn about like abandoned dolls. The darkness that enshrouded the building had also covered perhaps a third of the lot. It wasn't impenetrable—she could see into it—but it did obscure her vision, as if it were a ray of darkness instead of light darker than the night.

She hovered over the scene for perhaps two minutes. Nothing moved within her range of sight. Nothing made a sound. She realized that she'd have to get closer, to land and make a thorough inspection if she had the hope of discovering anything useful. Besides, she had been in the air for quite a while. Perhaps that was what was making her feel so weary. It would be good to feel her feet firmly planted on the ground again. She'd check things out, and then report back to Lohengrin. It was a plan. Maybe not a good one, but the only one she could come up with. She paused for a moment to check her cell phone again, but it was no good. If anything, the static and whiny electronic sounds were louder and more annoying. She put the phone away and descended, cautiously, glancing about carefully as she drifted earthward.

Her sense of unease increased as she dropped lower. By the time her feet touched the asphalted parking lot and her wings vanished to wherever it was that they went when she didn't need them anymore, her unease was almost palpable, but she could see no reason for it. Yes, of course the scenery was distressing and she'd just been through an uncomfortable experience—to understate it—but there was something wrong here, very wrong, if she could only figure out what it was.

There were, she realized, voices speaking in her head, but she couldn't understand what they were saying. She wasn't even sure if they were speaking words. Maybe they were talking in a language she'd never even heard, let alone could understand. She shook her head, but they were still there, vaguely at the limits of her consciousness, buzzing, chittering, laughing, screaming.

She crossed the parking lot slowly and cautiously, passing abandoned cars that looked perfectly fine, mostly, and a few that had run into each other or were oddly crumpled, as if something large had stepped on them or thrown them so that they'd rolled over and over again. She was a dozen feet in before she passed the first body. She'd smelled it first. It had obviously been there awhile. It was a woman in what looked like a white nurse's uniform, although it was stained with brownish splotches of what was blood, probably hers. A look of horror was still stamped in her swollen and darkened features and it looked as if something large had taken a bite out of her neck where it curved into her shoulder. The Angel said a quiet prayer for the repose of her soul as she passed her by.

She went by more wrecked cars, some rubble from adjacent buildings, more dead bodies. None had died peacefully, none were whole. Some were dressed like normal people in suits and coats, some more casually. Others were in uniforms, either holding weapons or with weapons lying nearby.

Soldiers or paramilitary troops of some kind, obviously. One, in a white uniform with a name badge, had been strangled with a stethoscope. Doctors? Nurses? She looked at the shadowy lines of the building before her. *Could be a hospital.*

All the corpses had one thing in common, all the ones who still had discernible features, anyway. Their faces were all stamped by the mark of madness. They were all twisted into a rictus of crazed insanity. The Angel's flesh crawled as she realized that. *What could cause such a thing?* she wondered. *Mind-destroying fear? Some kind of psychoactive gas?* She sniffed deeply and instantly regretted it as her stomach clenched and she gagged. If someone had released some kind of poisonous gas in or over the hospital, any lingering trace of it had been covered by the fetid scent of rotted flesh.

She finally stopped before the invisible wall of darkness. She almost turned away. But the voices in her head were becoming clearer now. She could almost understand them without really knowing what they were saying. They were, she felt, urging her forward, promising her enlightenment and companionship if she would just keep moving forward. She wiped away the sweat that was beading her forehead. The night was hot and she was thirsty, but still cautious. It looked cool and inviting inside the zone of darkness, but somehow she didn't think it was a good idea to enter it. She wondered what she should do. She still had a task to perform. She grasped what courage she had left and slowly extended her gauntleted hand and put it into the dark.

It tingled and she felt a light, almost pleasant shock go up her arm. Even through the thick leather that covered her hand she could feel it was definitely cooler in the dark. Definitely cool and welcoming. She took another step forward and was completely enveloped in it. She felt it wash over her body almost like a lukewarm shower on a hot day. She felt as if she should stand there and drink it in and it would nourish her and cleanse her body and her mind with clear and sharp knowledge it had never had before.

And then she heard the laughter.

It was not in her head. It came from outside her, from the rubble that surrounded the intact structure that was the epicenter of the dark zone. It was familiar laughter, feminine but unpleasant, like the cackling of a witch's coven or the insane hysteria of a pack of approaching Maenads. She remembered where she'd heard it before just when the first of the pack broached the rubble wall and stood atop it and looked at her.

It went back to the adventure when she'd first met Billy, when they'd set out in the Highwayman's rig through what he called "the shortcut" through an alien dimension of strange landscapes peopled by strange creatures. One kind of them were hunting spiders who ran in packs and who tittered like little girls who were denizens of Bedlam.

A decade later, she heard their horrible laughter again as they appeared among the structural debris. This was not just a smell, a whiff of something in the air that she could easily conflate with another faint half memory. This was something solid and real. There were a score or more of them, their white, hairless, bulgy bodies held high off the ground by too many spindly legs. Their bodies were the size of large dogs, their lumpy heads had disturbingly human-like features but for their large, protruding fangs that dripped a thick ichor that smoked and steamed when it hit the ground. The Angel knew that it was powerful poison. It had seared her before—only her thick leather jumpsuit and Billy's quick action saving her from permanent scarring.

What in God's name are they doing on this world? the Angel wondered, and then the lead creature lifted its head and screamed like a dying animal, a high-pitched cry that hurt the Angel's ears. It jumped down the wall it'd been perched on and the others followed it as it ran toward her, scuttling amazingly quickly on its spider legs.

For a moment the Angel stood frozen, staring at them as a great anger fastened upon her. The very sight of them sickened and offended her. They were obscene insects that should be wiped from the face of the earth, that should all die screaming, lingering deaths. She wanted to pick their legs off one by one. She wanted to see them curl up and shrivel under the blast of a flamethrower; she wanted a big-ass gun that she could use to blow chunks of ragged flesh off their bloated, squishy bodies. She wanted—

Overcome by her wildly running emotions, she staggered backward a step and sagged with sudden weariness as the overwhelming tide of hatred washed over her. She was suddenly appalled at what she'd felt. She wondered where those feelings had come from. She felt revulsion as she realized that they still plucked at her brain, begging to be released again.

It will feel so good to rend and tear and see their ichor run in rivers, the voices promised. *Their ichor, and the blood of all your enemies.*

"What is this?" the Angel asked aloud. "What—"

She looked out into the parking lot and saw that the pack was almost upon her. She had only a moment in which to act.

"Save my soul from evil, Lord," she cried aloud in a heartfelt voice, "and heal this warrior's heart!"

It was the wings that came to her, not the sword, and she sprang into the air just as the first of the beasts sprang at her. Its forelegs grabbed her around the knees as she rose, but the Angel kicked with almost hysterical strength. The creature's legs were many but weak. She felt more of them clutch at her as it sought to swarm up her body and sink its dripping fangs in her flesh, but her first kick freed her right leg and her second kick punted the thing right where its head met its suet-fleshed abdomen. It screamed brokenly and catapulted away from the Angel, falling among the rest of the pack that was trying with no success to leap up and grab her.

Whether driven by anger, frustration, hunger, or maybe all three, the pack fell upon their shrieking comrade, and tore it apart, devouring the ichor-dripping chunks of flesh while the Angel flew away to rejoin the Committee aces at the outskirts of the city.

Michelle stood over what was left of Aero. The noises and pounding in her head faded. The anger subsided. She began shaking. It was Mummy. It had to be Mummy. She'd never hurt Aero. *Oh, yes, you would. And you'd be right to. Killing him only makes sense.*

She no longer knew who she was. Something was inside her. And it wanted blood. Endless gouts of blood. Or maybe it was what she had wanted all along. Yes, if she were being honest, it had been a struggle not to kill. And now it made such sense.

"You've lost it," Ana said. It wasn't Adesina. It was Ana. But she didn't sound like Ana. She sounded a little hysterical. "You pulverized him. You just slaughtered him." She twittered. "Slaughtered." Then she put a hand up to her mouth. "Why am I laughing? Why am I laughing, Michelle? This is horrible. But so funny." Tiago had a murderous expression as he stared at the two of them, then a chuckle escaped him.

Michelle couldn't help herself. She began laughing, too. As she giggled, she wiped her hands on her pants. The blood grew tacky as it began to coagulate. It clung stubbornly and she couldn't get it off her hands. There was ichor under her fingernails. She didn't bother trying to get it out.

It was only a few blocks to the Jokertown precinct. Frank tried to run, but stopped after a few strides. It jarred the wound in his side, and pumping his arms tore at his shoulder, and his feet were screaming. Even walking he still arrived at the doors blown and breathless.

Wingman heaved up from behind his desk. "Shit! Franny! Where—"

Franny threw up a hand. "No time." He pushed through into the bull pen. There was an eruption of sound as everybody started talking at once, questions were thrown at him too many to understand much less answer, and then he was surrounded. Rikki, small and quick who resembled a human greyhound, Slim Jim the absurdly skinny ace, Beastie, big furry and lumbering, the claws on the tips of fingers practically dragging on the stained linoleum; Bill Chen, his first partner, who was almost as tall as Beastie, but an ace. Even Tabby and Bugeye, the men who had made his life a living hell, were grinning and pounding him on the back.

His partner, Michael Stevens, pushed through the crowd and grabbed him in a hard hug. Frank gasped and the black detective released him like he was a hot skillet. Maseryk strode out of his office.

"SHUT UP!" Everybody did. "So, our globetrotter returns," the captain growled.

"You can chew me out later, Captain. Right now I've got to get to the UN."

"Oh, excuse me. I'm taking orders from you now? I haven't even decided if you still have a job. My office!"

Franny, limping, followed him. Behind him someone began to clap. It was picked up until a hailstorm of applause accompanied him to Maseryk's office door. Franny's shoulders hunched with embarrassment and he felt his face burning. Maseryk's shoulders were hunching too, but Franny expected it had more to do with anger.

The instant the door shut Franny blurted, "Grekor's taken control of the Jokertown Clinic. He's threatening to kill people. The woman who kidnapped the jokers is there and she's directing everything, including me. Please, Captain, I have to get to the UN and bring the people she wants."

"Who are they and why does she want them?"

"Has any news about Talas reached the States?"

"Yeah. Nobody knows what the fuck is going on, but it looks like a wild card outbreak."

"It's not and Baba Yaga does know what's happening."

Maseryk leveled a hard stare on him. "Explain this. Slowly."

"We don't have time!" Franny yelled. Maseryk glared and Franny grabbed at the fraying edges of his temper. "The old lady says the world is ending . . . and . . . and, I think I believe her. Captain, please just let me go get these people before more innocents get hurt."

"Fine, go."

"I . . . I don't have any money or ID, nothing. I need a way to get there, and I . . . I don't think I can walk." Admitting that seemed to bring his exhaustion and pain into stark focus. Franny swayed, and laid a hand on Maseryk's desk for support.

Maseryk's expression softened. "Okay, I'll wait on that report for now." He opened the door, and started issuing orders. "Stevens, alert SWAT and get people over to the clinic. We've got a hostage situation. Tell them I'll meet them there. Beastie, get Black a squad car."

Bill Chen stepped forward. "I'll drive him."

Franny eyed the big Chinese-American ace. Bill had been his first partner when he'd arrived at Fort Freak, but Franny's early promotion to detective had angered the older man. They hadn't been on good terms since.

"You don't have to," Franny said.

"Yeah, I do. You look like shit."

"What does that have to do with anything?"

"You'll probably wreck the damn car."

"You two lovers work it out," Maseryk snapped and strode away surrounded by a phalanx of cops.

Bill and Franny exchanged measured looks; finally Franny nodded. "Okay."

"So where are we going?"

The traffic was maddening. Even with the cherry lit it was taking forever to reach the green and white slab rearing against the June sky. Franny's knee was vibrating. He gripped it with a hand to try to still the motion. It wasn't helping his nerves that so far the drive was taking place in total silence.

Bill's big hands gripped the steering wheel hard enough to whiten his knuckles. He stared straight ahead at the sea of brake lights. They crawled forward a few more blocks as cars tried to get out of their way.

"You did a good thing." The words emerged as a growl that wasn't easy since Bill had a ridiculously high-pitched voice.

"Excuse me?"

"You heard me. I just don't know why the fuck you didn't reach out to me instead of that damn Fed."

"So you know about—"

"Yeah, his body along with a bunch of Russian goons fell out of the ceiling a few days back."

"How the hell—Mollie," Franny concluded grimly. He shook his head. "I cannot figure that girl out. She strands me in Talas and then goes back?" A few seconds of thought and he had the answer. "Oh. Of course. The money."

"You done talking to yourself?"

"Sorry. Does Jamal's family know?"

"Yeah, they're in town to claim the body."

Franny closed his eyes. "I should see them."

"Yeah, they'd probably like to know how their kid ended up dead in Trashcanistan."

They fell silent once more. Fanny sucked in a deep breath. "I didn't reach out to you because I knew what I was doing was probably going to end my career. I couldn't ask that of anybody else."

Bill reached out, and gripped Franny's shoulder. Unfortunately it was the left and Franny hissed in pain.

"Sorry. Jesus, how fucked up are you? As for your career ending—" Bill gave his high-pitched laugh. "I suspect that you have once again fallen in a pile of shit and will emerge smelling like a damn rose. You brought those jokers back. That counts for a lot, and the press and the brass have a bad guy they can crucify. Mendelberg."

"What?"

"She was getting kickbacks from Grekor."

"Which means Baba Yaga," Franny said slowly. "No wonder she tried to shut down the investigation and left my ass hanging in Shymkent."

"Where the fuck is that?"

"Not the garden spot of Central Asia, I can tell you that much."

Bill saw an opening and shot through. He pulled a U-turn and they slid to a stop in front of the UN entrance. "I'm gonna head back. It's gonna be all hands on deck."

Frank leaned back in the car and gripped Bill's hand. "Thanks. For everything."

"Enough with the overly serious good-byes. I'll see you back at the station."

Frank stood and watched the squad car pull away. "Maybe," he said to the air.

The UN lobby was like a stirred anthill. People dressed in everything from business chic to Arab dishdashas and African dashikis were rushing past. Most of them with cell phones pressed to their ears. That was heartening to Franny. Their tight and fearful expressions were less encouraging. He pushed through the crowd, including a number of confused tourists sporting cameras and I HEART NYC T-shirts, and stepped in front of a fat man in a Hawaiian shirt, khaki shorts, black knee socks, and sandals at the visitors' desk.

"Hey, buddy! The line starts back *there*." He pointed to the end of a long line of people.

"Police business," Franny snapped, and his hand went instinctively to his breast pocket, except he was still wearing the now very rumpled tux jacket and his badge was somewhere in the hospital back in Talas. He also hadn't showered since the run-down hotel in Shymkent and he was aware of his own stink and the dark stubble sprouting on his face.

"Yeah, you don't look like a cop." The man thrust out his jaw and chest, except it was mostly his belly that bumped up against Franny.

"I'm undercover. *Now get the fuck out of my face!*" Something in his expression must have penetrated because the peckerwood deflated and stepped back. People were muttering, backing away from him.

Franny turned and summoned a smile for the pretty Asian girl behind the desk. It didn't ease her look of alarm. From the corner of his eye Franny spotted security drifting his way.

"Hi, I'm Detective Francis Black, my captain, Maseryk, from the Fifth Precinct sent me over. I need to speak to the Secretary-General and to the head of the Committee." It sounded insane even to him.

"Do you . . . do you have an appointment?" the girl fluted, clearly stalling for time.

"No, this is an emergency. It's about what's happening in Talas." He prayed she had a fucking clue that anything was happening in Talas. His prayer wasn't answered. She looked confused and even more nervous. The guards were closing in.

A big heavyset young man dressed in slacks and a shirt stopped, spun, and walked over to Franny. "Talas? Did I just hear ya'll say Talas?" He had a twanging Southern accent.

"Uh, yes. I was there. I've just returned and I have vital information."

"Well that just beats all. That's real helpful." He held out a soft, rather moist hand. "I'm Buford Calhoun. Toad Man," he added in a somewhat hopeful tone but with the air of a man who didn't expect a response.

But Franny had a guilty pleasure. He had been a devoted follower of *American Hero* and he recognized the name if not the man. (Buford had definitely packed on a few more pounds since his appearance on the show.)

"You were on Team Spades."

Buford beamed. "Sure was. That's when people saw my talent and realized I could be a help. I got recruited—"

"Talas," Franny reminded. "I really need to see the Secretary-General and/or the head of the Committee. Actually both of them would probably be best."

"Well, I don't know Mr. Jayewardeeni all that well, and Klaus is out of town, but I bet Babel will want to talk to you. Ya'll just come with me. *I'll* get you *right* in."

The Angel reached what she recognized as once being the command point— but it was deserted. Only the tents were left in mute witness to what was once a bustling hive of activity. Soldiers, doctors, patients—everyone was gone and the area was given over to the mists and tendrils of fog emanating from central Talas.

She landed in the deserted camp that was lit only by the greenish light cast by a swollen, miscolored moon that had risen while she was flying out of the center of the city. It was a bloated, diseased moon, shining lambent green like infected tissue. She avoided looking directly at it because it seemed as if a smiling skull leered back at her from its pitted surface. The Angel felt as though she'd come upon an abandoned ghost town lost for years in an unhealthy desert. She wondered how the feeling of age and decay could have come upon the location so quickly, and she realized that it was the silence, the smell of death and decay that already clung to it, as if it was inhabited by untended corpses left to rot.

She cautiously went into the hospital area. Some of the tents were flapping in the hot breeze that smelled like the breath of a dying animal, others remained standing and intact.

"Hello?" the Angel called. "Anyone here?"

Her voice croaked. She'd finished the last of her water a while back and it was thick with dust and dry as desert sand. She needed water, food, and medical attention. She quickly searched through the intact tents but in the first few found only what she'd feared she'd find, what confirmed her worst suspicions. Only bodies.

They had abandoned their patients, she thought, shocked. Some had tried to follow. Few were able to crawl more than a few feet before their torn and abused bodies had given up their impossible struggle. Some had not even made it out of their cots. All of their faces had expressions of terror on them.

Suddenly she couldn't take the horror anymore. She ran out of the last tent she investigated, and despite her weariness and pain, hunger and thirst, sprang up into the sky, and went back down the road.

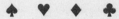

Buford was able to get him out of the public areas of the building and upstairs, but that seemed to be the extent of the ace's clout. Franny was left in an outer office with a bland-looking male secretary who alternated answering the phone with scrolling on his iPad. His response to most of the callers was, "Ms. Baden is in a meeting and can't be disturbed. She'll get back to you as soon as she can." A few of the calls went through.

Time ticked past. Outside the windows the skyline of Manhattan began to glow as the night came in. Franny lurched out of the overly low, deep chair and stalked to the receptionist's desk. Resting his palm on the top he leaned across.

"Can I get you something? Cup of coffee?" the man said with the air of someone who had placated a lot of waiting dignitaries.

Franny pointed at the closed door. "You can get me in there."

"Ms. Baden is—"

"In a meeting and can't be disturbed," Franny finished the sentence. "Would that meeting happen to be about Talas? Because if it is I know a little something about that, and I can connect her with somebody who knows a fuck lot more than I do. So, will you *please* get me in?"

"We have people on the ground. I'm sure Ms. Baden is well briefed on what—*Hey!*"

Franny reached the door and threw it open. There were a lot of people in the conference room. Some of them Franny recognized from *American Hero*. At the head of the table was a small dark-haired woman with shadows beneath her eyes and even deeper shadows haunting her dark eyes.

"What is the meaning—?"

"There's someone who wants to see you. If you don't come people are going to start dying. As a further incentive, she can tell you exactly what's happening in Talas." He paused, thought about it, and then added, "And probably how you've fucked everything up. She's really good at that."

"Where are we?" Tiago said to Ana. He'd dropped some of his armor, and trash littered the streets behind them like breadcrumbs in Hansel and Gretel.

"I have no idea," Ana replied. "Our tracking equipment is dead. So are these hazmat masks." She tossed hers aside.

The drizzling let up, but it didn't make anything better. The mist was getting thicker. They were walking blind now that their coms, phones, and trackers had stopped working. And nothing looked like it had on the map for the tracker. They should have been near Bugsy's last location, but the streets were all wrong.

Fuck him anyway, Michelle thought. *Can't do a simple reconnaissance mission. Idiot.*

A low moan floated to them. They came to an intersection. There was a dry fountain in the center with a pillar in the center. The broken pieces of some Kazakh hero lay on one side of the fountain. Ringed around the fountain were cages.

The fog thinned, and Michelle saw people in large dog crates. Naked people. They drew closer, and from out of the gloom came a woman. She wore an antebellum gown with a bloody apron over it.

"Welcome," she said with a smile. "I've been waiting for you. See what I've done. It's so educational."

She walked to the first cage and opened the wire door. Part of a body flopped out. It had stitches on its wrist where a hand from a different body had been attached.

They stared, fascinated as if they were in thrall by the scene before them. "This was my first attempt," she said. There was pride in her voice. Pride and amusement. "The hand transplant didn't work as well as I wanted it to. And the screaming. So much screaming. It didn't bother me, but I was concerned about the neighbors."

She moved on to the next cage. The person in this cage was alive, but his bones had been broken and had healed at unnatural angles.

"Kill me," he said in a pleading voice. "Kill me. For the love of all that's holy."

Then he began to change, his body morphing into a slithering mass of grey tentacles. One baleful eye glared at them. He began to ooze through the mesh of the cage.

The woman smiled, and then she began to change as well. Her face melted into a pulpy mass. Only black eyes remained of what had once been human. A gaping maw opened. Some kind of sound erupted. Something inhuman and agonizing to hear.

Michelle clamped her hands over her ears and felt a hot wetness. She pulled her hands away and saw her own blood there. Earth Witch and Recycler did the same.

The creature slithered to another cage and pulled out a young girl.

The creature opened an orifice ringed in razor-sharp teeth. Then another mouth sprang from the gullet of the creature. That mouth was festooned with sharklike teeth. It neatly bit the girl's head off even as the girl shrieked for her mother.

No, no, no!

Somewhere deep inside, Michelle recognized herself—her real self. *Adesina*. That girl could have been Adesina! But now she was almost entirely disconnected from her feelings for her daughter. It didn't matter anyway. She wanted the blood. She wanted to see the blood. It was right. The blood was everything.

A trench opened, expanding until it consumed the cages, the fountain, and the obscenity that had once been a woman. Ana at work.

I swear I'm going to kill that bitch.

"I wanted to see the other cages!" Tiago yelled. "Didn't you want to see? Didn't you want to help? We could have helped. We're supposed to help." He began coming closer to Ana. "You aren't helping."

A crater opened up and swallowed him, too. Ana smiled beatifically.

A black rage swept over Michelle. Fuck the mission. The mission didn't matter anyway. Bugsy deserved to die. His death was inevitable.

And Ana, well, Ana needed to die.

The red mist floated in Michelle's vision. The pounding in her head was back, and it grew worse. The hissing voices she couldn't understand were louder. She shook with bloodlust and rage.

She let a bubble fly. But before it hit Ana, a wall of earth rose from the ground, blocking its trajectory. So Michelle blasted the wall of dirt with a barrage of bubbles. It broke apart, but reassembled a moment later, larger, thicker, and taller. Then the earth flipped back—and like a fly swatter, smashed into Michelle and sent her flying.

She hit the building behind her and blasted out the other side. The pain knocked her out.

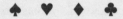

Introductions had been exchanged in the car, and now Franny and Baden were making their way through a phalanx of cop cars that surrounded the old building that housed the Jokertown Clinic. Spotlights glared off the windows of the hospital. A helicopter circled overhead. SWAT team members looking insectile in their helmets, goggles, and vests were positioned on rooftops and leveled high-powered rifles at the doors of the clinic.

An ambulance driver was remonstrating with Maseryk. "I gotta drop off this patient."

Maseryk was firm. "Take them to Bellevue."

"He's a *joker*."

"And the people inside the clinic have been taken hostage. You want to join them?"

"Uh . . . Oh. No."

"That's what I thought," Maseryk muttered to himself. He spotted Franny and Babel. He walked over, his erect bearing and the cadence of his steps forcibly reminding Franny that Maseryk was ex-military.

"I'd like to have ears on what happens in there," he said.

Franny shook his head. "They're going to search me. Let's not give them a reason to shoot me, okay? I'll report back to you."

"If they let you out."

"I'm sure Baba Yaga will have another chore for her errand boy." Babel gave him a sharp glance and he realized he'd probably revealed more than he wanted.

"What about her?" Maseryk jerked a thumb at Babel.

"I'm certain the lady didn't insist on seeing me unless she wanted me to do something. She'll have to let me leave if she wants that to happen," the diplomat replied.

Maseryk nodded and stepped aside, but he didn't look pleased. He spoke quickly into his radio, and waved Franny and Babel toward the front doors of the clinic.

Barbara glanced at the scowling Officer Black—Franny. His face was stern and angry as he leaned against the wall of the hospital room.

The room reeked, and it wasn't just the usual hospital miasma. Much of it seemed to emanate from the foul-mouthed old women in the bed in the center of the heavily guarded room. Rheumy eyes glared at Barbara from the wrinkled face. Barbara stopped short of what she hoped was the woman's spitting distance.

"So you're in charge of the Committee?" the woman asked in a broken, husky voice. "You're younger than I expected you to be. A mere puppy. So . . . tell me you haven't already sent aces to Talas. Tell me that we can still decide who to send and where to send them in order to end this."

Baba Yaga's harsh gaze impaled Barbara, and even though she thought her face would betray nothing, the woman on the bed gave a sigh and closed her eyes, her head turning on the pillow. When Baba Yaga spoke again, it was in Russian this time, and Barbara closed her eyes momentarily to release the wild card ability within her, putting Franny within the bubble of understanding while leaving the guards outside, though she knew some of them obviously spoke the language. "Ah, they've already gone. You're stupid as well as young, then. You've lost them, haven't you?"

"Our contact with the team has become . . . erratic," Barbara admitted, knowing that Baba Yaga would hear it as if she'd spoken fluent Russian. The old woman's eyes widened slightly, as if she hadn't expected Barbara to understand anything she'd said, then she laughed. Against the wall, Franny cocked his head, listening intently.

"You speak my language like a native," Baba Yaga said. Barbara shrugged; she didn't correct the woman's misapprehension. "You've lost them, your team," Baba Yaga repeated.

Barbara ignored that comment, though she felt the growing knot inside her stomach, her fear of what had happened with Klaus, the horror of what she'd seen and heard only a few hours before. "Officer Black tells me that you know this person called Hellraiser, and that he's the one causing the disturbance in Talas."

Now the old woman's eyebrows climbed her forehead. "Disturbance, you call it? That's what you would call the possible end of the world, eh? A fucking *disturbance?*"

"I'd call it hyperbole to be talking about the end of the world," Barbara answered, and again the old woman cackled mockingly.

"Oh, you *are* an idiot," Baba Yaga answered. "Believe me, it's not hyperbole, just the raw truth." Barbara shivered involuntarily, hearing that. She tried to read the old woman's craggy face, tried to pretend that Baba Yaga was lying, but she found she couldn't believe that. Those wrinkle-snared eyes stared at her, and through the scorn and derision, Barbara thought she saw a faint glimmer of sympathy. *Klaus, what have I sent you into? Why didn't you let me go with you? Why didn't I insist? Please be alive. Please stay alive.*

"Officer Black said—" Barbara began again, but Baba Yaga cut her off.

"Francis is afraid. He should be. We all should be afraid." Baba Yaga sniffed. "I have something you must listen to. Cassette tapes." Her rheumy gaze slid over to Franny. "Go bring us a cassette player, boy," she spat.

Franny's scowl deepened. "Give me the money to buy it, bitch," he answered.

Baba Yaga motioned with her head to one of the Russian guards, who reached into his suit jacket and pulled out a wallet. The man silently handed Black a hundred-dollar bill. He stared at it for several seconds, then spun and left the room. Barbara cocked her head toward the old woman on the bed.

"He's a pup, too—but a lucky one."

"Tell me about this Hellraiser," Barbara said, trying to bring the conversation back to something that might help Klaus, might give Barbara and the Committee something solid on which to hope and plan. The woman lifted her head a bit on the pillow.

"His name's not Hellraiser. It's Tolenka. He was my partner in the KGB:

a good one. And Tolenka isn't the one causing your 'disturbance.'" She coughed as she stressed the word. "It's the thing that is inside him doing that."

"The thing inside him?" Barbara asked.

"We went on a mission many years ago to . . . well, you don't need to know that. All you need to know is that it didn't go well. Tolenka went to use his power, and realized that he'd taken in something he couldn't control, something that had taken a foothold in his body and couldn't be banished—and that's why Talas has become what it is."

"What are you talking about? What took him?"

"Wait," Baba Yaga told her. "Be patient a little longer. When Black gets back, I will play the tape, and you will hear Tolenka. I would offer to translate, but . . ." She gave Barbara a mirthless smile. "You will understand the words, at least."

Miles later, the Angel came upon the vehicles they'd arrived in that morning, but hovering above the scene, could see no one to greet her.

She was exhausted, hungry, and hurting. Her shoulder throbbed from the injuries she'd sustained in the battle with the bat-beast. She thought the bleeding had stopped some time ago, but her side was still wet and tacky from the blood she'd lost. She could feel the semidried blood pulling off her flesh when she turned certain ways and she wasn't looking forward to removing the gore-soaked leather away from the wound.

She hovered for a moment, peering down at the vehicles. The foul-smelling, sticky green fog that had obscured her vision and made her nauseous and thickheaded as she moved through it had thinned and finally vanished as she'd moved down the road toward the airport they'd arrived in. But as far as she could see there was no activity on the ground below her.

She wondered if any of the Committee aces had made their way out of Talas. The Angel wondered if perhaps the army units had retreated as, as it seemed, the fog had advanced.

Suddenly, someone emerged from the front seat of one of the parked vehicles, holding a rifle and looking up at the sky. The figure waved vigorously and she finally recognized him in the leprous moonlight, more from the hat he wore than anything else. It was the Australian ace, Tinker. He gestured for her to land and she did so gratefully. She dropped tiredly to the ground, landing near the girl. Her wings vanished.

"You look like hammered shit," Tinker exclaimed in his broad Aussie accent as the Angel limped on cramping legs toward him. The heat of the day still wafted up from the pavement in unrelenting waves.

"Water?" she croaked through parched lips. The ace unsnapped a canteen from the web-belt slung across his narrow hips, and flipped it to her. The Angel caught it, twisted its cap open, and put it to her mouth. The water was hot and metallic-tasting, but at least it was wet. She drunk off about half the canteen and then held it back.

Tinker shook his head. "You need it more than me. 'Sides, we got more back in the SUVs." He frowned. "A little more, anyways."

"Thanks." The Angel took another gulp, swished it around her mouth, and spit it on the concrete. The water sizzled and after a very few moments was gone. She looked around the relative tranquility. "Where is everyone?"

"Gone," Tinker said. "There's just me 'n' Bugsy and that worthless Lama bloke, and now you."

"The army?" the Angel asked.

Tinker pulled a face. "They scarpered like 'roos when reports came back that the probing column Lohengrin took in got scragged. A few stayed on with me and Bugsy. Maybe figured it was safer. I tried to tinker together some listening equipment when the radios went out." He shrugged massive shoulders. "Didn't work. Getting some intermittent contact with Babel since we withdrew, but I dunno." He scowled back into the city center. "Looks like the crap is following us."

The Angel nodded. "Where's Bugsy?"

Tinker jerked a thumb over her shoulder. "In the back of the SUV. Probably still curled up in a ball."

The Angel questioned him with a look.

"Been a cot case pretty much since you took off."

"Did you get anything out of him?"

"Been jibbering like a hoon about this creepy shit he's seein' out there, stuff worse than the worst slasher movie you can ever imagine."

"I can believe that," the Angel muttered.

"Still small, too," the Tinker added quietly.

"Where is he?"

"Come on." Tinker headed over to the cars. "I got some tinnies in an ice chest. Guess you could use one."

"Tinnies?"

"Cans of beer."

"Guess I could," the Angel said.

Much to her relief, her gear seemed intact in back of the SUV where a still-diminished Bugsy was sleeping in the backseat. He was wrapped up in a fetal position and he looked like a little boy. She wanted to reach out and smooth his tousled hair, even though she still remembered what an annoying twit he was.

She pulled her duffel bag out a little awkwardly with her left hand as Tinker approached with a beer can he'd taken from a cooler in the front seat. She reached for it automatically with her right hand, winced, then took it with her left.

"What's the matter?" he asked.

"Dislocated right shoulder," she said. "I think. And a wound in my side I've got to dress."

"Ouch," Tinker said. "What happened?"

"Had to fight some flying rat-bat thing. He got a hold of me at one point, clawed me. I hurt my shoulder pulling away."

She decided not to mention the spiked red penis thing.

He handed her one of the beer cans he was carrying, watched her as she raised the can to her lips. It was magically cold. She drained the bitter liquid from it in a disappointingly few number of gulps, dropped it, and drew a sharp, wicked-looking knife from the belt around her hips. Slowly, carefully, and somewhat painfully she cut the top off her leather jumpsuit and pulled it down so that it hung at her waist. Under it she wore only a heavy sports bra. Both the bra and her torso were covered in blood. The slashing wound in her side had clotted, but she'd leaked more fluid than she'd realized. Her injured shoulder sagged.

"You got some muscles on you," Tinker opined. "Not like a man's, though."

Rather unconsciously, the Angel thought, he flexed his weight lifter biceps showing from under his short shirt sleeves.

"No," the Angel said. Gingerly, she slipped the bra strap off her damaged shoulder.

"And some boobies, too."

Sudden anger flared through the Angel, overcoming her weariness. She locked eyes with Tinker.

"You know who my husband is," she said.

"Yeah," Tinker said.

"And what I'm capable of."

"Just sayin'," he said with a poorly concealed gulp. "I mean, we're out here and all. Who knows if we'll be alive this time tomorrow?"

Her anger turned to something else as she regarded him closely. He wasn't exactly handsome and he stank. He had big muscles, though. Looked strong. She knew that she could break him if she wanted to. Who knows, indeed, what they could do, alone, out in the desert, to each other?

Her eyes closed momentarily and she swayed, barely catching herself before falling. *What am I thinking?* she asked herself. *How can I think it?*

"I—Sorry. Tired. Loss of blood." She was babbling.

"Better wash out that wound before you dress it," Tinker said, all business now.

The Angel looked at him with concern. "Is there enough water?"

Tinker laughed. "To clean wounds with? Right-o."

He went off toward the small group of Kazakhs encamped a little down the road and came back lugging a plastic jerry can that looked to be about forty gallons.

"Need a hand?" he asked, dropping it at her feet with an effort-full exhalation of breath.

The Angel just shook her head. She lifted it by a single handle with her left hand, hefted it experimentally. It was almost full. Virtually without effort she lifted it over her head, flipping it like a bottle of Coke when it was in the proper position, and poured the tepid, plastic-smelling water over her head as Tinker looked on, impressed.

It was heaven, almost as wonderful as the most luxurious shower she'd ever taken. It took an effort to cut off the flow of water, to make sure she had enough to cleanse her wound. It looked puffy, red-tinged. She patted it gently with a towel, cleaning it as best and as stoically as she could, slathered it with powder from the first-aid kit, and as a final precaution jabbed herself with a syringe that contained a wide-spectrum antibiotic, and taped it over. She looked up to see that Tinker was following her every movement with interest.

"How's your first-aid skills?" she asked.

"Nonexistent," Tinker replied.

"I'd better get this done by myself. God knows I've watched Billy do it enough times." At the thought of Billy she frowned, gritted her teeth, and slammed her shoulder back into its socket with the palm of her left hand.

There was a flash of white-hot pain that nearly brought her to her knees, and then, suddenly, it felt a lot better. Not perfect, for sure, but better. She went back into the duffel bag and removed a large ACE bandage and roll of tape.

"Wrap the bandage," she told Tinker. "Like this." She held one end of the bandage against her skin under her arm and showed him how to unwrap the roll under, over, and around her shoulder. "Tightly," she ordered.

Once he pulled it too hard, and the Angel sucked in her breath and winced.

"Sorry," he said automatically.

"That's all right." She took the end of the bandage from him and hooked it fast. "Now the tape."

Tinker nodded, bent down for the tape the Angel had set in the mouth of the duffel bag.

"Thanks," she said, flexing her shoulder experimentally, then gingerly reached into her duffel bag with her injured arm, found a shirt, and put it on, carefully.

"You gonna be all right?"

"After I get some food," she said. "Some rest."

He nodded judiciously. "You do that. I'll take the watch."

"We can pull shifts—"

Tinker shook his head. "You're a tough Sheila and game as Ned Kelly, but I got the feeling that the shit is just gonna get hotter. I've done nothing today, but play with the radio. Maybe I can fix it, somehow, anyway. You eat and rest."

The Angel nodded.

"And get ready for tomorrow," she said softly.

He had once again been sent on an errand. *"Go bring us a cassette player, boy."* The dismissive order from Baba Yaga.

"Give me the money to buy it, bitch," had slipped out before he thought better.

Fortunately Baba Yaga seemed more amused than inclined to turn him into a Barcalounger. She had nodded and one of the goons had casually peeled off a hundred-dollar bill from a roll he had pulled from his pocket.

Franny had gone straight to Nightingale's Pawn and old Nightingale had hemmed and hawed to himself and flopped off into the shadowed depths of his cluttered, jumbled store. Franny had amused himself by counting the number of guitars hanging in the store—thirty-two. Studied the watches and jewelry in the locked case. The abandoned wedding rings were especially poignant to him. Wondered why on earth Nightingale would have taken in turntables and speakers. Finally the old man returned with an ancient cassette player. Its white plastic case had faded to an ugly yellow like a fungus-infected toenail.

Still it played and it was doing so now. The speaker was tinny and crackled a bit, but the voice of the man came through clearly enough. It was a rich baritone, warm and almost buttery. Franny tried to reconcile it with the *thing* he'd seen in the hospital bed.

Baba Yaga was expressionless, just staring at the plastic box resting at her side on the bed as the story spooled out. Which Franny understood courtesy of Babel's power. He wished she hadn't been so courteous. The man had been trying to give a dry, factual report, but Franny could hear the fear and sorrow beneath the words. He'd heard it in the voices of cops who had been through a harrowing situation, in the voice of a high school friend diagnosed with a brain tumor and facing death.

". . . Help me. For the sake of whatever God you believe in, help me . . ."

". . . I don't know what entered me, Mariamna. I don't *want* to know what it is. Horrorshow, I call it, or Dark God, or . . . The name doesn't matter. All that matters is that it intends to move across all the realities, across all the boundaries between our world and the rest of the universes out there. It wants to own them, wants to devour them, wants to rule them. It wants all the pain and the blood and the agony to feed itself and grow stronger. It will create minor gods to worship it, but that won't be us. [Tolenka laughs, a bitter cough.] We're nothing to it, creatures hardly worth noticing . . .

". . . But I've found a way to keep it back, keep it inside and not be free to pursue its ends in our world. It feeds on death and fear, and that's what I have to give it. Not too much or it would become too powerful; not too little or it would destroy me in frustration and emerge anyway . . .

". . . I'm so sorry, Mariamna. I didn't want this . . .

". . . I don't know how long I can continue this, Mariamna. I've become loathsome to myself, a creature nearly as bad as the Master inside. I hear its voice and it's my own that I hear. I think of how pleasant it would be to just die and let it go, because I wouldn't be there to know what happens afterward. If I die, it will be free to enter our world . . .

". . . Help me. For the sake of whatever God you believe in, help me . . ."

Baba Yaga pressed the STOP button on the tape recorder. In the awful silence that followed, Barbara could hear her own breathing, ragged and too rapid. Her heart hammered against the cage of her ribs. *Klaus, what do I do now? I want you here, my love, because I'm terrified.*

"I did what I could for him," Baba Yaga was saying, and Barbara jerked her gaze to the woman on the bed. "That was recorded decades ago, not long after our botched mission. I tried to help him hold in that thing. I spent *years* nursing him as he became more and more twisted and awful to be near. I managed to keep him at least somewhat sane and docile . . ." She nodded toward Franny against the wall. "Until Black ruined it for all of us," she finished.

Her thin fingertips caressed the black buttons of the recorder, and Barbara thought that she would play more of the tape. Instead, Baba Yaga closed her eyes hard, as if Tolenka's voice amid the hissing of the ancient cassette had conjured up something terrifying in front of her and she wanted to shut out the vision. "Horrorshow is a monster from another place, another dimension. A terrible, awful god. It wants . . . it wants death and terror and horror. That's what makes it strong." Her eyes opened again. Yellowed pupils sought Barbara. "Now, there's little hope at all. It's growing stronger every day, and soon there will be no way to stop it. The whole world will become like Talas is now, and it will be the world's master."

"Then we need to find a way to get to Tolenka and kill him, if he's the one through whom this thing is going to come."

"*No!*" The word was a shriek, a scream. Baba Yaga lurched up in her bed, her hand clenched like a claw about to strike. "Didn't you hear what Tolenka was saying? That's what you *can't* do, you fool! Tolenka is the only thing holding back the monster now. He is trying desperately to keep shut the door the creature has opened. If he dies, if you or your aces kill him, then the monster will step through fully, in all its awful power. It will rip open the walls between its world and ours, and everything there, all the horror and all the filth, will spill over. There will be no place for anyone to hide or escape. Everything and everyone in our world will die. *Everyone.*"

She stopped. The truth of everything the woman had said was written in the lines of her face. Barbara felt sick. She imagined Klaus, caught up in the madness, or worse, already dead. *I did this. I sent Klaus and the others there. I let Klaus go without taking me along. I could have at least been there with him when . . .*

She stopped the thought before it could go further. *All the plans we've set into motion would end in Tolenka's death. How can I stop this from happening? How can I convince Jayewardene and the others?* "Is there a way to deal with this? Can we end this somehow and stop this thing? There has to be a way. There *has* to be."

At that, Baba Yaga only shook her head. "I know this: it is Tolenka that is holding back the Dark God. As long as he lives, the thing inside can't step through completely. For there to be any hope at all, you must keep my Tolenka alive. As for the rest . . ." Baba Yaga shrugged.

"Then that's what we'll do," Barbara told her.

She had no idea how they might accomplish that.

"How do we know he's not already dead?" Franny struggled to keep his voice level. To emulate the man on the tape. *Just the facts, ma'am.* "I was in that hospital room in Talas. People were going crazy then and that was days ago. Nobody's replacing the IV bags, or changing his Depends, much less feeding him. And judging from the pictures this thing has been gorging itself on pain and death and fear."

"If Tolenka were dead we would not be having this conversation. The madness would fill the world," Baba Yaga said. "He was a strong man. He knows what's at stake. He will fight to the end."

"We have no choice but to proceed as if he's still alive," Babel said.

"And whatever you do, you must do it quickly!"

"Then I best get to it."

Babel left.

"She's smart," Baba Yaga said. "She reminds me a bit of myself. I was prettier, of course. Well, we shall see. Perhaps she is clever enough for this."

Baba Yaga frowned at the tape player. She pushed it roughly aside. Franny felt a stir of pity.

"It must have been hard. Hearing his voice. How long has it been since you listened to those tapes?"

The cold eyes pierced him again. "You are a sentimental ass, Francis. Go away."

Nothing had made Marcus's case about the evil coming out of Talas like the creature Vasel's coin had turned into body waste. After that, when Marcus pleaded for the villagers to flee they had ears for it.

Baikonur. The Cosmodrome. The names passed from mouth to mouth in fervent whispers. It seemed as good a place as any, and a much better one than a village apparently in shuffling distance from a city of horrors. The entire village packed up and prepared for the journey in a frantic rush, all of them with an eye toward the bloodred sky that made a beautiful twilight somehow sinister. Though they worked quickly and with collective purpose, there was much to be accounted for: joker bodies of all shapes and sizes, some with debilitating deformities, arguments over what could and couldn't be brought and over how their precious few vehicles should be packed and passengers distributed. They didn't roll out until the dead of night.

Instead of joining the highway down in the valley on the Talas side, they fled via a smaller road up and over the ridgeline above the village. At the crest, Marcus turned and looked down the valley. Toward Talas, distant confusion, a strange glow that shifted colors and made the horizon roil with menace. The lights from planes or helicopters cut through air, fading in and out as if passing through banks of thick cloud. He thought he could see large shapes moving in the valley, but each time he tried to focus on one it seemed to blend into the mirk and vanish.

He knew, though. Horrors were out there. The certainty of it made his skin crawl.

He pulled his gaze in to what mattered, the people he cared about. The caravan of jokers crept upward under the bone-grey highlights of a full moon. The truck Olena had commandeered in Talas led the way, its engine rumbling loud despite the fact that it inched forward at a walking pace. The bed was crammed with children and the old, and those for whom walking was hard, or impossible. Behind it came the rest of the village's vehicles: Timur's truck, an old Russian-made van, a car missing doors on one side, another pulling a makeshift trailer piled high with supplies, and a motorcycle that looked absurd beneath the three teenage boys who shared it. In among the motorized vehicles, a procession of wagons creaked along, drawn by an old nag, a mule, and a joker who looked more like a white bull than like the man he'd once been. Many just walked.

Silently, Marcus wondered, *How are we ever going to make it? Five hundred miles* . . . It seemed an impossible distance, but it was the only way. He wouldn't leave them.

Neither, apparently, would Olena. She'd had a dustup with her father, both of them speaking machine-gun rapid Ukrainian. Marcus wasn't sure what she'd said, but she must've had him by the balls in some way or another. Instead of liquifying Timur and just taking his truck, Vasel had stood by impatiently as they packed. Now, he kept pace beside Olena's truck, continuing to lecture her, gesturing his frustration with his entire body. He still scared the hell out of Marcus, but not the way he had as the cool customer who had first shown up in a helicopter with a mini-army at his call. He was jumpy in a way he hadn't been before. There was fear in him. And just that fact chilled Marcus, underlined how real this all was.

As she rumbled past him, Olena smiled and waved. She was clearly enjoying her father's frustration. Watching her, it stunned him again that he was here, in some crazy-ass country he'd never even known existed, with a beautiful girl who he both knew and didn't know, with a gangster ace that might destroy them or save them, and with a procession of jokers he could barely talk to but felt willing to stake his life on. He thought of his family, a world away in the suburbs of Baltimore. A quick barrage of ancient memories flashed through his mind, times long gone. What would they think if they knew where he was? Nothing, he figured. They didn't want to know, wouldn't care if they did. *Forget about them,* he thought. *Only here and now and these people matter.* He pushed his past out of his mind.

He noticed Nurassyl gazing at him from the back of the truck. The joker boy held up a tentacled hand.

Marcus did the same. He mouthed the words the boy was fond of saying, "High-five, bro. What's up?" He couldn't help saying them with a Kazakh accent. He figured he'd hear those particular words in the boy's voice from now on.

The Handsmith, who was trailing behind the truck, stopped beside him. He turned and took in the scene a moment. He didn't give an indication he saw the vague shapes Marcus did. After a short silence, he said, "Moses."

"What?" Marcus asked.

The man turned to him. He smiled with one corner of his mouth, revealing the gap of a missing tooth Marcus hadn't noticed before. "You . . . Moses."

"Oh," Marcus said, "you mean I'm like Moses leading the Jews out of Egypt? Hardly." He smirked at the idea, though the compliment made him flush. "Like Moses taking you to a promised land called Baikonur . . ."

The man nodded. "Like Moses to Baikonur. Come, Moses, to Baikonur." He slipped an arm around Marcus's shoulder and eased him into motion. Sliding forward beside him, Marcus looked ahead into the moonlit valley on the far side of the ridgeline. The road switched back and forth as it descended, a silver shimmer so bright that the vehicles had begun to cut their lights and inch along it at one with the night.

Good, Marcus thought. This was one migration that was better done in secret. Better, as jokers, that they travel as far as they can unnoticed by the world. *Or unnoticed by a god that looks down on it and laughs.*

It was close to midnight when some impatient asshole with no sense of time simultaneously rang the doorbell and pounded on the farmhouse door. Mollie, half awake, welcomed the respite from her dreams.

Mom came downstairs a moment later wearing a dead look in her eyes. The same dead look she'd worn since Mollie had taken her to the hospital.

"Mollie." Her flat voice carried no emotion. "Get your lazy ass upstairs and answer the door."

"Why me? Who is it?"

"I dunno, but there's a lot of 'em and they're wearing suits." Rarely, if ever, was it good news when a suit showed up unannounced on a farm. "And they're asking for you. So go up there before you cause this family even more grief."

As Mollie mounted the stairs, she could hear Jeff calling a report to the rest of the family. His bedroom looked out over the porch. "They have a dog. And I think one of 'em's carrying a gun!"

Mollie stopped. The soft yellow glow of the porch light through the frosted glass of the storm door showed human silhouettes standing on the porch. She opened a hole in space to make sure the barn was locked up tight before opening the door. Then she reached through a portal to Bismarck and grabbed a silk scarf from the closet.

Three people stood on the stoop. Some sort of K-9 unit, apparently—the dog Jeff had seen from upstairs was a big-ass mastiff. The men wore suits, and they didn't make an effort to conceal their sidearms.

"Mollie Steunenberg?"

"Yeah. And you are . . . ?"

The dog stepped forward, leaned toward Mollie, took a long deep sniff, and stepped back. Weird.

The man who spoke had a face that looked like it had been sculpted in a hurry. Not the crowbar kind of sculpting, not like Jim and Troy had done to each other. At least this guy had a face, of sorts. But a network of faint scars ribbed his features, his eyes weren't quite on the same level, and his chin seemed the wrong shape for his jaw, almost as though it was lacking some bone. He wasn't hideous, but he seemed not quite right. She didn't recognize the Fed or his backup singers. She'd know if she'd met him before—his face was off just enough to be pretty memorable. She stopped staring at his face long enough to glance at the badge he flashed in her face.

Redundantly, he said, "William Ray, SCARE." He jerked a thumb over his shoulder. "These are my colleagues: Agents Moon, Huginn, and Muninn."

The scarecrow-tall guys hanging back behind the badge-flasher were twins. They shared the same pale complexion, the same sweep of inky feathers on the scalp instead of hair, and identical eye patches over their left eyes.

"You're either way early or way late, but Halloween is in October and we're all out of Tootsie Pops." Probably because it was the middle of the night, she hadn't slept well, and because he was being an asshole, it took a second for what he'd said to sink in.

"I only count three of you," she said.

The dog growled. *Oh.* Mollie suppressed a sudden urge to flee like a startled fawn. "Let me guess," she said. "You must be Agent Moon. Strays have to sleep in the barn."

The SCARE guy with the mashed-up face rolled his eyes. "What happened to your family, Mollie?"

"Nothing happened to my family." Mollie tightened the scarf around her neck, wincing slightly when it rubbed against her abraded skin.

"Is that the story you're sticking with? Because the hospital's telling us a very different story."

"We live on a farm. Sometimes people get hurt. It's dangerous work."

The Feds looked at each other. Agent Ray said, "Uh-huh. It must be even more dangerous than I realized. The occasional pitchfork stabbing, sure, I can see that. But bite marks? Human bite marks?"

Mollie wondered how they knew about that. So she shrugged again. The gesture tugged at her scarf; she reached up to catch it before it fell loose.

One of the backup singers, either Huginn or Muninn, piped up. In a voice that sounded like it was meant to be funneled through a beak, he asked, "How did you get those ligature marks on your neck?"

"What's a ligature mark?"

"The purple things you're trying to hide under that scarf," said Agent Ray. "If we found a corpse with those wounds we'd say she'd probably died of strangulation."

She said, "Uh-huh. Well I'm obviously not dead but I really appreciate the concern. So, hey, thanks for dropping by." She made to close the door.

Ray blocked the door with his foot. "Don't jerk us around. We've been to the hospital. I've seen entire platoons just back from their third tour in the most war-ravaged backwaters suffering fewer casualties than your family. So how about you fess up and tell us what the hell happened here?"

"Oh, yeah? Why don't you go take a long walk off a short pier? In fact, let me help you with that."

She reached for a doorway, something over the South Pacific, but the fucking thing kept slipping away because she couldn't quite picture it. Just as she got it fixed in her head, the dog leapt forward with a growl that could have felled the walls of Jericho.

Mollie retreated a step. "Whoa, whoa, whoa! Let's all calm down here."

She decided against dumping Fido and the Feds into shark-infested waters. Not because the portal wouldn't open, that wasn't the problem at all, but merely because it was prudent. She could have. She just chose not to.

"Can we come inside?"

"Nope."

Instead, Mollie joined them on the stoop and closed the door behind her. She beckoned them away from the house, where she knew Mom and the boys were listening to every single word. They walked a dozen yards toward where the rusted cattle guard spanned the culvert at the end of the drive. Wind whickered through the moonlit stubble in the adjoining field. It dusted Mollie's skin with a fine layer of grit.

Either Huginn or Muninn screeched, "We want to thank you, Ms. Steunenberg, for returning Agent Norwood's body to the States. That was thoughtful."

"Oh, yeah." Billy Ray yawned. "The way you dumped his corpse on the floor, that was super touching." He stretched an arm over his head, twisting until his joints popped.

The other twin continued, "But we won't lie to you. Plunking heavily armed gangsters into the middle of the precinct was less helpful. But Agent Norwood's family will be very grateful. You did the right thing there, so we'll call that one even."

"Jamal was, um . . . You know. He wasn't so bad. He deserved better than to be left—" Mollie cut herself off before she said something incredibly awkward. Something about abandoning people in Talas. In cannibal central. She shook her head, pinched the bridge of her nose until the tears went away.

Oh, screw it. Jamal had been working with SCARE, so maybe . . .

"Hey. Um. Do you guys happen to know a cop named Franny Black?"

"Are you kidding?" Ray laid a hand over his breast. "He's like a brother to me."

"Did he, uh . . . I was, you know, just wondering if he's back from Kazakhstan yet."

"You mean you're wondering if he made it home after you abandoned him in the middle of nowhere?"

Mollie shrugged. "Look, I'm just asking."

"Worry not. He got home safe and sound." Ray paused, then held up a pair of crossed fingers. "He's like *this* with your old pal Baba Yaga now."

"She's here? In the States?" Mollie tossed her gaze back and forth across the farm, looking for another passenger in the Feds' car, or for a flash of Baba Yaga's hair as she bulled into the house, or even ohcrapohcrapohcrap into the—

Mollie set off toward the barn at a fast walk. Moon leapt ahead and blocked her path. Ray said, "Relax, kid. She's in New York."

"Oh." The tension went out of her shoulders like a spring uncoiling. Her teeth actually squeaked when she stopped grinding them. "Okay."

"But just out of curiosity, what's in the barn that you don't want Baba Yaga to see?"

"Nothing. Just cows, cow shit, and hay. What do you expect to find in a barn?"

"Okay. In that case, how about you give us a tour? Because, you know, I've never been inside an actual working barn before and I'd just love to see it."

Mollie said, "I'd just love to see a warrant."

Ray chuckled. "Uh, you saw my badge, right? You think I couldn't get one?"

"So what? Even if there was something in the barn we didn't want you to see, and there isn't, we all know I could have it long gone by the time you came back with the paper. So you'd be wasting your time. And as tax-payers who pay your salary we'd call serious bullshit on that."

Oops. Ffodor had warned her that there were certain subjects a professional thief would be wise to avoid. But he was such a jerk, this Fed, he got under her skin.

Ray nodded. "Income taxes. Yeah. That's an interesting topic. But let's put a pin in that one and come back to it later."

Huginn or Muninn said, "Why the sudden interest in Detective Black?"

"I just, um . . ." *Don't think about the baby. Don't think about it. Don't think about pitchfork tines and people tearing into a twitching infant on iron spikes and desperately needing to pull out people's guts. Don't don't don't. Just don't.* "I, uh, I was just wondering if he saw anything weird when he was over there."

Quick as a rifle shot, the twin agents exchanged a look. The dog stood taller, its ears swiveling toward her like a pair of fuzzy radar dishes.

Ray glanced toward the barn again. The penny dropped. He slapped a palm to his forehead as though he'd just had a flash of insight.

"Oh. Got it. You went back to loot the casino, tossing the money in the barn as you went." He spoke to her, but looked at the others while he did. "You went back to Talas and something happened while you were there . . ."

One of the twins spoke again, his screechy voice pitched lower. "What happened in Talas, Ms. Steunenberg?"

Mollie shrugged. The wind tugged at her scarf. The loose end flopped over her shoulder. She didn't bother to hide her throat. Or wipe her watery eyes. "I dunno. Just some majorly fucked-up stuff."

She concentrated on breathing, filling her lungs with one long shuddery breath.

Ray said, quietly, "You witnessed some serious stuff going down. Different from the fight club. Worse. Right?"

Mollie nodded. Sniffled. She didn't bother to deny it. For one thing, she was too busy trying and failing not to weep, not to fall apart into a blub-bering mess. And for another, these assholes knew more than she did about what happened. And that was somewhat reassuring.

One of the twins asked, "And is what you witnessed in Talas related to what happened here?"

She couldn't talk. Her throat was too tight; her face was beet red now, she knew, for she burned with shame and fear. All she could do was keep nodding.

"Oh, my God," said Ray. The SCARE agents studied their surroundings again, looking slightly jumpy. The dog growled at the barn, fur bristling. Their agitation was less reassuring.

"It's over. It passed," she sobbed. "Why are you guys here, anyway? If you came to arrest me you're taking your sweet time. Do you understand what's going on?"

Ray sighed like somebody who very much disliked what he knew. "Yeah. Sort of," he said. "Things are not good right now. And we need your help."

Mollie shivered. How was it suddenly so cold out here? She crossed her arms. Hugging herself in a pointless attempt to ward off a bone-deep chill, she said, "No, no, no, *no fucking way* am I going back to that hellhole, not in a trillion years."

. . . a howling newborn, twitching on iron spikes while men and women tore into the baby fat like wolves devouring a felled deer . . .

Ray raised his hands, palm out. "If you want to understand what happened to you and your family, and if you want to prevent it from happening again—and I know you do, Mollie—your only bet is to come to New York with us." He took a deep steadying breath, as if preparing for something he didn't do very often. "I have . . . There's a lot on the line, okay? So I am asking you, one human being to another, to come to New York and hear us out. Please?"

He even ventured a smile. It was about as attractive as a cheap toupee on a hairless cat. But . . . goddamn. He really meant it. This was personal for him.

What if she'd known somebody had the power to prevent the rage-riot in the barn? What if somebody had had the power to prevent her brothers from pounding each other's faces into hamburger? She would have pleaded, too.

Mollie sighed. "Do you really know what's going on?"

"Yes."

"Do you know how to stop it?"

He hesitated. "Not yet. But we're working on it."

Well, at least he was honest.

"Very well. One red-eye express to New York, coming up."

She was so exhausted and emotionally wrung-out that creating another fold in space felt like trying to do a push-up with her tongue. But she managed to create a doorway to a Manhattan taxi stand on the third try.

After a moment's resistance, a shimmering doorway appeared in midair. A whiff of exhaust wafted through the portal. Traffic noise was light this time of night, but the loud rambling of a drunk echoed down the steel canyons. The hotel bellmen unloading luggage from a late-arriving tour bus stepped around the hole in space as deftly as though it were nothing but a dog turd on the sidewalk. New Yorkers: it was impossible to faze them. Mollie supposed that when you lived just a few subway stops from Jokertown you either got accustomed to the weird stuff pronto, or you moved.

Huginn and Muninn went first, followed by Moon. The dog hopped lightly from the moonlit gravel drive of an Idaho farm to the halogen glare of a New York sidewalk. Billy Ray waved her forward and followed so closely—practically grinding against her—that she couldn't have left him behind if she wanted to. But she was too tired to try.

He waved his SCARE badge at a sleepy taxi driver and ushered her into the backseat. Mollie was asleep before the driver had the car in gear.

Franny walked the streets of Jokertown.

It was a warm night and the streets were crowded. Jokers sat on stoops, passed cigarettes and conversations. Kids rode skateboards, tossed footballs. The flavors of a hundred different cuisines filled the night air. A pair of deformed joker lovers twined arms and stole kisses while orbiting each other in their wheelchairs. Through open windows the sounds of televisions, radios, and iPods spun their harmonies.

Occasionally there would be the serious tones of a news reader describing rape, murder, people eating their own flesh. And worse. People being changed. The way they had been changed on that long ago day back in '46 when the wild card virus had been released.

He hurried past those windows because now he had heard it all. And after hearing the tapes he realized the full magnitude of what he had done. The world as they knew it was ending. Knew that death or worse was coming for them all unless a young woman could find a solution.

If he had known would he still have gone to rescue the kidnapped jokers?

He thought about the beaten body of José Neto, the dead joker who had started this entire clusterfuck. The forgotten people had been first to be stolen. The dregs, the derelicts, people no one would miss. Then the losers like José whose family would be ignored when they reported him missing. Eventually Baba Yaga's claws had snatched away the worthy people, people whose absence would be noticed, and it had finally culminated with IBT and Father Squid.

Preserve and protect. He'd had to go. He didn't have a choice. And he'd really only accelerated the day of reckoning. The aging body of Hellraiser was going to die. Or Baba Yaga would die without passing on her formula to keep the monster at bay. Franny really hadn't caused this. The justifications rang hollow.

Organ music sang through the open door of the church of Jesus Christ Joker for indeed this was where his wandering steps had brought him. Word of the priest's death had clearly spread because there was a carpet of flowers all around the walls of the church and spilling down the steps. Franny hated that he hadn't thought to buy a bouquet. Of course he still had no money. Tomorrow he was going to have to start the laborious process of reestablishing his identity.

But really, why? What is the point? he thought.

He walked up the steps and into the church. Pausing at the holy water font he dipped his fingers, genuflected toward the altar, and crossed himself. There were a lot of people in the shadowed space, hunched over the back of pews or kneeling staring up at the Joker Christ hung above the altar. Others were lighting candles. The space smelled of melted wax and incense.

Franny slipped into a back pew and knelt. He said the rosary and the familiar cadence of the words were a balm to his bruised spirit. He covered his face with a hand and offered up a prayer for the soul of a good man then whispered, "God forgive me for what I've done. I may have destroyed your creation."

This time prayer offered no comfort. His guilt was too great. He left the pew but before he could reach the door he found himself looking down into a pair of eyes peering out from a face deformed by lumps and knobs of twisted skin. It was Wartface. One of the jokers he'd freed in Talas.

"Hey! It *is* you, man! Where were you? I looked around and you weren't there and that hole was gone, too."

"There was fighting. The girl who helped get us there . . ." *She abandoned me flat, the fucking bitch.* He swallowed the angry words. They shouldn't be uttered in this holy place. Instead he said, "She panicked and she ran." He remembered Mollie's upthrust middle finger and the look of bitter triumph. Yeah, some panic.

The organist stopped playing. People were starting to stare. Franny saw more of the jokers who had been Baba Yaga's prisoners. People stood and gathered around him. A gentle-faced man with a chitinous insectile body laid a hand on Franny's arm.

"Thank you," he said softly. He paused to push his glasses back up on his nose. "I thought I was going to die there. Thank you for giving me back my life."

Only for a handful of days, Franny thought. *"You destroyed the world. I hope it was worth it."* Baba Yaga's voice echoed in his head. He wanted to confess, to admit his sin to more than God, but he couldn't bear to destroy their joy and happiness however brief it might be. He just stood, accepting their congratulations and thanks though every grateful word seemed to scald his soul.

"Excuse me." A woman's voice, soft and husky.

Franny turned and found himself facing an older African-American woman dressed in a conservative woman's business chic. Her hair was lightly silvered and her eyes were red from crying. An older African-American man stood next to her. He was big and powerfully built. Franny saw echoes of Jamal Norwood's features in both their faces.

Standing next to them was a tiny perfect doll of a girl. She was beautiful enough to catch the breath in a man's chest, a golden blonde with dark blue eyes glittering with unshed tears . . . and maybe eighteen inches tall if she stretched. *How the hell did they ever?* Franny cut off that line of thought with a mental knife.

"Are you the police officer who was with our son in . . . in Kazakhstan?" the woman asked.

"Yes, ma'am. I'm Francis Black."

"Could we talk with you? We'd like to hear . . ." Her voice faded away.

The jokers, displaying that uncanny sensitivity that seemed to be a hallmark of all of them, moved away.

Franny led the couple and the tiny girl over to a corner near the wrought-iron stand of prayer candles. The flickering flames brought sections of their faces into momentary sharp relief, a jigsaw puzzle picture of grief.

"Did he die a good death?" Bill Norwood's voice grated like metal dragged across rock.

The question would have taken Franny aback if during conversations with Jamal while they had waited for a suspect to show up he hadn't learned that Big Bill Norwood had been a football coach. In fact his son's coach. It was the kind of tough, show-no-pain response Franny would have gotten from his maternal uncle who coached his hockey team up in Saratoga.

"I don't know that any death is good, sir," Franny replied. "He died brave, if that's what you mean. His actions saved a lot of people." He gestured toward the nave of the church. "A lot of them are here tonight. Reunited with their families because of your son."

Maxine Norwood and the tiny joker girl Julia were quietly crying. Julia fluttered over to him, her feet scarcely seeming to touch the ground. "Jamal was sick. Why the heck did he go?"

"Jamal was a law enforcement officer. He knew his duty and he did it." Franny swallowed hard. "I am sorry for your loss," he said formally. The recommended course for grief calls was to leave it at that, but he felt he couldn't. This death had been personal for him, too. "I didn't know Jamal long, but we became friends. I'm grieving for him, too."

Maxine gave him a quick hug, and Bill gave him a buffet on the shoulder. Julia hugged him around the waist. He accepted the comfort offered by this physical contact. He needed it after what he'd heard in Baba Yaga's hospital room.

Franny headed for the door. Bill called after him, "Don't know what you two did over there, but you seem to have unleashed hell."

Franny hunched his shoulders, dug his hands into his pockets, and fled.

FRIDAY

IT WAS A LONG and restless night, ending at first light. The Angel had slept fitfully, and was stiff, sore, and hungry when she awoke.

The fog glowed phosphorescent green, eerily energized by its unknown source, but it was shot through with other colors as well. Brief bursts of colors, acinetic white like a burst of fireworks, arterial red like a burst of blood from a severed jugular, pops of green like the lures of the fish who live so deep under the sea that the phosphorescence they themselves generate are the only light they ever see. Once during the night she'd awoken to what she thought was a rumble of thunder and saw a long, sinuous beast, a snake or maybe an eel, with fantastic mouth feelers twitching before its wide-opened jaws, swimming through the night, its lolling tongue lifting a human-sized and -shaped object. She thought she heard a feeble but terrified scream but she was tired and her eyes still smarted from the touch of the fog on the previous day and after she'd blinked both the shape and its perhaps imagined victim were gone.

"Hey, guys," a feeble voice came from the back, "I gotta pee."

"Well, go pee," the Angel managed.

"Can you give me a hand?" Bugsy asked. "I'm kind of tired. Really tired."

"I'm not?" the Angel said, but she got out of the SUV and went around to the back door and half helped, half dragged Bugsy from the vehicle.

"Why am I so tired?" Bugsy complained. "I didn't lose that many wasps."

He leaned on the Angel as they shuffled a few feet away.

"You can't afford to lose what little muscle you've got." Her face screwed up "You better not be peeing on my leg—"

"Sorry," Bugsy mumbled.

"It's this place," the Angel said quietly, looking around at the desolation. "It's sucking the life out of everything. Zip up."

"I gotta have something to eat," Bugsy croaked.

"I've got some food in my duffel," the Angel said. "Let's hunt up Tinker."

"Maybe we better get out of here. I mean, look at us, just three of us, here, and some Kazakhs—"

Tinker came striding from down the road and heard Bugsy. "Guess again."

"The Kazakhs are gone?" Bugsy repeated numbly.

"That's what I said, hoon." Tinker didn't look pleased. "I was up all night—couldn't sleep if I tried." The Angel thought he looked more haggard, more worried, and angrier than yesterday. "I didn't hear them bugger off last night, but I heard . . . things moving around us in the buildings."

"What kind of things?"

"Who the hell knows, sonny boy," Tinker suddenly yelled. "Awful, horrible, slimy, choking, killing things. And they're coming after us!"

"What about the others?" the Angel said quietly.

"The others?" They both turned to look at her.

"Bubbles, Earth Witch, Lohengrin, the rest . . . the ones who already went in."

Tinker bit his lip.

"How's the communications with Babel?"

"Not good," Tinker said. "There's plenty of interference. Static. Weird whistling sounds. Voices, almost, like someone else on the line . . ."

"Let's give it a shot," the Angel said. "Call Babel."

Tinker nodded and got on the radio, but it was worse than he'd said. All they could hear was a steady stream of sharp, staccato static with momentary instants of lucidity that produced a stray word or short phrase. Some words were not in Babel's voice; some were not even in English or any earthly language.

The occasional burst of insane laughter added a frission that crawled up the Angel's spine like a spider with icy feet.

"SSSSSSSSSSSSSSSSSSScomeSSSSSSSSSSSLohehenSSSSSSSSSSSSSSSSS.fghtag-nmwalwltSSSSSSSSSSSSSSHAHAHAHASSSSSSSSSSpleaseSSSSSSSSSSSSwrckg-gugghh . . ."

Tinker shut the radio down with a savage, jerky motion.

"It won't get better," he muttered.

"It won't," the Angel agreed quietly. She knew what she had to do. She didn't want to do it. She knew, in her heart, that Billy would never want her to go alone and unsupported back into that hell but she knew sure as hellfire and damnation that he, himself, would be the first one in. "I got out once. I can do it again."

She went around the back of the SUV and took out her duffel bag. She dumped all its contents on the ground. She divided her food and water into two piles, one twice the size of the other.

"You don't have to do this," Tinker said as Bugsy shuffled forward, eyeing the cache of food.

The Angel shook her head. "We all came on this journey together. You remain loyal to those you come with. Billy taught me that simple fact. If we can't stand for each other, how can we stand against the Adversary?"

"The Adversary?"

"The Foe. The Enemy. The Devil."

"There ain't no Devil."

"There assuredly is. I have seen him and I have battled him many times in his many forms. I have known him for many years, as have we all. In our own ways we rage against the Night. Otherwise, we wouldn't be here."

Tinker nodded.

"Keep trying to raise Babel to let them know what kind of hell this place has become. But for God's sake—get out if things get too dicey."

"Don't worry about us," Tinker said.

She remembered the spider pack from the day before. "Here's something important to tell HQ if you can get through. Tell them that I've seen things in Talas that I saw when Billy, John Fortune, and I had taken our ride with the Highwayman. Can you remember that?"

Tinker nodded. The Angel glanced at Bugsy, who was eyeing the stack of food on the ground. "Bugsy?"

"Yeah. Got it." He snagged a package from the bigger pile and Tinker reached down and smacked him in the head.

"Hey!"

"Don't eat it all," the Angel warned. "You don't know how long that'll have to last."

The Angel packed the smaller portion of supplies into her belt pockets.

It didn't take long, because there wasn't very much. She stood and hooked her last full water canteen on the belt next to the food. Food was one thing, but there had to be potable water somewhere out there in Talas. After all, millions of people inhabited the city only a couple of days previously.

"Take care, mate," Tinker said.

She smiled, said her prayer, and her wings came upon her. She smiled her good-bye and rose slowly and majestically into the air and was gone, as if borne away on a gentle wind.

After they arrived at the UN, Agent Ray herded Mollie to an office with a view of lower Manhattan from many stories up. The window faced south; the East River flowed to her left. A misty night, but she could make out the spotlights on Jetboy's Tomb in the far distance. The shingle on the office door read BARBARA BADEN.

Baden and Ray stepped out for a moment, so Mollie tried to rack out on Baden's leather sofa while they went to round up whomever it was they wanted Mollie to meet. Nice couch, but the anxiety had her curled into such a tight fetal ball that her back and neck ached like somebody had tried to use her vertebrae for a xylophone.

Somebody's executive assistant ("I'm Juliet, but call me Ink.") poked her head in to ask Mollie if she needed anything. Nobody seemed to care or notice it was the middle of the night. Working at the UN must suck if it meant keeping such hours.

"I'd lick a spider for a decent cup of coffee."

She expected it to come in a paper cup, like from a vending machine. But she got an actual ceramic mug. It even had a logo: THE UNITED NATIONS COMMITTEE ON EXTRAORDINARY INTERVENTIONS.

Two things went through her head at the same time. One: *The Committee has its own coffee mugs? That seems a little douchey.* Two: *Shit, shit, shit. Crapsticks. Shit.*

She should have realized the Committee would be involved. This was a problem. Noel Matthews had been working for, or maybe with, the Committee when he recruited her to help steal the Nshombos' gold. Were people still angry about how that went down? Crap.

The coffee wasn't terrible. Before she finished it, Agent Ray and Baden returned with a short man. The slightly tubby guy introduced himself as J. C. Jayewardene.

Baden said, "Thank you, Ms. Steunenberg, for agreeing to meet with the Secretary-General and me on such short notice. We appreciate it."

Mollie's mouth went dry. Bad enough that Ray had come all the way to Idaho just to put Mollie in a room with the de facto leader of the Committee. But the goddamned Secretary-General of the goddamned United Nations? Didn't he have diplomats and world leaders to harass? For somebody like him to make time for a stupid hick from potato country, she figured the situation had to be pretty fucking grim.

Was it ever.

Because, while the sun rose and Ray stood in the corner with his arms crossed, Baden and Jayewardene sat down and proceeded to tell Mollie the worst story she'd ever heard. Worst not because it was unbelievable—oh, she believed it all right, because only something absolutely terrible could explain what happened in Talas and in the barn—but because it was so fucking *hopeless*. The end of the world and supernatural evil and aces going batshit like the baby eaters in Talas . . . Jesus. Mollie and her family had nearly killed each other after just a few minutes. How long had that team been stuck over there?

Compared to this, Mollie's role rounding up jokers for the fight club was positively heroic. Sure, she'd been forced into it, and a lot of those people had died, but at least it had helped to keep the unstoppable world-consuming evil at bay, though she hadn't known it at the time.

Nothing the UN guys said made her the least bit interested in participating or helping. Helping meant *voluntarily* getting exposed again to that . . . that . . . whatever it was. Horrorshow. Hellraiser. Those were the names they used. She'd rather kill herself before she experienced that again. She'd kill her loved ones, too, if she had loved ones, before the malignant madness had a chance to take them. And not in a psycho face-eating pitchfork-murdering sort of way. Gently. To save them from something worse.

Despite having received the full download from Baba Yaga, Agent Ray and the others still thought there was a way to fight this. What an idiot. They couldn't understand. Not really. They hadn't been inside it. Hadn't embraced the madness as it took them. Hadn't welcomed the veil of scarlet rage as it settled over their minds.

She stood and crossed to the window again. The view of Jetboy's Tomb seemed fitting. A monument to failure. He at least had had a fighting chance. But against Horrorshow, nobody stood a fucking chance.

She tried to make them see. Pointing at the logo on her mug, she said, "Your team is dead."

So fierce was the look flashing across Ray's face that Mollie took a step back. He trembled as though tensing for a physical fight. "You don't know that! You don't know my wife! She could . . . Nobody knows what's going on over there."

"*I know!*" Mollie shouted. "I know. I've been inside it, okay? A rage-slave to mindless supernatural evil. You don't know what it's like! You have NO MOTHERFUCKING IDEA." People in the outer office turned to stare. She ignored them. "You can't imagine it. There's no fighting it. I don't care who you are. My dad and brothers put each other in the hospital in just a few seconds. At least two of them will never have normal lives, assuming they survive their injuries. Taking a crowbar to the face half a dozen times will do that to a person. And they're just nats, all of them! Chew on that for a moment. You're talking about trying to rescue *aces* who've been inside it for *hours*."

Baden said, gently, "We have to try to save them."

"And you're the only person for the job," said Jayewardene. He had a very gentle manner, quite welcome in contrast to Ray. "So will you please help us? You could save many lives."

"I understand," Baden said, "you have a rather, ahh, colorful record." (Agent Ray snorted. "That's one word for it.") She ignored him, continuing, "In return for your help, we could arrange to wipe the slate clean."

Wow. They really were desperate. But that meant Mollie had bargaining power. Leverage. Good. She could salvage something good out of this nightmare. Because she didn't give a runny shit about her "record"—she wanted something else, and these guys had the power to make it happen. So if they wanted her help so badly, they'd have to earn it.

Mollie said, "Here's my condition. I want to talk to Baba Yaga first."

That shut them up. After a moment's bewildered silence, Ray said, "A little while ago you looked ready to drop one in your pants when you thought she was at your farm."

She glared at him. "You said you needed my help. I've listened to your story, but now it's my turn. And I won't lift a fucking finger until you put me in a room with Baba Yaga." *And maybe not even then. Not if it means returning to the psychopath cannibal hellhole.* "But if that vodka-marinated cunt even thinks of hocking a loogie at me—"

"She won't," said Baden. "We're all on the same side here, okay?"

"Okay," Mollie said, not fully convinced. "Fine. Let's go and see that withered old bitch. Where is she?"

In a hospital, it turned out. *(Good.)* Ray recited an address in Jokertown. Mollie thought for a moment, did some arithmetic with cross streets. She had dozens of portal sites in New York, and she'd memorized locations at various hospitals and medical clinics after Ffodor had harped on her about it, but the Jokertown Clinic wasn't one of them.

Hospitals . . . She never could have gotten Dad and the boys to the doctors in time if not for Ffodor's advice, she realized. She shook her head so hard it wrenched her neck. Yet still the regrets clung to her like cobwebs.

To keep from crying again, she said, "I can't get us there in one shot. My closest site is about five blocks from there."

Ray looked impressed. "That's actually pretty close." Mollie didn't like the way his eyebrows hitched together, as though he were thinking through a puzzle. "How many sites do you have memorized in New York?"

"A lot."

The SCARE agent was a lot sharper than he looked. He said, "Wow. Rounding up all those jokers must have been hard work. I feel for you."

When Michelle woke, she was alone.

The fog curled around her like an obscene lover. It was misting again, but the cold had changed to a suffocating heat, just like the jungle in the PPA. She got up. It was difficult. The punch from Ana's dirt wall had given her a surge of fat. It wasn't as much as she'd handled before, but she hurt now. Really hurt. And that frightened her.

Looking around, she saw she was in the jungle. In the distance, she could hear Monster roaring. The last time she'd encountered him, she'd battled him to a standstill, but now she wouldn't be able to. Not when something as minor as Earth Witch's wall had thrown her for such a loop. She took a step and groaned.

No, no, no, she thought, a cold shiver running down her spine. *This can't be happening. How will I protect Adesina? Screw that freak. I wouldn't*

even be here if it wasn't for that creature. She should have left her in that char-
nel pit with the rest of those monstrosities.

Nononononononono. I love Adesina. Michelle clung to the thought, but it
only flickered in her mind for a moment.

And as she thought of it, the ground in front of her opened. *Ana. That
bitch.* But she didn't see Earth Witch. Rotting things began crawling out of
the hole. They were covered in the festering syrup of the charnel pit. The
stench made her gag. Around her the jungle began closing in. Pushing her
closer to the pit.

Across the pit, she saw Mummy.

"I just killed you!" she screamed. "I've killed you twice!"

Michelle held her hands, palms up, in front of her. A barrage of lemon-
sized bubbles flowed from them. They hit and blew chunks of Mummy
into the air. It didn't matter. The chunks reassembled and she grew larger.

"No," Michelle moaned. Terror surged through her. "No, you're dead."

Mummy began walking toward her. The creatures crawling from the
pit stopped crawling out, allowing her to walk over them. They lifted their
slimy tentacles and she stepped across them, moving inexorably toward
Michelle.

Run, Michelle thought. *Run.*

Jayewardene had messaged her that morning. *Need you. Great Hall ASAP.*
Barbara grabbed Ink and took the elevator from their offices down to the
main floors.

Jayewardene motioned to Barbara from the podium stage where he sat
in the main hall. She could hear the representative from Uzbekistan de-
claiming in Russian from the lectern set below the podium. ". . . great state
of Uzbekistan and our neighbor in Kyrgyzstan have little choice. If Kazakhstan cannot control this threat, we must deal with it ourselves before it
reaches our border. Surely the member nations and the Security Council
can understand this . . ."

"Stay here," Barbara told Ink, then slid past the guard at the foot of
the steps and climbed up until she stood behind Jayewardene. She could
see the curved rows of representatives and their staff, rising in tiers before her—most of the seats filled, which she gathered was unusual. She
crouched down next to him; from his headphone, she could hear the whis-

per of the translator's voice. "After him, Kyrgyzstan is speaking. They're both saying the same thing: if the infection is centered in the city of Talas, then Talas must be destroyed. They're making the case for taking action."

"We can't let that happen. If what Baba Yaga has said is true, that would allow the door to swing open entirely."

"I agree. But the mood is in their favor. They intend to ask for a resolution to be allowed to protect their borders."

"You'd let them bomb Talas?"

"It's not something I can allow or disallow, Ms. Baden; it's that I think they will have the votes. Russia will vote in favor, and will drag all their allies to vote with them. Everyone is watching the chaos spreading and worrying about how far it will go. If Kazakhstan's next-door neighbors are willing to be the first to act, they won't condemn them for trying. Even the United States and its allies might feel the same way." Jayewardene stared at her blandly. "Russia will call for a vote, if no one else. Probably soon. Unless I have reason to delay the vote." He continued to look at her.

She nodded and rose, walking back down toward Ink. Jayewardene turned back to the papers before him as the representative from Uzbekistan continued to rail and argue his case. "Well?" Ink asked her.

"I have just one thing to say, then we'll go back to our office," Barbara said. "And that's this: Bababadalgharaghtakamminarronnkonnbronnton-nerronntuonnthunntrovarrhounawnskawntoohoohoordenenthurnuk!" With that, she released her wild card power, letting it spread over the entire hall.

For a moment, nothing happened. The Uzbekistan representative was still talking, but now the words echoing through the chamber were nonsense: "Ghar thurka jallaci indum . . ." he intoned, then closed his mouth, looking puzzled. "Harek ilkad?" he said. Around the hall, representatives were tapping at their earphones, or taking them off to speak to the people around them. The uproar started softly, then grew into a roar. People were standing around the hall, gesticulating and shouting, as if sheer volume could accomplish understanding. At the podium, Jayewardene was hammering his gavel, the sound reverberating. Representatives began to leave the hall, still shouting nonsense.

There was nothing but chaos in front of Barbara. "I think it's time for us to go now," Barbara said to Ink, who was staring at the confusion with wide eyes.

"Bababadal—what, Mizz B?" Ink asked Barbara as they left the UN hall through one of the back exits. The sound of shouted gibberish still echoed in the hallways. "God, that makes me sound like them," she added.

"*Finnigan's Wake*," Barbara answered. "It's supposed to be the word God thundered out after the Fall of Man. At least that's what my English professor back in Tel Aviv claimed. It seemed apropos, somehow."

"And you *memorized* it?"

"It was college. You wouldn't believe how many drinks I cadged being able to recite that."

Ink nodded. "I guess," she said. She inclined her head toward the continuing clamor. "Will that help, you think?"

"It'll give us some hours at least, and gives Jayewardene an excuse to be slow reconvening the session. Maybe he can even hold them off until tomorrow. In the meantime, we can decide what we have to do."

"You'll get Klaus and the others back, Mizz B," Ink said. "I know you will."

Barbara managed a weary smile at that. "Thanks. I hope you're right. Let's get back to the office. We have a lot of work to do. I need you to get on the phone to the White House . . ."

The leaves of the shrubs and trees smacked her in the face. Creepers grabbed at her feet and tripped her. It didn't matter. Michelle kept going. Every time she looked back, she could see Mummy behind her.

Occasionally, she'd let a bubble fly, but all it did was blow off a chunk of Mummy, which was then reabsorbed and made her larger. After a couple of futile bubbles, Michelle gave up and ran as fast as she could now that she'd lost a chunk of her weight. She was still fat, though.

Sweat, dank and smelling of fear, rolled off her. Her thighs chafed as she ran. *Fuck,* she thought, hating her fat for the first time. It was slowing her down.

She stopped abruptly and turned. This time she didn't aim at Mummy, but at the jungle floor in front of Mummy. Michelle blew up a chunk of earth, making a huge hole. Mummy didn't have time to stop, and she tumbled into it. Then Michelle let another round of bubbles go as dense and heavy as she could make them, and they piled into the pit on top of Mummy.

Michelle was significantly lighter now. "Get out of that, you bitch," she panted. Then she ran.

She ran blindly until her sides ached and her legs burned. A mindless terror possessed her. The jungle wasn't just a jungle anymore. It was changing, turning to some nightmarish landscape. Sometimes she slipped in bloody pools, landing hard on her hands and knees.

She saw a small boy hanging from a tree, pinned there by an enormous knife through his chest. A few yards later, she came across a woman in a filthy and torn flowered dress, systematically cutting off pieces of herself. She'd taken most of her left thigh and was working her way through her bicep.

"Want to help?" she asked, holding the knife out to Michelle. It dripped crimson blood. Michelle stopped and reached for the blade. *Sounds like fun,* she thought. *Knives aren't my thing, but I could help.*

Then Michelle heard something behind her. She made an impulsive choice. She let a bubble go, and it caught the cutting woman in the chest. A scarlet flower of blood bloomed there. Then, despite her fear of Mummy, Michelle laughed hysterically. She'd solved the whole help-me-with-the-knife problem.

She began running again. Grotesque scenes of self-mutilation went past as she ran. A man was peeling the skin off his body. The bluish muscles gleamed in the low light. He looked up at her quizzically, but immediately went back to his work. She heard him letting out little shrieks. Pain or hysteria—she couldn't tell.

She came upon two women holding a third down. They were scalping her. They bared their yellow teeth at Michelle, but she let three bubbles fly and neatly ripped all their heads off. *No point in saving someone who might as well be dead. Nor two who deserve to be.*

Now her lungs were nothing but pain and fire. Each breath was like breathing in a hot poker. And then, abruptly, the jungle vanished altogether.

Michelle found herself once again on the devastated streets of Talas. The miasma blurred her surroundings until she couldn't see beyond a few feet. Unspeakable things moved just far enough ahead that she couldn't quite make out what they were, and she hoped never to see them clearly.

A thudding invaded her mind again. It was like a section of timpani had taken up residence in her head and was playing the entire catalog of Joker Plague turned up to eleven.

She grabbed her head. The pounding wouldn't stop. It was so loud it made her want to vomit. And she did.

"Hello, Michelle."

She looked up. In front of her was Earth Witch. But it wasn't Ana. It was some shape-changer who was wearing an Ana meat-suit.

Michelle frowned and narrowed her eyes. "You're not Ana," she said. Bubbles were already forming in her hands. She let them fly. Or she would have if the earth hadn't opened up and swallowed her whole.

The clinic smelled like antiseptic. As soon as the odor hit her nose Mollie realized it had been hours since she'd checked with the hospital in Idaho. Were Jim and Troy out of surgery yet? Were Mick and Brent recovering? Had they found the rest of Dad's ear? They probably thought she'd abandoned them again and that she didn't even care. They all thought so little of her.

Ffodor had been different.

Billy Ray flashed his SCARE badge as they passed the nurses' station outside the isolation ward.

Mollie said, "You really get off on that, don't you? Seriously, it's like a sexual compulsion or something."

He didn't respond. Instead, he took her by the elbow and directed her down one corridor and around a corner. Mollie's step faltered a bit when she saw the no-neck crew flanking the door to Baba Yaga's room. She didn't recognize their faces or tattoos, but she certainly recognized the type. Typical. Even here, halfway around the world, Baba Yaga managed to scrounge up a troop of fine upstanding citizens to attend her every kneecap-shattering whim. The goons let them pass with a nod after glancing at Ray's badge. ("Wank, wank, wank," Mollie whispered.)

Baba Yaga lay unmoving, as expressive as an ice sculpture in her hospital bed. And—*holy shit!*—one of her arms ended at the elbow. Somebody had done a real number on the hag. *Good.* But there was color in her cheeks and the machines connected to her emitted a steady series of beeps. Mollie felt conflicted about that. She wanted the old woman to die, though not before Mollie had a chance to apply her leverage.

Baba Yaga wasn't alone, Mollie realized. She noticed the man sitting next to the hospital bed and flinched.

"Shit," she said.

Franny looked up from his phone. "Surprised to see me?"

She'd last seen him several days ago, when he was embroiled in a fire-fight in the Talas casino. She'd taken advantage of the distraction to pick the lock on his cuffs and open a doorway to Paris.

Mollie tried to toss a bored shrug, but it came off a little shaky. So did her raspy voice. "Nah. I figured you'd be fine once you didn't have to drag me everywhere."

"Oh, well, when you put it that way, thanks so much for that. You're just a forward-thinking humanitarian."

"I don't see why you're bitching," she said. "It obviously turned out okay."

Franny stood, cleared his throat. Baba Yaga cracked one eye open. Mollie took a step back and bumped into Ray. *So much for the tough front.*

"Ah," said the witch. "The little thief returns."

"Cram it up your vodka-pickled twat, you bitch."

"Guttersnipe."

Ray muttered, "Oh, for crying out loud."

"Hey! How dare you—"

"How dare I? How dare *you!*"

Baba Yaga's jaw muscles twitched, as though she were conjuring up a big gob of saliva. Franny yanked Mollie aside and planted himself with arms raised between her and the woman in the hospital bed. Baba Yaga turned away and swallowed rather than letting spit fly at the detective.

Interesting. What was that all about? It was usually spit-first-and-ask-questions-never with her. She'd thought Ray had been kidding when he claimed Franny and Baba Yaga were tight. They must have had one hell of a trip back from Talas if he'd earned her respect. Insofar as she respected anyone.

"Ladies! Truce, okay? We're all on the same side."

Mollie crossed her arms. Baba Yaga poked the tip of her tongue into one cheek, bulging it. A moment passed while they glared at one another.

The Russian woman broke the silence. "The situation has been explained to you." It wasn't a question, but Mollie nodded. The other woman studied her face through narrowed eyes. Mollie wanted to squirm under the scrutiny. She looked away. Still staring at Mollie, Baba Yaga said, "She has been touched by it. I see she carries the taint of one who has been exposed to Horrorshow. It's in her eyes. It leaves a mark. Nobody is quite the same after that."

"Yeah. I've seen it." Mollie hugged herself.

"Aha. Was it when you returned to rob my casino?"

Mollie glared at Billy Ray. "You asshole."

He screwed his deformed face into something that approximated indignation. "Why do you assume I told her? We're not idiots, you know. And you do have a record of predictable behavior. The Committee and Interpol have been taking an interest in you for quite a while. You're real popular with the NYPD now, too."

"It's true," said Franny. "You're what we call a repeat offender."

"You don't have anything on me."

Billy Ray said, "Only about thirty counts of kidnapping."

"Well la-de-dah. You'll never make it stick. I mean, hey, the world's gonna end in a few days, right? So good fucking luck pressing those charges."

The SCARE agent massaged his forehead. He turned to Franny. "Where on earth did you find this kid? Because she is a piece of work."

"Tell me about it."

Baba Yaga raised her voice to cut through the muttering and bickering. "These men think you can help. But they say you demanded an audience with me." She flinched, slightly, as if she'd tried to make a gesture. "So here we are. Have you come to apologize?"

Apologize? To *her*? Had everyone gone crazy? Maybe Mollie was still stuck inside the evil insanity bubble and only thought she'd escaped it. "No fucking way. I owe you nothing, you evil hag."

"Mollie." Franny tapped his wristwatch. "We are sort of on the clock here, okay? So if you could speed it along a little bit."

"Fine." A doorway to Idaho opened in the middle of the hospital room. Perhaps because she was too angry to remember to be afraid, this portal didn't resist her quite as much as the others had over the past day. A cold wind ruffled her hair and set the wires of Baba Yaga's monitors to swaying. A whiff of manure permeated the room. Baba Yaga twisted her mouth in a moue of distaste.

"Hey, wait—" Mollie stepped into the barn, grabbed the Louis XIV chair, and popped back to the hospital before Franny could finish his sentence. "—a second."

Billy Ray blinked at the chair. "What. The hell. Is that?"

"This is my condition for helping you. You don't like it, you can go to hell."

But Franny knew. She could see it in his eyes. He looked genuinely sad for her. She didn't like it. "Was this somebody you cared about?"

"He *is* somebody I care about." Mollie lugged the chair to the side of Baba Yaga's hospital bed. "Change him back."

The Russian woman blinked at her. "This is your condition? You thought I would do this and then you would do your part?"

The goddamned tears had come back. Everything turned blurry. "Change him back. Make him a person again!"

The hag shook her wrinkly head.

"Change him back *RIGHT FUCKING NOW!*"

Franny tried to interject. "Mollie—"

"I can't," said the Russian woman.

"You will. Turn Ffodor back right fucking now or I swear to God I will dump your leathery old ass into the Pacific Ocean a thousand miles from the middle of nowhere."

"Mollie." Franny took her arm. He tried to pull her aside but she wasn't about to let go of Ffodor. "She didn't say she wouldn't. She said she can't."

Mollie rounded on him. "Of course she can. She has to." She wept openly now. "You have to turn him back."

"I can't."

Billy Ray said, "I think she's telling you it's one-way, kid."

No. No. No.

Mollie lifted the heavy chair, shook it at Baba Yaga. Sorrow made her strong. "You have to turn him back so that I can apologize to him."

Baba Yaga closed her eyes. Shook her head.

"Ffodor has to hear it." Somewhere a dam burst, a dam she'd built a long time ago, and now a rushing cataract swept away the last of her self-control. She convulsed, struggling to speak through the wracking sobs. "He has . . . to hear . . . my apology. Make him a human again . . . so he can hear it and . . . forgive me . . . and I can stop . . . I can stop feeling like this. It hurts so much . . ." She fell to her knees, blinded by tears. Her nose was running and her upper lip tasted like snot.

"Please," she whispered. "Please turn Ffodor back so I can tell him I'm sorry. The world is ending and I can't die without his forgiveness."

Baba Yaga stated, in a voice like a mausoleum door slamming shut: "Your Ffodor is dead."

"No. He needs to know I'm sorry." Mollie slumped lower on the lino-leum floor. Wrapped her arms around the chair legs. Laid her head on the cushion. "I'm sorry. I'm sorry. Oh, God, I'm so sorry. This is my fault. I'm sorry I'm sorry I'm sorry."

Snot dribbled from her nose, dripped on the cushion. That made her cry even harder. He deserved so much better. And then she realized she was having a complete breakdown in front of Baba Yaga, whom she hated more than anybody, and that humiliation made her cry harder still. "I'm sorry I'm sorry I'm sorry Ffodor. Ffodor please forgive me." She dissolved into a sniffling, sobbing wreck.

"Well," said Billy Ray. "This has been a fun visit."

Franny held her while she cried herself out. It took a long time.

She felt small and fragile as he held her shaking body. When they'd all headed off to be big damn heroes in Talas she'd been a rather zaftig arm-ful but the events of the past days had stripped all that away. Even the tough-girl act was gone. She wailed like a lost child and despite everything she had done—to the jokers, to him—Franny felt pity.

"Mollie. He knows. He knows," he said softly. That made her cry all the harder.

He wondered who this Ffodor had been. Boyfriend, lover? Clearly a partner in crime. He had obviously been the object lesson that convinced Mollie to work for Baba Yaga.

Baba Yaga had gone back to making phone calls. Billy Ray was mutter-ing into his cell phone. All of them oblivious to the devastated girl hud-dled on the floor. Anger stirred in Franny's breast, but he accepted the reality. Against a threat that could destroy the world this one suffering girl meant nothing.

Her sobs began to subside. Franny stood with a grunt of pain, went into the bathroom, and grabbed a handful of tissues. As he passed Ray, the man grabbed his arm, and hissed into his ear.

"You know what we need. Get it done."

Franny gave a sharp nod, tore free from the older man, and returned to Mollie. She accepted the tissues and mopped her face.

"Come on," Franny said gently. "Let's get out of here."

Michelle was suffocating.

That cunt had buried her alive. There was a limited amount of time before she ran out of breath. The last breath she had.

Blindly, she began a barrage of bubbles. They hurt as they exploded, but she didn't have time to think about that. About what that meant. She hoped like hell she was bubbling through to the surface.

She couldn't hold her breath anymore. It released and instead of a mouthful of air she drew in a mouthful of dirt and started choking. With the one last blast of the power she had left in her now skinny body, she punched through something and her lungs filled with stale air. She began coughing out sandy dirt. It felt as if she were suspended by her lower body, but that couldn't be right.

Then she fell.

She slammed into something hard. Rock, maybe, or concrete. It didn't matter because she couldn't see a damn thing anyway. She was in total darkness. Darkness so heavy it was like a weight on her eyes.

Not the dark, she thought. *Anything but the dark.*

Somewhere in the back of her mind, something said very softly, *Move.*

She got to her feet, then reached out. Her hands touched nothing. She took a step to her left, and her foot splashed into water. It almost sent her off balance and tumbling, but she recovered.

Where am I? she wondered frantically. And then she remembered hazily from that other place before Talas—that place that must be a dream—that there were catacombs under the city. She'd forgotten about them.

GodOhGodOhGod don't let me be stuck in the dark. Because she remembered what she had forgotten. No, never forgotten, just shoved away far and deep. They'd locked her in the closet. And left her there for hours at a time. No light reached inside. And things were in there with her. Things that only lived in the deepest, darkest blackness. She may have been a child, but she knew that much.

"Shut up," she whispered. She hit herself in the face. "Shut up. Shut *shutupshutupshutup.*"

And then things began slithering.

Fear and a sick rage combined in her. She didn't have much fat, but she could kill whatever it was in the dark. *Can you? Can you kill what you can't see?*

Whatever it was, she would make it bleed. And that made her smile.

Move, the voice said.

Michelle cocked her head the way a dog might at a confusing command.

Move.

Something scuttled in the dark. There was a whisper of air as it brushed past her. She shrieked and let a tiny bubble escape. It burst against a wall, and for a brief moment there was a tiny flash of light. What she saw was an eyeless creature. Its body was the shade of necrotic flesh. It had long, vicious claws, a dent where its nose should be, and razor-sharp teeth.

Can't hurt me. Can't hurt me. Yes, yes it can. No. No! NO!

The fear was like a live thing inhabiting her chest. It was sucking the air from her lungs and it felt as if a stone had settled on her chest.

Move, the voice said again.

She took a large step to her right; this time her fingers touched a wall. It was rough and the edges bit into her fingers. That was good. It hurt a little, but it gave her a minuscule amount of fat. *Little bubbles,* she thought hysterically. *Little bubbles are all I got.*

She took a tentative step forward. Then another. She giggled as she realized she could be stuck down here forever—or until she died of starvation. At least there was water. Foul-smelling, stagnant water. No doubt with some kind of blind fish living there. Or maybe something worse. Something with teeth and claws and malice.

The pounding in her head was still there. The buzzing was back, along with those chanting, humming voices that had never quite gone away. They made her furious, and she hit herself in the face again and again. Sadly, it didn't add any fat.

Stupid, she thought. *So stupid to come here.* Fucking Jayewardene. If she ever got out of here, she would kill him. But slowly. She might not even use her bubbles. There were so many more painful ways to kill someone.

It was Jayewardene's fault she was in here. His and that fucking Adesina. A faint whisper inside her said, *Adesina. I love her.* And then the thought was crushed by her fear and rage.

Move.

Down in the hospital commissary, Franny bought her a cup of burnt coffee and a slice of cheesecake. Mollie took one bite of the latter and pushed the plate aside. The cheesecake tasted like ass.

"Want to talk about it?"

"No."

She concentrated on stirring her coffee. Stirred half a shaker's worth of sugar into it. The commissary only had skim milk so the coffee had that disgusting not-quite-black-why-even-bother color and taste. She'd been with Ffodor the first time she'd had coffee with heavy cream in it, which had ruined her for anything less ever since. *Krémes kávé,* he'd called it. The memory of his weird Hungarian vowels tugged at the corners of her mouth. She licked her lips. Tasted salt from her tears.

"What happened?"

"I told you I don't want to talk about it."

"Okay. I'll talk about it. I think I can piece it together. Months ago you guys decided to rob Baba Yaga's casino—"

"It was my idea. Ffodor wasn't crazy about it at first. I'm not talking about this."

"—but it went wrong. And she caught you. How am I doing so far?"

"Wow. You could make a kickass detective someday. Oh, wait, there aren't any more somedays."

Franny continued in the same level tone of voice. "So what happened then?"

Mollie set her cup down so hard that coffee slopped across the table. "You want me to say it? Fine. I abandoned him. I left Ffodor behind. She caught us and I ran away."

"Can't say I'm surprised," he said. Sipped his own coffee. Grimaced. "Where'd you learn to pick the lock on a pair of police-issue handcuffs, anyway? That's supposed to be almost impossible."

"Ff—" Her voice hitched. "Ffodor taught me."

"You two must have been a hell of a team."

"He was good to me, you know? He was the only person who didn't treat me like a disappointment, like my parents do, and not like I was just somebody to be tolerated and used, like Berman did. He cared about me. Taught me stuff."

"He saw your potential." Franny gave up on the coffee. Jesus Christ. It had to suck if a cop wouldn't drink it. "There's a lot of it. But you keep channeling it in unfortunate directions."

"If that's a fancy way of calling me an asshole, I already know it." She sighed. "Escaping. That's my power. I can run away from anything, so I run away from everything."

"Well, nobody can run from this. Not forever. Not even you. Not unless we find a way to fix it."

"Well, then I'd say we're all fucked."

"Not necessarily."

She looked up from the mess on the table. "You guys have a plan?"

Mollie looked up at him and there was a flare of hope in her green eyes. *Fuck no, they don't have a plan!* is what Franny wanted to scream at the girl.

"Get it done." Ray's cold command. Franny didn't want to die in horror and madness, twisted and deformed like the people inside that spreading zone of darkness. Mollie was a Hail Mary pass, but he'd take any chance no matter how remote.

And there was only one way to accomplish that. He was going to lie to her and manipulate her and use her the way everybody had used and lied and manipulated her. He would be deformed, but it would be hidden from everyone except him. This deformity would twist his soul.

In that moment he hated himself.

"Nope. Not yet. And I'm sorry I can't do anything about your friend. He's past the point of being able to forgive you. You can't help him, either. But you can still redeem yourself. If you help us you'll be helping so many more people than you've hurt. Me included." Franny sighed, shook his head. For a moment, he looked much much older, as though a tremendous weight had aged him. He spoke like a man confessing to his priest: "I'm the one who caused all this . . . by blundering in there. Maybe you can help make it right."

Mollie squinted at him. He was always such a Boy Scout. But when she examined his eyes, she saw a shadow scudding behind them. The mark that Baba Yaga had mentioned. He worked hard to hide it.

"You've seen it, too, haven't you?"

He nodded. "But not from the inside. Not like you have. But it was touch and go getting out of Talas. I saw people do . . . very bad things to each other."

Mollie hugged herself. *Don't think about the baby don't think about the baby and pitchforks and intestines just don't don't don't think . . .*

"Franny, I . . ." Ah, screw it. "I'm sorry I left you behind. I didn't know it was going to be like that."

He dipped his head, a gentle nod. "I appreciate the apology. Not, you know, a *lot,* since you did strand me in a foreign country without my passport in the middle of a mob gunfight. But I guess it's something."

Mollie took a deep breath. Held it. Exhaled. Tried to calm herself. It didn't work. Tried to find something to hold on to, something that would keep the fear at bay. But she came up empty. She started to tremble. Her shivering rocked the table and sent rivulets of spilled coffee under the paper napkin dispenser.

Though she already knew the answer, and it filled her with terror, she asked, "This help you're trying to wheedle out of me. It means opening doorways into the evil insanity zone, doesn't it?"

"Probably."

The pressure in her bladder suddenly surged. For a moment it felt like she was going to wet her pants. But she'd already humiliated herself in front of Franny enough for one day. Gritting her teeth, she said, "Oh, joy. I can't wait."

Franny pulled out his phone. "I'll let Billy Ray know you're on board."

Marcus, Vasel, the Handsmith, and a joker named Bulat had gone ahead of the caravan to plan. They stood over a map laid out on the road, the edges of it pinned with stones to keep it from blowing away in the dry morning breeze. Before them, a crossroads. One track of parched pavement bisected a smaller dirt road, running over a flat stretch of scrubland that stretched all the way to the horizon in both directions. The dirt road was a continuation of the one they'd followed here. It meandered into a stand of hills and veered out of sight.

Vasel jabbed at the map with a finger and said something in Russian. The Handsmith and Bulat exchanged wary glances. Bulat, one of the village elders, was a thin man with a weatherworn face, black mustache, and hair. He wore a long Kazakh jacket and a hat that to Marcus looked like some variation on a sailor's cap. Glanced at in the right moment, he looked like a nat. But that's only if you didn't notice the small, lizard-like head that moved under the thin membrane of his skin. The head appeared and disappeared. It shifted from cheek to cheek, down the neck to his chest, up to protrude from his temple. It snapped flies out of the air whenever they got close enough.

Bulat said something that the Handsmith grunted agreement with. Vasel let flow with a string of words. The two men suffered his rant in silence, heads down. Clearly frustrated with them, Vasel turned to Marcus. Gruffly, he spoke English. "This way. To the A-2. Then M-32. Is the best way."

"To the highway?" Marcus asked. "You saw what it was like coming out of Talas. We get on the highway, going slow, most of us jokers and all the crazy shit that's been going on . . . That's asking for trouble."

Vasel scoffed. "Trouble I can handle. This snail's pace I cannot. We can't keep moving like this." He gestured down the road they'd traveled on, disgust in the flick of his fingers.

"I should never have agreed to this," Vasel said. "These jokers . . ."

"Don't forget *why* you agreed," Marcus said. "And anyway, they saved Olena, and they took us in more than once. You claim to love your daughter; if so, you owe every person in that village."

"Person? I hardly see a person among them." As the procession of jokers neared them, Vasel leaned in to Marcus and said, "And fuck you, black mamba. I know more about my daughter than you ever will. She is my blood. Don't forget it."

Olena's truck inched up to them, leading the weary group of travelers. They'd kept moving all through the night, many walking, others catching what sleep they could in the jolting vehicles. With the truck idling, Olena opened the door and half swung out of it. She looked between the two men a moment, one eyebrow crooked. She'd been up all night as well. Marcus knew she must be exhausted, but she made a point of not showing it. "So, which way?"

Fifteen minutes later, with the whole group caught up and with vehicles and carts, people and animals, clogging the intersection, the answer came to them. It rolled in from the far horizon in the form of two Kazakh troop transports. The vehicles came on hard and fast, and didn't slow until the last minute. The grid of the first truck pressed dangerously close to Vasel, who stood waiting for them. The driver of the first truck leaned on the horn and shouted out the window at the same time. Through the ripples of hot air billowing off the engine, Marcus saw a host of soldiers stand up in the back of the truck, all of them armed with machine guns. He muttered, "Shit."

Out of the corner of his mouth, Vasel said, "I smell no shit. Just opportunity."

The officer climbed down from the truck, gesticulating angrily, shouting in Kazakh and clearly telling them to move out of the way. Vasel listened for a time, face incongruously calm, as if the man was making polite small talk instead of ranting at him with a host of young, armed thugs at his back. His coin was in hand again. He placed it between his front teeth and bit down, lightly, on it. When the man paused, Vasel pulled the coin away and said something in Russian. The officer switched to that language and started up again.

Marcus had never felt more mono-lingually American. If he ever got out of this, he'd learn a second language, or three or four.

"They are going to the A-2," Olena translated, "rushing to get to Talas."

"My daughter is correct," Vasel said. "Very good of them, don't you think? Noble of them. They are going to save the day. So many noble soldiers. How many do you think there are?"

"What?"

"How many? Count them with me." Vasel palmed his coin in his left hand. The fingers of his right, held above it, tapped on his thumb. A coin appeared and dropped to clink against the others. "As many of them as we have walkers, I think." Another coin dropped. Clinked. And then another.

The officer shouted something, a single clipped word that brought all the soldiers' rifles up, aimed at point randomly at the jokers.

"Vasel," Marcus said. He moved closer, speaking low. "Come on. Let these dudes pass. Slow and steady, you know? We'll make it."

"Slow and steady," Vasel said. He dropped another coin into a hand that, to Marcus's surprise, was overflowing with coins. There were so many there now that it seemed incredible none slipped off. "The only thing I do slow and steady is fuck. Other things, I do fast and furious, like the movies, you know? Don't blink; you'll miss the moment."

Marcus didn't miss it, though it happened fast and furious, as the gangster promised. One of the soldiers fired, probably by accident, a nervous pull on the trigger that would've put a chunk of steaming lead into Timur. Vasel snapped a coin from his right hand. It moved so fast Marcus didn't see it, not until it and the bullet from the soldier's machine gun dropped dead in front of Timur, right before his large feet. The next instant Vasel flung his handful of coins. Some of them caught other bullets from the sudden barrage that followed the first shot. The rest flew like an angry swarm of hornets. They sliced through the soldiers, right through them, liquifying them and then curving into another and another. Bodies dropped. Machine guns shot uselessly into the air as they fell. A chaotic couple of seconds. When it ended, the transports carried only steaming piles of liquified humanity, the clothes they'd worn, and the weapons and gear they'd carried.

Into the stunned silence that followed, Vasel piped, "Like I said, opportunity."

Barbara stood at the front of the conference room, pointing at the map projected on the wall. Ink and Secretary-General Jayewardene were physically present in the room, as well as Snow Blind, Toad Man, and Wilma Mankiller—the B-team of the Committee, she thought unfairly. *How can you even think of sending them, when Klaus, Michelle, Ana, and all the others failed.*

The room had been swept for bugs; the blinds had been carefully drawn shut so that no one passing in the hallway could see what was being shown on the screen.

"Here's the Baikonur Cosmodrome," Barbara said, using a laser pointer to show the buildings outlined on the satellite map. Jayewardene peered at his laptop, where the photograph also appeared. "And here is our best estimate of the current edge of the Talas disturbance." The laser pointer skimmed the edge of a black arc to the bottom of the picture. She nodded to Ink, at her laptop, and two dotted lines appeared on the screen, both following the curve of the arc. The second and farthest of the arcs touched the buildings of Baikonur. "As you can see from this, at its current rate of movement, the disturbance will have reached the complex within thirty-six hours and overrun it in forty, at which point . . ." Barbara shrugged to Jayewardene. "Control of the nuclear missiles and material, as well as the airports, launchpads, and all military equipment there, will be lost. We don't know who might take them or what they might do with them."

Jayewardene nodded. "And what are you proposing, Ms. Baden?" the

Secretary-General asked. "The Committee has already lost several aces trying to control the crisis at Talas. That was a failure—and I'm very sorry
that Klaus is one of those currently missing."

He's not dead. He can't be. "It was a failure," Barbara admitted. "And no
one is taking that loss harder than myself." *That is more true than I want to
admit.* "But we can't afford the loss of the Cosmodrome on top of Talas."

"I've spoken directly to President Putin," Jayewardene said. "He assured
me that the troops already on the base are doing everything they can to
remove critical equipment from the Cosmodrome and render the site
harmless. A full Russian brigade is also on the way to help. He believes
the Cosmodrome will be secure before the disturbance reaches them."

"I've also taken the liberty of speaking directly to President Putin," Barbara answered. "He gave me much the same story. I've also reached out to
President van Rennsaeler in Washington, and with the intelligence she
allowed me to see, I'm afraid I find President Putin's claims difficult to
believe. At the request of Prime Minister Karimov, President Putin sent
a good portion of the Russian division based at the Cosmodrome to Talas
when this all started a few days ago. He sent yet more as the crisis escalated. All those troops have effectively been neutralized. The soldiers the
Russians have left there are demoralized and frightened, have heard rumors of Talas, and are too few to keep control of the compound or to move
away more than a fraction of the nuclear material and weapons stored
there. I believe—and understand that I am very reluctant to say this,
Mr. Secretary-General, but it's what the NSA chatter has indicated—that
President Putin intends to use the nuclear missiles at the Cosmodrome to
take out Talas."

Just saying the words made Barbara pause. *And if that happens, there is
no hope for Klaus, and if that Russian woman is right, no hope for anyone
at all.* "I don't need to remind everyone what Baba Yaga has told us: if
Tolenka dies, then the beast inside him will fully emerge, and what we're
looking at now will be only a mere taste of what's to come."

"And you believe her?" said Jayewardene.

"I do," Barbara answered. "She had no reason to lie to me. My staff
has verified most of the information she gave us, and Officer Black has
backed up the rest. Putin has no intention of neutralizing the Cosmodrome; he intends to use it, and within the next thirty-six hours. We
have no time to waste. His brigade, from the satellite photos we've seen,
are still mobilizing in Russia; the transports are still on the ground, and

are going to stay there because President Putin already knows he'll lose those as well. We don't have sufficient UN troops to put between the Russians and the Cosmodrome." Barbara saw Jayewardene nod at that. "But a Committee team might be able to stop them. The decision, Mr. Secretary-General, is yours, but we need authorization from the UN now."

Barbara waited, listening to the hum of the projector and feeling its warmth on her face. "I agree with you, Ms. Baden, if reluctantly," Jayewardene said finally. He stood. "You will have that approval within the hour, Ms. Baden. I will secure it now. I hope you are right. I hope that for all our sakes."

With that, Jayewardene gave everyone a brief nod of acknowledgment and left the room.

"That went well, Mizz B," Juliet said. "I think."

"Should we get ready, Ms. Baden?" Toad Man asked, looking at the others.

"Yes!" Barbara said, then realized how loudly she'd spoken. They were all staring at her. She closed her eyes, taking a long breath. "Yes," she said again, feigning a calm she didn't feel. Barbara turned to Juliet. "Get Ray on the phone for me. We need his help."

The Angel found flying slow and painful. She wobbled and wandered like a stoned butterfly and although she tried to maintain a straight flight path, she constantly found herself fluttering off course and expending vital energy.

Below her Talas was a devastated hellscape smothered in sickly green mist. Vague forms moved on the ground below her and she frequently heard muffled screams and cries and gunshots and explosions, but could make no sense of anything. She knew that she had to fly lower, despite the danger that entailed.

Familiar terrain, and a line of unmoving vehicles spotted below her, forced her hand. She swooped down low, recognizing the line of vehicles they'd driven into the city the night before. A quick reconnaissance showed her that they were silent and still. Nothing moved around them except for the tendrils of fog. Gingerly, she alighted on the lead tank.

She looked around the eerily silent cityscape; she cupped her hands and raised them to her mouth.

"Lohengrin!" she shouted. *"Lohengrin!"*

Her cries echoed back creepily and from somewhere, maybe everywhere, came maniacal shrieking laughter, inhuman in scale and volume, that devolved into insane tittering. Screams came from off in the thick mist. They almost sounded human, but bubbled away as if choked off by gobbets of flowing blood. She would have gone toward them, but she couldn't tell where they originated. Some things, she thought, were playing with her.

She tried again, though she realized that it was hopeless. *"Omweer! Earth Witch!"*

From behind her came the sound of cracking concrete and collapsing buildings. She whirled, staring. Someone had answered her call, after all.

Earth Witch stood atop a hill of naked dirt, fifty or sixty feet away. Her clothes were caked with it. It was smeared all over her horribly immobile face except for the two runnels down her cheeks cleansed by the tears that streamed constantly from her staring eyes.

"Ana!" the Angel screamed.

The young woman's arms were outstretched beseechingly and her lips moved constantly, but the Angel could not hear what she said, if anything. The Angel rose into the air with a single beat of her wings, but even as she moved, so did Ana.

The street below her rippled, the concrete cracked and parted like the Red Sea, and a fountain of dirt ran up to join the hill that the ace stood on. The dirt rippled, moved, like sand dunes blown at fantastic speed by an unseen wind. Her head turned, maintaining eye contact with the Angel as she fled down the street, surfing her wave of earth.

The Angel clenched her jaw and took out after her, willing all her strength into the task of keeping up with the fleeing ace. But the young woman was moving at an impossible speed as she zigzagged down the streets, and the Angel soon realized that she was losing the race. The ache from her injured shoulder spread throughout her body but she continued her pursuit until the Angel turned a final corner and the girl was no longer in sight. Nor could she hear the sounds of breaking concrete. She looked around, realizing that she was in a different part of the city.

She was no longer on the edges of Talas, but had come into the city center. The buildings were denser and taller, though more broken than those on the outskirts. Her nose twitched and she caught her breath at the stench of death that was everywhere. Hovering above the street, she was afraid to touch down because there were bodies everywhere, but to the Angel's horror, most seemed to be moving, twitching, and twisting unnaturally, as if trying to find a more comfortable position among the piles of sharply angular and hard debris that had become their final resting places. Their ragged clothing rippled, but there was no breeze.

Revulsion then threatened to overcome her as she realized that all the corpses were teaming with vermin of all sizes and descriptions. Their action had paused at the Angel's arrival in the vicinity, but as if seeing that she posed no immediate threat, they returned to their feeding.

There were beetles the size of roaches to that of small dogs, most with pinchers that ripped and tore into the heat-ripened flesh, ropy creatures limbless like snakes or with uncountable legs that burrowed into and out of the corpses like maggots in cheese, ant-like beings with curiously bulging foreheads and all-too-inquisitive eyes that often stopped and stared at the Angel ruminatively as they fed with small, clacking sounds of their mandibles, and the slimy, slug-like creatures that made no sound at all as they sucked out the eyes of the dead.

The Angel's stomach heaved, but there was nothing in it to vomit, not even bile.

She looked on in horror for a moment longer, and then the bigger scavengers came slinking and crawling and rolling out of the nooks and crannies to which they'd fled at the Angel's approach. She was too aghast at the furred and scaled and leather-skinned, at the sight of the things, to move, but when the humans joined them and fought them over the remains of the bloated, rotting corpses, she turned her head and arrowed up into the sky.

Michelle walked slowly forward, dragging her fingers along the wall to her right. She didn't know how long she walked or for how far. Time had ceased to move in any normal way. Her combat boots made scraping noises no matter how softly she tried to step. They echoed in the unnatural quiet. But there were other things down here with her as well. Every so often she heard something. Horrible gurgling noises. A choked-off cry. The sound of skin being torn and bones being crushed.

Sometimes she'd let a tiny bubble fly in the direction of the noise, and usually it would hit a wall. For a quick flash, she'd see something. The image would burn into her eyes from the shock of light in so much darkness.

In one flash, a man crouched naked, his distended genitals scraping the floor as he sucked the spinal fluid from a baby's neck. Michelle dry-heaved. And then she wanted to kill him, but she couldn't afford the fat. *Fuck it.* She let a bullet-sized bubble go. She heard the lucky hit. There was a satisfying thud as his body hit the floor.

She wondered if baby marrow was tasty. It'd been a long time since she'd had anything to eat. And then she began retching again. *NoNo-NoNoNoNoNONONONO . . .*

Move.

She staggered forward. She tripped over the corpse of the baby-eater and kicked him into the water. Her foot stepped on something soft and squishy. The baby. She kicked it into the water as well. There was a splash. It was next to her, and she pushed herself back against the wall. She felt the brush of air as whatever it was came out of the water. In her gut, she knew it was eating what she'd just kicked into the canal.

Quickly, she started moving. Once again, she had no idea how far she'd walked. Or for how long.

Finally, she came to the end of the wall. She put one hand out, keeping the other on the corner. Nothing was there. A tiny bubble flew from her fingertips. It hit something, and she saw in the flashbulb moment where she was.

Arching above her like a cathedral ceiling was the roof of the catacombs. Corridors came off this center room like spokes on a wheel. Her legs suddenly gave out, and she sat down hard on the walkway.

She was going to die, all alone in the dark.

Move.

Fuck you, she thought. For a moment, she had the urge to scream it out loud, but the fear of whatever might be down here with her was too great.

I'm the Amazing Bubbles. Nothing can hurt me. But that wasn't true, was it? In this nightmare, this hellhole, this unspeakable place, there were plenty of things that could hurt her. Bullets. Ana's wall of dirt. Mummy.

A spike of fear shot through her. And panic set in. A terrifying fear. She'd felt it with the rage before.

And then she heard the shuffling behind her. How far away it was she didn't know. But she knew the sound. She'd know that sound for the rest of her life. The thing in the dark. She knew what it was. And it was coming for her.

The Committee officers were much more crowded than when Mollie had departed a few hours earlier. Babel hadn't wasted anytime assembling her B-team.

"Whoa!"

Mollie, Franny, and Billy Ray emerged from folded space quite close to a petite woman slouching in the corner. Streaks of her hair were dyed brilliant red, almost crimson. She was even shorter than Mollie, but so thin she made Mollie feel like a blubbery sow. *Great.*

The other woman staggered back, but caught her balance after a step or two. "Neat trick. Who the fuck are you?"

"I'm your ride." Mollie sniffed, wrinkled her nose. Looking down, she noticed the German shepherd at the woman's side. She frowned. It growled, staring at her with one milky eye and another that appeared to have something wriggling in it.

"Problem?"

"Your dog. It looks . . ." *Like it's suffering from an acute case of roadkill.*

"Yeah, well, what'd you fuckin' expect? She's been dead awhile."

"Aha," said Mollie, trying not to use her nose. "I take it you're Joey." So far she matched the description.

"That's Hoodoo Mama to you, cocksucker."

Yep. Totally matched the description. *Oh, joy.*

Joey looked her up and down. Squinted. "Weren't you on *American Hero* a few years ago?"

Oh, Jesus Christ. "Don't remind me." Mollie sighed. "On the show I was called Tesseract."

Joey yawned, crossed her arms, and resumed scowling while she watched the assembled aces mill around. Franny and Billy Ray had gone off to find Babel, so Mollie decided to hang back and watch the swelling crowd.

She saw Agent Moon, the mastiff that had come to the farm with Billy Ray. There was a guy who looked entirely normal, relating in a Gomer Pyle accent some asinine anecdote about his uncle Raymond back in Florida.

The woman sitting next to him and politely chatting in a silky French accent had dyed her hair a brilliant magenta; if she'd stood next to Joey, the two could've blinded anybody foolish enough to look at their hair. A pair of large translucent black wings sprouted from the back of a guy dressed like a cowboy, with a bead necklace hanging around the collar of his unbuttoned red-and-white checked shirt. He was talking with a tall woman who looked strong enough to wrestle a bear; her jet-black braids were so lustrous that Mollie reached up and touched her own hair. Damn.

More Committee members arrived. The milling crowd spilled out of the atrium and into adjoining offices. Mollie wondered how many of these poor sons of bitches realized they were the expendable second-stringers, recruited for a pointless suicide mission to try to rescue the A-listers who by now were, at best, gibbering cannibals.

Joey saw her watching the crowd. She pointed to the couple on the couch. "That's Toad. He's okay, he gets it. That's Simone with him. She thinks her shit smells like a fresh-baked croissant just because she's French Canadian. Big fucking deal, you know? We speak French in New Orleans, too, but we don't act like the sun shines out our asses. That guy with the devil horns and red tights is Mephistopheles. Don't get alone in an elevator with him; they call him Randy Devil for a reason. That motherfucker tries anything with me I'll rip his dick off, though. The woman with the braids is Wilma—"

"It's, um, it's okay. Thanks. I appreciate it. But I don't need introductions."

Mollie could learn their names if they made it out. Then again, in a few days, nobody's name would matter. The only identity anybody had would be the howl of madness echoing among the uncaring stars and the click of teeth on bone as they devoured themselves.

Besides. She couldn't look them in the eyes. Not when she knew she was probably sending them to their deaths.

Joey squinted at her. "Oh. I get it. No point learning our names, huh?"

"I didn't say that."

"No. But your face sure as fucking did."

Mollie tried to change the subject. "I take it you're on the Committee. You must work with these guys."

"Hell no. I've been eavesdropping on these retarded cocksuckers for the past hour." She reached down, absently, to scratch her zombie dog behind its ears. It made a sound somewhere between a happy yelp and the outgassing of a dead barn cat on a hot summer day. Mollie held her breath. "I've never been good enough for the motherfuckin' Committee, but now all of a sudden they need a touch of the old bayou voodoo and suddenly, hey, holy shit, what do you know? All of a sudden I *am* good enough." She snorted. "Fuckin' knob-gobblers."

Joey asked, "So how come you don't go by 'Tesseract' anymore? It's a fuckin' badass name."

It'd been a long damn time since anybody had called her that. That had been her name on *American Hero*. (Come to think of it, maybe one good thing would come of the Horrorshow Apocalypse. She took vindictive comfort knowing the no-talent ass-clown who got her kicked out of the competition, Jake Butler, the "Laureate," would die screaming when a horde of spider-eyeballs sucked his brains out through his asshole.)

A few nearby members of the suicide squad looked at her more closely. "Ohhhhhh, yeah," said the toad guy. "I sure thought you looked kinda familiar."

"Because when I do," Mollie said, "that happens."

The cocktail party hubbub trailed off into ripples of senseless gibberish amid a sea of confused faces. Baden's voice cut through the nonsense, clear as a bell. "Mollie? Is Mollie still here?"

Oh. I get it. She looked at Joey and said, "I guess that's why they call her Babel."

Joey scowled at her. "Gkjj ybq ppjp xif aza bxb?"

Mollie sighed. She raised her hand and waved. "Yeah. Back here."

Baden wended through the crowd with Billy Ray in tow. Mollie wondered where Franny had gone. Baden said, "We're ready for you."

A twinge of panic softened Mollie's knees, as though they were soft candle wax. "Don't you want to wait for others to show up?"

"We can't wait any longer. This is the team we have."

Mollie followed Baden to a conference room, Billy Ray and Joey in tow. She felt as though she were walking to her own execution. It seemed a miracle her legs could even hold her up. But she made it to the conference room, where a pair of laptops had been plugged into the telepresence setup. An immense flat-screen monitor on the wall at the far end of a long table showed a split-screen image; the left half looked like either a satellite photo or high-altitude aerial photo; the right half, the grainier of the pair, had been zoomed in on a particular stretch of tarmac.

"So that's balalaika, huh? Big fucking deal," said Joey.

"Baikonur. A 'balalaika' is a Slavic musical instrument, like a triangular guitar," said Babel.

"What-fucking-ever."

The close-up showed a shaded corner where two warehouses met: the B-team's landing site. The wider view showed a sprawling concrete complex stippled with warehouses (the landing site helpfully circled in red), hangars, subterranean silos, spaceplanes, even a tank or two. Beyond these, in the bottom left corner of the image, a portion of what appeared to be a perimeter fence and a multicolored mass. Mollie's stomach did a flip when she realized it was a crowd comprising thousands of people.

It seemed pretty clear the people were pressed up against the fence, trying to get in. But were they fleeing the madness, or carrying it with them?

Now that she looked more closely, she realized there had already been skirmishes and fighting among the refugees. There were bodies strewn at the edges of the crowd.

. . . don't think about the barn, don't think about the barn, don't . . .

With trembling hands, Mollie poured herself a glass of ice water from a decanter on the conference table. When it no longer felt like her throat was plugged with ash, she asked, "How recent are these photos?"

"Six hours," Baden said.

"You don't have anything more recent?"

The Committee woman tensed. "Is that a problem?"

"No. No, I can do it. It's just . . . are you sure this place hasn't been absorbed yet? By the, you know . . ."

"Trust us. It's safe. We wouldn't use it for a staging ground otherwise. The whole point is to get in and out before it gets engulfed."

"Be smart, be safe, be quick," Mollie whispered. Hidden under the conference table, her knees shook.

"What?"

She shook her head. "Nothing. Just remembering something a friend used to tell me."

Taking a seat at the conference table, she gazed at the video screen. She squinted from the effort to absorb every detail of the image: the angles of the shadows, the color of the concrete, the rust spots on the hangar roofs, the faded Cyrillic lettering on the runways . . .

Baden said, "Will these images work?"

Mollie cleared her throat, twice. The bruises on her neck did their best to squeeze every last burr and rasp from her voice. "Well, they're grainy, but they'll do. In a pinch I've used some pretty blurry webcams."

But that was before she'd been to Talas . . . where people shoved broken bottles into their own eyes . . . and lobbed babies onto iron finials . . . and gnawed each other's faces . . .

Her concentration dissipated like a burst balloon.

The Angel desperately needed rest and sustenance. Luckily she spotted a flat-roofed building that looked to be in decent shape where she wouldn't be too deep within the fog's clutches. She made a graceless landing and came up against a small cupola that covered a staircase leading down into the building's depths.

Her wings vanished and she felt as if a great weight had been removed from her back and shoulders. She stretched gingerly and wished Billy were present with his powerful hands and awesome massage skills. His touch would be quite welcome now, she thought, even the slightest caress of his hand against her cheek.

"You always were a defiant child," a familiar voice said.

The Angel straightened as real fear knifed through her body, fear she hadn't felt in many years.

"Willful," it said. "Deceitful. Plotting. Conniving. Evil little brat."

She knew that voice. She knew it well. She turned and faced her mother.

She hadn't changed since her death. Not a bit. Her face was crisscrossed with still-bleeding wounds with remnants of windshield glass still embedded in the score of gashes, including the long, deep tear in her throat. The coroner had thought that that was the wound that had taken her life, but he wasn't sure if she'd bled out because of the broken windshield that'd sliced her throat or the impact of the steering wheel that had crushed her chest or maybe the collision of her flying body against the tree that had broken her back as the car hit it. The vehicle had left behind no brake marks on asphalt or turf as she'd plowed off the county road while going ninety miles an hour in a drunken stupor.

The words ran in an uncontrollable rush through the Angel's mind. She could only watch in helpless horror as her mother approached her. It was a miracle that she could stand upright let alone walk, if you could call her halting, shambling gait "walking." How, the Angel wondered, was she functioning at all, with quarts of blood soaking her tattered clothing and running down and dripping off her ruined body, leaving a thick trail behind. Much of it came off her face and head—she'd been half scalped by a sharp shard of the windshield that'd ripped half of the hair from her skull and left it exposing the bone underneath.

"You should feel quite at home here," her mother said, shambling to a stop before her. "You're an unnatural thing, like everything here. Born a bastard. Turned into a twisted genetic wreck by that unholy virus brought to this world to act as righteous vengeance against the unworthy—"

"It made me a hero—" the Angel dared to say, but her voice was that of the little girl she'd been before her mother had put the knife to her.

"*It made you a freak,*" her mother shrieked. "You were always a little liar, an unbeliever, though I tried so hard to bring you to God. It turned you into a glutton, always stuffing your face, on top of your whoring after boys—"

"I never—"

"*I saw you kissing him!*"

"Once—" the Angel said through her tears "—just the one time—"

"*You wanted them all!*"

The Angel slipped to her knees, able only to shake her head in denial. "I wanted someone to love," she whispered.

Her mother sneered. "Well, you found him. Another twisted freak, like you. And look at you now, in your slutty suit, crying and broken—"

"Angel . . ." The voice came from behind her, low and tentative, seeking. "Angel . . ."

It came again.

The Angel twisted her neck, gazing behind her and saw an old woman dressed in a black cloak, tall but leaning on a cane. The woman looked at her and the Angel was startled to see that she no longer had eyes, just empty black pits where they once were, the cheeks below them rimmed with faint red stains like the remnants of strange makeup.

"It's you," the old woman said breathlessly. "I can see you in my mind. My dreams *have* come true. I told you so. I told you all."

For the first time, through the thickening fog, the Angel noticed that there were people behind her. Or people-like things, anyway. One little boy stood behind her, peering around her and clinging to the speaker's cloak. He had little horns like a faun and hairy legs like a goat.

"In a dream I saw you, Angel of the Alleyways. We have suffered hard and sought you long, we beseech you to succor us in the hour of our need."

The Angel swiped at the snot running down her face with the back of her leather gauntlet.

Her mother laughed wildly. "What are these disgusting creatures?" she asked. "We would never allow such grotesque monsters into Mississippi State." She shook her head in despair, the flap of semidetached scalp dropping down to cover one eye. "I always knew that you'd end up in hell," she said.

Slowly the Angel rose to her feet. Her head turned back and she looked at her mother.

"Shut up, you drunken bitch," she said in a low, hard voice.

Her mother didn't seem impressed. "So you break another commandment," she said. "Will you break them all before you're done?"

"Shut up!"

Unbidden, the sword was in her hand. She took a step forward, a fierce scowl on her face and a fierce joy racing through her body. She swung her blade with an angry, wordless cry and it cut through her mother's neck right where the sliver of windshield glass had sliced. The head jumped away from the neck and the Angel watched it fly in a lazy arc. Interestingly, no blood splattered from either junction of the cut, but thick, green fog slowly roiled out in languid swirls.

When the head hit the roof it vanished in a puff of green smoke while the Angel watched as her mother collapsed into herself like a punctured balloon and neatly vanished.

"Madonna of the Blade!" the old woman cried. "Please come to our aid!"

The Angel turned to her. "Show me what you need!" she commanded.

The old woman turned without a sound. There were clicking and slithering and tittering noises as those behind her limped and slithered and flowed down the stairs under the cupola. The Angel followed them, for the first time realizing that the sword had come to her without her prayer. She thought about it momentarily, then dismissed it from her mind.

"Thanks to everyone for coming on short notice."

"Cut the fucking bullshit," Joey Hebert said. "All I care about is pulling Michelle outta Talas. You just gotta get me fucking there so I'm close enough to use my children. I can goddamn do the rest."

Barbara shook her head. "We'll get to that. Right now, I want to make sure that everyone's aware of the entire situation." Joey pushed off the wall, coming closer. The smell of rotting meat was coming off the zombie dog beside her. Barbara leaned back in her chair, as far away from Joey as she could get. "Joey, there are more people than Michelle in Talas that we have to worry about. What about them, the rest of the team?" *Klaus, especially,* she thought, but bit back his name. "Yes, I want Michelle back as much as you do, but we also need the others—all of them, if they can be found."

Joey was already shaking her head. Billy Ray watched the confrontation with an amused look on his face. "Fuck 'em," she said. "If those assholes are with Michelle and I can get 'em, fucking fine. If they're not . . ." She gave a shrug of tattooed shoulders.

Barbara could sense the desperation in the woman's voice, in her stance, in the way her face twisted with those last words. The disgust she usually felt around Hoodoo Mama dissolved, and she realized in that moment that Joey was grieving for Michelle in the same way that Barbara grieved for Klaus, that the emotions racking Joey were the same that were assaulting her every moment for the last few days.

The difference was Joey might actually be able to do something about Michelle, and maybe the others. *Not me. That's not a power I have, not my gift. And Klaus knew it.*

Barbara raised her hand. "We all want Michelle back," she said. "And any of the others you can find while you're there. We need them."

"You'll fucking get me to Talas, then?" Joey said. "When's the goddamn plane leave? I'm ready now."

"There's no plane. There's a better way." Barbara glanced at Mollie, who visibly shrank back against the plush cushions behind her. There was no sign of cohesiveness to this potential team. Barbara had to stop herself from shaking her head at the realization. "I don't know how much each of you know at this point," she began. "So forgive me if I start telling you things you already know—others here may not be aware of it."

Even to her own ears, that sounded too flat and too rigid, not like Klaus, who would have been all flaming emotion and passion. "This is what I've learned from Officer Black and Baba Yaga," she continued. "All that's holding back whatever entity is trying to cross into our world from this place is the person she knew as Tolenka or Hellraiser, now in the hospital that's the center of the disturbance. The man is dying. *Will* die, and soon. And when he does, Baba Yaga claims there's nothing to stop the thing inside him from crossing over fully. That's the situation that we're facing."

"Then we take out this fucking Hellraiser guy," Joey said. "Pretty god-damn simple."

"No!" That was Franny. "You don't understand. Kill him, and it's over. That horror steps on through then. Killing him isn't the answer."

"How about grabbing the guy and tossing him in one of those rockets at the Cosmodrome?" Ray asked. "Putin would gladly cooperate with that. We throw the bastard into orbit, or put him on the moon, or hell, drop him into the sun. Either way, he'd be far, far away from us—and do you think this thing can survive the sun?"

"That occurred to me also, Director," Barbara answered. "If we can't kill Tolenka, then maybe we can put him somewhere far enough away that it won't matter. But we don't know what this thing can survive. It might just put the sun inside the same darkness that's around Talas and Kazakh-stan now, and that takes care of all life everywhere in the whole damn solar system. We may make things worse."

Ray snorted a laugh through his nose.

"The Russians want this ended. Uzbekistan and Kyrgyzstan want to bomb Talas to rubble," Barbara continued. "Putin is willing to drop a nuke. President van Rennsaeler might even agree with that. Worse, the Cosmo-drome is within hours of being overrun by whatever started in Talas—at which point we don't know who or what will have control of the material and weaponry there."

"You're saying we're screwed," Ray said.

Barbara glared at him. "No. I'm saying that I have a plan. Maybe not much of one, but unless one of you has something better . . ."

Move.

Michelle was paralyzed. There were multiple ways she could go, and she didn't know if any of them was the way out. She gritted her teeth with anger and frustration. The only reason she was here was because of Ade-sina. That brat had been nothing but a burden since Michelle had brought her home. A faint voice inside her cried out against the thought, then was eclipsed by her anger.

And now she was stuck in the dark, with Mummy coming for her. The shuffling was closer.

There was a blink of light two passages down. It couldn't have really happened. It was some sort of hallucination. But all she had to do was cross the water to get to it. The water that had God only knew what in it.

The shuffling was getting closer.

She could feel how thin she was now. Her hands ran over her body. Ribs stuck out, her hip bones were sharp. About the only things with any fat were her breasts, which had never been large anyway. But large enough, maybe.

The flash again.

She strained to see it. The blobby remnant of the light floated in her vision.

Move.

Fuck you. I can't move. I'm stuck.

But she stood up and let another tiny bubble fly. Each one was one less that she could use to fight the shuffling thing coming after her. Mummy.

Shut up. She can't be down here. It has to be something worse.

There is nothing worse and you know it.

The bubble hit the floor on the other side of the water. The canal was about two and a half meters across. But she'd have to go into the water to cross it. And that made her shudder.

She decided to try to jump across. She might be able to make it. It seemed so reasonable.

She jumped.

In the dark, she miscalculated—not that she could have made it across anyway—and ended up slamming stomach-first into the opposite wall of the canal. She got a little fat from it, but it hurt like hell. Her hands slid off the wet stones edging the wall and she sank into the foul water.

It was deeper than she'd thought. She kicked hard and hoped she was moving toward the surface—when something grabbed her leg. She screamed, and noxious water rushed into her mouth. Whatever it was, it started pulling her down. She kicked and yanked, but the thing wouldn't let go. In desperation, she put her hand on the tentacle wrapped around her leg and let a bubble go.

There was a small explosion. It burned like fire, but the thing released her leg. Michelle kicked away and burst through the surface. She flailed around to find the edge, found it, then dragged herself onto the walkway.

She lay there panting, and then she heard the shuffle again. It was closer now. She began shivering—from the wet or the sound, she wasn't sure.

Move.

The only voice she could hear over the roar of everything else in her head.

Now it sounded like Adesina.

Only not like her. It was·close, but the voice was deeper than her daughter's. And she'd failed Adesina. She hadn't stopped anything. Only ended up here shivering in the dark, with Mummy coming for her.

Move.

Shut up. Shut up. Shut up.

Michelle was shaking all over now. She had no fat on her to keep her warm. But what was really making her shake was what was coming down the hall toward her.

Mom, move!

She wanted to cry. Adesina's voice. The only reason she was here was to keep her from dying. And now she was trapped in the dark with Mummy. And she'd failed utterly.

Then she did cry.

Hot, bitter tears rolled down her cheeks. Shaking and crying, she hit herself in the face again and again and again.

The faint light flashed once more. She scrambled to her feet and ran toward it. Her shoulder slammed into a wall, and she wondered whether she was in the right place or if she'd lost track of where she was.

The shuffling was closer. She could almost hear Mummy's wheezing.

There was a faint glow coming from the tunnel. Michelle ran toward the light.

It wasn't the most pleasant work, but they cleared the soldiers' remains from the transports, claimed the vehicles, and turned—as Vasel wished— toward the highway. For a time after connecting with the A-2, the going was easy. The road was wide and flat enough for the trucks to open up and for the miles to scroll by beneath them. The transports led the way, with the best of the village vehicles close behind them. Gone were the wagons and animal-drawn carts. They roared past the foot traffic on the edges of the road, and wove around slower vehicles, many of them piled high with people and supplies. Clearly, they weren't the only ones trying to put Talas far behind them.

Marcus rode in the bed of the lead transport. Sitting upright on his coils, he took in the barren landscape the road cut through, the dry air hot on his face. He had to admit that they were making better time, and the villagers were getting some much needed rest. Still, they were riding in stolen property that had been attained through murder. That didn't sit right with him.

He was one of many in the transport. They were jammed in tight enough that many of the jokers pressed against Marcus's coils. Nurassyl leaned back against him, his big eyes closed as he slept. A playmate of the boy's, Sezim, had actually climbed onto a curve of Marcus's tail and slept there, holding a stuffed rabbit cradled in her three small arms. Before Marcus would have felt embarrassed having so many people touching his deformity. In this case, it felt almost comforting. None of the jokers seemed to think he was deformed at all, and the press of bodies reminded him of something, some long-buried memory that he didn't try to dig up.

As they approached the city of Shymkent, the highway became increasingly choked with traffic. Vasel pressed forward, shoving his way through with vicious blasts of the horn. For a time that worked, too. People parted to let the big military vehicles through. But as they rolled past and they got sight of the joker passengers the other travelers' deference turned to indignation. They glared. Shouted. Gesticulated.

"Shit," Marcus whispered. "This could get bad."

It did. With the M-32—the road that would take them north to Baikonur—in sight in the distance, they came to a dead stop. The whole distance to the turnoff was jammed, vehicles stuck bumper to bumper. Vasel leaned on the horn, but it was hopeless. The cars in front of them couldn't have moved out of the way even if they'd wanted to.

Olena climbed out of the second truck and squirmed through the crowd. Stepping up on to the sideboard, she peeked her head over the side of Marcus's transport. "What is it?"

Squinting into the distance, Marcus said, "I think there's a blockade at the M-32. Soldiers, looks like. This is bad. Even if we get up to them how are we going to explain Kazakh military transports being full of jokers?"

"They'll never let us through," Olena agreed. "That's not our only problem, though."

There were murmurs coming from the vehicles around them. Whispered conversations. A few shouts. People, obviously, were noticing the jokers. They didn't look happy to see them.

Vasel's door opened. He jumped down to the road, stretched his back, took in the gathering crowd.

Marcus called down to him, "See? I told you the highway would screw us."

"We are not screwed," the ace said. He jerked his head to indicate the vehicles clogging the road in front of them. "They are." The coin appeared, this time spinning on its edge on the tip of Vasel's finger.

"No," Marcus said. "Vasel, what are you going to do? Kill everyone between here and Baikonur?"

The gangster shrugged. "Whatever it takes." He turned and began to walk forward.

Marcus lifted the little girl and set her next to Nurassyl. As carefully as he could so as not to hurt anyone, he flowed up and over the rim of the transport, grabbing the map through the open window of the cab of the truck in the process. He slithered around Vasel so quickly the man had to draw up. As he unfolded the map and scanned it, Marcus said, "There's been enough death already. There's a better way. Here. We backtrack on A-2. Connect to this smaller road. We passed it already and there wasn't a roadblock. It heads north and connects to the M-32 farther up."

Vasel considered the route he'd drawn, coin still spinning effortlessly on his finger. "That will take longer."

"But it'll save lives. You start flipping coins here, who knows what'll happen."

Marcus motioned at the crowd continuing to congeal around them. They were pointing now, a few of them trying to climb up to peer into the transports. Timur fended them off on one side. The Handsmith and Bulat tried to calm them on the other. Olena spoke rapid Russian to another group, arguing with beautiful passion.

"Why do you care about these people?" Vasel asked. "Do you know what they are saying? That you are contagious. That you are an evil to be destroyed. They would wipe you jokers from the earth without a moment's thought."

"I guess that makes me better than them," Marcus answered.

Someone from the crowd threw a glass bottle that shattered on the truck's railing, causing the jokers to cringe away from the shards of glass.

"Come on," Marcus said, "before things get out of hand. Let's go back to go forward, and nobody gets killed."

After a moment's more consideration, Vasel palmed his coin. "Okay. One last time we do it your way, if you can get us turned around."

"I can." Marcus shot back toward the trucks, just in time to confront a group of young men converging on the Handsmith and Bulat with clubs and lengths of pipe in hand. Marcus rose tall and writhed toward them, throwing his coils out in front of him to drive them back. One of them brought a wrench down on his tail. Marcus snapped forward and clocked him so hard the man's legs went to jelly and he fell. He hadn't meant to do that, but adrenaline was coursing through him now. They were all getting too close, looking too beastly and angry. He shouted that they weren't to blame. They were refugees just like anybody else. The commotion just grew, though.

He raced around to the other side of the truck to find Timur fighting a guy wielding a shovel. He took his legs out from under him with his tail. A second later the air was filled with thrown objects. Bottles and rocks pelted them. "Olena," he called, "tell them we're going to turn around. Tell them to just let us go!"

As she tried to do that, Marcus did what he had to. His tongue punched a man brandishing a pistol. He picked up another guy and hurled him into a group of approaching men. When one guy got up onto the side of the truck and lifted a pipe above the screaming joker women and children, Marcus careened around toward him. Before he knew that he was going to do it, he slung his tongue out, wrapped it around the guy's neck, and yanked him back off the truck. He was unconscious by the time he hit the ground. He'd never used his tongue quite like that before, but he didn't have time to pause and applaud himself.

Through pure hard work and force, constant motion and all the menace he could muster, Marcus managed to back the crowd enough so that the caravan could pull off the highway and swing around.

When Vasel finally pulled up beside him on the other side of the highway, Marcus answered the unasked question on the ace's face. "I said I didn't want anyone dead. That doesn't make a pacifist." He curved up into the truck bed, careful not to squash anyone as he did so. "Everybody all right?" he asked. Despite his English, they seemed to understand him. They made room, welcomed him, and, he thought, thanked him.

The Angel was astonished to discover that the building was actually a giant department store. The first level they went through was devoted to home furnishings—beds, couches, tables, sofas, chairs, tables. You name it, it was there. Most were in use, with people lying, sitting, crouching fearfully on them. They were the helpless, the sick, the wounded, the starving, and the dead. Other items were occupied by other beings, some at least partly human, but changed, horribly, in a parody of a wild card outbreak. The Angel had seen it all before. It was Jokertown writ small. They had too many heads or appendages or not enough. They had warty, leathery, bloody, oozy skin covered by fur, feathers, scales, or slime.

But it was the others, the utterly alien with little of humanity about them, that disturbed her. The things with hooves and tentacle-covered bodies, the sifting masses of protoplasm that had mouths all over them, the hideous creatures with rubbery-looking skin, sweeping bat-like wings, and blank faces devoid of features that looked as if they'd been carved out of blocks of ebony. They disturbed her the most. They had the scent of alien realms on them, and somehow the Angel knew that they'd never been human. They had come to earth, and they did not belong here.

Yet as she passed by them, led by the black-draped crone, they all turned to her. Even the featureless creatures of blackness turned their blank faces toward her, and a great murmur arose, a susurrus of awed voices whispered through the despoiled furniture showroom.

"What is this?" she asked the blinded crone, who looked at her with blank sockets that seemed as if they could still see.

"These are your people, my Angel. They have been awaiting your coming."

"How did they—did you—know about me?"

"I told them that I had seen you in my dream, perhaps my vision—I often can't tell now when I'm awake or sleeping. The dark and the light are all the same to me. But I saw you, Angel of the Alleyways, and I saw you protect us and rule over all."

"Rule?" the Angel asked, tasting the word, feeling it sweet on her tongue.

"Yes, my Lady," the crone said.

She nodded. "What do my people need most?" she asked. Her own stomach rumbled emptily. The Angel ignored it, as well as the wave of weariness and unease that washed over her. "Food?" she asked.

The crone nodded eagerly. "Yes, my Angel. There is a stock of it yet—but we can't break into it."

"Take me to it," the Angel said. She liked the tone of command in her voice. With her mother now truly and finally banished there was no one to rule over her, to order her about. She followed the crone down another flight of stairs.

The second floor had been devoted to clothing, but it had been so thoroughly looted that nothing remained but scraps and rags and occasional corpses lying in pools of blood or ichor, depending. She stepped around them daintily. Disturbingly, some looked as if they'd been partially devoured. She made a note in her mind to outlaw cannibalism among her people. Perhaps it was understandable during a time of emergency, but generally it was not a healthy practice. She wrinkled her nose. The bodies were starting to smell offensively. She'd have to detail someone to drag them out of the building, which, she was thinking, could serve adequately as her temporary headquarters. Later she could inspect the city and find something more suitable.

The Angel reached the ground floor, the crone behind her. She finally understood why a crowd had gathered here. The first floor had been a grocery store.

There were still maybe a hundred entities—most of them passably human—in the room. Most were aimlessly wandering up and down the looted, trash-filled aisles, some of them scouring the floor for crumbs and scraps of the bounty that had once graced the now-emptied metal shelving. Once or twice she noticed someone pouncing on a forgotten box of breakfast cereal or a can of beets in an obscure or hidden nook and someone else pouncing on the unlucky finder until a fighting, yelling scrum of hungry bodies had gathered. Casualties usually resulted.

She moved out into the room. Some noticed her and their random pacing through the devastated store ceased as they stood and watched her. She ignored them, moving to the store's front and looking out the glass windows.

Great gouges had been torn into what had been the parking lot, the asphalt dug up in huge cracked chunks and tossed about heedlessly. The city's underbelly had been exposed, the pipes running through culverts in the packed dirt beneath parking lot and city streets. Great trenches had been dug through that dirt, which had been flung and heaped against adjacent buildings. Some were almost entirely buried. The Angel idly wondered if this was more of Earth Witch's work, or the result of some barely glimpsed leviathan's anger or whimsy.

It hardly mattered. What mattered was the result of the colossal excavation. The Angel licked cracked lips. Thirst made as many demands on her body as hunger, and out there pipes extruded from broken culverts and from one, clear, clean water geysered up and fell back to the ground forming a muddy pool at the bottom of the excavation.

And around the pool a pack of the hunting spiders like those she'd encountered earlier stood and drank, as well as less savory things.

We need that water, the Angel thought.

"Who's this?" a voice behind her demanded in a childish tremulo. "Is this the savior you promised us?"

"It is," the Angel heard the old woman say in proud tones, and she turned to face the speaker and saw the last thing in the world, mad as it was, that she expected to see.

It was no child, nor was it human. At least, most of it wasn't. It was as high as she was tall, and much bigger around. It was more like a pile of protoplasm than a slug, but it had characteristics of both. Its flesh was translucent and you could see blurred things moving inside it as if caught in a slow-moving stream or perhaps more accurately, some kind of circulatory or digestive system. It, the Angel saw, had not lacked for food. Besides the human parts tumbling slowly around its body the Angel saw parts of some of its fellow alien entities. Obviously the thing was an undiscriminating eater.

The childish voice piped up again from one of the score of mouths haphazardly located around its eight feet of girth. "It looks a tasty tidbit to me," the creature said. Its voice made the Angel queasy and angry at the same time as she realized what it must have devoured to obtain it. "Why should I let it lord over me?" it inquired brightly.

"The question is," the Angel replied in a hard voice, "why should I allow such an abomination as you to live?"

She reached for it with empty hands.

It reacted suddenly, with frightening speed, rearing up on a stumpy base and stretching out two enormous tentacles, as to embrace and engulf her. The Angel realized that it was big enough to do so, but she didn't pause. Ignoring the tearing pain in her shoulder as best she could she suddenly gripped the sword in her hands.

The flames leapt from the blade. The creature tried to shrink away, but the Angel stepped within striking distance. Her blade had no problems cutting through the thing's rubbery flesh like it was Jell-O.

The tentacles thumped to the floor and thrashed around, leaking an abominably smelling ichor. She changed her grip on the pommel and rammed the blade like a spear into the creature's chest. It screamed horrifically in its childish tremulo and the Angel slashed left and right, the blade engaged to the hilt. The thing's flesh startled to sizzle.

The Angel panted in her killing frenzy. She didn't even think of a mercy blow, if she could figure out where to place one in the undifferentiated mass of the entity, but just kept whisking the blade around her opponent's interior, as if she were stirring some nauseous soup, and it kept burning from the inside.

It stank so badly that she would have vomited if there had been anything in her stomach to bring up. She could hear the onlookers' cries of disgust mingled with calls of encouragement. Apparently it had not been a popular figure. She wondered how many of their companions had fallen to its oozing embrace over the last few days, whose child had provided the voice and the knowledge of English to the predatory entity.

It started to shrivel up into itself and the piteous cries it emitted turned to wordless moans that grew softer and softer. Finally, it was a blackened lump of stinking protoplasm and it collapsed entirely into a greasy mass on the floor. When she pulled her sword away, it was still burning with a cleansing flame. She thrust her blade into the air and released a cry of triumph that was answered by the onlookers.

The old woman stepped forward. "Bow," she cried in a ringing voice, "bow to Our Madonna of the Blade! Our Savior who will lead us from this wilderness to a land of peace and plenty! On your knees, all of you!"

One, then another, then two or three more followed the shouted order and the Angel felt her heart leap as everyone fell to their knees before her. She could hear their murmured prayers and supplications, and it was good.

"Where is this food you spoke of?" she asked the crone.

"The back of the store," the old woman said. "In the storage lockers. The meat freezers, mainly. The walls are strong and we haven't been able to break into them—"

"I will," the Angel vowed.

Her people looked up, sudden hope on starving faces. She nodded, smiling, then thrust her arms out for silence. She was gratified to see that they obeyed almost immediately. The rapturous look in their eyes and on their faces was like nectar to her parched throat.

"This sword," she said, holding it high, "will break down any barrier!"

They might not have understood her words, but there was no mistaking the meaning of her gestures. They cheered.

"And then we will feast!"

Ensnared by the strength of her emotions, they cheered louder and crowded around her, but left an open corridor that allowed the Angel to be led to the storage locker that was built into the wall in the rear of the store. The only entrance to it was a massive iron double door held tightly shut by a thick chain looped tightly around both handles, secured by a large padlock.

The Angel laughed. She gestured dramatically and the crowd around her edged back, giving her more room. She demanded her sword to come to her, but for the first time ever it failed to appear.

Anger shot through the Angel like a tongue of fire and she cried aloud. She shook a clenched fist and somewhere, somehow, her soul or her mind touched something that was, she knew, watching her, weighing her, and, she realized, finding her worthy. A heavy weight came into her grasp, but it was not the blade that she had used all through her existence as an ace.

It was heavier, cruder, and somehow it tugged at her brain, seemingly whispering to it indecipherable but somehow insidious thoughts. It was all black, blacker than night with a dull sheen that threatened to draw you into its substance if you stared at it for too long, with sharp but jagged edges. The pommel was entwisted with thorns and barbed wire, holding her hands tightly within its grasp. The Angel was quite thankful for her leather gauntlets.

Awed gasps and whispers sounded from around her as she experimentally cut the air with it, testing its balance, and the leading edge of it coming perilously close to a man in the tattered remnants of a Kazakh army uniform. The Angel found herself twisting her wrist ever so slightly and the edge of the blade lightly passed across the skin of his throat. He stood there staring for a moment and then a fine bloody mist jetted from his severed jugular vein, whistling a high-pitched tune in the sudden silence.

He stood until he bled out, then he collapsed like a marionette with its strings severed. Again, gasps of awe broke out from the onlookers. A few applauded. The Angel, staring almost incomprehendingly at him, roused herself, laughed, turned, and severed the chain holding the door shut.

Eager hands reached out and stripped the chain from the handles and pulled the doors open. The meat locker was packed, but not for long.

Michelle could still hear the shuffling, and it was still coming closer.

But the drumming in her head had diminished a little. And the buzzing was almost gone. Those horrible voices remained and they had been the worst of it. And she began to realize what she'd done.

A wave of dizziness swept over her.

Aero. She'd killed Aero. And for no reason other than . . . no, she hadn't killed Aero. She'd killed Mummy.

No, Mom, you didn't.

Shame. Shame such as she'd never experienced in her life came crashing down. And guilt.

Oh, fuck that. She'd had to kill Mummy.

Move.

There was more light in the tunnel now and she saw Adesina. *Maybe this has all been a horrible dream. I'm going to wake up and . . .*

Aero appeared and snapped Adesina's neck. Her tiny neck. It snapped like a dry twig. And Michelle screamed. She didn't know how long she screamed. It felt like it went on and on and on.

Aero vanished before she could bubble him, and in his place Joey appeared. She smiled at Michelle, but it wasn't a smile Michelle had ever seen on Joey's face before.

"I can raise her up, Bubbles," Joey said. "I'll bring her back for you." And as she spoke, Adesina got up from the floor. Her head hung to one side and she tried to fly, but couldn't control her wings properly.

Mom. The voice came from Adesina, but it was wrong. It was so close. *Mom, that's not me. It's nothing. Move.*

Michelle stared at zombie Adesina. She took a step toward her daughter, but whatever it was didn't step toward her. And Joey still had that hideous grin on her face.

Even though she was gaunt, she still had enough for this.

A small bubble flew from her hand and gathered speed. It was as heavy and hard as Michelle had ever made. It sped up and smashed into Joey's left eye. Joey collapsed like a rag doll. Adesina fell to the ground, too.

Michelle walked forward and stepped over them, not bothering to look down. Now she knew something new and horrible about herself. She could walk over the corpses of people she loved and not turn a hair.

That's not you.

I think we have plenty of evidence to the contrary. Her mind was clearing as she followed the voice, and what she'd done began to come back in dribs and drabs. Her mind shied away from what had happened in Talas. What she'd done. What she'd done. What she'd done.

Michelle couldn't think of anything else to do now except press on. Occasionally, she would hit herself in the face, and she didn't know why. It hurt.

The tunnel began to slope upward.

We're almost there.

Who are you?

I'm your daughter.

She's dead. She died back there in the tunnel.

That's not me. I came for you. I'd never leave you, Mom.

I left you.

You had to. And now you have to move. It's coming for all of us. You have to save me now. I love you, Mom.

I love you, too.

Baikonur sat on a massive plain, a flat, featureless expanse. Marcus stared, trying to make sense of the geometric confusion of the place: rectangular wedges, domes white under the morning light, silos and towers that jutted up toward the sky. All of it like a scene from a Mars movie. But Mars was a lifeless planet. Not so Baikonur.

"Look at this place," Marcus said, to himself more than anyone else. "It's a fucking tent city."

For an isolated compound strewn across a barren landscape, the plain outside the compound's walls hummed with an incredible amount of activity. A whole army gathered protectively before the main gate and along the wall: khaki-clad soldiers by the thousands, trucks and jeeps galore. They weren't the same as the Kazakh soldiers they'd encountered before. They were white guys, grim-faced and bristling with weaponry. Russians, Olena told him. There were tanks spaced at intervals, all of them facing outward toward some coming, but as yet invisible, threat. To Marcus it felt like those silent barrels were aimed at him and the people he cared for.

Kept apart from the army but separated by a narrow zone patrolled by soldiers, the throng of refugees gathered. Tens of thousands of them. Men and women and children who must've rushed here for the protection—real or symbolic—of the old Soviet order. It was a makeshift array of tents and lean-tos. Numerous fires sent pillars of smoke rising straight up into a clear, windless sky.

The caravan nosed as far into the refugee encampment as they could, coming to rest pressed up against people too fatigued to clear the way. They disembarked. Marcus and Olena did the best they could to get the various vehicles arrayed in a protective ring around the villagers. They posted sentries to keep watch, got their own fire going, and helped any who needed it onto the blankets to rest. Marcus lifted Nurassyl down from a flatbed, feeling the soft, moist texture of his skin. The boy's large eyes stared into his. Despite the strangeness of the touch, the smile on Marcus's face was genuine. God, he wanted the best for this kid. He lifted Sezim down as well. He snatched up her stuffed rabbit when she dropped it, dusted it off, and gave it back to her.

"It's going to be okay," he said to both children. "We're safe here."

Once the children were settled and Aliya began sharing out portions of biscuits between them, Marcus asked Olena, "Where's your father?"

"He's gone to where the power is." She pointed toward the compound.

"Does he know people here?"

"Of course he does. If it's nuclear, corrupt . . . If there's power to be had . . . My father has a connection to it. Marcus, I think we should not have come here."

"It was a crazy ride, wasn't it? But at least we're all here together." Marcus, studying the wall behind the cordon of soldiers, said, "We get in there and find someplace out of the way. A room or something where we can lock the door and sit this out."

"They won't let us in," Olena said. "My father, yes. Me, yes, if I would go. But a village of jokers? No. They are here to protect Baikonur, not us. Anyway, that's not the point. I was so desperate to get away from Talas I didn't think why my father wanted to come here. Now I'm worried he wants to do something horrible. Marcus, this is Baikonur. Do you know what that means?" Marcus's expression must've indicated that he didn't.

"There are enough nuclear weapons in there to destroy the planet. All of it, Marcus. All of us. I think we've come to a bad place."

Babel set up her staging area inside one of the immense warehouses adjacent to their arrival spot from New York. It seemed a reasonable base of operations: a large contained space they could control . . . assuming the evil insanity zone didn't engulf it, and assuming the massive and constantly growing crowd of refugees didn't force their way inside the facility. Half of it looked like something from *Raiders of the Lost Ark*; aisle upon aisle of crates and shelves, stretching into the fluorescent-lit distance. The shelves reached a good twenty or thirty feet high in places; Mollie pictured cherry pickers and forklifts on steroids. The crates sported stenciled Cyrillic labels; for all Mollie knew, they might have contained anything from baby food to plutonium. Keenly aware that Ffodor could read Russian and could have explained what this warehouse was for, Mollie swallowed the tightness in her throat and concentrated on where the real work would happen.

In the far corner, Babel and Billy Ray liaised with a Russian officer. Decked out in pixilated tan-grey urban camouflage, he looked like his daily regimen included broken glass for breakfast and afternoon bear-wrestling for light cardio. Mollie wondered how hard it was to coordinate a three-way between the Committee, SCARE, and the Russian army.

Many of the SCARE guys and Russian troops wore hazmat suits. Mollie didn't know what to make of that. Would she get a suit? Did it even matter? Some cheesy Andromeda Strain suit wasn't going to do squat against a tidal wave of supernatural evil.

Joey sauntered up, zombie mutt—and its odor of putrefaction—in tow. Mollie changed her mind about the utility of a hazmat suit. At least some of them had built-in gas masks and rebreathers.

Thick black cable bundles threaded the site. Some were electrical, she assumed, because they connected to giant arc lights on stands, like the kind of thing they'd used on *American Hero* when filming on location. The lights were arranged in concentric rings. Massive overkill: the interior of the warehouse was almost painfully bright. But there were other cables, too, with unknown purposes. There were at least a dozen cameras, too, and gadgets Mollie couldn't identify. They weren't fucking around.

Just then, one of the Andromeda Strain guys came jogging up to the two of them. "Mollie Steunenberg?"

"Yeah."

The man graced her with a curt nod from within his suit. "Agent Vigil, SCARE." He spoke crisply and quickly, his diction as precise as his buzz cut. "The equipment's in place, so we're ready to begin when you are."

He looked at her, expectantly.

"Um, okay. So what happens now?"

"Agent Ray made it clear that you had the most experience with a crisis of this nature."

"What nature would that be, exactly?"

"Agent Ray chose not to divulge that information to me, miss." He continued to look at her as though he were the world's most obedient dog. As though she was about to leap into action and take charge. As if she knew what the fuck she was doing. As if she wasn't about to piss her pants.

Joey looked at Mollie, then the SCARE guy, then back at Mollie. Joey said, "Ohhhkay. Thanks for the sitrep, agent jarhead. I gotta say, you two are instilling me with heaps of fucking confidence right now."

Mollie said, "From your end, how does this work? What do you need?"

"You do what you do. Make a door to Talas. I'll round up the largest crew of toe tags I can manage."

Toe tags? Oh: zombies. Cute.

"Well. No shortage of bodies. So I guess that's useful, huh?" Mollie tried for a halfhearted laugh, a little gallows humor, but it turned into a sob that clamped her throat like a vise. Christ, it hurt. She ran the back of her hand across her eyes. When she could talk again without croaking like a frog, she said, "Once your, uh, guys are on the other side, do you need me to hold the portal open? Or can you control them without it?"

Joey looked at the SCARE agent. "How far are we from Talas?"

"Approximately five hundred miles, ma'am."

She frowned. Whistled. "That's not next door. I've never tried anything so remote. Getting anything useful from even a single toe tag over that distance . . . The headache would probably kill me, or give me a fuckin' stroke." Joey shook her head. "I'll need a shortcut if my shamblers are gonna do anything useful in Talas."

That was *not* what Mollie'd hoped to hear. She started trembling again.

"Are you absolutely positive? Maybe you could try it without the shortcut first."

Joey rolled her eyes. "Yes, I'm fucking positive. It's not like my god-damned card turned just this morning, you know."

"If I have to keep a portal open to Talas, that bubble of supernatural psychosis will leak through. It happens fast." Mollie hugged herself.

. . . don't think about pitchforks don't think about pitchforks don't think about Daddy's missing ear don't think don't don't don't . . .

"Well we don't have a lot of fucking choice, do we?"

"Are you even listening to me? You have no idea what you're getting into."

Agent Vigil stepped forward. To Joey, he said, "Miss. How large would the opening have to be in order to enable you to do what you need?"

She shrugged. "Not that big. I just need a connection, is all."

"Would a pinhole suffice?"

"Beats me. Maybe."

He turned to Mollie. "Miss. Could you do that? Make a portal that small?" She nodded. "Would that be acceptable to you?"

The portal from the family barn to the casino had been large enough for people, tools, slot machines, and loot. And the psychosis had taken over quickly. But maybe, just maybe, if the hole was small enough, Horrorshow's sphere of influence would seep through more slowly . . .

She goaded herself to answer before she lost her nerve. "Yes. I can do that," she said, in a warbly voice that undermined any pretense of confidence. "Where will you guys be?"

He pointed to a mobile command center parked on the far side of the warehouse, a hundred yards away. It looked like an armor-plated Winnebago, and utterly out of place outside a casino parking lot. The roof bristled with dishes and antennae. "We'll monitor the situation from there as long as the feeds hold."

Mollie noticed that most of the cables strung around the site ran in thick bundles back to the command center. She shook her head.

"Your electronics are gonna start to fail the minute I do my thing."

Vigil nodded. "Yes, ma'am. We've been briefed on that. The technical perimeter is our early warning sentry. We'll track the advance of the effect as the electronics fail. We'll stay outside the trouble zone and pull the plug when it threatens to expand beyond our control."

Clever. They'd actually thought this through. They'd actually listened to what she told Franny, Ray, and Babel, took her seriously, and come up

with a strategy. Mollie didn't know how to process that. It actually felt . . .
nice. Still, there was a problem.

Her voice trembled. *Breathe. Take it easy. Just breathe.* "How will you pull
the plug if I go off the reservation?"

"With this," he said. The lieutenant shrugged, unlimbering the rifle
slung over his shoulder. It was almost half as big as Joey. "We have shoot-
ers stationed around the perimeter."

Joey took a step back. "Jesus Christ taking a runny shit on a camel!
What the fuck? What the *actual* fuck?" She grabbed Mollie by the arm
and tried to pull her away. It was actually kind of touching. "C'mon. Fuck
these motherfuckers."

Mollie said, "Relax. It's just a tranquilizer gun." She paused. "Um, it is,
right? You're just gonna trank me and not blow my brains out, right?"

The corner of Vigil's mouth twitched. The guy was wound so tight that
this was probably the equivalent of a knee-slapping gut-buster on him.
"No, ma'am. My orders are to knock you out, nothing more. You'll have a
nice nap. Not even a hangover."

Mollie nodded. "Okay. But you should be ready to pull the plug even
before the danger bubble gets too large." She glanced at Joey. "We might . . .
I might . . ." She blinked, wiped her eyes, trying to clear away the nightmare images from the street in Talas and her own family's barn. "Look. If
I start acting weird, don't hesitate to dose me."

Vigil gave her his crisp little nod. "Understood." Then he cocked his
head, pressing a gloved hand to the side of his suited head; a little antenna
ran along his jaw. After a few moments of muttering to the other jarheads,
he said, "We're ready to begin."

Mollie and Joey passed through several concentric rings of cables, lights,
and electronics until they reached the center. Mollie turned, examining
the windows. Each had a hazmat guy with a rifle like the one Vigil had
brandished. Surprisingly, the hazmat suits made it difficult to distinguish
the SCARE guys from the Russian soldiers. Big difference, though, between
a Fed desk jockey who used firearms once a year during an annual requali-
fication on the shooting range, and a battle-hardened Spetsnaz killer who
slept with his rifle. Mollie wondered who'd be taking the shot at her, if it
came to that.

Vigil, stationed by the vehicle, gave her a thumbs-up.

"Okay," said Joey. "Gimme a minute."

Her gaze went a little distant, as though she was deep in concentration. Moments later, the dull murmuring of the crowd beyond the fence swelled into a white-noise hiss, as if storm-driven waves pounded rocky cliffs. Then came a flurry of shouts from inside the Cosmodrome perimeter. Past the command unit where Vigil stood, something shambled into the warehouse. And then Mollie understood. Joey was animating some of the freshly dead from around the premises.

Dead men and women filed toward them like the world's slowest, least enthusiastic conga line. The nat corpses among them had a chalky pallor broken with blackish-purple spots where blood had pooled; there were a few jokers among the recently dead, too. One toe tag shambled across the warehouse on feet like giant lobster claws. Eventually Joey managed to corral about a dozen corpses to the innermost ring of lights and cables where she and Mollie stood.

None of the dead were as ripe as Joey's dog, but the cumulative odor of death churned her stomach. She swallowed gorge. God, how did Joey stand it?

Joey snapped out of her glassy concentration, though she still looked fairly distracted when she said to Mollie, "Okay. Let's get this fuckin' show on the road."

Mollie slammed open a portal to the casino before she could think about what she was doing. Before she had time to chicken out. It was about the size of a pantry door, centered near where the slot machines had been. The space underlying the Talas side of the portal felt strange. Ripply, or jiggly. Almost organic. Mollie shuddered.

Wisps of oily, luminescent mist wafted through the hole in space. It smelled like rotting meat, and echoed with screams and non-Euclidean scuttling. Compared to the oppressive death-stink of the evil insanity zone, the diesel-fuel-and-zombies' odor of the warehouse was like a rose bouquet and twice as welcome. The casino had become a foggy hellscape, as if the deepest subconscious nightmares of Hieronymus Bosch, M. C. Escher, and H. R. Giger dropped a metric shit-ton of acid and then fucked each other blind in an amphetamine-fueled three-way. She couldn't recognize anything, much less tell if she'd hit the mark.

Mollie closed the portal. "Hold on a second. Let me try again. I can save you some time if I can get a portal on a street outside the casino." She pictured the streetscape as seen from Baba Yaga's window, just outside the casino, where she'd glimpsed the big snake guy.

The warped geometry inside Horrorshow's sphere of influence made it almost impossible for Mollie to know if she'd successfully moved the portal. It could've been fifty yards, half an inch, or a light-year for all the difference it made. But she did manage to get it open again.

"Okay. Hurry."

Joey closed her eyes. She fell quiet again. The zombies shambled forward at what, for them, seemed a bit of a hurry. But it wasn't fast enough. They weren't going to Talas faster than the evil was seeping through.

"Come on, come on," said Mollie. "Hurry."

"Keep your panties on," said Joey, through gritted teeth.

The first ring of lights dimmed, flickered. Why wasn't Joey hurrying? Didn't she realize this was important? Didn't she know what Mollie was putting on the line for her? Ungrateful little bitch. Mollie curled her fists. She ought to—

Joey slapped her across the face so hard it snapped her head aside. The portal disappeared; the lights came back to full strength. Mollie blinked away tears. Her ears rang. She rubbed her stinging cheek. It felt hot.

"Ouch! Jesus." Joey had walloped her but good.

Mollie shuddered. She'd started to slip away far too quickly that time.

"You were mumbling to yourself," Joey mumbled. "Didn't like the . . . sound . . . of it." She still had a faraway look in her eyes, as if eavesdropping on a conversation just at the edge of audibility. She frowned. When she spoke, the words came out slurred and distracted, as if she'd been to the dentist and shot full of novocaine. "I . . . uh . . . I can barely keep ahold of the toe tags."

Mollie shook her head, tried to dispel the ringing in her ears. "Okay. Here."

She concentrated on re-creating the portals she'd made a moment ago, but far smaller. Smaller than a horsefly, smaller than her pinky nail, smaller than a pinprick. The first hole in space came out the size of a basketball. She slammed it shut, tried again. The next was closer to the size of a plum.

Joey squinted. She leaned forward. Mollie flinched. The doorway blinked shut about a hairbreadth from the tip of Joey's nose. The woman rounded on her, ready to unleash abuse, but whatever she saw on Mollie's face defused her temper. "Fine. Fuck it. Let's keep going. Just try not to give me a nose job."

Mollie kept working to make the smallest portal she could. But she closed the new ones almost as rapidly as they opened—they were still too large.

"Fucking hell, I'm getting whiplash here," said Joey. "It's like the *z*'s are right in the room with me one second and then in a different country the next. Slow your roll before you give me fucking epilepsy."

But Mollie couldn't help it. Abject terror made it difficult to concentrate. But after half a dozen tries she managed to create a portal no larger than a pinhole. If she hadn't made it with her own mind, and thus knew where to look, she might not have known it was there. She pointed it out to Joey.

"How's that?"

The smaller woman relaxed visibly. She still spoke as if carrying on two conversations at once. "Okay. That's much better. Still . . . hard . . . keeping track of them all, but they're not so . . . far away now."

Mollie watched the lights. They hadn't begun to flicker. Yet.

There was a stone staircase leading up. Michelle climbed it. At the top was yet another set of stairs. They spiraled up out of sight.

They stopped at a metal door. She reached out and turned the knob. *It can't be this easy.* The door opened. Afternoon light poured through, blinding her. She put her arm up to cover her eyes.

When she could see, she discovered she was in a courtyard surrounded by a fancy metal fence. She looked around and saw a sign in Cyrillic. No help there.

There was still some mist here, but much thinner. She let herself out the gate. There was still something in her head, but for the most part, she knew what was real. and that was bad.

How many people had she killed? She didn't know. At some point she'd just killed because it felt so good. And it was so easy. And she knew she'd killed Aero. The way she'd killed him was terrible. And what she had done to his body afterward had been done with joy.

Her hands began to shake. There was a time when she knew who she was and what she was capable of, but now she had no idea. What kind of person could kill a kind person like Aero with such abandon?

She was as skinny as she'd even been in her life. There was carnage all around her. Dead bodies lay everywhere. There were cars and trucks aban-

doned in the road as if their drivers had suddenly just decided to stop for
no reason. Some had corpses at the wheel, some just had blood on them
drying in the sun.

She looked into the cars, hoping to find one with the keys still in the
ignition. And a lot of them did, but none of them would start.

Shit.

She started walking. She had to find someone she could tell what was
happening in Talas. But she wasn't sure it mattered. She was pretty sure
that whatever was in there was beyond the Committee's—or anyone's—
ability to stop.

She kept walking. There was nothing else to do.

The Angel leaned back with a sigh, licking grease from her fingers con-
tentedly. Her stomach was comfortably distended, and she felt a sleepy
lassitude washing over her. For the first time in days she felt full and well
fed. They had finished off all the meat. Of course, she had all she wanted,
while she watched in some amusement as some of her weaker followers
fought over the scraps of what was left. Tomorrow they would have to
search for food again, but tomorrow was tomorrow and they'd worry about
it when it was upon them.

Outside, night had fallen. The bloated greenish moon illumined the
shadowy things that still slunk around the water pool. At the start of
the feast the Angel had ordered her people to gather what utensils they
could—there were still plenty of pots and pans on the household section—
and she boldly opened a door leading outside, willed her new blade to her,
and stood guard while her people gathered enough water for their needs.

Nothing had dared to attack them. The Angel had smiled scornfully.
Even they recognized her power. Soon perhaps, they would willingly join
her clan. For now it was enough to have their fear.

She was tired. She was sore. The thought of sleep was upon her, but
she suddenly noticed a strange, somehow familiar figure stagger to the edge
of the pool, fall down, and stick his face in the water, drinking thirstily.

Things moved in the darkness around him, as the Angel watched with
interest.

One of the hunting spiders leapt high, but the figure at the pool suddenly rose to one knee and with a flourish of his arm pointed at the thing.

Thunder peeled in the otherwise still night and a lightning bolt leapt from his hand, incinerating the spider in midair.

The man suddenly stood and like a virtuoso directing an unseen orchestra, he gestured right and left, twisting and bowing his entire body in contortions that would have been ridiculous if the end result weren't lightning bolts, punctuated by the occasional clap of thunder, streaming outward, picking off attackers with amazing accuracy and efficiency.

A name suddenly came to the Angel. Doktor Omweer.

She stood, her people watching, and strode to the door. The attacking spider pack had either been entirely destroyed or discouraged by the time she reached the banks of the pool and Omweer stood on his toes, his arms thrust into the sky, his back dramatically bent backward like a bow.

He heard her approaching step and whirled to face her. His full head of grey hair thrust wildly in every direction, his face was smeared with dirt and what looked to be caked blood. One lens was missing from his eyeglasses that lay crookedly upon his face and his eyes, the Angel saw, were mad. Stark, crazy mad.

"What is," he asked almost conversationally, "the difference between the rational and irrational?"

The Angel edged a small step to her right. To her left was the open pool. To her right, the broken ground from which it was torn.

"I don't know," she replied, in a cunningly rational voice.

"The question is, which one are you?" Omweer replied. "There exists, irrational numbers a and b such that a to the power of b is rational."

"Of course," the Angel said.

"The square root of two is irrational, yet two is rational." He approached her carefully. "Consider the number q which equals the square root of two to the power of the square root of two. Either it is rational or irrational."

Omweer, she saw, was not going to take a chance. His right hand twitched at the wrist, giving her time to dive behind a pile of dirt that proved thick enough to protect her as his lightning bolt flashed outward, exploding it into a pillar of dust.

"If q is rational," Omweer screamed, "then the theorem is true, with a and b both being the square root of two!"

The Angel leapt, taking to the sky as her wings appeared. Her wings beat twice as she gained height, then she suddenly turned and swerved as Omweer tried to track her flight path.

"If q is irrational," he shouted to the sky, "then the theorem is true, with *a* being the square root of two to the power of the square root of two and *b* being the square root of two, since—"

She dodged a right-handed then a left-handed thrown bolt, though the latter singed the feathers of her left wing that were tightly clenched to her body as she barely rolled in a tight circle and willed the sword into her hand. Then they collided, the sword striking Omweer in the chest, and they tumbled together to the ground. She lay on his chest as her sword ripped through his body and the tip came out of his back.

"—the square root of two to the power of the square root of two to the power of the square root of two, in parentheses, equals two."

He looked at her as if that were the most important thing in the world, but she had no idea what he was saying. He was completely mad. But he was also dead and no longer a threat to her or her new position.

The Angel went back into the devastated store and hands reached out to touch her as she passed. She wore a grim smile on her face and her beauty was terrible to behold. She had never felt like this before, like an adored queen, like a beloved sovereign. True, her following was small, but she would call more to her side and they would answer.

She drank in their adulation like a fine wine, and it was good.

She Who Must Be Obeyed had come into her kingdom.

SATURDAY

THE PINHOLE SLOWED THE seepage of evil from Talas to Baikonur, but it wasn't foolproof. Sometimes the lights in the innermost ring would flicker. Sometimes the Andromeda Strain guys lurking at the edges of the warehouse with the big-ass guns would start to look fidgety. At those times, Mollie would slam the portals shut until everybody—mostly meaning her—could calm down.

But she wasn't very good about warning Joey, which led to friction. Juggling control of a dozen different toe tags in increasingly disparate locations—assuming physical distance even carried meaning in the depths of Horrorshow's sphere of influence, which was doubtful—taxed the ace from Louisiana. The closure of the pinhole portals effectively meant her zombies went from being in the same room with Joey to five hundred miles away in an instant, which, she explained, meant her reach over her scouts instantly became far more tenuous.

Actually, what she really said was, "God fucking damn it, you hare-brained quim. When you do that without warning me it's like snapping an overstretched rubber band against my brain. It fucking *hurts,* you cunt. Do you *want* to give me a motherfucking aneurysm?"

Michelle was heading away from Talas. At least she was pretty sure she was. Her sense of direction was completely screwed up. She supposed she should be using the sun as a guide, but she no longer trusted anything she saw or felt. *That's right,* she thought. *Maybe you didn't kill Aero after all.* But that was bullshit and she knew it.

The only thing she wanted was to get as far away from Talas as she could—and as quickly as possible.

Even this far away from what she thought of as the core of crazy, there was carnage. ("Crazy" was an adorably weak word for what was happening here. This madness was blocking out the sun.) Automobiles and trucks were scattered across the road like toy cars thrown by a toddler.

There were dead bodies everywhere. A young girl in a pale pink floral dress hung out of the window of a pale blue Lada. There was a bloody scalpel in her hands. She'd slashed her wrists and had gouged out her eyes, too. A small pool of blood coagulated on the road underneath her. Michelle wanted to feel something, but she was numb. Numb from what she'd seen already. And numb from what she'd done.

Glass from shattered windshields ground under her boots. The road here was buckled and cracked, too. And she tripped and fell occasionally.

There was a pile of corpses ahead. They were bloated and bruise-colored. Some of the bodies had already exploded, and maggots covered the entrails. With numb horror, she realized that festering dead bodies that hadn't been changed into grotesqueries was the most normal thing she'd seen in a while.

There were so many ruined vehicles that Michelle despaired of ever finding one that ran.

She came upon a relatively intact Gaz with its driver's-side door hanging off one hinge. She ran up to it and saw there were keys dangling from the ignition. The surge of joy she felt made her queasy.

She got in and turned the key. The ignition clicked, then nothing. She tried again, giving the gas a pump. Still nothing.

"Fuckfuckfuckfuck!" she screamed in anger and frustration. She pounded her hands on the steering wheel until they turned red.

She got out and kicked the one-hinged door three times, trying to make it fall off. All it did was make her foot throb with pain.

She wanted to kill someone. *Anyone.*

The influence of whatever was coming from Talas was still strong enough to be affecting her. She had to get all the way out of the corruption zone. Or Batshit Crazy Town, as she decided it should be called for now. Oh, the hysterical funny on that one. She was just distracting herself. Anything so she didn't have to think about killing Aero. About blasting his head open and then making a bloody paste of his body. In the faint, lingering, crazy buzzing, she was filled with grief.

It was like being hit in the gut. She'd done the unspeakable. And not just what had happened to Aero. She'd killed wantonly. And she wasn't even sure how many people she'd killed—or if they had even been people anymore. There were some she could remember, but she suspected—no, she knew—that there had been more. Given her power, there had to be so many more.

And Mummy. She'd killed Aero thinking he was Mummy. There had been multiple versions of Mummy, and she'd killed all of them. Or was it part of her madness that she'd imagined doing that?

It seemed as if space and time were being warped. Her memory was slippery and confused. How else to explain the primordial things she'd seen crawling through the city streets? The way normal people were being changed into other vile things? How else could she explain the self-mutilations and suicides, and the glee with which so much of the carnage had taken place?

And she had been part of it all. She'd killed Aero. She'd killed those women in the forest. Killed the man in the catacombs. (*Oh, he deserved to die,* part of her whispered. *They all did.*)

She shook her head. She wasn't out of the fog yet. Remnants of it lingered.

And whatever was causing the fog and the madness, she wasn't sure the Committee could fight it. She wasn't sure anything on earth could.

The hours dragged on. Mollie fed Joey orange juice through a straw to keep the semi-comatose woman hydrated while her zombies roamed an alien nightmarescape searching for survivors of the Committee A-team.

Mollie hated that she had to hold a portal to Talas open for so long. Even a minuscule one, even periodically closing it until the seepage of supernatural evil abated. She managed not to piss herself. It felt like an accomplishment.

But worse than the fallow time while Joey's toe tags stumbled across nothing interesting were the times when she perked up and announced, "I think I have something."

Because then Mollie had to open a larger portal to Talas, so that they could take a quick peek inside and investigate with eyes that weren't, well, putrifying. Sometimes she had to make the portal large enough so that hazmat guys could use the magnifying scopes on their rifles to scan the view through the hole in space. After the first time a crab-like thing hopped through the portal, scuttling into Baikonur on legs covered in eyeballs covered in mouths, the SCARE agents and their Russian counterparts made a point of keeping their weapons trained on each portal.

They were good shots. But the tranquilizer darts weren't terribly effective against the abomination; it didn't stop moving until they put several high-caliber rounds into it.

More than once Mollie had to snap a portal shut because something tried to hop, shamble, ooze, or hurl itself through to the Cosmodrome. Vaguely human shapes fused together at the face, perpetually eating each other; roving eyeballs slithering on a carpet of tentacles; once she even glimpsed through the fog something that she swore could have been a real-life human centipede.

As he dressed for work on Saturday Franny kept the TV on. Then wished he hadn't. It was filled with pictures and reports from Talas, actually now an area hundreds of miles outside of Talas because the troops kept retreating from the encroaching darkness. The networks replayed images of troops shooting each other, a general committing suicide on air, people or things that maybe had once been people gnawing on dead bodies, and occasionally a flash of some grotesque, inhuman shape in the drifting fog. Reporters speculated and yammered endlessly about the cause of the phenomenon.

Apparently no one in authority had seen fit to tell the fourth estate what was actually going on. After a moment of reflection Franny decided they were probably right. If you told people the world was going to end the resulting panic would . . . What? Make it worse?

The embedded reporters spoke in hushed tones about what they felt—fear, rage, lust. They tried to stay professional, but sometimes they lost control. Cold sweat broke out of Franny's chest and back as he remembered what he had felt in that hospital. He turned off the television and bolted from his apartment.

SATURDAY   393

The precinct was nearly deserted with most of the officers still occupied by the ongoing standoff at the Jokertown Clinic. Michael was already at his desk. Franny slid into his chair. There was a stack of files next to his battered old P.C., and a note on a Post-it stuck on the screen. It was from Maseryk telling him he might be needed to carry messages between the hostage negotiators to Baba Yaga and Grekor, but in the meantime he should start to clear the backlog on his desk. Franny rubbed a thumb across his forehead and squeezed his eyes shut. When he opened them Michael was staring at him.

"Headache? Already? You just got here," Michael said.

"Yeah." Michael looked tired, and his eyes were shadowed with grief. "You okay?" Franny asked.

"Family troubles." Michael fell silent. Franny waited, sensing his partner really did want to talk. The dam burst. "Kavitha, she left me! Took our daughter. Isai is confused, upset. Minal blames me one minute and Kavitha the next." He bowed his head and pressed a palm against his forehead. "Everything's just so fucked up."

You have no idea.

Michael looked up again and forced a smile. "But hey, at least you made it back."

"Yeah."

"So, shall we get into this?" He held up a file. "Somebody fire-bombed the offices of Ace Assurance. Given their habit of selling cheap insurance to jokers and then never paying up I'm surprised it didn't happen sooner."

Franny shook his head. "You've also got to question the wisdom of picking that name when you're selling insurance to jokers."

Michael gave a sharp laugh. "Yeah, hadn't even thought of that. Unfortunately the janitor was running late that night and he was in the building when it went up."

Franny turned to his phone. "I'll request a list of their clients. We can start there."

Fifteen minutes after his call to the company a long list of names came scrolling across Franny's computer screen. He and Michael divided up the list and worked for another hour. It was boring and tedious and so far nobody had jumped out as a mad bomber. Michael went and got them each a cup of the notoriously bad Fort Freak coffee, and settled with a sigh into his chair.

"What I don't understand is where she gets off leaving me. Kavitha, I mean. I mean, I'm the wounded party. She's the one who hid her brother from me . . . us. If we'd had that information what happened to you . . . well, it might not have happened."

"I guess people's first instinct is to protect the ones they love," Franny said and he found himself thinking about Baba Yaga and Tolenka and Ray and his wife.

"Yeah, maybe." Michael fell silent for a moment then added, "The bed just feels really lonely right now."

"Wait, I thought you said Minal was still there?"

"Yeah, but I'm used to getting snuggled from both sides," the detective said with a sigh.

Franny forced a smile when what he really wanted to do was deck Michael. The man was down to just one hot babe in his bed and was whining while Franny didn't even have a girlfriend. He found his thoughts straying to the young English ace and actress, Abigail Baker. He'd had the hots for her ever since he'd first found her naked on the sidewalks of Jokertown. He had even been pathetic enough to help her deal with her ex-boyfriend Croyd Crenson when the guy had been in one of his sleep-deprived psychotic rages. How much more of a sap could he possibly be?

He went back to cross-checking the list of clients with anybody who might have had the training to construct an incendiary device, or access to the materials used in this particular device. Once again the cruel irony of life struck Franny. Somebody gets fucked by their insurance company, acts out, and was now facing a murder rap. Franny was sure their unknown perp hadn't intended to kill Ben Wilson, but that had been the outcome.

Just like I hadn't intended to unleash hell on earth. But he had, and what did it matter if they ever caught Wilson's killer? In just a few more days Wilson would be just one corpse among thousands. Maybe millions. Sickened, Franny pushed back from his desk, the crooked wheels on his chair chattering like skeleton teeth on the stained linoleum.

"I'm gonna get some lunch. Want to come?" he asked Michael.

"Nah, I promised Minal I'd meet her for lunch. She's pretty upset, too."

Franny had managed to get a temporary ID, money, and a new phone. His replacement badge was going to take five working days. At which point it wouldn't fucking matter.

He stood on the sidewalk, bounced the phone, and dithered. He finally dialed Abby's number.

The morning was nothing but frustration. Marcus and Olena spent it moving through the growing crowd of refugees locked out of the Cosmodrome. He rode high on his coils, his torso well above eye level, fists clenched at his side in threats that didn't need translation. People cleared the way for them. That worked to get him through the fugitive camp, but they were searching for a way inside the barricades. On that they were striking out. Each time he approached the buffer zone, Russian machine guns honed in on him, warning him off. Once, he'd swallowed down his fear and kept going, thinking he'd just leap the barbed wire and the fence and make his case from inside. A quick barrage of machine-gun fire drew him up. The ground in front of him came alive with little explosions of dust. A ricocheting bullet flew past his ear, singing as it went. So much for that. He retreated, much to Olena's relief.

"These fuckers meant business!" she scolded. "You see the bodies strewn about sections of the buffer zone? Don't become one of them."

Truth is, he was lucky they didn't gun him down on sight and he knew it. There was more than the usual amount of anti-joker sentiment in the air. It was as thick as ripples in the evil miasma back in Talas.

He did flare with hope when he came upon a contingent of blue-helmeted UN soldiers. They were guarding a side gate away from the main refugee camp. Behind the entrance, big warehouses stretched into the distance. A bustling confusion of military and nonmilitary people came and went. Marcus approached the gate slowly, with his arms raised and as little menace in his posture as he could muster. Olena stayed at his side. The soldiers' guns came up just like the Russians.

"Hey, are any of you American?" he asked. "Help a fellow American out?"

"Keep back," one of them said. Not an American accent, but at least he spoke English. "This entrance is for Committee use only. No nonessential personnel. No civilians." Though, saying that, his eyes did linger on Olena as if he might reconsider this in her case.

"And no jokers," another guard said. Different accent on this one, but still not American. He stepped closer, looking jumpy, too ready to use a weapon.

A wasp buzzed around Marcus's head. He swiped at it, just faintly, with his upraised hands. "Committee? There are aces here? I need to talk to them. I know things about what's happening in Talas. Bad things are coming here, man. You gotta let me—"

The jumpy soldier cut him off. "Move away!"

Marcus froze, trying to ignore the wasp as it danced in front of his face. He whispered at it, "Fuck off!" To the soldiers, he said, "Look, my hands are raised. I'm not trying to hurt anybody. I have information—"

The joker-hating soldier raised his gun higher, sighted right at Marcus. "Permission to use force?" he asked out of the side of his mouth.

"Denied," the first soldier answered. To Marcus, he repeated, "This entrance is for Committee use only. Orders from on high. Move along. Now. This is your *last* warning. We will fire."

Marcus didn't doubt he meant it.

"Forget it, Marcus," Olena said. "Idiots. Let's go."

"Fuck 'em," Marcus said. "We should check on the villagers anyway." The two moved away, backtracking for a time before finally turning their backs on the soldiers.

Marcus had been chewing over the idea that if they couldn't get in to the protection of the Cosmodrome they should keep moving, get even farther away from Talas, maybe someplace secluded to wait this all out. He'd been reluctant to bring it up with Olena, the Handsmith, and Bulat and other village elders. He didn't know how they'd take it, after they'd gambled so much on Baikonur. But it was starting to seem like their only option. He began, "Listen, Olena, if we're trapped on the outside when the contagion reaches—"

He cut the words off when the wasp appeared again, right between his eyes, dangerously close. "Hey, what the—" It dive-bombed him, zigged to one side when he swiped at it. He'd never seen anything quite like it. An annoying, harassing green annoyance of an insect. He'd just decided to tongue tag the bugger when a swarm of other green wasps joined the first. For a second Marcus and Olena were caught in a swarm of them. Then they congealed, blended into each other, and took on human form. Not much of a human, though, just a half-sized, emaciated figure, small as a boy but with a face that looked a couple weeks past death. He was naked.

This fact only marginally less disturbing for the swarm of wasps that blurred where his genitalia should've been. His eyes, as green as the hornets.

"Infamous Fucking Black Tongue!" he exclaimed. "We thought you were toast back in Talas. You don't even look burnt. You're kind of in trouble, kid, though it won't really matter if we all go insane and . . ." He had more to say, but his eyes slipped to Olena. He studied her a long, lecherous moment. "Hello there. You know, from what I've seen the last few days the world's days may be numbered and counting down fast. Half of me is bugging out, but despite that a part of me wants to do nothing more than to get to know you better."

Olena smirked. "Which part of you is this? That doesn't care about the world, I mean."

"We should talk about that. Jonathan Hive, at your service. And yes, I mean *the* Jonathan Hive."

Dead-faced, Olena asked, "Why do you tell me you have hives?"

"No, no. Hive, from *American Hero*! Season one, back when it was real."

Olena scrunched up her nose like she was remembering the smell of something rotten. "I don't watch American television. Except HBO."

"Oh, you just haven't given it a chance." The ace stepped forward, one arm crooked as he rotated to slide it into Olena's and lead her away.

Marcus slipped in front of Olena, the flat of his palm halting Bugsy. "Are you kidding me? She's with me, and not to be rude, but you look like a shrinking dead man walking."

Jonathan scowled. "Fucking Talas. Lost half my wasps there." His gaze shifted from Olena to Marcus and back again, seemingly calculating the wisdom of continuing down this track. A green wasp crawled out of his ear and hung upside down on his earlobe, cleaning itself. "All right, whatever. We're here on business anyway."

A commotion came from back at the gate. A figure hovering in midair floated over the guards toward Marcus. Just behind him jogged a burly man clutching something to his chest. They came toward Marcus with the soldiers in tow.

"Bugsy, what the fuck?" the floating man said. He was olive-skinned, Asian-looking. He carried himself with a strange mixture of floating tranquility and nervous-eyed agitation. "Why'd you swarm and fly away like that? Scared the hell out of me."

"Everything scares the hell out of you," Bugsy said, about as snidely as Marcus had ever heard a person address another. "Meet the Lama. Not to be confused with the Llama." Gesturing toward the burly man huffing up to them, he added, "And my butler here is Tinker, maker of clever, useless machines."

"Bugsy!" the burly man called in an accent Marcus recognized straightaway. Australian. "What were you thinking? You forgot your clothes, mate."

"That's what I have you for." The emaciated ace snatched the bundle from him and began slipping himself into the comically oversized garments. "Comrades, let me introduce you to one Marcus Morgan. Aka the Infamous Black Tongue. Denizen of the sewers of Jokertown, keeper of Father Squid's underground crypts. A vigilante of considerable repute, illegal gladiatorial fighter. And all-around bad boy."

Olena wove an arm through Marcus's. "He knows you!" she said. "Even the bad boy part."

"Of course I know him," Bugsy said, cranking at the belt of the trousers that, thankfully, hid the swarming blur of his crotch. "Been writing features about him for *ACES!* magazine. He's good copy."

Marcus narrowed his eyes. "What have you written about me?"

Tinker grinned. "Probably better you don't know."

Bugsy didn't dispute it. He smiled lasciviously at Olena. "And you are?"

"Not interested," Olena answered. "And my name is Olena."

Tinker grinned again. "I like her. She's got you right sussed, Bugsy."

"You were in that horror, weren't you?" Lama asked Marcus. "Talas, I mean."

Marcus nodded.

"Us too," Bugsy said. "On the first team of aces the Committee sent in."

"Yeah?" Marcus couldn't help but show his eagerness. "What happened? Did you fix things?"

The wasp on Bugsy's ear dropped off. He caught it in a fist and popped it into his mouth. "Not exactly. Barely lived to tell about it, is more like it. Come on. We've got things to talk about then. You'll need to be debriefed. See if you know anything we don't. Let's get you inside."

"Ah," Tinker hesitated. "Babel might not like this."

Bugsy scoffed. "What, 'cause he's a joker? Screw her. All the better if it twists her nipples. Come on."

The joker-hating soldier began to protest, but his superior officer shut him down. He said, "They've just become Committee business. Let 'em alone, soldier."

As Marcus started forward, feeling the first sense of relief in days, Olena said, "Wait! Marcus, the villagers. We can't leave them."

"Oh, that's right." Marcus pulled up. "Hey, it's not just us. We've got a village with us. Good people. They helped us get here. We gotta get them inside, too."

The aces exchanged glances. "Not likely," Bugsy said. "We're not running a shelter here."

"Not a joker shelter, that's for sure." The hater again. Marcus felt like slapping him.

"Your villagers are jokers?" Bugsy asked. "In that case forget it, kid. There's not a chance in hell. Babel runs things by the book, and a bunch of useless jokers ain't in this particular book. Come on. And I'm not asking. Consider it a Committee order." He moved off, Lama trudging glumly beside him. Tinker shrugged apologetically and turned to follow them.

"Marcus, we can't just abandon them," Olena said.

"I know." He thought fast, watching the aces recede toward the gate. "I won't do that. I promise. But this is our best shot. Get inside. Talk to people in power. We'll find a way to get them inside."

"You are promising?"

"Yes. Straight up promise. Come on."

The sun beat down on her unmercifully. The last time she had eaten or had anything to drink had been in the Kazakh army camp. And now that she'd used the last of her fat, she was cadaverous and weak.

But, at last, she was out of the crazy zone. And the horror of what she'd done washed over her again and again. She relived every moment with ever-increasing shame and remorse. But even as she agonized, in some horrible part of her, remembering blasting Aero's head apart came with a deep glee.

And then there were tears. They rolled down hot and bitter. Who was she now?

And she hadn't saved Adesina at all.

That brat.

Shut up!

She kept walking. Step after staggering step. She didn't know why.

You do, too.

And she did. She was going back to see her daughter and Joey. She wanted to be with them when the world came to an end.

Joey said, "I've got something!"

The constant terror of flirting with madness, of opening portals into hell and closing them before the devil noticed, had left Mollie exhausted and numb. Hours and hours of endless dread melted together into . . . boredom.

She'd heard this before, too. But every time one of Joey's zombies glimpsed something that might have been a survivor, inspection with living eyes always revealed a gibbering vaguely human abomination that was too distorted to identify as a former Committee member.

"That's nice," said Mollie, lying on the cold hard concrete of the warehouse floor. The Andromeda Strain guys couldn't be bothered to bring her a pillow or blanket; they refused to get too close to the pinhole Talas portal.

"No, seriously. I'm seeing furrows in the earth and, and, it looks like what little remains of this building was torn apart by an earthquake."

"You know it's probably not even earth anymore," said Mollie. "Not really. It's—"

Ana Cortez.

The name leapt unbidden into Mollie's mind. She didn't think she'd absorbed any of the information about the A-team that Babel had given her. In fact, she'd consciously tried to disregard the briefing, knowing better than anybody that the aces who'd gone on that first ill-advised foray were forever lost. But now one name from the briefing echoed through her memory.

Ana Cortez. Earth Witch.

Mollie sat up, aching from the hard floor. "Show me."

As always, it took a bit of triangulation and negotiation before she zeroed in on the location that one of Joey's wandering zombies had shambled to. But sure enough, barely visible through the sepulchral non-Euclidean meat-fog, the ground—she'd never call it earth—had been torn apart as if ruptured with a giant machine. Machinery didn't work there, of course. The furrow cut through a nest of pulsing purple roots to an edifice that might once have been a building but which was now a shuddering blubbery massif covered in boils and suppurating gashes. The flesh structure had collapsed where it met the furrow, as though it had been shaken apart.

It was a tedious process, following the furrows through the zombie's eyes, constantly closing and opening new portals. But she eventually found a rent in the ground that looked as though somebody had physically peeled back a layer and laid it back down with a deliberate wrinkle. A shelter; a hiding spot.

Joey enlisted several more dead things scattered around the hellscape to help with the digging. If there was one thing zombies could do, it was scrabble at dirt, impervious to rot and ruin. Though it had been buttressed with stones and roots, the dead tore it open in short order.

It was a burrow. Maybe a crypt. It contained an unconscious woman, Joey reported. When the excavation was complete, Mollie gritted her teeth and widened the portal to Talas for a quick look. The woman in the burrow was barefoot. She looked to be in her late twenties. It looked as though the ground had simply swallowed her, as though taking her into its embrace. She'd hidden herself, Mollie realized.

Safe in the outermost ring of the warehouse, Babel looked at the unconscious woman through a high-powered rifle scope. "That's Ana!" she shouted.

Mollie opened a portal under Ana and dropped her in the lobby of the Jokertown Clinic. Then she slammed the connection to Talas closed again.

"Boston may be shit, hot and sticky, but the show is brilliant. Lovely reviews for the previews. I'm sure we'll get to Broadway."

Franny and Abigail the Understudy were seated at his favorite restaurant, Mary's Lamb. Mary herself, cloaked and masked, was lumbering about refilling coffee cups and asking how folks liked the food. Abby was slathering ginger jam on a scone, but persisting in talking with her hands as well as her voice so dollops of jam were falling like sugar bombs onto the white tablecloth.

"I just hope the producers don't decide to recast. I think I'm safe. It's a small part. But *pivotal*, absolutely pivotal. And one reviewer actually mentioned me." She gave a brief frown. "I do hope it wasn't because of all that flap at the circus."

Franny reached across the table and laid a hand over hers. The movement pulled at the stitches in his side and he winced. Abby didn't notice. He wasn't surprised. She was a terribly self-involved little person, but utterly adorable.

"I'm sure it wasn't that. I bet you were great. Let me know when you open. I'll be there on opening night." Except *there won't be a Broadway or a New York or a world by then unless Babel and Ray and Mollie and the others succeed.* He pushed away the thought.

"I'll get you a ticket, and I'm so sorry I didn't call. I got your messages, but it's just been so hectic."

"That's okay. I just got back into town yesterday. I was in Kazakhstan."

No reaction. "I do rather think the second act needs work. All the energy drops out, and we have to work all that much harder in the third act to build it back."

Franny tried to figure out how to penetrate the bubble in which she surrounded herself. He could tell her the first part of the story and seem like a big goddamn hero. Brilliant detective who broke the case, and then bucked authority to go and rescue the captured jokers. Make himself seem like a "movie cop" as Jamal would have put it.

Or he could focus on how he'd been wounded and play the sympathy card. But he didn't want her pity, he wanted . . . well, what he wanted was to get laid and this might be his last chance before the world ended. But first he had to break her out of her bubble.

He pulled his focus back to what she was saying. ". . . essential the other actor actually *listens* to what you're saying and not just sit there thinking about what *they're* going to say next. It can't always be about you, and this girl who's playing my older sister keeps stealing the few scenes I do have—"

"Abby." The urgency in his voice penetrated.

"Yes, what?"

"Have you caught *any* news?"

"I don't watch the news. It's all just wars and rumors of wars and there's nothing I can do about any of it so why make myself stressed over things I can't change?"

"So you have no idea what's going on in Kazakhstan? You know, that place where I was until just a few days ago? That place where people are going nuts and killing each other?"

"Well, no. Based on what you're saying I'm glad I haven't heard anything. It's a good thing you're not there any longer if that's what's happening."

He grabbed her hands. "Abby, something terrible is entering our world. Something that will drive us all crazy. Millions are going to die unless the Committee and others can stop it. If they fail there isn't going to be a Broadway opening for your play. Everything . . ." He gestured at the cozy restaurant. "Is going to change. The world as we know it is ending. I'll try to protect you. I want to, but . . . well, this might be our last chance." He tightened his hold on her hands. "Sometimes you just have to seize life. You know *carpe diem* and all that."

Thank God she didn't go *what* and misunderstand his meaning forcing him to spell it out in even more blunt terms. Unfortunately the conversation didn't go where he'd hoped. She pulled one hand free and folded his hand in both of hers.

"Oh, Franny, that's so sweet, and I can't tell you how flattering it is, but I just don't feel that way about you. You're such a dear friend, and I always know I can count on you to help me, which means so much to me. And really I'm not the right person for you. You're so serious and dedicated. You need a girl who will always be there for you and support you. I'm much too focused on my own career, but I'll always be your friend."

He felt his jaw aching as he clenched his teeth as the terrible, deadly words spooled out. Unfortunately she didn't just leave it there.

"As for this terrible thing. I'm sure the aces will take care of it. It seems like these horrible things never actually come to pass. Someone alway steps in to fix things."

The events of the past week crashed over him. Exhaustion and pain coupled with a gnawing guilt broke his fragile control. He leapt to his feet. So violent was the move that his chair crashed over backward. People looked up and Mary and her waitstaff who were carrying six plates froze.

"Like things got fixed on September 15, 1946? Thousands of people died when the virus got released. Nobody stopped that. Or like all the people who died in the People's Paradise just a couple of years ago? It doesn't matter if this other actress is stealing your scenes. In just a few weeks you're going to be ripping off your own face and eating it! And there won't be anything the police or the army or anyone else can do to protect you because they will have gone mad, too! Hell, they won't even be human any longer. People's bodies, not just their minds, are being warped, twisted."

He realized he was shouting. The only sound in the restaurant was the musac playing in the background. Everyone was staring at him. He shook his head, and made a helpless gesture. Everyone resumed talking and obviously turned away. Mary and her staff set six plates down in front of the lone man sitting in a corner booth.

"Oh, look, that must be Croyd," Abby said brightly. "Obviously just now waking up. I really should say hello. Thank you for lunch. Well . . . I guess." She stood and walked quickly away to the other table. Back to the ex-boyfriend. The ace.

Franny threw a bill down on the table, and bolted out of the restaurant. He pictured Abby twisted into the shapes described by retching reporters. Or raped and murdered by some madman. He had a horrible moment wondering if he might be that man. He was crazy about her. What if he lost all inhibition and acted on his desire?

He wanted to go back and apologize to Abby. To Mary. To everyone. For everything. For fucking up.

They'd been at it for hours, the sun closer to rising than setting, when Mollie reluctantly widened yet another portal for a quick survey of something Joey had glimpsed through her toe tags' putrefying eyes. Day and night seemed to carry little meaning so deep inside Horrorshow's zone of influence; the fell luminescent fog illuminated everything with a sepulchral glow. Joey pointed to damage in the barely recognizable remnants of buildings, streets, people. Here and there, craters pocked the surreal landscape, or what might have been blast marks.

"That's her trademark," she said. "Michelle was here." She glanced around the edges of the portal, as if triangulating. "I think she was standing over there when she threw that one. Try over there."

The lights flickered. In the far corner of the warehouse, Agent Vigil urgently waved his hand at his neck: their "cut it off" motion. Mollie fought to kill the portal; once the evil seeped through, they resisted her a bit, as though she were trying to uniformly compress a water balloon. But she managed to pinch off the incursion, then waited for the lights to return to normal operation. The SCARE team and its Russian counterparts monitored a bank of electronics inside the machoed-up Winnebago. She yawned hard enough for her jaw to pop while waiting for the all-clear. One of the Russian Andromeda Strain guys gave her the thumbs-up (who knew that was international?). Mollie rubbed her stinging eyes, steeled herself, and opened the bajillionth portal pair since entering the warehouse. The Talas side of this one opened on a site near where Joey had indicated.

After finding Earth Witch in her burrow, they'd come up empty on the rescue front. Mollie had been ready to pack it in hours ago. She could barely concentrate. But Joey was relentless in her search for Bubbles.

Here they found bodies strewn among the rubble. Vaguely recognizable human bodies. Some had been gnawed down to the bone by the significantly less human things scuttling through the mist. But Joey rubbed her hands together. "All *right*. About fuckin' time. Now we're in business. Hold it there."

"Um . . ."

"I said fucking hold it there. You're doing your thing, now let me do mine." The corpses shuddered, flopped, rolled, and shambled to their feet. Or what remained of their feet. Just a few days ago, Mollie would have been sickened by the sight. Now she found herself hoping like hell that the rest of her morning would be as quaint as this.

"Try to be quick, okay?"

Joey rolled her eyes. "We're a rescue party, not working the drive-through at a taco joint. So butch up, buttercup. But now that I have these guys—" She jerked a thumb at the portal and, by extension, her zombie henchmen. "You can pinch down the opening again."

Mollie braced herself for the incipient headache. But this time, shrinking the Talas portal was relatively easy. Compared to the crushing resistance that accompanied every other effort she'd made over the past several hours, it was almost a joy. She allowed herself a tired smile of relief.

On reflection, she nudged the portal a bit wider, from a pinhole to the size of a quarter. It sounded like Joey was on to something; the more easily she could work, the faster they could finish this pointless bullshit and the sooner she could take a twenty-year nap.

Joey muttered to herself, or the zombies, while she gathered an army to search for Bubbles. Mollie couldn't see what was going down on the other side but she didn't care. She concentrated on keeping the connection open.

It was easy. She didn't understand why she'd been so reticent about it before. Time passed.

Pop. Pop. Pop. The lights on the innermost ring blinked out. In the distance, Mollie watched a little flurry of activity take over the SWAT guys in their comical hazmat suits. They looked like plastic-sack hand puppets. She laughed. Joey looked at her, frowning. Mollie pointed, singing, "C is for cookie which is good enough for me."

"Yeah, uh, hold that thought. I think I just saw her."

Joey didn't get the joke. Oh, well. Screw her. Maybe the snot-nosed twerp would find it funny when Mollie doused her with gasoline and set her on fire. She had just begun to picture a gas station in Coeur d'Alene when another ring of lights went out. It actually made a difference; the warehouse was slightly dimmer now. That wasn't good. They needed to see what they were doing. But Mollie could fix that. In fact, now that she thought about it, it was actually quite simple.

She opened a new pair of portals. One up near the warehouse ceiling, just under the struts and beams, the other a mile over Australia's Gold Coast to capture the rising sun. It was far better than the shitty artificial lights. She widened the portals to let nice natural light flood the warehouse. The interdimensional hole in the ceiling exploded to thirty feet in diameter. Beautiful sky. Mollie did this all while maintaining Joey's doorway to zombie Talas.

Two pairs of portals, simultaneously. It was incredibly easy. She couldn't understand for the life of her why she'd struggled so much with something so simple. A baby could do it. From the corner of her eye, she saw more plastic-suited mannequins gamboling about like puppets in the distance. She giggled.

Joey said, "Uh . . ."

"Eyes in the sky!"

"You sure you want to be doing this?"

Mollie stopped laughing. Fucking ungrateful bitch. "I'm helping you, you stupid cunt!"

"Hey! Looney Tunes!" Joey wheeled on her, jabbing a finger in Mollie's chest. Mollie traded the sunlight portal for one just before her sternum, just large enough for Joey's finger.

"I'm just about out of patience with you—" Jab, jab. "—you ugly-ass bi—"

Mollie snapped the portal shut. It blinked closed on Joey's finger, then blinked open again to catch the precious severed digit before it fell into the sea off the coast of Queensland.

Joey doubled over, screaming, clutching the bloody stump where her finger had been. Red spray misted Mollie's face and doused her shirt—*that wretched little bitch fucking ruined Mollie's shirt*—where she hugged her hand to her stomach. Her finger made a tink-plop sound as it hit the concrete floor, first the fingernail side, and then the raspberry lollipop side. Mollie snatched it from the ground—five-second rule—lest the maggots swarm it and carry it back to their queen before it could be sanctified. Between licks of the stump of Joey's finger, she said, "Don't fucking touch me. Don't you EVER FUCKING SMEAR YOUR FRANKENSTEIN GOD-MACHINE FILTH ON ME AGAIN!"

She kicked Joey in the nose. It knocked the little cunt down, sent her sprawling. Mollie wound back and slapped her across the face for good measure.

Mollie took her shirt off. It had been befouled and couldn't be cleansed. Balled it up, threw it into the air, caught it with a portal that opened on the garbage incinerator in the basement of her apartment building in North Dakota. The finger went with it.

Joey rolled to her feet. Time passed slowly, smoothly, like a magenta crayon dropped in a meat grinder.

More lights blinked out. The next ring, and then the next. No matter. Mollie re-created the Australian sunlight portal. It was bright and warm in the warehouse. The plastic-suit guys looked really worked up about something.

Two portal pairs at once. God, it was easy. How had it ever been hard? Ffodor, that shitbag Ffodor, *he* was the problem. He'd clouded her mind, working against her, stifling her abilities, that miserable son of a bitch. She'd show him.

A Louis XIV chair plummeted into the warehouse to shatter on the floor.

She kept the Talas portal in place, of course; she didn't want to interrupt the mission. The mission was important. The mission was her gateway to rebirth in a new world, a world carpeted with Joey's flesh.

One of the fakey plastic hazmat Mummenschanz puppets aimed his popgun at Mollie. She moved the sun portal again to intercept the dart and sent the projectile right back at the shooter, like she'd done with the

Taser-happy frog cop in Paris. In seconds he slumped over, the electric-blue feather of a tranquilizer dart protruding from his cheap-ass Halloween costume. Fucking assholes. She'd fucking teach them not to attack her. She opened a portal under the Winnebago and dropped it on the shooter. Then—

Something slammed into her ribs. Mollie tried to turn, but something clamped on her shoulder like a vise made of needles. She screamed.

Joey's zombie hound wrenched its head back and forth, giving off a burbling growl as it tore a chunk out of Mollie's arm. She screamed again. She opened a portal underneath herself, dropping through the floor to escape zombie Fido.

A trio of eyeball crabs scuttled through the Talas portal. Joey kicked one aside; it ruptured, splashing her with black ichor.

"Where'd you go?" she screamed. "Come back here, you fat greasy shit-stain, so that I can tear you apart!"

Mollie crept up behind Joey, beside the broken chair. Blood streaming down her arm, she picked up Ffodor's femur. (Suppressing another giggle as she did: *Ffodor. Femur. Alliteration. Alligator. Antidisestablishmentarianism.*) She wound back for a blow that would open the little cunt's skull.

"I FUCKING TOLD YOU NOT TO SMEAR YOUR FILTH ON ME! *I TOLD YOU!*"

Billy Ray tackled her hard enough to steal her breath and send them both skidding and rolling across the hard concrete floor. She dropped Ffodor's femur. A rabbit punch snapped her head back. Ray wound up for a more powerful blow, one with his shoulder behind it. Mollie threw up a portal shield to intercept his fist, but his reflexes were too fast. He threw wide before she could chop his hand off at the wrist. Fine. She dropped him through a wide floor portal twinned to one in the ceiling; the SCARE agent fell from ceiling to floor over and over again, faster and faster, until he was a blur.

All these motherfuckers did was try to distract her while she held the connection to Talas. It'd be easier to hold the line once they were all buried in the maggot queen's stomach.

Mollie turned just in time to see Joey's zombie mutt crouching for a lunge at her throat. She moved the portal in the ceiling. Billy Ray pancaked the zombie pooch when he hit the warehouse floor at terminal velocity, about 120 miles per hour.

Joey screamed with inchoate rage.

What was the crack the bitch made about *American Hero*? She deserved to get her eyes shoved down her throat for that. But Mollie could do even better. She hurled herself on the smaller woman. Pinned her to the ground—easy peasy, Mollie outweighed her, let's hear the little shit make fun of her weight now—and clamped her teeth on Joey's eyebrow ridge. She craned her neck. Flesh tore with the sound of a wet bedsheet ripping in half. Joey screamed. Mollie swallowed warm rubbery flesh stippled with bristles.

Joey's remaining fingers tore a furrow in Mollie's face while an icecold hand reached around from behind to clamp on her throat. Squeezed. Mollie couldn't breathe. Needed air. Mollie clawed at the arm but couldn't loosen its grip. The vise on her throat squeezed harder. The room got darker.

Thwip. A bee stung her in the ass. *Thwip, thwip.* Then two more followed suit, one in the small of the back and the other just under her left breast. The opportunistic motherfuckers.

Spinning shadows engulfed the warehouse. The last things Mollie saw before it all went black was a severed corpse arm falling free of her neck; Joey clutching one bloody hand to her chest and the other to a hamburgerraw spot over her eye while more blood sheeted down her face; and a gang of toe tags shambling through the portal as it closed on them.

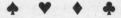

The Russian goon leaned against the wall, his chair canted onto the back legs while he picked his teeth with a well-chewed toothpick. He gave Franny a casual nod of greeting reminiscent of the nods he'd received from his fellow cops who ringed the clinic. It bothered Franny that this criminal treated him with the same acceptance and familiarity.

Before he reached the hospital door it was opened and five men in expensive bespoke suits walked out. They all carried briefcases that cost as much as a year's salary for a lot of people. Franny recognized two of them—they were the top criminal defense lawyers in New York and they only represented high-profile, high-dollar clients.

He couldn't help but contrast his appearance with these men. Franny might have a law degree, but that's where the resemblance ended. He was dressed in blue jeans and a T-shirt and instead of a twenty-thousand-dollar

Lederer de Paris briefcase he carried a bag of take-out Chinese food. They probably thought he was the delivery boy.

And wasn't that exactly what he was? He'd delivered Baba Yaga to New York. Delivered Babel. Delivered Mollie.

He almost tossed the food into a nearby trash can. Food he'd brought for the old lady because . . . He tried to analyze why he had brought her a late-night dinner and realized it was because he felt a strange bond to the old bitch and if he was honest he had no place else to go.

The back of the hospital bed was elevated and the old woman was flicking from news channel to news channel.

"I see you had company," Franny said.

Baba Yaga grunted. "Hardly a social call if you have to pay them. What have you brought?" She nodded toward the sack.

"Chinese. You didn't strike me as the pizza type."

He pulled over the rolling table and started setting out containers. Baba Yaga watched him, frowning. "Why are you here, boy?"

"I'm not sure. I felt like I ought to check on you, I guess." He glanced up at the television.

"You have no sweetheart to fuck before the world ends?" she asked. Her tone implied that she knew damn well he didn't.

"You don't seem to think it's ending," he said as he dished out General Tso's chicken. "Not if you're preparing for your prosecution."

"I thought there might be a chance." She gestured at the television. "Until I saw how badly you people have messed up. America proves once again to be a disappointment." She snorted and folded her remaining arm across her chest.

"If you had leveled with me on the plane I could have called. Kept them from sending the aces. It was the right move based on what they knew. You don't get to criticize them because *you* fucked up by playing for leverage." Franny realized he was on his feet and shouting.

The guard appeared in the door. Baba Yaga waved him away. Her next remark surprised Franny. "I suppose that is true." She took a few bites of the food he'd set out for her. "And it is human nature to grasp and cling to life and to hope. If they can keep Tolenka alive they may buy enough time to find a solution." She tried another bite of General Tso's chicken. "I also understand you have retired from the hero business."

"Huh?"

"When that UN person and the ugly man came with maps and wanted me to pinpoint the location of the hospital. They said you had declined to help. I'm surprised. I would have expected you to leap onto your white horse."

"Maybe I learned something from you. It should be all about me and my stuff."

"I would have gone, Francis. I offered, but the doctors say I might not survive the journey, and Mr. Ray seems not to trust me."

"Trying to guilt me?"

"Trying to understand why you're fool enough not to try and save yourself." Baba Yaga gestured up at the now muted pictures flicking by on the television screen.

It was showing a loop of a Kazakh general drawing a gun and shooting an interviewing journalist in the face. Blood and brains sprayed out the back of the man's skull.

"That will soon be your fate, Francis. Who will you shoot? Or perhaps what happens to you will be worse. Some survivors have slithered out of the affected area. I believe some troops beat one of them to death before they realized it was a human. Or used to be."

Guilt lay on the back of his tongue, an oily horrible taste. "I'm an ordinary person. Just a normal guy. What could I possibly do in that?" He gestured at the screen.

"Die fighting to live instead of cowering."

"Good-bye, Mariamna, it was interesting meeting you. Maybe I'll get to testify at your trial."

"If the world survives I doubt it will go that far. My legal team seems rather confident the blame will fall on the underlings who undertook this terrible criminal operation beneath the nose of a fragile and senile old woman." The sharp expression in her eyes died and her face went slack. She suddenly looked like a woman lost to dementia. She shook it off and gave him one of her wintery smiles. "I will never see the inside of a jail. I have millions in Switzerland and the Caymans, and money can fix anything."

"Except the end of the world," Franny said and he left.

"Don't be stupid, Marcus," Olena said. "Eat. When was the last time you had a hot meal?"

"When was the last time anybody from the village had a hot meal? They should be in here with us. There's room enough."

He said this without managing the certainty he intended. The warehouse-like space they were in was crowded with people, buzzing with activity. There were bureaucrats with their air of importance, suits gathered in clusters, cell phones to their ears, gesturing to underlings who darted back and forth on various errands. There were the few aces he recognized, Bugsy and Tinker and the Lama, who were themselves engaged in a high-profile briefing at a table some distance away. Among all this even more people milled around. Military and civilian alike, they grazed the buffet tables, chowing down donuts and inhaling coffee. Worse, some stood with glazed expressions on their faces. If that was unnerving enough, there were the ever-present Russian soldiers, machine guns hung over their shoulders. They didn't look happy to have any of the foreigners here, but they stared with particularly withering animosity at Marcus. He couldn't tell what they hated him more for, being a joker or being with Olena.

For her part, Olena didn't seem the least bit intimidated about them. "Russian pricks," she'd called them. She shot a few choice Russian words at them on several occasions. Marcus assumed she was responding to insults to him. He couldn't understand a word of it, but he didn't have to. Their disdain for him was clear enough.

Olena picked up the spoon that Marcus had so far ignored. She scooped up a dollop of mashed potatoes and waved it before his mouth. Ignoring it, he said, "There must be someplace secluded in here. That's all I'm talking about. Just let us have the corner of some old warehouse somewhere. Is that too much to ask? I should talk to—"

Olena shoved the spoon in his mouth. She grabbed his chin and encouraged him to chew. "Eat first. Then save the world."

Despite feeling guilty he was eating when the villagers were still locked out, he did as she ordered. Doing his best not to enjoy the food, he tucked into potatoes, sausages, and overcooked peas. For a time he got lost in doing one simple thing, lifting a spoon to his mouth and eating. He didn't even notice how much of a relief it was. Nothing he'd heard since entering the Cosmodrome had been good news. From things Bugsy, Tinker, and the Lama had said, he gathered that not only were things still fucked up in Talas, but that the nightmare world he'd seen there had continued to spread. A whole team of aces had gone in and hadn't been able to do a thing about it. Fucking depressing. He and Olena had been debriefed by some nondescript suit whose face Marcus forgot the moment he left him. Guy hadn't really seemed interested, and Babel hadn't deigned to speak with him herself.

As soon as he wiped the tin plate clean, all the miserable facts fell back on him. They were inside, but so what? There was nothing but bad news, and the only people he cared about were still locked outside, with the contagion heading toward them like some all-consuming nightmare of a dust storm. It was coming; of that Marcus was completely sure.

"I gotta talk to Babel," he said. "Just talk sense to her, you know?"

"I don't think she wants to speak to you," Olena said, with a flatness that Marcus read as sarcastic.

"What are we going to do, then? We can't just sit here. Maybe we should get the fuck out. No one would stop us from leaving. Let's get the others and keep moving. There's got to be someplace we could hold up, just be by ourselves."

"And let the world go to hell?" There was that flatness again.

"I'm just trying . . . to . . . to do something!"

She slipped an arm around back and leaned her head on his shoulder. "I know, Marcus. You're right. We should go. Get supplies. Water. All the food they'll let us take. Fuel. Whatever we can get, and then go."

"Should we tell your father?"

"Fuck him," Olena said. "He doesn't care about me. I'm better off without him." And then, with a deeper level of conviction, "*We're* better off without him."

Marcus pressed his lips, gently, to her forehead. "All right. I'm gonna go see if they'll help us." He jutted his chin toward where the aces were milling about after their briefing ended. "Tinker, at least. He seems decent."

Slithering through the crowd toward them, Marcus noticed someone who made him pull up. A black woman—the first he'd seen in a long time— had just emerged from one of the many corridors leading out of the main warehouse. It wasn't just her race he noticed, though. It was the pained expression on her blood-smeared face and the way she held a hand wrapped in bloody gauze clamped at the wrist with her other hand. She met Marcus's gaze, paused a moment to stare at him, but then carried on as several people helped clear the way through the crowd for her.

Bugsy seemed to be waiting for him when he approached the aces. Marcus asked, "That woman, what happened to her?"

"Joey?" Bugsy asked. "Also known as Hoodoo Mama. Tesseract happened to her. Bit off her finger."

"Hoodoo Mama, that's right," Marcus said. "And . . . Wait. Tesseract? You mean Mollie? The bitch that snatched the jokers and brought them here?"

Bugsy swiped his longish hair away from his face. "That would be the one. See how desperate we are?"

"Damn," Marcus said. His eyes found Joey again. She was seated now, with medical aides buzzing around her.

"Too right," Bugsy said. "She's a real piece of work on the best of days, but from what I hear she's pretty much batshit crazy. Which is a problem since she's pretty much the only ace in this deck that Babel really had a plan for. Possible savior of the world, but she'd rather bite people's fingers off. Joey's not getting that finger back, either."

Marcus kept staring at her, feeling the shape of an idea turning to face him. When he had it, he said, "Actually, I think maybe she could." Without another word, he turned and slithered toward Joey and the swarm of activity around her. He got as near as he could, pausing to watch a doctor snap on his rubber gloves.

She said, "Let's have a look." She gently peeled the wrapping from around Joey's hand, ribbon by ribbon until the bloody mess of it was revealed. One finger was cut clean away. The stump pulsed blood that immediately began to trail down her wrist. "Is there any way to get the missing digit?"

"No," Joey said. "It's fucking gone."

The doctor inhaled. "Sorry to hear that. We'll get this sterilized and—"

"Hoodoo Mama!" Marcus called. But that sounded weird, like it might be an insult. "Or, Joey . . . Look, this is going to sound strange, but you gotta come with me."

She looked up and through the people attending her. Her face was raw and bruised, the flesh above her eye torn ragged and oozing. A nurse dabbed at it with a bit of gauze, but Joey yanked her head away. To Marcus, she said, "You're IBT, huh? I been meaning to look you up. Next trip up to Jokertown, I thought, but no. Fucking Kazakhstan instead. Believe this shit?" She paused, her attitude slipping. "You ain't exactly seeing me at my best."

"I've got someone you need to meet. He'll make you feel better."

"Are you for real? Do I look like I'm up for it? Another time, sure, but—"

"No, I mean I know someone who could heal you. Like really heal you. Give you your finger back."

Joey's eyes narrowed. "Nigga, you playing with me? I don't stand for being played. You got a pretty face, but I won't hesitate to have some old shriveled up Russian zombie fucker eat your face off."

"No, I swear it. I know a jo—I mean, I know an ace that can do it. I'll take you to him."

"This ace, he's gonna give me my finger back? 'Cause shit if I know how to find it. Probably got a crab chewing on it right now."

Marcus swallowed. Hoping it was true, he said, "He can do it."

Numbness. Drifting. An unconscious entity floated on a formless sea, devoid of thought, memory, sensation, consequence. She was a disembodied mind, adrift and unconscious.

From somewhere a million miles away, a woman's voice said, "Wow. She did a number on you."

A man's voice, equally distant. "Yeah, well. I've had worse."

It sounded like he was missing some teeth. Like he'd fallen face-first from a great height.

"How is she?"

"Not good. Not good. She's been practically comatose like this since . . ." A sigh. "The shrink says she might have had a permanent psychotic break."

"Damn," said the woman's voice. There was a name attached to it, a sound, a babbling brook. Babbling. Babel. "It must be awful, seeing this and wondering about your wife."

Again, a man's sigh. "She's been over there awhile."

"She's a fighter. She's tough."

"Yeah."

"Thank you, Mollie," whispered the woman. "We saved Ana because of you."

A warm pair of lips touched her forehead. Trembling. Compassionate. Revolting.

The touch of flesh brought memories of severed flesh and bone, the taste and texture against her tongue . . . The thought of a mouth reminded her of crab-things scuttling through the shadows, hideous human-sized spiders covered every inch with suppurating wounds that licked themselves

with scaly tongues and suckled with baby teeth. Of mouths that opened
to scream but could only choke on the squamous eyeballs within.

The touch of flesh. Sick, suppurating flesh.

Again, the compassionate kiss. Horrifying, disgusting, unwelcome
touch of flesh.

A scream parted the formless sea. It persisted until the sound shred-
ded her throat and she coughed on blood.

But then she remembered what she had done to Ffodor, how she'd des-
ecrated his body—shattered him, used his broken mutated arms and legs
as clubs—and she wailed anew.

"Look," Joey said, "all I'm saying is that the little mollusk has a magic
touch. Wasn't more than five minutes caressing my hand before he grew
me a new digit. Felt good, too. Kinda like the best finger work ever, if you
know what I mean." She pointed her newly restored finger at Nurassyl.
"This kid. Shit, when he's growed and learns what he can do to a girl with
them tentacles he'll be swimming in pussy."

Nurassyl, who was standing flanked by Marcus and Olena and facing
a contingent of international aces, flushed suddenly crimson.

"Really, Joey!" Babel said. "I'm translating. There's a little boy here."

Joey shrugged. "Truth is truth."

"I'm up next," Bugsy said. "For the healing, like, not the weird joker
kid-sex stuff."

Babel ignored him. She looked to Marcus, who grew instantly uneasy
under her gaze, more so than with any of the other aces who huddled
around them. She wasn't impressive-looking, and he knew her powers
weren't deadly. But still, she scared him the way his high school librarian
always had. She made him feel like he was about to do something wrong
and she knew it before he did. "I appreciate what the boy did for Joey, but
the situation with Mollie is graver than a single finger."

Joey smirked. She held up a single finger, but not her pointer.

"This information is above your pay grade, but it's nothing about her
body that truly needs healing. It's her mind, and that's a complicated thing.
I don't—"

"Not complicated," Olena said. The ace didn't seem to invoke the same timidity in her. "Simple." She placed her hands on either side of Nurassyl's head, roughly where his shoulders should have been. "He's a healer. Body. Mind. No difference to him. I know this. He took the madness out of me. I don't even remember it. Nothing."

"You don't remember it?" Babel didn't seem to think that was a good thing. "That won't do. Mollie needs to remember. She needs to know what's happening and why and how urgent the situation is. If this healing results in amnesia, there is no deal."

Marcus found his voice. "Screw that! The deal is already the deal. We brought him to you, showed you what he could do. We've held up our side of this." Looking to Nurassyl, he said, "You can heal more people, right? Make Bugsy better? Soothe Mollie's mind? Not take away all the memories, but just make her a little better?"

The boy blinked his large eyes. He smiled. In what sounded to Marcus like perfect mid-Atlantic American English, he said, "Yes, Marcus. I can do it."

"Good boy," Marcus said. He wanted to hug the kid. And why not? He *did* hug the kid. "So, Babel, we've got a deal. Nurassyl heals your aces. You let his family and his entire village in here. We'll stay out of your way. That's the deal, though. Right, Nurassyl? It's the village or nothing."

Nurassyl nodded. "Village or nothing," he said. He primly folded his tentacles together and waited, his big eyes on Babel, making it clear just where he stood.

Bugsy laughed. "He's a cheeky little negotiator, this one. Admit it, Babel, he's got a good hand here."

"You want to save the world?" Marcus asked, feeling the momentum of it. "Then you need this kid. What other choice do you have?"

Babel was a long time trying to come up with one before she snapped, "Fine. Bring her in."

Bugsy began, "Hey, I said I was—"

"Bring her in!" Babel repeated. "Mollie first. Lesser actors after."

Olena said, "Wait. You didn't say you agreed. You must say it. Nurassyl does his part. The village is safe. Say it."

For some reason, Babel seemed to dislike Olena as much as Olena was uncowed by her. She grimaced, but eventually said, "As you say, I agree."

When they brought her in, Marcus barely recognized Mollie. Last time he'd seen her, in the casino, she'd been a cocksure countrified bitch who had looked the jokers she'd transported straight in the eyes. She flipped off any who returned her gaze too long. Not anymore. Now she was as scratched and bruised as Joey had been. She looked drenched in fatigue, barely able to walk with the aid of two nurses. Despite that, her eyes bounced around the room with a crazed energy. Every time they touched on something she flinched. She looked ready to jump out of her skin, ravaged and frightened, remorseful and on the verge of both rage and utter collapse.

Anyone could see that. Marcus saw more, though. He recognized the horror that wafted off her. It hit him in the gut, made his skin crawl, shot his long tail through with adrenaline, with the urgent desire to flee. His mind flared full of horrible thoughts, the sort of things that had clawed at him in Talas, brutal, senselessly violent, grotesque. He wanted to consume each thought, but he also felt like vomiting. All of this, brought on just by the sight of her.

Fortunately, she didn't have the same effect on Nurassyl. Full of compassion, the boy said, "She is not well. Come. Bring her to me." He peeled his tentacled hands away from his chest and beckoned to her.

"What the fuck is that?" Mollie snapped. "What the fuck are you doing?" With a sudden burst of energy, she tried to squirm away from the nurses. A big man closed on her from behind, trying to calm her even as he gripped her in the vise of his burly arms. This was not starting well.

"Don't hurt her," Nurassyl said. He looked at Babel. "I will be her friend. Let me talk to her. Just me. Can you do that?"

Babel pursed her lips. That was all the answer she gave, until the auditory ambience of the room changed entirely. Marcus hadn't been able to understand half the people around them before, but now he couldn't understand *anybody*. Every voice speaking became a garbled jumble that didn't even resemble language anymore.

"What the fuck?" Marcus turned to Olena. She looked back at him, opened her mouth, and let out a barrage of nonsense. It must have been Babel using her power. He tried to explain this to her, but Olena grimaced and put her hand over his mouth, shutting him up. Together, they turned and—like everyone else—watched Nurassyl and Mollie. They, apparently, were the only ones who could still communicate.

Nurassyl was speaking. Though his words were as incomprehensible as anybody else's, Marcus could imagine the gentling effect of them. He spoke as much with his round eyes and with the gentle motions of the tentacles.

He seemed to float toward Mollie, propelled by the hundreds of nodules he had instead of feet. For her part, Mollie stopped fighting and started listening. She said something, and after a few exchanges her face relented. She let the nurses guide her to a low stool, and soon Nurassyl was right beside her. Mollie flinched back when he reached for her, but didn't really pull away. The moment his tentacles caressed her temples, her mouth dropped open, her face softened, and her eyes took on a faraway glaze.

The world snapped back to normal when Babel said, "Remember, only ease her troubles. Not too much."

Nurassyl turned and looked at her. "She has so much pain," he said.

"I know. She's got pains that began before any of this. Just don't go too far."

Nurassyl turned back to Mollie. He spoke to her, low enough that Marcus couldn't hear what he said. Mollie listened. She nodded often. At some point, tears welled in her eyes and cut tracks down her cheeks. Watching, Marcus knew they were the good kind. He glanced at the aces and the watching nurses and soldiers. They were all transfixed, even Babel.

Eventually, Nurassyl plucked the tentacles of one hand away. A moment later, he withdrew the others.

Mollie grabbed him, desperately. "Please, don't stop!" she gasped. "Take it all away. Please . . ."

"No!" Babel snapped. "That's enough, Mollie. I need your mind sharp. I need you to remember. It's the only way you'll understand the things you'll need to do." There was something close to compassion in her voice as she said this, but it dropped away when she began to give orders. "Take her away. Let her rest. Give her something to eat. And then we go at it again."

Mollie wailed as the attendants started to lead her away. "Afterward," she said. "After I've done it, then you'll take it all away. You will, won't you? Tell me you will."

"Yes, Mollie," Nurassyl said, "I will do that for you. After."

That calmed her enough that she let herself be led away. "Hey," Bugsy said, slipping his emaciated form into the seat Mollie had just vacated, "I'm up next! Return me to my normal grandeur, please."

Babel rolled her eyes and started to leave.

"Hey!" Marcus called. "Nurassyl did his part. Now you do yours. Let my jokers in."

"*Your* jokers? What are you—Moses?"

"It's something to aspire to." For some reason, Marcus didn't feel as intimidated by her. Maybe it was the look of awe he'd seen on her face as Nurassyl worked, the knowledge that she'd needed a joker and knew it.

"Fine."

As Babel issued orders for the jokers to be brought inside and located somewhere remote, Marcus bent to be closer to Nurassyl's level. "When just you two could talk, what did you say to Mollie to make her calm down?"

"Just who I was and what I could do for her. Nice things. I made her not afraid."

Marcus smiled. "Yes, you did. You did more than that, too."

Babel cleared her throat. When Marcus looked at her, she waved her phone, impatient. Marcus said the last few things he wanted to before the language barrier dropped down between them again. "Nurassyl, you did good. For the village. Maybe for the whole world. I told you that you were an ace. See? Today you proved it."

Marcus looked at Babel. She nodded, looking at him differently than she had when she first saw him. She walked away, and Marcus prepared to go with the soldiers to get the villagers. Olena started to come with him, but stopped. "Shit," she said.

"What?"

"My father."

Following her gaze, Marcus spotted him. Vasel had just entered the big room, propelled by a phalanx of suits and officers. Russians, he imagined. They cut through the crowd in a wedge, making people clear the way for them. He barked something at Olena, motioning for her to come to him.

"What does he want?" Marcus asked.

"I don't know." Olena considered it for a moment. "Go ahead and get the villagers. I'll talk to him."

"Wait. What are going to say?"

She smiled, leaned up onto her toes, and kissed him. "Don't worry. I'll tell him to piss off. Him and all the goons." And then she was gone, walking toward the Russian contingent at a leisurely pace that obviously annoyed Vasel.

That's my girl, Marcus thought, and then he squirmed to catch up with the soldiers waiting for him.

Later, she remembered her name. Remembered other stuff, too. Remembered everything she wanted to forget. Like licking the stump of Joey's severed finger like a lollipop, the sensation of eyebrow hairs caught in her teeth—

Mollie rolled over and vomited explosively into a wastepaper basket. Stomach acid scorched the interior of her throat, while the convulsions irritated bruises on her neck. She probably had a new set of throat bruises, she realized, where a zombie had damn near choked the life out of her. The need to retch didn't subside quickly or easily. But it did, eventually.

She could hear her own breathing. The blood pulsing through her ears in time to her heartbeats. When she shifted, the bandages on her face rasped across a blanket, loud as a gunshot.

The sane world was so quiet. So calm compared to the howling madness.

Strange that the world could be so quiet in its final hours. She'd have thought the end of the world would be louder.

Footsteps. The floor creaked under a man's weight. He crouched on the floor beside her. A whiff of aftershave tickled her nose, roiled her stomach: Billy Ray. That was his name. He touched her shoulder, gently. Mollie pretended not to feel it. But he persisted. "Hungry? The Russians brought MREs, the very best dehydrated borscht rubles can buy. And we found some instant lunches stashed in one of the cabinets. You should rehydrate."

He had a slight lisp. But it was already less pronounced than earlier, when he'd been talking to Bubbles.

Mollie was in the warehouse, she realized. In the Cosmodrome. She lay on a cot, beneath a scratchy wool blanket.

Steam wafted against her face, carrying with it the umami scent of instant noodles. In her mind, it became a moist tendril draped across her face, grasping, wafting corpse-stink eddies of an otherworldy fog against her unprotected flesh. Mollie screamed. Flailed. Sent the Styrofoam cup tumbling. It splashed on Billy Ray, Mollie, the blanket. Most of it ended up on the floor. He cleaned the mess without comment, after which he left the container for her. She drank what little broth was left. It was salty. She vomited it into the basket almost as quickly as she ingested it.

A while later, he tried again: "How're you doing, kiddo?"

"How . . ." Mollie trailed off, coughing. The screaming had given her a voice like Tom Waits. She swallowed blood, and a gobbet of she-didn't-know-what, and tried again. "How the fuck do you think I'm doing? I ate somebody's eyebrow. Her *eyebrow*, for God's . . ." Mollie rolled over, retching. Her empty stomach had nothing to offer, but she coughed up dark bitter bile. The violent heaving splashed acid into her sinuses.

Billy Ray handed her a Kleenex. She blew her nose, wiped her mouth. Frowned. Tried to fish out whatever was caught in her teeth. Pulled a bristly eyebrow hair from between her incisors.

Threw up all over again.

Even Billy Ray looked a little ill.

When the urge to vomit finally subsided, and Mollie's body couldn't force another drop of fluid past her lips, she lay on the floor limp as a rag doll. Billy Ray took the sloshing, stinking wastebasket and disappeared. He returned a few minutes later, and set it down next to Mollie's elbow. Giving the room a few sniffs, he wrinkled his nose.

What a pussy. A little bit of human puke? That was a fucking rose garden compared to the eldritch-charnel-house smell washing over the world in Horrorshow's wake. It was getting closer, every second, tick tick tick, but she could already smell it, as though the evil had permanently etched the insides of her nostrils.

Her face ached. It had for a while, she realized. But she'd been too busy sicking up to notice. Mollie touched the bandages. She only vaguely remembered hands raking her face. Didn't really feel it at the time, but then she had been hopped up and giddy with supernatural ultraviolence. The bandages were bigger than she realized at first—shit. She frowned, and felt something tugging at her skin. Stitches. Joey had probably torn off half her face. Even if she hadn't been wreathed in Horrorshow's influence, too, Mollie had given her plenty of incentive.

Still rubbing the bandages, Mollie asked, "How is she?"

Billy Ray swallowed. He knew whom she meant. "Joey'll be okay."

"But she isn't right now."

"You'll both need some surgery when this is over. If you want it."

Mollie sat up. Hugged her knees.

"If I want to not look like somebody tried to tear my face off, you mean? Gee, that's a tough one. I'm sure Joey is right now weighing the pros and cons of looking like somebody took a giant fucking bite out of her face."

The SCARE agent sat at the foot of the cot. He didn't try to hug her or touch her or even try to talk. He just sat there, breathing the same air and asking nothing more, because he understood that was the best thing he could do.

He was thinking about his wife. Mollie could tell. The worry lay over him like a pall.

"It happened again," she said.

"What did?"

"The part where I became a murderous cannibal rage monster fueled by supernatural evil."

"You knew it was going to happen, but you overcame your fear and you helped us anyway. And it worked. We rescued Ana Cortez."

"That has got to be one of the least convincing pep talks in history. I dropped a goddamned Winnebago on one of your guys. Did he . . . is he okay?"

"No." He didn't hedge, didn't hesitate, didn't clear his throat. Mollie reminded herself that above all else he was a federal agent. And that she was a criminal. Then again, distinctions like that meant fuck-all when the world was soon to be absorbed into the Face-Eating Cannibal Flash-mob Dimension.

"The others? Did I kill anybody else?"

"No. They're fine. A little freaked out, but they're fine. You scared the hell out of them."

"Yeah, well, those pussies can man up. It's not exactly a Disney movie of unicorns and rainbows playing on the insides of my eyelids right now, you know."

He nodded. "You said something strange at one point."

"You don't say."

"It sounded like something about the filth of a Frankenstein god-machine, or some such. Do you remember? I was just wondering what that meant."

Grasping for understanding. He was desperate to understand what his wife was experiencing.

"It meant I'd gone so incredibly batshit that I was completely and ut-terly out of my fucking mind. I can't begin to figure out what that might have meant and I sure as hell don't care to try. But you can bet it made complete sense to me in the moment. And that's part of what's so horrible about this." It took several deep breaths before she could get her raspy voice and the tears under control. "You don't know the darkness is taking

you because you're so mad—crazy mad, furious mad—that you don't realize anything has changed. The rage makes *so much sense* when you're
drowning in it." She hugged her knees tighter, folding herself into the
tightest ball she could. More memories came rushing back in horrifying
detail. A sob escaped; the struggle to hold it in felt like pulling a muscle in
her chest. Several more followed in its wake. Mollie had to swallow down
gorge before finishing her thought aloud. "Cutting off Joey's finger, then
snatching it off the floor and licking—" She reached for the basket. Dry-
heaved. "—licking the stump clean made the utmost sense in the moment.
It was what I had to do, the only thing I could do. I did it because from
within that fishbowl it was obviously—*obviously*—the only sane thing to
do." Another bubble of gorge stung her acid-raw throat. She coughed.
Though her voice was but a rasp, she continued. "But you know what makes
it even worse? Knowing that I savagely and gleefully mutilated somebody
with you and God knows who else watching. I feel naked, like the entire
world saw me lose my shit. It's worse than naked. Naked would be just my
body, but you, Joey, and SCARE and Babel and the Committee and the
even fucking Russian army, you all saw the inside of my mind at its most
broken."

The satellite map projected on Babel's wall showed a large swath of
Kazakhstan. Somebody had superimposed a large oblong crosshatched in
red and black; this was labeled SHADOW ZONE on the PowerPoint slide. Best
estimates put it less than a day from engulfing the Baikonur Cosmodrome
and the nuclear weapons stored there.

"Hold on a second," said Mollie.

She hadn't really thought it through until now—it seemed like nobody
had—but now that she was paying attention to the plan for dealing with
this part of the crisis, she realized it was stupidly overcomplicated. Babel's
people, the second-string Committee aces, were trying to dismantle and
move the weapons before the shitstorm hit. This over the objections of the
Russians, whom Babel and Jayewardene were trying to placate.

That was stupid. They needed to work faster. Better to act now and beg
forgiveness later, and so on and so forth.

She said this to Babel. And then she continued, "My point is, you're
doing this the hard way. Just move them out of the danger zone. Plunk

them somewhere far away from Horrorshow's encroachment. Then take
all the time you need to disable them. Or, hell, I don't know, hold them in
reserve in case you need them later."

"We can't just waltz into a sovereign country to steal a bunch of nuclear missiles and spaceplane bombers."

"You can't. But maybe I can."

"Oh, no. No, no, no." Babel shook her head. "Not a chance. That would
be an act of war."

"Listen up, Super Bureaucrat. It's becoming obvious to me that you *still*
don't understand what a shitstorm it'll be when Horrorshow engulfs the
site. Nobody's going to give a shit about international law when they're
all too busy feasting on each other's intestines."

"We're working in a grey area, legally, as it is. Taking another country's
nuclear assets is not grey."

"Oh, yeah," muttered Mollie. "We sure as hell don't want to offend
the psychopath bloodrage crowd. Better to let them keep their nukes." She
shook her head, felt a stick pop under her bandages, and winced. "If you're
worried about getting caught by the international community," she said,
"I know all about dumping loot, too. I'm not an amateur thief, you know.
I could open portals under the missiles and twin them to portals over the
ocean. Or, I dunno, Nevada. I could dump the missiles and the bombers in
the middle of nowhere. No fuss, no muss, no need to toss people into the
meat grinder. And it's not like the cops could barge in and catch you red-
handed with a pile of Kazakh nukes stashed under your bed like so many
unopened Blu-ray players and crates of Swarovski crystal."

"That is a rather specific analogy," said Babel. She sighed. "Anyway, no.
We looked at this, okay? If the missiles go on alert, they automatically get
pumped full of fuel." She slapped at a sheaf of papers on her desk, some
sort of technical report from the look of it. "The fuel is very, very nasty.
Grandchildren-with-flippers nasty. And the airframes on those old missiles are paper thin. If you start throwing the missiles around they're prone
to rupture. Then we have a much bigger problem. Even if the leaking fuel
doesn't explode outright, which it could very well—leaving us with nuclear
warheads basted in burning rocket fuel—the chemicals would poison everyone and everything in the area. We're talking a ten-thousand-square-
mile dead zone in the middle of the ocean. And that's not even accounting
for the nuclear material in the warheads. Let's try to leave a planet to enjoy after we've vanquished our current problems, okay?"

Sneer at me, you fucking cunt?

A snow globe paperweight on the desk blinked through a small trans-dimensional rift to plummet from the ceiling over Babel's head. It clocked her square on the crown hard enough to make her cry out and stagger. The glass bounced from Babel's head and shattered on the floor. It happened so quickly that the snow globe water was seeping into the carpet before Mollie even consciously realized she was angry. She clapped a hand over her mouth, too late to stifle her gasp. "Oh, God."

The dig at her criminal history had upset her, and she'd instinctively, reflexively retaliated with violence. She'd never done anything like that before. *Never.* Not while in her proper state of mind. She'd thrown punches and taken punches from her asshole brothers, but that was just family stuff. She wasn't a violent person. She wasn't.

A rivulet of blood trickled through Babel's hair to dribble down her forehead. Leaning against her desk, she felt the tickle and touched her scalp. She winced. Her fingertips came away stippled with blood. The confusion on her face became a frown when her gaze fell upon the shattered snow globe. She looked at her desk (pristine, unbroken, blameless), then the acoustical tiles over her head (ditto), then Mollie (shamefaced and humiliated).

"Oh, God, oh, my God," Mollie mumbled through the fingers still draped over her mouth. "I'm so sorry. I'm sorry. I'm not like this. I swear I'm not. I'm not a violent person. I'm a good person." She started to cry again. It hurt the zombie-bruises on her throat. "I'm not evil. I'm not violent."

Well. She didn't used to be. But now . . . now the madness had taken her twice. The propensity for supernatural rage, the drive to visit profound violence on those around her, had worked its tendrils so deeply into her that perhaps she'd never be free of them ever again. Horrorshow's influence had left a mark on her, warped her psyche. She'd spent too much time in the abyss. Looking at the shards of snow globe misted with Babel's blood, Mollie realized—it felt like a kick in the gut—that she'd never again walk in the light, not fully, after thinking, feeling, and doing the things she had. She wasn't the same woman she'd been a week ago.

The tears blurred her vision and made it impossible to unpack the calculating expression on Babel's face. The Committee woman appeared to come to a decision. She shrugged.

"It's okay," she said, unconvincingly. "We're all on edge right now."

Mollie sniffled. "Oh, God . . . I'm never going to be normal again, am I?"

Babel opened her arms. It was the most calculated invitation to a hug Mollie had ever witnessed. It was like getting embraced by a robot. And about as warm. But at least the Committee woman was trying.

"It's okay," she whispered. "You'll be okay. We'll get you all the help you need. I swear it. We have resources. After this is over, I'll see to it that the entire weight of the United Nations is thrown behind anything you or your family need."

"Give them to the family of the guy I squashed with a Winnebago. And Joey. She's the one I mutilated."

"Yeah, well, I probably deserved it," said a new voice.

Mollie clamped harder onto Babel. Pressed her face to the other woman's shoulder. Her bandages rasped against Babel's lapel. She didn't want to turn around. Didn't want to see what she'd done to Joey.

The zombie wrangler said, "My memory is sort of fuzzy, but I do remember thinking some wickedly fucked-up shit. I've never been that angry in my life. And I admit that's saying something."

Babel broke off the hug. She stepped away from Mollie. But Mollie kept her head down and her back to Joey.

"I'm sorry," she whispered. "I'm so sorry for what I did to you. I wasn't myself. I'd never . . . I'm not . . ."

When did her entire life become nothing but a litany of apologies? How did it get this way? When did she stop being a woman with an actual life, and instead became a woman with an insoluble burden of contrition?

"Enough with the motherfucking waterworks," Joey said. "We'll buy a few bottles and get epically shit-faced together and scream and carry on and cry our eyes out when this is over. But that's for later. Right now let's do this fuckin' thing and get Michelle home."

Mollie wiped her nose on her sleeve. After a few steadying breaths, she turned around.

Joey looked ghastly: a huge sapphire-blue gel bandage wobbled over her eye, where her eyebrow used to be. She caught Mollie staring.

"Don't flatter yourself. I gave as good as I got. You look like five miles of bad fuckin' road, sister."

Mollie changed the subject. "What's this about Michelle?"

Joey rolled her eyes. To Babel, she said, "Jesus H. Christ. You haven't even told her yet?"

"We were distracted by another matter before you entered."

"Told me what?" Mollie asked.

"They found her," said Joey, bouncing on her toes with so much excitement she practically levitated. "They found Michelle."

Yeah, they'd found Michelle Pond all right. At least, Mollie took their word for it when they showed her the satellite photos of the gaunt woman limping down the highway. She didn't look like a supermodel, though. If Mollie looked like five miles of bad road, the woman in the grainy image looked like fifty miles of even worse road.

There was, of course, a problem.

The image projected on Babel's wall was now a split screen. Michelle on the left, the map of Kazakhstan with the superimposed "shadow zone" on the right. A bright green dot had appeared on the map: Michelle's location.

Right on the hairy edge of the evil insanity zone.

And she was on foot. Moving too slowly to outrun the bubble. It would overrun her, if it hadn't already.

Mollie shook her head and waved her arms as if trying to flag down a passing airplane. "If either of you think I'm going to create another portal to the kingdom of the psychopath cannibals, you can fuck yourselves with a chain saw."

"Spread your legs, sweetheart. Because if you try to refuse," said Joey, "we won't be the only ones getting a Black and Decker crammed up her twat."

Babel cleared her throat. "This photo is less than two hours old," she said, in a tone that should have caused the snow globe water in the carpet to ice over. "We know where she is. This won't be a blind expedition, like the search for survivors. That worked for Ana, but you were lucky to find her. No luck here." She tapped the screen. "We know where she was two hours ago. She's moving slowly. She knows she needs to get away from the shadow zone, so we even know what direction she's moving. This road is a straight shot, her best bet. She's still on it."

She drew her finger across the map, suggesting the road from the other image. "You could open a sequence of small scouting portals, starting here"—she tapped the abandoned truck at the edge of the road in the photo of Michelle—"for just a few seconds, then jumping down the road a hundred yards at a time. Once you find her you could drop her back to us."

Mollie said, "You're assuming she's acting rationally. How do you know she hasn't already gone completely bugfuck?"

"She's stronger than that," Joey said. She made the pronouncement so simply, so directly, it brooked no argument. A statement of fact and nothing less.

Mollie wondered what it would be like if somebody believed in her so resolutely. Wondered what it would be like to deserve such simple, unshakeable faith in her character.

Babel saw her wavering. "You could save another life," she said. "This would be a major win for us."

Mollie chewed her lip.

"Please," said Joey.

I never learn. I never ever fucking learn.

Billy Ray met them in the warehouse.

He looked Mollie over. Took his time about it. Every shameful detail of her recent history played across his stupid face. It was even more mashed-up than usual. He was thinking about their fight. The way his gaze flicked from Mollie to Joey's bandages and back confirmed it.

It made her feel naked and ashamed all over again. Ashamed of what she did to him. Ashamed that he tried to beat her senseless, ashamed that she deserved it. She felt the heat rising on her face as she blushed.

He kept staring.

"Hey, G-man. You plan to keep eye-banging me all day, or what?"

He clenched his fists. But he said, "How are you feeling?"

"Like a zombie mutt took a chunk out of me, somebody used my face for a punching bag, somebody else tried to tear it half off, and then another zombie choked the shit out of me like something out of undead bondage porn."

"Yeah. I guess it's been one of those days."

He was hard to read, the SCARE agent.

She turned to Joey. "Let's do this before I lose my nerve."

The SCARE guys, or maybe their Russian counterparts, had more or less reassembled the rings of cables and equipment that had been destroyed or displaced during the chaos in the warehouse. Mollie could feel their eyes on her as she and Joey returned to the epicenter, the innermost ring of lights. They were all watching her, wondering how quickly she'd lose her shit this time, and how bad it would get before they took her down.

Babel denied it, of course, but Mollie was absolutely certain that this time some of the hazmat guys weren't packing tranquilizer guns. They'd have rifles trained on her. Real rifles, the kind that could shoot through a church. Maybe right now a Spetsnaz sniper was centering crosshairs on her temple.

Maybe that's why Mollie agreed to this. Maybe she wanted to go crazy one last time, just so that they'd put her down like a rabid dog.

Mollie stared at the photo of Michelle limping down the road until she could close her eyes and still see every detail of the barren fields, the dusty pavement, the abandoned truck with the tattered canopy. Imagined the smell of thin soil blowing on the arid wind, the flapping of the truck's canopy, the whisper of a breeze through the scrub. She held that image in her head as she looked at the center of the ring of lights. A fist-sized hole appeared in midair.

In her imagination, the smell of arid soil became the smell of viscera; the whistling of the wind became the keening of a thousand voices raised in howling madness and the skittering of squamous abominations across a landscape of shattered bone—

Mollie swallowed a scream. It wrenched the bruises on her throat. The doorway disappeared.

She shook her head and ran her hands through her hair, trying to hide the fact that she was hyperventilating and pretending she didn't care that everybody was staring at her.

"Just making sure that spot would work," she said. "Looks good." It might have been the most unconvincing lie she'd ever uttered. This time she concentrated on not thinking about Horrorshow, not thinking about a baby impaled on a wrought-iron fence, absolutely not thinking about the taste of Joey's eyebrow.

The hole in space reopened; it looked down on a wet road lined with telephone poles. It was raining on the other side. Joey trotted toward the portal, zombies in tow.

—Coppery warmth flowing over her tongue as she lapped at Joey's severed finger . . . the rubbery texture of human flesh between her teeth . . . eyebrow bristles raking her lips—

The doorway snapped shut again.

"Hey!" said Joey. "What gives?"

Mollie tried to lie but the pebble in her throat had become a boulder.

She ran the back of her hand across her eyes. Somebody laid a hand on her shoulder, but she knocked it away.

"I'm fine," she croaked, though obviously she was anything but. "Stop distracting me. It's hard to do this from satellite photos."

That was a lie, of course. She'd used satellite photos to get everybody to Baikonur.

It used to be a snap. It's also how they first arrived at Baba Yaga's casino when scouting for the theft: Google Earth had made it trivial to get on the roof—

Oh, shit.

Remembering that was a mistake. It reminded her of Ffodor, and what a horribly ungrateful bitch she'd been to him—before and after the Russian hag killed him—and then Mollie couldn't see anything.

"I just need a minute," she cried. And ran blindly from the warehouse.

Heat shimmered up from the road. Michelle was pretty sure wherever direction she was heading, she was going the wrong way to get back to any kind of civilization.

In the distance, she saw figures heading toward her. The closer she got, the more they looked like something from inside Talas. *Corpses*, she realized. *Walking dead.*

"Oh, God," she moaned. She'd never gotten away from Batshit Crazy Town after all. This was just another fucking nightmare. She tried to bubble, but nothing happened. She was all out of fat.

So this was it. She wouldn't see Adesina or Joey again. She was stuck. Trapped here with whatever new monstrosity had come for her.

They came for her, and she kicked and bit and flailed. Her strength was giving out, and the dead things were on her now.

And then she heard Joey say, "Stop fighting, you dizzy bitch! Can't you see I'm fucking saving you?"

Ten minutes later, after another wave of tears diluted the terror and guilt to the point where she could focus, Mollie managed to open a stable portal over a rainy road somewhere in Kazakhstan. After the toe tags shambled through, followed by Joey herself, Mollie decided it was better to keep herself distracted. So she sat in a far corner of the Cosmodrome warehouse—far enough from everybody else for the distance to say leave-me-the-fuck-alone—and called a farmhouse in Idaho.

The phone rang. And rang. And rang. Eventually, the answering machine picked up. Her folks never made the transition to voice mail like the rest of the 21st century, so they still had one of those machines with the little cassette tape in it. Embarrassing.

A tinny approximation of Mom's voice came down the line. "Howdy. You've reached the Steunenberg farm. If you're hearing this then we're all working hard and can't come to the phone." *Or laid up in the hospital with crowbar and pitchfork wounds,* thought Mollie. "Please leave a message with your name, number, and the time you called—" (Mollie rolled her eyes. "For the millionth time, just get voice-mail service, for Christ's sake.") "—and we'll call you back just as soon as we wash the good earth from beneath our fingernails."

Beep.

"Uh, hi. Momma? It's me. Mollie. Is anybody there? Can you pick up, please?" She waited exactly as long as it would take for somebody to cross the porch pantry, mud room, and dining room to reach the kitchen phone. Nobody did. She sighed. "I'm, um, I'm in New York right now. I was just calling to see how everybody is doing. Are Jim and Troy out of the ICU now? What about Daddy and Brent? What are the doctors saying? When can they all come home?" She hadn't thought about why that seemed so important, but upon reflection it was obvious. "I just, uh, I think maybe we, well, you all, you should all be together. There's, uh, there's some stuff going on . . ." No point explaining how the psychotic rage that briefly engulfed them was soon to sweep over the entire planet like a tsunami of madness. They'd find out for themselves in a few days. But they could be an actual family for at least a little while. "And it's just, you know, we should stick together. As a family." Jesus Christ, she sounded lame. Fuck it. "I want to come home, too. I really really want a place I can call home again. I miss you all so much and I'm sorry. I'm sorry, Momma, and Daddy, and to all the boys, if you're listening. I can't tell you how sorry I am that I caused you all such suffer—"

Beep.

She pressed redial. But when the answering machine *beep*ed again, she didn't know what more to say. So she hung up.

For somebody whose entire life had become a litany of apologies, she really sucked at delivering them.

Sliding through the gates of the Cosmodrome with the joker girl, Sezim—and her doll—cradled in his arms, Marcus felt better than he had in a long time. Before him and behind him, the other jokers walked, shuffled, or squirmed. A few were carried in. They moved through a channel of soldiers that protected them from the masses rumbling angrily outside and from the unkind eyes of the various soldiers—UN, Kazakh, and Russian—who weren't exactly welcoming them in.

Let them stare, Marcus thought. It didn't matter. The only thing that did was that—with Nurassyl's help—they'd delivered on their promise to get the villagers inside the Cosmodrome. They were about as safe now as they could be.

The Handsmith strode beside him, holding his wife's hand. "Thank you," he said, touching Marcus on the shoulder. "Thank you."

Marcus shook his head. "Not me. Nurassyl. He did it." He wished he could explain it all to him. He'd make sure that Olena did. Saying he'd go and get the boy, he handed Sezim to Aliya and started toward the Committee's warehouse. He didn't get more than a few yards before a swarm of wasps shot out of the warehouse, curved in the air, and swept toward him. Bugsy formed in front of him, looking quite a bit more substantial than he had when Marcus had left him with Nurassyl. He was naked again, but this time not even modest enough to blur his genitalia.

"Something's up with your girl," he said. "She was talking to this guy for a while, and then they started arguing. Next thing you know a bunch of Russians grabbed her and dragged her away. She went screaming bloody murder, man."

"You let them take her?" Marcus asked.

He swiped his limp hair from his face. "*Let them?* What could I do? Have you not noticed that Russians run this place?"

"Where'd they go?"

"Come on. I got a hornet following them."

Bugsy swarmed, and Marcus squirmed after him. *Vasel*, he swore, *if you hurt her I'll kill you. If you take her away* . . . He couldn't finish that thought. If Vasel vanished with her what chance did Marcus have of ever seeing her again? The gangster seemed capable of anything, and he had all of the vastness of Russia at his disposal.

They went around the warehouse, between two others, and then shot past an open hangar where Tinker was at work on something. Bugsy reformed. "Tinker, there's a damsel in distress. What's that?" He pointed at the contraption Tinker had built. It had the treads of a tank, but with a body that looked cobbled together from oil drums and scrap metal, creating the base for a swiveling artillery gun that appeared to be manned by a Homer Simpson bobble head.

Tinker grinned, looking at it proudly. "I'm calling it a Think Tank. A tank with a programmed artificial intelligence. It's all right here in the noggin." He set the bobble head bobbling with a brush of his fingers. "Really simple intelligence, though. We can send it into the beasty swarm without worrying it'll go mad and start—"

"Bring it! They're getting into a plane, supersonic bomber it looks like."

"Fuck," Marcus said, knowing they were doing more than just making an escape. "Vasel thinks we should destroy Talas. He might try to bomb it on his way out of here."

"That would be a very bad idea." Bugsy swarmed again and was off, Marcus squirming so fast he almost got ahead of him. Tinker shouted some protest, but when Marcus glanced back he saw the big man lumbering along. The tank kept pace with him like a well-trained dog.

The airstrip was massive. A maze of crisscrossing runways and airplane hangars and several towers that stretched to the horizon. One plane was landing. Several others were taxiing. A bunch more—in various shapes and designs—cluttered the area as far as Marcus could see. "Which one is it?"

"There," Bugsy said, suddenly his naked self again. He pointed at a sleek number just turning onto one of the runways. It was smaller than Marcus expected, more like a billionaire's private jet than what he imagined a bomber to be—if the billionaire happened to like packing nuclear warheads attached to its underbelly. It was heading away from them, toward the end of the runway.

"What now?" Tinker asked.

Marcus pointed toward the plane, which was making a slow turn at the far end of the runway. "We stop that plane. Can this thing do it?"

"I wouldn't count on it," Bugsy grumbled.

Tinker was more confident. "You bet. Homer, acquire target. Take out that Russian plane."

The tank started toward the runway over a rough patch of grass. The bobble head bobbled, spun, and dipped. The gun lowered.

"No!" Marcus shouted. "Don't shoot it! Olena's in there."

The gun boomed, sending a mortar round scorching across the tarmac and right into the tail section of . . . an entirely different plane, one parked innocently outside a hangar.

"I should've known," Bugsy said. "Another Tinker original."

"No, not that plane!" Tinker shouted. "The other one!"

The barrel of the gun swung around, shot again, this time taking out a helicopter.

"Homer, that's not even a plane!"

"You know," Bugsy continued, sounding ruminative, "it's not really a matter of *if* his gadgets will screw up. It's more a matter of how monumentally."

Next down was a shuttle bus, a mobile staircase, and a fuel tanker. The blast from that explosion nearly flattened Marcus. All of this while Vasel's plane completed its turn and started down the long stretch of runway. Marcus hoped the explosions might make them pause. Just the opposite. The plane rolled forward, starting to take off.

"Fuck!" Marcus squirmed onto the tarmac. He slammed into the back of the tank. The bobble head rotated and looked at him. Homer's big eyes went wider. Marcus swiped the head so hard it flew away and landed in the grass. *Okay*, Marcus thought. *That's the brain of the thing gone.* That still left the plane, which was coming toward him, picking up speed every second. If he didn't do something now, it would be past him and unstoppable. He bunched the muscles of his tail and leaned into the tank. *Damn this is heavy!* He pushed harder, coils churning and flexing against the scrubby ground. The plane got nearer, the roar of its engines loud now. Marcus pushed with every muscle of his body right down to the tip of his tail. The tank rolled forward, a slow bastard but . . . He got it to the center of the runway. He turned to face the oncoming plane, staring right into the pilots' frantic faces. One of them gesticulated wildly at him, telling him to move out of the way. Marcus didn't. He didn't know much about planes, but he was pretty sure this one wasn't going fast enough to take off. Second by second, it got closer, the whine of its engines in his ears and vibrating through his scales. *Oh, no . . .*

Then they swerved. The plane veered off the runway and into the scrubby grass beside it. The nose wheels caught in a dip and the momentum of the plane wrenched the gear back. The nose dived, churning up soil and grinding through shrubs. The plane ground to a halt, a cloud of dust billowing around it.

Marcus watched, gasping, as Bugsy and Tinker rushed up to him.

"It worked!" Tinker said.

Bugsy guffawed. "Yeah, that was exactly what you had in mind, I'm sure."

The plane's door slammed open. Vasel leapt out on to the ground. A torrent of armed guards poured out after him. Red-faced with anger and throwing Russian expletives, the gangster took in the damage to the front wheels. Olena jumped from the plane as well. She didn't look at the plane, though. Her eyes found Marcus. She ran to him and threw herself into his embrace. The feel of her slim body, her arms around him, her hair tickling his collarbone, and her forehead pressed to his neck: it was gorgeous. But it didn't last long.

Vasel wheeled on Marcus. "You!" he roared. "You did this!" He strode toward him, flanked by the armed guards.

"Marcus, let's go!" Olena yanked on Marcus's arm, but he didn't budge. If he was going to die here at least he'd meet it front on, not with his back turned.

"You!" Vasel said. "You . . ." He cut himself off, unable to find the words and instead just grinding through a full-bodied roar of anger. His eyes were crazed, his motions as jerky and savage as when he'd stomped on the creature back at the village. Marcus's mouth flooded with saliva. His tongue bunched and twisted inside his mouth, a living thing ready to explode if he let it. He didn't, though. Even with Vasel so near, ranting and insane, he didn't know if he could actually kill him. He was an ace, for one thing. More important, he was Olena's father. There was stuff between them that Marcus would never understand. He'd do anything to defend her. That would be easy. But she wasn't the one in danger.

Then Vasel's expression sharpened. His eyes came into focus, searing into Marcus. He said, "You will not stop me. There are other planes, other missiles. So fuck you, black mamba." His fingers danced and there was the coin, sliding through and over them like a living thing. "Heads or tails? Call it whichever way you like . . ."

The coin was in the air before Marcus even saw the motion that flicked it. He watched it turn over and over as it moved toward him, flashing bright and then dark. Bright and then dark. He knew it was his death, and yet there was something undeniably entrancing about it. He knew the horror of it, and he wanted to flee, to just wriggle for it, to just give in to panic. But his eyes couldn't help but follow it. Like a fish drawn to the lure that will be its death, he stared in awe and hunger. He began to lift his arm, instinctively, to catch it.

Olena beat him to it. She swung in front of Marcus, the flat of her palm upraised. So fast. She snatched the coin just before it would've hit his face. Marcus stared at her upraised fist, right there in front of him, a small, white-knuckled fist, gripping the coin. The wail of misery inside Marcus began so deep it had a long way to rise. He felt it, though, coming, raging up, taking shape as his grasp of what was about to happen did.

Vasel knew as well, and he found his voice faster than Marcus. He bellowed something in Russian. Two words, over and over again.

Olena opened her hand, turned it to reveal the coin. It was there, stuck fast to her palm, pulsing with energy. That stopped Vasel's shouting. Olena shook her hand, trying to drop the coin, but it was stuck fast, embedded in her skin. She stared at it again, as did Marcus and everyone else. The moment stretched, long and silent. Nobody moved. Marcus held his breath, afraid that if he marked the passage of time the fate that awaited those on the receiving end of Vasel's coin would fall on Olena as well.

Olena said, flatly, "I'm not dead."

As if freed by the words, Vasel approached her. He opened his mouth to say something, but didn't get a word out. Olena—her words as hard and compact as stones—said, "I hate you. I wish you were dead." When he tried to speak again, she smacked him. The hand with the coin flew with such speed and fury that it cut Vasel off mid-word. The blow snapped his head to the side. When he looked back, an oval-shaped slash had been burned into his cheek. "Die, Papa! Die."

An expression of utter grief possessed Vasel's features. His flesh shriveled and squeezed taut against the bones of his skull. His eyes hollowed and his lips drew back, revealing teeth that looked instantly ghastly. Before their eyes and in just a few seconds, the life drained out of him. He reached out toward his daughter with a now skeletal hand that clutched at the air but didn't reach her. Then he crumpled to the ground.

"Whoa," Bugsy said, "that was a serious bitch-slap."

Michelle held Joey's face gently in her hands. They were in the hangar that served as a base for the Committee and the remnants of the Kazakh and Red Crescent forces. Soldiers and what Michelle assumed to be black ops were engaged in various make-ready activities. All armed to the teeth, and even the doctors wore sidearms.

"What are you doing here?" Michelle asked. She was shaking. With happiness or fear she couldn't tell. "Where's Adesina? You shouldn't have brought her here." A hot stab of panic went through her. Adesina had to be safe. What was the point to any of this if her daughter wasn't out of harm's way?

Joey laughed, then winced. "I left her with Wally. You think I'd bring the niblet here? I swear, you are so cocksucking . . ."

Michelle leaned forward and kissed Joey on the forehead where it wasn't covered in bandage.

She didn't care that she stank and was covered in gore. For now, she was happy that Joey was here and that her daughter was in good hands.

"You're right, he'll protect her—as long as anyone can." He'd protect her right until they were consumed by the fog.

"And what on earth happened to your face?" she said, stroking Joey's unwounded cheek.

Joey shrugged. "We were trying to find you. Mollie had a portal open near Talas, and then we both went pretty batshit insane. She cut off one of my fingers, with her fucking portal, then bit off my left eyebrow." Joey lifted up her bandaged hand. "Then this joker kid grew it back. The finger, not the eyebrow."

"I bet you gave as good as you got," Michelle replied with a tight smile. Then she had a moment where she thought about killing Mollie, but her joy at seeing Joey stamped it out. For now.

"I'd like to say I gave as good as fucking got," Joey said, shaking her head. "But that bitch is crazy. She's insane and in a very *bad* fucking way. I'd be careful around her, Bubbles."

"I've never been so happy to see you," Michelle said, ignoring Joey's warning. She noticed that the other people in the room were staring at them, but she didn't care.

"Of course you're happy to see me," Joey said. Suddenly, the scowl she constantly wore was replaced with a mischievous grin. "You're my bitch."

Michelle laughed. "Yes. Yes, I'm your bitch. And you're mine."

Joey reached up, pulled Michelle's head down, and began kissing her. It was urgent and hard, then soft and sweet.

Tasting Joey again made Michelle feel dizzy and alive and sane. It was perfect.

"Are you two done?"

Billy Ray.

"Director, always a pleasure," Michelle said without turning around. She pulled Joey closer. "And no, I'm pretty sure I'm not done."

"Well, you have to be. Babel is waiting for your debriefing."

Michelle dropped her head. The last thing she needed was to have a conversation about what had happened in Talas.

"Let's go," Joey said, pushing Michelle away. "For once those dicklickers are doing something good. We gotta figure out how to stop this."

"I don't want to . . ."

Joey crossed her arms. "Don't think anyone has a choice about it now."

"Balls," Michelle said dejectedly.

"Not into them."

Michelle smiled wanly.

"Lead on," she said as she turned to face Billy Ray. "But first you've got to feed me."

Babel was standing at a fold-out table. Behind her, flat-screen TVs took up part of the wall.

"Have a seat," Barbara said. There were circles under her eyes, and she looked exhausted. "Have you had something to eat and drink?"

Michelle nodded. She held up the water bottle in her left hand and the sandwich in her right. It was her fifth bottle of water since she'd gotten to the Cosmodrome. She felt as if she could drink five more.

She hoped Billy Ray would help her put some fat on later. In the past, he'd been happy to beat the shit out of her. It was part of their history.

What if I can't take a punch without it hurting anymore? she thought with a surge of panic.

"We have some intel from Mollie about what's happening inside the zone, but we were hoping you could give us a better idea of exactly what's going on," Barbara said.

"Yeah, I imagine Mollie isn't a reliable narrator," Michelle said. She took a bite from her sandwich and began talking as she chewed. "From what Joey said, she's pretty unstable. And if Joey's face is any barometer there's no doubt about that." She gave a hollow laugh, grabbed a folding chair, and sat down. The metal was cold against her ass.

"I'd like to tell you more, but at some point things become fuzzy." She was dancing around what she'd done to Aero now. Trying to distance herself from what had happened. Trying to get away from her murderous glee.

"I wasn't me anymore," she continued. "I no longer had control over anything. We *all* lost control of ourselves." Yes, that was it. Share the blame. "And it wasn't just us going mad. The city is changing for the worse by the second. I can tell you that however bad you think it is in there, you can't imagine how much more awful it is."

Michelle wasn't going to tell them about Aero. She hadn't seen Earth Witch or Recycler or Doktor Omweer after Joey had brought her back. They were the only ones who could tell what had happened.

It was her burden to bear. She had so much shame and guilt. *But you liked it. It felt good. You could do what you wanted. And the blood. You bathed in the blood. You barely wiped it off your hands.*

She thought she was going to vomit.

Puking seemed like a very good idea. It might get in the way of the crying. Because now she really wanted to cry. But she wouldn't let that happen. She didn't deserve to cry after what she had done.

"I'm not even sure I know what was happening because at some point, I didn't know what was real and what wasn't." *Don't say anything about the people you killed,* she thought, even as the desire to confess was rising up inside her. *Never tell what you did. They don't need to know. No one needs to know.*

"People ate each other. They committed suicide. They murdered each other. It was carnage. Blood ran in the streets like water." She was panting now. There was nothing she could do to stop her memories. Talking about it made it real. She would get the story out, then never talk about what had happened in Talas again.

"It's okay, Michelle," Billy Ray said. "We've been tranquilizing Mollie just to get her stable enough to use her portals without killing herself or anyone else. Anytime she opens one close to Talas, well, it goes badly."

Joey started giggling. "Oh, fuck me," she chortled. It was bordering on hysterical. "I'm giving you the award for Most Understated Assessment of a Fucking Insane Person, Billy Ray."

Billy Ray's eyebrows drew into a line and for a moment, Michelle thought there might actually be a fight.

"Can we please table the whole beat-the-crap-out-of-each-other thing right now?" Barbara asked. "Let's get Mollie in here and figure out what our next move is."

"I'm done," said Mollie.

But Babel wasn't paying attention to anything Mollie said. She just used Mollie to get what she wanted, to send her people around the world, like Mollie was some kind of charity taxi service, and then she couldn't even have the courtesy to listen. What a fucking ungrateful bitch. She'd be a lot more respectful after Mollie opened her—

Oh, God.

She was doing it again. Giving over to rage. Mollie looked around to convince herself that Horrorshow's malign influence hadn't seeped through the portals. But the portals were closed and folks weren't trying to nibble on each other's eyeballs. No, it wasn't so simple.

She was tainted. Repeated exposure to the madness had changed her. It was as though her brain had been rewired, lowering her threshold for anger—no, not just anger, but incandescent rage—until anything could set her off. It no longer took a nudge from supernatural evil to push her thoughts in wickedly violent directions. Her emotional barometer had been destroyed. Her emotional state had only two readings: teetering on the verge of becoming a useless blubbering heap, or fantasizing about tearing people apart in retaliation for the most minuscule of imagined slights.

Mollie shuddered again. She counted off the days on her fingers. Six. Had it really been less than a week ago when her biggest problem was dealing with a couple of trigger-happy Paris gendarmes? That couldn't be true. That had been a million years ago. A different planet. A different Mollie.

"Did you hear what I said? I said—"

Babel's phone rang. As the Committee leader lifted it to her ear, Mollie glimpsed the caller's name on the glassy screen: Ink.

"Sorry. I have to take this," Babel said.

"Sure. Whatever."

Mollie checked her own phone. Nothing. Nobody from Idaho had called her back.

She thought about going to the hospital to see for herself how Dad and the boys were doing. She even started to call up a doorway to Idaho, but then she imagined the naked disdain on their faces when they saw her. The nascent portal disintegrated.

"Fuck this," she said. And decided to distract herself with some shoplifting. She stepped around the corner and opened a doorway to Half Moon Bay.

The cold walls of the building in the Baikonur Cosmodrome surrounded them, adorned with peeling curls of green-grey, thick paint. Barbara wasn't quite certain where in the huge, sprawling complex of buildings, launch pads, and mission control areas they were in; the building into which they'd been ushered looked to date back to the Soviet era and didn't appear to have been updated since. The curtains of the meeting room where they were gathered were simple white cotton cloth unrolled from hangers along the top of the windows. The table in the room was thick oak ringed with the residue of a thousand coffee mugs. On the walls, posters in Cyrillic script overlaid images of serious, uniformed soldiers, reminding onlookers of the need for discipline. A row of ceiling fans twirled lazily overhead, and the room was lit by a phalanx of inset ceiling floodlights, the fan blades throwing sweeping shadows around the room.

To Barbara, it looked like a shot from a film noir set. That seemed apropos enough.

The only other person physically present in the room was Billy Ray, now in his white fighting suit, as if he were anticipating action. Two cameras had been set on tripods in the center of the table, one pointed toward where Barbara sat, another facing Billy Ray. Several flat screens, looking as if they'd just been unboxed a few hours before, faced them and trailed wires over the table to a server on the floor; in them, solemn faces were arrayed: Secretary-General Jayewardene, in Brussels; President van Rennsaeler in Washington; President Putin in Moscow; General Ruez of NATO; President Karimov of Kazakhstan.

"Thank you all for being here," Jayewardene said. "Your cooperation is greatly appreciated in this crisis. We are facing critical decisions that must be made quickly, and it's imperative that we all understand and realize the consequences of those decisions before we proceed."

"It's simple enough," Putin said, his translator (unnecessarily for Barbara) relaying his words in English a few moments later. "We must take out the hospital and this Tolenka."

President van Rennsaeler brushed greying hair back from her face, shaking her head. "Your own agent said that would only release the creature that is trying to come through Tolenka."

Putin shrugged. "She and this Tolenka were associates. She is trying to protect him. We have no assurance that any of her claims are true. Are we to just wait? I say that we move now to take out the center in Talas. Now. Waiting any longer is foolishness."

That started everyone talking at once.

". . . not even possible. The drones we sent in all failed . . ."

". . . my government absolutely would protest the use of nuclear weapons . . ."

". . . no guarantee that bombing would take out the man . . ."

". . . and if Baba Yaga is right, then what? We will have no other options . . ."

Bill Ray gave a sigh and leaned toward Barbara. "Bureaucrats," he said. "Everyone trying to cover their own ass."

Barbara managed a quick smile at that: it was something Klaus would have said. She waited for the furor to lessen, then spoke loudly into the opening.

"I appreciate your point of view, Mr. President," Barbara answered.

Which is not something Klaus would have said. "And yours may yet be a tactic we have to attempt, if there are no other options left to us. But Director Ray and I believe there's another way, one that both he and I agree upon. If destroying Tolenka isn't the answer—and I do believe Baba Yaga, as everything else she's told us has been verified, and she has no reason to lie—then there's another way. If we can't simply kill Tolenka, then we must take him elsewhere."

"To where?" Putin scoffed. "Assuming you can find and capture the man—and I would remind you that the Committee's last attempt at that was a miserable failure, Ms. Baden—where would you take him? Where would you send him?"

"To hell itself," Ray answered.

"Via the Highwayman," Barbara hurried in to say. "John Bruckner."

"I've ridden with the Highwayman," Ray said. "I've seen the dimension that the man opens up, and everything about it says Talas: the twisted, deformed figures, the monsters, the fog. That's where that beast inside Tolenka is from, and if we toss Tolenka back there and leave him, then . . ." Ray clapped his hands together dramatically. "Everything closes up. Let the beast come out of Tolenka—the passageway into our world would be gone, because Tolenka *is* that portal."

"This is all just supposition," President van Rennsaeler said.

"Yes, Madame President," Barbara told her, "but everything fits: what we've seen in Talas, and the dimension through which the Highwayman travels. It's no worse a supposition than killing Tolenka or reducing Talas to radioactive rubble will also solve the problem. And if we fail . . ." Barbara shrugged. "Then the other option is still on the table. At least let us try."

"Bruckner is in St. Gilles, serving out his sentence," Jayewardene said. "We would have to contact the authorities in Brussels and work with them in order to release him."

"Did you not hear what we've been saying?" Ray spat. "We don't have time to waste."

"There are protocols, rules, and legalities we still have to follow, Director Ray," Jayewardene responded.

"Then do that, Mr. Secretary-General," Barbara told him. "Now."

Jayewardene's solemn gaze seemed to traverse the screen in front of him, looking at each of them. "President Putin, President van Rennsaeler, President Karimov, General Ruez? Are we in agreement here?"

"Twenty-four hours," Putin said immediately. "No more. And we need Committee aces to help defend Baikonur."

"Done," Barbara told him.

The others murmured agreement. Putin's screen went to black; the others quickly followed. "I will contact Brussels now," Jayewardene said before he broke contact. "I will do my best. You will have to do yours, Ms. Baden." He said the last sentence with a strange emphasis, and Barbara nodded to him. With that, his screen flickered and went dark. The only sound in the room was the hum of the fans.

"They'll never get it fucking done in time," Ray said to Barbara. "Bureaucracies are like old dogs; they don't like being pushed, and they bite when you do."

Barbara carefully put her power around the two of them before she answered, suspecting that the room might have live microphones; if so, they would hear only gibberish.

"Jaycwardene knows that," Barbara told Ray. "We'll give him eight hours. No more. And we'll make our own plans based on him not getting Bruckner released. If he hasn't given us Bruckner by tonight, we'll get him ourselves."

SUNDAY

IT TOOK SEVEN TRIES to get a portal into the cash register. Even when she was looking right at the damn thing from across the aisle, pretending to browse a rack of ugly-ass souvenir T-shirts intended for tourists with worse taste than a colorblind five-year-old with a kawaii fixation. Space refused to twist and fold to her whims like it used to. It used to be so easy. Now creating a pair of openings in space felt like trying to nail Jell-O to the wall. That she eventually succeeded offered little consolation. What was the point? Soon enough the money would be worthless, and there'd be nowhere to spend it. But she was bored and scared and didn't know what else to do. Anything was better than sitting around with nothing but her own thoughts for company.

I guess at heart I really am just a petty thief, despite Ffodor's insistence that I could be so much more.

Her phone rang just as she was wrist-deep in the cash drawer. It shattered her concentration. She yanked her hand free of the opening just as it blinked closed. She lost her balance and stumbled into a spin-rack of miniature vanity California license plates preprinted with boys' and girls' names. The rack toppled over with a resounding crash. Tammies, Quentins, Siennas, Ambers, Johns, and Dakotas skittered across the floor. Everybody in the store stopped to stare at Mollie.

"Hey!" The joker shopkeeper came trotting over on a pair of faun legs. "What's the big idea?"

Mollie ignored her. Heart fluttering with relief, she instead looked at her phone, which was still buzzing. But it wasn't a call from the farmhouse. It was a New York area code. Mollie sighed. Answered.

"What the hell do you think you're doing?" said the shopkeeper.

Into the phone, Mollie said, "Whoever you are, you can kiss my ass, because your timing blows chunks."

It was Ink. She didn't bother with hello. "Mollie! Administrator Baden needs to see you immediately. Can you please go to Bai—"

Mollie didn't hear the rest, because the shopkeeper chose that moment to reach for her elbow, which meant it was also the moment when the man started screaming at the top of his lungs. A portal pair blinked into existence, one side hovering just beyond her elbow, just large enough to accept his arm. The portal lasted just long enough for him to get elbow deep before she slammed it shut. A severed arm fell to the platform in a Tokyo train station.

Blood fountained across the T-shirts. It spewed from the severed shoulder like something in a Monty Python skit, except nobody was laughing. Instead, the other shoppers joined in the screaming. Several ran for the door.

Motherfuckers. Mollie stationed a new portal to intercept one of the stampeding shoppers, its twin *inside* another. An instant later viscera geysered across the display window as two bodies tried and failed to occupy the same space all at once. The wet explosion sounded like the world's wettest fart. Teeth, vertebrae, and shattered ribs clattered against the walls, floor, and ceiling like so much hail. It was annoying as hell.

A tinny voice hollered, "Hello? Hello? Mollie, are you there?"

Mollie still held the phone to her ear. Irritated, she stepped from Half Moon Bay back to the Committee offices at the United Nations. Ink started, broke off in mid-sentence when Mollie emerged from empty space to stand next to her desk.

Mollie hung up. "I'm busy. What?"

Ink's face twisted in a scowl. She covered her nose. "Oh, my God! What happened to you?"

"Nothing happened to me. I'm fine," said Mollie. But then she caught a whiff of something nasty. She frowned. The residual shit smell of ruptured viscera had followed Mollie from California. And now the draft from the AC felt especially cold against her skin, as though she were damp. She looked down and realized she was drenched in blood. What the hell? A second ago she was swiping a handful of cash from—

Oh, Jesus. Oh, God, ohGodohGodohGodwhathaveIdone?

The phone fell from her nerveless fingers. It bounced under Ink's desk.

"I . . . I . . . I need help. I'm not myself anymore. Even when I'm here, I'm not myself. The evil, it's touched me too many times . . ." Mollie crumpled to the floor. Rolled into a fetal ball. "I think I just murdered three people. Oh, God, somebody help him."

Ink practically vaulted her desk. She crouched beside Mollie, cradled her head. "Help who?"

Mollie tried to open a doorway to California. She couldn't. "The rage, it took me again. I didn't mean it," she sobbed. "I didn't mean it. I'm sorry, I'm sorry, I'm sorry . . ."

Ink stood and slapped a button on her phone. "I need paramedics here, now! Administrator Baden's office!"

"No, no, not here," said Mollie. She tasted strangers' blood, and worse, when the tears trickled into her mouth. "Help him instead. Please! You have to help him."

"Who?"

"There's a man with a severed arm bleeding out in a T-shirt shop in Half Moon Bay. He's going to die. He needs help. His arm . . . I don't know where I left it. And the others." She tried to talk but somebody was wailing and sobbing with her voice and she could only speak in little gasps. "The others . . . oh, God, the others . . . I . . . I don't know how I did that . . . Somebody help them!"

She tried again to fold space but it slipped through her fingers. She couldn't get a grip on it. Couldn't concentrate. Couldn't breathe. The shame and horror were too heavy. Like elephants mating on her chest. They crushed the air from her lungs and didn't stop. They squeezed and squeezed until everything went dark.

The Angel awoke, not quite sure where she was. Her head was buzzing with an almost subliminal noise, a buzzing like a herd of Bugsy's wasps stirred up and angry, and it was making it difficult to think. The heat washed over her like a furnace.

She sat up, leaning on one elbow. She was in a small room, once an office. All the furniture in it—a desk, uncomfortable-looking plastic chairs, a cheap, worn sofa, and filing cabinets that had definitely seen better days— were pushed to the room's edges, clearing an open space for the mattress she was lying on. It was fairly clean with only a couple of blood and some less identifiable stains on it and she'd been tired as a dog, so she'd fallen asleep immediately. Even the bad dreams she'd had all night hadn't woken her, nor could she now remember their content. But they still bothered her, fragmented images from them still popping up disconnected in her mind.

The events of the last evening now flooded into her mind, of her coming into her kingdom and defending it from the mad interloper who thought only in terms of mathematics. He'd gotten only what he deserved from her hands. In fact, his death had been merciful. She was recalling it in intimate detail when the first explosion rocked the foundations of her headquarters.

The Angel sprang to her feet and ran into the great room of her headquarters. Her subjects were running in panic and crying out for help. The sight of her only seemed to increase their distress. They ran to her, imploring her aid, threatening to overwhelm her. Shrieking at them, she struck out with her fist, hurling them away with her superior strength. She knew that she didn't need her sword to deal with this rabble. They fell to the floor, scrabbled aside, ran to escape her wrath.

The Angel made her way outdoors and climbed to the top of the earthen ridge Earth Witch had left when she'd scooped out the parking lot in front of the store. She turned, facing west from where she thought the initial explosion came, and lifted her face to the sky. The buzz of giant insects was in the air and she could see a group of half a dozen helicopters hovering over Talas, raining down death and destruction in the form of rockets and bombs.

She didn't know where they came from, she didn't know why they were attacking, but she was driven by some primal, previously unfelt need to protect the city. There was something precious at its heart, something that whispered an urgent demand and promised unutterable delights as a reward.

Anger tinged with unholy anticipation took control of her. Wings sprouted from her back, but not her normal ones. These were leathery, bat-like, mismatched in size but seemingly more powerful. She swooped up into the air and from the roofs and dark crannies of adjacent buildings other winged creatures joined her—faceless devils seemingly carved from jet, moths with death-skull markings, lizards of every size and hue, swarms of insects from the size of ants to dogs. She led them toward the choppers, her black sword pointing the way.

The faster creatures overtook her. She let them, and they bore the brunt of the rocket and machine-gun fire. She swooped low, dodging under the flight of bullets and the gunners aimed at what they thought were the most dangerous targets. And they were wrong.

Saurians and moths fell from the sky in droves as the Angel came in low and unseen under the copters, turned, and came at them from behind. She braced herself in the sky and swung her black sword. It punched through the shiny metal armor of the copter's tail assembly and the chopper twisted and tumbled in the sky. The pilot of one of the other choppers noticed her and pulled up. She dodged the machine-gun fire coming from the open side door but the hail of bullets followed her as she jinked and twisted in the sky, leading it to fire into the nose of one of its companions. She laughed aloud as the bullets stitched a path across the airship's fuselage and it spiraled down in a path of death, exploding when it hit the ground.

The pilots of the remaining craft panicked, but the Angel was not going to let them escape. She came up from underneath one, cutting a way into the fuselage with her black sword. She levered the sword to peel back the metal floor panel and pulled herself into the cabin. Inside, four armed men stared at her with disbelief as her wings disappeared and she was among them with her sword before they had a chance to react. She laughed in sheer delight as heads and limbs flew. One got a shot off with a sidearm and the bullet burned her side as it passed by. She stuck her sword into his gut and twisted, laughing as he floundered in his own intestines. The last crewman jumped out the door and fell to his death rather than face her.

Bloodied and frenzied she stormed into the cockpit and chopped left and right at the seated pilots. As the copter dove earthward she hurled herself forward, sword first, and burst through the shattering plastic dome that shielded the cockpit. One of the giant moths banked low and she fell onto its man-sized thorax, took a deep breath, and leaped off as her wings disappeared.

Only one helicopter was left in the air and it was turning and heading for the desert that surrounded Talas. An armed force of vehicles and troop columns was waiting out there to attack the city after the choppers had softened it up, but the plan hadn't worked. As the Angel watched, swarms of countless tiny insects caught up to the copter as it tried to right itself and flee. It barely got away from the city limits before the bugs caught up to it and enveloped it within the dark haze of its million little bodies. The chopper swerved, jerked, and then dove.

The ground forces beneath it tried to escape but it crashed hard and exploded into a ball of flames and metal shrapnel that cut through flesh like bullets. The troops broke, heading back to wherever they had come from.

The Angel let them go, chased by what was left of her airborne flotilla. She wanted to return to the heart of the city to claim the prize that had been offered her.

The message from Jayewardene had been terse: *Earliest Bruckner release two days. Not earlier. Will keep working, but . . .*

The trailing ellipsis said all that Barbara needed.

Barbara and Billy Ray, now joined by Michelle Pond, were back in the same conference room Barbara and Ray had been in earlier, but no one watched the flat screen, and Barbara let her wild card power wash out over the entire room, putting them in a safe bubble of understanding that anyone outside wouldn't be able to understand. Billy Ray, in his immaculate white outfit, looked almost half bored as he leaned back. Michelle stared into empty space.

"I've heard from the Secretary-General," Barbara said without preamble. "The earliest Bruckner can be released from prison is two days from now. We don't *have* two days. We have eighteen hours at the most. We need Bruckner, which means we're going to have to go and get him. Then convince him to drive to Talas."

"I just fucking got *out* of there," Michelle said. "What a bitch."

"I know," Barbara said, knowing she would be thinking the same thing if it were Klaus sitting there discussing their options. *I don't want you to go back there,* she'd tell him. *Please don't go back.* And Klaus would shake his head. She could nearly hear his voice. *"I have to. I must . . ."* he'd say.

The debate continued all around her. She closed her eyes, letting her power seep out, and they were all shrieking nonsense to each other. Slowly, the hubbub died down as they realized that they could understand nothing of what anyone was saying. When the room was silent, she let the power dissipate.

"We have a plan that we believe—we *have* to believe—has some chance of success, and we know who we need in order to complete it, and that's all of you here in this room. Now—does anyone have anything concrete to say?"

There was silence around the table until Ray leaned forward, elbows on either side of the report in front of him. "I've already seen everything that you've all described inside the disturbance," he ventured. "I've seen it before—because I've ridden with the Highwayman and I've seen what's outside the windows of his truck. Whatever dimension he travels, it's the same place that Hellraiser has tapped into. It *has* to be."

"Yeah. Fucking *maybe*," Michelle said.

"Maybe's the best we have," Barbara said. "But we need the Highwayman, and we need him now."

Ray nodded. "Babel's right. We break him out without asking 'em. We don't have time for negotiations and bureaucratic red tape and legalities. And if the fucker doesn't want to help, well, we don't give him a choice."

Barbara looked around the table. "Anyone got something better?" No one spoke, and Barbara nodded.

"I'll be going with you," she told the others. "I can make sure that the guards won't be able to coordinate well enough to stop us. Michelle, we'll need you: for St. Gilles, and for Talas." Michelle's face showed distress at that, but Barbara didn't let her interrupt. Not now. Not when things were at least moving somewhere. Klaus would have just bulled through without a plan, without support.

"We act *now*. I had Ink send us maps and photographs of St. Gilles, and of the hospital in Talas from before this happened. We'll find Tolenka easily enough without him."

"Finding Tolenka isn't the problem," Michelle said.

Barbara let herself smile at that. "No, it's not," she said. "But we'll manage it. We have to. Let's get started."

"What about Jayewardene?" Ray asked.

"He already knows what we're doing," Barbara said. She glanced at everyone. "Let's go over everything one more time, so we all know our parts and what to expect."

"Fucking bureaucrat," Ray said, but a smile creased his face.

"Just making sure we're all on the same page," Barbara told him. "Including me."

Babel was pacing with her back to the door of her makeshift office at the Cosmodrome, talking to somebody on a speakerphone, when Mollie stumbled in with her arm over Ink's shoulders. The tattooed woman was stronger than she looked, and thank God for it; Mollie could barely open the portal from New York to Baikonur, and wouldn't have been able to stumble through it without help. Like everything Mollie touched, Ink was smeared with blood.

The administrator turned at the sound of their entrance. The first hints of a smile were tugging at the corners of her mouth, but they fled at the sight of Mollie. A shadow fell behind Babel's eyes; it snuffed what might have been a spark of optimism.

"I'll call you back," Babel said, killing the call.

Ink deposited Mollie on the cot in the corner of the trailer. Mollie collapsed there and watched, blearily, while the UN women hissed at each other in urgent whispers. She'd always thought it was merely a figure of speech, some overblown artistic expression, when people wrote about the color draining from somebody's face. But it wasn't. Babel's face did exactly that just then.

Mollie knew what that meant. She knew why they'd called her in California *(don't think about the T-shirt shop, don't think about what happened there, don't think about WHAT I DID TO THOSE PEOPLE don't don't don't think about portaling two people into the same body don't don't don't think about the torn-sodden-bedsheet sound they made when they exploded like an overfilled water balloon oh God oh God oh God don't think about all the blood fountaining down the shop window for everybody to see and hear the sounds of teeth and shattered ribs hitting the ceiling fan blades don't don't don't just DON'T FUCKING THINK ABOUT CALIFORNIA)* even before she heard Ink's voice. She hadn't wanted to accept it, or admit it to herself, and maybe that stoked the murderous rage that erupted in . . . in . . . that place. But it was obvious.

Babel needed Mollie's help. And from the way she and Ink stared at her and whispered, she needed it desperately. Even a person half out of her wits with grief and fear of herself could see that.

She couldn't stand it. The naked fear on their faces. Not the fear for themselves—though that was present, too—but fear that Mollie was too far gone to do whatever it is they needed from her. They were wondering when she'd blow up again, when she'd try to murder them in a fit of pique.

"Oh, Jesus, stop whispering. I might be losing my mind, and increasingly prone to random acts of violence, but I'm not stupid. You need me for another taxi ride."

They stared at her. Shared a look. Then Babel gave Ink some minute sign, and the tattooed woman departed. Mollie realized she hadn't closed the New York portal. That was getting harder, too. She waited until Ink was back at the UN before clenching her eyes shut, concentrating hard until the damn thing closed.

" 'Increasingly prone to random acts of violence'? What exactly do you mean by that?"

Only then did Mollie realize there was another person in the room. Billy Ray, the SCARE guy with the mashed-up face. He'd been sitting in the corner the entire time. Probably chiming in on Babel's phone call. He sat next to the door, and Mollie had too much blood caked in her eyes *(strangers' blood don't think about it don't think about it don't think about what they didn't deserve)* to see him when Ink carried her through. The question had come from him.

Mollie said, "I, uh . . . I never used to get so angry. But it's like . . . it's like after being exposed to supernatural rage so many times I can't ever really leave it behind, you know? I'm tainted and I can't get clean. And now I'm stuck in limbo and I get angry so easily and when I'm furious I start doing things with my power and when I'm back I don't even understand what I did or how I did it. I'm dangerous. I need to be put away." SCARE. That meant he was some kind of fancy federal cop, right? He could do that. "Look at me. I'm a mess because I just killed two people—fuck, it's three by now—just because a shopkeeper chided me for knocking over some merchandise. I deserved to get thrown out of the store. They didn't deserve anything at all except to live their lives. But he reached for me, and it reminded me of the way Berman would touch me, and it made me so mad . . ." She tried to wipe her eyes with the back of her hand, but it just smeared the blood stippled on her face.

Ray and Babel shared another look.

Mollie said, "And now you're scared shitless. Which tells me you're up to something important."

Babel said, "We think we know how to stop this."

"Stop me from losing my shit? Stop me from becoming a murdering lunatic?"

"Stop Horrorshow. We have a plan for putting an end to this."

Mollie's heart tried to chisel through her breastbone. Her pulse tripled. First in exhilaration, but then in dread. "And I'm the transportation."

"Yes."

"It means going back to Talas again, doesn't it? Because that's where . . . Because that's the epicenter."

Babel shook her head, waving her hands for emphasis. "No. No, no, you don't have to worry about that. That's the great part. We don't need you to open a doorway to Talas. Instead, we need your help breaking somebody out of jail. He's in Belgium. Very far from Kazakhstan."

Mollie blinked. "I know I'm losing my mind, but still, I have to admit that is not what I expected you to say." She shrugged. So far, it didn't sound so bad. "Jails are easy. Who is he?"

"This jail won't be," said Ray. "Ever heard of the Highwayman?"

"Nope. Wait a sec—highwayman? As in robbing people on horseback?"

"Not exactly."

"What's he doing time for?"

"Ah." Babel cleared her throat. "War crimes."

Mollie leapt to her feet. "Are you fucking serious?"

Ray was out of his chair, too. Wow, for somebody whose face looked like badly sculpted clay he was spooky quick.

The entire world was getting absorbed by the evil insanity zone but instead of dealing with that problem these fucktards wanted Mollie to break some war criminal out of jail? What, so he could make the inevitable atrocities even worse? It was disgusting. It enraged her.

(Even as a meek little voice in the back of her churning mind said, *What right have you to be so high and mighty? So what if he's a war criminal? You just murdered three people in cold blood.*)

She said, "What the fuck are you two playing at?"

"Calm down," said Ray. He cracked his knuckles. "Calm down or I'll put you down."

Babel said, "Ray, that's not helping!"

He dropped his fists. But Mollie wasn't fooled.

"Do you think you're faster than I am? I could dump you in the ocean right now. I could send you to Talas. I wonder how long you'd last, tough guy, all by yourself in Cannibal Flashmob Central. Think you could find your wife before the madness claims you? Take one more step and you'll find out." So many possibilities. A hole opened in space. It orbited Ray like a dancer around a maypole, showing glimpses of Icelandic ice and fire. A cold wind howled through Babel's office, rifling the papers on the planks that passed for her desk.

"Mollie, please listen to me," said Babel.

Mollie had never noticed how mellifluous the UN woman's voice could be. It was almost pleasant. She held off on sending Billy Ray to hell just for a few more seconds, just to hear what else Babel had to say.

"I know it's confusing and counterintuitive. But we'll explain it to you and you'll understand. We're not breaking him out of jail because we like him or support the terrible things he's done. We're doing it because he's our only hope for banishing Horrorshow."

Why was she standing? She'd been so angry a moment ago. Why? Over what? She could hardly remember now. All she wanted was to hear Babel speak a little more. The portal disappeared.

She sat on the sofa. "Tell me your plan."

They did.

Mollie was still turning it over in her head when one of Ray's SCARE guys came in with a change of clothes for her. She recognized him—Agent Vigil. Babel said, "There are showers next door. Hurry, okay?"

Mollie stood. She started to follow Vigil, but stopped. "This plan of yours. You're not yanking my chain, are you? You're serious about not returning to Talas?"

"Completely."

"Okay. Good. Because as far as I'm concerned, Talas is a permanent no-go zone. I don't care who might be stuck over there. I'm never *ever* opening another doorway to that hellhole. No matter how small, how short-lived, how compassionate the cause."

She was a broken lonely coward, and she cried in the shower until the water ran cold and somebody complained in Russian.

Marcus and Olena didn't talk about what happened. They would eventually, but Olena made it clear she wasn't ready yet. They'd disengaged with the rest of Vasel's men, both sides backing away from the ace's remains in an uneasy truce. Olena had kept her coin hand clenched in a fist. Back at the Committee compound, she'd rifled through a first-aid kit, found an ACE bandage, and wrapped her hand with it. Then she found another and wrapped it again. Marcus watched silently, there for her, waiting for the touch of her eyes on his. That touch didn't come, but neither did she push him away. Together, they'd done the things they had to for the people who still needed them.

The jokers spent the night in a dilapidated hangar. Marcus had protested. He wanted something safer than the sprawling outdoor camp the other refugees were housed in. But Babel had handed them off to the Russians and they claimed the hangar was the only place they could spare. It was an old structure, like something out of a black-and-white newsreel or something. Musky. Dark and dingy, with only a handful of working lightbulbs. One wall had half collapsed, leaving an opening to the outside, and the other walls looked like they were about to give it up at any moment. Hardly the safe haven Marcus had hoped for.

Determined that one night in the place was enough, Marcus rose in the predawn, intent on getting them better accommodations. He left the jokers in seclusion—Olena there with them but silent, staring, holding her bandaged hand a little away from her body, like it wasn't part of her—and he went looking for a better place, or for someone who could direct him to one.

Despite the early hour, the entire compound thronged with purpose, people and cars and transports and tanks all on the move. Planes arriving and leaving, choppers thwacking through the sky: the place was a confusion of massive proportions. Lost within it, Marcus could barely get within shouting distance of anyone in charge. When he did, it didn't do any good. At best they ignored him; at worse he found himself staring down machine-gun barrels. The message was clear enough. The jokers were on their own. Still, he kept trying.

He was gesticulating with arms and shoulders and tail, trying to make himself understood to a cadre of Kazakh soldiers, when a smooth, Southern voice asked, "Hey, IBT, you know them fuckers can't understand you, right?"

Joey. She stood watching him, looking at ease despite being out of place, urban casual. At first Marcus didn't know what to make of the mildly predatory look on her face. When she opened her mouth slightly and ran the tip of her tongue along her teeth, he kinda figured it out. He flushed, and was glad to be able to look behind her at the rows of the walking dead that had paused with her. They stood crooked and deformed, vacant expressions on their hollowed, worm-eaten faces. Marcus slid close enough to catch the scent of them.

"Who are your friends?" Marcus asked.

Joey shrugged. "Fuck if I know. Dead meat is all. You'd think there'd be more bodies buried around here." She considered Marcus again. "Heard you stopped some crazy-assed Russians from nuking Talas."

"I guess," Marcus said.

"Is that humility I hear?" Joey squinted. "You did it for the girl, didn't you? What's her name?"

"Olena."

"You hitting that?"

Marcus didn't know what to say. He tried, "Uh . . ."

"All right," Joey said, smiling. "You don't have to answer. Of course hitting it. International style. Got you a little Anna Kournikova."

"Who?"

Joey shook her head. "Anyway, what was all that hollering about with the soldiers?"

"Just trying to get some help," he said. "The Russians have my villagers staying in a ruin."

Joey raised an eyebrow. "*Your* villagers?"

"Not mine, exactly, but . . . you know, I owe them. They saved my life more than once."

Raising her hand and wriggling her full set of fingers. "I hear you. They did me a solid, too. I didn't thank you properly for having the little guy heal me. I should do that. Thank you, I mean. Must be some way . . ." A number of things about the way she said this was suggestive: her tone, the pauses, the way her gaze slipped from his face and moved across his chest. Marcus was on the verge of squirming—literally and figuratively—when her eyes popped back up to his. "Fucking Russians. Some coldhearted bitches, ain't they? Tell you what. Take me to this ruin." She cocked her head toward the zombies and then swiped the blaze of red hair back from her face. "I'll get my crew on it."

She ought to have taken a nap while Babel and company assembled images of the Highwayman's prison.

Instead, Mollie had gone to Idaho to check on the family. Farmhouses could be quiet at night, but they should never be empty. But hers was. She didn't know where everybody had gone. Some were still in the hospital, she supposed. Maybe the rest were visiting. Whatever they were doing, they hadn't bothered to tell her about it. Mollie even checked her phone to see if she'd missed a call, but of course she hadn't. She wandered the empty Steunenberg farmhouse like a lonely ghost.

Ffodor had been great at times like this. She wished she had never heard of that stupid casino. She wished she hadn't badgered him into agreeing to rob it. She wished none of this had ever happened. She wished she hadn't tried to steal that gold, and got Todd killed as a result. She wished Noel had never approached her. She wished she had never gone on that stupid TV show in the first place, because if she hadn't Noel wouldn't have found her later and none of this would have happened.

She was still roaming the farmhouse and rehashing her life's regrets when Babel called.

"Mollie. We're ready for you."

She didn't ask where she'd gone, didn't ask if she was okay, didn't ask if she'd changed her mind. Babel acted like Mollie's participation was a given, as though Mollie's word were an inviolate covenant. Nobody believed that, not for a millisecond, but it was a nice gesture of trust.

"I'll be there," said Mollie.

And, after six attempts to open a portal back to Baikonur, she was.

"I swear to God, Director, you hit like a tiny, fuzzy kitten," Michelle said. Billy Ray had just delivered one hell of a roundhouse to her chin. It hadn't hurt a bit, so now she just wanted him to go on hitting her. Even though it didn't put on fat as quickly as the truck that had just run over her, knowing she could take a beating and have no pain was a relief. *(But you're going back into Talas,* came a soft voice inside her that wouldn't shut up. *You know what happens there. Pain. So much pain.)*

Billy Ray stopped his next punch a fraction of an inch before he slammed it into her gut. "You're really weird, Michelle," he said with a hint of dismay. "You're kind of taking the fun out of this."

Michelle looked around the makeshift headquarters at her companions and tried not to despair. Babel looked confident enough. But she always did. Mollie was shaking like a junky getting off meth. Joey looked pissed, but that was reassuringly normal.

"I dunno, Billy Ray," she replied as she released a little bubble and sent it bouncing across the floor. "My standard for weird has gotten pretty skewed of late."

He nodded, then pulled back to punch her again. "Michelle, for once, we see eye to eye."

Getting a portal inside the Belgian jail was shaping up to be a monumental pain in the ass.

Utterly unsurprisingly, there wasn't a conveniently placed webcam pointing at the Highwayman's accommodations. Not even one showing the yard. Assuming war criminals were afforded the right to use an exercise yard; that seemed like a crunchy-socialist European thing to do. But St. Gilles might as well have been the center of the Australian Outback for the dearth of useful webcams.

Even Babel couldn't pull enough strings to get a blueprint or floor plan of the place. Not on such short notice, anyway. And the Belgians sure as hell weren't sharing information about all the anti-ace contingencies they'd undoubtedly worked into the building.

So Mollie would have to get the team on the premises, and portal them inside once she got the lay of the land.

Probably while guards shot at them. Awesomesauce.

Street-view images only showed the gate to St. Gilles prison, which huddled between two hulking towers complete with crenellations, turrets within turrets, and arrow slits—goddamned *arrow slits*—everywhere. It looked like something from HBO, or a history book. Very Gothic, this place. But the gate was closed in the street view, and the walls were thirty feet high, offering no way to see inside the prison grounds.

Satellite photos showed the gate fronted an avenue along the north side of the prison. The walls enclosed a massive complex. The prison was built around a tall central tower from which radiated six long spokes. The space between the spokes housed a bit of green space and what might have been an exercise yard. One spoke connected the central tower to the main gate, suggesting they were built in a similar style. The other five looked more modern, or at least like they hadn't been built during the fucking Crusades.

Better yet, the modern spokes had skylights. That, and the layout, gave her the beginnings of a plan.

"Okay," she said. "I think I know how to get us inside. But it's gonna take two steps, and then we'll have to work our way to whatshisface's cell."

"You mean Highwayman? His name's Bruckner."

"Your plan rests on convincing him to effectively commit suicide. If he doesn't help, we're all dead. If he does, I'll never meet him again. So I really couldn't give two runny shits about his name."

"Wow, kid. You're just a beam of sunshine," said Ray.

Bubbles said, "Tell us your plan, sweetie."

"First, we get on the roof." Mollie tapped the screen with her finger-nail. "There, I think. Near the skylights. Once I'm there I can peer through the windows and make a portal inside. We step from the roof to inside this long corridor."

Babel asked, "But how do we find Bruckner?"

"I'm guessing this central tower controls everything. There must be a master alarm or security station. If we can get there, we can find him. We might even luck out with a CCTV feed, in which case I open a doorway right to his cell." She shrugged. "It'd be a hell of a lot easier if I could create a shortcut straight to the tower. But once on the roof I'd need a high-power telescope on a tripod and time to study the windows before I could try it. They'll make us long before that. The skylight is farther away but it'll get us inside a lot faster."

Or so I hope, she didn't add. *Assuming I can keep my shit together. Assuming I don't lose control.*

"Huh." Ray crossed his arms, frowning as though in grudging approval. "That's . . . not half bad."

The others concurred. Mollie wondered how much of the agreement was tactical encouragement directed at her. Ray looked around the room. Babel and Bubbles nodded at him. "We're ready when you are."

Mollie stared at the screen, concentrating.

At least this time there wasn't an imminent danger of the site getting absorbed by the Psycho Cannibal Flashmob Evil Insanity Zone. Hell, no. That was at least two days away, three at the outside. Why, if this idiotic plan failed, the world might persist for entire *week* before the last unsul-lied patches were overrun by the squamous rugose incarnations of malig-nant madness. And this time around the potential drawbacks of the plan going wrong didn't involve nuclear weapons going off like a string of fire-crackers. So the pressure on Mollie to get the ball rolling was considerably lessened, comparatively speaking.

Didn't help.

The first shortcut she created inadvertently opened on an empty barn in Idaho. It was silent, too, but for the keening of the wind. Not even the shuffling of hooves or the lowing of cows to break the eerie quiet. Where had the livestock gone? Where was everybody? She gave the wind blowing in from halfway around the world a quick sniff, testing it for fresh manure, but couldn't be sure.

Ray said, "Oh, so *that's* what a barn looks like on the inside." He looked pointedly at the pile of dented battered slot machines lying abandoned on the dirt floor. The chipped Cyrillic lettering, the shattered teeth, and the blood-crusted crowbar gave the scene a postapocalyptic grace note. "I always thought barns contained things like hay and animals and maybe a tractor. The things I learn on this job."

"Oh, fuck off," Mollie said.

She killed the portal. Tried again. And got slapped in the face by a very confused koi riding the water that gushed into Babel's makeshift office from the basin of a Paris fountain. In seconds the torrent doused everything. It rose to ankle level while everybody climbed the furniture and cursed at Mollie. The fish that smacked Mollie with its tail wasn't the only one flopping on the floor when she finally closed the spacetime rift.

Nobody said anything. The only sound was the wet slapping of koi convulsing on a ruined carpet. The office stank of fountain water and pigeon shit. The AC kicked in, causing Mollie to shiver. Soaking wet and humiliated to the bone, she could feel the others' eyes on her, feel the judgment raking her flesh. She wanted to pluck their eyes out. How dare they judge her failures? She—

"It's okay, sweetie." Michelle laid a hand on her shoulder. Mollie started, hard enough to bite her tongue. "We're all scared. You're not alone. We know you're doing the best you can. We know you can do this."

Babel said, "Do you want to try the sedative?"

Mollie shook her head. "No. Save those for the people who'll really need them."

Save the drugs for the Talas Suicide Squad.

A crowd of Russian soldiers and SCARE agents gathered outside Babel's door. They'd traced the torrent to its source. A few chuckled when they saw the koi. It was the dull, forced laughter of men on death row.

Babel shut the door. "Just ignore them."

The next shortcut opened on a T-shirt shop in Half Moon Bay. Police tape fluttered on the ocean breeze while a crime-scene cleanup crew scrubbed blood from the ceiling.

Mollie screamed.

Light spilled from Babel's makeshift office in Baikonur to the rooftop of a prison five time zones to the west. A humid Brussels night wafted into the Cosmodrome.

The extra illumination didn't threaten to give them away—the spotlights bathing the prison would do that. The lights revealed a centrally peaked metal roof sloping away on both sides. The patter of rain beat a soft tattoo on the metal and sent little rivulets of water trickling down the roof. A few yards past the hole in space, the raised boxy panes of a skylight straddled the apex. It looked a bit like a greenhouse. Rainwater beaded the glass. It reminded Mollie of rainwater beaded on the windows of a French police car; she'd seen that once, a million years ago.

Ray stepped through first. The metal gave little creaks of protest under his feet. He crouched with one foot on each side of the apex and crab-walked halfway to the skylight. It looked uncomfortable. "Careful," he whispered. "It's really slippery."

Bubbles went next, then Babel. They waddled past Ray to the skylight. The trio stared expectantly at Mollie through the portal.

You don't have to do this, said the small selfish coward voice in her head.

Actual voices now. That was new.

It went on: *This is pointless and stupid and it's not going to work. You could let these motherfuckers twist in the wind. Get as far away from Talas as you can and try to enjoy the earth's final hours.*

"Shut up, shut up, shut up," she muttered, stepping through the hole in space. At least the rain was warm.

But she was too preoccupied with trying to close the portal to pay attention to her footing. She stepped to one side of the peak, rather than straddling it as the others had done. Her shoes had no purchase on the rain-slicked metal. Her feet flew out from under her. Her hip and head slammed against the roof hard enough to ring the metal like a gong. She slid toward a long drop. Woozy, head spinning, she scrabbled pointlessly for a fingerhold.

Bubbles yelled, "Mollie!"

A *clang,* a *thud,* and then a hand clamped around her wrist. She jerked to a halt. Ray lay sprawled over the roof, one ankle hooked around a pipe. "Careful, kiddo."

Spooky quick, that guy.

Somewhere nearby, an alarm Klaxon pierced the silent night.

"Well, shit," said Mollie.

St. Gilles prison smelled of testosterone and anger, of urine and fear.

"Hey! Who are you people?" someone shouted in Belgian French: a man in a guard's uniform, down below. Barbara opened her power, spreading it as widely as she could but leaving an untouched space around the four of them. The guard's shout turned to gibberish as he touched the mic velcroed to his shirt, as Ray—moving faster than Barbara thought possible—slammed into the man, shoving him up against the nearest wall and hitting him twice, quickly. The man crumpled, and Ray stepped back, brushing at the front of his suit as if flicking away lint.

Around the prison and in her head, Barbara heard prisoners calling out and guards shouting for clarification, but none of them could make themselves understood by anyone else. The chaos was spreading. Somewhere down on the first floor, an alarm continued to howl. They heard locks clicking shut on all the doors around them.

They also heard the barking of dogs. "Dogs," Ray said. "Why didn't we know they had dogs? Do you speak Dog, Babs?"

Barbara shook her head. "Fuck," Ray muttered.

Dogs. Michelle *liked* dogs.

"You didn't say anything about dogs," she said. "I'm not killing dogs." *This is where I take a stand on killing things?* Michelle thought. *I may be as crazy as Mollie.*

"Then shut the fuck up and do something about them," Billy Ray snarled. He looked like he was about to barrel straight for the guards and dogs.

Michelle opened her arms wide. Twenty bubbles the size of oranges flew from her hands. They sailed through the air, soft and rubbery. They blobbed about like soap bubbles as they landed in front of the dogs, bouncing erratically. As she had hoped, the dogs went nuts. They shied away from the bubbles, barking and snapping at them.

The guards tried to control the dogs, pulling on their leashes and yelling commands in French. But by now the guards were tripping over leashes and the bubbles themselves.

Michelle released another wave. These were marble-sized. Several hundred bounced across the balcony, clacking like castanets as they hit. There was nowhere to step that wasn't covered in bubbles. The guards and dogs that weren't already going ass-over-tea-kettle began retreating down the grey metal stairs.

Michelle glanced over the railing. Bubbles rose from her palms and began raining down on the courtyard below. The courtyard wasn't that big, and she had plenty of fat. She filled it chest-high with iridescent bubbles so it looked like the largest, and prettiest, plastic-ball pit ever—minus the snotty, germ-filled kids.

The guards and dogs were floundering in the bubbles when the marble-sized bubbles began rolling off the balcony, causing more mayhem below.

Michelle had a small moment of pride. She'd managed not to kill another living thing this time.

The floor shifted underfoot in the manner of a bathroom scale coming to a slow decision. The doors issued *thunk-thunk-thunk* sounds, suggesting a sequence of heavy bolts slamming into place.

Mollie said, "What the fuck was that?"

"I think we're locked in," said Babel.

Ray cracked his knuckles. "Great. That means everyone else is also locked *out*. So let's find Bruckner and get out of here."

Mollie joined him and Babel as they examined the control panels. She looked for anything that might enable the guards to switch between views from the roughly eight bazillion security cameras scattered throughout the prison.

A faint *tink* echoed from the louvered air vents. The HVAC kicked in, blowing hard.

"Uh, guys . . ." Bubbles pointed to one of the vents. A faint yellow mist gusted through the grate. Similar gas spewed from all the vents.

Mollie gasped. That was a mistake. It felt like a grizzly bear had just shit lava in her throat.

She fell to her knees, realizing at that moment why the floor felt like a scale: it was. This must have been some kind of precaution in case a group of prisoners tried to storm the security station. Normally the four of them shouldn't have outweighed half a dozen guards. But with Bubbles in her current state, not exactly heroin chic at the moment, they did.

Ffodor had never mentioned anything like this in their talks about security systems and, more importantly, how to defeat them.

Babel doubled over, coughing, snot running from her nose. Billy Ray clenched his eyes, groaning. He started kicking at the door. It dented the frame but the door didn't budge. Michelle flung bubbles at the vent, but the stinging gas had temporarily blinded her, too.

Mollie's eyes were on fire. Closing them didn't help—it was as though her very tears had become battery acid.

Clean air, she thought. *Need clean air.*

Just before she passed out, she remembered encountering Vaporlock at the casino.

A large rift opened in the air above the security station. Its flipside faced an observation deck on Mount Rainier, about 12,000 feet above sea level. The lower air pressure on the mountainside sucked the gas through the portal.

"So much for the element of surprise," Ray said. His fighting suit was ripped and spattered with blood, most of which didn't appear to be his. "Which damn cell is Bruckner's?"

Barbara had to concentrate to answer, to keep the space around them clear of Babel's power while she tried to match the floor plans that Ink had pulled to the reality around them. The retreats and flights they'd already made only made things more confusing. *I always followed Klaus. I was never the battle leader . . .* Babel forced herself to concentrate, to place herself in the map that Ink had given them. "That one," she said, pointing to a door two down to the left. "At least, I hope so. Does the guard have keys on him?" She looked at the body slumped against the wall, blood drooling from one nostril.

"This is easier." Bubbles had already moved, two ponderous steps. They saw an iridescent sphere rise from her hand. "Barbara, can you make Bruckner understand me?" she asked.

Barbara nodded and shifted the power so that Bruckner's cell was clear of her power. In the distance, they could hear garbled, indecipherable shouts.

"John," Michelle called out. "Move to the back of the cell. Now!" The sphere floated away from Bubble's hand, gathering speed as it moved. When it touched the steel door, there was a percussive clap that had Barbara involuntarily flinching, even though she'd been expecting the explosion. Dust and pebbles of splintered steel showered down, then Ray dashed forward, sticking his head inside the hole in the prison door.

"Hello, Bruckner," he said, "your parole board's here. Come on out and talk."

"Why do you always step on my lines?" Michelle asked Billy Ray, poking her head through the shattered door. "Hello, Mr. Bruckner, please get your ass out here as fast as possible. Billy Ray is twitchy, and honestly, what I just did to your door should definitely get your attention."

Bruckner coughed and waved his hand to clear the debris smoke in front of him. "Jesus," he said in a thick cockney accent as he stepped forward. "Billy Ray, you're still a faggot in a jumpsuit, I see. Oh, and look, you've brought along an enormous cow. You a dyke, honey? Most of you fat cunts are. I'd've rather been rescued by a nig . . ."

Michelle stepped into Bruckner's cell and let a baseball-sized bubble fly at him, hitting him in the chest as hard as she thought he could take without killing him. He sat down like a toddler surprised to discover it was walking.

"Asshole, please," she said as he tried to get to his feet. "Bad day. Getting worse. Billy Ray loves that jumpsuit, and you've just insulted it. Now me, I'd just as soon leave you where you are, but we need you, you sorry excuse for a human being. Now get up and move, or I will encourage the director to kick your ass in all the creative ways I know he has in him."

She grabbed Bruckner's arm and yanked him up from the floor.

"I said, MOVE!"

Bruckner looked as if he were about ready to run, and Ray grabbed the man's arm, shaking his head. "Uh-uh," he told him. "You're coming with us." He glanced around at the array of cells. The prisoners were nearly all well back from the bars, huddled in corners away from the uproar. A bullet pinged from the wall near them. "Any ideas?" he asked Barbara.

The block door had closed them off from where Molly's portal had been: a solid steel door. She pointed to it, hoping she was right. "We need to go that way," she said. "Michelle, we need a door."

"It's coming," Michelle told her. Another bubble was already rising from her open hand, a larger one this time. It sped away as if pushed by a wind none of them could feel; when it impacted the wall, the *thump* of the explosion was a hard punch to Barbara's chest, and for a moment, her concentration wavered. They could hear shouts in French as a hole appeared in the wall, with sunlight glimmering through the curtain of dust as concrete and rebar continued to tumble down. Barbara quickly put the barrier back up.

"Let's move," she said with the roar of the explosion still deafening her, with the effort of altering the barrage of words in her head causing her temples to pound. "Hurry!"

The quartet went through the hole, Barbara marveling at the thickness of the steel, which only emphasized Bubbles's power. "Up there!" Barbara pointed: a small window of silver shimmered on the wall a floor above them.

A guard came running up the stairs toward them, shouting nonsense orders. Evidently someone had taken the initiative to open a weapons closet, as this one brandished an automatic rifle. Ray gave him no chance to do more than shout and gesture with the weapon. He leapt at the man: a kick tore the weapon from the man's hands, a following punch sent the man tumbling backward down the steps ahead of them. As they reached the ground floor, Ray ripped away the rifle, dangling from its strap, from the unconscious guard. He pointed the muzzle at the guard.

"We're not here to kill anyone," Barbara reminded Ray. "Just to get the Highwayman." The confusion of the situation threatened to overwhelm them. She felt lost here, but tried to show none of it. She doubted that she was successful.

"Yeah," Ray was saying, "but they don't exactly seem to mind trying to kill us, and I'm not intending to let them." Hefting the rifle and setting it against his shoulder, he sent a spray of gunfire chattering down the length of the prison hall. "Just saying hello," he told Barbara and Michelle. "Maybe the rest of them will keep their heads down now."

"Seriously, Director, what's up with the ultraviolence?" Michelle asked tartly. After they got Bruckner out of his cell, they encountered more guards on the way to Mollie's portal. Billy Ray didn't hold back meting out punishment to the guards. Michelle winced as flesh met metal grating.

"You know I can take care of that without anyone getting hurt," she continued. Chunks of plaster flew off the wall as bullets hit. Bruckner and Babel both ducked, but Barbara caught a piece of flying plaster on her neck. It sprayed blood onto her white shirt collar.

Billy Ray looked over his shoulder at Michelle. There was a gleeful expression on his face.

He's really loving this, she thought.

"I need you to protect Bruckner and Babel," he replied. "How I get my job done isn't up for debate."

"I know, but I can do two things at the same . . ."

"Are we going to have a discussion or are we getting the hell out of here?" he asked. He'd already turned his attention back to the guards. His muscles flexed under his jumpsuit as he threw another guard over the railing into the courtyard below.

"Get behind that corner," she commanded Barbara and Bruckner. To Billy Ray she said, "Then let's give them a target."

She stepped out into the line of fire. Instantly, a barrage of bullets blasted her. It was glorious. All of the power and none of the pain.

Explosions, gunfire, and shouting were not conducive to Mollie's concentration. Every time she got a handle on the Cosmodrome another concussion would echo around the corner to slap her silly and shatter her concentration.

"We can leave anytime," said Ray.

Mollie had always thought Belgians were supposed to be levelheaded international diplomacy wonks. But they pretty much lost their shit when they realized Bruckner was the target of the jailbreak. It seemed as though every prison guard in northern Europe wanted to keep Bruckner in his cell. Mollie could only guess, but she imagined "time off for being a shitbag" wasn't part of his sentence.

Michelle leaned around the corner and sprayed the guards with exploding bubbles large enough to blow chips from the masonry. That seemed a little extreme until Mollie glimpsed a foolhardy guard who charged around the corner; in the moment before Ray sent them sprawling, she saw they'd anted up with riot gear. Good. Nobody wanted to kill them. They were just doing their jobs, after all.

"Wotcher!" Bruckner flinched from the explosion. He crouched, fingers in his ears. "Are you lot going to faff about all night?"

Michelle ducked back into cover. She touched Mollie's shoulder. "Anytime you're ready, sweetie."

"Uh-huh. Working on it."

Mollie tried again to picture the Cosmodrome. The brutalist Soviet architecture, the echoes in the cavernous hangar, the bloodstains on the concrete where she'd dropped a Winnebago on some poor fuck—

Four guards rushed their hiding spot. Ray put his fist through one guard's Lexan face shield, twisted, and planted his heel just above the other guard's navel. The body armor absorbed the worst of it but it still knocked the man down. Michelle threw down another line of bubbles, deftly knocking back the other two guards.

Ray said, "Seriously. Now would be a *really good* time to leave!"

Oh God oh God oh God they're depending on me oh God and I couldn't even get a shortcut to Brussels right and don't think about Half Moon Bay don't don't don't think about the sound of teeth hitting the ceiling fan and now I'm supposed to get us out of here and I can't concentrate DON'T THINK ABOUT THE BABY—

A hole opened in space. It was dark on the other side. Clearly audible through the gunshots and explosions came the lowing of frightened cows and the overpowering odor of manure and cow piss. Mollie suddenly wondered who had been taking care of the livestock while half the family was hospitalized. Son of a bitch, she hadn't even thought about helping—

Ray said, "That's not the Cosmodrome!"

"It's fine, sweetie, it's totally fine," said Michelle. "That's plenty good for now." She ducked around the corner to toss a few more bubbles, shouting, "Everybody in! Go!"

"You're not bleedin' serious, doll," said Bruckner, pinching his nose. "Stinks worse than a spearchucker's bunghole in there."

Ray grabbed him by the collar and physically tossed him through the portal to Idaho.

"Babel, your turn," Ray said.

There was a chatter of gunfire from near the gate, and pouts of dust erupted near the truck. She heard the whine of a bullet passing overhead and the *t-chink* of several hitting the metal of the railings. "I'd hurry if I were you," Ray added. Aiming high, he let out a one-handed burst from the rifle he'd taken from the guard while still holding on to Bruckner's arm.

Barbara shook her head. "I'm not going with you," she told him. "I have to stay here."

"What?" Ray sputtered. "Are you insane? After this?"

"I knew it would have to be this way from the start. Jayewardene will need a scapegoat. And if nothing else, all of this proved that I'm better dealing with your bureaucrats than in a firefight." *As Klaus knew.* Thinking of him made the fear knot her stomach again.

Ray shook his head. "You're insane. You could be stuck here in St. Gilles for years taking the blame for the rest of us."

Barbara managed to smile wanly at that. "Not altogether a bad outcome, assuming that the rest of you manage to save the world." She waved her hand at him, not moving. Ray, still shaking his head, pushed Bruckner ahead of him through the portal and went through himself. The portal shimmered, pulled once, then vanished. There was nothing but a concrete wall behind her.

She was alone in the prison. With a sigh, Barbara let the barriers drop in her mind and closed off the wild card power, feeling the usual exhaustion that followed. Forcing herself to stand erect, she lifted her hands in the air.

"I surrender," she called out to the nearest guards in French as they began to cautiously approach her, weapons at ready. "You must call Secretary-General Jayewardene of the UN for me. Bring me to the Secretary-General."

The Angel's heart was beating heavily in her chest as she flew through the streets of a devastated Talas, twenty feet or so above the ground. The surrounding destruction no longer made an impression on her. It was just

the way things were. Perhaps, once this danger was past, she would orga-
nize her people to clean things up a little, make them nice again. She had
no desire to rule from a ruin. She wanted a palace, bright and shining and
clean. She *deserved* a palace . . .

Certainly, it worried her but at the same time she felt her anger rising
as she considered the fact that the outside world was interfering in her
domain. They'd fled, abrogating all rights to this realm, and now they
were trying to destroy it? *They dare attempt to attack my domain?* the
Angel thought. *Fuck them.* She would teach them the meaning of destruction.

She flew on, ignoring the pain and weariness that the last few days had
brought. She tried to keep her mind focused on her task. She couldn't be
distracted by thoughts of her recent actions or by the vague notions that
troubled her mind about earlier days she'd spent in a world that was now
more dream than reality. She was the Madonna of the Blade, the Angel of
the Alleyways, She Who Must Be Obeyed and this was her world. No one
or no thing would take it from her.

She flew on toward the heart of the city where something was, vaguely
but persistently, calling to her. It was pleased with her, it wanted to reward her, and she wanted to give it the worship it so deserved.

Reality was crumbling all around her, but she was so eager to get to
the heart of the darkness that called to her that she didn't notice the
nature of the buildings or the streets or the things that inhabited them.

The call got stronger and more insistent in her mind and she knew
when she'd arrived at her goal.

A single building stood higher than the rest, but it seemed no longer to
be made of stone and steel, but rather flesh and blood like a giant, static
creature. Things crawled in and out of its windows and doorways, things
like the worms of the earth and even more alien places. The beings that
loitered around it were cone-headed creatures with bloodred tentacles in
place of faces, and sentient slugs with transparent flesh, and armor-plated
insects that crawled, hopped, and slithered on mysterious errands like no
earthly creature.

Most impressive, though, were its two guardians. One stood in bloodred
armor that shone so bright you could barely look upon him, fifteen feet
tall. His name, the Angel dredged from some far recess of her memory,
was Lohengrin. The other was even bigger, twice the knight's size, and was

an impossible conglomeration of garbage and worms and corpses, all of which flowed incessantly, never still but not alive, either.

They were marvels to behold and the Angel wanted to be one with them and the love that she felt wafting off them in palpable waves for their god who dwelt in the building behind them. Their dark, wonderful god who had promised her her heart's delight.

"What is my reward, my lord?" she begged aloud and she felt a sudden twisting in her body, a sudden racking pain in the middle of herself. She fell to her knees, her arms clenched around her stomach. A hand sought the knife, forgotten until now but still belted about her waist. She pulled it out and slashed, not deeply, at her abdomen, though her skin sliced and blood came. She pulled away the leather jumpsuit from about her stomach, panting.

Her eyes closed and she fell and rolled to her back. Her stomach burned as a weight pushed down on it. She screamed as a woman giving birth and a head pushed through the unbroken, smooth flesh of her stomach, followed by a chest, shoulder, arm, and hand. Another hand popped out with lesser pain lower and nearer her side, but no more than a tiny hand and a forearm appeared above her own flesh.

She stared down at the little face, screwed up and wailing, at the fair hair, and plump-lipped mouth. It was a baby, a boy, she somehow knew. It cried angrily, but then a red tongue slipped out from between its Cupid-like lips and licked at the Angel's blood that flowed from the shallow cut she'd given herself as she'd cut away the restraining jumpsuit. The lips worked eagerly. The tongue sought more blood.

A great love dawned over the Angel. Yes. This was something she'd always wanted. Something to love.

She rocked happily and cooed to her baby. She took her knife and cut her forearm and held it to her child's mouth. As it eagerly sucked at her blood she fervently thanked her lord for his gift while all around her beings howled and clashed, fought and coupled frenziedly through the black night under the green, grinning moon.

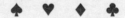

They were back in the command room in Baikonur. If Michelle never saw another propaganda poster, walls with grey-green peeling paint, or crummy fluorescent lights again, it would be too soon.

"We need to keep this simple," Billy Ray said. Michelle thought she could have led the mission, but she knew Billy Ray was the better choice. Also, he'd keep trying to take charge anyway, and it was easier to just give it to him.

"I agree," Michelle said with a nod. "No one extra along. No one to slow us down. Light and fast. Surgical."

Billy Ray smiled at her. She cocked her head at him and frowned. He never smiled at her. "So let's break it down," he said. He extended his index finger. "One, obviously, we need Bruckner. But we need a truck for him—or any kind of transport like that—but none with computers or anything that relies on electronics. We should be able to find something in this Soviet-era shithole."

He sneered at Bruckner. "Think you can handle finding the right kind of vehicle, toots?"

"If you think I'm going into that place, you're even more insane than that little slit," Bruckner replied.

Michelle knocked him off his chair with a hard, fast, softball-sized bubble. "Color me indifferent to what you want or don't want. You're taking us into Talas, and none of us care about your feelings about that." Another bubble formed in her hand, but Billy Ray grabbed her arm. She let it pop.

"You're getting a truck. You're going into Talas," Billy Ray snarled. "Or I'll let Hoodoo Mama have some fun with you.

"Now where was I? Secondly," he continued. "Obviously, Michelle and I are going. We're the strongest ones here. We should be able to protect Mollie, Bruckner, and Black."

"Why the fuck would you need Black?" Joey asked. There was a baffled expression on her face.

"He's the only one who's actually been in the hospital. He knows what Horrorshow looks like, and he can help guide us once we're inside."

"He's not going to go back in there," Joey interjected.

Billy Ray's mouth set into a grim line. "I don't really give a shit what that candy-ass does or doesn't want."

Michelle stared up at the ceiling. Someone had sprayed grey insulation in the rafters. *It's so bad in Talas,* she thought. *What if what we do doesn't make any difference? What if I can't make a difference. I'm the Amazing Bubbles. I'm supposed to make things different.* It felt like a lie. But since she'd killed Aero, her life was going to feel like a lie anyway. Whatever was left of it.

There had never been any question in Michelle's mind that she was going back into Talas. It was the only way to even have a chance of saving Adesina. Where things ended up afterward didn't really matter.

"I'm going, too," Hoodoo Mama said.

"No, you're not," Michelle said flatly. She stood up and went over to Joey, then took her by the shoulders. "You're just not strong enough."

Joey looked like she'd happily strangle Michelle. "There's nothing *but* fucking dead people in there! I'd have an army!" She smacked Michelle's arms away.

"And you'd go batshit crazy, and then we'd be dealing with an army of toe tags," Michelle replied tersely.

"Mollie could hold a pinpoint portal open for me like she did before. Then I could control a few meat sacks. Enough to help without losing it."

Oh, yeah, Michelle thought. *I can totally see this happening.* "Are you sure, sweetie?" she asked. Having some of Joey's zombies would be an advantage. Dead people didn't go crazy.

"That'd work!" Joey said. "It'd work like a fucking charm. That's how we got you out, Bubbles. God, you cocksucking bitch." She glared at Michelle. Michelle stared back with dismay.

She grabbed Joey's arm and pulled her to a corner of the room. "You don't get it," Michelle whispered intently. "I don't want you anywhere near this mission. Odds are we're all going to die. And then who will take care of Adesina?"

Suddenly, Joey reached up and put her good hand on Michelle's cheek. Michelle almost jerked back. This wasn't like Joey at all.

"I know why you don't want me to go," Joey said, softly stroking Michelle's cheek. "I know. But if this is the last fucking stand, then I want it to be here with you. And if we don't come through, it won't matter because everyone will be dead anyway."

A horrible lump formed in Michelle's throat. Joey was right. If they didn't succeed, her daughter was dead.

They walked back to the others. Bruckner's mouth was pulled into a grim line. Billy Ray's expression was unreadable, and Michelle suspected that was because he was already in command mode.

"Okay," Billy Ray said. "It's go time. We get Bruckner his truck, get

Franny back here, and then we go. No screwing around. We need to be moving as soon as possible."

For one long moment, they all just stood there looking at each other. Even Bruckner managed to shut the fuck up.

Then Billy Ray said, "Michelle, go get Mollie, get us Black. Bruckner, get a truck. And Hoodoo Mama," Billy Ray turned toward Joey. "Go get some good corpses."

The trailer floor creaked under a light footstep. Mollie cracked one eye open.

Michelle stood in the doorway, mostly back to her supermodel figure. "Oh. I expected you to be napping."

"Yeah, well. I'm not so good at it these days. When I close my eyes I see, uh, things . . ."

Michelle nodded. "Uh-huh. I have the nightmares, too."

"I'd give anything to never again see the things I've seen. And I'd give more if it meant I could undo all the fucking awful things I've done."

"Oh, sweetie."

Michelle sat on the cot and draped an arm over Mollie's shoulders. Mollie tensed. Michelle and Joey were close.

Mollie whispered, "You know about what I did to Joey, right?"

"Yeah."

"I'm so sorry about that."

"It wasn't your fault."

Mollie remembered the sensation of eyebrow bristles stuck between her teeth. She suppressed a gag reflex and said, "Of course it was."

Her breath came in little gasping sobs. Michelle hugged her until it no longer felt like she was going to hyperventilate. Mollie rested her head on the other woman's shoulder, wincing when her bandage tugged at the stitches on her cheek.

"Let me guess. You came to find me because you guys just realized your plan won't work without Franny. You need him to get into the hospital."

A look of surprise flashed across the other woman's face, but the corners of her mouth twitched up in a faint smile. "Yeah, actually."

It was confirmation and a question. Mollie shrugged.

"This ace I can barely control anymore? There's a little part in the back of my mind—or there used to be, back when I wasn't three-quarters batshit—constantly thinking about stuff like this. How to get from *A* to *B*, do I know where *B* is, on and on and on."

"It's second nature to you. Not to the rest of us."

"Hmm."

Michelle rubbed her hands together. "We'll probably find him at the precinct house. They'll know where to find him if he's not there. I think you're familiar with the place, yes?" Sometimes Michelle had so much tact it practically dripped out of her ass. But Mollie appreciated how she made no issue of dumping Jamal Norwood's body, and a handful of mafia thugs, into the center of Fort Freak. "We should go get him now."

Mollie stood. The aluminum poles in the cot frame were digging into her shins. "No offense, but I think it's gotta be me and Ray in New York while you keep an eye on Bruckner. I give him shit for flashing that badge around like he gets off on it, but let's be honest. The director of SCARE is probably the only thing that'll stop them from arresting me the second I set foot in Fort Freak." Mollie looked away, her face turning hot as she remembered all the shit Berman made her do for Baba Yaga. Every terrified joker they snatched. She didn't want Michelle to glimpse the full brunt of her shame. Lamely, she concluded, "I'm not real popular with the NYPD right now."

"No," said Michelle. "I suppose you wouldn't be."

Franny had pulled the graveyard shift. Franny was at his desk trying to clear the files and waiting to see if he'd catch a murder call. He was also obsessing over Baba Yaga's certainty she would escape justice.

He grabbed his cup and headed for the coffeemaker when a hole appeared in the center of the bullpen. Through the opening Franny saw daylight, dust, jeeps, trucks, troops, and jokers—in short a scene of frenzied activity.

It was a testament to the unflappable nature of Fort Freak cops that nobody freaked. Or maybe they were just getting used to Mollie opening doorways into the station. The girl wasn't alone when she walked through. Billy Ray was with her.

He wasn't dressed in impeccable Armani. Instead he wore his fighting whites and ceramic insert body armor. There was a pistol at his belt and an assault rifle slung on his back. His expression was grim and determined. Mollie was white-faced and her eyes shadowed and bloodshot. Her hair looked like it'd been combed with a hand mixer. Frank soon saw why. Her fingers writhed through her hair, twisting strands of hair into virtual knots.

"Let me guess. I'm coming with you whether I want to or not," Franny said.

"You gotta come. You've gotta. You gotta make it stop. FUCK OFF!" This was directed at Rikki, who was just walking past.

Rikki started to snap back, but Franny held up a restraining hand. The joker cop moved on after bestowing a glare on Mollie. Mollie drew even closer to Franny. He had to resist the urge to back away. There was so much crazy packed into that small body.

"You can make everything better. I'm trying but I keep making . . . mistakes."

She yanked hard and a clump of hair came away with her flailing hand. Franny winced. Now that she was so close he could see bare patches dotting her head where other tufts of hair had been pulled out. Blood caked a few of them.

Ray took Mollie by the shoulders and tried to move her aside. She bared her teeth and snapped at his hand. "Don't touch me, cocksucker!"

"Easy, Mollie," Franny said gently.

"Like Mollie said, we really need you." Then to Franny's surprise Ray added, "But I'm not going to force you. I'm asking for your help." All around Franny the room had gone silent, everyone listening intently.

"We're going in. We'll do our best to find this hospital, but time is running out." Ray suddenly looked old, old and devastated. "Believe me, I don't want to do this. My wife is on her way here . . . well, there . . . Baikonur . . . leading an army of monsters. I want to stay and try to pull her back from the madness. Save her. But I know that would only be a temporary fix. If I'm really going to save her I have to go to Talas."

Isn't there somebody you love? Somebody you'd risk everything to save? The words were unspoken but implicit. Franny thought about his mother and Abby and his friends and companions at the precinct. He thought about the father he'd never known. A police officer like himself and a man who had died trying to protect New York from madness and destruction.

Franny glanced back at Michael. "Tell the captain not to fire me until I get back."

"I don't know what he's saying? What is he saying? What does he mean?" Mollie implored Ray. Her hands were back in her hair, clawing at her scalp.

"Wait," Franny said to Ray, whose look of hope died at that single word. Franny ran over to the cabinet where the precinct kept a supply of sedatives. They were there to help the cops deal with any particularly violent or dangerous aces' powers.

"Mollie, this may help you deal with . . . things."

"You're not going to hurt me?"

"No, you've been hurt enough," he said.

As they walked through the Tesseract opening Franny said to Ray, "Sure hope you've got some extra body armor available."

Like worms the whispers crawled about the underside of the Angel's skull and insinuated themselves into her brain and she slowly began to understand their meaning. She understood it and was awed. This building in Talas was too small to house the form of her dark lord, as was Talas itself, and even the garbage dump called Kazakhstan. All the world was too small for him, but it would serve as a staging place for his dark majesty to enwrap the solar system, the galaxy, and eventually the entire universe. And she, the Angel, would carry his banner forth and forever glory in his dark realm.

The time for words was over. Words signified nothing. They were ripples on the air without meaning or substance. Only the worship of the dark lord and the devastation wrought in his worship had meaning and she would be the one to lead the vanguard of his unstoppable army.

She stood. Her child gurgled, pawed at her angrily. She knew it was hungry, so she fed it again with blood drawn from her forearm. As she walked down the streets of Talas, the fighting and the killing stopped behind her, and all creatures, great and small, fell into line behind her, she, the tip of the unbreakable spear of her lord's will.

Follow the light, it spoke silently in her brain, and she did. The shining knight in the bloodred armor did her obeisance as did the Trash Man who guarded the resting place of the lord. Those bound in place, remaining behind as a lesser guard, cried salt tears if they were capable, rent their flesh with their own talons, claws, or teeth, if they were not, weeping and wailing inconsolably to be left behind, but the Angel neither cared nor noticed.

She took half a dozen running steps, following the light, and took to the sky. The others followed as best they could behind her. She had no idea how long it was she flew or how far. The light came closer and closer, brighter and brighter, and for a moment she felt as if she were eaten up, bit by bit, but she had faith in her dark lord, and bit by bit she was put together again and she realized that she was in a different place where by sword and fire she would bring the blessings of her lord. It was, the sudden revelation out of the past she once lived in came to her, Sunday.

Franny held a syringe.

Mollie asked, "So you're just planning to funnel that shit into my veins?"

"It won't put you under. It'll help you stay calm. It'll take the worst edges off the anxiety."

"Listen, Boy Scout. Nothing short of a full goddamned frontal-lobe lobotomy is going to make me sanguine about returning to Talas: *Noth. Ing.*"

"None of us are keen on it," said Michelle.

"Keen? You're not keen on it? Well, I'd say you're doing pretty well, because me, I'm fucking terrified. I'm about one halfhearted 'boo' away from peeing myself."

Franny pointed at the syringe case. "These should help with the wanting to pee yourself."

"I don't care how mild it is. I'm going to be doped to the gills if you pump all of that into me."

He shook his head. "I thought it might be a good idea if we all take a dose before we depart." He zipped the case. "We'll have spare doses, too. For, well, the rest of it."

Michelle looked directly at Mollie. The eye contact actually made her feel a little better. It was as if Michelle was looking to her for confirmation, or as though in this particular thing she saw Mollie as a peer. And perhaps they were because Mollie knew exactly what she was thinking.

"I dunno," said Michelle. "My experience in the, what did you call it again, sweetie?"

"The Psycho Cannibal Flashmob Evil Insanity Zone."

"Yes. My experience inside the PCFEIZ makes me doubtful that anything could ward off the madness." She shrugged. "But what the hell. I'll give it a shot. Even if it only helps a little, or for just a few minutes . . ."

Baikonur was like a stirred anthill. Jokers, nats, soldiers, aces, and *zombies,* fucking zombies, were moving in every direction. Franny hoped there was some order to their peripatetic movements and they didn't signify just random panic. The day was hot and dry and off in the distance a large cloud of dust was rising marking the approach of the monster army. Ray stood gazing toward a distant flying figure. Franny turned away, not wishing to impose even by a look on the man's naked grief, worry, and longing.

While he was being supplied with weapons and body armor Franny had learned that IBT had made it to Baikonur. That was one small piece of guilt removed from his conscience. Even though Baba Yaga's information had been critical it had still eaten at Franny that he had abandoned the kid. Fortunately IBT was part of the effort to defend the Cosmodrome so Franny wasn't likely to run into him until this was all over . . . one way or the other. If they failed it wouldn't matter. And if they succeeded . . . well, Franny could only hope an apology would keep IBT from laying that poisoned tongue on him.

Bubbles was in a huddle with the angry-faced young black woman who had glared at him when they were introduced, turned her back, and snapped at Bubbles, *"So, bitch, you're taking this motherfucking pasty white boy and not me?"*

"Yeah, because he fuckin' knows where this hospital might be and what this cocksucker looks like," Bubbles had shot back. Bubbles had then shaken his hand and introduced herself. Despite the seriousness of the situation Franny couldn't help but be thrilled that he had now met three of the most kickass ladies of *American Hero.*

Right now Bubbles and Joey were flanked by three walking corpses. Apparently Joey's "zombies" would accompany them to Talas. Franny was not happy about that even though the skinny young ace Bugsy had said cheerfully that "at least they were fresh." Somehow it seemed disrespectful if not down right blasphemous to Franny.

Franny spotted Mollie standing next to the battered and clearly vintage military truck. It had a canvas cover over the truck bed, four doors, handholds on the front hood and sides, and running boards. It had once been desert camouflage. Now it just looked leprous. Bruckner, the heavyset older Brit who apparently had the power to drive through other dimensions, was circling the vehicle and literally kicking the tires.

Mollie was standing stock-still, hands clenched at her sides. It had been only a little over a week since he'd been handcuffed to the girl, but the ensuing days had taken their toll. On all of them, Franny thought as he touched his side. He walked over to her.

"Hey," he said softly as he laid a hand on her shoulder. She shied violently away, then seemed to focus and actually see him. "Easy, easy, You need another hit?"

"No. Yeah. Maybe. I don't know." The green eyes were raised to his. "We're never coming out. One-way trip," she whispered and she no longer seemed to be talking to him. She didn't even notice when he injected the other half of the first syringe.

"Okay, let's saddle up," Ray called as he turned his back on the approaching army and his wife and walked to the truck.

The zombies did a decent job shoring up the hangar. It wasn't pretty—and the villagers watched the undead with alarm more than gratitude—but they made up for craft with the pure bulk of beams set in place, crates stacked and abandoned bits of hardware and containers shoved up against the crumbling walls. By the time Joey called them off the hangar was half hidden within a mound of debris.

As the jokers filed back in, Marcus parted with Olena. When they hugged she gripped him hard, but only briefly. Her lips brushed over his so quickly it barely counted as a kiss. Then she disappeared into the hangar.

It didn't seem enough. There was so much more to say and so much he wanted to ask. She still hadn't said a word about the fact that she killed her father, or that she seemed to have some variation on his power stuck right in the flesh of her palm. He might never see her again. Considering that, shouldn't he tell her everything he might ever want to? It seemed like he should, but that was the problem. There was too much to say and ask and wonder, to promise and hope and swear to. Too much, and no time to do any of it.

As a final measure the zombies shoved an old shipping container in front of the door, sealing them in. Marcus would rejoin them if he could, but first he wanted to see what the Committee had planned. He snaked his way back into the chaos with Joey and her zombie soldiers. Near the Committee's warehouse, Joey stopped walking. Standing still as her undead army marched into the area they were going to defend, she pinched the lower end of Marcus's T-shirt and tugged it playfully. "You're a good man, Marcus. You know that, right? The things you been doing for them jokers . . . Shit, I'll be direct. It puts me in the right kinda mood. We make it out of this, you and I should spend some time together. You ever been to the bayou?"

"No."

"You'd feel at home. You'd feel like you never knew what home was. All this length on you . . ." She smiled and trailed her hand over his scales. They lingered just above his conveniently hidden groin. Her fingertips drew slow circles there. Marcus was beginning to see what she was getting at.

She was about to say something else, but the pronounced sound of a throat clearing interrupted her. A voice said, "I hate to interrupt this moment of intimacy, but, Joey, they need you in the Committee briefing room." It was the Lama. Or, not exactly the Lama, but a hazy, incorporeal version of him. He stood right beside them, looking grumpy and put upon.

"Tell them we're coming," Joey said.

The Lama looked down as if to inspect his translucent fingernails. "I'll tell them *you're* on your way. The snake-boy is not invited." The image of him faded.

"How can you tell he's really gone?" Marcus asked.

Joey shrugged. "Fuck if I care. Look, I gotta go deal with this shit. Stick around. Someone will fill you in. We're not all assholes. And think about what I said. Most likely, we're all gonna die horribly in an hour or so, but if we don't . . . I wanna fuck you cross-eyed. And I'm not hating on that little Russian girl of yours."

"Ukrainian," Marcus corrected. It was lame, but it was easier to respond to than the *fuck you cross-eyed* part. "Or . . . half and half."

Smiling, she backed away. "Whatever. Bring her. If we can open up her mind a bit maybe we'd all get along. All three of us. We live through today . . . it's a new world. Who knows what could happen?"

She turned and walked away. Despite the clean thoughts he knew he should be summoning, Marcus watched her for as long as he could, wondering, *Would Olena ever . . .*

They were rolling across the plains of Kazakhstan. The three dead people were clinging to handholds on the hood of the truck while a small opening floated in the air over their heads. Through it Franny could see a portion of Joey's bandaged face. Franny was in the passenger seat clutching a shotgun. Standing on the running board on his side was Michelle. She was at full fighting weight, and she was holding a kinetic bubble in her free hand. Ray stood on the driver's side running board holding a sawed-off shotgun. Mollie was in the backseat muttering to herself. When Franny used the rearview mirror to check on her he saw sweat running down her face and she was shaking. She had her eyes fixed on that floating portal.

Just some aces and zombies and one fucked nat off for a pleasant Sunday drive, Franny thought.

He wondered how long this trip was going to take. Several hundred kilometers separated Baikonur from Talas. Supposedly Bruckner could get them there fast. So far the fast part hadn't materialized. The old Soviet truck was rattling and groaning, slowly gathering speed, but it was no Tesla. Bruckner seemed to be on Franny's wavelength.

"Piece of shit, Russian crap," he muttered. His cockney accent was very evident.

They rolled on. Bruckner gave a small jink of the steering wheel and trees appeared on the horizon where there had been no trees before. Raindrops pattered against the windshield. It had been a cloudless day at Baikonur. Another subtle turn of the wheel and they were driving on red pavement rather than dirt and it was night. Five misshapen moons hung in the sky. A tall plant covered in spines loomed up on their left. Franny swallowed hard and sucked in a deep breath.

Bubbles noticed. "You okay?" she asked over the rumble of the engine.

He thought about blowing her off. Doing the guy thing. *"Nah, I'm fine. Piece of cake."* Instead he told her the truth.

"Scared." He gave her a wry smile.

"I don't blame you." The reply surprised him. "I don't want to go back. I barely got out of there. But I've got a little girl and . . . Look, if it's any help I'm going to do everything I can to keep you safe. We need you if we're going to have any hope of pulling this off."

"I'm afraid I won't be able to hold it together," Franny admitted. "I was there at the very beginning, and it was almost overwhelming then. I saw parts of myself . . . well, let's just say I really wish I didn't know they were there."

"From what Ray told me you were right in the room with this thing. I can tell you from experience that the effects lessen the farther away you get. And it doesn't hit all at once. It comes over you slow. We're just going to have to go like hell, get to the hospital, grab the guy, and get the fuck out before we're overcome."

Talking with Bubbles had taken his mind off the journey. He looked through the front window and realized they were in a city of squat, rounded buildings and signs in a script he didn't recognize. Something large flapped past overhead, the beat of the fleshy wings bringing a stench like rotting flesh into the truck.

Mollie whimpered. "Shit," Franny said.

The Zil's shocks were shot. Michelle could hear Bruckner muttering under his breath about what a shitcan it was. She saw the others wince as the truck hit potholes. She didn't feel the pain of the jolts, but she knew that as soon as they got into Talas, she would.

Bruckner was cursing about not being able to get the truck up to speed. As long as he wasn't calling her a dyke, Mollie a slit, or Billy Ray a faggot, she could ignore his bitching. She tried to stay calm. Someone had to be steady with Franny and Mollie looking like they were both going to freak long before Bruckner even got them into the hospital.

Three of Joey's corpses sat in the back of the truck. Occasionally, one would smile at her. She knew it was Joey smiling, but it was still pretty disgusting.

"You could give me a smile back, Bubbles." There was nothing like the sound of your girlfriend's voice coming through a toe tag to make you feel loved. *How much whistling past the graveyard can you do?* she wondered. *As much as it takes, apparently.*

She saw the land around her begin to change. It wasn't a quick slam like the portals Mollie made. It was just a few things here and there.

The terrain began to undulate, then turned more mountainous. Then it changed back to a steppe, but now there was a luscious carpet of grasses covering it. But instead of being verdant, the grass was a deep blue-violet. The sky took on a strange greenish color, as if a tornado was about to touch down. Then the world shifted again. It was disconcerting, and had she not been in Talas before, Michelle might have found it overwhelming. But now it was just an interesting ride.

The world continued to shift and change. Then, abruptly, they were in Talas again.

"I'm sorry, Mr. Secretary-General," Barbara said, not knowing whether any of this was being recorded or not. Her voice echoed in the interview room within St. Gilles prison. She lifted her cuffed hands and let them drop again. The sound of them on the metal surface of the table at which she sat was terribly loud and final. "Everything that was done was at my orders, no one else's. We had to release the Highwayman before President Putin's deadline; this seemed to be the only way. I take total and full responsibility for what happened here."

"Ms. Baden," Jayewardene said softly, with a hint of a smile on his thin lips, "I've made very sure that there's no one recording this. But I thank you for your . . . candor."

Barbara gave a brief smile at that, but she also let her wild card pulse out to cover the two of them, just in case Jayewardene were wrong: any recording device now would record only nonsense syllables from the two of them, while she and Jayewardene understood each other perfectly. "Have you heard from Director Ray? Are they . . . ?"

"Yes," Jayewardene answered. "A truck was stolen from Baikonur Cosmodrome. The guards there say they saw it vanish."

Barbara nodded, but Jayewardene continued speaking. "There have been other developments as well while you've been here, Ms. Baden. Kyrgyzstan sent in six attack helicopters to bomb Talas."

Barbara sucked in a breath. "No. Did they take out the hospital? Is Tolenka dead?"

Jayewardene's brown face remained impassive. "They did not. Their copters were taken out of the air by a winged woman and a flight of horrors."

"The Midnight Angel."

Jayewardene nodded. "Yes. The same woman who is at this moment leading a horde of monsters toward the Baikonur and the Cosmodrome. President Putin has informed President van Rennsaeler and myself that he intends to wipe out Talas with a nuclear strike before the Cosmodrome is overrun."

"Then get me out of here," Barbara said. "We need to meet with Putin, talk to him."

"You won't convince him."

"I don't have to," Barbara told him. "I just have to make it impossible for him to give the order. *That*, I can do—at least, hopefully long enough for Ray and Michelle to succeed or fail. All I have to do is stop them for a few hours. Hopefully that should be enough. What's a few hours, Mr. Secretary-General? If three hours from now this isn't over, then let Putin drop the nuke, for all the good it will do. Three hours, Mr. Secretary-General. Give my people three hours, then you may do whatever you want with me."

Jayewardene stared at her. Looking at the flat expression on his face, she thought she'd lost. *I'm sorry, Klaus. I tried. I did all I could and I'm sorry it wasn't enough. I'm sorry that I never got to talk to you and tell you everything . . .*

Jayewardene stood up and went to the door of the room. He knocked, and a guard opened the door, with another standing behind him with a hand on the butt of a holstered sidearm. "Tell the warden that I will be taking the prisoner with me," he said. The guard nodded and closed the door again.

"I will handle President Putin and get him to honor the window he gave you, Ms. Baden," Jayewardene said. "You'll get your hours—as long as Putin believes that the Cosmodrome is being adequately defended. That's *your* task and your burden."

Michelle looked at the hellscape before her and despaired. Bruckner's truck had gotten stuck again, and now she, Billy Ray, and Joey's zombies were going to have to push through that sea of perverted flesh and writhing, unspeakable horrors to get Franny to the hospital and Horrorshow.

Why did I think we could do this? In what universe could you stop this madness? The anger began to boil in her. *Shit.*

They had to move, because otherwise they'd be too crazy to do anything but kill each other. Or themselves.

Michelle opened her arms, and a stream of bubbles flowed from her hands onto the uneven road. The bubbles drove a path through the ichors, tentacled monstrosities, and spiders. Blood and viscera sprayed into the air. It wasn't a perfectly clean path, but she thought the truck could get through now.

"Let's go," she said.

Sweat was making it hard to hold the shotgun. Franny switched it from hand to hand, and wiped away the wetness on his pants' leg. Not that he'd had to use it yet. Talas was a city of the dead filled only with fog and that incessant drone like a dentist's drill to the brain.

"It's like my shortcuts have invaded our world, and brought bloody hell with them," Bruckner muttered.

Brought hell. Brought hell. Brought hell. The older man's words repeated over and over in Franny's head. The tone and timbre changed. It was Sister Theresa Anthony from Holy Ghost Elementary School telling the second graders about hell. Her voice was very loud, ringing in his ears. *Your fingers will burn away, and your eyes will melt, your skin will turn black and peel from your body. There will be no water or Kool-Aid. Nothing to drink to ease your agony* . . . Franny looked to his left. She was sitting on the divider between him and Buckner, but there was no face inside the folds of her wimple, just shadows.

Behind him one of those damned souls was whimpering. Franny started to turn around, drive the butt of the shotgun into the face of the tortured soul. Ray's voice jerked him back.

"Black!" Ray's voice sharp and commanding. "Where now?"

Sister Theresa Anthony was gone, and Franny remembered the whimpering was Mollie's. Franny tried to pretend it hadn't started. That he wasn't already losing control, going mad. A new sound overlaid the droning. Singing. High-pitched and unearthly. A group of children, perhaps fifty of them with elongated heads and massive mouths, walked past the truck. They were in a perfect diamond formation, a choir of monstrous angels singing the praises of a diseased god.

There was a tall structure ahead of them. Once it might have been a multistory office building. Now it was a tower of bleeding flesh. In places the glistening red viscera pulsed as if great hearts were beating beneath the oozing tissue.

"I . . . I'm not sure." The road opened up into a plaza. Fog drifted past, and briefly lifted to reveal other roads branching off the plaza. Giant dykes of dirt, asphalt, and cobbles blocked three of the roads.

"Earth Witch was here," Bubbles said.

A burning wind that carried the stink of smoke, cordite, and rot ripped the fog into tatters. An equestrian statue appeared. "I remember that," Franny cried. "Go left."

The Highwayman spun the wheel. He had begun to drone an unceasing litany of curse words.

"Stop it! Stop it! Stop it! Fucking shut up!" Mollie screamed, and she punched Bruckner in the back of the head.

The truck slewed wildly from side to side. Franny grabbed the steering wheel. Bruckner was digging out his pistol. Franny released the wheel, and wrestled the gun away before Bruckner could bring it to bear on Mollie. In the few seconds it had taken him to disarm the driver the truck had jumped a curb and plowed into a building. Ray yelled, zombies fell from the hood like overripe fruit, and Michelle lost her grip on the truck, and tumbled to the ground.

Franny heard her murmur "Adesina," as she started walking away. Bruckner's nose was bleeding from where his face had hit the steering wheel and he was weeping, tears mingling with blood and snot.

Franny shoved open the door and ran after Michelle. The ground felt strange as if he were running in taffy. "Michelle, Bubbles, wait! You promised. You have to keep us safe."

Ray had joined him. "Michelle, the kid's right, we can't do this without you." She stretched out her arms toward nothing but fog, and gave a cry of joy. "Shit we're starting to lose it." Ray mumbled and checked his watch. Franny followed his gaze, but the hands of the watch were spinning, changing into spiders and running across the numbers that were melting.

"Not much time. Not much time," Franny whispered. He groped in his pocket for his father's rosary, felt the carved beads and the arms of the crucifix cut into the palm of his hand.

The pain gave him a moment of clarity. He looked around, tried to reconcile the strange and twisted surroundings to what he had seen only a few short days before. He'd always had a good memory, and his years on the force had made him even better at observation. He had a sudden overlaid image of what the area looked like and realized they were only a short distance from the hospital.

"I remember. I know. I know where we have to go." He tugged on Michelle's arm, but couldn't budge her.

"Baby, Mama's here," she crooned. A figure shambled out of the fog and tried to accept Bubbles's offered embrace.

Franny gave a cry of disgust and stumbled back. Sucking mouths covered the entire head. There were more mouths on the palms of the thing's hands. Suddenly the zombies were there, interposing themselves between Michelle and the monster. They moved stiffly, but with surprising strength. They pushed the thing away, then two of them picked up bricks and battered it into a bleeding pulp while the third held it still. The arrival of the zombies broke the illusion. Michelle gave a shudder, and murmured, "Thanks, babe."

They returned to the truck. Ray clapped Bruckner. "Kid says he knows the way. Let's go."

Franny climbed back into the cab, and the two aces took up their positions on the running boards.

Mollie concentrated on maintaining a pinhole connection to the Cosmodrome for Joey while Bruckner rolled the truck to a halt. The idling engine chugged along, puffing diesel-scented exhaust into the same Bosch/Escher/Giger three-way acid trip Mollie had glimpsed when Joey was searching for A-team survivors. The landscape around the casino had become a forest of bone trees, the pustule-stippled boughs hanging low with pulsing organ fruit. A trio of twenty-foot millipedes reared like cobras before the truck, mandibles opening wide to reveal shrieking mouths bursting with dozens of shiny black spider eyes. A bubble came winging from where Michelle huddled in the canopy. It cratered the road—for lack of a better term, because the ground under the truck looked and smelled and jiggled like something hacked up by a lifelong five-pack-per-day chain-smoker—and sent little gobbets of singed nightmarepedes raining on the truck. They sizzled on the windshield glass. The other two monsters undulated away, leaving a trail of fizzing slime as they skittered on legs that looked like prehensile tongues.

Franny hastily rolled down his window, leaned out, and vomited. His puke was just about the best thing Mollie could hope to smell here. The zombies were a close second.

Ray clung to the running board flanking Bruckner's window. He squinted, trying to peer into the fog. He had to speak loudly to be heard over the diesel engine and background noise of screams, gurgling, and mindless gibbering that ever pierced the fog.

"Is this the casino? I can't see anything."

The darkness, shadows, and the creepy fog that disregarded the wind obscured everything more than forty or fifty yards from the truck. Baba Yaga's casino, if this was the casino, was a vaguely non-Euclidean silhouette glimpsed fleetingly through the shifting miasma. It took a heroic effort of imagination to see the shambling misshapen massifs and pulsing valleys as buildings and streets.

Mollie struggled to reconcile the landscape with her scant knowledge of the area around the casino. But that came mostly from glancing out the window from Baba Yaga's personal apartments (—OH SHIT OH SHIT DON'T THINK ABOUT THE BABY DON'T THINK ABOUT IT DON'T THINK ABOUT A WROUGHT-IRON FENCE AND MADMEN FEASTING SHIT SHIT FUCK—) to see the source of the wild commotion . . .

They had to work fast. Faster than fast. Despite the injection, Mollie felt panicky, desperate, rushed. The madness would take her any moment.

Mollie pointed. "There! That's where the entrance should be. We're on the north side of the casino, facing west."

"As if the bleedin' compass rose has any meaning here," muttered Bruckner.

Franny wiped a sleeve across his mouth. "The hospital—" He paused to make a strangled urking sound, but forced it back. "Should be to our east. Behind us."

Bruckner put the truck in gear, cranked the wheel. The nightmare landscape pirouetted around them. The truck lurched on the squishy ground. Mollie gripped the windshield, thinking for a moment the whole thing was going to topple over. Michelle yelped; the zombies shambled to keep their balance. The truck lurched again, harder, and then the engine squealed.

Bruckner slammed his fist on the steering wheel. The short toot of the horn sounded incongruously mundane in the surreal hellscape. "Bugger! We're stuck. Everyone get out and push. That includes the monster mash back there."

"If you think I'm setting foot out there," said Mollie, feeling the soft edges of her drug injection crumbling away, "you're crazier than I am."

Franny said, "Mollie. The sooner we get moving again the sooner we can get the hell out of here." His voice fairly vibrated with strain; she knew it was from the effort to keep from screaming.

"Fine."

She followed him out of the cab. Her shoes squelched when they hit the ground. She slipped. And then she saw why the truck was spinning its wheels: thousands of hairy, hissing, blood-colored millipede things were boiling out of the ground under the truck. They surged across the ground and over her legs like a blanket. Mollie screamed.

From somewhere nearby came the chittery shrieking of full-grown nightmarepedes.

"We can't get you to Baikonur," Jayewardene had told Barbara. "There's no time, and travel would be too dangerous at this point, in any case. You'll have to coordinate strategy from my office in Brussels . . ."

Once more, Barbara was sitting before an array of flat screens, this time in a conference room in Jayewardene's UN offices in Brussels, and this time there were no individual faces looking back at her, only a series of views from security cameras around the Cosmodrome. Keyboards linked to each screen gave Barbara control over the cameras feeding the views, allowing her to swivel or zoom in. There was Gagarin's Soyuz rocket on one screen, upright at the entrance to the complex near the Kazakh highway and the railroad station, and beyond it the rest of the Y-shaped complex spreading out into the distance over flat, tan earth, concrete buildings clustering like grey mushrooms here and there, and launch towers rising from the landscape like metal trees. Another showed Launch Complex 81, another the refugee encampments, and yet another the Area 95 buildings, and on and on as the other screens gave her the outside scenery around the Cosmodrome.

And the last screen, from a security camera at Krainy Airport looking east to the Kazakh highway: it was there that a dark fog bank lurked, and from under the green-black wings of the fog emerged what looked like an insect swarm of writhing creatures from a Boschian nightmare slithered and humped and wriggled forward toward the complex and the cameras, spilling over the highway on either side like a dark flood, an onrushing wave of deformed humankind. Babel was glad for the lack of audio on the screens; she could imagine the sound from the thousands of throats screaming as they rushed forward.

She wondered, terrified, if among the horde might be Klaus, but she saw no gleam of ghost steel and armor in the masses.

In her ears, from a set of headphones attached to an array of toggle switches, she could hear voices in several languages: Capitaine Lefévre, directing the NATO forces that had arrived the day before; Colonel Kutnesov, the Russian officer in charge of the troops stationed there; the feeds from Earth Witch, Bugsy, Glassteel, Wilma Mankiller, Toad Man, Tinker, the Lama, and Snow Blind, who were arrayed near Area 51, where the nukes were stored and where the joker refugees were encamped. "Artillery, commence firing!" she heard Kutnesov say over his command channel, and a moment later, Lefévre gave the same order to the NATO forces.

A few moments later, the screens overloaded with bursts of light as explosives tore into the ranks of the creatures, ripping into their disordered ranks. Babel was glad for the distance. She could see dark shapes hurled into the air from the force of the mortars and rockets, but the shapes were indistinct and blurred—like toy soldiers thrown about by the hands of children.

Not people. Not torn, severed limbs and gouts of blood. Not Klaus.

The flashes continued, but the mass of hell-creatures continued to advance, running now, and more emerged from the fog behind them. "Advance!" Kutnesov called to the troops stationed near the entrance, and from the bottom of the screen, Barbara saw a phalanx of tanks rumbling toward the invaders, and behind them, soldiers firing automatic weapons.

And above the hell-creatures, emerging from the fog, was a small figure in flight: a winged woman, with a sword of flame.

Bruckner gunned the engine, which sent more nightmarepedes sidewinding into the shadows. A pair of hulking shapes loomed out of the fog.

"There," said Franny. "That looks familiar. Follow this between those buildings."

Smaller figures coalesced from the fog, too. They stood to the sides as the truck blurred past them, alien limbs extended like hitchhikers thumbing a ride. Hitchhikers sculpted entirely from pulsating brain tissue, their arms replaced with gigantic dragonfly abdomens, each eyeless face nothing but a gaping maw filled with needle teeth long enough to curl back and pierce the head like a crown of thorns. One hurled itself at the truck.

Ray ripped it from the canopy, hurled it into the shadows. "I don't like it here," he said.

They neared the buildings Franny had pointed to. The fog parted. Mollie swore. They weren't buildings any longer. They were mountainous piles of suppurating flesh. Pus cascaded down folds of quivering blubber from open wounds that used to be windows. Dark, hairy, segmented bristles like tarantula legs stippled the festering meat.

"I really don't like it here," said Michelle.

The mountain of rot on their right started to jiggle as Bruckner drove them closer. Suddenly it lurched back as if leaning to release a pent-up fart and unfurled a curtain of hook-tipped tentacles. They shot toward the truck, clacking and slavering. Franny and Mollie screamed in unison.

Fuck this, thought Mollie. *I'm out of here.*

She dropped the connection to the Cosmodrome and pictured a space-time rift in the dashboard, just big enough for her to leap through and land on the soft warm sand of a beach outside Perth. Instead a hole opened in the space between the truck and the tendrils, then blinked shut the instant she recognized she'd gotten it wrong yet again.

The quivering mound of ex-building emitted a chorus of screams from a dozen hidden mouths as it yanked back the stumps of its tentacles. The severed appendages sprayed electric-blue ichor over the truck. Ray emitted an unintelligible sound something between a squeal and a groan. Bruckner flicked the lever for the windshield wipers and gunned the engine. They blurred past the whimpering massif of putrefying meat.

Oh, shit. I'm too fucked up to make a shortcut back home. I'm stuck here.

Bruckner glanced sideways at Mollie. Gave her an appreciative nod. As if she'd meant to protect the truck all along, and hadn't been trying to abandon them.

She didn't look at Franny. Instead she scrambled to reestablish the pinhole portal to Joey at the Cosmodrome before the toe tags became useless.

They had gotten away from the millepede things, and the octopus building after Mollie had chopped off its tentacles. Now the tires were bumping and the truck swaying as they drove over obstacles. Franny managed to discern that the speed bumps were in fact bodies. Lots of them. Some seemed normal. Others were figures out of a Hieronymus Bosch painting. Blank faces devoid of any features, legs fused into a single fleshy pillar, multiple arms lining a torso.

"Not all that different from Rwanda," Bruckner grunted with forced bravado.

"Yeah, bullshit," was Ray's response.

"I *hate* macho bullshit," was Bubbles's response.

Mollie was whimpering. The small portal floating over the hood of the truck contracted, fluxed, and twisted. Franny reached back and grabbed her shoulder. "Don't look." He'd hoped to make it a firm order. Instead his voice wavered and broke. He coughed, trying to clear the obstruction in a throat made raw from vomiting, but fear was not so easily banished.

"Okay, Tonto, which way?" Bruckner grunted.

Fuck if I know, Franny thought, but instead he just gestured vaguely in front of them. "Just drive until I see something familiar."

"Jesus Christ," Bruckner said with an edge of hysteria in his voice. Under his arms, large sweat stains soaked through his shirt, and even over the smell of Joey's zombies and the festering stench of the Talas corruption, he gave off the ripe odor of fear. "It just doesn't end."

Mollie giggled, and Franny blanched. But they were actually holding it together better than Michelle had expected. *Wonder drugs,* she thought. Magic cocktails of godonlyknewwhat. Probably Xanax, Thorazine, and a touch of good ol' Valium. Now that she thought about it, none of them should still be standing, much less barreling through Dante's last Ring of Hell, given the amount of drugs they'd been pumped full of.

She knew she'd been feeling the effects of Batshit Crazy Town for some time now. The drugs had muted them somewhat, but not enough. Something slimy was poking around in her head. Or it felt like it was. Maybe not. She wasn't really sure, but she knew things were getting slippery for her mentally.

"Which way?" Bruckner asked Franny. "Tell me fast, you scared little rabbit man."

"Lay off," Michelle snapped. She'd hated him out the gate. It would be so easy to kill him. A tiny bubble formed in her hand.

"Nothing looks right," Franny muttered, peering through the mist. Michelle closed her hand, and the bubble gave a soft crack and was gone.

"Don't worry about it," Michelle said, trying to comfort him. She was still having moments of being herself. The self she used to be. "Just take a deep breath and sort it out."

Billy Ray glared at her. "We don't have time for breathing exercises," he said. The scars on his face, normally pale pink, were bright red now.

"That way," Franny said, pointing to their right.

Bruckner jammed the truck into gear, swearing as it crunched and lurched. "Can't take it any farther, you shiny dick weasels."

There was nothing Michelle recognized as Talas left anymore. She was amazed that Franny could navigate at all. Everything was a mass of seething tentacles, pus-filled sacks of skin, dead-eyed creatures with hungering mouths covering their bodies, fetuses hanging from spiny silver trees, and an ever-evolving host of monstrosities.

"There it is!"

Michelle peered through the haze. Something that looked roughly like a building, but built out of meat, stood about two hundred meters ahead. Dead bodies surrounded the steps leading to what appeared to be the entrance. If a door that occasionally turned into a gaping maw ringed with knife-sized teeth was an entrance.

"Oh, fuck," Michelle said as the mists parted.

Standing at the bottom of the steps leading into the meat palace were Lohengrin and Recycler. Recycler stood behind Lohengrin, a towering mass of rotting flesh encasing his body. And Lohengrin's armor was no longer gleaming white. It glowed a hellish red.

And fire so hot—so hot Michelle could already feel it—encased Lohengrin's sword. He towered over them all.

A phalanx of monstrosities surrounded the hospital. The sound of teeth snapping and spiders chittering greeted them. A wave of foul odor came off the horde. A combination of shit, blood, pus, and death. Michelle gagged.

"How're we supposed to get past that?" Franny asked, choking on the smell.

"The way we always do," Billy Ray growled. "The way we always do." He leapt forward, pulling his pistols from their holsters. Joey's zombies jumped out of the truck, shockingly nimble. *They must have been really fresh,* Michelle thought.

"Stay here," Michelle said to Mollie, shoving her back into the truck cab.

"Are you fucking nuts?" Mollie yelled. Her stringy hair was sweat-plastered against her skull. She was panting, and Michelle knew the tranq shot was wearing off. "I didn't come all the way back into the Psycho Cannibal Flashmob Evil Insanity Zone just to bail out." Michelle was pretty sure that was bullshit. But she had to trust Mollie—it was the only choice.

"Then at least stay far enough back that you're not straight in that line of . . . of whatever the hell this is."

Michelle turned and started running toward the two aces who were now the defenders of the great perversion. Bubbles streamed out of her hands. Chunks of festering flesh flew off Recycler's armor. She had to force herself to hold back because part of her—a growing part of her—wanted to make sure he didn't live. After all, dead men tell no tales. And she certainly didn't want Tiago telling hers.

Tiago. Oh, Jesus. She'd left him behind, and this was what had happened. And now she wanted to kill him. Oh, God.

She looked over and saw Billy Ray had started picking off the monsters.

She released a barrage of bubbles at them. They exploded and she watched with grim satisfaction as viscera, black ichor, and chunks of suppurating meat spewed into the air. Billy Ray's perfectly white jumpsuit was covered in gore. She felt the spray of unspeakable fluids covering her. And she tried not to glory in it.

Lohengrin took a swing with his sword at Billy Ray, and Billy Ray neatly dodged it. Michelle threw some bubbles to distract Lohengrin. Mollie was using her portals to decapitate the horrors. Michelle didn't want to speculate on how Mollie was managing to use her portals and still keep the pinpoint open for Joey without going mad.

But then a new wave of perversions was upon her, and she didn't have time to think about it.

Mollie looked at the aces defending the hospital. One was unrecognizable, a mountain of corpseflesh. But the other, the one in the shining armor, had been a semipermanent fixture on magazines, billboards, and television for years: Lohengrin. She'd never seen him in person, but she'd recognize him anywhere. Except.

The images always depicted his gleaming ghost-steel sword a brilliant silver. It wasn't. It shone the dark scarlet color of pitchfork tines shoved through a man's gut.

Shit, shit, shit.

Franny stood by the passenger door, and desperately clutched the shotgun. Churning, fear-induced nausea filled his gut. His chest ached as he tried to draw in panting breaths, but it felt like his lungs were trying to expel the foul air, filled as it was with the reek of smoke and rot.

Franny forced his legs to move.

Each stroke of Lohengrin's sword cast a flashing incarnadine light over the surreal battle. In the pink half-light Mollie saw Franny sprint across the pustule field that passed for ground here. A shrieking nightmarepede saw him, too. It slithered across the battlefield. It was far faster than he was. Its slimy body barricaded the cop from the hospital entrance. He tried to dodge, but the 'pede was fifty feet long if it was an inch. Without thinking, Mollie opened a hole in space directly in front of Franny. He lunged for it, and emerged on the hospital stairs. He might have raised his fist, flashing a thumbs-up gesture over his shoulder as he disappeared inside the suppurating fleshpile that used to be a building. But Mollie was distracted by the cough of a diesel engine.

She turned just in time to see Bruckner in the truck cab, heaving on the shifter. The transmission clanked as the truck lurched into gear. Bruckner cranked the wheel. The empty truck squished a trio of spider-shamblers while inching through a tight circle.

Electric-blue ichor spurted from their ruptured bodies; it sizzled, steamed, and bubbled on everything it touched. The splash raised a line of smoking green-black blisters across a swath of the Recycler's putrefying flesh. It howled.

A pair of zombies tottered before the truck. They raised their rotting arms as though to wave down a ride. Joey was trying to stop him from leaving.

Bruckner floored it. The truck smashed through the toe tags and bounced over the pulsating fleshroad.

"You fucking asshole!"

Abandoning people in their hour of need? That's my role.

She folded space. Bruckner slammed on the brakes. The skidding truck ripped bleeding gouges in the fleshroad with the sound of a wet bedsheet torn in half. It slid through the portal only to reemerge on the other side of the battlefield, headed back into the fray.

"Nice try, motherfu—"

A pair of tentacles whipped around Mollie's arms and yanked her off her feet.

Franny wiped sweat onto his forearm and took a firmer grip on the shotgun. The things on sentry duty didn't look human any longer, but he still didn't want to kill them. Not unless he had to. He had enough on his conscience.

He tried to generate some spit to ease his desert-dry mouth and burning throat. It didn't work. A few more of the monsters marched away, heading toward the fighting. Franny saw his opportunity and darted out only to draw back when the children's choir of the damned came drifting past singing in their eerie piping voices. A shiver ran through him and for a moment Franny thought he understood if not the meaning of the grotesque words at least the intent. It was a song of praise to a new god, rising in darkness, eating the light. Glorious nothingness beckoned. He once again groped for the rosary, but this time it brought no comfort. What power did the Christian God hold against a deity that could twist the very fabric of reality?

The singers moved on and Franny remembered his task. He hung the rosary around his neck as if it could ward off the doubts and the fear. The way forward was clear and a shattered door, hanging loosely on its hinges, beckoned. He ran for the hospital and ducked inside. It seemed to be a delivery area judging by the cases of canned goods trapped like bugs in amber by the transformed walls that had turned into red crystal.

Franny moved on, searching for anything familiar. He finally located the entryway where he'd run after Baba Yaga and her goons a lifetime ago. The floor was littered with bodies. Overhead chandeliers of branching crystal tipped with growths that seemed to be sometimes flowers and sometimes grasping fingers were forming on the ceiling. It seemed the new God was making himself a palace.

The lobby was filled with floating papers buoyed up by the overheated air. Franny took a breath and started running across the bodies. One of them moved and Franny lost his footing and went down. The man crawled his way from beneath the actual corpses and threw himself on Franny. His hands were at Franny's throat, his teeth snapping. Oozing sores covered his face and hands. Franny tried to bring the gun to bear, but the barrel of the shotgun was too long. He dropped the gun, and tried to hold off his attacker while he felt and heard the bones in his throat creaking. The only thing saving him was that the pus on the man's hands made his grip unsteady. A weapon, Franny thought. He needed a weapon. He wished he'd thought to equip a knife.

He released one hand, and groped frantically at the rotting bodies next to him. Black spots were dancing in front of his eyes when his palm hit a set of keys. Franny snatched it up and jammed a key deep into the man's eye. He screamed and fell back clutching his face. Franny scrambled to his feet, snatched up the shotgun, and swung it bat-like against the side of the man's head. There was a sickening crunch and the side of his skull depressed. He flopped onto the other bodies and didn't move again.

Sparks were arcing in the one elevator that was in the lobby so Franny headed for the stairs. With each step it became more and more difficult to lift his foot, force the muscles to respond. A crushing weight rested not just on Franny's body, but on his heart and spirit. All was lost. Nothing remained but fear and death. An image of Abby with the skin flayed from her body rose up before him. His mother twisted into one of those slug creatures, his comrades at Fort Freak dismembered. And he was a murderer. He was damned to hell. He gasped on a sob and sank down on the stairs.

Franny stared at the shotgun. Better to end it now, by his own hand. Not end up like those monsters in the street. It would keep himself from killing again and again and again. He went to place the muzzle beneath his chin, but the rosary got tangled on the barrel of the gun. He tried to shake it loose and it swung before his eyes, the carved onyx beads, the silver crucifix. His father's image filled his mind. All he had were pictures, a box holding his medals and this crucifix. John F. X. Black had died doing his duty fighting to protect Jokertown from an ace of terrifying power. What would he think of his coward son?

He struggled against the hopeless lethargy that held him in its grip, but shame was not enough to break its hold. It had brought him to the point of understanding that this was an exterior force eroding his hope and courage, but not how to fight it.

"Suicide is a mortal sin," he whispered and dropped his head onto his folded arms. The shotgun rested on his knees. He found himself remembering Father Squid's final sermon just before he was kidnapped. The priest had spoken on inequity, of the unfairness of the wild card virus, the unfairness of life itself. How some folks ended up with the ability to move mountains, and others were twisted and suffered, some were rich and some were poor, but the priest had concluded that there was a power that transcended the strength of aces or the affliction of jokers or the power of money—love. He had ended with First Corinthians—*Bear all things, believe all things, hope all things, endure all things, but know that love never fails.*

Franny let the shotgun fall onto a step. He grabbed the railing with his hand, noting it was blackened with soot and stained with blood, and pulled himself to his feet.

"Just a little farther now. I can do this."

He climbed.

The tentacles dragged Mollie across bursting pustules and splashed her through puddles of steaming ichor. It burned. She writhed, first trying to wriggle free, but struggling only lured more of the slimy vines to come snaking across the ground and loop around her arms, legs, neck, mouth. The demon limbs were segmented with bristly black hair like tarantula legs, adorned with a cluster of tiny eyeballs at each joint. Mollie clamped her mouth shut, but one slender shoot wriggled past her lips and teeth to explore her mouth with its pulsating bristle hairs. The taste of sulfurous death filled her mouth; an odor like five-day-old sunbaked skunk roadkill wafted into her sinuses. She vomited. Yellow spume splashed against her face, but the tentacles only squeezed more tightly. Still she bumped across the putrid ground, moving faster and faster as more tentacles joined the effort to pull her . . . where?

Mollie flopped like a trout on the bottom of a canoe. Straining against the pressure, against the feel of a thousand needle-like bristles piercing her skin, she righted herself and glimpsed her destination. A slavering maw, like the shared acid trip of Bosch and Giger—

Another tentacle slapped around her head like a wet towel. She couldn't see.

She couldn't see.

She couldn't fold space to intercept the tentacles; she couldn't put a portal beneath the monster mouth; she couldn't get away. The chittering grew louder, like the rattling of a thousand dice.

The bristly tentacles secreted a foul slime that stung her skin. *Oh God oh God ohGodohGod it's salivating in anticipation of devouring me.*

She scrabbled for a mental handhold on any of the dozens, hundreds, of portal sites she'd used over the years. But every time her panicked mind landed on one, she couldn't make it manifest. She tried to fold space just a few feet away, in the direction the slime ropes seemed to pull her, but the bumping and splashing across the pulsating earth fouled her sense of direction and prevented her from creating new doorways. She couldn't sever the tentacles dragging her toward the maw because she couldn't picture her surroundings.

The chattering teeth grew so loud the ground shook. Hot sour breath gusted across her face like a sepulchral Santa Ana. Acid saliva burned her skin. But she didn't dare scream because then the nest of wriggling tarantula legs planted on her lips would scuttle past her teeth and into her throat.

"Mollie!"

A thunderous roar shook the pulsating earth, then again in close succession, like lightning striking the same tree twice. The tentacles wrapped around Mollie went slack, and then a hot rain pelted her. Mollie shook off the amputated slime ropes and leapt to her feet.

The maw was now a smoking crater, thanks to the bubbles Michelle had pitched into it. But even as she watched, a new crop of tentacles wriggled from beneath the maw corpse like a hundred snakes birthed at once. They slithered across the ground toward Mollie all over again.

She folded space under the nest and over an Icelandic volcano. Gravity tore away a chunk of the perverted landscape and sent it tumbling into lava thousands of miles away.

Billy Ray was insanely fast, but Michelle saw even he was having trouble keeping up with the swarm of noxious creatures flowing toward them.

Fuck it, she thought. She could feel the dark rage sliding over her. She needed to channel it. *Let me finish these things off.* She raised her hands over her head, splaying her fingers out as she did.

She rained bubbles down like so much fire from heaven. Each one hit and blasted holes into foul bodies. It felt as if her fat was pouring off. When she finally stopped, she looked down at herself.

She wasn't as thin as she'd been while getting out of Talas, but she wasn't too far from it. She needed to get fat on, fast.

"Director!" she shouted. "I need you!"

Billy Ray spun around, then leapt to her side and began pounding her. It hurt like hell, but still wasn't enough damage fast enough.

Suddenly, she was falling so fast and it was like jumping off a tall building.

The portals. Go one place—come crashing out another.

Michelle slammed into the ground. The pain almost knocked her out. "Again!" she cried.

The zombies were sluggish. Lohengrin's sword cut clean through the last two shambling undead as though they were scarecrows stuffed with wet paper towels.

Mollie tried to open a connection to the Cosmodrome so that Joey could animate more corpses, but just then Recycler raised a massive fist that bristled with plastic syringes and biohazard bags—it had absorbed the stinking medical waste dumpster behind the hospital into its body. The fist cocked back, ready to pound Billy Ray into the ground like a tent peg. But the SCARE ace was too busy fending off a nightmarepede to notice the killing blow.

"Ray!" she cried, opening a hole in space just above his head. Recycler's fist came whooshing down, disappearing just over Ray's head and plunging into the Indian Ocean just off the coast of Perth.

"Behind you!"

Still wrestling with the immense 'pede, Ray glanced over his shoulder to glimpse the mountainous Recycler rearing back for another attack. He tore the monster in half, spun, and flung half of the still-scrabbling beast into Recycler's face. Smoking electric-blue ichor splashed into his corpse-eyes. The demented ace howled, clapping hands of medical waste bags and used syringes to his face.

Oddly there were no bodies in Tolenka's room.

The IV bags were flaccid and empty, the room smelled of piss and feces. The monitors were just blank screens, but Franny had the horrible sense that faces were peering out at him from the blackness. The droning hum had become almost a scream. It clawed at his mind, trying to find purchase to elicit the rage and violence and fervent faith. Exhaustion, mind-numbing fear, and prayer formed fragile bulwarks against the compulsion. Franny alternated between the Hail Mary and the Lord's Prayer as he approached the bed.

The shriveled body of the old man had coiled into an almost fetal crouch. His lips were cracked and bleeding from dehydration, and he barely seemed to breathe. The eyes were open, and a fearsome intelligence filled with malice and hate gazed out at him as Franny reached him.

Franny took hold of the body, and then the throat pulsed, and an ululating cry burst out. The Dark God was summoning help. Franny pictured misshapen things loping up the stairs. He looked around desperately. Time was ticking away. It was uncertain how long Ray and Bubbles could continue the fight. Monsters were coming. He had to move.

Franny wiped away the sweat that was pouring down his face and stinging his eyes. He glanced toward the window. "How about we take a page from Bruckner?" he whispered to Tolenka. "Take a shortcut."

He staggered out of the room, searching for something to fashion into a rope. The counter at the nurses' station had become a strange nautilus-shaped thing. Franny feared something might actually be living inside the shell so he gave it a wide berth. He found a linen closet and pulled out an armful of sheets.

Back in the room he slammed shut the door and backed it with a chair beneath the handle. He began frantically tearing the sheets. Blows began to hammer on the door. It flexed under the pressure from outside. With almost numb fingers Franny fashioned the sheets into a rope. He then created a sling and tied the dying joker against his chest like a father carrying a grotesque and ancient baby. The stink of shit and death hung on the body, and Franny gagged and began breathing through his mouth. The malignant intelligence seemed aware of these moves because the joker began to feebly kick his legs, but there was no strength behind the kicks and Franny could ignore them.

Franny slung the shotgun, locked down the wheels on the hospital bed, tied off one end of his makeshift rope to a leg of the bed. He secured the other end around his waist and bashed out the window. He had hoped to back slowly out the window and pick his route, but the metal legs of the bracing chair bent, and the door came open with a screech. Franny twined the material around his hands and flung himself backward out the window. He swung violently back toward the wall of the building, and caught it with his feet. The shock vibrated through his body and tore at the wound in his side. He began to rappel down the building, grateful that he'd spent some time wall climbing at his gym.

Tolenka's teeth were clashing together as he tried to bite Franny. Fortunately he was slung low enough that he was simply biting Kevlar.

What if he dies while I'm carrying him? Franny thought. He pushed aside that horrible thought.

They were surrounded. Mollie again felt the edges of her chemically induced stability crumbling away.

She stood with Michelle and Ray within a contracting ring of nightmarepedes, shambling things that once were human, scuttling eyeball spiders, and worse. The Recycler loomed closer, shaking the ground with every footstep.

Michelle tried to summon more bubbles to hurl at him but she was too gaunt.

She yelled, "Ray! Punch me again!"

To Mollie he said, "Cover us, kiddo."

He did. His fists slammed into Michelle's stomach with a steady rhythm, her body bloating just a bit with each impact. But he was tired and slowing, each punch slower and weaker than the one before.

Meanwhile, Mollie struggled to maintain a flickering sequence of portals to intercept the monsters that lunged for them. Keeping the smaller beasts off prevented her from concentrating on the walking pile of putrid garbage and corpseflesh that the Recycler had become.

Michelle, slightly more zaftig than she'd been moments earlier, broke off from Ray and hurled everything she had at the mountainous ace. The explosions cratered his armor but he kept coming. In seconds she was gaunt again, her bubbles depleted.

"It's not enough!"

"Hold on," said Mollie. She opened a hole in space directly under Michelle's feet. Gravity pulled the ace through the hole and out through its flip side, which Mollie had situated hundreds of feet above the hospital battleground. Seconds later, Michelle's impact sent shock waves rippling through the pulsating earth, violent enough to knock down the shambling abominations surrounding Ray and Mollie. When the model stood again, she was five times larger than she had been a moment earlier.

"Again!" she cried.

Ray did his best to fend off the circling menagerie of nightmares while Mollie repeated the process. The second time, she aimed the egress hole so that Michelle pancaked a troop of abominations. She wobbled to her feet, nearly as corpulent as the Recycler himself.

A fleshfall of jowls wriggled when Michelle nodded at her. "Thanks," she said, and unleashed a spectacular stream of bubbles at the Recycler, the rapid-fire concussions knocking him to his knees.

But Mollie ignored her. Instead she wondered how she could cleanse herself of the Frankenstein god-machine filth before throwing herself on the maggot queen's mercy to plead for sanctification.

Michelle and Billy Ray were ankle-deep in carcasses. Now only Lohengrin stood between them and the hospital.

She'd peppered Recycler with bubbles until all his flesh armor was gone. The kid underneath was gibbering in some tongue Michelle couldn't understand. All she knew was she'd give anything to make him stop talking.

Billy Ray gave him a quick punch to the jaw, and Tiago fell to the ground unconscious.

Now they just had to keep Lohengrin busy until Franny got out with Horrorshow.

A soccer-ball-sized bubble formed in her hand, and she sent it speeding toward Billy Ray. It caught him in the back, thrusting him out of the arc of the burning red blade. He tucked into a ball and was up on his feet before he hit the ground. Then he pivoted back toward Lohengrin. Michelle saw Lohengrin lift his sword again.

She knew his armor was almost impenetrable. But he wasn't immune from getting the shit beat out of him in that form. And thanks to Mollie, she was now incredibly heavy and had loads of bubbling power.

She held her palms up, her fingers curled, and began to grow a massive bubble between her hands. It would be heavy, and hard, and right after it hit, it was going to explode. She hoped Lohengrin was as tough as he seemed, because she didn't need another death on her conscience.

But it'd be fun to see him die now, wouldn't it?

Something moved in the corner of her vision. She looked up and saw Franny climbing out a window on the second floor of the hospital. He had tied sheets together to form a rope. Swaddled to his body was a grotesque form. Horrorshow.

Lohengrin began to turn toward the hospital, and Michelle released her bubble. It wasn't as powerful as she'd meant it to be, but she needed his attention back on her and fast.

The bubble caught him in the chest, and he went down hard just before it exploded. Michelle staggered back as the blast wave hit her. It hurt. It hurt bad.

Billy Ray appeared at her side. He was covered in gore. "You think he'll stay down?" he asked, wiping his face with the back of his hand. It didn't help clean his face at all.

As if in reply, Klaus struggled to his feet. Billy Ray immediately jumped toward him. But Klaus was faster. He threw his hand out, swatting Billy Ray away like a gnat.

Billy Ray crumpled to the ground. Michelle was shocked. She never would have believed he could be defeated by anything.

And now she was alone.

She was the only thing between Lohengrin and the rest of them having a chance to get Horrorshow away.

"C'mon, Klaus," Michelle shouted as she began to move to his right side. If he followed, it would turn him away from Franny and Bruckner. "I've always wondered which one of us would win in a fight."

It wasn't fair odds. Klaus was filled with some otherworldly power and towered over her by at least two and half meters. But the only hope she had of saving Adesina was to keep him occupied.

She blasted the ground underneath him. Chunks of dead monstrosi-

ties and fleshy ground blew into the air. Lohengrin stumbled and fell to
his knees. Then bubble after bubble exploded against him. Even with
the massive amount of fat she had on, she was beginning to thin up. But
there was nothing else to do but keep at him. Every time he tried to get up,
she slammed him down. He was getting angrier, but so was she. The red
mist was falling over her mind. There was only one way to end this. Only
one way she could think of to take him down and give the rest of them the
time they needed. Only one way to save her daughter.

The tranquilizers had worn off. So she stopped resisting and let the terrible rage slide in. She released a hail of bubbles at Lohengrin, pouring
every last ounce of rage she had into them.

He collapsed, dropping his sword, which lost its bloody fiery sheen as
it fell from his hands. The ground shook as he landed and Michelle staggered backward. He didn't get up.

The other supplicants hurled themselves before Mollie. Seeking to impede
her approach to the Maggot Queen, they attacked her, wave upon scuttling wave: gaunts, nightmarepedes, shambling suppurating mountains of
flesh. But she held them at bay, portaling them into each other's roly-poly
bodies. Three at once, twelve at once, thirty-seven at once, until they
erupted in fountains of gore. She strode through a landscape punctuated
by geysers of blood and ichor. Not far to the Maggot Queen now. Not far
before Her Putrid Majesty rechristened her with the robe of flesh like a
second womb from which Mollie would be reborn. She licked her teeth in
anticipation and tasted salty blood. It made her giggle. She was an invincible indomitable merciless goddess. She was a MOTHERFUCKING
GODDESS wading through a lake of SCARLET TAINTFILTH, feasting on
the jelly orbs of—

A bee stung her on the shoulder.

Somehow, a bee slipped through the nonexistent gaps in her armor to
sting her in the arm. It STUNG her in the fucking ARM and tainted her
with its SLIMETOUCH. She swatted the little fucker away—it had taken
the form of a syringe, as though that would deceive her—and spun. A nest
of broodcrabs had piled upon each other like a quivering tower of sinew
and blood in caricature of a human fleshform.

A cool numbness trickled down her arm, to the hand that carried the fate of all who crossed her, to the fingertips black with the ichor of her enemies. The crab tower looked less and less like a crab tower and more and more like a human, an actual human. The deception—the gall!— angered her, stoked her fury. But the righteousness, the need to smite her enemies and bathe in their gore, felt just out of arm's reach, dangling just past her filthy fingers. It was as though the bee venom had become an impenetrable one-way window keeping the hottest fires of her rage brightly visible yet just out of arm's reach.

Bee? No. That was a syringe.

The crab tower, in fact, looked more and more like a person. It looked like Billy Ray, if somebody had tossed him into a stump grinder and then coated what came out the other end with blood and slime and shit for which there were literally no words. He swayed on his feet like a prize fighter who'd just gone the distance in extra rounds.

Behind him, Michelle looked scrawnier than a concentration camp victim. She raised her hand at the galloping three-legged slimegaunt bearing down on them, but the bubbles that emerged from her fingers were the size of champagne bubbles. Flat champagne.

Billy Ray clamped his hands to either side of Mollie's face. She staggered. He was leaning on her, she realized. He couldn't stand on his own any longer.

"Please, kid, get us out of here . . ."

His eyes rolled back in his head. He collapsed.

And then she saw it. Nightmarepedes and eyeball crabs, thousands of them, an enemy army stretching past the horizon in every direction. Hundreds of suppurating flesh mountains shook the ground as they converged on the five doomed aces.

Part of her wanted to join them.

Part of her wanted to fight them. Destroy them.

The rest of her wanted to GET THE FUCK OUT OF THERE.

One last time, Mollie embraced the madness. The madness that let her do things with her ace she couldn't do when she was sane.

Five portals opened simultaneously. One each beneath Bubbles, Billy Ray, Lohengrin, Recycler, and Mollie herself.

She fell through a ceiling.

For the second time that week, Fort Freak erupted in pandemonium.

Marcus grabbed Bugsy as he came out of the Committee meeting. "Hey, what's going on?"

Bugsy wore headgear of some sort, with a mouthpiece and a tiny camera perched on the side of his head. He frowned at Marcus and kept walking. "Shit's about to hit."

Marcus kept up with him. "Which means what?"

"It's coming. All of it. The whole nightmare of Talas, times a hundred and ten."

"But you all have a plan, right?"

"Such as it is," Bugsy scoffed. "Fucking long shot if ever there was one. Fate of the world in Tesseract's hands? We're all screwed." He placed a hand to his ear and, confusingly, he added, "Oh, come on, Babel. Fuck confidential. He's here, he might as well know everything."

Marcus didn't hear the Committee leader's response, but whatever it was Bugsy went on. He gave Marcus a quick sketch of the plans, of Tesseract's mission and the Highwayman's role in it. None of it made much sense to Marcus—the old dude was the cause of all of it?—but he clung to every word. It had to work. These were aces, the world's best. Their plan simply had to work. Just the fact that they had a plan at all was comforting. But only for a scant few moments.

Marcus followed Bugsy up a concrete staircase, his tail switchbacking as he climbed. The roof was crowded with people, loud with two helicopters whose engines were on, rotors turning. Bugsy gripped the railing and shouted to be heard over the commotion, "Behold, the coming apocalypse."

That's exactly what it looked like, something conjured up out of a fevered, ancient mind, one filled with images of hell. The end of the world, roiling toward the compound across the great dusty expanse of the plains. The cloud billowed and glowed. It ate up the distance with unnatural speed. Marcus could see shapes moving inside it, but what was worse was knowing that its vapor hid much more than it showed.

"They might as well," Bugsy said, obviously speaking through his microphone. And then, with a change in the pitch of his voice, to Marcus, "Let's see what the boys in uniform can do."

Please, Marcus said silently. *Please stop them. You have to, for Christ's sake . . .*

So, when it all came down to it, he could pray after all. Was he talking to God? Yes, but he was also talking to every ace here to protect the Cosmodrome. He was praying to the soldiers—UN and Russian and

Kazakh—and to pilots of the jets and helicopters and the men in those tanks. He was praying to more than the God he didn't believe in. He was praying to the entire world, asking all creation to see what was happening and to stop it.

Please, stop them . . .

The tanks opened fire. The muzzles spouted destruction, deep, thrumming blasts that Marcus felt right through his tail. The blasts tore into the cloud, exploding on impact, tearing creatures apart. In one spot, a tall, lumbering thing ripped in half, his upper body twirling away even as his legs stumbled forward a few more steps. In another, a mass of shapes disappeared in a spray of cloud and dust.

Yes. Keep killing them . . .

The machine gunners strafed the oncoming horde with wild abandon. Here and there Marcus saw the deformed bodies dance and jerk as bullets tore through them. Creatures fell, writhing, clawing their way forward, wailing as they died. Those that got out in front of the others took the brunt of it, soldiers training their aim on them and shredding them until they fell in bloody pulps.

Yes. Stop them!

Jets roared out over the plain, iron daggers that sliced through the sky at incredible speeds. They dispatched their missiles, banked before they got too close, and shot off to either side as the resulting blast lit the cloud from within with booming eruptions of light and fire and, hopefully, death.

Yes!

And the combat helicopters. What deadly beauties. When the tanks began to back toward the Cosmodrome, they flew in over them, a cordon stretching all the way across the oncoming mass. They opened fire with their mounted machine guns. The horde came on but the helicopters backed as they did so, chewing them ragged.

Yes, we're doing it.

Each death seemed a small victory. A tiny burst of hope. The monsters were dying. There could only be so many of them, right? Marcus turned to Bugsy, who was staring at the scene as he spoke into his mouthpiece. He clutched him by the shoulder. "We're doing it!" he cried. "We're gonna fucking beat them!"

Bugsy yanked his shoulder out of his grip. He turned on him, pushed away the mouthpiece, and pointed. "I've got wasps in that shit. If you could see what I can you'd—"

A collective gasp cut him off. Both men looked back just in time to see something low and long-limbed racing out of the cloud. It crawled forward with incredible bursts of speed, like a desert lizard. It jumped and caught one of the helicopters from underneath. It clung there pounding and tearing at it. The helicopter stayed in the air a few frantic seconds, then it tilted and then fell like a rock. It hit the earth and became an instant ball of fire. Rotors chopped into the ground until they broke apart. Bits and pieces of them sliced through the air. Some of the debris hit the next nearest helicopter, which swerved wildly, trailing a billow of black smoke. It turned and retreated. It managed a crash landing, but creatures were on it the moment it touched down. The whole line of other helicopters turned, presumably on some order, and tried to pull back. The first few made it, but others began to teeter and weave. They fell one after the other. Some crashed. Some landed only to be overcome by the raging horde.

"No," Marcus whispered. Just like that, the hope he'd clung to vanished. It got worse.

One of the jets flew too far. It disappeared into the cloud. It carved out of it a moment later and turned back toward the Cosmodrome, skimming just over the heads of the nearest creatures. The plane wobbled, its nose dove and then righted. Dipped again, tilted over to one side. It looked like a dead thing, a wedge of steel limp in the air instead of propelled by its engines. It went down a little ways out from the barricades. It tore a trench through the ground, collided with a tank and spun end over end until it crashed into the earthwork barricades, ripped through fencing and barbed wire. It exploded. Everyone on the roof hit the deck. The building shook with the force of the blast. Marcus stayed down until the cloud of debris that rained down on them lessened, then he rose up on his coils to survey the damage. It was bad. The jet had cut a jagged route right through all their defenses.

"Shit," Bugsy said. "We just left the front door open." He shouted, "Ana! Close the door, please!"

A woman—one of the other Committee members judging by her matching headset and mouthpiece—shouted back, "I need to get nearer. To see the ground better."

"IBT," Bugsy said, "help her. She's Earth Witch."

For the first time since coming up to the roof, Marcus realized he could do something other than just watch. With liquid, muscular speed, he slipped through the crowd. He swept the woman up, and as she cried out, he flowed over the railing and off the roof. It took all his strength to curve out of the plummet smooth, hitting the ground and churning forward with everything he had. He deposited Earth Witch near the trench.

"Thanks," she said, stepping away from his embrace. "You might ask first next time." That said, she went straight to work. She pointed. "There. That whole section of ground. Get everyone off of it."

Marcus did, yelling and gesticulating to the soldiers. When the space was clear of everyone but himself, Marcus felt the earth beneath him trembling, a low-level vibration that made his tail tingle. "You, too," Ana said, her voice tight with concentration. "Get on the other side of me."

As he slithered around her, he caught sight of the trench again. It wasn't empty anymore. Panicked soldiers were swarming through, in full retreat now and running as fast as they could. Behind them, the cloud loomed, and the creatures out in front of it were taking more horrible shape every minute. Marcus could hear them now, a cacophony of wails and roars, of misery and ecstasy and bloodlust. There were deeper sounds too, bellows of prehistoric dimensions.

Ana cursed. "Fools! The gates are still open for you."

It didn't matter. The soldiers looked crazed. Desperate. Soon the first of them were running past Marcus and Ana. They were so heedlessly frantic that Marcus placed himself in front of Ana, towering above the soldiers on his coils to keep them from trampling her. From on high, he could see over the mass of soldiers. The first of the creatures were in the mouth of the trench now. They were attacking the running soldiers, jumping on their backs and pulling them down, ripping into them with fingers and claws and teeth. "You have to close it," he said. "They're coming."

"Let me see," Ana said.

Marcus curved around and hoisted her up. She stared at the scene, lips tight. "Hold me steady," she said. Marcus propped her against his chest so she could see, clinging to her torso to hold her in place. Intimate, but he wasn't even thinking about that. He craned around and watched the horde approaching. Creatures he could only describe as monsters. They came in all shapes and sizes, no two the same. All of them marred by deformity. Massive jaws on that one. A too tiny head on another. Legs and arms that jointed in the wrong places and made their rapid progress grotesque. Many of them looked broken, but on they came. Masses of deranged humanity, people baring their teeth and shouting, driven by a rage that Marcus recognized all too well. He felt it now, wafting in on the hot breeze buffeted by the oncoming cloud. One of the creatures pulled out in front of the others. It was human-like but not quite, ghostly white, skeletal, with arms that curved like meat hooks. Its eyes were fixed on Ana.

"Put me down!" Ana shouted. When Marcus did, she dropped to her knees. She gripped the crucifix hanging from her neck and slammed her other hand down onto a patch of hard-packed dirt. The earth moved. Like an earthquake, the ground beneath them trembled and shifted. Marcus, standing high again to see, swayed. He felt for a moment like the earth was going to disappear beneath him. It didn't, but that's exactly what it did underneath the trench. The torn-up earth dropped away, creating a sudden, deep cavity. A massive protrusion of dirt and rock surged up into the cleared space, a tower rising as the earth was sucked from one place and thrust up in another. Most of the attackers—and more than a few fleeing soldiers—fell screaming into the abyss. The meat-hook creature managed to claw forward with his arms digging into the falling earth. He leapt clear of the trench, screaming. He flung his arms wide to pierce into Ana from both sides. Marcus lunged forward. He caught the creature by both arms and slammed his forehead into its face with enough force to smash the creature's nose and snap its head back. He shoved it into the trench, bloody-faced as its limbs lashed at the air.

And then the tower poured down into the hole, a tidal wave of earth and stone that swept the falling creature away and buried everything and everyone it fell upon. A moment later, Ana pushed a wall of earth forward, a sheer block that more than plugged the breach in the defenses.

She was slow in getting up from her knees. When she spoke through her panting, Marcus knew she wasn't speaking to him. "Thank you . . . I did what I could . . . It's not going to hold them for long, Barbara. That's for sure." She listened a moment, and then said, "Okay." To Marcus, she said, "Thank you. You just saved my life. I owe you one."

Marcus rubbed his forehead. "Don't worry about it."

The NATO and Russian soldiers were falling back in an unorganized retreat, with Kutnesov and Lefévre shouting orders to their officers in Barbara's ear. Barbara toggled from screen to screen; it was all the same. She reached for the toggles in front of her; the shouting voices died in her earphones. "Barbara?" she heard Ana—Earth Witch—say.

"It's time," she spoke into the microphone, to all of them, all the aces. "Do what you can to hold them back for as long as you can. Don't let them have the weapons, and give Michelle and Ray the time they need. Beyond that . . ." There was nothing more. The plans they'd already made would work, or not. "Stay as safe as you can, and good luck to you all."

She bit at her lip as she heard their assents. *More lives risked on my orders. More deaths. How many more do I have to send?*

There was no answer to that, and she could do nothing but watch.

The vapor hit them with a tangibly physical force. It was warm and rancid and horrible, a sickly touch that flooded Marcus with a whole host of nightmare memories. He fought back the desire to turn and flee. He told himself there was no escaping. Not anymore. They were here and now they had to do whatever they could to keep the monsters at bay. He hoped the aces had plans, but he wasn't an ace. He was just himself, but he could and would fight.

That's why he was there in the front ranks with the soldiers, all of them on the same side now, ready to defend the place if—when—the creatures got through the barricades. The sound from the host outside was tremendous, a discordant misery of howls and bellows and roars. There was fighting there, soldiers trapped outside and dying because of it. Machine guns mounted in towers strafed the whole scene indiscriminately. Marcus couldn't blame them. He'd be doing the same in their place. The thought made him realize he didn't have any weapons. Why hadn't he asked for a bazooka or something?

The first creatures to scale the barricades and leap over were spiderlike climbers, things with hooks at the end of their long, many-jointed legs. None of them were quite the same. Each was a variation of a similarly grotesque form, with a hard plating over its front portions and on its legs. One of them landed not far from Marcus. Its mouth parts cackled its pleasure as it reached a leg out and pierced a nearby soldier. It shoved the man into its mouth, chomping into his legs and eating up his body as the man screamed and gibbered. Other soldiers opened fire on it, but their bullets thudded uselessly against the armor. The creature darted into them, eviscerating men even as it continued eating.

Marcus carved around behind it. There. Its bulbous backside was unprotected. Marcus slammed into it with all the force he could churn up. He pressed into its bristled skin and began pounding it with his fist. Once. Twice. Again and again. He kept squirming forward to keep it from turning, growing more enraged with each blow. And then one of his punches burst through the skin. His fist went deep into the thing, spraying him with a yellow gook fouler than anything he'd ever smelled. He pulled back, retching.

At least it was dead. But it wasn't the only one. Others had dropped into the soldiers all around him, hooking and piercing and eating. Marcus grabbed one of the dead thing's legs and twisted the joint until it snapped. A weapon. Holding it in a two-handed grip, he went to work. He killed three more by getting behind them and ripping them open with the hook. With another he slid up the wall and under its belly just as it came over. He sunk the hook in, sliced, and shoved the body away as its fluids gushed over him. This time, he didn't even retch. He twisted around and looked over the wall.

God, there are so many of them! All shapes and sizes. Each one ghastly in its own way. Many of them were tangled in sections of barbed wire, but others used the dying bodies to climb over. One creature that looked like an elephant drawn by a child who had never actually seen an elephant used its trunk to pull down one of the towers, casting it sideways over a section of barbed wire. Instantly, others swarmed over it.

Marcus was about to intercept them when he caught sight of movement in the haze too large to pass over. The being he called the Harvester emerged through the rippling vapor, taking monstrous shape all too quickly, moving with its deceptively slow-looking speed. It was even more massive than before, with yet more legs, and a body pocked with hundreds of those torture chambers. One of the tanks shot at it. The shell tore a portion of the creature's amorphous head away, but it reshaped immediately. It flipped the tank over with a leg and kept coming.

Marcus couldn't tell if what happened next was planned, or if the other creatures just realized on their own that the walls and barricades and barbed wire would do nothing to stop the giant. Hordes of them rushed toward it. They leapt unto its body. They climbed up using the divots as foot and handholds. Some just grabbed its passing legs and clung on. The Harvester walked right through a section of the fortifications, impervious to the hail of gun and mortar fire it walked into. Its legs crushed portions of the wall, dragged barbed wire and beams forward, and churned through

Ana's earthworks. As soon as they were clearly inside, the hitchhikers began to leap off. And behind them, others swarmed to follow the newly cleared route in.

Jesus, Marcus thought. The "keeping them out" portion of this was over. Now, it was just the fight to survive. He had to keep those he cared about alive for as long as he could. No thought but that one. No action but things to make it so. Clutching his leg-hook, he peeled away from the wall and shifted it as fast as he could back toward the hangar. Toward the villagers and, mostly, toward Olena.

Barbara tapped frantically at the keyboards, trying to keep some sense of the action as it spread out chaotically all over the south end of the complex.

TAP: Near Gagarin's Soyuz, Earth Witch opened yawning chasms in the midst of the frontal mass of the attackers. Barbara saw the creatures falling, flailing claws and tentacles and flapping wings as they cascaded into the long pit, which then closed over them.

TAP: The trio of massive, twenty-foot-tall robots were Tinker's, cobbled together from spare military parts, derricks, gantries, and rockets, looking like an invading alien army from a fevered H. G. Wells novel. They strode into the ranks of the hell-creatures, fire spewing from nozzle-tipped, multiple arms, their massive feet crushing those beneath. They cut three burning, smoking, and gigantic swaths through the invaders.

TAP: Near the joker refugee camps, Toad Man's tongue lashed out, grabbing creatures and pulling them into the maw of his mouth. As Barbara watched, the ace spat out his tongue once more, this time to a four-armed creature with a face like a squid and waving a Russian-made Kalashnikov. The tongue wrapped around its neck, and the great toad reeled it back quickly. The Kalashnikov went flying; the creature went flailing into Toad Man's mouth. She saw the bulge moving down the Toad Man's throat.

TAP: Wilma Mankiller's black braids flew as she reached for the snarling bear-headed joker from the mob around her. Its claws slashed at her, but too late; she lifted the creature as if it weighed nothing and threw it back into the crowd of attackers.

TAP: Snow Blind's magenta hair nearly glowed in the camera. Barbara's camera caught her standing in the doorway of the Space Museum, confronting a wave of attackers led by a humans lizard whose skin was aflame and whose breath pulsed out gouts of blue fire. Where it walked, its footprints left behind puddles of fire. But Snow Blind's power was already active, and as it approached the museum, the lizard and its followers went suddenly blind. They staggered, confused and lost, and the lizard's flame-breath wheeled around, setting some of its own people afire. Snow Blind lifted an AK-47; she pressed the trigger . . .

TAP: Glassteel's liquid form lurked by the gantries for the Saturn measurement post, with a squadron of NATO soldiers around him. On the screen, Barbara could see the gantries alive with dark movement, as if a swarm of red and black ants were overrunning the area. Glassteel looked impossibly small against the thousands, but Barbara saw the gantry suddenly melt under Glassteel's ace, sending the swarm plummeting to the ground amid the steel girders. The NATO troops opened fire on the stunned creatures.

For a moment, Barbara felt a fleeting hope. Surely the Highwayman must have reached Talas by now; surely they must have snatched Tolenka—surely, or there was no hope at all. Surely between the aces and the troops guarding the Cosmodrome, they could hold off the assault: if not forever, at least long enough.

There was movement in the screen that drew Barbara's eyes back: the Midnight Angel, swooping down from above, her sword aflame. "No!" Barbara screamed, fumbling with the toggles for her mic. "Glassteel! Above you!" In the screen, she saw Glassteel raise his head, but it was already too late. The Midnight Angel's sword moved.

Headless, she saw him fall.

Marcus cursed himself for ever having left Olena and the villagers alone. He should've been there with them, locked away and protecting them. What mattered more than that? He refused to let anything stop him from getting back to the hangar. He squirmed past creatures devouring people. He kept moving around and over bodies. He ignored anything that ignored him. Each passing second seemed too many, and the distance back to the hangar—and route to it—was longer and more confusing than he remembered.

Keep your mind clear, he told himself. He kept shaking his head, trying to focus. But in addition to all the hideousness around him, he had to fight back vile notions of his own: how sickeningly enticing the smell of viscera was, the way the sounds of a woman's desperate screams stiffened his cock and made him want to stop and watch her being raped by the twisted men who were fighting over her. *It's not you,* he thought. *It's fucking Horrorshow. Don't give in to it. Just remember Olena.*

He was still saying that, a mantra, when he came in sight of the hangar. What he saw took away all thoughts but one. *Kill it.*

The "it" was a creature similar to the canine pack animals that had followed him and Olena out of Talas. It perched on top of the hangar, clawing at the metal roofing. It had one piece bent back already. Marcus dropped his leg-hook and churned toward the canine. He rose and hit the rooftop. His coils zigzagged behind him, and he crashed into the creature full on, slamming it and careening over onto the far side of the roof with it. They rolled together. Marcus managed to get his hands around the creature's neck and did his best to bash its head against the rusty metal. They just avoided a unit of piping protruding from the roof. And then they went over the edge. Marcus fell partway, but he managed to coil his tail around the piping. He strained to hold on to it as he tightened his grip on the canine's neck. A moment of incredible pressure, his hands clenched and every muscle in his tail straining, and then he felt the creature's neck snap as its weight broke it. He dropped it, dead, to the ground, and curved around to check on the damage done to the roof. It wasn't that bad. Not yet, at least. He did what he could to bend the metal back into shape.

When he was as satisfied as he figured he would be, he looked up. The turmoil all around him went on. The place swarmed with invaders. He thought, *Come on, you fuckers. Any of you, try to get in here.* The moment he thought it he wanted it. He wanted someone to try it. He'd kill them. More than that, he'd fuck them as he killed them. Maybe he'd do more than that. He'd—

He caught sight of a figure swooping down from the sky. A woman. She dropped down into the center of the refugee camp. The moment she touched the ground, a sword of black fire appeared in her hand.

Marcus knew who she must be. *The Midnight Angel.* He'd heard she'd been lost in Talas when the first ace team went in. But there she was, still living. The flare of hope this gave him was enough to beat back his crazed thoughts. Maybe there were other aces alive also! He remembered that there was a mission in the works. There was a way to end this. Her being here seemed like proof of it.

Hope only lasted until the Angel swung her sword. She sliced down the people nearest her. She leapt, wings flapping, from one place to the next. Her blade lopped off heads. It severed arms and cut panicked refugees in half at the torso. She twirled and spun and struck again and again.

"No!" Marcus shouted. "You're killing the wrong people! Those aren't the monsters." He hesitated a moment, but then he decided. The hangar was intact. The villagers were safe for now, and he couldn't just stand watching as innocents got slaughtered. Hitting the ground, he retrieved his leg-hook. Then he went to meet the Midnight Angel.

. . . and before her, alone and hissing, was her adversary, the Great Snake. The Angel raced to meet him, leaving behind the honor guard of gaunts, werewolves, and thousand-legged armored centipedes the length of large dogs that had formed just behind her.

The snake demon was approaching quickly. He was a young black man from the waist up, otherwise a serpent that seemed to go on forever. There was a certain beauty in the brightly colored bands of his pebbly-textured tail, but the Angel knew that it was beauty that masked evil.

"Midnight Angel!" it called out. "Why are you doing this?"

But she had left words behind.

She snarled at him. He was an agent of the Father of Lies and she was determined not to let him snare her in a web of deceit. She charged, her hands clasped around the hilt of her black sword.

He was fast, she gave him that. She chopped at his tail and, snake quick, it flicked out of the way. He looked as if he wanted to say more, but knew her ears were closed to his entreaties. She did not deal with demons, she didn't negotiate with them. She slew them.

He skimmed across the ground, the Angel chasing him, and slithered around an abandoned truck that had crashed and tipped over on its side. She pursued hotly, though her legs ached and her shoulder felt beyond pain. She wondered if it had partially slipped out of its socket again, but she could do nothing but clench her teeth, pursue the serpent, and send him back to hell, all for the glory of her dark lord.

She rounded the front of the truck and something lashed out like a whip, inches thick, caught her across her torso, and flung her against a wall. She smashed into it. Her vision blackened for a moment and she fought to regain her breath as her sword vanished. Her baby wailed and anger burned even deeper, if that were possible.

She could smell his snake odor somewhere nearby and she punched out, half blind, with her right hand clenched into a fist. It connected against a rough, pebbly hide, but it was her weakened left arm and she couldn't put her whole strength into the blow. Nevertheless, she heard an agonized gasp and felt bones break under the rough hide.

Her lungs worked spasmodically, desperately trying to draw in oxygen.

For a few frantic moments as Marcus darted away, just barely escaping that black sword, he tried to reason with the Angel. She didn't need to attack him, he said. They were on the same side. She had just been in the shit too long and wasn't thinking right. Before long, he stopped trying. She *had* been in the shit too long. *Way* too long by the looks of her. She was supposed to be beautiful; this woman was monstrous. She was a gaunt, twisted version of herself, with crazed eyes and shriveled lips that she held in a perpetual snarl. Her teeth bit the air as she swung at him. Her wings were dark and leathery, lopsided and bat-like. They gave off a stench when they flapped that was almost as bad as the spider-thing's guts. The worst thing was the baby jutting out of her chest. It hissed and gnashed its tooth-less mouth. It writhed against the flesh that contained it as if it was try-ing to break free and attack him itself.

No, whatever the Midnight Angel had been, this creature wasn't her anymore.

That means one thing, Marcus thought. *Kill it. Kill it,* he repeated, in that voice that was his and not his inside his head. The voice of the arena, of the fury that had taken him over in proximity to Horrorshow. It was on him again, and he reveled in it.

The next time she landed near him, coming in with her sword slash-ing at him, he batted away the blow with the leg-hook. The Angel spun away with the deflected force of her attack. Marcus gripped his weapon in imitation of a Japanese swordsman. He could do this. He'd fucking kill her. He kept his tail seething beneath him. He made it a writhing, multicolored, and confusing mass of coils. From above it, he parried each strike of the sword. That just seemed to drive the Angel to greater fury. She screeched and attacked again and again. Her blows were powerful and savage, but also wild and sloppy.

Once, after she'd missed him with a downward strike, he got the hook behind one of her legs. He yanked it back. The point dug into her hamstring and pulled the leg out from under her. She spun in the air, wings flaring, and nearly took off his head. The black blade scorched by so close that his hair caught fire. For a moment he could only fight on, desperately, head on fire and the scent of burning hair and flesh in his nostrils.

He got a moment of reprieve thanks to a creature that looked like a giant, wingless fly. It attacked the Angel, its snout seemingly intent on sucking in the baby. The Angel sliced it in half horizontally, and then vertically just out of rage. The thing fell to the ground, quartered.

Marcus had enough time to slam his hand frantically across his burned scalp, tamping out the flames. His head smoldered and some part of him felt the pain of it, but he was too filled with his own murderous anger to care. He hated her like he'd never hated anyone or anything. And he hated the thrashing baby in her chest. Staring into its tiny, murderous eyes, he acted before he even knew he was going to. His tongue exploded from his mouth. It thwacked the baby dead in its face. Marcus felt his venom splash all over it, into its eyes and nose and mouth. He lingered like that, loving that he was poisoning it.

Die, he thought. *Die you little fucking monster from* . . .

He lost the thought when the Angel's sword flashed up and sliced off his tongue.

Marcus screamed. He screamed in pain and fear and misery, only he did so silently. He couldn't make a sound other than the wet mumblings and moans his mouth managed. He dropped his leg-hook and probed his mouth with his fingers, desperately searching for his tongue. But it was gone. Only a raw mangle of flesh remained where it had been.

He couldn't believe it. She'd cut off his tongue. *His tongue!* He shouted the affront of this at her in wordless, silent misery.

Somehow, she seemed to hear him. She looked up from her chest. Her eyes found him. They locked on his with a trembling malevolence that had a physical force to it. She started toward him, her sword suddenly in hand again. Marcus didn't have time to bend for the leg-hook. Instead, he turned and fled.

He heard the Angel's cry of rage following him, and it drove him all the faster. He scrambled to find something—anything—to fight her with. But he didn't have anything. No tongue. No weapon. He snatched up a machine gun and squeezed the trigger. Nothing. He tossed it away.

He cut between two buildings, squirmed through an underpass, and came out at the edge of one of the runways. He turned, trying to get his bearings. He couldn't tell where he was. This wasn't the same set of runways as when he chased Vasel. Or maybe it was, but in the weird light and filled with chaos nothing looked the same. The scene across the flat expanse was even more hellish than ever. Everywhere men and women, monsters and beasts, were tearing each other apart. The dead had risen and fought as well, despite the injuries that killed them—crushed and broken limbs, body wounds and bites. Was that Joey's doing? Probably, but at the moment it just looked a part of the madness.

Above everything, the Harvester reigned triumphant. Its arms sweeping out to snatch up unfortunates and slam them into the misery that are the pits in its mountainous body. It was almost enough to stop Marcus right there, so filled was he with despair.

The Angel leapt up and over one of the buildings, coming toward him. Not knowing what else to do, he leaned forward and took off, right through the pandemonium. Right toward the Angel.

He wrapped his coils around her, and squeezed.

Barbara swept her gaze from screen to screen. Everywhere she looked, there was destruction and death. The fog had already enveloped Gagarin's Soyuz and the museum nearest the entrance to the compound; the hell-creatures roamed freely in front of it. Tinker's robots and drones were all smashed and gone. Snow Blind and Toad Man were retreating together along with most of the remaining NATO and Russian troops toward the Energia launch pads, well to the north. She couldn't find Wilma Mankiller at all. Earth Witch, looking exhausted and ragged, was erecting a massive rampart around the refugee camp, but Barbara couldn't imagine it stopping the hordes that were coming.

She toggled the switch to talk to them all. "Hang on," she said. "A little longer—that's all we need. A little longer . . ."

She released the switch. She sobbed, unable to stop the grief, the pain, and the guilt.

My fault. My fault. I've killed them all.

The Angel and IBT were locked in an embrace like a statue born out of Greek tragedy, his snake part wrapped around her body, her hands clenched around his throat, preventing him from spitting his venom in her face. Now her weak arm was almost useless. With the length of tail wrapped around her and holding her mostly off the ground, she couldn't get much in the way of leverage.

She felt her rib cage constrict, press upon her internal organs, and flexed her muscles as best she could to keep the pressure off her dying baby, but still, it was coming down to a test of strength and she knew that she was stronger than the snake. She could see his face darken.

Shrieks of laughter rang from behind them distracted her, though her grip relaxed not one iota. A glance at her foe showed sudden horror on his face as he tried to shrink back from the dozen or so approaching creatures, claws and fangs ready to rend.

The Angel felt her vision darken to black. Unbearable pressure clamped onto her chest. Clarity and coherence returned for a nanosecond.

So this is death, she thought.

Marcus squeezed and squeezed and squeezed. It felt euphoric. Homicidally euphoric. Every muscle in his body was flexed, trembling with the joy of killing. He felt the Angel's horrid body being crushed. He felt the tremors of ribs snapping, and he knew the moment that the baby's skull popped. It was all glorious, and would never have stopped if not for the part of his mind that was conscious of the Harvester's bulk sliding by above him, and of the monsters and walking dead of all kinds moving around him.

Finally, knowing she must be dead, he relaxed his grip. His coils slackened and slid from around her. His torso rose and he looked down on her crumbled, lifeless form. For a moment, seeing her in death, he felt sated. Full. Satisfied in his exhaustion. And then he looked around. The chaos was as before, only it looked less chaos now and more like the world that was and ever would be. It was, he realized, a world he could triumph in, as he just had. He had only to kill. To kill and eat and take what he wanted and think of nothing else. Such a pure way to be. He felt it all so clearly. Not fear at all. Just bloodlust.

Keep killing, he told himself. *Keep killing forever and ever.* It was just a matter of who was next. He looked about, searching. There were so many to choose from. The killing would be very, very—

The impact was so complete that at first he didn't know what had hit him. Something crashed into his side, lifted him in a viselike grip, and swept him up from the world with such force his brain rocked in his head. The world went black for a second, and then came again, all motion, him above the ground, everything a blur until the grip loosened and he was slammed into a tiny compartment, jammed in with the bunched length of his tail. He looked out on the raging battle now far below him. He saw those giant arms working below him and he knew he was in the Harvester. Panicked, he tried to push himself out, like a person leaping from a balcony. But he couldn't. Something held him in place.

The monster began to suck life out of him. It felt like every bit of fluid was being sucked out of him. His cells were being broken down, his flesh melting away from within. It was painful, but the worst part wasn't physical. It was the utter desolation that came with it, the suffering, the longing for existence to just end, and the certainty that it would go on like this forever. He knew now why the faces inside these cells had looked so utterly desolate. It wasn't just the agony of life being sucked out of them. It was because this world thrived on the misery of unending suffering. It had begun, he understood now, ages ago, and would continue forever onward. Never ending. He would die, yes, but the misery would go on. Misery triumphant. Every noble ideal or belief, every notion of love and right and good . . . all of it defeated by the world that now was and always would be.

He thought of Olena, and the anguish was even worse.

There had been no monstrous sentries left to impede his return to the truck. The fight against Ray and Bubbles had drawn them all off. Franny reached the truck and looked toward the front of the building. What he saw terrified him.

Bruckner reminded him of their purpose. "Let's get this done, mate! Old fucker looks like he's about to croak."

Bruckner gave Franny a boost into the back of the truck and slammed shut the drop gate. Franny untied the makeshift sling and rolled up the sheets to form a pillow beneath Tolenka's head. The old man had stopped struggling and the sunken chest seemed to be barely moving. Franny laid a hand on the age-spotted skull and the few remaining wisps of hair were greasy beneath his fingers.

"It's going to be over soon. One way or the other," he said and wondered if the Russian could hear him or even understand.

Bruckner slid open the window that divided the cab from the truck bed. There was a lurch as he threw it into gear and they reversed away from the hospital. Once he could, Bruckner turned and started down a street where all the buildings seemed to be weeping a strange viscous blue material. As the truck passed the buildings swayed and bent as if looking down to regard the passing vehicle. Franny shivered. He wasn't sure Bruckner was seeing this.

"Drive faster!"

"I'm *trying*. Bloody piece of shit."

"Or at least get us off this street! *Now!*"

Bruckner threw them around a corner. Franny grabbed Tolenka and buffered him so he didn't hit the side. He feared what such a blow might do to his fragile grip on life. The slack mouth worked and a grating sound emerged, "Ma . . . ma . . . ma . . ."

Was this it? Was he dying and calling on his mother? Then Franny took a wild guess and said, "Mariamna? She's fine. Safe. I got her to the States."

A clawlike hand gripped Franny's forearm. Tolenka's eyes shifted colors and for an instant they seemed the eyes of a man and not windows into darkness. Franny kept talking, hoping to keep whatever remained of the man present.

"She told me about you. Dancing at embassy balls, and . . . and missions together. She still wears your medal." The slack lips moved—a smile or a grimace? "She told me you were brave. I heard your voice on those tapes. You got the warning to us. We listened. We're going to make it right."

An exhalation of breath that might have been a sigh, though Franny feared it represented the final breaths of a dying man. He gripped the Russian tighter and whispered, "Hang on, sir. Just a little longer."

The old engine on the truck groaned, the wheels vibrated as their speed increased. Frank held Tolenka tightly to try to ease the jouncing. The view outside was uncanny but were they still in Talas or in that other place?

"Bruckner, you gotta tell me once we're . . . there."

"Gonna be a bit hard to tell, mate, since *there* now seems to be *here*."

"We've got to be sure."

"I *know!*"

They drove on. Tolenka writhed in Franny's arms, but the movements didn't seem directed at the cop. He fought some other battle. A sibilant whisper wove through the truck. Words on the edge of understanding. It raised the hairs on the back of Franny's neck.

A thread of violence began to weave and dance through his thoughts. He looked down at the misshapen horror he held in his arms. Such perversion shouldn't be allowed to live. A new majesty was waiting to be born. Only this abomination held it back.

Franny watched with bemused interest as his hand crept toward the ropy, wattled neck. The truck veered and he had to grab for purchase and it broke the spell. He noticed their surroundings. They were driving through a deep valley washed by a poisonous greenish-yellow light. The source of the light was a massive bloated moon that filled the sky and kissed the horizon. All around were colossal mountains whose unnaturally sharp peaks were like jagged teeth rending at the sky, trying to devour the moon.

Franny didn't need Bruckner to tell him that it was time. Cradling the old man in his arms Franny crawled on his knees to the drop gate of the truck.

"It's now or never, mate!" Bruckner shouted.

Franny looked down into the ravaged face and tried to see the vestige of the handsome man from the picture. "You did it. You can rest now."

He heaved the wizened body out the back. It hit the slate-grey ground hard and exploded. At that moment a thousand mouths opened on the face of the moon and began to scream. The mountains walked, and out of the mist of blood rose something that defied words and understanding. A swirling blackness that began to rapidly swell until it was a towering twisted figure. Sparkling red glyphs ran through the body. An inchoate howl of rage like a gust of hurricane winds struck the truck. Bruckner fought for control as he downshifted and floored it.

The mouths of the moon became eyes and they wept filling the valley with a heaving sea of decay. The smell of burning rubber joined the other stomach-churning smells as the liquid ate at the tires. The canvas cover was starting to burn. When the acid reached him Franny would burn, too.

Franny flinched as liquid pattered through the holes in the canvas, but it was only water that struck his upturned face. Outside the pus slowly shifted into black water and the mountains transformed into trees trailing beards of moss.

Franny collapsed onto his back and stared at the canvas roof of the truck but all he could see was the shadowed face of the god. The god he had defied and thwarted. It would find him someday and a reckoning exacted. He began to shake.

New sounds broke through the fear that gripped him. Voices and car horns, the sounds of traffic. He managed to sit up. They were on a street circling a tall pillar with the figure of a man on top.

"Where . . . where?" It was all he could manage.

"Trafalgar Square. I don't know about you, mate, but I could use a drink."

Barbara could *feel* the moment of change, even through the screens and the headphones. The grim, stormy fog melted away, as if being sucked in by some gigantic vacuum. Many of the horrors that had been marching on the Cosmodrome vanished with it: creatures that had emerged from whatever place Horrorshow had tapped. And the rest, those that the fog had changed and twisted and deformed, whose minds had been taken and used . . . they were returned to what they'd once been. She saw them in the viewscreens: staggering, lost, confused, dropping the weapons they bore as if in disgust and horror, falling to their knees or raising their hands toward the sky as if in thanks.

Barbara sank back in her chair with them. "It's over," Ana's voice whispered in her earphones, and she wanted to answer: *No. Now the hard part starts . . .*

But she said nothing. She closed her eyes. *The hard part. Waiting to know if I will ever see Klaus again . . .*

532   HIGH STAKES

Marcus was screaming again. Silently, mouth full of blood, with frustration beyond anything he'd experienced before, he cried for his own death.
He wanted nothing more. Only for everything to be over, for him and for
the world itself.

He was so caught up in that that he kept screaming as the cell around
him dissolved. He felt himself falling, but he thought it some part of the
Harvester's torment. He fell through flesh that disintegrated as his body
pushed through it. He flailed. He lashed at the air like a drowning man.
His tail searched for purchase that wasn't there, and still he plummeted.
He hit the ground hard, in a rain of filth. Himself, and a thousand
others. The living and dead. Foul things, thudding to the earth on and
around him.

Arms raised protectively over his head, Marcus squirmed upright. *What
had happened?* he asked, and he beheld it. He saw it. Heard it. Felt it. Understood it. The Harvester had disappeared. All the beings trapped inside it
fell to the earth in whatever state of life or death they'd been in. He
watched other monsters vanish as well. A hog-like thing as large as a bus
raised its head and bellowed as its legs disappeared. The rest of its body
vanished before it hit the earth. Worms writhing on the ground undulated themselves into nothingness. Lumbering monsters became insubstantial mid-stride. Many of them howled as they vanished, but they may
have been the lucky ones. They weren't of this world. They were, Marcus
thought, being transported to whatever hell they belonged in.

Not so the mutated humans. He could spot those because no matter
what form they took they didn't vanish. Instead they writhed and bellowed
and trembled as their bodies shifted back toward what they'd been. The
agony of the transformation was clear. It was ghastly, watching them, but
in so many ways it was beautiful, too. Humans were becoming human
again! The air had a clarity it hadn't had since the horde arrived. Creation
itself shimmered. The world glistened like the entirety of it dripped with
the newness of . . . creation. Marcus blinked in the sudden brightness. It
was glorious. Amazing.

Yes, he caught glimpses of even more massive and horrible creatures
fading as the day brightened. They were the things that would have come,
the leviathans of the other dimension, bigger even than the Harvester, but
they had no hold here anymore. They faded to nothing as the world—the
world Marcus knew and loved with a sudden, complete devotion—came
back to its own.

God, it felt good. He stood panting. Injured and burned and half dead as he was, he felt flushed through with ecstasy. It swelled in him until he wanted to sing it out loud. He didn't have the tongue to do that, but the world did. It sang. Creation was, in that moment, a chorus of an uncountable multitude of voices.

This, he thought. *This is like witnessing the birth of a world. This,* he thought, *was seeing God work.*

The euphoria—as beautiful as it was—vanished as soon as Marcus remembered Olena and the villagers. He'd never gotten back to them! Anything might've happened to them. If another one of those dogs sniffed them out . . . Suddenly, it seemed a bad, bad thing that he hadn't been with them the whole time. *Please, God, let them be alive.*

He squirmed toward the hangar. He pushed through the crowds of stunned people and weaved around the carnage of the dead bodies and the destruction and debris. He ignored all of it, full of dread, his heart pounding, scared now as much as he had been in the worst of the miasma.

It only got worse when he finally got a view of the hangar. Corpses littered the ground all around it. Human and joker, clear evidence that the refugees had been caught up in the madness. Survivors stumbled through the carnage, looking shell-shocked and wary. All of them bore scars of the ordeal in some way: clothes torn, faces scratched, bite marks on their arms. A few cradled broken limbs or limped along or lay moaning if their injuries were severe enough. Many of them were red and brown with blood and filth. Their own or others, Marcus didn't want to think about.

The sight of the hangar itself made his heart sink. It looked like a mound of rubbish, like flotsam from a flood or the ruination left in the wake of a tornado. For a moment he was afraid to go any nearer. *It doesn't matter what it looks like,* he reminded himself. *It looked like shit to begin with. Maybe they're all right.*

He squirmed to it and went to work. He yanked boards away and shoved objects, first just trying to locate the door. When he found it he struggled to shove the container and other random objects away. He shouted for Olena and the villagers, calling them by name and identifying himself and telling them it was all over now. They were safe. Nobody answered. He hated that silence. *Maybe they're scared,* he thought, *staying quiet and hiding. Maybe . . .* He worked even more frantically.

When he finally had the door cleared, he stood panting, staring at it. The structure really did seem intact, but he realized it might have just become a prison of trapped madness. As quickly as he thought that, the idea curdled. Even if they hadn't been discovered, anything might have happened locked inside a sealed chamber. The madness didn't honor walls and concrete and steal. They wouldn't have been themselves. It wouldn't even be their fault if they'd attacked each other. He might find as great a slaughter inside as there was all around him. He tried to shake off the thought. It was no use speculating. He just had to find out. He gripped the handle, turned it, and stepped inside.

Coming from the bright of day into the dimness, Marcus couldn't see anything at first. The few lights that had worked last night were all out. *Olena?* He tried, but he barely produced a mumble. He tried other names. Jyrgal. Bulat. Timur. Nobody answered. The silence of the dark chamber seemed full of menace. Marcus slithered forward cautiously, his arms extended before him. He wove through the clutter of long unused planes, bits and pieces of discarded machinery. Gradually, his eyes adjusted and made the best of the dim light seeping through cracks in the ceiling and walls. Hulking things took shape, all of them motionless. In the silence, the scraping of his scales across the moist concrete seemed absurdly loud.

Coming from around a stack of crates, he saw them and thought, *No, God, don't do this . . .*

But he had. The proof was right there in front of him, the soft curves of people, all lying together. Their joker bodies were entwined, leaning against each other, arms interlocking, woven in an intimate tapestry. Completely still. As still as . . . death. He knew that's what he was seeing. The truth of it twisted his heart, squeezed it so that he felt it physically, something dying in the center of him. Of course they'd turned on each other, driven mad, trapped in here in the dark. He should never have left them. Maybe, if he'd stayed, he could've . . . But what he could've done he couldn't say.

He slid forward slowly, afraid of seeing the details, but knowing he had to. As he got closer, he began to make out individuals. Timur's big frame hulked larger than the rest. There was Sezim, the little girl, still clinging to her doll with her three arms. And Bulat, flat on his back, the tiny lizard that lived below his skin just as still as he was, its head jutting out of the man's cheek. Jyrgal leaned shoulder to shoulder with his wife, and Nurassyl was not far away, at the center of the entire group. It was too much to bear. Marcus ducked his head and, fingertips pressed against his closed eyes, he bawled out his misery. He was some time at this, as there was a lot of misery, and he didn't want to do what he knew he still had to.

When his tears were dry and he couldn't put it off any longer, he raised his head, took a deep breath, and continued looking for Olena. He found her all too quickly. She was at the far end of the group, lying on her back. One hand—the one wrapped in the bandages—she cradled close against her belly. The other stretched out to one side, the fingers of it interlaced with the stubby digits of one of the other joker children. Marcus pressed his body against hers. He felt the tears welling up again. He tried to blink them back, but they escaped him as he leaned over her.

Olena, I'm so sorry, Marcus thought. *I should've been here. I'd rather have died with you.* He suddenly remembered Father Squid screaming his long-lost lover's name at the moment of his tortured death. Would he be the same? Years later, when he left this world, would it be Olena's name on his lips? Yes, he was sure of it. And every day between this one and that would be a misery for not having her with him. *I love you. I always will.*

Thinking he would carry her outside, he slipped his arms under her. That's when she opened her eyes and looked at him. She studied him a moment, and then asked, "Is it over?"

Marcus stared at her, stunned and uncomprehending. She sat up. Her arms slipped around him and pulled him against her. He felt the warmth of her breath and the brush of her lips against his neck, and he heard the emotion in her voice as she said, "You're so bloody. Oh, God, you're so hurt. But it's over, isn't it? That's why you're here. Tell me it's over."

Marcus wouldn't have been able to answer even if his tongue-less mouth hadn't been full of blood. He was too elated that she was moving, talking, holding him. He brought a hand up and hesitantly stroked her hair. *She's alive*, he thought.

And not only her. Others began to move as well. Timur rose and stretched out his long arms. Jyrgal, waking suddenly, turned and whispered to his wife. She opened her eyes and answered him. One by one, all the jokers stirred. They sat up and began talking. They hugged each other. They smiled. They cried joyful tears.

How? Marcus wondered.

As if she heard him, Olena pulled back. She turned and watched the

awakening with him, and she answered his unspoken question. "Nurassyl
did this."

Nurassyl. Of course. The boy was right there at the center of the group.
Villagers crowded around him, touching him, thanking him. Some even
bowed. The boy smiled and answered them softly, but his large, round eyes
were fixed on Marcus. There was so much compassion on his face, so much
beauty in his joker-blessed features. The boy lifted his arms and held his
tentacled hands outstretched toward Marcus.

"Go," Olena said. "Be healed. Be healed, Marcus."

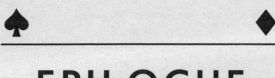

EPILOGUE

THE ANGEL WOKE IN a hospital bed, with a breathing tube down her throat, and an IV in her arm. A heart monitor beeped beside her head.

When she ripped loose the tubes and wires, the monitor began to scream. She remembered the battle she had with . . . the snake . . . like something out of a particularly nasty dream, but her body felt as if it had been real. Just breathing was agony.

And speaking of nasty dreams . . .

She glanced down to her stomach. The only marks on it were bruises and an incision, little more than a scratch from a sharp knife. She leaned over and vomited, but nothing would come out of her stomach, not even bile. She was racked by dry heaves, then heard her name being called.

"Angel!"

It was Billy.

Ray was as battered and bruised as he always was after a fight. He dragged a leg behind him as he entered her room. But the pain on his face was overshadowed by a solemn joy as he caught her up and hugged her tightly. It hurt like hell, but it was a good hurt.

"I wasn't sure about this one, babe," he said into her hair. "The only thing that kept me going was the thought . . . the desire to see your face." He frowned, held her at arm's length when she didn't respond.

"Oh, Billy." She discovered that she couldn't meet his eye.

He pulled her close again. "Hey, Angel, what's the matter?"

She was unspeakably weary. "I betrayed you, Billy," she said. "I betrayed my world. I betrayed my God. I did terrible things and had terrible desires. I lusted. I blasphemed. I put myself above all others—"

"It wasn't you," he said softly, stroking her cheek with his fingertips. "We're good now. Everything's okay."

"Is it, Billy?" She finally relaxed, leaning against his dirty and torn fighting suit.

"In time, babe."

She nodded, though she knew that, if ever, it would be a long, long time. *Save my soul from evil, Lord,* she prayed humbly, *and heal this warrior's heart.*

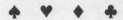

"Stop! Do you have clearance to be here?" the soldier asked. He was tall and fresh-featured, with blond hair showing under his blue UN helmet. He held his gun a little snugly, earnest instead of with the casual swagger he was used to seeing on the Russians. Marcus placed him as Scandinavian.

Marcus didn't answer immediately. He gazed past the soldier at the entrance to the casino. There it was, not looking nearly as menacing now as it had the last time he saw it. Nothing in Talas looked like it had. Now everything was drab, fatigued, like even the stone and steel and cement had been through hell and back. Well, he had been, too. "Clearance?" he asked, speaking with a tongue that still felt shiny and new and perfect, a gift from Nurassyl. A pink tongue. Olena had already joked that people would start calling him IPT. "Come on. With all that happened, you still want to check people's papers? It's a war zone, all of it, and we're the survivors. That's all the clearance I need."

"Yes but this isn't just anyplace."

"I know," Marcus said. "People will vouch for me. I was at Baikonur with the Committee. Call them if you need to."

The soldier considered this for a moment, and then let his official sternness fall away. He smiled. "I don't have their number. I know you, though. I saw the video footage. Before all this started, you were here in Talas, weren't you? You took part in the fights."

Marcus inhaled. *Oh, great.* "Look, that was not like it seemed. I didn't have much choice."

"I know," the soldier said. "I saw the one where you wouldn't fight."

Marcus met his grey eyes. "You saw that one, huh?"

The soldier said something, likely *yes* in Swedish or something. "I saw. You made me think about what I would do or not do to stay alive. It's not an easy question. You know what I'm saying?"

"Yeah," Marcus said. He exhaled, a long, tired breath. The soldier was probably a similar age as Marcus, but standing before him Marcus felt himself much older. Too old, really, for the years he had to his name. "I don't think a person can know until they face it. I'd like to think that everybody has some limit, though. Something they won't do. Someone they care about enough to die for. Most people, though, they never have to find out."

"You think it's better that way? Not having to find out."

Marcus shrugged. "Yeah, probably. But . . ." He craned around enough to see back to Olena waiting with the Kazakh driver assigned to take them to the airport. "I don't know. It's complicated."

The soldier nodded. "This is true." He stepped to the side and motioned that Marcus could pass.

The inside of the casino was a rubbish-strewn mess. Pretty much everything that could be overturned had been. Clothes and bottles and broken glass littered the floor, poker chips and bits of paper and stuff that wasn't exactly anything but debris. He wove through the betting tables, the roulette wheels, passed the rows of slot machines. He paused for a moment at the mouth of the tunnel that led to the arena, a rush of memories coming back to him. He pressed forward. He was here for a reason. He was going to see it through.

The tunnel opened out onto the arena. The rows of seats, the glass enclosing the fighting ring, the netting above it. All of it looked smaller, more decrepit than he remembered, run-down like some amusement park that had seen better days. Baba Yaga's box still hung over everything, but Marcus only glanced at it. He didn't want to think of her if he could avoid it. He slithered down toward the ring and entered through a door that had been left open.

And there he was. Knocked over on his side, half covered in debris. Marcus righted the strange, twisted, achingly beautiful prayer bench that had been—and still was—Father Squid. He hefted it up and walked through the rubble toward Olena and a waiting truck and driver. The man helped him slide the prayer bench into the bed of the truck. "Hey," Marcus said, "careful. This isn't just a bench." He almost said more, but he didn't know how to say it. The man couldn't understand him anyway.

He slithered over to Olena, who stood taking in the destruction with awed eyes. When he stopped next to her, she said, "It really all happened? Just like you said."

"You still don't remember?" She shook her head, and Marcus was relieved all over again. Just as she didn't remember the nightmare of Talas, she'd been spared the ordeal of Baikonur. Back at the Cosmodrome, hidden in their ramshackle hangar, Nurassyl had come to their rescue. When things got bad and the beasts were howling around them and the villagers themselves began to lose their minds, he'd urged them to all hold hands, or tentacles, or flippers, or whatever. Once they were all connected, he opened his power to them, letting it flow from one person to the next until they were all soothed by it, letting them forget. He'd dropped them into a sleep so deep that none of the turmoil outside the hangar woke them. He'd gone with them, and thus they'd slumbered through a dream of forgetting as the world raged around them.

Afterward, Nurassyl had offered that same forgetting to any who wanted. Many did. Refugees and soldiers. Nat and ace and jokers alike, Kazakh and Russian soldiers, even a few Committee members. All of them, in their own way and for their own reasons, saw Nurassyl for the wonder that he was and deigned to ask for his healing touch. Marcus had been sorely tempted himself, but he chose to keep the memories. As much as he would've liked to forget, he knew he needed to remember: both the horror of the other dimension and the beauty of seeing this one return. And he'd promised to remember for Olena, to tell her everything so that she'd know, but wouldn't have to live with the firsthand horror of it. Hopefully, she'd never have nightmares like Marcus was sure he would. No posttraumatic stress for her. And if she was sane, he stood that much better a chance of staying sane himself.

"Yes," Olena said, "but you haven't told me about my father. And this." She held up her hand, the one with the coin imbedded in it. She wore a snug-fitting cyclist's glove over it. Mollie had got it for her. Bought it legal-like and everything, she'd assured them.

"We've got a few long flights ahead of us. Let's save it for there."

"When we're up above the world and all the things of it look tiny?"

Marcus liked the sound of that. "Yeah."

"Let's go, then," she said.

"You're really coming with me?"

She nodded her head. Leaning toward him, she tipped herself up on her toes and kissed him. "I always said I wanted to, didn't I? First time I met you I said it. I knew. Now you know, too."

"But I don't know what's going to happen," Marcus said. He wasn't really sure why he kept talking, but he couldn't stop himself. "I might be in trouble. You know . . . all the stuff in the arena. I killed people. For all I know there'll be cops waiting for me on the other end."

"If there are I will give them an earful," Olena said. "I'll tell them you are Infamous Black Tongue, who helped save the world. It's true, and soon everyone will know. You shouldn't worry. You are a hero." She climbed into the truck and fell into instant banter with the driver.

Marcus settled in the truck bed. As the vehicle began to move, he set a hand on Father Squid. "Father, I hope you don't mind flying. I never asked you about that, but I guess you've been around the world already. This is just one more trip. Maybe the last one, all right?"

With his hand gripped around the prayer bench, Marcus looked up and took in the landscape scrolling by around them. This place, that had seemed so foreign at first, didn't seem that way anymore. It occurred to him like it never had before that he was at home on the earth, even far away from the places he knew. The world just didn't seem quite as large anymore, not when he could come all the way around the globe and find people he cared about, and who cared about him.

Still, it felt good to be going home, no matter what awaited him there. If the cops didn't grab him he'd head straight to Jokertown. He'd take Father Squid to Our Lady of Perpetual Misery. Father Squid had said it was a sanctuary. Now it would be his sanctuary forever after.

Maybe, Marcus thought, *it'll be mine, too.*

"Father," Marcus said, "I'm taking you home."

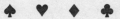

Michelle opened her eyes. Looking down at her was Joey. There was a fresh bandage on Joey's forehead where Mollie had taken a bite out of her eyebrow.

"About fucking time you woke up."

Michelle started to sit up and discovered that she was weak. Her hands instinctively went to her body to check for fat. She felt hipbones and ribs, then stopped. Time enough to put fat on later. But she hurt. She still hurt.

"There's someone here to see you," Joey said. There was an odd tone in her voice.

Michelle shoved herself up. She saw a joker girl sitting in the corner. Michelle took her to be fourteen or fifteen, about the age Michelle had been when she'd been emancipated from her parents. The girl wore faded jeans, low-cut Converse Chucks, and an *American Hero* T-shirt.

She had high cheekbones, wideset brown eyes, lush, full lips, and coppery dreads down to her waist. Her skin was the color of obsidian. Antennae rose from her forehead. When she stood, large, iridescent wings partially unfolded from her back.

"Adesina?" Michelle asked. It couldn't be. This couldn't be her daughter. But she knew in her gut that this strange girl was Adesina.

"Hey, Mom," her daughter replied, walking to the edge of Michelle's bed. Her voice was recognizable as Adesina's, but it was deeper and more resonant. Instead of a puppy-sized insect body, Adesina's figure was human in size and shape save for four vestigial insect legs along her torso. She'd cut slits into her T-shirt to accommodate them.

"You're so different," Michelle said. She reached out and touched Adesina's cheek. It wasn't soft and warm anymore. It was cold and hard.

"I'm still the same on the inside. I'm still your daughter. You're still my mom."

"And you saved me," Michelle said as her hand fell away from Adesina's face. Guilt washed over her. "In the catacombs. You shouldn't have been there. All the things you must have seen . . ."

"It's okay, Mom." Adesina gestured to her body. "See, I'm fine. And you're okay now, too." But there was a slight tremble in her voice.

She's not fine at all, Michelle thought. A hard lump formed in Michelle's throat, and she tried not to cry.

All Michelle had wanted was to protect Adesina. That was her responsibility. It's what mothers did. They kept their children safe. That was what everything had been for.

Going to Talas. The terror. All the death. Aero.

But she hadn't protected Adesina at all. If she had, then there wouldn't be this stranger standing next to her bed. The stranger her daughter had had to turn into to survive.

"I'm sorry, baby," Michelle said. She couldn't stop the tears now. "I'm so sorry."

"We'll talk later, Mom," Adesina said. Her antennae twitched. "Everything will be all right. See, I'm safe now." She paused, and when she spoke again the tremble was gone. "I'm who I'm supposed to be."

The word had come to Barbara in Brussels. "Barbara, he's alive." Ink's voice crackled over the speaker, and the words nearly made Barbara drop the phone from stunned fingers, that Lohengrin was alive.

"Klaus . . . ?"

"Yes. Klaus. Tesseract sent him back to Jokertown. I made arrangements through the Secretary-General as soon as I heard. There's a UN troop transport plane leaving from Brussels in an hour; I have you a seat on it . . ."

Now she was back in New York under a sky that was mockingly cloudless and blue, and she saw him, no longer Lohengrin but just Klaus, standing alongside a window, staring blankly outward to the bustle and confusion of the the city.

She felt all the fears, all her terrifying images of what might have happened to him and the nightmare of thinking he might even be dead, dissolve in that instant. She felt light suddenly.

"Klaus! My God . . ." Barbara rushed to him.

She ran to Klaus and embraced him, pulling him hard into her. "Klaus . . . I was so afraid that you were . . . you were . . ." She kissed his neck, his mouth, her fingers snared in his golden hair.

And she realized that his arms weren't holding her in return, that she might as well have been kissing a stranger. "Klaus?"

He looked down at her, his single eye focusing slowly. His black eye patch was gone—he wore a makeshift white one with an elastic string tangled in his hair. A hint of a smile touched his lips, then vanished. He opened his mouth, but what emerged was a sob. He choked it back with an effort, his throat moving, and his hand reached out to touch her cheek. She clasped it, holding it there. "So awful," he said. His voice was cracked and rough, as if he'd spent days shouting and roaring in the madness that had taken him. "Barbara, what I did . . . *Es war schrecklich*," he finished in German: *it was terrible.*

"It wasn't your fault," she told him. "You know that."

He shook his head mutely. His gaze searched hers, and she saw the moisture gathered in his eye. "I was right," he said. "You needed to be in

New York. You put together the team that saved us. You did what I couldn't do."

She shook her head as she hugged him again. She didn't want to talk about it, didn't care. "Klaus, I never knew what it was like for you, not really. I didn't listen to you closely enough, didn't hear what you were trying to tell me underneath all the words, and I'm sorry for that." She took a step back from him, still holding his hands. "From now on," Barbara said, "we will keep nothing from each other. We'll be the team we were meant to be. We'll tell each other what we're feeling, what we're thinking. There will be no secrets between us. Promise me that."

Klaus's hands shook. She tightened her grip. He shook his head. "No," he said, his voice dead and empty, his face slack. When his gaze finally came back to her, there was no affection there, only pain. "No," he repeated. "I can't make that promise, Barbara. There are things that I will never tell you. There are things that must always remain hidden."

She nodded, not wanting to agree but knowing that she had no choice. Not now. "Then we should talk about the Committee, what we need to do going forward from this, what we need to do to recover."

His head was shaking before she finished. "Do what you feel you need to do, Barbara. Whatever seems best. As for me . . ." He took a long, slow breath as his good eye closed, as if he wanted to shut out the entire world. "I don't know if I can do this anymore. I don't know."

"Klaus . . ." she began, but he let her hands drop away.

"I'm so tired," he said, and he began to walk back toward the hospital wards. "So tired," she heard him repeat, speaking to the air.

She watched him go, wanting him to stop, to turn, to reach back for her, but he did not.

After a moment, she followed.

Maseryk hadn't fired him. Instead Franny had been placed on administrative leave. Told to take as long as he needed.

As he was leaving the office the captain had clapped him on the shoulder. "Ray told me what you did over there." Franny cringed, waiting for the tally of all his sins and failures. "Kind of ironic, isn't it? All these damn aces and it's a nat that saves the day."

"It wouldn't have happened without all those aces." He had almost left the office when he remembered and turned back. "What about Baba Yaga, sir?"

"D.A. won't file charges. Lack of jurisdiction. And apparently a handful of jokers don't rise to the level of a crime against humanity so Brussels won't touch it either."

"So she skates?"

"Looks that way."

Franny had just shaken his head, but it gnawed at him. Filled every waking hour and even invaded his dreams driving away the gasping nightmares of Talas and the Dark God. In the brief intervals when he did sleep he alternated between terror and fury.

He had decided Baba Yaga deserved to know that Tolenka's last thought was of her, and indeed his final word as well so he was back at the Jokertown Clinic. She hadn't noticed him yet standing in the door of her room. She was dressed in a chic businesswoman's skirt and jacket. There was a full set of Louis Vuitton luggage. She had clearly replenished her wardrobe.

Did the means justify the ends, Franny wondered as he watched her place a final item in the largest bag. Yes . . . probably when literally the fate of the world had hung in the balance, but—

And then he saw the cassette tapes and the old player in the trash can. A cold certainty came over him, but he decided to give her a chance.

"Heading out?"

She turned. "Back again, boy? I thought you'd have had enough of me."

"I have, but I wanted to tell you about Tolenka."

She shut the suitcase and struggled to zip it closed with her one hand. "He didn't die here. That's clear. What more do I need to know?"

"He tried to say your name. His last thoughts were of you."

She gave a derisive snort and said, "A hero and a romantic. You're a—"

"A sentimental ass, a fool, yes, I know. What did you do with his medal, Mariamna? Is it in the trash, too?"

"I gave it to Grekor. He collects such trinkets. Relics of the old days when Americans feared us. We should have beaten you. You are all such sentimental fools."

"You called out to him when you were delirious."

"Concern that he'd finally died and I was doomed." Her voice was harsh. There was no softer emotion that Franny could discern.

"Deflection? Or do you really not give a fuck about a man you worked with, made love with, protected for decades?"

"First sentimentality and now psychobabble. You really are pathetic, Francis." She read something in his face and her brows snapped to gather in a sharp frown. "What, boy?"

"Nothing. Thank you for clarifying things for me." He turned and headed to the door. Paused and looked back.

"May I ask where you're going?"

"Going to come visit?"

"You never know."

"Paris. I haven't been there in a while and I like it."

"Bon voyage, Mariamna."

The gravediggers didn't understand why they were burying a chair, but they were happy for the work.

Mollie relished the feel of the sun on her skin. She stood, along with her supervisory entourage, at the edge of a cemetery in a remote Hungarian village. At least, the GPS anklet said it was Hungarian. Ffodor had been born close to a wrinkle in geography where Croatia, Slovenia, and Hungary came together. He had planned to bring her here, just for the hell of it.

But that had been a million years ago. Before Horrorshow. Before Baba Yaga. Before the fight club, before the botched robbery at the casino. Before she'd lost control of her power. Lost control of her mind.

Her ankle itched. The anklet was specially designed to detect any discontinuities in her GPS location, such as if she stepped through a portal. If it did detect a problem, it would tase the living shit out of her (which made showering a little nerve-racking) and then drug her unconscious long enough for a recovery team to collect her.

She snaked a finger under the band to scratch the itch. One of her minders frowned. For a few heartbeats a rage boiled so hot within Mollie she thought she might erupt like an Icelandic volcano, despite the raft of antipsychotics the docs had prescribed for her. But Mollie remembered her centering exercises and caught herself in time.

They wanted to keep Mollie an emotional zombie. That was for the best. Bad things happened when she got angry.

Her doctors had referred her to the cosmetic surgeon who worked on Joey, but Mollie had declined. She couldn't afford elective surgeries. Her own family's medical bills were fucking insane, and all the money raised by the auction of the stolen property in her North Dakota apartment, all sixty-eight thousand dollars, had gone to Jamal Norwood's family and the families of the people whom she'd murdered in Half Moon Bay.

Besides . . . Mollie deserved the scars. And so much worse. Compared against everything she'd done to—to Ffodor, to Joey, even to Berman—a few physical scars were a slap on the wrist.

But she'd measure her mental scars against anybody else's.

Dr. Swanson yawned quietly behind her hand. She was jetlagged. They all were. They'd traveled from New York the long way around. The primitive way. Using machines.

Mollie used her ace only on rare occasions, and some Committee bureaucrat had to sign a sheaf of papers for each of those. The jobs usually involved opening shortcuts between dingy warehouses in disparate parts of the world so that aid workers could ferry food and water.

The head gravedigger called a halt to the excavation. They knew what they were doing. The square edges went straight down. Deep enough to bury a Louis XIV chair.

True to the time-honored traditions of their profession, the gravediggers wandered off a short distance to give the mourners space, and promptly lit cigarettes. The strange scent brought a sad smile to Mollie's face. That had been Ffodor's brand.

Mollie waited for a nod from her minders before climbing into the grave. They offered to help her lower the deceased, but Mollie insisted on doing it herself. The chair was painfully heavy, but she did manage to lift it over the lip of the grave and set it softly in the dirt. It didn't list or wobble. Part of her therapy involved learning to work with her hands and learning new (honest) skills, so she'd repaired the damage Ffodor's transmogrified body had taken during her fight with Joey.

Just glue. No woodscrews, no staples. She couldn't bear the thought of drilling into Ffodor like that.

She didn't cry. She'd already cried enough tears for one lifetime. Crying was the easy part. What came after the tears? That was the hard part. The frightening part. The part with apologies and reparations and guilt. She wasn't ready to face her family yet. Dr. Swanson had warned her that might take a while.

Mollie knelt in the mud. She laid her head on the seat. Sighed.

"I wronged you, Ffodor Mathias," she said. "You died because of my arrogance, my hubris, and my greed. You were very very good to me. You deserved better. And I am so deeply sorry. I will carry this regret for the rest of my days. That is my pledge to you."

Franny had finally made it to Paris.

He had glimpsed it briefly when Mollie had abandoned him in Talas, but now he was finally here. The guy who had never traveled any farther than Florida to visit his grandparents had now been in Talas and Tehran and Paris. He had to say Paris was better.

Figuring that Baba Yaga would only stay at the best, Franny had downloaded a list of the most expensive hotels in the City of Light. He had worked his way through sixteen of the twenty-five listed by Forbes. Hôtel Fouquet's Barrière was next. According to the article the cost was $1,487 per night and that was before taxes. He couldn't imagine spending that much on a place to sleep. Just buying a plane ticket had depleted his meager savings.

Shifting the floral bouquet into one hand he fingered the vial of Trump virus in his coat pocket, then touched the syringe in his breast pocket. He wasn't killing her. Not really. There was a reason the trump was normally only used in Black Queen cases. Using it on a stable ace risked four possible outcomes—nothing would happen, their powers were stripped away, the virus reactivated and turned them into a joker, or death. Administering it to her wouldn't make him a murderer. He was giving her a chance. It was more than she'd done for her victims.

Of course, once he found her he would have to deal with her guards. She *would* be guarded, he was certain of that. Even if all her mob competitors had died in blood and madness in Talas she still wouldn't feel safe.

The hotel was on the Champs-Élysées. In the distance loomed the Arc de Triomphe. The building was white with a blue roof and shaped like the Flatiron Building in New York City. He walked past a line of black lion statues, under the red awning, and entered the hotel. The lobby flashed in shades of gold with crimson throw pillows and crimson rugs on the gold marble floor as accents. He approached the front desk that was fronted by gleaming crystal panels.

The supercilious desk clerk gave him the hairy eyeball. "I have a delivery for Mariamna Solovyova."

"We will have it delivered to madam," the man said. The disdain dripped off the accented words and Franny wanted to slug him.

He didn't argue, just handed over the flowers. He walked away and used a fall of gold drapery as cover. A few moments later a bellmen arrived at the front desk and took the bouquet. Franny took a position where he could see the elevators, and watched the numbers light up. The elevator stopped on the fourth floor.

He then ducked into the bathroom and dialed 17. He had ascertained that was the emergency police number for France. He assumed what the operator asked him was *What is your emergency?* so he started talking.

"I'm staying at the Hôtel Fouquet's Barrière, fourth floor. I came out of my room and saw armed men. I managed to get away, but I think something is happening."

"Un moment s'il vous plaît."

That he understood. A few seconds later a new voice came on the phone. "You have an emergency?"

Franny repeated the lie.

"Your name, sir?"

"Oh, shit!" Franny whispered.

He then drew his pistol and fired a shot into the toilet bowl. He dropped the burner phone he'd purchased, stepped on it and tossed the broken pieces into the toilet, and flushed it away.

The gunshot had been deafening with all the marble so he quickly ducked out, knowing someone would come to investigate. He hurried to the front door of the hotel and was satisfied when he heard the ululating cry of approaching sirens.

The few individuals in the lobby were looking confused. The desk clerk was alarmed as police cars pulled up outside. Franny ducked into the stairwell and ran up the stairs. As he reached the fourth floor landing he heard booted feet pounding up behind him. He pushed into the hallway.

An unmistakable thug stood outside a door. Even better, he had drawn his gun. When Franny suddenly emerged he fired, but Franny had been expecting that, and threw himself to the side. The bullet clipped his side, but the vest he wore beneath his shirt sucked the force.

That meant he was cowering on the floor when the cops burst out of the stairwell and came boiling off the elevator. They saw a man with a gun and reacted as Franny expected. One guard down. Another popped out of the hotel room. He was smart and threw down his weapon. While he was being arrested Baba Yaga emerged from the room.

She was spitting mad, but fortunately not actually spitting. She was shouting at the police in French. They were starting to look confused. The first goon was bleeding on the floor. More sirens as an ambulance arrived. Guests were emerging from their rooms. The scene was becoming chaotic. Franny loaded the syringe and joined the crowd. He edged in until he was next to Baba Yaga. She suddenly noticed him. Understanding flared in those cold eyes. Her mouth began working. Franny jammed the needle into her thigh and depressed the plunger, then leapt back.

She screamed and began to convulse. People drew back as she fell to the floor. Her back was contorting, trying to twist her into a circle. Med techs raced out of an elevator carrying a stretcher. There was massive confusion as everyone talked at once in five different languages and the EMTs dithered between the bleeding goon and the convulsing old woman. The old woman won out.

They had to strap her down to keep her on the stretchers as the violent tremors continued. Grim satisfaction and guilt warred in Franny's breast as he watched the transformation. The stump of her arm began to swell. A grotesque claw began to form. It was flailing and snapping. Bony plates emerged from her back like the spines on a stegosaurus. Her brow ridge became a horny shelf. She held the claw up to her face. A look of horror twisted her face and she began to scream.

Franny walked away. Justice had been served. For Jamal, and Jose, Tolenka and Father Squid. The dark, kindly eyes of the priest swam before him and Franny was shaken by doubt. The priest would not be grateful. He would have urged Franny to forgive. Regret and guilt washed over him. He had become as monstrous as the woman he'd punished.

Franny leaned against a wall and wept.

Closing Credits

STARRING	created and written by
Marcus (Infamous Black Tongue) Morgan	David Anthony Durham
Barbara (Babel) Baden	Stephen Leigh
Bathsheeba (The Midnight Angel) Fox	John Jos. Miller
Francis Xavier (Franny) Black, NYPD	Melinda M. Snodgrass
Michelle (Amazing Bubbles) Pond	Caroline Spector
Mollie (Tesseract) Steunenberg	Ian Tregillis

CO-STARRING	created by
Mariamna (Baba Yaga) Solovyova	Ty Franck
Horrorshow (Tolenka, aka Hellraiser)	Ty Franck
Josephine (Hoodoo Mama) Hebert	George R. R. Martin
Billy (Carnifex) Ray	John Jos. Miller
Olena Davydenko	David Anthony Durham
Vasel Davydenko	David Anthony Durham
Adesina Pond	Caroline Spector
Klaus (Lohengrin) Hausser	George R. R. Martin
Jyrgal (The Handsmith)	David Anthony Durham
Nurassyl, son of Jyrgal	David Anthony Durham
Jonathan (Bugsy) Tipton-Clarke	Daniel Abraham
Pakash (the Lama, aka Han) Bhandary	Royce Wideman
Hal (Tinker) Anderson	Carrie Vaughn
John (the Highwayman) Bruckner	George R. R. Martin
G. C. Jayewardene	Walton Simons

FEATURING	*created by*
Ana (Earth Witch) Cortez	Carrie Vaughn
Marcel (Doktor Omweer) Orie	David D. Levine
Cesar Antonio (Areo) Clerc	Walton Simons
Tiago (the Recycler) Goncalves	David D. Levine
Samuel (Vaporlock) Palmer	Stephen Leigh
Juliet (Ink) Summers	Caroline Spector
Wally (Rustbelt) Gunderson	Ian Tregillis
Yerodin (Ghost) Gunderson	George R. R. Martin
Abigail (the Understudy) Baker	Paul Cornell
The Mummy, deceased	Victor Milán
The Family Steunenberg of Coeur d'Alene	Ian Tregillis
Captain Chavvah Mendelberg, NYPD	Melinda M. Snodgrass
Detective First Class Michael Stevens, NYPD	Mary Anne Mohanraj
Detective Third Class Joan (Razor Joan) Lonnegan, NYPD	John Jos. Miller
Ivan (Uncle Ivan) Grekor	John Jos. Miller
Inkar (the Tulpar) Omarov	Caroline Spector

WITH	*created by*
Ricardo (the Lhama, aka Juan) Nunez	Victor Milán
Buford (Toad Man) Calhoun	Royce Wideman
William (Tinkerbill) Chen	Ty Franck
Dr. Bradley Finn	Melinda M. Snodgrass
Temir Bondarenko	Stephen Leigh
Andrii	David Anthony Durham
Stache, the Otter, Baldy	Melinda M. Snodgrass
Aliya, Bulat, Sezim, Timur	David Anthony Durham
Andrei, the Ice Man	John Jos. Miller
Shadow, a Russian hit man	John Jos. Miller
Jeanne (Moon) Duff, SCARE agent	Walter Jon Williams
Huginn and Muninn, SCARE agents	Ian Tregillis
Lorra (Cocomama) Juarez	Kevin Andrew Murphy
Juan (Curare) Leal	Kevin Andrew Murphy
Ibrahim (Messenger In Black) Montalvo	Kevin Andrew Murphy
Amare (Peregrine) Sweet	Gail Gerstner Miller
General Nabiyev, Dr. Rahal	Caroline Spector
Dr. Asil Basar	Caroline Spector
Nurlan, Dasha	Caroline Spector
Jamal (Stuntman) Norwood, deceased	Michael Cassutt

Deputy Inspector Thomas Jan Maseryk,
  NYPD   Chris Claremont
Sergeant Homer (Wingman) Taylor, NYPD   Steve Perrin
Patrolman Benjamin (Beastie) Bester   Kevin Andrew Murphy
Tom (Brave Hawk) Diedrich   Steve Perrin
Glassteel   Daniel Abraham
Wilma Mankiller   Daniel Abraham
Simone (Snow Blind) Duplaix   Walton Simons
Mephistopheles, aka Randy Devil   Ian Tregillis
Jimmy, Margaret, Mrs. Klein   Caroline Spector

BRINGING NEWS FROM OUR WORLDS TO YOURS . . .

Want your news daily?

The Gollancz blog has instant updates
on the hottest SF and Fantasy books.

Prefer your updates monthly?

Sign up for our
in-depth newsletter.

www.gollancz.co.uk

Follow us  @gollancz

Find us facebook.com/GollanczPublishing

Classic SF as you've never read it before.

Visit the SF Gateway to find out more!

www.sfgateway.com

ABOUT GOLLANCZ

Gollancz is the oldest SF publishing imprint in the world. Since being founded in 1927 Gollancz has continued to publish a focused selection of bestselling and award-winning authors. The front-list includes **Ben Aaronovitch**, **Joe Abercrombie**, **Charlaine Harris**, **Joanne Harris**, **Joe Hill**, **Alastair Reynolds**, **Patrick Rothfuss**, **Nalini Singh** and **Brandon Sanderson**.

As one of the largest Science Fiction and Fantasy imprints in the UK it is no surprise we have one of the most extensive backlists in the world. Find high-quality SF on Gateway written by such authors as **Philip K. Dick**, **Ursula Le Guin**, **Connie Willis**, **Sir Arthur C. Clarke**, **Pat Cadigan**, **Michael Moorcock** and **George R.R. Martin**.

We also have a strand of publishing in translation, which includes French, Polish and Russian authors. Gollancz is home to more award-winning authors than any other imprint, with names including **Aliette de Bodard**, **M. John Harrison**, **Paul McAuley**, **Sarah Pinborough**, **Pierre Pevel**, **Justina Robson** and many more.

The SF Gateway
More than 3,000 classic, rare and previously out-of-print SF novels at your fingertips.
www.sfgateway.com

The Gollancz Blog
Bringing you news from our worlds to yours. Stories, interviews, articles and exclusive extracts just for you!
www.gollancz.co.uk

GOLLANCZ
LONDON